YAF LFG

# PRAISE FOR *FURYBORN*

"Legrand's epic feminist fantasy is scary, sexy, and intense, set in a world made rich with magic, history, and a gorgeously imagined literary tradition."
—Melissa Albert, *New York Times* bestselling author of *The Hazel Wood*

"*Furyborn* is an addictive, fascinating fantasy. Truly not to be missed, this story…will have you on the edge of your seat."
—Kendare Blake, *#1 New York Times* bestselling author of the Three Dark Crowns series

"A veritable feast of magic: mystical beings, ruthless power struggles, and gorgeously cinematic writing that will sweep you off your feet."
—Traci Chee, *New York Times* bestselling author of the Sea of Ink and Gold series

"Immersive and intricate, *Furyborn* is a kick-you-in-the-teeth and grab-you-by-the-heart tale of two queens."
—Roshani Chokshi, *New York Times* bestselling author of *The Star-Touched Queen* and *A Crown of Wishes*

"Lush, riveting, and full of intrigue, *Furyborn* is a gripping read that grapples with questions of power, fate, and our abilities to change the world."
—S. Jae-Jones, *New York Times* bestselling author of *Wintersong*

"Epic in scope, endless in imagination, this book will grab hold of you and refuse to let go."
—Amie Kaufman, *New York Times* bestselling author of the Illuminae Files series and the Starbound trilogy

# KINGSBANE

ALSO BY CLAIRE LEGRAND

**The Empirium Trilogy**
*Furyborn*

# KINGSBANE

## THE EMPIRIUM TRILOGY · BOOK TWO

## CLAIRE LEGRAND

sourcebooks
fire

Published by Sourcebooks Fire, an imprint of Sourcebooks, Inc.
P.O. Box 4410, Naperville, Illinois 60567-4410
(630) 961-3900
Fax: (630) 961-2168
sourcebooks.com

Library of Congress Cataloging-in-Publication Data
Names: Legrand, Claire, author.
Title: Kingsbane / Claire Legrand.
Description: Naperville, Illinois : Sourcebooks Fire, [2019] | Series: The
    Empirium trilogy ; book two | Summary: Sun Queen Rielle faces new trials
    as she tries to maintain the Gate and is tempted by the angel Corien,
    while centuries later, Eliana must choose whether to embrace the crown or
    reject it forever.
Identifiers: LCCN 2018052449 | (hardcover : alk. paper)
Subjects: | CYAC: Fantasy. | Kings, queens, rulers, etc.--Fiction. |
    Angels--Fiction.
Classification: LCC PZ7.L521297 Kin 2019 | DDC [Fic]--dc23
LC record available at https://lccn.loc.gov/2018052449

Printed and bound in the United States of America.
LSC 10 9 8 7 6 5 4 3 2 1

*For Erica,*
*my light in the darkness*

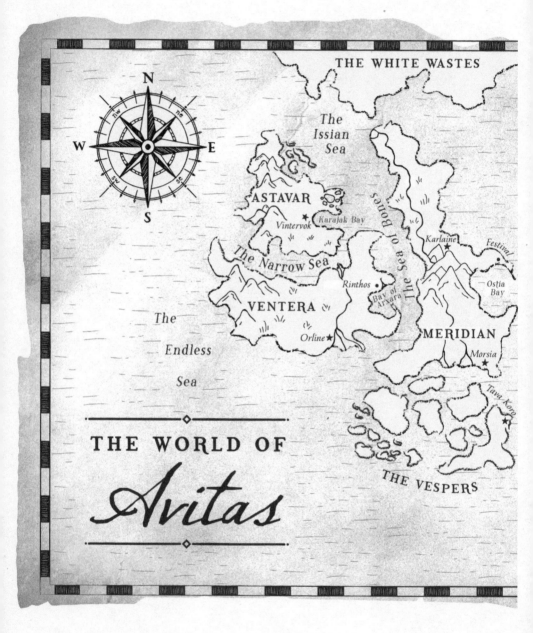

THE WHITE WASTES

The
Issian
Sea

ASTAVAR

*Vintervok* ★ *Karajak Bay*

The Narrow Sea

*Rinthos* ★

VENTERA

*Orline* ★

The

Endless

Sea

The Sea of Bones

Bay of
Arxara

*Karlaine* ★

*Festival*

*Ostia
Bay*

MERIDIAN

*Morsia* ★

*Tava Koro*
★

THE VESPERS

# THE WORLD OF
## *Avitas*

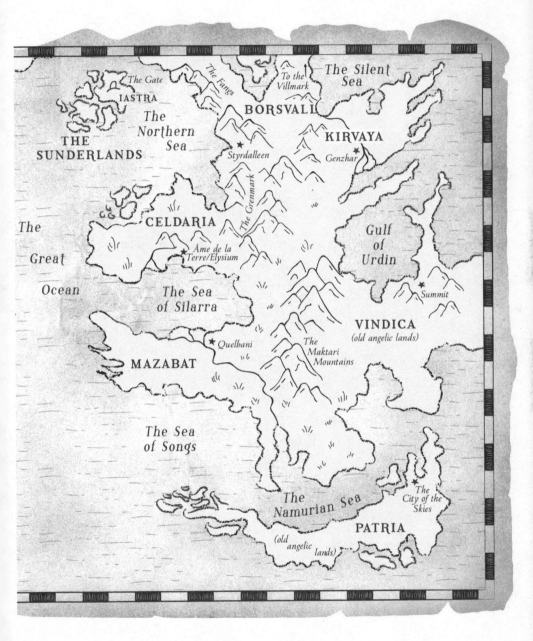

# A TRAVELER
# AND A STRANGER

*"The dangers of threading through time are many, but one often overlooked is the danger it poses for the traveler. The mind is fragile, and time is pitiless. Even powerful marques have lost themselves to the ravages of their temporal experiments. Perhaps it is best, then, that over the course of recorded history, only a few hundred beings have ever possessed this power, and that most of them are now dead."*

—*Meditations on Time*
by Basara Oboro, renowned Mazabatian scholar

W hen Simon awoke, he was alone.

He lay flat on his back on a scrubby plain veined with brown rocks and white ribbons of ice. The sky above him was the color of slate, choked with sweeping clouds that reminded him of waves, and from them fell thin spirals of snow.

For a few moments he lay there, hardly breathing, the snow collecting on his lashes. Then the memories of the last several hours returned to him.

Queen Rielle, giving birth to her child.

Simon's father, his mind no longer his own, throwing himself off her tower.

Rielle thrusting her infant daughter into Simon's arms, her face worn, her eyes wild and bright gold.

*You're strong, Simon. I know you can do this.*

Threads glowing at his fingertips—*his* threads, the first ones he had ever summoned on his own, without his father's guidance, and they were strong and solid. They would carry both him and the child in his arms to safety.

But then…

The queen, behind him in her rooms, fighting the angel named Corien. Her voice, distorted and godly. A brilliant light, exploding outward from where she knelt on the floor, knocking Simon's threads askew and summoning forth new ones—dark and violent, overtaking the others. Threads of time, more volatile than threads of space, and more cunning.

He'd tightened his arms around the screaming child, clutched the blanket her mother had wrapped around her, and then, a rush of black sound, a roar of something vast and ancient approaching.

Simon surged upright with a gasp, choking on tears, and looked down at his arms.

They were empty.

The only thing left of the princess was a torn piece of her blanket—slightly singed at the edges from the cold burn of time.

All at once he understood what had happened.

He understood the immensity of his failure.

But perhaps there was still hope. He could use his power, travel back to that moment on the terrace with the baby in his arms. He could move faster, get them both away to safety before Queen Rielle died.

He pushed himself to his knees, raised his skinny arms into the frigid air. His right hand still held the child's blanket. He refused to let it go. It was possible to summon threads with a cloth in his fist, and if he released the blanket, something terrible would happen. The certainty of that tightened in his chest like a screw.

He closed his eyes, his breath coming shaky and fast, and remembered the words from his books:

*The empirium lies within every living thing, and every living thing is of the empirium.*

*Its power connects not only flesh to bone, root to earth, stars to sky, but also road to road, city to city.*

*Moment to moment.*

But no matter how many times he recited the familiar sentences, the threads did not come.

His body remained dark and quiet. The marque magic with which he had been born, the power he had come to love and understand with his father's patient tutelage inside their little shop in Âme de la Terre, was gone.

He opened his eyes, staring at the stretch of barren, rocky land before him. White peaks beyond. A black sky. The air held nothing of magic inside it. Pale, it was, and tasteless. Flat where it had once thrummed with vitality.

Something was wrong in this place. It felt unmade and clouded. Scarred. Scraped raw.

Once, his marque blood—part human, part angel—had allowed him to touch the empirium.

Now, he could feel nothing of that ancient power. Not even an echo of it remained, not a hint of sound or light to follow.

It was as if the empirium had never existed.

He could not travel home. He could travel nowhere his own two feet could not take him.

Alone, shivering on a vast plateau in a land he did not know, in a time that was not his own, Simon buried his face in the scrap of cloth and wept.

—◆—

He lay curled in the dirt for hours, and then days, snow drawing a thin carpet across his body.

His mind was empty, hollowed out from his aching tears. Instinct told him he needed to find shelter. If he lay for much longer in the bitter cold, he would die.

But dying seemed a pleasant enough thought. It would provide him an escape from the terrible tide of loneliness that had begun to sweep through him.

He didn't know where he was, or *when* he was. He could have been thrown back to a time when there were only angels living in Avitas, and no humans. He could have been flung into the far future, when there were no flesh-and-blood creatures left alive, the world abandoned to its empty old age.

Wherever he was, whenever he was, he didn't care to find out. He cared about nothing. He was nothing, and he was nowhere.

He pressed the piece of blanket to his nose and mouth, breathing in the faint, clean scent of the child it had once held.

He knew the scent would soon dissipate.

But for now, it smelled of home.

—◆—

A voice woke him—faint but clear.

*Simon, you have to move.*

He cracked open his eyes, which was difficult, for they had nearly frozen shut.

The world was thick and white; he lay half-buried in a fresh drift of snow. He couldn't feel his fingers or toes.

"Get up."

The voice was close to him, and familiar enough to light a weak spark of curiosity in his dying mind.

An age passed before he found the strength to raise his body from the ground.

"On your feet," said the voice.

Simon squinted through the snow and saw a figure standing nearby, wrapped thick with furs.

He tried to speak, but his voice had disappeared.

"Rise," the figure instructed. "Stand up."

Simon obeyed, though he didn't want to. He wanted to tuck himself back into his snow bed and let it gently shepherd him down the path toward his death.

But he rose to his feet nevertheless, took two stumbling steps forward through snow that reached his knees. He nearly fell, but this person, whoever it was, caught him. Their gloved hands were strong. He peered into the folds of furs covering their face, but could see nothing that told him who they were.

They wrapped an arm around Simon, bolstering him against their side, and turned into the wind.

"We have to walk now," they said, their voice muffled in the furs and the snow, but still somehow familiar, though Simon's mind couldn't place it. "There's shelter. It's far, but you'll make it."

*I will.* Simon agreed with their words. They slipped into his mind, firm but gentle, and gave him the strength to move his legs. A sharp gust of wind sliced across his face, stealing his breath. He turned into the furs of the person beside him, seeking warmth in their body.

He wanted to live. Suddenly, passionately, he wanted to live. He craved warmth and food. He clutched the baby's blanket in his trembling, half-frozen fingers.

"Who are you?" he asked, finally able to speak.

The person's arm was a reassuring weight around his shoulders, their gait steady even in the snow. For a strange moment, so strange it left him feeling unbalanced and not quite within his own body, it seemed to Simon that perhaps this person was not even truly there.

But they answered him nevertheless.

"You may call me the Prophet," they said, "and I need your help."

# RIELLE

*"Her Majesty the Queen is delighted to announce that Lady Rielle Dardenne—recently anointed Sun Queen by His Holiness the Archon, with the support of the Magisterial Council and the Crown—will be arriving in the town of Carduel on the morning of October 14 to introduce herself as Sun Queen, pay homage to the Saints, and demonstrate her abilities for those who were unable to attend the holy trials earlier this year."*

—A proclamation sent from Genoveve Courverie, Queen of Celdaria, to the magisters of Carduel, September 20, Year 998 of the Second Age

Apparently being anointed Sun Queen did nothing to diminish the pain of monthly bleeding.

Rielle had spent half the morning in this bed, and she had decided she was never leaving it. It was a good bed, wide and clean, adorned with piles of pillows and a quilt so soft she felt tempted to steal it. According to the proprietor of the Château Grozant, who had been beside himself with nerves as he escorted Rielle and her guard to their rooms the night before, this was the finest bed at the inn. Really, she owed it to the man to luxuriate in the room he and his staff had so meticulously prepared for her.

She told Evyline as much.

Evyline, captain of the newly formed Sun Guard, resplendent in her golden armor and spotless white cape, stood at the bedroom door, raised one inscrutable gray eyebrow, and replied, "Sadly, my lady, I don't believe lying in bed all morning is part of our schedule."

"You can make it part of my schedule though, can't you?" Rielle threw an arm over her eyes and grimaced as her cramps returned with a mighty vengeance. She shifted the hot-water bottle Ludivine had brought her, pressed it to her lower abdomen, and muttered a curse. "You can do anything you set your mind to, Evyline. I believe in you."

"I'm touched," came Evyline's dry voice. "However, my lady, we only have fifteen minutes before they'll be expecting us downstairs."

A knock sounded on the door, followed by the muffled voice of Ivaine, one of Rielle's guards. "Prince Audric to see Lady Rielle."

Rielle peeked out from under her arm. "I'm staying in bed! Forever!"

"Ah, but I've brought cake," came Audric's reply.

Rielle grinned and pushed herself upright. Before she could reply, Evyline rolled her eyes and opened the door.

Audric entered, in his trim formal coat of emerald-green, looking entirely pleased with himself. He strode to the bed, knelt at Rielle's side, and presented a silver dish bearing a tiny slice of chocolate cake.

"For the Sun Queen," Audric murmured, his dark eyes dancing. "With the chef's compliments."

From the door, Evyline clucked her tongue. "Cake for breakfast, my lady? We have a long day ahead of us. Surely something heartier would be more suitable."

"Nothing is more suitable than cake when you've been traveling for a month and your body feels like bruised mush." Rielle placed the cake on her nightstand and returned to Audric with a smile. She held his face in her hands, relishing the sight of his warm brown skin, his dark curls, his broad smile. "Hello, there."

"Hello, darling." He caught her mouth softly with his. "Should I leave you to your cake?"

"You absolutely should not. You should sit with me and order everyone to leave us alone for the rest of the day." She wrapped her arms around his neck and whispered against his ear, "And then you should kiss me, everywhere, over and over, until I tire of it, which I never will."

Evyline cleared her throat and left the room, shutting the door quietly behind her.

Audric laughed into Rielle's hair. "And here I thought you weren't feeling well."

"I'm not. I feel awful." She closed her eyes as Audric kissed her cheeks, her brow, the hollow of her throat. "That helps though," she murmured. She threaded her fingers through his curls and pulled him gently closer, a smile melting across her face. She shifted closer to him, fisting his shirt in her hands. One of his palms slid down her back, his touch so gentle that it painted soft shivering ripples across her skin. His other hand cupped her breast through the thin fabric of her nightgown, and she arched up against him with a soft cry.

From the courtyard outside the inn came a distant burst of noise— firecrackers, chiming bells, the cheers of children awaiting their first sighting of the Sun Queen.

But Rielle ignored it all, instead letting Audric press her gently back into the pillows. She curled her fingers around his, scraped his jaw lightly with her teeth, and then smoothed over his skin with her tongue.

"Rielle," he said hoarsely, his mouth finding hers. "We don't have time."

*I do so hate to interrupt,* came Ludivine's prim voice. *But what excuse, exactly, should I give the lovely people of Carduel who are waiting so eagerly to see their Sun Queen? That she is indisposed at the moment? That their prince has his tongue down her throat?*

Rielle pulled away with a groan. "I'm going to kill her."

Audric looked up from where he had been lavishing her neck with kisses. "Lu?"

"She's admonishing us."

*Would you rather Tal come admonish you instead?* Ludivine suggested.

Rielle nearly choked at the thought. *No!*

*I'm happy to sit here under this canopy, enjoy my tea in peace, and send him up in my place.*

*No, no, we're coming. Just give us a moment.*

Ludivine paused, and then said gently, *This is our last stop. We'll be home soon enough.*

*I know.* Rielle sighed. *Thank you.*

She touched Audric's cheek. "You need a shave."

He smiled. "I thought you liked me like this. What did you call it?"

"A bit of scruff. And yes, I do like it. I like the way it looks, and I like the way it feels against my thighs when you—"

With a groan and a kiss, Audric cut her off. "I thought we were meant to be responsible now, go greet the adoring masses."

"We are, we *are*, yes, fine." Rielle gently detached herself from his arms, allowing him to help her out of bed. When she turned to look at him, the sight of him so fine and poised—his lips swollen from her kisses, the sunlight through the windows gilding his curls—made her lose her breath.

Ludivine's words from weeks ago returned to her, sharp and searing: *And you lied to Audric about his father's death. We are well suited.*

Her chest constricted around her heart, and she suddenly wanted more than anything to wrap Audric in her arms and never again let him out of her sight. Instead, she blurted out, "I love you."

He cupped her face in his hands as if to imprint the sight of it forever in his memory. "I love you," he replied softly, and bent to kiss her once more. Then he murmured against her mouth, "My light and my life," and left her.

Before the door closed, as Evyline returned to the room with Rielle's two maids flanking her, a page arrived on the landing, breathless from the stairs. "My lord prince," he said to Audric, "I have a message for you, from the north…"

But then the door closed, and Audric's reply was lost.

"What gown today, my lady?" asked one of Rielle's maids—the younger of the two, Sylvie, in the white-and-gold shift that all of Rielle's new attendants wore.

In Audric's absence, Rielle's abdominal pain returned to her. She cupped her lower belly with one hand and stuffed the cake into her mouth with the other.

"Something comfortable," she declared. "And red."

—◆—

They had been traveling for a month through the heartlands of Celdaria, introducing Rielle as the recently anointed Sun Queen, and the reception in each of the thirteen cities and villages they'd visited so far had been, as Ludivine wryly put it, *amorous*.

The town of Carduel was no different.

When Rielle stepped out of the Château Grozant and onto the stone road that led up to Carduel's House of Light, the wall of sound that greeted her nearly knocked her off her feet.

Carduel's population was just under one thousand, and every one of its citizens had turned out for Rielle's introduction. They lined the road dressed in their most formal attire—embroidered coats edged with gold, the cut of the fabric a few seasons out of fashion; brocaded gowns stiff with disuse and faded with age; jeweled hair combs that caught the morning sunlight and sent it flying across the road in trembling bursts. Children sat on their parents' shoulders, tossing white flower petals and waving golden sun-shaped medallions. Acolytes from Carduel's House of Light stood every few yards, their castings softly glowing.

Audric led the way, Ludivine on his arm in a summer gown of lavender and pearl, and his guard surrounding them in a loose circle.

Rielle watched them, a slight unease nicking at her breastbone. Though there had been no official announcement, the truth was plain. It was impossible for anyone who paid attention not to notice the Sun Queen and the crown prince sneaking up to each other's rooms night after night, and word of that had traveled quickly throughout the country. Someday soon, they would have to address how to move forward, appease House Sauvillier, officially share news of the broken betrothal, and introduce the idea of Rielle as Audric's paramour.

But not today.

She ducked out from the vine-crowned trellis marking the courtyard entrance and smiled at the gathered crowd.

A sharp cry from above turned her smile to a beaming grin.

At Atheria's descent, the townsfolk nearest Rielle cried out and hastened away, making room. The massive godsbeast landed at Rielle's side with hardly a sound and folded her wings neatly against her body.

"There you are," Rielle cooed, stretching onto her toes to plant a kiss on Atheria's velvet muzzle. "Have you been hunting?"

In response, Atheria chirruped and peered about curiously, bright-eyed.

Rielle laughed as she began the ascent toward Carduel's humble House of Light, Atheria at her side. She felt the eyes of the crowd upon her and stood straighter, her cheeks flushing with pleasure. Some she passed met her gaze; others smiled and looked away; still others bowed, kissed their fingers, then touched the lids of their eyes—the sign of prayer honoring Saint Katell and the House of Light.

By the time Rielle reached the temple entrance, her arms were full of flowers, and soft white petals dusted her hair.

Tal, waiting at the doors in his magisterial robes of scarlet and gold, plucked a petal from her collar. "You're late."

Rielle wrinkled her nose at him. "Sun Queens can be tardy if they want to, Lord Belounnon," she replied, and then bowed low. He gathered her hands in his and kissed her brow.

"Last one," he reminded her softly underneath the din.

"And thank God for that."

He glanced down at her red gown, lifting an eyebrow. "I'm not sure it was wise to wear red, of all things."

Rielle rolled her eyes. She had guessed he wouldn't approve of this gown and its skirt of deep crimson. On him, it was a firebrand color.

On her, it could be interpreted as a color of the Blood Queen.

She took Tal's offered arm and accompanied him inside to the temple altar. As he began the ceremony of greeting—so familiar by now that she could have recited the entire thing from memory—she let her attention wander. It was, she knew, a disrespectful thing to do.

But if she had to listen to Tal praise her courage and heroism on the day of the fire trial one more time, she would scream, or start confessing things she shouldn't.

She maintained an expression of placid humility as he spoke of the tragedy—the innocent civilians who had lost their lives. The executed Sauvillier soldiers, who had been tricked into treason by Lord Dervin Sauvillier, who himself had lost his way in the face of ambition.

*Ambition*, Rielle thought. *That's a word for it.*

*Pay attention*, Ludivine scolded. *You look bored.*

*I am bored.* Rielle drew in a breath. *We should tell them the truth.*

*Ah, that an angel took over the minds of their fellow citizens? That angels are returning? That the Gate is weakening? Yes, that sounds like a splendid idea.*

*For how much longer do you think they'll believe these lies and omissions?* Rielle looked steadily around the sanctuary, into which so many townsfolk had crowded that the air had already grown damp and hot. *Our people are not stupid. We should stop treating them as if they are.*

"…And, of course," Tal continued, his already solemn voice taking on an extra weight that made Rielle tense where she stood, for she knew what came next, "we still mourn the deaths of Armand Dardenne, Lord Commander of the royal army, and our beloved late king, Bastien Courverie, a compassionate and courageous man who led our country into an era of unprecedented peace and prosperity."

Rielle lowered her gaze to her hands, swallowing hard. She would not think about her father, or King Bastien, or Lord Dervin. She would not think about the glorious moment just before she'd stopped their hearts, when the empirium was hers to command.

She shut her eyes against the memory, but still her mind summoned it forth: the sensation of the world splitting asunder at her command. Heat crowding her palms. A detonation of unseen power blowing her hair back from her face. The empirium, raw and blinding, reflecting her own fury and fear.

Corien, crawling away from her, his ruined body glistening with burns.

Three men, lying still at her feet.

Her father, using his last breaths to sing her mother's lullaby.

A mother, and a father. Both dead at her hands.

Rielle opened her eyes, stared at her clasped white fingers. Every time Tal's words forced her to recall that awful, wonderful day—the day her father died, the day she transformed fire into feathers, and killed a king, and began to understand the true scope of her power—every time, she was forced to reckon with the truth she could not avoid: If given the choice, she would do it all again. She would change nothing that had happened that day, for doing so would mean giving up that brief moment of radiant understanding—touching the raw empirium, tasting its sizzling, storm-flavored power on her tongue.

Even if it meant that her father would still be alive, and Audric's father too. Even then, she would change nothing, and her heart stewed in its own black delight—ashamed, but resolute.

Then Ludivine spoke: *Four men are approaching through the crowd, with the intent to kill you.*

Rielle flinched. *What? Who are they?*

*Men who lost loved ones at the fire trial. They blame the massacre on you. They distrust you. Don't act until I tell you. We must wait until the right moment.*

Rielle's fingers became fists. *Tell me where they are, right now, and I'll flay them where they stand.*

*That would certainly ease the minds of all who doubt you,* said Ludivine dryly.

*Do they have weapons?*

*Yes.*

Rage dragged its eager claws up her spine. *Audric is here, and Tal. You're putting their lives at risk.*

*A woman is about to interrupt the ceremony. Let her speak. Be ready.*

In the next moment, a dark-skinned woman in a high-collared azure gown, standing near the front of the crowd, moved forward until Tal's acolytes barred her way.

"My daughter was killed," she called out, interrupting Tal, her voice cracked and thin. "At the fire trial, she died. She was killed. My *daughter*."

The room fell silent. Audric rose to his feet.

"She had come to watch the fire trial," the woman continued, her eyes bright with tears. "She had come to pay homage to the Sun Queen. She was killed by a soldier from House Sauvillier." The woman pointed at Ludivine, her hand shaking. "*Her* house. And yet there she stands, alive and whole."

The crowd shifted, murmuring. Ludivine rose to her feet, the expression on her face one of eloquent pity.

*Here it comes,* warned Ludivine.

Rielle's body tensed. She resisted looking around the room. *Here what comes?*

"You brought her back to life." The woman locked eyes with Rielle. "And you should bring all the others back too. If you don't, you're worthless to us. A coward, and a fraud."

The crowd's voices grew into a low roar—insults thrown at the woman, a few angry cries of agreement.

Rielle took one step back from them. *You shouldn't have lied to them. We should have told them the truth.*

*That I'm an angel?* Ludivine scoffed. *Yes, they would have accepted me wholeheartedly.*

*They would have. I would have made them.*

*I need to be able to protect you, not spend my time fending off the fears of small-minded people everywhere I turn—Rielle, now! Left!*

Rielle whirled, throwing up her palm. The fire from the altar's prayer candles flew to her—a dozen flames coalescing into a single ball of fire. She caught it in her hand, then flung it toward a curtained balcony affixed to the far wall.

The knot of fire consumed the arrow zipping toward her, dissolving it to ash.

The crowd exploded with noise. Some ran for the doors. Others shoved their children to the ground and covered their bodies with their own.

Audric darted before Ludivine, unsheathing Illumenor. The moment the great blade hit the air, it flared to brilliant life, and the air around Audric snapped with sudden heat.

Evyline shouted orders, Rielle's Sun Guard—seven women strong—dispersing in flashes of gold to form a protective perimeter. Rielle heard a sharp twang and spun around to face the opposite wall. She felt the arrow more than she saw it, the empirium directing the instinctive power in her blood faster than her mind could form commands. She summoned a gust of wind from the air over her head and used it to slam the arrow against one of the sanctuary's high arched rafters, where it snapped in two and dropped harmlessly.

A third man was running up the altar steps, a long dagger flashing in his hands. Audric intercepted him, Illumenor blazing, and knocked the weapon to the floor. Defenseless, the man fell at once to his knees.

"Mercy, Your Highness," the man begged, hands clasped, eyes darting back and forth between Audric and Rielle. "Mercy, I beg you!"

A cry from the crowd made Rielle turn in time to see the fourth assassin tackled to the floor by a group of young women. Three held him flat against the polished tile; one kicked a dagger out of his hand. A fifth delivered a sharp kick to his head with her brocaded boot. The crowd cheered; the woman kicked the man once more.

*Show him mercy,* Ludivine suggested. *The ones here who love you—and there are many—will love you even more fiercely for it.*

Rielle raised her hands, flames sparking at her fingertips. "Stop! Hold him, but don't hurt him."

The women obeyed at once, bowing their heads as Rielle approached. She doused the fire in her palms and knelt beside the man.

"I'm sorry for the loss you have suffered," Rielle said, gentling her voice even as she itched to recall her fire and frighten more tears out of him. "I am still learning, and I hope that, one day, none in Celdaria will endure the grief of needless death. I will work tirelessly at the side of Our Majesty Queen Genoveve to achieve this."

The man stared furiously at Rielle for a moment, blood trickling down his forehead and nose—and then, as Rielle watched, his face softened and his eyes dimmed. His expression shifted into something sly and familiar.

One of the women pinning him to the floor cried out and scrambled away from him.

Rielle's skin prickled.

The man opened his mouth to speak, but Rielle did not recognize the words. It was a harsh tongue, yet somehow lyrical, and though Rielle did not know the language, she caught the meaning well enough.

It was a taunt. A tease.

An invitation.

And underneath the man's voice hummed another, familiar one that Rielle had not heard for weeks.

She stiffened. *Corien?*

The man grinned, and then, abruptly, his eyes cleared. His body stiffened, jerked, then fell still.

Rielle rose to her feet and backed slowly away from him, the wild drum of her heart drowning out the sounds of onlookers shoving closer to get a better look, shouting questions at Tal, at Audric, at each other.

The Sun Guard swarmed, forming a tight circle around Rielle and ushering her quickly out of the temple, Audric's guard following close behind.

Ludivine's voice came urgently. *We need to leave. Now.*

Rielle murmured a protest, shaking herself free from her shock as they moved outside. Atheria was prancing nervously in the garden just outside the temple, wings out, ready to fly.

Rielle turned, found Ludivine leading Audric toward her. The crowd pressed close, barely held back by the circle of guards.

"We have to stay," Rielle protested, looking round. A man shoved forward his small child, who reached for Rielle's skirt, sobbing. "They're frightened!"

*No.*

*Climb.*

Ludivine's voice cut like a blade. Rielle stumbled forward, catching herself on Atheria's chest. The godsbeast knelt at her feet. In a daze, Rielle mounted her. She heard Audric and Ludivine climb up behind her, felt Audric's arms wrap around her waist.

"Make her fly," came Ludivine's tight voice. "We're leaving."

*He won't touch you.* In Rielle's mind, Ludivine's voice was low and tremulous, like the roll of nearing thunder. *Never again will he touch you.*

Distantly, Rielle realized she was not in control of her mind. Ludivine was there, in her thoughts, stifling her, calming her, even though she did not want to be calm.

And yet, she gathered Atheria's mane in her hands and croaked, "Fly, Atheria."

The godsbeast obeyed.

# ❧ 2 ❧

# ELIANA

*"The Emperor favors dreams most of all. Here, you are at your most vulnerable, and therein lies the appeal. Before sleep, clear your mind. Say your prayers. Recite to yourself the following: I am myself. My mind is my own. And I am not afraid."*

—The Word of the Prophet

A t first, the dream was familiar.

Eliana searched through the smoking ruins of the Empire outpost where she had dined with Lord Morbrae. Prisoners still trapped in the rubble screamed her name, an agonized chorus.

*Eliana.*

Their voices overlapped, shattered, surged. She ran with her hands clamped over her ears, but the screams pierced her palms and burrowed inside her like animals scrambling for shelter.

*Eliana.*

Quivering flakes spun down from the sky, a gossamer gray curtain of ashfall. Soon she was inhaling more smoke than air. She stumbled over a pale-brown arm jutting up from a black drift.

She wanted to shout a protest, but her voice had vanished.

She wanted to run, but her body did not obey. Her body was not her own.

She grasped the cold hand, stiff with death, and pulled, dislodging her mother's body. It was monstrous, deformed, frozen in a state of convulsion—not Rozen Ferracora, but the bestial crawler into which the Empire had made her.

"Eliana."

This voice was near, and singular. A cool breath puffed against her shoulder. A faint, perfumed scent—spice and incense.

She whirled.

She was no longer in the field of ash.

She stood at the end of an eternal corridor, its carpet red as a raw mouth.

Galvanized lights, affixed to the walls with wrought-iron brackets, buzzed quietly between closed doors. The walls were wood-paneled, polished to a gleam. As Eliana walked, her blurred reflection accompanied her.

She tried the first door she came to. Tall and narrow, its arched frame formed a point that reminded her of knives.

She reached for her belt, but found she was without her weapons. She wore a simple dark nightgown; her bare feet were wet.

She glanced down at the plush red carpet, testing her feet. As her weight shifted, so too did the carpet's color.

Red bubbled between her toes.

Her stomach tightened, and the sudden high whine in her ears told her to run, but, as before, when she tried to move, she stayed right where she was. Her feet were pinned to the soaked carpet. When she tried to cry out for help, only silence emerged.

Then, with a great slam, as if from the drop of some unseen mammoth blow, the door nearest her shuddered in its frame.

Eliana stared, her skin an icy shell of sweat.

The sound came again, and again—faster, louder, until it was a pounding heartbeat, and then the rhythm degraded, and it was a hailstorm of two frantic fists, then a dozen, then two dozen, all beating against the locked door.

Eliana pulled at her legs, desperate to dislodge them from the floor.

Silent screams lodged in her throat like food too sharp and hot to swallow. And still the door shook, rattling in its frame. A scream began. Distant, deep, and rising, it joined the cacophony of fists until it drowned them out entirely, and the door was shaking then, not from the weight of hands but from the sheer anguish of the wild, furious howl now bearing down upon it.

Eliana stared, her vision watery, her legs stinging from the scratches of her own fingernails. Not long ago, she had summoned a storm from the skies and used it to sink a fleet of Empire warships. On that frosted beach in Astavar, in the cold shallows of Karajak Bay, her blazing fingers had crafted angry wind and furious waves, and every muscle in her body had bloomed with pain as a strange new power ricocheted up the ladder of her bones.

But here, in this corridor, the world remained unremarkable and closed to her eyes. Her hands shook and her knees trembled, and she couldn't gather her thoughts well enough to reproduce that terrible moment on the beach, her mother dead at her feet, when her scream of grief had torn the world apart.

The door would fly open at any moment, and when it did, whatever was on the other side would find her, sweating and barefoot and defenseless and alone—

Eliana awoke.

Her eyes flew open. Five ringing seconds passed before she was able to catch her breath. The alien angles of the world slowly turned familiar—the vaulted ceiling above her, painted a rich dusk-dark violet and spangled with silver stars. The thick, beaded quilt of her bed. The arched sleeping alcove lit quaveringly by an inch of melted candle.

She was in her bedroom, in the Astavari palace called Dyrefal—the home of Kings Tavik and Eri Amaruk, and of their son, Malik, and three other children, working to aid Red Crown in distant waters, far from home.

And their youngest daughter, Navi.

*Navi.*

Eliana pushed herself upright, swung her legs out of bed, and padded across the midnight-blue rug toward the far wall. She peeked through a door that stood ajar, and at the sight of Remy sleeping peacefully in the adjoining room—embers glowing softly behind the fire grate, fur-trimmed blanket pulled up to his chin—some of the tension in her shoulders abated.

Soon, she would have to tell him about their mother's death—some of the truth, if not all of it. He deserved to know, even if she couldn't find the courage to tell him how Rozen had died.

But not yet.

She pulled the door closed, slipped on her boots, threw on a heavy velvet dressing gown over her sleeping shift, and steeled herself before opening her bedroom door.

The two guards stationed in the corridor, standing against the opposite wall, snapped to attention and bowed their heads.

One of them, a short, solid woman with dark-brown skin and close-cropped white hair, stepped forward.

What was her name? Eliana searched her memory for the answer, but could only think of dream images: A scream behind a locked door. A soggy carpet foaming red between her toes.

"Is there anything we can help you with, my lady?" asked the guard. "Shall we send for the captain?"

At the thought of seeing Simon in her current state, Eliana blurted out, "God, no!"

Then, collecting herself, she managed a polite smile. "I simply wanted to go for a walk. Please, as you were."

But as Eliana walked away, the guards followed her.

She turned to face them. "As you were, I said."

"Begging your pardon, my lady," said the guard, "but we've been ordered to accompany you, should you need to leave your chambers."

Meli. That was the woman's name.

With considerable effort, Eliana softened her expression. "Meli, isn't it?"

The woman straightened, clearly pleased. "Yes, my lady."

"Well, Meli, while I do appreciate your devotion, surely, after everything I've done for your people, you can allow me this one small thing?" She placed a gentle hand on Meli's forearm, which made the woman flinch. She stared at Eliana's hand as if it were a star that had fallen expressly for her to enjoy.

"Of course, my lady," Meli said, bowing her head once more. "I apologize."

"I don't need your apologies. I simply need an hour or so to roam the halls undisturbed."

With that, Eliana left the guards behind. She felt the press of their awestruck gazes upon her back long after she had turned the corner and tried to stifle her annoyance. If they insisted upon looking at her that way—as if she really were some long-awaited queen come at last to save them from the world's evils—then they could do so. Their adoration did nothing to change the truth: the power she had summoned that night on the beach had not returned.

And she was in no hurry to find it.

✦

After three-quarters of an hour, having wandered through the palace's corridors, each one dark and velvet soft, dimly lit by candles from within and the night from without, Eliana stepped into the windowed gallery that connected the palace proper to Navi's tower. The ceiling arched high overhead, bracketed torches throwing shivering arms of light across the polished stone floor.

She hesitated.

Then, in the corner of her eye, a flutter of movement. A flash of color against the obsidian glass.

Eliana turned, and a body slammed into her, knocking her to the floor. She managed to twist, landing on her side, but then a fist connected with her jaw. Her head snapped back against the floor.

She lay there, gasping. Once, she would have been able to clear her vision with a swift shake of her head and launch herself to her feet, but now she remained breathless and immobile. Bright stars sparked across her eyes. Pain reverberated through her skull, sharp and hot. She touched her scalp; her fingers came away red with blood.

Remy's words from the previous week returned to her: *Your body could heal itself, and we never knew why. But it was because all that power was trapped sleeping inside you, and it didn't have anything to do, so instead it fixed you up whenever it could.*

And now?

She tried to push herself up, but her head was spinning viciously, an unfamiliar and utterly disorienting sensation, and she stumbled back to the floor.

A wild shriek cut the air, just before a weight slammed into her once more, smashing her flat. A body straddled her; two hands closed around her throat.

Eliana blinked until her vision focused on Navi, glaring down at her with glittering eyes, her face rage-twisted.

"Navi?" Eliana gasped.

Navi's hands tightened around her neck, her fingernails digging into Eliana's flesh. She growled gibberish words, and Eliana clawed at her friend's arms, tried to push her off, but the pain in her own head was a spreading fog, dumbing her senses. Her head filled with blood; her face felt ready to burst.

Running footsteps approached. Someone seized Navi, yanked her away. Eliana gulped down air, coughing and gagging. She looked up, eyes watering, and saw Navi crouched several feet away, teeth bared in Simon's direction. He circled her slowly, hand hovering at the holster hanging from his belt.

"Don't," Eliana croaked. "Don't hurt her."

His gaze flicked sharply toward her, and that beat of time gave Navi her opportunity. She launched herself off the floor and flew into Simon.

He slammed into the nearest window, cracking the glass, then staggered away, shaking his head with a slight snarl.

Navi ran back for Eliana, but she was ready. She let Navi pin her once more to the floor, keeping her arms still at her sides.

"Navi, it's me," she said. "It's Eliana."

Navi's gaze flickered across Eliana's face, animal and unseeing.

Simon lunged for Navi once more, but Eliana shouted at him. "No, wait!"

He obeyed, fists clenched at his sides.

"Listen to me," Eliana said firmly to Navi, blinking away the black crowding her eyes. "'Tell me something real.' Remember?"

A wave of recognition shifted Navi's expression.

Eliana clung to the sight. "I came to you, in Sanctuary. I'd had a nightmare. You held me. You comforted me."

Navi's grip loosened. The scowl on her face uncurled.

"You told me to tell you something real. I told you about Harkan."

Navi's eyes brightened, twin candles flaring to life in a dark room. She scrambled away, shaking her head.

"No, no, no." She raised shaking fingers to her temples, drew her knees to her chest. "Oh, God, what's happening?"

Unsteadily, Eliana crawled toward her. "It's all right. I'm here, I'm right here, I'm fine."

"What did they do to me?" Navi huddled against the stone pillar dividing the cracked window from its unbroken neighbor. Shivering, her face drawn and hollowed from fatigue, her shorn head still bearing the marks of Fidelia's knives, she turned imploring eyes toward Eliana. In the silence, her single sob broke like the crash of glass.

"What did they *do* to me?" she cried.

Down the gallery, past Simon, four guards turned the corner and hurried toward them, but Simon—hair tousled, weapons belt hastily thrown on over his trousers and sleep shirt—stopped them in their tracks with a single icy glare.

Eliana approached Navi as she might a wounded animal, her neck still throbbing. Blood trickled down her cheek. She wiped it away, realizing with a sick lurch, belly to throat, that, for the first time in her life, a wound wasn't closing.

But then Navi looked up and cried out, and Eliana forgot everything but the sight of her friend's tear-streaked face. Navi reached out for her, and Eliana gathered her tightly against her chest.

"Send for Princess Navana's healers," Simon instructed the guards.

Eliana tucked Navi's head under her chin and met Simon's furious blue gaze. She could see the reproach there—and the pity.

"Don't say it," she told him quietly. "Not tonight."

He inclined his head and turned away to stand watch until the healers arrived.

But Eliana heard his unsaid words as plainly as if he'd whispered them against her ear: *there is no hope for her.*

*The Navi we knew will soon be gone.*

# 3

# RIELLE

*"Saint Grimvald the Mighty was the first to tame the great ice dragons of the far north, though in those days he was neither saint nor mighty. He was a dreamer, a metal-master whose heart had not yet been hardened by war. He traveled the dark slopes of the Villmark, determined to see a godsbeast with his own eyes, though the creatures had not been seen in half an age. And it was this wonder, this purity of spirit, that brought him to their nests hidden high in the ice, and spared him his life."*

—*The Book of the Saints*

They had been in the air for the better part of an hour before Rielle's mind cleared at last.

Behind her, Audric called out over the wind, "Where are we?" He sounded startled, groggy, as if just woken from a hard sleep.

Too angry to speak, Rielle guided Atheria into a small woodland lining a ridge of low hills. The godsbeast responded at once to even her slightest movements, and as soon as Atheria's hooves hit soil, Rielle slid off her back, jumped to the ground, and rounded on Ludivine.

"How dare you? You forced us to leave. I didn't want to, and you entered my mind without my permission and *forced* me." She watched Audric dismount. He looked a bit dazed, but still managed to shoot

Ludivine a glare of his own. "You were in Audric's mind too, weren't you? Lu, I'm so angry I can hardly look at you."

Ludivine dismounted last, and once she'd stepped clear of Atheria, the chavaile snaked her head around and hissed, baring her sharp mouth of teeth and fluffing up her great black wings to look twice their normal size.

Smoothing down her skirts, Ludivine hurried away. "That's a bit dramatic. You could have stayed, if you'd wanted to. I would not have *forced* you to do anything."

"Perhaps," Audric said, his voice tight and low, "as we'd already agreed, you could refrain from entering our minds unless in moments of absolute necessity. Such as giving us ample warning when people are approaching with the intent to kill?"

"There's something to be said for theatrics," Ludivine replied, unperturbed. "I wanted everyone gathered to see an unrehearsed demonstration of your power." She glanced at Rielle. "Both of you, together. The people of Celdaria need to be reminded of your strength and your friendship as often as possible."

Audric's mouth twisted. He crossed his arms over his chest. "They need to be reminded that Rielle is loyal to the crown, and that the crown trusts her."

Ever so slightly, Ludivine's rigid posture relaxed. "Precisely."

"A message that no doubt lost much of its impact when we fled five minutes later," Rielle snapped, "leaving the people of Carduel to fend off whatever danger approaches on their own."

"The danger in Carduel was for you, not for them," said Ludivine, regarding Rielle calmly. "That was the first time Corien has spoken to you since the fire trial. Isn't that right?"

Rielle felt Audric's eyes upon her, and her face grew hot. She lifted her chin, meeting Ludivine's gentle gaze without blinking. "Yes. He's been completely absent from my mind."

Which was the truth—and one that left Rielle's chest knotted with too many contradictory emotions to untangle.

"And that he chose to speak to you through that man today is an announcement." Ludivine touched Rielle's hand. "He is proclaiming his return. If not an immediate return, then an impending one. So, no, I don't regret fleeing. Putting distance between you and Corien is one of the most important things I can do to protect you, and everyone else."

"Even though fleeing may have given him the impression that I'm frightened of his return?" Rielle pointed out. "That I'm vulnerable and easily affected by him?"

*Aren't you?* Ludivine said gently.

Rielle walked away before the fury building behind her eyes manifested in a fashion she would regret.

She placed her hand against the trunk of an oak with shivering leaves and looked out over the riverlands below them—empty and verdantly green, save for dark clutches of woodlands, a lonely road, and a small village on the horizon, huddled on the banks of a narrow river. In the distance, the Varisian Mountains, at the southern end of which sat the capital of Âme de la Terre, reached solemnly for the afternoon sky.

For a long moment, no one spoke.

Then Audric cleared his throat. "Though I don't condone your actions, Lu, it's possible this is working in our favor. I was wondering how we would slip away from the others without causing a terrible scene. And," he added wryly, "without Lu having to interfere."

Rielle glanced over her shoulder as Audric withdrew a piece of paper from his pocket and unfolded it.

"What is that?" she asked. Then she remembered. "Your page came earlier with a message for you. From the north, he said."

A few paces away, Ludivine stiffened. Her gaze turned hazy, then cleared. She looked sharply at Audric.

"Yes, from the north," he said before Ludivine could speak. "A message from Prince Ilmaire of Borsvall. He and I have been corresponding in secret since Princess Runa's death. *About* her death, in fact, among other things."

Ludivine watched him closely. "Is that wise?"

"I'm surprised you didn't already know we'd been talking," Audric said, a note of bitterness in his voice.

Ludivine's shoulders squared. "I told you I don't go rifling around in your mind unless it's absolutely necessary, and I meant it."

*I'm sorry, truly.* Ludivine's voice came to Rielle abashed and muted. *Directing you away from Carduel was a misstep. I was frightened to see Corien on that man's face. Forgive me.*

But Rielle lacked the patience to coddle her. "Why is Prince Ilmaire writing to you about his dead sister?" she asked Audric.

"Whatever is attacking our border outposts is attacking Borsvall's as well," Audric replied. "He wants to stop the bloodshed and determine its cause as much as I do. Though our countries are not the allies we once were, Ilmaire and I both want that day to come again. He therefore thought it wise to begin a correspondence and pave the way for future friendship."

He glanced first at Rielle, then at Ludivine, seeming to steel himself. "There's something else. Violent storms have been ravaging Borsvall's western coast for weeks now, and with increasing severity. Their cities and ports are in ruins. They're sheltering as many citizens as they can in the capital, but even their food stores are running low, with most of their trade ships damaged and merchants avoiding Borsvall waters at all costs."

Audric paused. He glanced at Rielle. "In his latest letter, he's asking us for help. He's asking *you* for help."

Ludivine made an incredulous noise, but Rielle ignored her.

"Can he be trusted?" she asked.

"I believe he can. Everything I've heard about his character has been confirmed through the contents of these letters, the style of his writing, the ideas he communicates. His passion for peace."

Ludivine shook her head. "Belief is one thing, Audric. Given the history of our two countries, some might consider what you're doing treason."

"And I consider it diplomacy," he said sharply. "Not to mention that helping a country full of innocent people, regardless of whether or not we are on friendly terms with their leaders, is the right thing to do."

Rielle smiled at him, shaking her head a little, and then brought his face down to hers. Against his mouth, she murmured, "When you say things like that, your brow turns serious and grave, and I find myself unable to resist kissing you."

He caught her wrists, brushed his lips against each of her pulse points. "A distraction I welcome."

"Audric," Ludivine said slowly, "I understand why you want to do this, but I think it unwise. Perhaps Ilmaire is a friend, but we cannot guarantee that of the people around him. His father, his advisers. His sister, who commands the royal army."

And suddenly Rielle couldn't bear to hear Ludivine speak another word in that cautious voice of hers—as though they were children she was trying to work out how to let down easily.

"We'll go at once," she said to Audric. "We'll help them, and if that's treason, then I'll proudly face your mother and the council to receive my punishment."

His solemn expression melted into one of such adoration that Rielle flushed. "And then you'll threaten anyone who dares attempt to enforce said punishment?"

She took his hand with a slight pout. "You say that like it's a bad thing."

"On the contrary," he replied, lacing his fingers with hers, "I find it exhilarating."

Reminding herself that soon they would be home, and her bleeding would be finished, and she could have Audric to herself for an entire uninterrupted night, Rielle turned a triumphant smile toward Ludivine. "Well? Will you come too, or will you stay here and sulk in the woods?"

Ludivine frowned at them. "Tal will be furious when we return."

"I can handle Tal."

"Not to mention the Archon."

"I can handle him too." Rielle stepped onto Audric's laced fingers and climbed atop Atheria's back. "I can handle anyone."

Ludivine said not another word until they had all mounted the enormous godsbeast once more.

Then she said quietly, "At the first sign of trouble, I'll take control of you both and get us home."

Rielle looked back at her and snapped, "If you do that, you'll be just as bad as Corien."

Ludivine's mind jerked as if struck, but Rielle didn't wait for her response. She leaned forward, winding her fingers through Atheria's mane.

"Fly, Atheria," she commanded, and the chavaile ran through the trees to the hill's edge, opened her wings, and launched herself into the air. Audric's arms tightened around Rielle's middle; he kissed the back of her neck.

*I'm sorry, Rielle,* came Ludivine's whisper. Her remorse lapped against Rielle like an apologetic sea. *You're right. Of course I won't do that. I'm not like him. I just…*

*You worry.*

Ludivine nodded miserably. Rielle could see her clearly in her mind's eye—pale face, mouth in a tight line. *I do.*

*And I love you for it.*

Then Rielle imagined that they were all home, in Audric's rooms at Baingarde, nestled together before the fire as they had done for years before their world became the strange, frightening thing it now was.

She sent the image to Ludivine, and felt her sigh in reply, and whisper, her voice trembling with relief, *Thank you.*

◆

Ilmaire had requested they meet in a coastal village near the Borsvall capital of Styrdalleen. Atheria landed on a flat-topped hill encircled by stunted trees, and then Rielle, after kissing her nose, sent her away into the nearby twisted woodlands. They had decided that the sight of a godsbeast might ruin any diplomatic efforts before they began.

The village was situated a washed-out stretch of land, where mudslides had clearly ruined what had once been roads and pastures. Only a few toppled buildings remained, the beach's dunes had been flattened, and the air was wet and howling.

The whole beach was sopping with mud and ruin: shattered dishes, toppled chests or clothing gone black with rot, paintings bleached pale by the sea, ravaged corpses of livestock and birds. Abandoned stone houses high above the beach in the hills stood in utter disrepair.

But Rielle's attention was soon drawn out to the sea. The capital, safely tucked away in the nearby mountains, stood tall and white against a sky quilted with knots of storm-yellowed clouds. And the sea stretching out before the mountains like a black carpet was angry and roaring. Waves crashed furiously against the rocky shore. White sprays of foam towered high as houses throughout the broad harbor, connected to the city proper by neighborhoods at lower elevations that had been completely demolished. Along the horizon, a wall of black clouds loomed, threatening more wind.

Audric muttered a low curse as he came to stand beside her. Ludivine joined them, her face tight with worry.

"I hope the villagers managed to get to higher ground in time," Rielle said, her voice nearly swallowed by the wind. The air was choked with salt and silt; tiny granules of sand spat sharply against her skin.

"Some did," replied an unfamiliar voice. "But not nearly enough."

Rielle spun around to face it and saw a slender man with elegant bearing approach from the doorway of what Rielle assumed, given its stone columns and the engravings of wolves upon its obsidian doors, was the village's House of Night. The man was pale-skinned and clean-shaven, half his long blond hair pulled back and tied with a leather cord. He wore a cloak of shaggy white fur across his shoulders and thick silver bands at his wrists. Rielle sensed the weight of them, the taste of the magic left behind in their metal—alpine and sharp, fleeting and changeful. This man was a windsinger.

"Ilmaire," Audric said, beaming. He strode toward him and knelt. Rielle and Ludivine echoed him, and then Audric rose to his feet and embraced the Borsvall prince fiercely. Ilmaire returned his embrace, but his arms were stiff, his movements stilted. Over Audric's shoulder, his eyes locked with Rielle's. They were blue and grave, and they held her gaze for only a moment before glancing at something over her shoulder.

She turned but saw nothing. Only the eerie village, the wind-battered, salt-crusted hills. The gleaming white capital beyond. The black water and the black sky.

A delicate, scratchy feeling began climbing up the walls of her body, like the drag of a fingernail against rough stone.

*Lu?* She sent an echo of the feeling Ludivine's way.

*I know,* Ludivine replied. *Something's not right. Be on your guard.*

"Since they began," Ilmaire was saying, pulling away from Audric, "the storms have hardly let up for an hour. They're unnatural. Relentless." His voice was hollow, and when Rielle looked more closely at him, she saw the weariness of his expression, the haunted look in his eyes. "I wouldn't have asked you to such a dangerous place, Audric, if we hadn't lost all hope."

"Luckily for you, the three of us are accustomed to danger." Audric gestured for Ludivine and Rielle to join him. "This is Lady Ludivine Sauvillier, my mother's niece. And this..." He caught Rielle's hand, his face softening. "This is Lady Rielle Dardenne, recently anointed Sun Queen and my dear friend."

"And your lover," snapped a new voice—female, thin, and sharp as the relentless wind. "Or did you think we simple barbarians in Borsvall too far removed from the world's gossip to know about that?"

A young woman emerged from the ruined temple's shadows to stand beside Ilmaire. Lithe and glowering and nearly as tall as Ilmaire, her every movement snapped with energy. She had the same pale skin, the same elegant jaw and nose, the same fair hair kept in tight braids. Her long fur coat swept the ground, and the leather jerkin beneath it resembled a suit of armor.

This was Lady Ingrid Lysleva, Rielle assumed—Prince Ilmaire's twin sister. At twenty-one years old, Audric had told them, she was the youngest commander to ever lead the Borsvall army.

Ludivine bowed her head in greeting, her face troubled. *Something is preventing me from reading them.*

Rielle bristled at the smug hint of a smile Ingrid wore. "You have an interesting way of introducing yourself, whoever you are."

Audric gently touched Rielle's arm. "Lady Ingrid? I didn't know you would be joining us today."

Ingrid's smile hardened. "There are many things you don't know, Your Highness."

Then Ingrid bellowed furiously in the Borsvallic tongue.

Ludivine screamed "No!" and threw herself in front of Rielle.

A dozen soldiers in leather and furs jumped out of the bushes and down from the sea-worn statues adorning the half-collapsed temple roof, swarming to surround them. Swords and axes flashed.

"Ingrid, stop!" Ilmaire cried out, followed by several harsh Borsvallic commands.

But the soldiers weren't listening to him, and a horrible realization sank into Rielle's chest: these soldiers were loyal not to their prince, but to their commander.

Audric drew Illumenor, the blade so brilliant Rielle had to shield her eyes. A fierce wind gusted, sharp with windsinger magic, and knocked Rielle to the ground before she could turn on their attackers. Her head slammed hard against stone. Audric cried out in pain; Illumenor's light flickered out.

Rielle looked up, her vision wobbly. Another soldier grabbed Ludivine and wrenched her arms behind her back. When Rielle struggled to her feet, palms sparking angrily to life, mountain wind gathering fast around her fingers, Ingrid roared, "Stop right now, or I slit his throat!"

Rielle turned slowly, dread falling fast in her stomach.

Audric was on his knees, Ingrid standing beside him with his own sword at his throat and her hand tangled cruelly in his hair. Rielle met Audric's eyes; he shook his head as much as he could.

Soldiers pounced on Rielle, seized her arms, and pinned them at her sides.

Ingrid's smile was lupine. "Don't think of throwing that power of yours at us, *Sun Queen*, or I'll carve your lover to pieces before your eyes."

"Ingrid, stop this," Ilmaire said, his voice the only spot of calm in the tense ocean air. "This isn't you. This isn't us."

"This is who they've made us become," Ingrid argued, jerking her head in Rielle's direction. "Killing our sister. Ordaining some girl no one's ever heard of Sun Queen without consulting the holy leaders of any other country."

Fury boiled red in Rielle's heart. "How dare you. Soldiers from your kingdom attacked Audric months ago, and now you attack him again when he comes to you on an errand of friendship?" She stepped forward, dizzy with anger. "You are not worthy of touching him. Release him at once."

"Keep ordering me around, and I'll start a proper war right here, right now."

"You're already dangerously close to that, Lady Ingrid," Audric said, his voice tight. He tried to look left, but Ingrid pressed the blade closer. "Lu?"

"I'm here," came Ludivine's tearful voice from a few paces away. A soldier was binding her hands behind her back. Then he shoved a cloth sack over her head, and she let out a terrified cry.

"Lu?" Audric shouted, struggling in Ingrid's grip.

Ludivine choked out, "I'm all right. Please, Audric, don't anger them further. It's all right."

*Stay calm,* Ludivine instructed, her angelic voice much steadier. *Ilmaire is still our friend and ally.*

*Which is worth nothing to us, as his own soldiers are ignoring him,* Rielle seethed. *Take control of their minds. Make them release us.*

*I will not.*

*Ludivine...*

*No, Rielle. It isn't as dire as that yet. We can still win their friendship.*

Rielle's nails dug into her palms. *As soon as Audric is safe, I will burn Ilmaire and his sister, and their soldiers, and their entire rotten kingdom, to the ground.*

*You will not,* Ludivine said sternly. *This is exactly what Corien wants—for war to divide your countries so it will be easier for him to ruin you.*

"What's the meaning of this, Ilmaire?" Audric snapped. "We came here to help you!"

Ingrid spat on his face. "Fuck your help. We need none of it."

"A war will tear our nations apart. We must forget the old, bad blood between our countries and unite against whatever is killing our soldiers. And the storms that have ravaged your coasts cannot be a coincidence." His gaze flew to Rielle. "The prophecy—"

Ingrid kicked his spine, then pressed her mouth against his temple and smiled cruelly up at Rielle. "You should have thought about your precious prophecy," she snarled, "before you murdered my sister."

Audric's expression was so ferocious that Rielle hardly recognized him. "Commander Lysleva, Celdaria is not responsible for Princess Runa's death."

But before Ingrid could reply, one of the Borsvall soldiers let out a sharp cry, soon picked up by the others. Ludivine's captor released her roughly. She stumbled forward, catching herself hard on the rocks at her feet. Rielle hurried to her, helped her up, and then looked at the horizon, where the soldiers were pointing, their frantic voices overlapping and their faces drawn with sudden fear.

Abruptly, the anger clouding Rielle's vision fell away.

That line of black clouds at the horizon hadn't been clouds at all.

It was a tidal wave, rushing fast for the shore—so monstrously tall that it blacked out the sky. Even from this distance, Rielle could see that it would easily crest the mountains and destroy the capital in one fell blow.

Rielle's mind cleared, a slow tingle warming her body as she faced the sight of a disaster too mighty for anyone but her to prevent.

That is, if she cared to. And she wasn't sure that she did.

*Do it, now,* Ludivine urged her, her presence sharp and eager in Rielle's mind. *This is the perfect opportunity to win their allegiance.*

Then, distantly, curling and coy, another voice echoed Ludivine's: *Do it, now. This is the perfect opportunity to show them the power of the woman they've crossed.*

Ludivine's presence turned cold. Her deft fingers started pulling closed the doors of Rielle's mind.

But Rielle stiffened and held fast to the sly voice that so sweetly caressed her. *Where are you?*

Corien did not reply.

Ingrid roared at her soldiers in the Borsvallic tongue, silencing their panicked cries. Ilmaire hurried to her, his words swallowed by the wind. Ingrid glanced at Rielle, then down at Audric, whom she still held pinned by his own blade, then back at Rielle.

Scowling, she released Audric. Once he had risen to his feet, she thrust Illumenor toward him, refusing to meet his eyes.

Audric took it from her, his expression cold and hard, and came at once to Rielle.

She turned away from him. "Don't ask me to. I won't do it."

"This is why we came here," he insisted, coming around to face her. "We came to help them."

"That was before they attacked us and held a sword to your throat. Don't ask me to help the people who would have killed you."

*If you don't, any chance of friendship with Borsvall will be lost forever,* Ludivine said quickly.

Ilmaire approached cautiously. "Audric, I don't know how I can ever apologize to you for what's happened here today."

"You can't," Rielle spat, whirling on him. "If it weren't for Audric and Ludivine advising me against it, I would have already burned you and your sister to ashes."

"Please, Lady Rielle," he shouted, the storm's eerie light casting wan shadows across his skin. "The situation in my court is...complicated. But the plight of my people in this moment is simple." He faced her, his words thick with despair. His eyes traveled to the white city sitting high in the nearby mountains. The narrow ivory towers of the castle Tarkstorm, the city streets winding like bands of pearls through the mountains. "If you don't save them, they will die."

She turned away from him. If she looked for one more moment at his face, she would punch it. The sky opened and rain began to fall in gray sheets.

"If we leave them now, when we could have saved them," Audric said urgently, "it will surely start a war."

"They invited war when they attacked us," she replied. "They invited war when they threatened your life."

"And if you save their capital, they will have no choice but to accept our terms of peace." He cupped her face with his free hand. The rain plastered his dark curls to his forehead. "And accept you as the queen you are."

As she looked up at him, angry tears filled her eyes. She knew he was right, she *knew* it—and yet she imagined these people's bodies swept up by the water, bashed against the mountains until their skulls shattered. She imagined their grief when the wave crushed their city flat and drowned their families, and felt nothing but gladness at the thought.

But Audric was right, and if she turned away from this opportunity now, he would never forgive her for it.

She whistled for Atheria, and a few moments later, with a hawklike cry, the chavaile landed beside them and knelt at Rielle's feet.

Rielle stepped on Audric's clasped hands and clambered onto Atheria's back, and when she threw one last glance back at Ilmaire and Ingrid, she was gratified to see them cowed by the sight of her astride her godsbeast. How small they looked, and pathetic, their furs drenched.

She bit down on the terrible things she longed to say to them, turned to face the oncoming wave, and shouted for Atheria to fly.

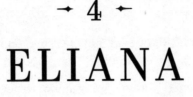

# ELIANA

> "Vintervok, the capital of Astavar, is a city well-guarded, its borders difficult to penetrate. It sits in a high valley between thickly forested mountains scattered through with glacial lakes. Nearby is Karajak Bay, its waters littered with rocks and ice for much of the year. In fact, this is the element that has made Astavar impossible to conquer. For years we have battered its doors, and yet they stand tall."
>
> —A report from Admiral Ravikant, commander of the imperial fleet, to His Majesty the Emperor of the Undying

The next morning, in the kings' council chambers, Eliana shifted uncomfortably in her chair and graced the polished table with a scowl.

"I hate this dress," she muttered.

Remy, in the chair beside her, watching the kings and the queen consort and the commander of the Astavari army file in with their advisers, trembled with excitement. Eliana wouldn't have been surprised if he'd actually started bouncing in his chair.

"You like dresses," he argued.

"I like other dresses. I hate *this* dress."

Hob, on Remy's other side, glanced over. "Why? It's a nice dress."

"It's too fine for me." She gestured at the intricate embroidery on the bodice, the soft velvet folds of the satin-trimmed indigo skirt. "It's too fussy."

"It's fit for a queen," Hob pointed out.

"I'm no queen."

"Of course you are," Remy said, now perched on the edge of his chair. "You're the Sun Queen."

Eliana barely refrained from snapping at him to never call her that again. The memory of Navi's deranged screams from the previous night lingered alongside the echoes of her nightmare. And the strength of Remy's faith in the destiny Simon had prescribed for her—the ancient, fervent heft of that destiny; the centuries of murmured prayers, including her own—left her feeling breathless, nauseated.

Cornered.

Not to mention starkly aware of how her skull still throbbed from Navi's attack. She had styled her hair to hide the scabbing cut, which would ensure that intrusive rebel captains didn't pester her with questions about it. But hiding the wound did nothing to assuage her own relentless, burrowing worry that this—this fragility, this low, humming presence of pain—was the beginning of a horrible new reality.

The royal secretary rapped his gavel against the table, making Eliana jump.

"This council meeting is now in session," he announced, and then put his pen to paper to begin recording.

King Tavik, tall and thin, with golden-brown skin and graying black hair, smiled warmly at those gathered—though the shadows beneath his eyes and the tired lines around his mouth belied his true state of mind. He glanced at Eliana's neck, where the bruises from Navi's hands marked her skin.

She did not drop her gaze, but she regretted not wearing a scarf. Everyone present knew what had transpired the night before; it would have been kind to spare them the reminder.

A gentler person, perhaps, would have remembered that.

She swallowed against the tightness in her throat, keeping her expression neutral.

"Good morning, everyone," King Tavik began. "I hope you don't mind if I get straight to the point. As you'll recall, the intelligence brought to us by Princess Navana warned of a second, smaller Empire fleet, which planned to launch from the northwestern coast of Ventera and strike us on our southern border, near the mouth of the Ulioqua River. You'll be pleased to learn that our defenses have easily dispatched said fleet, sinking seven warships and sending the remaining four retreating back to Ventera."

Murmurs of celebration drifted around the table. One of the queen consort's advisers clapped Commander Lianti Haakorat on the back. He smiled tightly, his gaze cutting to Remy.

Eliana bristled at the annoyed expression on the commander's face. She fisted her hands in her lap.

Simon sat back in his chair and propped one long leg atop the other. "That was lucky."

King Eri frowned. He sat to the left of his husband, shorter and more muscular, with pale skin and dark-brown hair. "Did you wish to add something, Simon?"

"How fortunate," Simon said, "that you were able to dispatch an entire armada of Empire ships in the span of, what, two days?"

"Navi's intelligence was accurate and thorough," King Eri replied, a flicker of sadness in his voice. "We were fortunate, yes, but also well prepared."

Simon shook his head. "It was far too brief and bloodless a conflict. They are testing you, lulling you into a false sense of security."

Lady Ama, the queen consort, folded her hands atop the table. "To what end, Captain?"

Eliana could hardly look at Lady Ama. Her face was too similar to Navi's—elegant and finely boned, with wide hazel eyes, warm brown skin, and a full, expressive mouth. Instead Eliana glanced around the table, reading the expressions of the gathered officials as Simon spoke. The secretary scribbled furiously, his pen flying. Several other advisers took notes; others stood at the room's perimeter, sifting through papers.

Commander Haakorat was rigid in his chair. His gaze flitted irritably to Remy, to Hob, to Remy again. When he looked at Eliana, she held his gaze, defiant, until Hob cleared his throat and broke her attention.

"To keep you distracted," Simon answered Lady Ama. "To keep your forces spread thin. To catch you off guard." He shrugged. "It could be any number of things, but to assume that this latest victory was anything but a calculated loss on the part of the Empire is a mistake."

The queen consort's mouth quirked. "Yes, and God forbid we take a moment to celebrate even that."

Eliana glanced once more at Commander Haakorat. The man seemed increasingly agitated—shifting in his chair, drumming his fingers against the table.

One of his advisers hurried over. "Shall I bring you a glass of water, my lord?"

"No," he muttered, glaring at Remy. "I need no water."

"Even if you're right," King Tavik was saying, "autumn is coming, with winter fast on its heels. The ice should protect us from further onslaught, at least until the spring thaws. We'll spend the next few months drilling our troops, replenishing our stores—"

Simon scoffed.

King Eri said sharply, "Right hand of the Prophet you may be, Captain, but in this palace, you are a guest. You will demonstrate the proper respect, or you will no longer be welcome at these meetings."

Simon inclined his head. "I must point out that there is a danger no one here has yet addressed, not once in the nine days since we arrived."

"And what is that?" asked King Eri.

"The Kaavalan Passage."

Light laughter scattered across the table.

"Our scout ships have reported back that the passage is frozen solid," Lady Ama pointed out. "The ice is thick, and it will only get thicker during the coming months. Ships can't break through thousands of miles of icebergs the size of palaces, Captain. Not even Empire ships."

"They won't need ships," Simon argued.

"Ground forces?" King Tavik did nothing to hide his incredulity. "Simon, not even adatrox can survive temperatures that frigid."

"Can't they?"

Commander Haakorat slammed his hands on the table, making several people jump.

"Forgive me, my kings, my lady," he snapped, "but does anyone else here care that we have a *child* in our midst?"

Eliana sat back, smiling. Suddenly all her nervous energy had a target. Her mind flushed hot and clear. "I was wondering when you would say something, Commander. I've been watching you stew and wagering with myself how long it would take for that vein in your forehead to burst."

"I'm overjoyed that I can provide entertainment for you, Lady Eliana," said the commander, "but this is not a joke. My kings, not two weeks ago, these people were completely unknown to us. Is it wise to speak of such sensitive matters in front of them? Especially when one is a child, likely to spill secrets whenever it suits him?"

Remy surged to his feet, face screwed up with indignation. "Just because I'm a child doesn't mean I can't keep secrets!"

Hob touched Remy's shoulder and gently directed him back to his seat. "You needn't worry about Remy, Commander. I'd wager he has as stout a heart as anyone seated here, if not more so."

"Ah. The word of yet another Venteran stranger." Commander Haakorat flung his hand at Hob. "Truly, I am reassured."

Simon's voice held a dangerous edge. "I've vouched for them. And my word is as good as the Prophet's. Is that not enough?"

"Not to mention," Eliana bit out, "that, were it not for me, Commander, your miserable ass would be half-eaten by crawlers and frozen at the bottom of the sea by now. If that isn't enough to prove my worth and loyalty to you, please do let me know, and the next time your country is invaded, I'll be sure to sit back and put my feet up rather than fly to your rescue." She rose to her feet. "If you'll excuse me."

In the hallway, she brushed past the guards flanking the council chamber doors and stormed east in the direction of her rooms.

Behind her, quick footsteps followed.

"We need to leave," murmured Simon, catching up with her. "As soon as possible."

His words were hardly a surprise, but Eliana nevertheless felt a swell of dread to hear them. Leave. Leave and go *where*, and do *what*?

"I'm not going anywhere until Navi is healed," she said.

"Navi won't be healed," came his blunt reply. "We thought the Fidelia physicians hadn't begun the transformation procedures. We were obviously wrong. Her body has been mutated, forever changed. There is no cure." His voice softened. "It would be better for you, and for Remy, if we were gone by the time she gets worse."

Eliana's eyes filled with tears. Unable to speak, she stared straight ahead, imagining she could use her eyes to drill holes in the floor.

They walked in silence for another few moments before Simon spoke again. "Have you read the books I retrieved for you?"

"Some," she replied, lifting her chin.

"But not all?"

"No."

Simon blew out a sharp breath. "Have you at least read the passages I marked?"

"Some."

"But not all?"

Eliana smiled to herself. "You sound irritated."

Simon cut in front of her, forcing her to stop walking. "And what of your power?" he asked, searching her face. "Has it surfaced again, even for the slightest instant? How are you feeling?"

"I don't know, and no, and I was feeling much better before this interrogation began."

She would not allow herself to quail, no matter how intensely he looked at her, no matter how heated his gaze. They hadn't yet spoken of the night she'd awoken after the battle—his hands reverently touching her face, his soft pledge of loyalty.

How close she had come to joining him in his bed.

They hadn't spoken of it, and she preferred it that way, and would maintain the silence for as long as she could.

She had been full of grief that night, exhausted and lonely. She had craved the comfort of a lover's hands—even if those hands were scarred, cruel, and murderous.

Never again.

At last, Simon looked away, his mouth twisting. "We have so much work to do. I thought that after the battle, after your storm, that your power would have fully awakened, and we could proceed to refine it."

Eliana stepped past him. "I'm terribly sorry to have disappointed you."

Simon hurried after her. "The disdain you hold for me, while entirely charming, is neither shocking nor productive."

"You can't imagine how little I care about your assessment of my disdain."

Simon laughed as they rounded the corner into the narrow hallway that led to their rooms. "My imagination is boundless, in fact."

His words plucked a taut wire in her belly, sending a shiver of heat down her arms. She ignored it. "I need to practice using my power, isn't that correct?"

"Yes, of course, that's what I've been trying to urge you toward."

"Surely, then, it is safer for me to do that here in Vintervok—under the protection of the kings' army, with the entire catalog of the royal libraries at my disposal, in a kingdom untouched by the Empire—rather than on the road with only you for company."

Simon exhaled sharply. "Eliana…" he said as if to begin some fresh new diatribe, but then he paused, and the sound of his voice saying her name lingered in the air like the last chords of a song.

Desperate to shake it from her ears, Eliana whirled to face him. "You claim I am your queen."

Simon stopped. "Yes."

"And you are a soldier. My adviser, and my protector."

"Yes," Simon answered quietly. "Always, Eliana."

"Then advise me, as you have done, and protect me, as you will no doubt continue to do—at least until I have no further use for you—and until then, get out of my way."

With that, she pushed past him and left him standing alone in the shadowed hall.

—◆◆—

That night, Eliana sat at the desk in her room, unable to sleep, with a pile of ancient books lying open before her.

She glared at the nearest page of tiny text, trying for the fifth time to read the opening paragraph of the chapter Simon had marked for her:

> *Parents who are curious about a child's elemental leanings may begin lessons with the child, under the guidance of temple acolytes, as early as the Church deems appropriate. Every child's capabilities are, of course, unique. One child may be capable of accessing the empirium as early as the age of eight (though this is rare, and such tutelage should only occur under strict Church guidance). Another child, even one in the same family, may not do so until some years later, or may never exhibit elemental powers whatsoever. A young windsinger from the Mazabat capital of Quelbani, for example, was not able to access the empirium, and therefore use her God-given power, until the age of seventeen—*

With a muttered curse, Eliana slammed the book shut. Dust puffed into her face, and she sneezed and cursed again, more loudly, and kicked the nearest leg of the desk.

"I know a way to save Navi," came a voice from just behind her.

Eliana whirled, hand flying to Arabeth at her hip before her mind caught up with the truth.

She glared up at Zahra's drifting dark form, the wraith's inscrutable face hovering some four feet above Eliana's own. Zahra's body shifted from one moment to the next—first a shapeless cloud; then the echo of the stately, eight-foot-tall angel she had once been, magnificent wings of light and shadow fanning out from her back; then flickering into nothingness.

"Also," Zahra continued, her sonorous voice a balm to Eliana's tired mind, "I should tell you that Simon is, as we speak, storming about the palace in a remarkable temper. Well done, there. I heartily enjoy watching him fume."

"Really, Zahra," Eliana scolded, "you've got to stop drifting in and out of rooms just because you can. It isn't polite."

"Coming from you, a paragon of manners and etiquette, that means almost nothing."

Eliana smiled, so grateful for the interruption that at first the wraith's words didn't truly register. Then she stood, her heart pounding. "Wait. Did you say you know a way to save Navi?"

Zahra looked inordinately pleased. She pushed a ghostly bundle of her long, white hair over her shoulder. "I do. I know of a place that will, in all likelihood, have at least a small supply of the crawler antidote."

"In all likelihood."

"I must admit the possibility that I am wrong. Though I don't believe I am."

"Is it far?"

"Not so very far, no."

"Is it dangerous there?"

"Extremely. In fact, my queen, it is with great reluctance that I speak to you of this now, for it is not a place I wish you to visit. But..." Zahra drifted closer, reaching for Eliana's shoulder. The wraith's touch was a gentle breeze, chilled and silken. "I know she is dear to you, my queen, and that her condition pains you."

"Thank you." Eliana returned Zahra's touch as best she could—a brush of her hand against Zahra's arm, her fingers dipping into icy water, smooth as honey. "How long will it take us, to travel to this place?"

"A few hours. We will need to move carefully."

"What is it called?"

"In Astavari, it is called Annerkilak. In the common tongue, it is referred to as the Nest. One of the most dangerous underground markets in the world, and one of the few that deal in stolen angelic goods."

Eliana nodded. "Such as the crawler antidote."

"And as you can imagine, such a place is heavily guarded, and not only by humans. By wraiths as well. A contingent of them, loyal to no one but themselves—not Red Crown, not the Emperor. They oversee everything within the market's borders. Only those they wish to find the Nest are able to. It is a game for them, making trades and bargains, tormenting thieves, reveling in riches. A distraction from their misery."

Eliana turned away to stand before the windows. Beyond them, the night sky stretched across the snow-capped mountains. Morning was beginning to touch the far eastern sky.

"Do the kings know about this place?" she asked after a long moment.

"Yes. It is a difficult balance they must strike—allowing the Nest to exist and its wraiths to play as they will, but preventing it from rising up and swallowing the city whole. A place like the Nest is inevitable in such a world as ours, and the kings have bigger battles to wage."

"And Simon? Does he know?"

"As far as I can tell, no," Zahra said archly. "Though, as you know, my queen, my ability to read that horrible, clawed-up mind of his is less than reliable." She paused, scowling. "I hope you won't ask me to tell him, or ask him to join us."

"On the contrary. If we go there—*when* we go there—we will leave him here to stew and wonder where we've gone."

Zahra's words stretched around a dark rib of a smile. "A most excellent plan, my queen."

"You'll hide me from him? Ensure his ignorance?"

"He will not be able to follow us, my queen. I can promise you that. But there is something I must tell you."

Hearing a note of hesitation in Zahra's voice, Eliana turned, eyes narrowed. "I'm sensing I won't like this next bit."

"You sense correctly. You see, my queen, I refuse to take you to the Nest until I know you can protect yourself."

Eliana raised her eyebrows. "Have I not proven that a dozen times over by now?"

"That was before." Zahra's bottomless dark gaze shifted to Eliana's scalp, where the wound from Navi's attack throbbed faintly beneath her hair. "You are no longer the Dread of Orline. You are breakable. And my ability to protect you goes only as far as my unpredictable strength. Particularly as I will be expending considerable effort to mask our movements, both from Simon and from the wraiths who live in the Nest."

Eliana opened her mouth to protest, but Zahra drifted lower to meet her eyes.

"No arguments, my queen," Zahra said. "This is not a point on which I will capitulate. Your safety is paramount, and now you are compromised."

"Can't you retrieve the antidote yourself?" Eliana waved her hand. "Possess a body, put it through the motions of a theft?"

"You know it is difficult for me to do that. I would not be able to successfully control a body long enough to steal from this place. And, besides, I would be found the moment I attempted it. The Nest wraiths are especially sensitive to the presence of those like them. I will accompany you to protect you, but I must remain as discreet as possible to avoid detection."

Eliana bit down on the first five responses that came to her mind. "Well, then. What must I do to pass this test you've set for me?"

"As much as it pains me to say so, you will do as Simon has instructed you," Zahra replied. "You will read, and you will practice, and you will learn."

There again came that hard knot in Eliana's throat, a constant companion in recent days.

"You want me to develop my power," she said, her voice catching on spikes of anger. "Just as he does. You want to make me into something I'm not."

"I want you to understand who and what you really are," Zahra countered. "I want to protect you against yourself and prevent the power with which you were born from consuming you, as it did your mother."

The unexpected mention of the Blood Queen jolted Eliana like a sharp blast of cold. "And if I refuse?"

Zahra's stare was pitiless. "Then I will not take you to the Nest and to the antidote. And, very soon, Navi will die."

# RIELLE

*"When the wave came for our city, brother, Lady Rielle tore through the skies for it. She faced the fury of our doom with no fear in her heart, her body burning gold as the sun, her godsbeast blazing with fire. I knew then that the Celdarian Church had been right to appoint this girl Sun Queen. Once, my nightly prayers were for the saints. Now, they are for Lady Rielle. May God protect her from all evil."*

—Journal of Reynar Pollari, Grand Magister of the House of Night in Styrdalleen, capital of Borsvall

A s Rielle tore across the sky, the howling wind and the roar of the approaching water soon swallowed her every thought but one.

*Stop the wave.*

The faster Atheria flew, the more eagerly Rielle's power licked along her veins, hungry and seeking. It had been restrained unfairly in the village while Ingrid's soldiers had attacked her beloved ones. It had been aching to leap to their aid, to destroy, and now it flared alive like flames across an oil-soaked field. Rain lashed her body in cold sheets. The force of the wave, and the swirling storm above, sucked the air from her lungs.

But none of that mattered, not with this wall of water crashing toward her, and her power leaping to life at her fingertips, and the beach below her—the ravaged, white-pebbled beach, crowded with the debris of wrecked ships. And the roads above the beach, soaked and flooded, and the people running frantically up the sea-ravaged city streets toward the castle, desperate for higher ground.

She couldn't resist. She directed Atheria along the winding beachside roads and smiled into her rain-soaked mane as she heard the cries of those below. They marveled at her and her godsbeast, stopping to stare and wave and shout, even with death fast approaching them.

*As it should be,* Corien murmured, his voice so faint in her mind that it could have been a mere silken thread dragged unsteadily along the back of her neck.

Rielle shivered, and pushed Atheria out to sea.

The wave groaned as it moved, sucking greedily at everything it touched—the shore, the mountains bordering the water, the air scraping against Rielle's cheeks. She looked down once more, her eyes watering from the wind, and saw crowds gathering at the seawalls to watch her, heard their faint screams of terror.

Bitter and horrible, to have to save them—these barbarians, these *fools*. She could turn around, force Audric and Ludivine to mount Atheria, and take them home. If Ludivine tried to stop her, she would injure her just badly enough that her mind-speak would be useless and ask forgiveness later.

And if war broke out because of her actions, Rielle would simply lead the army that had once belonged to her father into Borsvall's ruined cities and bring her surviving enemies to their knees.

But she could not ignore Audric's words: *If you save their capital, they will have no choice but to accept our terms of peace.*

She curled her fingers more tightly in Atheria's mane.

She hoped Audric was right.

The wave was upon them, a churning black mountain of spray and foam and furious energy. With a twinge of fear, Rielle recalled the avalanche she had faced in her first trial. The wave's rage was that of a thousand avalanches. It seethed, rumbling inexorably closer, consuming all other sounds—her own gasping breaths, the heavy beat of Atheria's wings. Rielle drove Atheria as close to the wave as she dared, the chavaile's great gray body trembling as her drenched wings desperately fought the wind.

Rielle closed her eyes and let her power bloom. *Come to me*, she thought, letting her mind unfocus, imagining her body expanding out past its fragile lines and curves to the air beyond. The wind whipped water against her skin; salt burned her eyes.

But she was immense. She was of the wave and wind, and yet she was more than either of them, and she could control them as she pleased, and she *would* control them. She would make them her own. She sensed their energy, their sheer unthinking force, like the silent pull of desire, tightening her skin.

*I do not break or bend*, she prayed, the memory of Tal's voice accompanying her, guiding her through her prayers. Her five-year-old self, safe in his lap. His hands helping hers turn pages in *The Book of the Saints*.

*I cannot be silenced.* She slowly opened her eyes. The world was outlined in infinitesimal grains of gold. The wave was full of them, spinning ferociously bright. They illuminated the howling air like stars. Rielle reached out with her mind, embracing every scrap of wind she could find. Eager gusts crowded at her fingertips.

She inhaled, and the air bent and bowed, echoing her lungs. *I am everywhere.*

Then she snapped open her eyes and thrust out her rigid palms.

The molten air rippled, exploding out from her hands to slam against the wave and lock into place like a dam. Water crashed against a thousand interconnected nets of gold. A blast of wind shot back from the impact, nearly knocking her off Atheria. But the chavaile bowed her head against the trembling force of the collision, pumped her wings and legs hard, and kept them both steady in the air.

Rielle gritted her teeth and held fast, fighting the urge to drop her arms and let the wave shatter. Despite the searing connection of her bones to her blood to the shimmering world beyond her fingertips, her shifting vision darkened; her muscles screamed in protest. Their message was plain: she was one mere girl, and this wave was a force unconquerable.

*No*, she told her aching body. *I am a force unconquerable.*

The gilded wall rippled, shifting—first invisible, then an array of countless shimmering gold specks, then invisible again. The wave spun, slid back into the ocean, then crashed forward again, smaller now.

"Gently," she whispered over and over, her body trembling. "Down, down, down." She doubted the words helped the water settle any faster, but if she didn't speak, she would collapse. Hearing the hollow sound of her own voice reminded her of the world beyond this wall and this wave—the people below her whose lives depended on her strength.

Audric and Ludivine, watching from the hills.

Ilmaire and Ingrid, hopefully brought to their knees by the magnificence of her power.

Her eyelids drooped, her vision flickering. She was not a girl shivering with rain and anger—no, she was a conduit. The world passed through her body, and by doing so, it grew sharper, bolder. It listened to her will and obeyed. She breathed, and it breathed along with her. She shook, then held fast; so too did the wall of her creation. She moved her fingers, like stroking the spine of an upset hound, and watched the water diminish.

At last, when the wave had flattened and the sea calmed, debris strewn across the shores and the call of gulls returning tentatively to the air, Rielle lowered her aching arms. The movement made her cry out, her muscles stiff and her blood rushing painfully back down to her fingers. She longed to collapse against Atheria's neck and let the godsbeast take her to some quiet mountaintop cave, as she had done that first day when she had saved Rielle from death, and wrap her in the nest of her wings.

But instead she whispered into Atheria's sea-soaked mane, "Take me to Audric, my dear."

Atheria obeyed, diving back down toward the city. Rielle watched through watering eyes as the drenched streets neared. Buildings of white stone tucked into the mountains; sharp, narrow towers piercing low clouds; rooftop gardens, elaborate and green in the diminishing mist; trees pelted flat by wind and rain. The sky was dark, and lanterns flickered tentatively to life throughout the city. Hours had passed, Rielle realized with a dim note of alarm. The edges of her body returned to her—her fingers wind-chapped and swollen, her mouth parched and sour.

They broke through a mist of cloud and approached a wide, flat stone plaza near what appeared to be the castle's main gates. Hundreds of people had gathered, crammed into every spare inch of space. They followed Atheria's progress, and as she descended, the crowd's wild roar grew deafening.

But Rielle, shivering with cold, could only concentrate on one thing—Audric hurrying toward her, and Ludivine just behind him. A group of uniformed soldiers followed them, including Prince Ilmaire and Commander Ingrid.

Rielle tightened her raw, aching fingers in the tangles of Atheria's mane. "If they try to hurt us again, we will show them no mercy."

Atheria whickered doubtfully, and the moment her hooves touched stone, the crowd pressing close around them, Rielle dismounted and dropped unsteadily to the ground. Ingrid's soldiers directed the crowd away from her, giving her and Atheria room, and as Prince Ilmaire approached, Rielle lifted her chin and prepared a cutting remark that she hoped would erase the smile from his face.

But she did not have the chance to so much as say his name.

Before she could, he knelt before her, bowing his head, and the others around him followed suit—the royal guard, the soldiers who had threatened them in the village hills, a group of people in elaborate robes whom Rielle assumed were Borsvall's Grand Magisters.

Last to bow was Commander Ingrid, with a murderous glare—but bow she did, as the gathered crowd cheered in response. They flung their sodden scarves and hair ribbons upon the plaza's stone. Along the rooftops surrounding the plaza, spilling out of windows and onto terraces, they stamped their feet and waved their arms, reaching for Rielle as if desperate to win even a glance from her.

Rielle turned to Audric and found him smiling down at her. Only at the sight of his face did she realize how exhausted she was, how close to collapsing. She had stopped a tidal wave in its tracks. She had tamed the sea.

She laughed a little, breathless, and when Audric and Ludivine moved to kneel like the others, she shook her head and took their hands in hers.

"Not you," she said. "Never you."

Then, with Audric and Ludivine at her side, her fingers laced through their own, Rielle lifted her arms to the sky and listened with satisfaction as the crowd's cries of adulation shook the stone beneath her feet.

—◆—

Rielle dreamed of waves as big as the world—endless waves, with voices that yawned and wailed.

She walked through them easily, a child splashing through puddles. They subsided at her touch. She dwarfed them. She towered over the world. She held it, curious, in her palm.

Then Ludivine's voice—soft, regretful—coaxed her awake, back to the spacious apartment to which Ilmaire had escorted them hours before. They had bathed and rested, all of them sprawled together in the apartment's largest bed, and now Ludivine was speaking, brushing Rielle's damp hair back from her face.

*We must go quickly*, she said. *We cannot linger here. I've had time to read the air while you slept, and now I understand.*

*Go?* Rielle raised herself up, rubbing her eyes. *Go where?*

*Ilmaire's coming, and Ingrid, and an escort of guards.*

Rielle tensed. "Audric," she said, shaking him gently. "Wake up."

*There's no need to fear them. You've won their loyalty.* Ludivine paused. *Well. Truthfully, Ingrid's is still to be won. But she won't make another move against us. Not for now. But, Rielle, the Gate...* Ludivine's fear crowded the edges of Rielle's mind like a new, gathering storm. *That wave, it was of the Gate. And more waves will come, more storms, as each day passes.*

A slow-crawling chill pushed Rielle fully awake. *What do you mean?*

"Rielle?" Audric murmured, voice hoarse from sleep. "What is it?"

*I will tell you more,* said Ludivine, *and Audric as well, once we're alone. But for now—we need a ship. Their fastest ship.*

Rielle touched Audric's arm. "Lu says Ilmaire is coming, and Ingrid too. They'll be here soon." *But Tal, Queen Genoveve, everyone at home, they'll be worried, they'll want us home at once.*

*They will have to wait,* Ludivine said firmly. *We must visit the Gate as soon as possible and assess the damage my kindred have done to it. Before it's too late. Before anything more disastrous happens.*

Rielle swallowed with difficulty. *Before more angels escape?*

*We cannot delay* was Ludivine's quiet reply.

Then, a knock on the door. A guard announcing the arrival of Prince Ilmaire and Commander Ingrid.

Rielle stood, wincing at the stiffness of her body. Still sluggish from the poppy tea Ilmaire's servants had offered to soothe her abused muscles, she nevertheless managed an expression of supreme disdain as Ilmaire entered the room, Ingrid and four guards just behind him.

"Prince Audric, Lady Rielle, Lady Ludivine." Ilmaire smiled widely, his eyes bright and the color high in his cheeks. "I hope you're feeling refreshed after a few hours' rest."

Beside him, Ingrid's shoulders sat tensely, her jaw square.

Audric's anger had always been a subtle thing, tightly controlled, but Rielle heard it thrum in his voice nevertheless. "Your servants," he said, his eyes snapping dark fire, "are to be commended for their hospitality and care."

Ilmaire seemed oblivious to the dangerous edge in Audric's voice. "I don't know what to say. I feel as if I've wandered into a tale of the First Age, when the magic of the empirium burned brightly in all things."

"This is not a children's tale, Ilmaire," Ingrid muttered, with the air of someone who had said that very thing countless times before. "This is reality."

"It is not a reality I've ever known." Ilmaire looked to Rielle, wonder soft on his face. "Lady Rielle, is there any limit to this power you have?"

"If there were," said Rielle, "I certainly wouldn't tell you about it."

Ingrid's mouth thinned, but before she could reply, Audric stepped forward. "We must speak of what happened yesterday."

At last, Ilmaire's expression dimmed. "I know. It was a rash decision, and an abominable one, made by people who have been frightened by what our kingdom has suffered in recent weeks and months, and have allowed that fear to rule their minds."

He didn't look at Ingrid as he spoke, but a rope of tension pulled tight between them. Rielle braced herself, preparing for it to break.

But a beat of silence passed, and then another. "I hope," Ilmaire said, "that you'll allow us a second chance."

"You attacked us," Rielle said. "We'd done nothing to you."

*Don't do this*, Ludivine admonished. *We have more important things to address.*

Rielle ignored her, glaring at each of the royal siblings in turn. Ilmaire met her gaze, his own steady and sad, but Ingrid looked away, her sharp, pale cheeks coloring though her mouth remained frozen in a scowl.

"Is that what the mighty nation of Borsvall stands for?" Rielle continued. "Lashing out at innocent visitors when you feel frightened? No wonder your kingdom's in such a state. You're all blindingly stupid."

Audric said quietly, "Rielle, this isn't helping anyone."

"I don't care." Rielle walked to the windows and looked out at the sunrise. The city was a wash of pink light and white snow, tiny lights quivering along the winding streets. "I almost wish you *had* done something to us. Merovec Sauvillier would have lost his mind with wrath if you'd hurt Ludivine." She tossed a cruel little grin over her shoulder. "The Shield of the North would have come for you in the night and killed everything you love."

Ingrid stood stiffly at her brother's side. "I am quickly losing any scrap of patience I might have had."

"Stop this." Audric stepped between Ingrid and Rielle, blocking their view of each other. "If we are to move forward from this moment with any hope for peace, we must truly strive for it and not merely pretend understanding." He paused. "And while we have much left to discuss about how our two nations will begin working toward friendship, I have one request I must make of you immediately."

Rielle frowned, startled. *What is he doing?*

*I told him we must travel to the Gate,* Ludivine replied.

That startled Rielle, as though she had stumbled over a step she hadn't realized existed. *You speak to his mind as you do to mine?*

*Not as often. And not as easily. But when I must, I do.*

Rielle folded her arms over her chest. Crossly, she thought, *Why did you speak to him just now?*

Ludivine's reply was gentle. *Because you are still too angry to be trusted with diplomatic relations.*

An obvious truth, but Rielle still bristled to hear it.

*Oh, Rielle.* Ludivine's surprise moved gently. *You're jealous that I would speak to him in that way. In our special way.*

*I'm not,* Rielle lied—knowing Ludivine could sense the lie nevertheless.

*You are, and I adore you for it.* The faint sensation of Ludivine kissing her cheek floated through her thoughts, a cottonseed on the wind. *My darling one.*

"We need a ship," Audric said. "Your fastest ship, and manned by sailors you would trust with your most sensitive missions. You are welcome to accompany us, if you wish it, but we must leave soon. At dawn, if possible."

Ilmaire looked surprised. "Why?"

"My Magisterial Council has reason to believe that the Gate has weakened," Audric continued, glancing at Ludivine, "and that it is the cause of several strange occurrences throughout the world—the out-of-season storms that have damaged coastal cities in Meridian, Ventera, and Astavar. The months-long drought in the Vespers. And," Audric added, "the storms that have ravaged your own country."

Silence filled the room. Outside on the terrace, Atheria echoed a bird's cry with her own chirruping neigh.

"How can your magisters possibly know if the Gate is weakening?" Ingrid asked, her voice sounding smaller and less cutting than it had only moments before.

"Magisters Saksa and Pollari and I were discussing this possibility days ago, in fact," said Ilmaire, the light returning to his eyes. Rielle recognized that look. It was one Audric wore when lecturing her and Ludivine on some obscure piece of knowledge obtained during his hours in the library.

"The three of you see catastrophe in a single fallen tree," Ingrid snapped at Ilmaire. "You long for it. You crave it."

"No harm can come from visiting the Gate," Ludivine pointed out. "If it stands strong, then it stands strong, and we dismiss the waves, the droughts, the storms, as unfortunate but meaningless."

Ilmaire watched her quietly. "And if it doesn't stand strong?"

The answer was one Rielle had been considering for weeks, since the days before King Bastien's funeral: *then I must remake it.*

"Then, as the two nations closest to the Sunderlands," Audric replied, "it will be even more important for Celdaria and Borsvall to unite in peace."

Ilmaire nodded, rising to his feet. "The *Kaalvitsi* can make the trip in a little over a week, given good winds."

"Why one of our ships?" Ingrid gestured irritably at the terrace. "Can't you ride your godsbeast out to the Sunderlands?"

"We could, yes," Rielle replied at once, "but I would prefer to travel in luxury, as it will take some time for my body to recover after saving your city from total destruction."

"I will prepare the *Kaalvitsi*," Ilmaire said before Ingrid could reply. Rielle thought she even saw him stifle a smile. "I would ask my father to join us, but as you know, he has taken ill in recent years and is not strong enough to make the trip. My sister and I will accompany you instead. While on board, you will enjoy every comfort we can provide."

"We're grateful, Ilmaire," Audric said with a small smile. "Thank you."

"While you prepare our ship," Rielle added, enjoying the mutinous expression on Ingrid's face and unable to resist, "I wonder if I might meet with your Magisterial Council. I understand they were perturbed to learn of my anointing—thinking, perhaps, that I did not deserve my title of Sun Queen, or that I was given it unfairly."

"Lady Rielle," Ilmaire said quickly, "I don't think anyone who witnessed what you achieved yesterday has any doubt that you are indeed the Sun Queen."

"Nevertheless, I would very much like to meet with them. To reassure them, and give them a chance to apologize for any part they may have played in the attack on Audric months ago and the attack on us only yesterday." She smiled sweetly at Ingrid. "Surely you can understand how important that is to me."

Ingrid opened her mouth to reply, but Ilmaire stopped her with a hand on her arm—a hand she abruptly shook off.

"Certainly, Lady Rielle," he said. "I will see to it at once."

She inclined her head. "I'm grateful."

*Was that necessary?* Ludivine asked wryly.

And then came an echo—faint with fatigue, delighted, and only for her: *Well done, Rielle.*

Rielle stiffened, an icy heat gliding up her torso.

Ludivine noticed at once. *What is it?*

*Nothing,* Rielle lied—and she knew the moment the words formed that Ludivine could not sense the lie. That something distant and sly was shielding her from it.

And Rielle found that she was glad for it, and relieved.

She squeezed Ludivine's hand, reassuring her. *It was only a small chill.*

# ⤙ 6 ⤚

# ELIANA

*"My brothers and sisters, my friends and compatriots, do not let these humans deceive you! They promise peace, but what they want is our destruction. You can feel it in their minds as well as I can, but you have let your desperation for peace, your exhaustion, get the better of you. I say to you now: Reach inside your ancient minds for the strength I know you possess. I say to you now: Stand with me, here on these icy shores, and fight for our homeland! This is our world! We were born to it, and we will not let these humans, with their weak minds and feeble hearts, send us running like cowards into the darkness!"*

—A speech delivered by the angel Kalmaroth
to angelic forces at the Battle of the Black Stars

Below the palace of Dyrefal and the dark-cobbled streets of Vintervok, buried far below the snow-dusted mountains, was a world of stone and shivering shadows.

As Zahra escorted her through the soaring obsidian halls, Eliana marveled. Each new chamber was different from the last—some vast and lofty, lined with rows of pale-gray stone arches boasting carvings of the saints at war. Others were narrow and still and padded with shelves of books, as if the mountains themselves were crowding down close to hear the pages whisper secrets.

Slender torches mounted to the walls in elaborate iron casings threw shifting shapes across every surface, creating the illusion that Eliana was traveling beneath the canopy of a forest shaken by soft winds. Enormous tapestries decorated the walls, warming the cold stone passages with depictions of Saint Tameryn, daggers in her hands and shadows writhing in her curls. Prayer smoke sweetened the thick air. Scholars in blue-and-black robes conversed in low tones; commoners come down below the mountain to pray knelt before gleaming black statues of Saint Tameryn in combat, in meditation, in repose.

There were no idols of the Emperor here, as had dotted the streets of Orline—no razed temples, no shattered statues.

This was a world untouched by the Empire, and Eliana did not know how to exist inside it.

She averted her eyes from Saint Tameryn's blank stares and placed her right hand on Arabeth at her hip to remind herself of who she was. She was not a coward, no matter what insinuations blazed in Simon's eyes. Nor was she a queen, the lost heir to a dead kingdom.

She was Eliana Ferracora. Daughter of Rozen and Ioseph. Sister to Remy.

She was the Dread of Orline.

Her strength lay not in her blood and not in magic but in her muscle, in the agile way her feet lit upon the ground, in her skill with her blades.

She said it ten times, like working her way through her father's prayer beads—words she didn't really believe, but that brought her comfort nonetheless. Then she imagined her doubt as a small creature sniveling in a damp room, and closed it away behind an iron door.

She would have to ignore her doubt, swallow her resistance to the idea of magic in her blood. If she wanted to save Navi, she would have to satisfy Zahra. She would have to summon her power again, just as she had on the beach at Karajak Bay. Prove herself capable of wielding it, deft and deliberate, in defense of herself.

Somehow, she would have to control it, and be able to do so with ease and at will.

The thought left her stomach in knots.

"Remember, stay in my wake," Zahra murmured, drifting just ahead of her. "Keep your voice low, and don't fall behind. We must hurry. If my strength fails me, and you are left to fend for yourself without me to shield you from sight—"

"Fend for myself against these people whose home I saved from Empire invasion?" Eliana said. "I think I'll be all right."

"Not everyone in Astavar delights at the knowledge that you are in their palace, my queen. What you did on the beach frightened many."

*Including me*, Eliana thought darkly.

As she followed Zahra for what felt like hours, down winding stairs and through stone passages, each one more unfinished than the last, she drew a map in her mind. But as the air grew colder, the weight of the mountain pressing upon her shoulders, her mental map disintegrated. Wherever they were, their route was too labyrinthine for her to find her way back alone.

When the shadows grew so thick that Zahra vanished within them, Eliana withdrew the small gas lamp from her cloak pocket and turned the catch on the base.

"Stop," Zahra said quietly.

But Eliana had already stopped, the sight before her leaving her speechless.

The small flame in her lamp illuminated the edge of a black lake. High cavern walls rose around them, glittering with gemstones. Rocky crags jutted out from the walls, creating cliffs over the water. Small islands rose from the lake's center like the humps of a beast. Eliana squinted through the dim lamplight.

"Don't be afraid, my queen," said Zahra, sounding amused. "This is not the dangerous place I spoke of."

Eliana followed her along the lake's edge. The ground was hard black stone, peppered with tiny amethyst flecks that glittered in the lamplight. "Where are we, then?"

"We are far below Dyrefal," Zahra replied, "in a private retreat that your Saint Tameryn requested her companions help her construct for Saint Nerida. Once, when magic still thrived, this was a refuge of light and greenery."

That sounded familiar to Eliana. She sifted through her memories for one of Remy's many stories about the saints.

"They were lovers, weren't they?" She caught sight of a shadowed structure tucked in a shallow cove. "Nerida and Tameryn?"

A low wall of stones connected the structure to the shore, and it was here that Zahra paused and looked back. The lamp's flame could not fix upon her; she was a void of gloom in the dim amber light.

"They were," she replied. "Come, my queen. Watch your step."

Eliana hesitated, then followed Zahra across the slick stones to the structure. The lamplight slowly revealed it to be an elegant circular belvedere—the smooth stone pillars discolored and rank with slime, the tiled roof shimmering with shards of crystal. Water lapped gently against the steps, pushed by some faint subterranean breeze.

"I believe it important for you to have a place of your own to practice your magic," Zahra said, at last coming to a halt between two of the pillars. "A place far from prying eyes, with ties to the Old World in which your mother lived. That is why I have brought you here."

Eliana moved gingerly around the belvedere, inspecting its pillars, the flecks of stones glimmering across its floor. A childish impulse told her that if she trod too heavily, she would awaken ghosts.

An even more childish impulse made her want to run from this place—from Vintervok, from Simon, even from the responsibility of Navi—and never look back.

Then a thought occurred to her, and she grabbed hold of it eagerly. Anything to delay the inevitable moment of sitting there, before Zahra's expectant gaze, and trying to work magic she did not understand.

"This was a retreat built for Saint Nerida," Eliana said slowly, dragging her fingers along the smooth stone of the nearest pillar. "Given to her by Saint Tameryn."

"Yes, my queen," Zahra replied.

"And how does it feel to exist in a space constructed by those who condemned your kind to the Deep?"

The silence that followed her question expanded to fill the entire cave. She took three measured breaths before turning to meet Zahra's gaze.

The wraith shivered blackly. She seemed to take on a texture, as if she had recently emerged, soil-rich, from the earth. The lamplight carved strange shadows into the air around her, creating dark slopes of nothingness.

"How it feels is irrelevant," she said at last, her voice as even and cool as the stone beneath Eliana's feet. "Being here is the best way I know how to help you, and helping you is what I have resolved to do since emerging from the Gate."

"But why? Why wouldn't you resolve to hurt me? To hurt all of us?" Eliana's heart pounded, but she had gone too far to relent. "Why help me when I should be your enemy?"

A ripple of emotion shifted across Zahra's face and then was gone.

"Because the Emperor is insatiable in his quest to find you," Zahra replied evenly, "and if he does, he may accomplish with you what he failed to with your mother. If that happens, it may spell doom for us all, in this world and in others."

That startled Eliana. "In others?"

Zahra was still for a moment. Then she sighed, drifting to the ground as if deflated.

"It would be easier, my queen, if I could show you, as I did in your Fidelia cell. My words are inadequate. I lose myself in them. Would you allow me this?"

Eliana hesitated, then settled across from Zahra on the stone floor and placed the lamp beside her. She squared her shoulders, willing herself not to be afraid. She had started this; she would finish it.

"Yes," she said. "I will allow this."

"I shall be brief, my queen. What you will see may shock you."

Eliana nodded once. "I understand." She gripped her knees hard, barely managing to swallow.

Then, as before, Zahra moved swiftly toward her, like the rush of exhaled smoke, and disappeared.

—◆—

Eliana opened her eyes to a vast green world at sunrise: cheerful woodlands, fields of quivering wildflowers, a quilt of slim silver rivers.

Above, in a cloudless blue sky, swirled a bruise. As Eliana watched, furious veins sprouted from its heart and raced across the sky, multiplying like cracks in glass.

She stepped back. "What is it? Zahra?"

Zahra appeared beside her, tall and whole, ebony-skinned. White hair to her waist, resplendent in gleaming platinum armor. Wings of light and shadow trailed from her back, flickering as she moved—smoky and dark one moment, brilliant the next.

"It is the Gate, my queen," Zahra answered, her voice thin and tired. "And on the other side of it is Avitas and your beloved saints."

"Then that means…"

"Yes. We are in the Deep."

Eliana gazed wonderingly upon the idyllic green world around her. "But this is no prison. It's an entire other world. Zahra, is this what you meant?" Her skin tingled, as if her body were stretching to accommodate this new information. "The Deep is another world like our own?"

"So we were led to believe during treaty negotiations," said Zahra. "Never mind that we were first to live in the world of Avitas, and that humans evolved later. Humans were weaker, they told us—the saints, and our own leaders. Humans could not survive outside the world in which they came to exist. But we angels were older, more advanced forms of life. We could adjust to existence in another world, and our departure would bring an end to the war. Both sides had lost many. Both sides were eager for peace. This seemed the easiest way to achieve it. So we were led to believe."

Then she pointed at the sky's bruise. Her voice lowered, thick and bitter. "We arrive."

In the next moment, something ruptured—something deep within the fiber of the ground Eliana stood upon, within the air she breathed. The sky rippled as if struck, and its bruise darkened, rushing across the canvas of morning sunlight like the flood of an angry sea.

"Look, my queen," said Zahra gently, and Eliana obeyed, not realizing until that moment that she was clinging to the angel's arm like a child gone to its mother after a bad dream.

She looked up at the sky and watched it open.

Out of it poured a great black cloud, thick and streaming, the fall of a dark river. It expanded in the open air—blooming, magnifying—and from within it came sounds like none Eliana had ever heard. Angrier than war cries, more unbearably lonesome than the howl of wolves.

And the world itself, green and verdant, waiting for a race of angels to build a new home upon its rolling hills, quaked and collapsed.

It happened quickly, as if the structure of the world had been hastily constructed and the arrival of the angels had triggered its demise. The sky shrank, no longer a luxurious expanse but instead a mere pinprick of light, retreating to an unreachable horizon. Green meadows and silver rivers faded abruptly to blackness.

The terrible cries in the air burrowed into Eliana's skull. She sank to her knees, gasping for breath, but her efforts were futile. She couldn't breathe in this place. There was no air, no water, no sense of depth or distance. She clawed at her chest and realized it no longer existed. She had no chest, no lungs. She was still alive. She had thoughts, and she knew her name.

But as she groped through the air, she found nothing—no legs, no hips or hands. She searched with her mind, which seemed the only thing left to her. She wanted to sob, but the idea of crying remained trapped in her mind.

It was then that the pain slammed into her.

Even without a body, she could register it. Her body hadn't simply disappeared. It had been taken from her, ripped away by this place in which she now found herself—not a fresh, green world, ready to be remade into a new homeland, but rather a void, a nothing space between the world of Avitas and whatever lay beyond.

The human saints had lied.

Eliana added her own furious voice to the millions around her, all of them crammed into a space both endless and caged. She wanted to beat against the walls that held her. She would tear them apart, burst back into Avitas, and destroy the saints from the inside out.

Except...she was nothing but a mind. A consciousness, bodiless and impotent.

She howled and wailed. She raged for centuries, and then—

The world changed. She was herself again. She was Eliana.

She gasped, clutching her own arms, her stomach. She touched her face. She was *alive*. She was whole.

"Zahra?" she sobbed.

"I'm here, my queen," came Zahra's voice, soft and regretful. "Watch."

Seven brilliant figures looked down upon that same vast green world, untouched and peaceful. A false world, a lie constructed to deceive the angels into submission.

And a good lie it was, a skillfully crafted one. Otherwise, the angels, with their powerful minds, would have never believed it.

Eliana reached for Zahra's hand; she grasped it gently.

"How did they deceive you?" she breathed. "Why did you believe them?"

"They were excellent liars," Zahra replied. "And they had help."

She gestured at the seven figures, standing at a ripped-open seam in the fabric of the world. Eliana's mind cleared, her heart still racing, for now she recognized them, from long years of Remy's stories: Tameryn, dark-haired and golden-skinned, her daggers trailing shadows. Pale, white-haired Marzana, her shield wreathed in flame.

*The saints.*

Eliana would have fallen to her knees once more if Zahra had not been there to hold her up. There were Saint Ghovan and his quiver of arrows,

Saint Nerida and her trident, Saint Grimvald and his hammer, Saint Tokazi and his staff.

Saint Katell, the sunspinner, her skin a rich, dark brown, her black hair coiled in a tight braided knot, carrying a blazing sunlit sword.

And beside her, tall and lithe, dazzlingly beautiful, was an angel—warm brown skin, wings of light and shadow framing his body.

"Aryava was a great leader of my people," Zahra said quietly, "and had many who were blindly faithful to him."

Eliana remembered Remy telling her the story of Aryava and Katell: an angel and a human saint, bound by a forbidden love.

"He died in her arms," Eliana murmured, recalling Remy's voice. "He died in the final days of the war."

Zahra nodded. "He died fighting angels who understood his betrayal and the deception of the saints, and who led a final insurgency in an attempt to save us." A beat of silence. Zahra's voice was careful, deliberate. "This rebellion did not succeed. They were cast into the Deep, along with the rest of us."

"And Aryava's last words..."

"'Two Queens will rise,'" Zahra said. "'One of blood, and one of light.'"

Saint Grimvald stepped forward, looking out over what Eliana now knew was the Deep, disguised to seem otherwise. "If we send them here, we doom them. They cannot survive here, not as they are."

Saint Katell nodded, her expression unreadable. "And if we do not, then they will destroy us." She glanced at Aryava, a flicker of doubt on her face.

He took his hand in hers, his eyes soft. "This is the only hope for you," he told her, quietly, "and for us."

Then the saints and the false green world of the Deep disappeared into a swift, dark fog.

Eliana returned to herself, gulping for air as tears streamed down her face. On her hands and knees in Saint Tameryn's cavern, she fumbled for Zahra's hand and found nothing there. The loss of Zahra's body struck her hard in the chest.

"My queen, please breathe," came Zahra's worried voice. "I know it is a great deal to understand. Perhaps I should not have shown you—"

"No, you should have." Eliana breathed for a few moments, then sat back against one of the stone pillars, trembling and nauseated. "Humans were losing the war against the angels, and they discovered how to open a doorway into another world."

"Not another world," Zahra corrected gently. "Not even the saints were powerful enough for that."

"So other worlds do exist?"

"Yes, my queen. They lie beyond the fabric of this one, beyond the reach of any being that has yet lived." She paused. "Except—"

"Except for my mother," Eliana said flatly. "And perhaps for me."

Zahra inclined her head. "The Deep, however, is the farthest your saints could manage to delve beyond our world. They used their elemental powers to craft a lie, a false promise of a new world for my kind to inhabit and mold into a land of our choosing."

"And then they forced you into this false world, where you were..." Remembering, she had to swallow against a surge of sickness. "You were stripped of your bodies."

"The realm between worlds is a mere liminal space," Zahra said. "The empirium functions differently there. It is distant, cold. It leaves a void in its wake. No physicality, no sensation. No sight or sound."

"A prison. Just as we've always been taught. But you thought it would be a new home." She looked up at Zahra through a film of tears. "You were willing to give up your own home in order to create peace between us."

Zahra said nothing, her dark eyes full of a sadness so immense that Eliana could no longer look at her. Instead, she gazed beyond the small circle of light her lamp provided, over the black lake she could hardly see.

"How could you want to help us after we did such a thing?" Eliana whispered. "You fight for Red Crown. You fight against your own kind for *us*, who lied to you, who banished you into this terrible place where your body was taken from you."

She closed her eyes. It was a monstrous act, too horrific to be believed. And yet she had seen it. She had lived it.

"I wouldn't blame you if you fought at the Emperor's side to destroy us," she said.

"And I don't blame your saints for doing what they did," Zahra replied. "They drove us into the Deep to save their people. It was the only option left to them. And you…"

Zahra cupped Eliana's cheek, creating a pocket of soft, cool air against her skin. "For all your power, you are fragile creatures. We would have won, had the war continued. If your saints had not created the Gate, had not forced us into the Deep, then it is probable that you, and Remy, and Simon, and the Lightbringer and the Blood Queen would never have been born. The human race would have been crushed into oblivion."

Eliana shook her head, fresh tears gathering angrily. "But they deceived you. They *murdered* you, all of you."

"And yet here we still exist, even if differently than we did before. And I shall not blame an entire race of beings for the crimes of a few." Zahra's fingers caressed Eliana's forehead. "So frail, and so dear. Your lives blink in and out of this world like the lights of fireflies. And I will do what I can to see that you continue to."

"How can you bear it? How can you even look at me, much less fight for me?"

In the lamplight, Zahra's smile was soft. "I bear the life I have been given because it is the only one I have. And I fight for you, my queen, gladly, because the things that have been done to your people since your mother tore down the Gate and released my own are equally as atrocious as what your saints did to us, if not more so. The debt has been repaid, and yet still the Emperor kills. Still he terrorizes and destroys. And I do not believe he will stop at the destruction of humanity. I believe he will venture beyond Avitas, beyond the Deep, to the worlds that lie past the farthest reaches of what we now know to be true." She paused. "If, that is, he obtains the power to do it."

The clammy air had cooled Eliana's sweating skin. She shivered, crossed her arms over her chest. "You mean, if he finds me."

Zahra's silence was all the answer she needed.

"Why does he do this?"

"Because he wants answers he has not yet found."

"What answers? And to what questions?"

Zahra hesitated, then said slowly, "Will you forgive me if I delay that particular discussion? It is not a light one, and you look rather drained of color just now."

Eliana gave her a wan smile. A profound weariness sank into her bones. She touched the scabbing wound from Navi's attack.

"You'll help me practice?" Her voice sounded small and foreign to her own ears, as if Zahra's vision had remade it.

"I will, my queen."

"I'd prefer to practice with you, rather than Simon."

Zahra's mouth twitched. "I can't imagine why. He's such a pleasant person, after all."

Eliana laughed a little, rising unsteadily to her feet.

"However," Zahra continued, hesitant, "I do encourage you to consider forging a casting for yourself. And that I know very little about."

"And Simon might know much more. Is that what you think?"

"It is."

Eliana sighed, scrubbed a hand over her face. "The moment I'm ready, you'll take me to the Nest? You won't delay?"

"No, my queen. I pledge this to you." Then she paused. "And might I suggest we return to your rooms for now? I know you are eager to begin practicing, but after what you've just experienced, perhaps a few hours of rest would be of more benefit."

Eliana nodded unhappily. "Very well."

They crossed the narrow bridge back to the shore. Eliana watched her boots cross the slick stones.

Gently, Zahra answered her unspoken thoughts. "You asked me why

I fight for you—for *you*, specifically. I do so, my queen, because in your mother's veins lived the power to save not just one world, but many. Not just humans or angels, but both, and perhaps other races we do not yet know about, in worlds we have not yet found. She had this power, but so do you. And I believe you will triumph where she could not."

Eliana let Zahra's words ring in silence. She bore the weight of them back through Tameryn's cave and up into the palace, as if they were a pack of stones bound to her body, slowly pressing deeper and deeper into her skin.

◆◇◆

When Eliana returned to her room, Remy was waiting for her.

He whirled as she entered the room, his flushed face streaked with tears.

Eliana froze, ice flooding her limbs. *He knows. Someone told him.*

"El, you'll never believe it," he said breathlessly. "You've got to come. Come *now*. They won't listen to me or Simon. They'll only listen to you."

He grabbed her hand, tugged her desperately out the door and down the hall. She allowed him this—dumbstruck, her relief making her stumble—and didn't recover her voice until they'd reached a suite of rooms on the palace's first floor, outside of which stood two guards. They bowed at her approach and opened the doors at once.

Behind her, having followed them downstairs, Zahra drew a sharp breath of surprise.

Eliana stepped inside the room, where several people had gathered—King Eri, King Tavik, Lady Ama. Hob, and a passel of royal guards. A woman in healer's robes, tending to the leg of someone hidden from view.

Simon turned at Eliana's entrance, an unreadable expression on his face, and then stepped aside.

Beyond him, filthy and battered, sat a ghost.

Eliana's shock rooted her to the floor.

*Harkan.*

# RIELLE

*"Not for love or church,*
*not for country or crown,*
*Only to the Gate do we pledge our hearts*
*Until the end of days, until the skies crash down."*

—*The Vow of the Obex*

Rielle awoke in the warm nest of Audric's arms and immediately regretted opening her eyes.

It had become grossly apparent, over the last few days aboard the *Kaalvitsi*, that her power was no protection against seasickness, and without sleep to bring her respite from the rolling sea, her stomach pitched with the waves.

She groaned, curling her body against the sensation, and hid her face once more in Audric's chest.

He laughed, groggy with sleep. "You can fly on a godsbeast and stop a tidal wave in its tracks, but the sea bests you."

Rielle grunted in protest. "Nothing can best me."

Audric kissed her brow, the warmth of his hands soothing her. "Our last day on the water. We should arrive this morning."

"And then we'll have the return journey on this horrible, stinking death trap."

"The *Kaalvitsi* is a fine ship."

"I hate it," she declared, "and I hate you for loving it."

"For someone who claims to hate me, you certainly do kiss me a lot."

Grinning, Rielle moved up his body to kiss his neck, his jawline. "I don't hate you. I could never hate you. I love you like the moon loves the sun. I love you so much I could die from it."

Audric groaned at her touch, a smile playing at his lips. "Your seasickness is making you talk nonsense."

Rielle giggled, her body stirring in that sweet, urgent way that it always did around him. She climbed atop him and pinned his arms to the bed, delighting at the flare of want in his eyes. "I'm tired of waiting, darling. I feel fine. I really do. My strength has returned, and I'm no longer bleeding, and I need you." She circled slowly against him. "What do you think?"

Audric cupped her hips, helping her move. His voice darkened, sending a delicious thrill down her body. "I can't imagine a better cure for seasickness."

She relished the sight of him leaning back against the pillows, his eyes drifting shut. He groaned low and slow, in that deep, chest-rattling way that made her belly tighten.

"You'll be gentle with me, won't you?" she said softly. "Given my tender stomach." She leaned over him, unbuttoned his tunic, kissed her way across his chest. He murmured her name and slid one hand up her thigh, raising the hem of her nightgown. The other hand he moved into her hair, winding his fingers through the wild waves and tugging slightly—as they had discovered, over the past several weeks, that Rielle very much loved.

She smiled in approval. "Ah, but not too gentle."

Audric moved the hand on her hips between her legs and rubbed his thumb in soft circles, his gaze intent upon her. "Just the way you like it."

Rielle clutched his shirt in her hands, moved her hips against his fingers, bent lower to kiss him—

And suddenly Audric was gone, and the room around Rielle had changed.

It was a dark chamber, lushly appointed, with a wall of square windows overlooking an icy landscape, mountainous and unfamiliar. Perhaps a northern country—Borsvall? Kirvaya? Astavar? She looked down at her body and saw she was no longer wearing her sleeping shift. Instead, a gown of black velvet, spangled with gold embroidery in abstract shapes, hugged her body like a soft glove. The neckline was low and wide; the wintry air pricked her exposed skin.

And in a chair by the windows, overlooking the ice, sat Corien, alive and whole, wearing a long black coat over a fine vest and trousers, and holding a glass of red wine.

At once, Rielle wanted to both move toward him and run from him. Her indecision kept her frozen.

Corien glanced at her, his eyes glittering with tears. Rielle's breath caught in her throat.

"Having fun?" he murmured.

She managed a step toward him. "Where are we?"

"You're in bed with your lover," he mumbled into his glass. "And I'm far away, scheming how best to ruin him."

Heat flared in her chest. "Impossible. He's too good for you to ruin. And besides, he has me to protect him. Touch him, and I'll burn you again." She raised her chin, approaching him slowly. Her palms itched with the urge to punish him for speaking of Audric in such a way. "Was it fun for you, when I burned you? Do you crave more pain from me?"

Corien watched her, unmoving. "I crave you, and anything you can give me."

As Rielle continued her approach, she remembered to observe the room—the landscape out the windows, the stars in the sky, anything of note in the room itself. Papers, paintings, artifacts that would give away Corien's location. Audric would want her to gather information.

Corien chuckled into his drink, knocked back the rest of it, and set the empty glass on the small table beside him. "Spying on me, are you? You'll see what you can see and then take it back to him like a faithful dog?"

Rielle marched over, her vision suddenly sharp and gold-tinged, and slapped him.

Corien bore it silently, then looked up at her, his cheek reddened, unafraid and unabashed. "I've missed you."

As she stood there, her hand stinging from the blow, Rielle could not decipher any of the feelings racing through her mind except one. She had missed him too, with a desperation she didn't understand. Though she refused to utter the words, they sat heavily on her tongue, and Corien must have sensed their presence, for his small smile broadened.

He rose, not touching her. Every line of his body looked as tense as Rielle herself felt. "Was it fun for you, being forced to save people who don't deserve you? Driving yourself to the edge of death for a kingdom of simpletons?"

Rielle raised her chin. "I enjoyed subduing that wave."

"I know you did."

Unnerved by the fondness in his voice, Rielle forced her own calm. "Establishing and maintaining a friendly relationship between Celdaria and Borsvall is crucial in these uncertain times. By saving them, I did my part in the name of peace. I'm proud of that, and you can't take that away from me."

Corien hesitated, then moved closer and cupped her cheek. She leaned into his palm, the cool softness of his skin making her shiver.

"Yes," he murmured, bitterly. "You were a dutiful Sun Queen that day. You served your kingdom well."

Now he held her face in both hands, his fingers unsteady against her cheeks. He leaned closer, lips hovering above her own. Rielle held her breath, every muscle in her body drawn tight and hot. If she moved an inch, she would kiss him.

"In my kingdom, in my world," he murmured, his breath hot against her lips, "you would serve no one."

Rielle placed her hands on his chest, but not to push him away. She stepped into the bend of his body, her eyes blinded with sudden tears—because she was afraid to be so near him, terrified of what she might do, and because his words resonated within her like the first notes of birdsong after a hard winter. As he wrapped his arms around her, she melted into his embrace. She closed her eyes, breathing him in. On the stiff, fine fabric of his coat were traces of the cold winter outside and some kind of spiced oil that reminded her of leather and smoke. He buried his face in her hair with a muffled sigh of her name, and his fingers dug painfully into her shoulders, but the sensation made her blood hum alive, and she found herself wishing for more of it.

Frantic for clarity in this moment she did not understand, she closed her eyes—and with that small movement, the world shifted beneath her.

She faltered, her eyes flying open.

She was on the *Kaalvitsi*, straddling Audric. Suddenly, his arms were around her instead of Corien's, his voice was groaning her name.

He sensed her unease at once and steadied her with gentle hands on her hips. "Are you all right, darling?"

She hesitated, breathless and feeling newly vulnerable in his arms. When he reached for her face, she flinched away from him.

He drew back, not quite masking the hurt in his eyes. "What's wrong?"

She shook her head, tears rising fast. Real tears, not creations of Corien's imagination. Tears she could trust. She wished she could go back to a few moments ago, when she was happy and content in the warm familiarity of Audric's love and her own desire—and yet she couldn't. Now, Corien's voice lingered in her ears, and she welcomed it.

*In my kingdom, you would serve no one.*

Furious with herself, her skin flushed and crawling, she settled beside Audric and curled against him like a child. He turned on his side to face her, waiting patiently.

Rielle's chest tightened. She did not deserve him, and she could not meet his eyes. She grabbed his hand, held it to her heart.

"What can I do?" Audric whispered. "What happened?"

She shook her head, unable to speak.

After a still moment, Audric asked, "Was it Corien?"

The question jarred her. Was she that transparent? She finally managed to look at him, fearing disgust on his face. But as he regarded her warmly, with no judgment or anger, the tension she held within her melted away. She wrapped her arms around his neck, her face pressed against his curls.

"I'm sorry," she whispered. "I couldn't see anything. I didn't... I don't have anything to report. All of a sudden he was there, and *I* was there, wherever he was, and I was so surprised, I didn't pay attention. I'm sorry, I'm sorry..."

"Please don't apologize." Audric cupped the back of her head, his touch so tender it made Rielle ache. She held him like someone lost at sea, clinging to the only steady thing in an ocean of storms.

She spoke against his neck. "I should have paid better attention."

"That doesn't matter. You're here now, and safe. That's all I want."

A sudden, terrible fear took root in her heart, and she clung even more tightly to him. "Don't let me go, Audric. Please."

"Never. I'd never do such a thing. I'm here." He drew the bed's quilt over their bodies, creating a warm cocoon.

"I don't understand what he wants. He speaks in riddles and half truths. He frightens me."

And that was the truth, but not the entire truth, a fact that made her hate herself—even as part of her balked at that hatred and rejected it, defiant.

*In my kingdom, you would serve no one.*

Was that such a terrible thing to crave? Was that a desire deserving of hatred?

"I've got you," came Audric's voice, low and soft. His lips brushed her temple, and she closed her eyes, concentrating on his warmth, his solidness. "Hold on to me. Stay with me."

Shouted words from the deck above pierced their quiet nest, followed by an echoing cry from Atheria, who had spent much of the last week circling the ship from the air, diving happily for sharks.

Rielle waited for Audric's translation: "We've arrived."

❖

From the long white shore, a company of two dozen archers in long gray robes watched their approach, hooded and still. They hadn't yet raised their weapons, but as Rielle stood on the main deck of the *Kaalvitsi*, snarls of tension twisted hotly in her shoulders.

Audric came to stand beside her, and Ludivine on her other side—both of them attired, as she was, in fur-lined traveling clothes and heavy woolen cloaks that fastened at their throats with silver clasps in the shape of the legendary Borsvallic ice dragons. Even so dressed, the sea winds cut bitterly.

"The Obex," Audric said, a thrill of excitement in his voice.

*The Obex.* The sacred guard, loyal to no kingdom or country, and instead loyal only to the legacy of the saints, to the protection and maintenance of the Gate. Rielle wished, for Audric's sake, that circumstances were different. He had longed to make the journey to the Sunderlands and meet the Obex guard for as many years as he'd known of their existence.

But inspecting a damaged Gate in danger of falling was surely not the visit he'd always dreamt of.

"We sent word of our arrival," snapped Ingrid, standing rigidly a few feet in front of them, hands tight around the hilt of her sword. "Why this aggressive stance?"

"Because they guard the Gate," Ilmaire replied, watching the shore with a wondering gleam in his eyes. "A message means very little to them, even a message from a prince. In their eyes, this could be a trick." He glanced back at Audric, and a pang twisted Rielle's heart as she noticed a similar excitement on her beloved's face. Two bookish, peace-loving princes who could have been true friends—were it not for Ingrid's warmongering soldiers, whatever evil plagued the Borsvall borderlands, and the long years of ill blood between their kingdoms.

"We must be cautious, Audric," Ilmaire urged. "They will not hesitate to protect the Gate."

Ludivine spoke quietly, so the others couldn't hear. "We aren't in danger. They do not intend to shoot." She paused. "For now."

"That's not very reassuring," Audric muttered.

"Ilmaire is not wrong. They will not hesitate to protect the Gate from any perceived danger."

*So I have to control myself?* Rielle thought, bristling. *Is that what you're implying?*

*Should I be worried that you won't?* Ludivine replied mildly.

The mysterious northern chamber returned to Rielle in flashes of sensation and sound: Corien's voice, whispering her name. His arms tight around her. The frigid air, the velvet hugging her body. The thrill of his words and the promise they contained:

*You would serve no one.*

Freedom. Control. The empirium—hers to explore and possess, unfettered.

*Did you speak to him recently?* Ludivine's thoughts felt startled. *Rielle... You saw him. You touched him. You didn't tell me.*

Rielle's surprise rattled them both. *You didn't know? You didn't sense him?*

*No. I felt nothing.*

*But what does that mean?*

Ludivine had no answer, and as they traveled across the choppy gray water in small dinghies, the sea spray misting their faces, she remained quiet, her mouth pinched and her thoughts closed to Rielle in a way that felt like reproach.

*I don't owe you every part of me,* she told Ludivine.

Instead of answering, Ludivine clasped Rielle's gloved hand more tightly in her own.

When they reached the shallows, they climbed out of the boats and walked ashore through thin sheets of foam that clung to the white sand—Rielle, Audric, Ludivine, Ilmaire, Ingrid, and a contingent of six guards.

Ingrid led the way, her blond braids and white fur cloak snapping furiously in the wind. The glower on her face was spectacular. She had wanted to bring a larger company, but Ilmaire had insisted they keep their party small to seem less threatening.

A few yards from the line of archers, they stopped, and Ilmaire made a show of laying down his sword. He raised his wrists, his castings catching the sunlight, and subdued the sea wind until he could easily speak over it.

"My name is Ilmaire Lysleva, crown prince of the kingdom of Borsvall," he began, "and I come to you humbly in the name of Saint Grimvald the Mighty, and in the name of my father, King Hallvard Lysleva, requesting access to the Gate."

The archers stood motionless, unresponsive. The foremost archer wore a long horn carved out of bone on a link of chains slung around his torso. Embroidered on his robe was a single symbol—a high, square tower capped with a single, unblinking eye.

Ingrid shifted restlessly.

Ilmaire gestured back at Rielle. "I bring with me Audric Courverie, crown prince of Celdaria; his cousin, Lady Ludivine Sauvillier; and Lady Rielle Dardenne, recently named Sun Queen—"

"We know who Lady Rielle is." The foremost archer's cold gaze flicked to Rielle, then Audric, and then to Ludivine. He stiffened. His eyes widened.

With a sharp gasp, Ludivine jerked as if struck.

Swiftly, the archer raised his bow and let a strange, copper-tipped arrow fly. Ludivine dodged it in time; instead of striking her heart, it hit her left shoulder. The impact sent her staggering back with a cry.

The air shimmered around her body, like faint ripples on the surface of a lake. The space around her body jerked and tightened before violently reversing course, like a swift, raging current. All the light and life seemed to rush out of her. The arrow glowed white-hot for a moment, then darkened.

She dropped flat to the ground.

Audric ran for her at once, Rielle just behind him. With a furious cry, Ingrid drew her sword and stepped between them and the line of archers.

Audric fell to his knees beside Ludivine and gathered her in his arms.

"Lu? Lu!" He brushed the sand from her face. "Say something!"

The archers raised their bows in unison and fired.

Rielle spun round, lightning in her veins. She flung up her arms and crossed them, forming a shield. The wind gathered at her command, forming a wall between her party and the approaching arrows. The gusting wall lit up, a gold sheet of fire, and when the arrows impacted it, they dissolved into ash and drifted in dark whorls to the sea.

Rielle smiled coldly at the archers, her arms rigid. The golden wall she had created shimmered in rhythm with her breathing. "If you move against any of us even once more, I will kill you where you stand."

The head archer lowered his bow, the others following him.

"Ingrid, watch them," Rielle snapped. "If they look like they're going to shoot again, shoot them first."

Ingrid gestured at her own archers, readying her sword with a hard grin. "With pleasure."

Rielle knelt at Ludivine's side. "Is she all right?"

Audric looked up at her, eyes bright, hands covered in Ludivine's blood. "She's not breathing. She's gone utterly cold."

"That's not possible. She couldn't have..." Rielle shook her head, her throat closing painfully. She could not believe it; she *would* not. "Even for an ordinary person, that shot wouldn't have been fatal. Would it?"

"Nor would she have lost so much body heat so quickly."

Ilmaire joined them. "An ordinary person? What do you mean?"

Audric peered at the arrow in Ludivine's shoulder. "This arrow is odd."

"What do you mean?" Rielle asked.

"Look at it."

She did, noticing that the arrowhead was unusually long and hadn't disappeared entirely into Ludivine's body. Perhaps three inches of it protruded from her flesh. On its bright copper planes swirled shifting clouds of darkness and light, as if the arrowhead now contained a tangle of storms.

Rielle rose to face the head archer, barely stifling the urge to destroy him. "What did you do to her? What is this weapon?"

The archer approached, his expression flat as he regarded Ludivine's prone form. "Were you ignorant of what she is, or did you know and keep the truth from us?"

Rielle's stomach dropped.

Ilmaire looked back and forth between them. "What truth? What is he talking about?"

Rielle went still, flabbergasted, and the archer smiled grimly. "Ah. So you did know."

"Audric, what is he talking about?" asked Ilmaire.

Audric ignored him. "Is she dead?"

"No," the archer replied. "She is trapped." He reached for the arrow, as if to pull it from Ludivine's body.

Rielle moved to block him, the wind spinning angrily around her and the beach trembling beneath her feet. "You will not touch her."

The archer raised one cool eyebrow. "It won't hurt her. This body means nothing now. The creature you love is contained in this blade."

Rielle stepped back, aghast.

"What?" Audric breathed.

Ingrid spat a quiet curse from a few paces away. "If someone doesn't explain what's going on right this instant, I'll start shooting indiscriminately."

"You'll do nothing of the sort, Commander," Ilmaire replied, the ferocity in his voice startling Rielle. "I'll remind you that I am our father's heir, and that you obey my orders."

Ingrid stared, her mouth parting in surprise.

Ilmaire knelt beside Ludivine. "Audric, please explain this to me. I know I haven't yet regained your trust, but if my soldiers are in danger, I must know."

"Ludivine is an angel," Audric said at once. "My cousin Ludivine died of a fever when she was younger, and an angel inhabited her body. We were unaware of this until several weeks ago, when Rielle was anointed Sun Queen." He glanced at Rielle. "She is our friend. We can trust her."

Ingrid stepped back, horror plain on her face. Even Ilmaire seemed struck speechless, though he stared at Ludivine's body with a new curiosity, as if she were a specimen he was eager to examine.

Corien's gleeful voice arrived. *My God, this is entertaining.*

An image of him lounging in that chair by the windows flashed across Rielle's vision.

"Quiet," she hissed aloud, distracted. "Leave me alone."

"Who is she talking to?" Ingrid demanded.

The archer raised an eyebrow, considering Rielle. "Who indeed?"

She ignored the question. "Explain this to me. What is that arrow?"

"It is a blightblade," the archer replied as tonelessly as if describing the weather. "It is forged from a combination of a copper alloy and the blood of monstrous beasts known as the cruciata. The cruciata originate from the Deep. Their blood, which is venomous to angels and extremely potent, gives the blightblades their power. When used against a body possessed by an angel, the blightblade extracts the angelic spirit from the body and traps the angel within it, leaving the body empty and free to die naturally."

Rielle looked at him in horror. Audric shut his eyes and turned away.

Ingrid was horribly pale. "What is he talking about? How can this be true? *Angels?*"

Ilmaire gazed at Ludivine's body in astonishment. "Can she be removed from the blightblade?"

The archer hesitated.

As Rielle advanced on him, the sand crackled beneath her feet as if flames were gathering inside it. "Well? Can she?"

After a moment, the archer nodded. "Yes. The blightblade, if shattered, will release the trapped angel."

"And then she can return to her body?" Audric replied.

"It's not her body, I'll remind you. She stole it, as have any angels who now live in this world."

"Once the blade is shattered," Audric repeated angrily, "she can return to her body?"

"Yes."

"And her body will be whole and well?" Rielle added.

The archer's expression tightened. "Oh, yes. Her angelic nature will ensure that this body is restored. Blightblades do, however, leave a scar that is, apparently, quite painful even for an angel to bear." His hard mouth quirked in a tiny smile. "And no amount of angelic might can cure it."

"So she'll be in pain forever?" asked Audric.

The archer inclined his head.

"She won't," Rielle declared. "I'll mend her scar and take away her pain. I'll make her whole again."

"Is that truly possible?" Ilmaire asked. "Can you heal wounds as well?"

Rielle stalked back to Ludivine and, ignoring Audric's protests, yanked the arrow from Ludivine's body. Her body jerked, inanimate, and Rielle's throat soured with revulsion.

"Blightblades are very difficult to shatter," offered the archer.

Rielle smirked. Her vision burned gold. "Not for me."

Then she flung the arrow to the ground and flicked her wrist, tugging sharply on the air.

Hot jolts of power surged down her arm and out her fingers, making the air quiver with heat. The blade shattered into dozens of tiny shards; the bright copper metal turned dull.

A shifting dark shape, fainter than a shadow, long and patchy, rose swiftly from the arrow's ruins and surged across the white sand toward Ludivine's body, like a parched creature desperate for water. From within it, an alien voice cried out mournfully, uttering words Rielle could not comprehend. They held Ludivine's voice and also another—deeper, older, and heavy with sadness.

A canvas of shadows shifted across Ludivine's body, like a woman-shaped mask hugging its mate, and then, in an instant, the shape disappeared. Ludivine's eyes flew open. She gasped for air in Audric's arms.

"I'm sorry you had to see me like that," she sobbed at once, her eyes wide and frantic. She clutched Audric's arms as if struggling not to drown, and her cries of despair tore at Rielle's heart.

"Careful now." Audric wiped his face with his sleeve, then ripped the sash from his coat and used it to clean the blood from her neck and shoulder. "Gently, Lu. You'll hurt yourself."

"Oh, God help me, I'm so sorry." Ludivine turned into his chest, shivering. "Don't let them... Not again, not ever again. Rielle? Where are you, my darling?" Blindly, she reached back for her, and Rielle moved past her shock to kneel at her side. Ludivine grabbed her arm and pulled both her and Audric close. "Don't leave me," she whispered. "Please don't let them take me from you. Not again, not again. I can't go back, I can't be that again..."

Rielle held her awkwardly, unable to speak. Perhaps she should have been repulsed, or concerned about what the Borsvall contingent would think of these revelations. But she cared only about this—her, Ludivine, Audric. Together and safe. She pressed her lips to Ludivine's golden head, trying to ignore the horrific shimmering bruise she could see blooming on Ludivine's shoulder beneath the torn fabric of her gown.

Audric looked back at the archer. "You have healers here, I assume?"

The archer was watching them thoughtfully. "We do."

"Then take us to them at once."

"They won't be able to eliminate her pain," the archer replied, sounding pleased. "She will carry that with her for all her endless, stolen days."

"They will do what they can until..." Audric glanced at Rielle.

"Until I can do it instead," she finished for him. "Which I will, with time. I'll do it. I'll learn. I know I can do it." She glanced up at the others—Ilmaire, watching in fascination; Ingrid, suspicious and horrified; the archer, wholly unimpressed. Rielle set her jaw. "You doubt me."

"No, Lady Rielle," the archer replied. "I fear you."

He stepped aside, gesturing toward the dark tree line. "Follow me. And fear not. My archers won't shoot again."

As they moved away from the water, Corien's appreciation brushed against Rielle like a caress of cool fingers. Every time he touched her, every time he spoke, his presence felt stronger in her mind, as if he were slowly regaining his footing.

*I almost wish they would shoot,* he murmured. *Just to see what you'd do.*

Rielle, imagining it, smiled to herself, and avoided Ludivine's curious, bleary gaze. *So do I.*

## ~ 8 ~

# ELIANA

*"The first human to manifest elemental powers was a girl, a sunspinner only nine years of age, and though her name has been lost to the passage of time, you will find her spoken of often in ancient texts from the First Age. In those pages she is known only as the Child of the Dawn."*

—*A Concise History of the First Age, Volume I: The Early Days of Humanity* by Alistra Zarovna and Veseris Savelya of the First Guild of Scholars

For a moment, Eliana could neither speak nor move. The impossibility of seeing Harkan sitting there in Navi's palace, looking so very much himself—the same golden-brown skin she had grown up seeing every day, the same black hair and large dark eyes—left her feeling as if she had stepped out of her skin to hover somewhere above the ground. As she had existed in the Deep of Zahra's memory—stripped of her body, but this time without pain and without fear.

"El?" Harkan's voice was hoarse, and familiar and beloved, and when he smiled, the new shadows under his eyes diminished. "El, you're staring."

With a small cry, she hurried forward, crashed to her knees at his side, and wrapped him in her arms so fiercely that he hissed in pain. "El, that's a bit tight."

Beneath the stench of travel and sweat was the familiar warm smell of

Harkan's skin, and suddenly, with her eyes squeezed shut, Eliana was back home in Orline, in the candlelit haven of his bedroom. Knots buried in her chest and shoulders loosened, pulling tears from her eyes.

"I don't care," she said, her voice muffled in his collar. "And I'm never letting go, either."

"So I'm to exist for the rest of my life with you hanging off my neck?" He cupped the back of her head with one hand, found her fingers with the other. With her cheek pressed against his throat, she felt his voice, thick with emotion, rumbling in her bones. "I think I can live with that."

Faintly, she heard King Tavik urging everyone out of the room, and looked up just as Simon turned to follow them. Remy bounced at his side, tugging on his arm.

"Did he tell you how he escaped Orline?" Remy's eyes shone. "Did you see that revolver? He stole it from an adatrox lieutenant."

Simon seemed not at all perturbed to have Remy dancing around him like an overexcited puppy. "Is that so?"

"Did you know Harkan used to write stories with me? Did you know Saint Tokazi is his favorite saint?"

"No, I hadn't heard that." Simon placed a hand on Remy's shoulder to direct him gently out of the room.

Just before he stepped into the corridor, Simon glanced back at Eliana. For a beat, their eyes met over Harkan's shoulder, and she felt a dull twist in her chest that she would have named guilt or embarrassment or some combination of the two—if such a reaction weren't completely absurd. There was nothing untoward about embracing an old friend, and even if she and Harkan had started kissing right there in front of everyone, as they would have been well within their rights to do after so long apart, there would have been no reason to hide.

And yet, shame climbed hot up her throat, as if she had been caught doing something illicit. This was not a betrayal; there was nothing to betray.

But Simon's declaration from that first night in Dyrefal circled through her mind, unwelcome and unasked for: *I care about nothing else but you.*

She tightened her arms around Harkan, refusing to be the first to look away.

Simon, with that strange, unreadable expression still on his face, was the one to do it. He turned his back on them, Remy still chattering away at his elbow, and shut the door quietly behind him.

—◆—

Later that night, her room lit by a dozen candles, the windows on the far wall cracked open to allow in a slight chill breeze, Eliana lay in bed beside Harkan, tensely curled against his side as she waited for him to respond.

Her whispered words hovered in the air like dead leaves taking an eternity to fall from their branches, and now that she had uttered them, she found herself wishing she had kept her mouth shut.

Instead she could have simply lain beside him, fallen in and out of sleep until the morning, fetched him fresh poppy tea if he needed it for his leg. She could have left him sleeping peacefully and returned to the stacks of books sitting on her desk. She could have pushed past the discomfort humming quietly below her skin, which left her feeling awkward in his presence, in a way she had never felt back home, and kissed him. She could have kissed him until it became something more, even though he was tired and in pain, even though she didn't particularly *want* to kiss him—which was a startling realization that had come upon her earlier in the evening, when she had first joined him in her bed.

But instead she had told him the truth, about everything: She was, according to Simon and Zahra, the foretold Sun Queen, the daughter of the Kingsbane and the Lightbringer. The Furyborn Child. She had many names, it seemed, and she had chosen none of them for herself. She had destroyed the invading Empire fleet by calling down a storm from the sky.

She had killed Rozen with a dagger to the throat.

She waited, her cheek against Harkan's chest, until his arms around her began to feel like a cage. Then, with a slow breath in and out, he resumed smoothing circles across her upper arm.

Eliana directed her muscles to unclench. He hadn't shoved her away or extracted himself from her embrace. That was something.

"Have you told Remy?" he asked.

"No." She glared at the nearest flickering candle until her eyes stopped stinging. "He thinks Red Crown is out there right now, searching for her."

"And you believe Simon and Zahra?"

"About my parentage and my power? I don't want to."

"But you do anyway."

"You weren't there that day." She shut her eyes against the memory of the battle in Karajak Bay, but that made the images even more vivid. "The things I saw—the things I *did*—shouldn't have been possible. And yet they happened all the same."

Harkan made a thoughtful sound. "Couldn't it have been an ordinary storm? And, perhaps, since you had endured so much, you were susceptible to Simon's suggestion? He offered an interpretation of what was happening, and you accepted it in the moment because the stress was so immense."

"You're asking if I was simply hysterical?" Eliana interrupted sharply.

Harkan's reply was as gentle as his circling thumb. "I'm trying to find an explanation that makes sense."

"I've tried that already. While it was happening, there on that beach, I felt something moving inside me. A force. Every lightning strike, every gust of wind, tore through my body like blows of pain. Like..." She paused, considering how to describe this impossible thing to him. "Like when you awaken the morning after a hard job, and your muscles ache—except a hundred times more painful, and it was as though I could feel every ounce of my blood, every inch of every muscle, and it was all erupting, all *scorching*. I could feel the ache being made. I thought it would tear me apart."

She realized she was clutching Harkan's tunic and released it at once.

"Could it have been someone else doing that?" he suggested. "Maybe someone else nearby, conducting magic, and you were simply feeling the effects? Maybe Simon—"

"No. It was me."

"But how can you be sure, if you'd never experienced anything like that before?"

Eliana sat up, resisting the urge to shove his arms away. Her body itched to move. She pressed her palms hard against the bed.

"If you were standing in a crowded room, where everyone was talking," she said, "and the layers of sound were so immense that you could hardly hear yourself think—if, in such a place, you heard me calling for you, you would recognize my voice, wouldn't you? And you would follow it until you found me."

"Yes. I would follow you anywhere." He found one of her hands, kissed her rigid knuckles. "I *did* follow you."

That voice, that tender touch, would have once melted her. Now, she bristled at it. His gentle presence inexplicably grated against her nerves.

"Well, it felt like that for me, on that beach," she said sharply. "I knew that power belonged to me, even though it felt unfamiliar, even though it frightened me, just as I would know your voice anywhere and know the rhythm of my own breathing."

That made her think of something, and she did soften then, and could hardly look at him, remembering the years of his quiet loyalty. "We never talked about it, and I thank you for not ever pressing the matter, but surely you noticed that any injuries I sustained while on a job didn't last. You heard the rumors, just as everyone else did. The indestructible Dread of Orline."

Harkan's gaze was steady. "I did."

She pulled away from him, wishing their conversation would rattle him. Only moments ago she had been steeling herself against the possibility of him pushing her away, of his disgust and judgment. Now, with him gazing up at her, acceptance plain and soft on his face, Eliana found herself craving a fight. How could he still look at her that way, just as he'd always used to, when everything had so utterly changed?

It would be easier if he recoiled, if he accused her of keeping secrets. If he lashed out at her, distrusting this new creature who looked like his oldest, dearest friend but had become something else entirely.

But instead he watched her, waiting for her to speak, and in the unbearable silence, Eliana wished suddenly for Simon to come storming in and say something nasty or scornful, so she would have an excuse to jump out of bed and hit something.

She rose and began to pace. "Remy thinks the reason for that indestructibility was my power. For years it lay dormant inside me, and its presence protected me from harm. It repaired me when I needed it, gave me incredible strength and resilience."

"And now that your power is no longer dormant?" Harkan asked.

She stopped to look out the windows, the mountains rising dark beyond the glass. She touched the tiny lump on her skull, still tender from Navi's attack, and was mortified to feel tears gathering in her eyes once more.

"God, what's wrong with me?" she muttered. "I've cried more in the past two weeks than I have for the whole rest of my life. I've been reduced to some kind of weepy child."

"What can I do, El?"

She wiped savagely at her face. "Now that my power is no longer dormant, it appears I'm no longer as invincible as I once was."

"You mean, now you can get hurt?"

She moved her hair aside to reveal the still-healing cut. "I'm fragile. I'm vulnerable." She spat out the word. "I could forget myself in a fight and get badly hurt, leaving Remy unprotected. And…"

But then came a thought she couldn't bear to voice. That the pain she had craved for years, had relished, had sought out with every job, every fight and kill—the pain that had reminded her she was alive, that she was untouchable, that she could not and would not break—was now something she must guard against.

Harkan came to her, reaching for her face, but she jerked away from him. Immediately, he withdrew. "I'm sorry, I didn't mean to—"

"It's fine." She resumed pacing. "I'm fine."

"You don't seem fine."

"Simon and Zahra told me that my mother—the woman who gave

birth to me—is the Blood Queen. Queen Rielle Courverie of Celdaria, of more than a thousand years ago. The Kingsbane. The Lady of Death."

"I know who Queen Rielle is." Harkan smiled softly. "Remy has told me many stories about her."

Eliana closed her eyes at the mention of Remy. Harkan touched her hand, and she once again flinched from him.

This time, he could not hide his hurt. "I'm sorry, El, I just thought—"

"That we would fall into bed together," Eliana said harshly, "just like we used to?"

"I wasn't trying to take you to bed, El. You're shaking, and I wanted to hold your hand."

"The hand of a monster."

"What?" He laughed, incredulous. "You're no monster."

"Were you there on the beach? Did you see what I did?" She flung an arm at the windows. "My storm left the bay in ruins. It destroyed dozens of ships, both Empire and Astavari. They're still cleaning up the beach. It's littered with the corpses of crawlers, adatrox, Astavari soldiers. People I killed, and I didn't even know what I was doing as I killed them!"

"Simon told me many more would have died, were it not for you," Harkan pointed out. "Astavar would have fallen."

"Don't you understand? Her blood is inside me. I didn't ask for it, and yet here it is." She gestured at herself and laughed bitterly. "I've been reading about her, you know. Simon retrieved books for me from the royal archives—not that there are many left from those days. She made sure of that, didn't she, when she died and took so much with her? She had years of training before she had to perform magic in anything other than a temple classroom. She had a whole city's worth of magisters helping her. She had the support of the crown. She lived in a world where magic actually existed, and people knew what it was about. And still she fell. She ruined everything. She destroyed everything."

"She didn't destroy everything," Harkan pointed out.

"She destroyed enough."

Harkan ducked down to meet her eyes. "You are not her. You are Eliana Ferracora, not Eliana Courverie. You are my friend. You are Remy's sister."

Eliana looked away. She had told Zahra she would practice using her power. In order to help Navi, she had resolved to do it, to swallow her revulsion.

But the memory of Zahra's vision still swirled thick as bile in her head, and Harkan's presence made her feel young again, and small. A child calling to her friend across the gap between their houses.

She shook her head, panic brimming sick and hot beneath her skin. "I won't be like her. I won't. I won't do this—"

"You don't have to." Harkan cupped her face in his hands. "You've done enough for this war. This isn't your fight. You are Eliana Ferracora."

She closed her eyes, unable to speak.

"You are my friend," Harkan continued, his voice soft and urgent. "You are Remy's sister. You are the daughter of Ioseph and Rozen Ferracora. You are the Dread of Orline."

"But don't you see? It's already begun." When she looked back up at him, her eyes were dry, but her body was a clenched tangle of worries. "The day my power awakens, I kill the woman who raised me, the woman who was more my mother than any ghost from the Old World could ever be. What does that tell you?"

From beyond Harkan came a soft cry.

Eliana's heart crashed against her ribs.

She turned to see Remy standing in the middle of the room, having just entered with a teetering stack of books in his hands.

The look on his face left Eliana feeling as though all the air had been sucked out of the room. She gaped at him, utterly frozen. The world was tumbling down around her, and she had no idea how to stop it.

Harkan took the books from him cheerfully, as though nothing had happened. "Hello there, Remy. Did Simon send some more books? How considerate of him. Can you ask him if, next time, he would be so kind as to jump up his own ass instead?"

But Remy ignored him. He allowed Harkan to take the books and then stood there, looking so small and frail in the shadows that the sight of him made Eliana's chest hurt.

"Is it true?" he asked, both his expression and his voice eerily calm, though his eyes were bright. "You killed her?"

Eliana forced herself to meet his gaze. "She wasn't herself anymore, Remy. They had turned her into a monster. She was attacking Simon."

"No." He shook his head, backing slowly away from her. "No. *You're* the monster."

Then he turned and hurried out of the room.

◆

Two days later, in the early evening, Eliana sat hunched over a table in the royal archives, staring dully at the book lying open in front of her.

She had tried to talk to Remy several times, and each had been a disaster. He had screamed at her, declared his hatred, wept so viciously that he'd made himself sick, and now he wouldn't speak to her. He saw her coming and ran the other way. She searched the castle for him and ended up chasing shadows. He was a small, sly thing, her brother. He had grown up in the twisting, narrow streets of Orline, and if he didn't want to be found, he wouldn't be.

So, now, utterly heartsick, feeling ill down to her toes, Eliana had retreated to the archives, spending most hours of the day there and letting Remy have the space he obviously craved—and hoping that Harkan would somehow be able to reach her brother when she had not.

A soft movement from the shadows made her glance up to see Simon sliding into the chair across from her. She returned to the book and pretended to read for a few moments while he sat with his hands folded on the table.

When she could bear his silent presence no longer, she looked up once more. "Yes?"

"You sent for me," he replied.

She flushed a little. "Oh, right. I'd forgotten."

"If it's so unimportant to you, perhaps my time can be better spent elsewhere."

"You have something better to do than serve your queen?" she snapped.

Simon's smile came slowly. He leaned back in his chair, considering her. "Royalty suits you."

The sight of him looking so quietly delighted unnerved her, which made her want to push back from the table and kick her chair into the bookshelves, but she was afraid she might start crying again if she moved with too much violence.

Slowly, she began stacking her books. "How does it suit me?"

"You're a snob," Simon replied, "and you have a terrible temper, not to mention an unshakable belief in your own worth."

An ugly laugh burst out of her. "My own worth." She slammed the topmost book shut. "I look in the mirror, and do you know what I see? I see the daughter of a cruel woman who nearly destroyed the world. I see a girl who doesn't understand one fucking thing about any of this nonsense." She gestured impatiently at the books. "And I see Remy, staring up at me, calling me a monster because I killed his mother."

She glared at the table for a long, fraught moment, and when she looked up, the sight of Simon watching her so quietly—his eyes piercing and unwaveringly focused—shook something loose inside her. He wasn't trying to comfort her; he wasn't showing her a scrap of sympathy, or moving to touch her, or hold her, as Harkan would have done. He knew very well what she was, she realized, and understood that she neither deserved comfort nor craved kindness.

She was suddenly, savagely, glad for his nearness.

It took her a moment to find her voice and remember why she had summoned him—to convince him of her loyalty so it would be easier to leave with Zahra for the Nest.

"I need your help," she said at last. "That's why I sent for you. I haven't wanted to attempt using my power again because I've been afraid of what might happen."

"Another storm," he guessed.

"Or worse. But if I had some physical assurance that that wouldn't happen—at least not as easily as it did on the beach—it might be easier for me to open my mind to this entire idea." She took a deep breath and met his gaze. "I want to forge a casting for myself, and I need your help to do it."

He nodded slowly. "I'm not well-versed in metalwork."

"But you're well-versed in the Old World. You can come with me to the Forge, help me speak to the acolytes. I want someone I trust by my side when I do this."

He raised an eyebrow. "Would you rather not have Harkan by your side, then?"

"This is not Harkan's world," she said. "It's yours. And I want to shelter him and Remy from as much of it as I can."

Simon searched her face for a long time, his expression impassive.

She glared at him. "Have you quite finished staring at me?"

"I'm understandably suspicious of this change of heart," he replied. "Two days ago, you were ignoring the books I gave you and barely acknowledging your power's existence. Now you want to forge a casting so you can try using that power again."

"Two days ago, my brother was speaking to me."

"Give him time," Simon said quietly.

"He won't ever forgive me."

"Perhaps not."

"And yet part of me is glad he overheard me. Now he can live under no illusions of what I am."

"He has long known what you are, and yet he never stopped loving you."

"Until now."

Simon inclined his head. "I suppose that's possible."

Eliana gripped the back of her chair, hard, and shot him a sardonic smile. "You know, I must thank you."

"For what?"

"For your cruelty. One word from you, and I feel furious enough to forget the rest of my troubles."

Simon smiled tightly, looking as though he were about to respond. Instead, he gestured at the books.

"As I'm sure you've read by now," he said, "when an elemental forged their casting, they usually melted down an artifact of personal significance to add to the mixture."

Eliana nodded. "The stronger the personal attachment to one's casting, the greater ease with which an elemental could use it to manipulate their magic. Luckily I have just the thing." She removed her necklace and tossed it onto the table. The scratched surface of the Lightbringer caught the flickering lamplight and gave the horse's wings the illusion of movement.

"You're not her, Eliana." Shadows cloaked the long lines of Simon's body, shrouding all but his eyes in darkness. "You're not your mother."

"No, but I'm her daughter. Or so you say. What makes you think I'll be any different from her?"

"Because I knew her. And I know you."

Eliana scoffed. "You hardly know me."

"I know enough," came his low reply. "No one can decide what you become except you. Not me, and not your parents. You have a choice ahead of you, just as she did, and I have faith that you will make it wisely."

He rose, straightening his jacket. "Shall we visit the Forge tonight, then? Or wait until tomorrow?"

His words left her feeling shaken more thoroughly than she had felt even in her Fidelia cell with Zahra's proclamation ringing in her ears: *You are the Sun Queen, and I've come to bring you home.*

But she would not allow him the satisfaction of seeing her rattled. She kept her voice cool and retrieved the necklace from the table as if it were a mere trifle, easily discarded.

"No," she replied. "We begin tonight."

# → 9 ←

# RIELLE

*"Together, in the war-ravaged plains of the land that would someday become the nation of Celdaria, the saints began carving a door out of this world and into the next. What they found, however, was not a new world, for not even they were powerful enough for so far a reach. What they found was the Deep—a void, eternal and narrow, a sea of hollow space just beyond the curtain of our world. And it was then that they began to understand what they must do, and how they would at last bring the angels to ruin."*

—*The Last Days of the Saints*, a study of the Gate and its construction, by Kristo Niskala, Borsvall historian

The archer who had shot Ludivine was named Jodoc, and as he led their party through the woodlands of Iastra, the largest island of the Sunderlands, Rielle glared at the back of his head, wondering if she could crack it open without even touching him.

Part of her very much wanted to try.

Ludivine walked beside her, making a valiant effort to keep up with the group's pace, but new, thin lines of pain framed her mouth and eyes, as if she had aged in the terrible minute between the blightblade piercing her and Rielle shattering it.

Rielle glanced at Ludivine's hastily mended dress. Tendrils of darkness—midnight-blue, indigo, the scaly brown-black of rotting flesh—snaked out from beneath her furred collar, following the delicate lines of Ludivine's upper arm.

Rielle quickly looked away, her throat tightening. She returned her gaze to the back of Jodoc's head and recited to herself that she mustn't kill him, reminded herself dozens of times over that she mustn't kill him, until her fists unclenched and she could breathe without feeling made of fire.

Over the past few hours, the bruise from the blightblade had spread down Ludivine's left arm, encasing it in a dark lattice of uneven lines that shimmered in the light as if tiny jewels had been embedded in her skin. Rielle would have thought it beautiful, were it not for the memory of Ludivine's muted screams as it bloomed. In the healer's rooms, she had clung to Rielle, muffling her pained cries in Rielle's cloak.

Thankfully, the bruise appeared to have stopped growing, the gown covered most of it, and Ludivine bore whatever discomfort remained without complaint. But Rielle was not fooled by her silence. Ludivine's pain was a faint presence in the back of her mind, like the remnants of an unsettling dream she couldn't shake loose.

And the farther they walked through the dense woodlands of Iastra, the greater became Rielle's feeling of uneasiness.

They could no longer hear the waves lapping against the island's broad beach, nor the seabirds' cries. The woodlands grew close and tangled, the trees' trunks large enough to serve as towers of a woodland fortress. Their branches sprawled like ancient black serpents across mossy hollows, their bark lined with silver lichens. Some bore clumps of white flowers that glowed faintly as if they had each swallowed a piece of a star. Torn petals hung suspended in the air alongside dark oak leaves, grains of sand, flakes of crushed seashells, and tiny white shards that Rielle thought might be bits of animal bone. The air was thick, heavy with a slow, spinning weight.

With each step, she felt as though she were moving farther away from her body and into a new realm. Her vision shifted, and she could see more clearly the gossamer net connecting everything around them—a delicate golden sea, forever undulating, forever seeking new shores, on which the rest of the seen world floated.

She smiled, drawing her fingers through waves of light no one else was powerful enough to glimpse.

Ingrid at last broke the silence. "What's happened to this place? Why is everything floating?"

Ilmaire and Audric answered simultaneously—Audric's voice hushed with awe, and Ilmaire's nearly giddy: "It's the Gate."

Ingrid cut an irritated glare Audric's way.

"The nearer the Gate," confirmed Jodoc, "the higher the concentration of the empirium. And in such a place, the world is not what it is else-where." He held aside a branch so the others could continue unimpeded.

But Rielle didn't follow. Jodoc, she sensed, was taking them the wrong way.

Well, not the *wrong* way, but certainly the *long* way—to confuse them, she assumed, and to make it more difficult for them to retrace their steps. She moved away from them, drifting farther into the trees, and as she walked, she observed how the entire endless woodland was lined with dozens of winding paths. The Obex had doubtless created these paths, treading upon them over and over for centuries, until they had become dirt tracks worn smooth. It was a maze; unwanted visitors would easily get turned around in the trees and never find their way out.

Rielle supposed that she herself was an unwanted visitor. But the call of the Gate pulled her like a distant light through a dark tunnel. She would not lose herself in these trees, no matter how earnestly they tried to confuse her.

Humming quietly to herself, her eyes unfocused, the world dreamy and slow-moving around her, she turned down a particular path that was a little more shadowed than the others, lined with floating browned petals. She pushed them aside, the movement lazy and supple, as if she were drawing her hand through water. She blinked and saw only her hand moving through the air, lightly bumping the petals out of her path. She blinked once more, and the world of the empirium appeared to her—every leaf, every petal, every faint breath of wind, every pore of her skin, painted with stipples of gold.

With her boots on, she could not feel the earth under her feet, so she removed them, discarding them in a nest of roots. Large iridescent beetles emerged from the shadows, skittering away from her presence.

The still, damp air grew charged and sour, as if from a nearing storm. The fine hairs along Rielle's arms stood up. Each inhale felt like trying to breathe with a hand clamped over her mouth and nose.

Then, finally, her feet hit something cold and hard.

She blinked, clearing her vision of the empirium, and saw an enormous flat plinth of stone, square and gray, immaculately clean, surrounded on three sides by the woods. On the far side of the plinth rose sheer black cliffs that disappeared into a thick veil of low gray clouds. A slender set of stairs had been cut into the stone.

Rielle began to climb them, and at the top, she emerged onto a rocky black plain, slick and gleaming. Flakes of ash floated in the air, slowly turning. A gray and endless fog surrounded her, and what the landscape looked like beyond that, she could not determine. She heard the distant crash of waves but could see no trees, no sky, no water.

She saw only a broad stretch of craggy black rock, as if something terrible had permanently scorched the ground.

And there, in the center of the burnt plain, stood the Gate—an angular structure of unadorned gray stone framing a dim, shifting blue light.

Trapezoidal, the Gate stood on yet another flat plinth of stone, this one circular. The two pillars that formed the Gate's sides, and the singular piece of stone connecting them at the top, were enormous, each slab as thick as twenty men standing with arms outstretched, finger to finger. The height of it made Rielle's head spin. It must have stood some five hundred feet in the air, and another five hundred feet across—and even that, Rielle thought, was an underestimation.

She approached it, her breathing slow and thin, as if approaching a wild animal she wished to tame and claim for her own. From her reading, she knew the structure itself was merely for show, to demonstrate the clear boundaries of where the Gate ended and began. The Gate itself was in the air—an opening into the Deep, carved out of the empirium by the saints before they banished the angels inside and sealed the opening shut.

But that seal, Rielle saw at once, was breaking.

She saw it as clearly as if someone were holding before her a piece of glass cracked by the impact of a stone. Shifting her thoughts outside her body to the eerie world around her, she unfocused her eyes and imagined her blood and bone extending beyond her fingers and toes, beyond the reach of her tongue, and into the ground—along the rocks beneath her, skimming the flakes of ash floating in the air. She tilted her head, inhaled, exhaled, and the picture of the breaking Gate sharpened before her eyes.

The empirium was a white-hot sun at the Gate's center, a solid wall of light—except for thin, dark cracks, fine as the threads of a spider's web, that drifted through the empirium's light like the alien shapes that floated across Rielle's vision after rubbing her eyes too hard. One moment, they existed, long and delicate; the next moment, they had faded, only to reappear seconds later in a different location.

It would be easy, she thought, to mend these holes. All she would need to do was sew them back together, as her father had tried and failed to teach her with a needle and thread long ago. She had been terrible at mending clothes, and impatient, pointing out that they had servants to do such things for them, and now she found herself wishing she had paid more attention during those long hours bent over her father's worktable.

She swallowed hard, dislodging the hot lump in her throat, and closed the door on her father's memory. She stepped toward the Gate, her hand outstretched.

Then a terrible scream pierced the air.

Rielle stumbled back from the Gate, just as Atheria landed on the rocks before her. The chavaile looked more ferocious than Rielle had ever seen her—ears flattened, sharp teeth bared, head lowered as if preparing to bite. She held her wings fully extended on either side, enormous and dark.

Rielle's tongue tingled; the air around the Gate had numbed her. "Atheria," she managed, holding out her hand. "Come here, my sweet girl."

Atheria's eyes narrowed. She pawed the ground, snorting.

"Darling Atheria. Are you watching out for me?" Rielle went to her, trying to ignore the Gate's insistent pull. She embraced the chavaile's great head, pressed her face against her velvet muzzle.

Atheria relaxed, whickering gently.

"You don't want me to touch the Gate?" Rielle murmured.

Atheria nudged Rielle's face with her own, folded her into the bend of one of her wings.

Smiling, Rielle stepped back to meet the godsbeast's enormous eyes. "But I must," she said simply, and then, stepping back, she gathered a clutch of air in her palm, thrust her fist at Atheria, and shoved her away.

The air rippled with the shock wave, but Atheria was apparently too powerful to be cast away completely. She simply staggered back a few steps before sinking to her knees. Another flick of Rielle's wrist, and a golden net encased Atheria, pinning her cruelly against the rocks.

Rielle made her way back to the Gate, ignoring Atheria's furious screams as she struggled to free herself. "It's all right, Atheria," she murmured. "I'll release you in a moment or two, once it's done. I can mend it. I see it so clearly."

She stepped onto the base of the Gate, squinting past the brilliant light contained between the enormous pillars of rock. The light vibrated, drowning out Atheria's frantic cries. Rielle could hear only the deep thrum of the Gate in her bones and the wild pounding of her heart.

She reached for the first crack she saw, floating before her like a dark river etched across a map. The solution was clear: she would gather this fissure in her fingers and pinch together the two golden expanses that flanked it, binding them into place with her own power until the crack was sealed.

She reached for the tear, her fingers buzzing. A great invisible force pushed back against her, the air dense and hot. Too dense and hot for a human to move inside it?

But, then, she was not entirely human. She was the Sun Queen. She was *more*.

Distantly, she heard a man call her name, pleading with her to stop.

Ludivine's voice came next. *Rielle, no!*

But Corien was delighted. *Keep going, my marvelous girl*, he told her, and for a moment she could see herself facing the Gate, and Corien standing behind her—his arms guiding hers toward the light, his lips caressing her neck.

*I can mend it*, Rielle told him.

*You can do anything*, he replied. When he kissed her throat, his teeth scraped her flesh, making her shiver.

She touched the crack in the Gate.

Lightning struck her—a thousand bolts, simultaneous. Too much light, too much power, as if all the sun in the sky were trying to force its way inside her. The feeling consumed her, convulsing her body; she could not see or move.

*Step back!* Corien screamed, no longer amused. *Break free of it!*

But Rielle couldn't move. The power of the Gate would not allow it, knitting her bones to the rock under her feet.

Another cry arose, closer than the others. "Rielle, stay with me! Listen to my voice!"

*Audric.*

The sound of his cries shook her. With monumental effort, she took one step back, pulling free of the Gate's hold.

A burst of energy erupted, flinging her off the plinth and back several yards into Audric's arms. Ilmaire caught them both, and they all went stumbling to the ground. Rielle shook against Audric's chest, her body steaming and crackling, her hands blazing gold.

"My God," Ilmaire murmured.

"Don't touch her hands!" Ludivine cried. "Audric, be careful!"

Rielle's eyes fluttered. She tried to focus on the image hovering above her—Audric's face. He cupped her cheek in his palm. "Are you all right? Say something."

Rielle forced out a word. "Something."

His laughter was fragile. "What were you thinking?"

"I can mend it," she replied.

"Forget the damned Gate, Rielle. Forget all of this. What good is any of it if it kills you?" He kissed her temple. "You're still a human, my darling. Still breakable."

Rielle gazed past him at the Gate, her vision spinning. She struggled to rise, Audric helping her up. "But I can mend it."

"What is she doing?" Ingrid snapped.

"Let her go," said Ludivine quietly. "She has to learn."

Rielle struggled against Audric's grip. When he held fast, she snapped at him, "Following in Corien's footsteps, are you?"

He released her at once, looking as though she had slapped him.

Jodoc approached, drawing an arrow from the quiver on his back. "I'll shoot her if I have to."

Audric unsheathed Illumenor. It crackled to life, casting brilliant sunbursts across the ground. "Make one move against her, and I swear to you, I will cut you in two."

Rielle took the opportunity to break free of him and make unsteadily for the Gate, the world tilting around her. Atheria had stopped screaming, and she wondered, her mind distant and distracted, where the chavaile had gone or if she had given up fighting or if she had died.

Scrambling up onto the plinth, Rielle found a crack at once, and seized the planes of light on either side of it, trying to press them closed. Instantaneous pain ripped up her body, as if some burning creature had possessed her, determined to rip her open from the inside out.

She stepped away, more easily this time, and gasped for breath. Hot ropes skipped across her skin like miniature bolts of lightning.

On her hands and knees she crawled back toward the Gate, reaching for the same tear that had eluded her—and saw, her stomach dropping, that even more tears now existed than there had been only moments before.

She hesitated, heat gathering helplessly behind her eyes.

*Do you see?* Ludivine's voice was full of pity. *You're making it worse.*

*I can mend it,* Rielle insisted.

*I believe that you can. But not like this. Not yet. You must be stronger.*

And that, Rielle decided, was entirely unfair. To be so powerful, to be such a rarity—the subject of a prophecy, for God's sake—and yet to be unable to do this one small thing?

Her temper ignited. She pushed herself to her feet, charged at the Gate with a scream that ripped her voice in two, and slammed her fists against the field of light that so mocked her.

The resulting shock wave threw her back off her feet and into blackness.

—◇—

She awoke lying on her stomach in a candlelit room, on a bed of soft white linens.

Audric slept in a chair beside her, his hand holding hers, and Rielle herself lay with her head on a pillow in Ludivine's lap.

Ludivine combed her fingers through Rielle's hair. "How are you feeling?"

Remembering everything that had happened, Rielle set her jaw against a rising tide of shame. Her head pounded; her body felt beaten by a thousand angry fists.

She glared at the aged wooden floor. "Don't you know?"

Ludivine's finger caught on a tangle, which made Rielle wince. "I do, but I would like to hear you say it."

"Fine. I feel like shit."

Ludivine said primly, "I expect that you do."

"Leave off, Lu," murmured Audric. "She's been through enough."

At the sound of Audric's voice, Rielle turned toward him and squeezed his hand. "Are you angry with me?"

He brought her fingers to his lips. "Yes. But more than that, I'm glad you're all right. And I understand why you did it."

Then she remembered. Panic punched her upright. "Atheria. Where is she?"

Audric hesitated. "She is not wounded, at least not that we could see, but she flew away shortly after the Gate threw you and hasn't been sighted since."

"I was mad," Rielle whispered, tears sewing her throat shut, fists clenched against her thighs. "I lost my head. If she doesn't return, it's what I deserve."

"Please don't worry. She'll come back to you. Just give her time." He bent to kiss her, and Rielle cupped his face in her hands and pressed her forehead to his, devouring the sight of his steady dark gaze, so close to her own.

"I just wanted to help," she said.

"I know," he replied softly.

*And you wanted to show off,* Corien pointed out, sounding sulky.

*And you urged me on,* she shot back, *even knowing that it would hurt me.*

He paused. *I didn't know it would hurt you that badly.*

*Audric would never do such a thing to me.*

*No, I don't suppose he would,* Corien replied, his voice curling. *Not yet, anyway.*

Rielle ignored him, preparing to apologize once more—but before she could, Jodoc burst in, accompanied by four Obex in plain gray robes. Beyond them, Ilmaire and Ingrid and three of their own guard stood at the ready.

Jodoc began speaking without preamble. "In the twenty-four hours that have passed since your foolish and perhaps disastrous attempt to repair the Gate—"

"Twenty-four hours?" Rielle glanced at Audric. "It's been that long?"

"In those twenty-four hours," Jodoc continued sharply, "I have already received a dozen reports from Obex around the world."

He glanced at the stack of thin papers in his hands. "An earthquake in Astavar. A typhoon in the Vespers, which has destroyed six fishing villages on the eastern coast of the main island. A blizzard in the Mazabat city of Zamar—a tropical city, mind you—which has completely incapacitated the Ferej Canal, an important shipping route for that part of the continent. A tidal wave, even more enormous than the one you recently encountered, off the coast of Vindica—which is largely uninhabited, thank God. And in your own country, in the coastal city of Luxitaine, a flock of birds, thousands strong, dropped dead from the skies, killing several and terrorizing many."

Audric closed his eyes and looked away.

Jodoc folded up the papers and placed them in his coat pocket. "And these, Lady Rielle, are only the events we know about."

Rielle sat in silence as he spoke, ignoring the temptation to lower her eyes in shame. Instead, she met Jodoc's flat gaze. "How could you know about such things so quickly?"

*They have marques in their employ,* Ludivine answered at once. *They have offered them asylum from their governments in exchange for their service.*

Jodoc raised an eyebrow. "That's the question you would ask of me right now?"

"It's a fair question," said Ilmaire. "How are we to know you aren't falsifying these reports?"

"And why would I do such a thing?"

"To frighten us into doing whatever you demand?" Ingrid snapped.

"Or to shame Lady Rielle?" Ilmaire added.

"She should feel shame, and you should feel frightened." Jodoc faced Rielle. "What you have done has exacerbated the problem that already existed. The elemental scholars in our order, who have spent lifetimes studying the empirium, have now counted an additional thirty-three fractures in the Gate. The catastrophic effects of its accelerated collapse cannot be overstated and will touch all of Avitas."

Ludivine's grip on Rielle's hand tightened.

"Have any additional angels emerged in the past day?" Rielle managed, after she had found her voice.

Ludivine shook her head. "No. Not yet."

The look Jodoc threw at her was one of utter disdain. "But they certainly will. And we are equipped to fight them, for now. But our blightblade stores are not limitless and cannot be replenished. And when the Gate falls at last and all the angels return, our meager weapons will mean nothing."

Ludivine fiddled with the end of her left sleeve, beneath which the blightblade scar glistened.

Ilmaire regarded Jodoc thoughtfully. "You said blightblades are forged using the blood of beasts called cruciata, and that cruciata come from the Deep. How did you obtain this blood?"

"A single cruciata escaped through the weakening Gate many years ago," Jodoc replied. "We were able to subdue it, at the cost of many lives, and conducted experiments with its remains, which yielded us the first blightblade. We have access to only this one corpse, and when our supply of its blood is depleted, we will have no means of forging additional blightblades." He paused, looking grim. "At least, not until the Gate truly collapses, and everything contained in the Deep comes pouring out."

Into the ringing silence that followed Jodoc's words, Audric spoke. "For how long can a blightblade contain an angel?"

"It depends on the strength of the blade," Jodoc answered. "Some for only minutes; some for years."

Audric began to pace. "So the question remains: How do we repair the Gate?"

"There is no way to repair the Gate. The kind of magic the saints possessed, the sheer power they used to create it, no longer exists in this world. The empirium is fading, and has been for years." Jodoc glanced at Illumenor, now sheathed at Audric's waist. "The kind of power you possess, Your Highness, is an anomaly now, as you well know. And even that is not enough to repair the Gate." He glanced at Rielle. "Nor is the Sun Queen's power, apparently."

"There has to be a way, some method no one's tried," Ilmaire insisted. "Texts, journals from the saints—"

"Journals are no use without the proper power to implement their teachings."

"I have enough power to do it," Rielle interrupted quietly. "I know I do."

"As we have already seen," Jodoc said, "that is not the case, Lady Rielle, no matter how dearly you wish it were."

She lifted her chin to meet his glare. "Maybe I can't do it *now*, but I think I will be able to someday."

"And when will that day arrive? Tomorrow? Next year? Twenty years from now? Have you no understanding of what's happened? The Gate is a volcano waiting to erupt, one large enough to obliterate us all, and we have no way of knowing when it will do so, no way of knowing what the angels are doing on the other side in their attempt to break free of their prison. No knowledge of how many cruciata they themselves have encountered, and subdued, and bound to them in service. And you," he added, "have merely stoked the building fire."

A moment of silence passed. Then Ilmaire said thoughtfully, "Perhaps she needs a casting."

Rielle laughed. "As you've seen, castings aren't necessary for me."

"Maybe not for stopping arrows or tidal waves, no," Ilmaire said. "But to repair a Gate sewn into the very fabric of the empirium? A Gate that required seven of the most powerful humans the world has ever known to create? For that, I think, you might need some help."

Beside Rielle, Ludivine tensed. *He has an idea, but he doesn't want to say it. Who does?*

*Jodoc.* Ludivine hesitated. *Ah. It's an excellent idea.*

"You have something to suggest, Jodoc?" she said out loud.

The man's face closed at once. "Poking around in my head, are you? Can't help yourself?"

"When you are withholding information that could assist Rielle," Ludivine replied, "then yes, I will poke around as I see fit."

After a moment of tense silence, Jodoc spoke. "Some of our scholars have theorized that the original castings of the saints might be necessary to achieve any sort of true repair of the Gate." He glanced at Rielle. "As with all castings, even after their user's death, they hold some residual power and will contain the memory of the Gate's creation. They are familiar with the fabric of it, with how it was originally constructed."

Audric's expression brightened. "You think that if Rielle wields the saints' castings—"

"That might provide her with the tools she needs to make the repairs," Ilmaire finished.

"As Magister Cateline Thoraval wrote in *A Treatise on the Inner Life of Magic*," Audric continued, "even for the most naturally talented elemental, structure is key. In the execution of any elemental task, especially those foreign to the elemental, or particularly dangerous—"

Ilmaire snapped his fingers, finishing the sentence for him. "A strong foundation of support—from knowledge to memory to the casting itself—is essential for success."

Ingrid cast a look of disgust at them both. "That was frightening, and I beg you to never do it again."

Rielle turned the idea over in her mind. *Is this possible?*

*I can't say,* Ludivine replied. *Jodoc seems to think so. And he has spent his entire life studying the Gate.*

"If I wanted to attempt this," Rielle said, "where would I find these castings? They are guarded by your order, are they not?"

Jodoc raised his eyebrows. "I cannot give you that information, Lady Rielle."

"But you just said—"

"Guarding the saints' castings and protecting the Gate are sacred duties that have been entrusted to the order of the Obex for centuries by the saints themselves. The information we hold cannot be shared."

Jodoc's gaze cut sharply to Ludivine. "Nor can it be easily extracted. We have worked for many centuries to close off those parts of our minds, thanks to the teachings left to us by the angel Aryava. And if you move against us, Lady Ludivine, I will blow this horn"—he gestured at the horn of bone he wore at his waist—"and every member of my order who possesses this information will hear me and, without hesitation, will ingest a poison that each of them keeps on their person, and so will I. We will die in a matter of seconds, and the knowledge we hold will die with us. The marques in our employ will travel the world and bring the rest of our order into deep hiding, and you will never find us."

"You would rather die than help us?" Ingrid said tightly. "You would sooner leave the Gate's defense incomplete?"

"I would rather die than have sacred information fall into the hands of an angel I have no reason to trust," Jodoc replied.

A tense silence filled the room.

At last, Ludivine said smoothly, "Very well. I will attempt no such thing."

Rielle threw up her hands. "So we're meant to wander the world, with no direction whatsoever, and somehow find seven hidden castings before the Gate falls?"

"We will watch the Gate closely," Jodoc replied, "and give you information if the situation requires it. But until then, Lady Rielle, you have proven yourself to be untrustworthy and unpredictable. And I therefore don't care to make your burden any lighter. If you are to wield the castings of the saints to whose legacy I and my companions have devoted our lives, you will have to show me you are worthy of wielding them.

"And I must note," he added, glancing at Audric, "that you aren't beginning this task aimlessly. The first piece of information you need, to find the casting of Saint Katell, lies in the castle Baingarde. I suggest you leave the Sunderlands and return home to Celdaria as quickly as you can."

With that, Jodoc and the other Obex exited the room, leaving Rielle's group of five alone. Ilmaire walked to the window and looked out over the moonlit forest. Ingrid sat heavily by the fire and filled a plain metal goblet with wine.

"Anyone else need a drink or three?" she mumbled.

Ludivine raised her hand. "Yes, please."

"Do you know what he meant by that?" Rielle asked Audric. "What's in Baingarde?"

"I don't know. But Mother might." He sat beside her, scrubbing a hand over his face. "Are you well enough to leave tomorrow?"

Rielle smiled wryly. "Does that matter?"

Audric's gaze was soft. "It does to me."

She could not bear to look at him for one more second without touching him, so she kissed him, softly, beneath the murmur of the others' voices. But that was not enough. Restless, exhausted, she knew of only one thing in the world that could grant her the peace she craved, and it was not a single kiss, no matter how lovely.

She rose, Audric's hand in hers, and led him quietly down the hall to a small, clean room that stood empty, faintly lit by the night sky. Once inside, Rielle closed the door and kissed him again, harder, until she could barely breathe, until he stopped treating her as if she was made of glass. He turned her away from him and pressed her gently against the door, and Rielle reached back to tug him closer, impatient. He kissed her neck and raised her skirts, and for those glorious blazing minutes while he moved inside her, one hand teasing between her legs and his voice hoarse and urgent in her hair, Rielle did not feel like a girl upon whose shoulders the fate of the world rested.

She felt, simply, like a girl lucky enough to know what it was to be loved, and she clung to that feeling as fiercely as she could, until Audric's murmured words and tireless hands pushed her past her lingering fears, and she could think no more.

# ~ 10 ~

# ELIANA

*"The importance of mental intimacy during the forging of one's casting cannot be overstated. You must treat these hours as the beginning of your new life. It is a rebirth. It is a transformation. Into your casting you must pour every-thing you carry inside you—even the darkness, even the cruelty, even the parts of yourself you wish you could cut away and burn."*

—On Castings: A Complete Study
by Eko Kaarat, renowned Astavari metalmaster

As Eliana stepped inside the Forge of Vintervok, the scents of smoke and oil filled her lungs, and her chest constricted around a swell of memory.

Before war had come to Ventera, before her years as the Dread, she had loved the stories of the Old World as fiercely as Remy still did—stories of the saints, the godsbeasts, and the magic that had filled the world before the Blood Queen's Fall shattered it.

Every year, she had visited the Forge in Orline with her parents on Saint Grimvald's naming day and murmured the Metal Rite alongside the other visitors—tourists come to marvel at the Forge's architecture; those who considered the old legends to be simply that, and tossed their prayers casually; and true followers of the saints, like Remy, who believed that the stories about the Old World were as real as the air in their lungs.

As Eliana herself had once believed, before she first donned her Dread mask and began shedding the fanciful skin of her childhood.

*And now?* Eliana thought, walking through the starkly decorated halls of Vintervok's Forge. *Now what do I believe?*

Before the invading Empire forces had destroyed the Forge in Orline, it had looked something like this—all right angles and gleaming dark surfaces, stark iron filigree barring every window. Artwork portraying Saint Grimvald in his pewter armor and fiery orange cloak hung alongside landscapes of war—battlefields glinting with swords, soldiers bearing brilliant bronze castings, bright-winged angels falling from storming skies with metal shards protruding from their chests.

One painting boasted a particularly dramatic spectacle. A dragon, gray-scaled and white-bellied, a mane of dark hair cresting its neck, rode toward a blinding door of light, which hovered just above a great chasm in the earth. Water surged up through the chasm, churning with foam. Saint Grimvald himself rode the dragon's back, his hammer raised to meet a regiment of swarming angels. Each armored angel carried a sword; each of their exquisite faces blazed with rage.

Eliana hurried past, averting her eyes. Like every child she had ever known, Remy loved the godsbeasts, and the ice dragons of Borsvall had always been his favorite.

*Give him time,* Simon had told her.

But there wasn't enough time in the world for them to come back from what she had done. Eliana felt the certainty of that reverberate through her body with every step.

Their escort—a scholar named Ikari—led them deep into the Forge's honeycomb structure to the enormous central forging room. Shallow steps sloped down into a circular pit at the heart of the room, where a wide coal hearth blazed day and night. A stone statue of Saint Grimvald stood in the hearth, his hammer raised toward the ceiling, where a series of windows allowed ventilation. A dozen others milled about the room—scholars dressed in plain floor-length coats and ceremonial acolytes wearing the more elaborate and old-fashioned dark-gray robes.

Ikari, a petite, plain-faced woman with kind eyes and pale-brown skin, led Eliana and Simon toward the hearth. As she did so, everyone gathered in the room paused in their work—tending the hearth fire, tidying the prayer candles, scrubbing the smoke stains from the floors—and turned to stare.

Ikari cleared her throat. "You all have tasks to complete? As does Lady Eliana."

The scholars and acolytes quickly resumed working, the air thick with their sudden, focused silence.

Below the crackle of the hearth flames, Simon murmured, "We can leave, if you want."

Eliana threw a glare at him. "I don't relish the idea of sitting around Dyrefal twiddling my thumbs for the rest of my life."

"Nor do I."

"Then stop trying to make me feel better."

"I'd never presume to do such a thing. I'd just rather you not embarrass yourself in front of these people."

"Embarrass me? Or embarrass *you*?"

"If you're going to panic, you shouldn't let them see it."

Eliana gritted her teeth. "I'm not panicking."

Ikari smiled warmly at her. "I thought I would show you around the forging hearth, my lady, and familiarize you with the traditional process. I hope you will forgive us our excitement. We have studied this practice in great detail, of course, but only in theory. This will be our first time to witness an actual forging."

Eliana nodded, not trusting herself to speak. The curious gazes of the people around the room sat upon her skin like hot coals.

"It is important for the person who will use the casting to carry out each step of the forging process themselves," Ikari began. "We will be here to guide you, of course, but it is your hand that must hold the hammer, your arms that must pump the bellows."

Eliana followed Ikari around the hearth. "I understand."

"First, you will use the bellows to pump air through the tuyere and feed the flames. Once they are at their purest heat, you will place each piece of metal you selected into the crucible"—Ikari pointed at a cylindrical vat of stone quietly cooking in the embers—"and melt them down. Their Majesties have told us you may have your pick of artifacts from the temple archives, my lady. Anything you wish to add to the mixture is yours. The archives include relics from as long ago as the Second Age—"

"I won't raid your archives for my own purposes," Eliana interrupted.

"But, my lady—"

"I won't use relics. I'll use scraps only. Bits of refuse. Metal left over from your own workings. The finery of precious artifacts would seem ill-fitting on me."

Ikari inclined her head. "Very well, my lady. I will take you to the scrap room after we're finished here, and you may peruse our stores. I suggest holding each piece in your hand and, as you examine it, listening to what your heart tells you."

A response to that came to Eliana's mind at once. Her heart was telling her she should have stayed in Orline. That this was futile, that Navi would die before she was able to help her.

That she was frightened of what would become of the self she knew, once she held a casting in her hands.

But she bit the inside of her lip and followed Ikari's slow progress around the hearth. Simon, a silent shadow, followed closely behind her.

"Have you given any thought as to what kind of casting you would like to fashion?" Ikari asked.

In fact, Eliana had known what the shape of her casting would be from the moment the idea first occurred to her.

"I have," she replied. "I would like two identical pendants—small, thin, smooth-edged." With her right finger, she drew a circle on her left palm, to illustrate the size. "I would like to wear one in each of my palms, to be held in place by slender chains."

Ikari nodded, then gestured at a young acolyte, who was hovering nearby. The boy hurried over with a pen and a curling leaf of paper.

"We can easily design such molds for you, my lady, and have them ready by tomorrow evening." Ikari moved to a stone shelf and quickly sketched out a design. "Like so?"

Eliana considered the sketched hand. A round disc sat in the palm, with thin chains connected to it in a cross shape. One chain hooked around the middle finger. Another wrapped around the back of the hand. A third chain connected the bottom of the pendant to the final, fourth chain that would form a bracelet around her wrist.

"Yes," she said, pleased at the elegant design. "Yes, that's exactly what I imagined."

Simon peered over her shoulder. "They won't be easy to remove."

"Good. I don't want them to be. I'll sleep more easily knowing my hands are bound. That I won't wake from a nightmare to find I've torn down the castle while I slept."

"We do not fear you, my lady," Ikari said softly. "You saved us from invasion. Astavar still stands free because of you."

"Some of you fear me, and you should. I do."

Ikari's gaze was gentler than Eliana felt she deserved. "You mentioned you have a personal artifact to add to the mixture?"

Eliana removed her necklace and gave it to Ikari without hesitation.

Ikari turned the necklace over, examining it. Her eyes widened. "Oh, my lady. This is—"

"I know. The Lightbringer. My father, apparently." The words felt brittle on Eliana's tongue. They were a betrayal to Ioseph Ferracora; she wished them unsaid. "Well, and he's long dead, isn't he? I don't think he'll care if I melt down his necklace."

"No, my lady. This is not the Lightbringer." Ikari pointed to a series of markings on the back of the necklace, near the bottom rim—which Eliana had of course noticed before but had never deciphered. "This is the mark of the metalmaster artisan who crafted this necklace. The three slanting lines, and the arching half-moon underneath, mark it as the work of an artisan of the royal house of Lysleva. And the markings below that—Borsvallic script. Numbers." She squinted. "From the year 999 of the Second Age. The year before the Fall."

A few scholars and acolytes had gathered, quietly crowding close for a look.

Ikari, eyes bright, pointed at the figure riding the winged horse. "And this, my lady, is the Blood Queen."

Eliana frowned. "But the Lightbringer rode a chavaile into battle. That's what Remy told me. And there was a statue at the eastern edge of Orline that depicted the Lightbringer on that very godsbeast."

"Yes, by all surviving accounts, the Lightbringer rode a chavaile into battle against the angels," Ikari agreed. "But before that, the chavaile did not belong to him. It belonged to the Blood Queen, as much as a godsbeast can belong to anyone. In the two years before her death, this image appeared on jewelry, armor, and castings across the kingdom of Celdaria. Across the entire *world*. We have one such surviving artifact in our archives, in fact." Ikari glanced up at Eliana, her expression one of pure delight. "I can show you, my lady, so you can see what a clearer engraving of this symbol looks like."

Eliana, her mouth gone sour, pointed at the battered line of script arcing across the bottom of her pendant. "And this? What does this say?"

"It is an ancient Borsvallic dialect." Ikari's voice was reverent. "I am not fluent, but I know this phrase, at least. It says, *May the Queen's light guide you.*"

The Sun Queen's prayer. As Eliana stared at the necklace, her thoughts filled with a memory that was not her own: the beautiful woman from the vision Zahra had given her. A woman in black-and-crimson armor, standing on a blood-soaked battlefield, kissing the Emperor.

She did not look at the necklace again.

The next night, Eliana and Simon returned to the Forge, where the fire of the hearth still burned.

The three pieces of scrap metal Eliana had selected from the Forge supply waited for her at the hearth—a piece of brass piping, a thick copper chain, a chipped bronze bell.

Beside them was her necklace, sitting innocuously by the other scraps as though it hadn't been engraved with the visage of an evil, traitorous bitch.

Ikari approached, her hair gathered into a tight bun, her face scrubbed clean. She wore plain, utilitarian clothing, a heavy apron, thick gloves.

Eliana herself would wear no such attire; the traditional forging process did not allow for it. The risk required of the elemental was thought to enhance the connection with their casting, and Eliana had decided to keep to that tradition—much to Simon's irritation.

He stood behind her, his tense presence pulling at her like an angry tide. She relished his anger. It sharpened her grief at Remy's continued silence, left her feeling hard and bright, like one of her grinning blades.

"Are you ready, my lady?" Ikari asked.

"Nearly," Eliana replied airily. She was already beginning to sweat in the hot, still air. Light as it was, the gown she wore clung to her skin. So she peeled it off, shimmying free of the cloying fabric until she stood in only her boots and thin shift.

Ikari seemed unperturbed, though the nearby young acolytes gaped as if Eliana had decided to forge her casting while standing on her head.

She looked back at Simon, silently daring him to reproach her, but instead he took off his own coat, rolled up the sleeves of his shirt, then folded both her gown and his coat into a neat pile and moved them aside. The light from the hearth fire made the lattice of scars on his sweat-slicked forearms gleam.

Eliana looked quickly away from them. "Now I'm ready."

Ikari gestured at the bellows. "Then, my lady, I ask that you begin to feed the flames."

Eliana obeyed, pushing down the dark lever of the bellows pump and listening to the subsequent hiss as the tuyere fed air into the hearth. The flames snapped and popped, blooming. She pushed the lever again, and a third time, a fourth. So close to the fire, the heat enveloped her like a second shimmering skin. Sweat dripped down her back, her neck, her forehead; her nostrils burned from the smoke, and her watering eyes itched terribly.

With each pumped breath of air, the heat became more unbearable, and her instinct screamed at her to move away. It was too hot by these flames, too dangerous. She needed cool air; she needed water.

Instead she gritted her teeth and pushed down the bellows pump.

"'A sword forged true with hammer and blade,'" she began reciting, "'flies sure and swift.'" She raised the pump and pushed it down once more, timing her movements with the words of the Metal Rite. She had tried hard to put such prayers out of her mind over the years, but hadn't been able to because Remy wouldn't ever shut up about the goddamned saints.

*Remy, Remy.* But she couldn't think about him. Not now, not tonight.

"'A heart forged in battle and strife,'" she continued, "'cuts deeper than any blade.'" Another lift, a push, a hot hiss of air into the flames. "'A sword forged true with hammer and blade…'"

The acolytes stationed around the room, including Ikari, began to recite the Metal Rite along with her. The only one to remain silent was Simon, standing near enough that Eliana could have reached back and caught his fingers in hers. She was grateful for his silence. It was the fulcrum upon which she balanced her work.

"'…Flies sure and swift.'" She followed the paths of the sweat coursing down her arms and back, using them to trace the lines of her muscles as she worked. "'A heart forged in battle and strife…'"

"'Cuts deeper than any blade,'" came Ikari's steady voice.

Beside Eliana, Simon shifted. She recalled what he had told her as they walked to the Forge earlier that evening: *Remember what you felt that day on the beach. Remember it, and channel it into every movement you make tonight.*

She had read as much in the books he had retrieved for her, as well as others she herself had worked with the royal librarians to find. She had to keep her mind clear and focused during the forging, direct her thoughts along every muscle and bone in her body, and dig deep within herself for the memory of how her power felt on the beach—a memory she had been working diligently to stifle.

But she could stifle it no longer.

With the Fall of the Blood Queen, the magic that had once illuminated humanity's path to the empirium had vanished.

And, somehow, Eliana had to find it again. Find it, and control it.

"'A heart forged in battle and strife...'" she muttered.

"'Flies sure and swift,'" Ikari and the acolytes echoed.

Eliana had read that a true forging process, back in the First or Second Age, might have taken many days, many fires.

But Eliana did not have that kind of time—and neither did Navi.

"A heart forged in battle and strife," she said, eyes stinging, "cuts deeper than any blade."

Ikari held up her hand, signaling Eliana to stop.

Eliana moved toward the hearth, each breath a scorching gulp, her thoughts an urgent haze of heat and memory. With a pair of tongs, she picked up each metal scrap and deposited it in the crucible. First, with a dull clang, the bronze bell. Then the long length of thick copper chain and the brass pipe.

Then, last of all, her necklace.

It hung from the tongs, turning slowly, the chavaile's wings glinting in the firelight.

She shouldn't think of them—she shouldn't, she *wouldn't*—and yet the memories rushed at her, eager and cruel: herself, in Rozen's lap, running her fingers across the necklace's engraving. Falling asleep against Ioseph's side as he read to her from a battered copy of *The Book of the Saints*. Remy, proudly presenting her with a sketch of her necklace—except, in his version, it wasn't the Lightbringer riding the chavaile. It was Eliana herself.

She faltered, nearly dropping the tongs.

"Simon," she said hoarsely.

He stepped closer, his overheated arm brushing against her own. "I'm here."

"Tell me I won't be like her."

"No. Say it yourself."

Fury snapped through her at his words, pure and clarifying, but he was right and she knew it.

"I am not like her," she said, through her teeth. "I am like no one but myself."

Then she dropped the necklace into the crucible and returned to the bellows. She pushed past the ache in her muscles to feed the flames and prayed to the ruthless saints her brother worshipped.

—◆—

With each pump of the bellows, she recited the Metal Rite.

Then the Fire Rite, then the Sun Rite.

She recited each of the seven rites, which she remembered because first Ioseph and later Remy had carved them into the walls of her heart.

She prayed until her voice grew whisper-thin, her throat an aching column of fire, and as she prayed, she imagined pushing her words down her arms, through the bellows, into the flames. She imagined herself as a beast made of fire, licking up the sides of the crucible, heating it. She imagined her necklace melting, the lines of the Blood Queen's scarred face morphing into ruin.

*I am not like her.*

Her mind unraveled and narrowed, both at once. A vision came to her, shimmering with heat: Herself, walking along a narrow ledge across a deep chasm. She had to breathe just so and step just so, or the ground beneath her would crumble, and she would fall.

She would not think of Rozen or Ioseph.

She would not think of Remy's voice condemning her as monstrous.

She instead remembered the beach—the world erupting at her fingertips, the sky tearing itself open at her command.

She revisited that moment of abandon, when her hands steamed hot

—126—

with Rozen's blood. She remembered it and then pulled back from it, holding the memory in her palms like a crystalline creature. She hardly breathed for fear of shattering it. Treading lightly along the chasm yawning beneath her, she bore the treasure of Rozen's death in her cupped hands, and then, opening her fingers, dropped it into the abyss.

She was not sad to see it go. Instead she pushed against the walls of her mind and held the feeling of her body's perfect blazing balance like a full cup in the valley between her shoulders.

*I am like no one but myself.*

Ikari's voice came like a breath on the wind. "It is time, my lady. It is done."

—◆—

Eliana lived in a humming cloud of fire.

She was afraid to move, so she kept her breathing shallow and thin. Light-headed, she used the tongs to lift the crucible. It was too heavy to move easily, even with her mind swimming in its strange overheated euphoria, and her arms trembled. But when Simon moved to help her, his hands cupping hers, his breath hot against the back of her neck, she shook her head.

If he joined her on this thrumming ledge, it would crumble.

Distantly she realized tears were streaming down her face, the flames pulling heat from her eyes.

She poured the molten metal—a dirty gold color, smoking and glossy—into the mold the acolytes had fashioned for her, and lowered the crucible back into the hearth. Then she used the tongs once more to lift the mold away from the fire and set it on a stone ledge to cool.

"My lady," said Ikari gently, "might I suggest going to wash your face while the metal cools?"

"No." Eliana shook her head. "I'm not leaving until it's done."

—◆—

She sat silently beside the mold, hugging her legs to her chest. Beyond her blurry field of vision, the hearth fire blazed, ecstatic and vicious.

Without a word, Simon set a cup of water beside her.

She ignored it. The balls of her bare feet balanced on the rocky ledge. A sly wind butted against the backs of her knees, trying to unbalance her.

But she was not afraid.

She sat beside the Forge's hearth, its flames dancing against her skin, and pushed the air out of her lungs, down her arms, into the cooling metal—strengthening it, gilding it with her mother's blazing blood.

The world was suffused gold with light. The shimmering air undulated around her.

Eliana breathed, and for a wild instant, her weariness so complete her mind felt stretched thin as fine paper, she thought she felt the world breathe with her.

—◆—

Two hours later, the metal was cool enough to remove from the mold.

Eliana rose, shoulders and legs and chest aching, eyes burning. Using the tongs, she removed the twin pendants from their molds and placed them on an anvil the acolytes had provided for her. Then she sat beside it and, with a charcoal pencil, drew shapes on the pendants' rough surface.

She was no artist; her lines were crude and uneven. But she refused to let anyone else touch the pendants. They carried the weight of her inside them. They were hers to use, and perhaps, someday, if she wished it, hers to destroy.

Her exhaustion was so complete she hardly understood her own actions. But she continued working, hunched over the anvil. Once her drawings were complete, she retrieved a small hammer and chisel from the array of tools the acolytes had spread out for her and began chipping away at the metal, along her clumsy sketched lines. Each strike of the chisel jarred her bones.

For hours she worked, refusing Simon's silent offers of water. She accepted only the rag he offered to wipe her face, and when at last she had finished, one of the pendants boasted a crude etching of a sun.

On the other, a jagged-bladed dagger—her Arabeth, her beloved. The mother killer.

One of the acolytes brought her a honing stone. Bleary-eyed, dry-mouthed, heartsore, she used the stone and thick, soft rags to file down and polish the unadorned sides of the pendants and their rims until they gleamed.

At last she sat up, her shoulders cracking, her back muscles screaming, and she thought she heard the Eliana sitting by the hearth fire let out a soft sob of exhaustion.

The real Eliana, however, was standing on the edge of the cliff upon which she had balanced for an age.

She peered down into the chasm that awaited her to find that it was no longer a chasm, but a river, near and roaring and golden. It didn't look like blood, but she knew that it was, and she craved it as she had craved nothing else in her life. Not Harkan, not the tongue of the Orline woman Alys, nor the girl she had given her first kiss at the edge of seven. Not Simon, not finding Rozen. She dipped a toe into the river's swirling gold eddies, and a charge ripped up her leg, pinning her where she stood.

She looked up, dazed. The forging room was hot and quiet, the flames dying. Morning light shone through the room's high windows, illuminating Saint Grimvald's stern face. Shapes moved through the room, shadowed and gentle.

"My lady, are you ready?" asked Ikari, very near.

For answer, Eliana held up her hands.

Using lengths of chain so slender and cool that they felt like ribbons of silk against Eliana's skin, Ikari and two young acolytes settled the pendants in her palms. The chains hooked over her middle fingers, along the backs of her hands, around her wrists.

When they had finished, Eliana's pendants sat against her palms like twin drops of fire. The metal had cooled long ago, and yet the pendants jolted her, branding her, and she wondered how she had ever existed without these chains around her wrists. They were a part of her, and always had been, that much was obvious. She had carved slivers of bone from her ribs and fashioned them into these discs now cradled in her hands.

A sharp energy swelled within her, drumming eagerly against the husk of her skin, and it felt both strange and familiar. Familiar, because she had lived a long time with the knowledge that she was ill-fitting in the world.

Strange, because at last she understood why.

She blinked, returning to herself with a sharp lurch, as if awakening from a wild dream. Her hunger, her thirst, her fatigue, the throbbing pain knitting her muscles to her bones—it all crashed down upon her at once, and she staggered forward with a cry.

Simon caught her before she could fall, and she was too tired, too overcome, too angry to fight him. She hadn't asked for this—being born to the Kingsbane; escaping death on the night of her birth, only to be flung into a doomed future by a frightened little boy.

Bitter tears rose to her eyes as she considered the awful truth that beyond finding the antidote that would save Navi, she knew nothing of what the future held for her, nor how to face it.

Feeling ill and fevered, her shift soaked through with sweat and stained with soot, she turned into Simon's chest and allowed him to fold her into his arms. Though she fully intended to disappoint him in the end, she decided she would allow herself this one small moment of respite, for he smelled like smoke and sweat and hot metal. He smelled of death, and that comforted her, for death was one thing she still understood, even as the rest of her world had changed before her eyes.

"Now what?" she mumbled against his shirt, her hands trapped between them. Her voice sounded worse than she felt, and she hoped that would make him pity her.

Simon's hand cupped the back of her head, and when his fingers grazed her neck, gently stroking in small circles, she shivered and nuzzled her cheek against his chest without quite realizing what she was doing.

"Now," he replied, his voice as weary as her own, "the real work begins."

# -11-
# RIELLE

*"My father's illness is not abating. He speaks of things I do not understand, his words jumbled and angry. Sometimes he knows my face. Sometimes he shrinks from me, screaming in terror, as if I am some nightmarish monster come to claim him for death. I beg you to visit Styrdalleen and assess his condition for yourself. We are fast losing what hope we had left."*

—A letter from Ilmaire Lysleva, prince of Borsvall, to the headmaster of the School of the Healing Arts in the Mazabatian city of Damezi

Upon returning to Styrdalleen, their party was met at the lower yards of the castle Tarkstorm by a pale man in a plain gray tunic and coat, flanked by four wide-eyed attendants.

"My lord prince," the man said, breathlessly, "your father has asked to see you at once."

"Is he dying?" Ingrid's words fell flat as stones.

"No, Commander. But..." The man glanced at Rielle, uncertain. "Perhaps it would be best if we spoke in private, en route to His Majesty's rooms."

"Our friends deserve to know the true health of their ally," Ilmaire said, his voice heavy with a new weariness. "Take us to him, Arvo."

The man looked helplessly at Rielle, then Audric, then tightened the line of his mouth and turned sharply on his heel.

They followed him up the terraced yards of Tarkstorm, their pace swift with some barely contained panic Rielle did not understand.

"Ilmaire," Audric said quietly, "if you must attend to a family affair, we'll happily wait in our rooms."

"It's as I said," Ilmaire replied, his worried gaze trained on the ground before his feet. "You deserve to understand the true desperation of our plight here in Borsvall."

*What does that mean?* Rielle asked Ludivine, all thoughts of the Gate and Ludivine's scarred arm and Atheria's whereabouts flown from her mind. The air buzzed with a fear she could not name, as if gray clouds had fallen over their group, though the sky was bright blue, the sunlight crisp and cold.

*He's lying,* Ludivine answered, her voice thoughtful but unafraid. *He wants our help, our insight, but he doesn't want to say that aloud. He knows I'm reading his thoughts. He is confused and afraid, but he has a theory. He…*

She paused, and then her presence in Rielle's mind sharpened, as if newly awake.

*Be on your guard,* she instructed, with an icy edge to her thoughts that sent fear skipping down Rielle's arms. *I can't pinpoint it. Something is preventing me from doing so. But I know this: we are not alone.*

◆

The king's apartments were quiet and dark, drapes pulled shut against the afternoon sunlight.

The king's healer, Arvo, insisted that the light hurt His Majesty's eyes, that the sight of the mountainous vista outside his rooms distressed him, for it reminded him of all that he could no longer enjoy—his city, his people, his morning rides with Runa.

Ilmaire, apparently, did not care.

Rielle watched as he strode across the room and opened the drapes. Sunlight poured in, bright and pale, tinged with snow.

From his bed, the king cried out softly. Ingrid, watching from the bedroom's threshold, flinched at the sound. She seemed smaller in these rooms, shrunken by the stale, sick-smelling air, as if the presence of her ailing father had reduced her to the girl she had once been.

*Why are we here for this?* Rielle asked, tense at Audric's side. She fought the childish urge to hide behind him. Something about this room—its shadows, the smell of it, the sight of the king's body beneath his blankets—crawled inside her like disease.

*He wants us to see something,* Ludivine said. *Be ready to run if I tell you to. Take Audric and run. Fight, if you must.*

"Hello, Father," Ilmaire said, a forced brightness in his voice. "How are you feeling today?"

Rielle's father had described Hallvard Lysleva as a mighty man, tall and proud. But now the king of Borsvall lay shriveled beneath a pile of blankets—muscles atrophied, skin hanging off his bones. He squinted against the sunlight, gesturing feebly to shield his eyes.

"Too bright," he croaked, his chapped mouth twisting. "No more!"

Ilmaire wedged open one of the terrace windows. A thin slice of frigid air punched its way inside.

"Sorry, Father," he said cheerfully. "You need fresh air, and you need sunlight. It isn't healthy to lie here in the dark day and night."

"How dare you." Hallvard glared at Ilmaire as he approached. "I am the king. You are no one."

Ilmaire sat in a chair beside the bed. "Now, Father," he said mildly, "you know that's not right. I am the prince. I am your heir."

"You? Danzdyrka?" Hallvard laughed, long and wheezing, letting loose a trail of discolored spittle.

"Danzdyrka?" Rielle whispered.

"A title given to junior dancers at the royal theater," Audric muttered in reply.

*But, in this case,* Ludivine said, *not a title of honor. A title of scorn. He has long been scorned by his father. His heart aches from it.*

"Runa," the king continued, his voice a thin rasp. "Runa is my heir."

Near the door, Ingrid turned away, fingers clenched at her sides.

Ilmaire touched his father's hand. The man's skin looked cracked, brittle. Rielle had the wild thought that if Ilmaire pinched two fingers together, he could pull off an entire piece of the king's flesh, like a hunk of stale bread.

"Father, Runa is dead," Ilmaire said gently. "You know this."

"Lies! You lie to me!" And then, abruptly, the king began to weep—thin, keening sobs that reminded Rielle of the sounds a wounded animal might make before its pain pulled it under.

She felt pressed flat beneath the weight of a rising panic. Audric's hand found hers, and squeezed.

*We shouldn't be here*, she told Ludivine. *We should leave now.*

"Father, if you'll indulge me." Ilmaire cleared his throat. "Perhaps you'd like to hear about my trip to the Sunderlands with Prince Audric of Celdaria."

The king's wailing came to a shuddering halt. "What?" He struggled to position himself against the pillows piled along his headboard. "You did what?"

Ilmaire's smile was wry. "You heard correctly, Father. I recently journeyed to the Sunderlands with Celdarian guests—Prince Audric, Lady Ludivine of House Sauvillier, and Lady Rielle Dardenne, recently anointed Sun Queen by the Celdarian Church."

Now sitting rigid against the headboard, King Hallvard stared silently at his son. There was a sudden stillness to his body and his expression, as if some phantom power had scraped away all his excess.

"And what did you do there, in the Sunderlands?" His gaze moved slowly across the room, sliding across first Audric, then Ludivine, then landing at last on Rielle. A thin smile curled across his face.

"Lady Rielle," he said softly, his voice cracking.

Audric's hand tightened around Rielle's.

*It can't be*, came Ludivine's voice, a note of fear ringing inside it.

"The Gate is falling, Father," Ilmaire was saying. "You remember this. I told you as much before we disembarked."

Instead of a response, silence stretched on. The king's red-rimmed gaze remained locked firmly on Rielle. His smile twitched. At the door, Ingrid shifted uneasily.

"Lady Rielle and Prince Audric requested that we visit the Sunderlands to assess the Gate for themselves," Ilmaire continued, hesitant now. "I could see no harm in it, and after all, Lady Rielle saved our capital from a tidal wave of enormous destructive power. A wave caused by the weakening Gate. It seemed only proper to grant them this request."

For a moment, silence. Then the king drew his knees to his chest and wrapped his arms about his legs, like a child eager to hear a story.

"And then what?" the king asked.

Dread crept down Rielle's back on narrow feet.

Ilmaire grew very still. "Are you all right, Father? You're acting strangely."

"I'm merely waiting for the end of your story. Go on. What did Lady Rielle do? She saw the Gate, did she? Was she able to repair it?"

"No." Ilmaire glanced Rielle's way, obviously uneasy. "In fact, her attempts to do so seemed to have further weakened the Gate's structural integrity. So said Jodoc Indarien, speaker of the Obex."

The king leaned toward Rielle. Though they were separated by several feet, she felt invaded by him. Ensnared.

She wanted to move away, but her feet were made of stone. *What's happening, Lu?*

"We should leave," Audric said quietly.

But Ludivine was held rapt, her brow furrowed. She examined the king as if trying to dissect him with her mind.

"By how much did she weaken it?" King Hallvard asked.

"I'm not certain," Ilmaire replied.

"Pah. Yes, you are. You can do very few things well, boy, but you do at least listen. By how much did she weaken the Gate?"

After a moment, Ilmaire relented. "Jodoc counted an additional thirty-three fractures—"

"Only thirty-three?" Hallvard made a disgusted sound. "The bitch is a fool."

The words had hardly left his mouth when, with a sharp cry of pain, he was jerked across the bed as if by an angry, unseen force. His body snapped to the left, then to the right; his head smacked against one of the bedposts.

Ingrid rushed forward, her sword drawn.

Ludivine shoved both Rielle and Audric behind her. She snarled something in a foreign tongue.

Ilmaire reached for the king's flailing limbs. "Father, stop! What are you doing? What's wrong?"

But the king jerked away from his son's touch. His wild movements carried him off the bed and onto the floor. He twisted violently on the rug, his back arching until it seemed he might snap in half.

Audric started forward, but Ludivine held him fast. Rielle saw his eyes glaze over slightly and could not even be angry with Ludivine for taking control of his mind.

Behind Ilmaire, the door opened. Several guards rushed in, then halted abruptly when they saw Hallvard convulsing on the rug.

"Commander?" the foremost guard barked.

But Ingrid stood unmoving, face pale, eyes wide, sword hanging uselessly at her side. Her gaze was perfectly clear. The horror of the moment had simply rendered her motionless.

"Fetch Arvo," Ilmaire cried, finally managing to subdue his father's arms and barely avoiding a swift jab to his jaw in the process. "Find the healers!"

The guard ran out at once.

Hallvard wrenched himself away from Ilmaire's grasp and prostrated himself on the floor, reaching feebly across the carpet for Rielle.

She flinched back from him, grateful for the shield of Ludivine. Her hand clung to Audric's, clammy with sweat.

"I am sorry," the king moaned. "My apologies, my lord. I do not think Lady Rielle a fool. Forgive me. I have rotted for too long in this corpse, and it is has weakened my mind. Please, my lord, let me come home. I ache for the north, for your presence and wisdom. I ache for the great work."

Ice gathered at the small of Rielle's back. "What are you?"

Hallvard lifted his head to smile at her. In a low, thin voice, he spoke words she did not understand. They were not in any of the Borsvallic or Celdarian dialects, nor the common tongue.

"Lissar," Audric whispered, his eyes still cloudy with Ludivine's hold.

Rielle's mouth went dry. She knew that word. It was one of the old angelic dialects.

In her mind, Ludivine translated the king's words: *I am infinite. I am invincible.*

Ingrid cursed softly and backed away from her father, raising her sword. Her eyes trembled with tears.

Ilmaire held up a hand. "Do not harm him, Ingrid."

Hallvard continued muttering, the unfamiliar syllables rattling across his teeth.

Ludivine's translation continued: *I am splendor, and you are dust. I am glory, and you are ashes.*

A grim look settled on Ilmaire's face. A look of resignation as if, at last, a question had been answered. "What is your name, angel?"

One of the guards let out a soft cry of terror.

King Hallvard drew himself up to a height that seemed taller than his body should have allowed. The lines of expression on his face morphed into something haughty and furious.

"I am Bazrifel," Hallvard replied, his voice no longer muddled with disease and exhaustion. "Second lieutenant to the third imperial brigade serving His Majesty the Emperor of the Undying."

"I've never heard of this emperor," Ilmaire replied.

Hallvard smirked. "Soon you will meet him for yourself. You will behold his glory as he flattens your pathetic kingdom under the boots of his armies."

"Why must he do this? What is it that he wants?"

King Hallvard's smile widened. He approached Ilmaire slowly, his body hobbling with every step. Ingrid inched closer, her sword a glint in the corner of Rielle's eye.

But Ilmaire, sad-eyed, square-shouldered, stood his ground.

The king cupped Ilmaire's face in one cracked, pale hand.

"To watch you burn." Then he leaned close and rasped four words. "Long live the king."

A shift in the air. A reshaping of the unseen planes of the world around Rielle's body. She staggered, unbalanced. She fell hard against Audric, and he against Ludivine, who stood firm, her eyes blazing with fury as King Hallvard's body dropped, suddenly heavy, as if every drop of his blood had been replaced with stone.

Ilmaire caught him before he could hit the floor. "Father?" He gently touched the king's cheek, brushing aside matted locks of silver-blond hair. "Father, can you hear me?"

But Hallvard Lysleva did not respond, and in his wide, staring eyes—no longer so clouded, but rather a glassy, brilliant blue—Rielle saw no glimmer of life.

$$\text{---}\diamond\text{---}$$

Two hours later, Rielle paced before the crackling hearth, struggling for patience.

Audric sat on a nearby divan, elbows on his knees, gazing pensively at the fire.

Ludivine huddled on a chair by the windows. She hadn't spoken since they'd been escorted to their rooms after King Hallvard's death—not aloud, and not in Rielle's mind.

But the silence had stretched on long enough, and Rielle had just decided to tell her as much when a knock on the door and an announcement from the stationed guards signified Ilmaire's arrival.

He entered alone, looking as if the past hours had scraped layers of color from his skin.

"Ilmaire," Audric began, "I'm so sorry for what's happened."

Ilmaire shook his head, silencing him. "Leave us," he quietly told the guards over his shoulder, and when they were alone—the four of them, Ingrid nowhere to be found—Ilmaire fixed his eyes on Ludivine.

"Did you know the angel Bazrifel?" he asked.

Ludivine shook her head, gracefully unfolding her body from her chair. "Not well. He is unremarkable in everything but his devotion to Corien."

"And, it would seem, his ability to occupy a human corpse for a considerable amount of time," Rielle observed.

Ilmaire shot her a glare. "Perhaps you'll reconsider, Lady Rielle, before speaking in such blunt terms about my dead father?"

Rielle flushed, but lifted her chin to meet his eyes. "Of course. Forgive me."

"Please tell me you didn't sense Bazrifel was here, Lu," Audric said.

"No, though I did sense an oddness, a wrongness, when we returned from the Sunderlands, though I couldn't name it." Ludivine frowned at the floor, and Rielle at last understood why she had been so silent. She was ashamed; she was frightened. "Bazrifel should not have been able to hide himself from me so successfully."

"Unless he had help," Rielle suggested.

Audric stiffened. Ludivine fiddled with the sleeve of her scarred arm, her brow furrowed with worry.

"You mean, from this emperor he spoke of?" Ilmaire asked, looking at them curiously.

"His name is Corien," Audric replied. "I didn't know he was calling himself emperor now."

"Neither did I," Rielle said quietly. Her gaze met his and held it for a beat of silence. She remembered how he had watched her on the *Kaalvitsi* in the aftermath of her vision. How patiently he had listened. The warmth on his face, the trust so plain on his features.

Did he believe her, that she hadn't known?

Or did he wonder what else she might have seen in her vision? Seen, and kept locked away from him.

She dropped her gaze to the floor, focusing instead on her hands clasped in her lap. She was being ridiculous. Audric had given her no reason to doubt his faith in her. The day had shaken her. She was exhausted; she was rattled.

The door opened without warning.

Ilmaire turned, frowning. "Joonas, I ordered no interruptions."

"Apologies, my prince," said the woman entering the room, "but this cannot wait."

The woman looked stalwart, humorless, and wore robes of deep charcoal, hemmed in fiery orange—the colors of the Forge. She was, Rielle assumed, the Grand Magister of the Forge, whom she knew was the senior-most member of the Borsvall Church. They had no Archon; traditionally, it was the Grand Magister of the Forge who held the highest religious authority, in honor of Saint Grimvald.

Six others flanked her, all in magisterial robes—and then there were three more, bringing up the rear. A man and two women, each of them wearing gray robes boasting a symbol Rielle recognized at once: a single, unblinking eye resting atop what she now knew was not simply a tower, but the Gate itself.

The sigil of the Obex.

Rielle's heart thumped hard against her ribs. She moved toward Audric, Ludivine following close behind.

The magisters moved aside to allow the Obex passage, and the three of them stepped forward as one.

In their outstretched hands lay a familiar object—worn and immense, its shaft engraved with countless minute carvings, its head a chiseled block of metal bearing the sigil of the Forge amid ice dragons in flight.

Ilmaire drew in a sharp breath. A chill moved slowly across Rielle's skin.

This was Saint Grimvald's hammer. Not a replica, but the actual casting of the long-dead saint himself.

A heaviness descended upon the room, like the rolling pressure of a black sky ready to break. Every person gathered, every pane of glass, every tile embellishing the floor thrummed, as if responding to the residual power the hammer still contained.

Rielle approached the casting at once, pulled toward it inexorably, following the call of the power that lapped against her like waves.

But then one of the Obex, flanked by her comrades, began to speak, and the words stopped Rielle in her tracks.

"'The Gate will fall,'" the woman intoned. "'The angels will return and bring ruin to the world. You will know this time by the rise of two human Queens—one of blood, and one of light. One with the power to save the world. One with the power to destroy it. Two Queens will rise. They will carry the power of the Seven. They will carry your fate in their hands. Two Queens will rise.'"

Rielle waited for the silence to end, apprehension bubbling in her throat. When no one spoke, she forced calm into her voice and arched an eyebrow. "Is there a reason you've come to recite Aryava's prophecy for me? Do you doubt that I'm as familiar with it as I am with my own body?"

"Lady Rielle," the Obex speaker continued, "we are aware of Jodoc Indarien's directive. You are to search for the castings of the saints on your own, without aid. We are aware of his reasons for declaring this. We are also aware that you saved this city from destruction when you could have abandoned us to it. We are aware that the Gate is falling, that darkness is rising. In the east, in the north, in Celdaria, in our own streets and mountains. It is our belief—that is, the belief of the Obex who live here in Borsvall and have devoted our lives to protecting the casting of Saint Grimvald—that there is simply no time left to any of us. Not for games or puzzles, not for anything but swift action."

The three Obex stepped forward once more and knelt before Rielle, offering up Saint Grimvald's hammer on the altar of their hands. "This is a gift, Lady Rielle, and a powerful one," the Obex continued. "We trust you will use it wisely and in good service."

Rielle gazed at the hammer, her head spinning. So close to the worn metal, her palms prickled as though she were holding her hands too close to a fire. And yet she hesitated to take the hammer for her own. Everything was happening so quickly. She glanced at the gathered magisters, at Ilmaire's astonished face. Was he really to allow the Obex to gift her with Grimvald's hammer without ceremony, behind closed doors, with his citizens kept ignorant?

*Do you care?* Corien asked.

Rielle bit down on a small smile. It was a fair point.

*Take it, my love.* He urged her gently, his words as cool and soft as a kiss of breeze. *They're offering it with no conditions. Take it. It belongs to you more than them. It belongs to you more than anyone.*

*More than it belongs to you?* she could not resist asking.

*I care nothing for human trifles,* he replied. Then, softer, the sensation of his mouth against her neck so near that she could almost pretend he was there beside her: *I want only you.*

"Take this, Lady Rielle, and hurry home," said the Obex, shaking Corien's voice from Rielle's thoughts. "There are six more castings for you to find, and other factions of our order will not feel as charitably toward you as we do. Hurry home and hunt swiftly. The angels will not wait. Even now, they are coming."

Rielle hesitated, glanced back at Audric, then grasped the hammer in both hands and lifted it, with some effort. The air around her pulsed with an invisible resonance she could feel in her veins, like the heady bite of adrenaline, and she knew with a sudden ferocious certainty that even if the council, or the Obex, or Ilmaire himself, suddenly decided to take the hammer from her, they would fail.

The casting of Saint Grimvald was hers now, the property of the Sun Queen, to wield or not as she saw fit.

And God help anyone who tried to wrest it from her grasp.

# ~ 12 ~

# ELIANA

*"When performing elemental magic, it is crucial not to think of the act as forcing the empirium to obey your will. It is a union, not a conquest. Think of this: How can I slip inside the rhythm of the song the empirium is already singing? How can I match its gait?"*

—The Path to the Empirium: A Meditation on Elemental Practice
by Velia Arrosara, Grand Magister of the Firmament in
Orline, capital of Ventera, Years 313–331 of the Second Age

Eliana waited for Harkan to respond for as long as she could bear the silence. Zahra floated nearby, her great black eyes fixed on his face.

He sat on the edge of the divan in Eliana's bedroom, brow drawn in an expression she didn't like.

She had no time for his worry, or his doubt.

"If you won't come with us and help me," she said when he still hadn't spoken, "will you at least keep Simon and Remy from finding out? Will you not say a word about any of this?"

"Magic, thievery, and a secret mission to a black market run by wraiths?" Harkan gave her a tired smile. "I can't let you have all the fun alone."

Zahra cleared her throat. "May I remind you that, even without your company, she wouldn't be alone?"

Harkan's expression tightened. "Of course not. My apologies, Zahra."

His uneasiness—with Zahra, with the entire situation—was palpable, and sat uncomfortably around Eliana like a layer of dirt she couldn't scrub from her skin. Briefly she wondered if she should insist he remain behind to help cover her tracks. The sight of her using her castings could forever change things between them.

But that change had already occurred. She knew this, even if she wasn't ready to accept it. There was no path left to them but the one leading forward.

She took Harkan's hands in hers, trying to ignore the ache of regret in her heart and smile at him as she had always done. "Thank you. I could do this without you, but I don't want to."

He kissed her fingers, avoiding her castings. A flicker of darkness moved across his face, as if the sight of the discs and their chains was distasteful, something he longed to wish away. Eliana considered admonishing him for that, but decided against it. After all, she wasn't yet comfortable with the chains binding her wrists. Why should she expect Harkan to be?

"When do we begin?" he asked.

"First I must practice using these," Eliana replied, raising her hands—and not meeting Harkan's eyes. "And when Zahra says I'm ready, we'll leave."

◆◇◆

The next night, as the castle slept, Eliana sat on the cold, damp stone of the belvedere in Saint Tameryn's cavern. With Harkan sitting beside her, she lifted her arms into the air, palms rigid, and began to pray.

The Wind Rite seemed appropriate for her first practice. She would pray to the wind and call upon her power just as she had done at the beach.

She could see it clearly in her mind. The air would open for her as easily as a door. She would gather it in her palms, and miniature storms would bloom in the cradle of her fingers. She would send them flying, like messenger birds, and then call them back to her. Their arrival would blow the hair back from Harkan's face, cool her own hot cheeks. Zahra would approve and take her to the Nest. Eliana would return triumphant to the palace, and Navi would live, and Remy would love Eliana again, if only because she had saved the friend he so adored.

After a few seconds of expectant silence, Harkan asked quietly, "Is something supposed to be happening?"

Eliana cracked open one eye.

The cavern remained still and silent. The air did not so much as quiver against her skin.

She dropped her arms. "I feel absurd doing this."

"You have tried for only forty-seven seconds, my queen," Zahra pointed out.

"Is there something I should be doing to help?" Harkan asked. "Shall I pray as well?"

Eliana didn't think he was mocking her, but she nevertheless bristled. "If you pray with me, I'll kill you. Doing this alone is bad enough."

"I'll sit quietly, then."

"That's all I ask."

Zahra's voice was patient. "Try again, my queen."

Eliana shifted, feeling the reassuring pressure of the knives strapped to her body. She exhaled sharply, closed her eyes, and raised her hands once more. With her eyes shut, she shifted her imagination, pictured something new. Instead of miniature storms, a set of strings. An instrument. She would pluck threads of air from the cavern, sculpt them into a new shape with mere taps of her fingers, compose a symphony using the power in her palms.

She slowed her breathing, measured each inhale and exhale. Long minutes passed, during which she forced her mind through memories of Remy's incessant ramblings about the empirium—how it was a power left behind from the creation of all things. The footprints of God. A power that bound the air to the earth to the water, wind to sunlight to time and space. The command *Obey me, obey me* cycled through her mind until her thoughts became a muddled fog. The muscles in her arms, sore from forging her castings, burned hot as fire.

At last she dropped her arms, spat out a curse, pushed herself up from the ground, and walked away.

For a few moments, the only sound in the cavern was the occasional drip of water into the vast, dark lake.

"We'll keep trying," Harkan said, his voice cheerful. "You can't give up after only a few minutes."

"I agree, my queen," added Zahra.

Eliana scoffed. "It won't work. The only time this has worked has been…"

She hesitated, an idea forming slowly. As it did, her mind cleared, and a grim sort of satisfaction overcame her.

Zahra made a reproachful sound.

"What is it?" Harkan asked.

"Twice my power has surfaced," Eliana said, turning back to them. "Once on the beach, and once last night as I forged my castings. In the Forge, nothing happened. I didn't summon a storm or crack open the earth or anything so dramatic. But I felt something. I felt near a precipice, an understanding. For a moment, my body opened up as if to receive a new light, and I could see beyond the world as you see it, to something greater."

Zahra nodded. "You glimpsed the empirium."

Eliana glanced at Harkan. "You think this is mad."

Harkan hesitated. "I do. But here I am, and here I'll stay."

*How generous of you,* Eliana wanted to snap. "In both instances," she said instead, "I was exhausted, hungry, parched. My mind was stretched thin, my body close to breaking. In the Forge, the heat and strain were unbearable. On the beach…" She hesitated, pushing past the mental wall that kept her grief from consuming her. "On the beach, my hands were hot with my mother's blood. And my power awoke."

Harkan searched her face. "You think that by returning to such a state, you can summon your power again."

"My queen, I must advise against this," Zahra said. "My knowledge of elemental magic, and your own mother's practice, is not complete, but I know this much: magic forced through duress is unstable, unkind, and bound to break."

But Eliana had already decided. "I have no other choice, and neither does Navi. We'll come here again tomorrow night, at the same time. And the night after that, and the night after that, until it's done."

Then, with one last glance at the silent cavern, Eliana turned away and began the walk back up through the mountain.

—◆—

The next day, after a bath so frigid it was painful and a breakfast she did not eat, Eliana tied her hair back into a severe braid and joined Simon in a corner of the palace's central library.

A table and two chairs awaited them by an open window that let in the morning breeze. On the table sat a bowl of water, five metal scraps, a chunk of rich black soil, a squat candle and matches, a pitcher of water, and two glasses.

Eliana looked away from the water, her throat dry as she swallowed.

In silence, they read the passages the temple scholars had marked. They attempted small exercises with the materials spread out before them—Eliana muttering prayers as she directed her castings at the water, the earth, the flickering candle; Simon reading notes scrawled in the margins of various texts.

Lunch arrived, brought by wide-eyed servants. Simon wolfed his down immediately; Eliana ignored hers, and her dinner too.

Night fell. Nothing had responded to her—not the candle flames, not the water in its bowl.

"Disappointed in me?" she asked, ignoring her growling stomach.

"I don't expect you to learn how to use your castings in a day." Simon glanced at her uneaten dinner, but said nothing.

—◆—

The next day brought more of the same, as did the day after that.

At night, with Harkan and Zahra at her side, Eliana tried and failed to conduct magic in Tameryn's cavern, and in the small hours before dawn, she sat in her room, alone, and relived the moment of Rozen's death. She recalled Rozen's last words: *Finish it.*

In the mornings, her sleepless mind heavy with the weight of grief and guilt, Eliana exercised her body.

In the afternoons, she met Simon in the library, and on the third day of this, as she stood in a pool of sunlight, reciting the Sun Rite, her vision shifted and darkened.

She staggered, dizzy.

Simon hurried toward her, but she shook him away, catching herself on a nearby chair.

"It's fine," she told him. "I'm just tired."

He was watching her, in that still, keen way that always left her feeling too seen. "You're not sleeping."

"I am."

"There are shadows under your eyes."

"I always look like this."

He laughed, a soft, bitter sound. "I know what you look like."

Eliana shook his words from her skin. "Read me that passage again."

"Which passage?"

"I don't know, the…" But she could not gather her exhausted thoughts well enough to remember.

"You can't think if you don't eat."

She glared at him. "I'm eating."

"You're not." He slammed his book closed. "Eliana, I don't know what you're trying to do, but—"

"I can't sleep. Is that what you want to hear?" Her voice cracked, but she refused her eyes their tears. If she cried, she would realize how hungry she was, how tired and frustrated, and her magic, her useless castings, would have defeated her. "I try to eat, and it makes me sick."

She turned away, her jaw clenched.

After a moment, Simon asked quietly, "Is it Remy that's keeping you from sleep?"

She nodded. It wasn't entirely a lie.

"You should try talking to him again. It's been days. Neither of you will heal like this."

"I can't," she whispered. "I can't bear to hear him tell me yet again how much he hates me."

"I won't tell anyone. Just…" Navi struggled to move closer.

"Stay still, please." Eliana shifted to the bed's edge. "I'm right here."

"Promise me it isn't dangerous," Navi whispered.

"I can't do that."

"You are more important than I am, Eliana. You must protect yourself."

"Because I'm the Sun Queen?" Eliana muttered.

"If I die, my family and people will mourn me. If you die, the world will fall."

"The world may fall anyway. It's fallen before."

"The people suffering under the reign of the Empire need hope more than they need me. And you are that hope."

Eliana turned away. "I don't know how to be anyone's hope."

Navi touched her cheek, turning her back. "You're mine already. Did you know that? I've prayed to you all my life, before I knew your face. And since I learned who you are, I've prayed to you instead. You, Eliana, the Sun Queen of my prayers and my dreams. I lie here in this stinking bed as Fidelia's poisons eat me alive, and I think of you and pray to you, and when I do that, I feel a lightness in my heart that helps me bear the rest of it. For even if I die, you will live on, and you will ride into the Emperor's city on a steed of light and burn down every one of his towers until all that remains is ashes."

Eliana blinked back tears, blotting Navi's brow with a soft white rag. "You need to rest. You're talking like a madwoman."

"I know what I see when I close my eyes. I know what my prayers tell me. My prayers are of the empirium, and the empirium doesn't lie."

"The empirium is dead. It died long ago."

"And now it lives again, in you." Navi kissed Eliana's hands, her face tightening with pain, and Eliana realized, her stomach turning, that Navi lay bound to the bed with cushioned ties. "Go, before I become something other than myself. And be safe, Eliana. Wherever you go, whatever you do for me, it is not as important as what you can do for them."

"Them?"

"Everyone else," Navi replied, beginning to pant.

Eliana could no longer bear to watch her. She left quickly, sending the nurse back inside. As she walked away from Navi's room, she heard her friend's terrible cries of pain and covered her mouth with her hand.

—◆◆—

In the small eastern library, Eliana found Remy sitting at a window beside one of the royal librarians—a young man, fair of skin and hair, with two canes to help him walk propped against the table. He was opening a book for Remy to see, and from her hiding spot, Eliana saw on the tome's binding the familiar colorful sigils of the ancient elemental temples.

Remy pointed at the open book, his eyes alight. "Saint Ghovan! I've read his eagle had a wingspan of eight feet."

"Only eight?" The librarian smiled, shaking his head. "This is a godsbeast we're talking about, my friend. The imperial eagles had a wingspan of up to twenty feet. Saint Ghovan's was especially grand. This particular account"—the librarian gently turned the brittle page, skimming down the lines of text with one gloved finger—"ah, yes, here it is. This account, written by Saint Ghovan himself, reports his godsbeast to have a wingspan of twenty-two feet."

Remy's eyes widened. "Saint Ghovan wrote this? This is his actual writing?"

The librarian grinned. "His very pen marks, little one."

From behind a towering case of books bound in dyed leather, Eliana watched them, numb. She had resolved to try speaking to her brother again, but now, so near to him, her courage vanished.

How would he react to seeing her, after their days apart? More tears? More of that dead-eyed stare, his pale face drawn with hatred?

She turned away from them, retreating to the shadows with her hands in fists. She tried to will her cowardly, aching heart into something black and unfeeling. The words sat unused on her tongue:

*I love you, Remy. I'm sorry, and I love you.*

—◆◆—

Unsteady and aching, she returned to her rooms to continue her punishment—no water, no food, no rest.

Only memory would sustain her now—the memory of Rozen's blood.

Rozen's throat, punctured and gaping.

Rozen's body, limp in her arms.

Remy's quiet voice: *No. You're the monster.*

Over and over, Eliana forced herself to watch each terrible moment. She mercilessly pushed her body through exercises in her room—practicing punches and kicks, using the bar of her bed to pull up her body. When Harkan arrived at the appointed time, she whirled on him, sweat-drenched and shaking—and her vision, at last, rimmed with gold. She swayed, but she did not fall.

Harkan's face was grave. "El, you look terrible."

"I know," she said, her voice hollow and dreamy.

Zahra drifted at Harkan's elbow. "Are you ready, my queen?"

Eliana existed in a golden forest, dense and unkind, where pushing past every brambled branch sent shocks of lightning flying up her spine. The world tilted. The way through this strange wild was painful and stifling, but it was hers.

Without hesitation, she reached for the candle flickering on the bedside table. The casting in her palm buzzed and thrummed, as if it had freshly emerged from the Forge's hearth fire.

And then the candle's flame flew to her, coming to rest at her fingertips.

She stared at it, turning her hand around it, caressing it. The flame hovered, trembling, on the back of her hand, across her knuckles, in the bend of her palm.

She closed her fingers slightly, dimming the flame. She opened them, held her palm flat. The flame sprang to brilliant life. She cupped both hands beneath it, spread her fingers wide. As if following the steps of a dream, she thrust the flame toward the ceiling. It slammed into the rafters, spreading fast, until it had outlined them in strips of fiery gold.

Harkan cried out in alarm.

A jolt of heat shot up her fingers into the joints of her shoulders, as if twin wires connected her castings to the flames, and they were tugging on her, calling her away from her body to join the flames instead.

She stepped back from that pull, her skin going cold and clammy with sudden dread. An answering spike of heat shocked each of her castings, singeing her palms. The flames were stubborn, clinging to her. They were insatiable in their desire—both for her and to break free of her. Controlling them felt like wrangling a herd of wild animals using only her uncertain will.

"You created them, my queen," came Zahra's voice, low and calm beneath the fresh snap of fire. "You can unmake them as well."

Eliana sank to the floor, needing the solidity of the stone to anchor her to the incandescent sensation of her own body. She didn't know how to douse these flames, other than to follow the taut thread of instinct vibrating inside her. She held her hands out, palms down. Slowly, she lowered them to the floor, imagining that she could press down on the fury of those flames and cow them into submission. Her castings grew hotter the closer her palms came to the floor, as if they were absorbing the fire's heat. The flames overhead began to shrink; the room slipped into darkness.

Eliana flattened her hands against the stone. She bowed her head, breathing deeply through her nose.

The flames diminished. The room was still and black.

She looked up—stiff-shouldered, nose burning—and, through the acrid haze of smoke, found Harkan's wide eyes.

She nodded at Zahra, smiling faintly. "I'm ready."

Zahra's mouth was a dubious black line.

But Eliana held her gaze. *I won't wait any longer. You will take me to the Nest. Now.*

Zahra relented, with a slight, unhappy nod. "Then we'll leave tonight."

◆

As Zahra led them down to Tameryn's cave, Eliana held on to the strange sensation firing through her veins. She was feeling the beginning of near-death, she suspected. If she didn't eat soon, if she didn't sleep, it would be her end. With every step she took, her mind suspended in its fevered state, the discs in her palms blazed hotter, like twin stars turning.

When they reached the shore of the black lake, Zahra said quietly, "Wait here," and then disappeared into the water. The glassy surface swallowed her without sound or splash.

Harkan caught Eliana's arm. "This is a terrible idea. You're not well enough to go to this place. You need sleep and food. You know now what it feels like to summon fire. You can recover that feeling easily, after you've taken some time to rest."

Eliana watched the lake without blinking. "You don't know that. I have the feeling now, and I must take advantage of it while I can."

Harkan came around to block her view. "El, you can't defend yourself against whatever awaits us if you can hardly stand."

She blinked, glared, stepped away from him only a little unsteadily. "I can do much more than stand."

Zahra reappeared. "The way is clear. Are you prepared to swim?"

Harkan stared furiously at Eliana for a moment longer, as if that would somehow dissuade her.

She placed a hand on his arm. At the touch of her casting, he flinched—barely, but enough.

Once, she would not have had to ask him to trust her.

Times had changed.

"Trust me," she said—a command, not a request.

Then she walked into the lake, not stopping until it rippled black at her shoulders. She held her breath, heard Harkan do the same, and pushed out beneath the water.

# ⇀ 13 ↼

# CORIEN

*"He began in the far north, all those years ago, when the
one they called Kingsbane was still alive. He carved an
army out of the ice and black mountains. He taught himself how to build monsters. This was the beginning of his
Empire. The dawn of our great enemy."*

—The Word of the Prophet

On a flat stretch of frozen land, crowded by mountains and overlooking an icy black sea, the angel who had named himself Corien sat in
the bones of an evolving fortress, drinking himself into a stupor.

Or at least, as much as he could drink himself into a stupor, given the
fact that even as powerful as he was, he still did not quite fit into his stolen
body, and he never would.

He gulped down the rest of his drink, examined the empty crystal
goblet, and then hurled it against the far stone wall, hoping the sound of it
shattering apart would satisfy him, bring him some momentary relief from
his raging dark thoughts.

It did not.

He stood up, only a little bit woozy, even after seven glasses of wine.
To amuse himself, he exaggerated the unbalanced sway of his body, as if
he were ready to topple over.

"I'm drunk," he announced to the empty room, which was a lie.

Everything about him was a lie—his drunkenness, his outward calm, even his name.

*Corien*. After finally battering his way through the Gate and escaping the Deep, he had, in a fit of pique, shucked off the mantle of his angelic name. That name belonged to his previous life, the one tainted with exile. He had not spoken the abandoned name since. Some days, if he searched his memory for it, he returned empty-handed.

It was just as well. That angel had been a prisoner. A victim and a failure.

This angel, reborn, was a visionary.

◆

In those first giddy days after escaping the Gate, nameless and liberated, he had begun his search for a body to possess.

He had hunted for years, determined to be particular. If he was going to inhabit a human body, then he would settle for nothing less than the most beautiful one he could find—which he did, at last, on a tussocked hilltop in Celdaria. Some pathetic, lonesome shepherd who neither understood his own beauty nor recognized how it drove every living soul in the nearby village mad with desire.

Corien didn't even remember the man's name. He paused only long enough to note the fine lines of his cheekbones, the full curve of his mouth, the lean strength of his body, forged over many years of herding sheep in the mountains.

Herding sheep. Even now, Corien often felt a twinge of shame and wounded pride, imagining the humble beginnings of his assumed form.

But, then, it was a rather marvelous joke, wasn't it? Once a human shepherd, now the angelic emperor of the new world. There was something immensely satisfying in that dichotomy. When his pride bristled, Corien thought of that delicious contradiction and was soothed.

He approached the windows on the far wall, which allowed him a breathtaking view of the arctic vista outside. Or it would have been breathtaking, perhaps, if he had true breath to take.

He leaned his forehead against the cold pane. His exhalations painted the glass with tiny infant clouds. He wiped them away with the end of his sleeve. Lies. Falsehoods. A manufactured pretend.

Bitterly, he looked down upon the network of industry sprawling across the ice: His kin, inhabiting human bodies of their own, swathed in furs, directed hundreds of human slaves to haul rocks, clear snow, forge weapons, add rooms of stone and iron to the fortress. Other angels worked deeper in the mountains, some distance away, in underground laboratories. Still others, in cavernous chambers that offered some respite from the merciless wind, ran new adatrox through training drills. They taught the dull-eyed brutes how to move and fight once more, now that their minds were no longer their own.

Corien rubbed his aching temples. His generals and a few trusted lieutenants took on a generous portion of the mental burden—directing the adatrox, managing the recruiting efforts in Kirvaya, overseeing the logistics of the laboratories.

But this was his enterprise, his great work. His nascent empire. He could only stomach relinquishing tiny pieces of control. He considered it crucial to demonstrate his power to the angelic ranks. Show them that he was worthy of their loyalty and of his self-styled title. Keep them fighting and devoted, even as the days turned relentlessly on. Even as the Gate remained standing, separating them from the millions of angels still stranded in the Deep.

More importantly, Corien reminded himself, he was indeed powerful enough to maintain control over this frozen base he had named the Northern Reach, as well as the efforts in Kirvaya, and in Borsvall, and...

He closed his eyes, reaching out with one tentative overture, like the stretch of a fledgling wing: *Rielle? Are you there?*

She did not answer.

Instead, a sharp rap sounded on the door to his rooms.

He turned his thoughts away from Celdaria, tucking them safely into the deepest layers of his mind, before snapping over his shoulder, "Yes? What is it?"

His favorite servant entered with a low bow—Alantiah, a young angel with great potential. She inhabited the body of a sharp-eyed young woman with pale skin and rich, auburn hair.

"The angel Bazrifel has returned from Borsvall," Alantiah announced, "and seeks an audience with Your Majesty to deliver his report."

Corien examined his reflection in the glass. His mouth was chapped and discolored from too much drink. His hair fell over his forehead in unkempt, greasy strands. He needed to bathe. He needed a distraction, and to feel like himself again.

He needed to not think about Rielle for a few hours.

He certainly did not need to talk to the fool Bazrifel. He already knew, from a cursory sweep of Bazrifel's thoughts, everything he needed to know: King Hallvard Lysleva was dead at last. His son and heir, Ilmaire, a milquetoast sop of a man, would soon take the throne and was losing his mind with panic at the prospect. The general sentiment in Borsvall was one of fear. Lack of faith in the royal family—in Ilmaire, specifically. Worry about the mysterious sickness that had bedridden their king. A lingering grief over the mysterious death of their beloved princess, Runa.

A hatred toward their southern neighbor, Celdaria. A hatred that was beginning to change. Celdaria remained the enemy, its leaders still the likeliest suspect in Runa's murder.

But the Celdarian Sun Queen, Lady Rielle Dardenne...well. She had saved the capital from destruction, after all. *She*, at least, deserved loyalty. Trust. Maybe even affection.

Corien glimpsed all of this in Bazrifel's mind, and his spirits lifted. All was unfolding as he had engineered it to.

"Tell Bazrifel to return to his post," Corien said unnecessarily, for he had already tossed a thought of dismissal Bazrifel's way. But he enjoyed barking out commands. He relished the sensation of words sliding across his stolen tongue.

"Yes, Your Majesty," said Alantiah, turning to leave.

"But you, stay." Corien glanced at Alantiah's reflection, noting how her face lit up with anticipation—and how her thoughts bloomed against his mind, deferent but delighted. "I require a bath and your company."

He shrugged off his coat, then his vest and silk shirt, then his boots and trousers. He opened another bottle of wine and took it with him into the bathing room, Alantiah's bright gaze following him, rapt and eager.

As Corien watched her prepare his bath, distantly admiring the plump lines of her body, he allowed himself to look once more toward Celdaria. Like cracking open a door to peek inside a room he knew he shouldn't enter, he reached for Rielle, and though only an instant passed before her image manifested before him, it felt like an endless, unbearable age.

Through Rielle's eyes, he saw the scene. She, Ludivine, and Audric were traveling home to Celdaria by horseback, accompanied by an entourage of Borsvall soldiers. The chavaile Rielle had named Atheria had not shown herself since the incident at the Gate. Corien sensed Rielle's heartache, her longing to make amends with the godsbeast, and nearly sent her a feeling of comfort. A press of affection, a mere brush of his thoughts against hers.

But he refrained—barely. He clenched his fists and stepped back from the desire as if it were a physical entity too dangerous to approach.

He knew it was wise to limit his time with Rielle. Doing so enhanced her longing for him, her curiosity, her frustration.

It also prevented him from doing anything foolish that would turn her forever away from him—such as inspiring her to stab the sniveling traitor Ludivine while she slept or slip poison into the besotted Audric's supper, or taking control of her mind entirely, forcing her to leave her home and come to him.

"Shall I leave you to bathe alone, Your Majesty?" came Alantiah's gentle voice. "Or do you require company?"

He blinked, struggling to clear the fog of Rielle from his mind. Alantiah stood before him, loosening the laces of her dress. Her boldness pleased him; theirs was a practiced dance. One that would distract him for an hour or two, and then leave him feeling hollow once more.

Rielle's party had stopped to rest in a sunlit woodland. The Borsvall guards formed a perimeter, their backs turned. Audric stretched out on the grass, yawning, and rubbed his hands over his face. Rielle curled up beside him, and when he cradled her head in his hand and kissed her brow, her subsequent happiness blossomed, tender and warm, until Corien could hardly see for his despair.

Alantiah's mind was nearby, open and willing. He grabbed her by the arm and yanked her against his body, kissing her with such force that she cried out into his mouth.

Before he lost himself in her desire, Corien sent Rielle a final thought, sly and thin, as she watched Ludivine examine her blightblade scar. Its ugly blue lines glittered in the sunlight, like the blade-strewn ruins of a battlefield.

The idea was already there, in Rielle's mind. She had proclaimed her intentions before the Obex. She had spent many hours, as they traveled, quietly examining the possibilities. She simply needed encouragement, and that, Corien was only too happy to give.

*Repair*, he murmured to her.

*Restoration.*

And then, unable to resist touching her, he drew the trailing end of his thoughts down the soft length of her spine, and whispered, *Resurrection.*

# ⇥ 14 ⇤

# RIELLE

*"How did you bear the death of your father? How did you come to live with your grief? My own sends me violent dreams. Unlike Ingrid, I don't have the command of an army to distract me. I have only the endless stack of petitions on my desk. The skeptical eyes of a kingdom upon me. Instructions for my impending coronation whispered to me by bitter magisters who loved my father and my late sister, Runa, and who have no affection for me. I would laugh, if I wasn't afraid it would make me cry. In conclusion, did I mention that my capacity for self-hatred is limitless?"*

—A letter written by Prince Ilmaire Lysleva to Prince Audric
Courverie, dated October 25, Year 998 of the Second Age

Âme de la Terre buzzed like a sticky hive, every courtyard lining the central avenue packed to the brim with citizens eager for a glimpse of the Sun Queen's return.

Rielle hardly noticed, her nerves singing in anticipation of seeing Tal, and Sloane, and Queen Genoveve. And Evyline, Dashiell, Maylis, the rest of her Sun Guard. Poor Evyline would have been absolutely beside herself since they fled Carduel.

*You should wave at them,* Ludivine suggested, *and smile.*

*I'm rather busy at the moment,* Rielle replied.

*You can worry about Tal and Evyline, and wave and smile at the same time.*

Rielle obeyed, begrudgingly. *There, is that better?*

*Your smile looks rather like the painted-on smile of a ravenous doll,* Ludivine observed, *but, yes, that's better. It's important that they see you happy to return home. Many rumors have been circulating since we left Carduel.*

Rielle glanced at Audric, who waved at the gathered crowds with a broad grin on his face. A child broke free of her father's arms and rushed forward, a bouquet of wildflowers in her arms. The Celdarian royal guard, who had replaced their Borsvall escort at the city border, tried to intercept her, but Audric waved them aside.

He knelt to meet the girl's gaze. When she thrust out her fistful of flowers, he accepted the offering with a smile. "These are lovely. Did you pick them yourself?"

The girl nodded, her brown cheeks dusted with gold powder. She bit her lip, as if considering her options, and then flung herself at him, hooking her arms around his neck. The force of her affection nearly knocked him off his feet, but he nevertheless returned her embrace before gently redirecting her back to her father, who watched, mortified, from a few paces away.

Pride bloomed in Rielle's chest, clearing her thoughts of the erratic, faint visions of Corien she'd seen on their journey home. Since then, a word had sat coiled in the deepest hollow of her mind—eyes open, breathing steady. A watchful reptile.

*Resurrection.*

She glanced at Ludivine, who was absently fiddling with the end of her left sleeve. She tugged it farther down her arm, even though the blight-blade scar was completely obscured.

*They all adore Audric,* Rielle told Ludivine, determined to distract them both. *This sort of thing suits him, beautifully.*

Ludivine was silent.

*What is it?*

*They do not all adore him*, Ludivine replied.

*The ones who don't are unworthy of him*, Rielle said at once. Then, after a pause: *And me? How do they feel about me?*

Ludivine hesitated. *Many are pleased to see you return.*

*And some*, Rielle guessed, *are not as pleased.*

*We'll have to talk about this later, I think.*

*Why?*

With a gentle press against her mind, Ludivine directed Rielle's attention up the road, toward the grand outer gates of Baingarde's lower yards, where a group of people awaited them: Sloane, in her blue-and-black House of Night robes. Evyline, and the rest of Rielle's gold-armored Sun Guard.

And Tal.

Despite the clamor of the crowd, the cries of her name, the flowers thrown at her and Audric's feet, Rielle felt Tal's anger as clearly as if someone had taken a knife to the fleshy underside of her arm.

Her throat clenched up at the sight of him. She should never have abandoned him in Carduel without so much as a message explaining herself.

They entered the massive stone yard that separated the lowest reaches of Baingarde from the city's upper neighborhoods. The yard glittered with fountains, adorned with dramatic sculptures of the saints. Rielle held her breath and bowed low before Tal. Behind her, the gates clanged shut. At once, the crowd pressed against the iron flourishes—banging their fists, waving their silken gold banners, chanting her name, Audric's name, Ludivine's name.

"Did you really stop a tidal wave, my lady?" called out a jubilant male voice.

Rielle smiled hopefully up at Tal. Implacable, he opened his mouth, most likely to admonish her, but before he could, she jumped to her feet and threw her arms around his shoulders. The smoke-sharp scent of his clothes and the soft press of his blond waves against her cheek were such familiar sensations that a burst of homesickness, irrational and surprising, overwhelmed her.

"If you yell at me in front of everyone," she teased, "they might tear down the gates to rescue me and carry you screaming to the nearest dungeon."

His embrace was stiff. "My office," he murmured. "One hour."

—◆—

Rielle had known Tal would be furious with her, but she hadn't realized just how furious.

She arrived at his office ten minutes early, after convincing Audric to stall their meeting with Queen Genoveve. Taking her customary seat at the scarlet-curtained window, she waited, hands folded tightly in her lap. The clock on the mantel, crowned with gilded flames, ticked away her every breath. Tal's shield sat on its stand near the hearth, grinning a demented, polished grin.

Beside Rielle's feet sat a padded wooden crate, which their Borsvall escort had helped carry on the journey south. The crate's contents quietly hummed, a phantom energy that she felt more than heard, like an arm drawing shapes in a dark room.

The clock chimed a single golden tone—half past four—and the door flew open, admitting a glowering Tal. He slammed the door shut behind him, unclasped his scarlet-and-gold day coat, and tossed it onto his chair. For a long moment he leaned hard against the desk, his back to Rielle.

"It's lovely to see you too," Rielle remarked when she could no longer bear the tense silence.

Tal turned, his eyes bright and anguished. Rielle's froze, staring. She had not expected tears. She had expected him to yell at her or, even worse, to tell her in that soft, wounded voice of his how deeply she had disappointed him.

Instead, he sank to his knees before her, gathered one of her hands in his, and kissed their interlaced fingers. His mouth lingered against her skin, hot and urgent, as if it were his last chance to show her affection. The afternoon sunlight slanted against his skin, illuminating lines of exhaustion around his eyes and mouth.

Rielle struggled to find her voice. With her free hand, she touched his hair. "Tal, I'm so sorry."

He shook his head against her knuckles, then rose to sit beside her. "Rielle, may I hold you for a moment? To convince myself that you are in fact here, and safe?"

Rielle could not remember a time when she had felt more taken aback. "Of course."

Without hesitation, Tal's arms came around her. When he exhaled into her hair, his hand cupping the back of her neck, the sound came out torn. Rielle's body sat at an awkward angle, but she did not dare move to ease her discomfort. She spared a fond feeling toward her younger, smitten self, who would have been giddy to have Tal touch her in such a way.

"Now that I've reassured myself you are in fact not a dream here to torment me, I must ask you a question," he said at last. Dry-eyed, he straightened his tunic and then fixed her with a glare as hard as sunlit nails. "What in God's name were you thinking, leaving us all in Carduel like that? And taking Ludivine and Audric with you? My God, Rielle."

He dragged a hand through his hair. "No one knew where you had gone. No one knew if you were even alive, until we received word from our spies in Borsvall that, yes, you were alive, though you'd barely avoided capture by the Borsvall commander and her soldiers, who had been plotting to do so for weeks. And don't think I won't take our own spies to task for that blunder—if they survive Queen Genoveve's fury, that is."

Tal rose and began to pace. "And, of course, the fact that you abandoned frightened citizens in Carduel hasn't exactly increased your popularity among those who deeply distrust any power that could accomplish what you've achieved, and therefore distrust *you*."

"Tal—"

"No, I'm not nearly finished yet. Then, a tidal wave threatens the Borsvall capital, and you fly out on Atheria to stop it, with no regard for your own safety."

Rielle bristled. "I'll have you know—"

"I said, I'm not finished yet!" Tal snapped, his voice cracking. The sound of his anger seemed to deflate him; he rubbed a hand over his face. "And then, after all of this, you journey to the Sunderlands, still not sending word to anyone in Celdaria of your health, your whereabouts, your intentions. You visit the *Gate*, of all places, and attempt to repair it, without any preparations or assistance, and thereby weaken it dramatically."

He whirled on her. "You heard, I suppose, of the thousands of birds that lost all their navigation abilities, thanks to the shock waves from your efforts, and dropped dead across the streets of Luxitaine? Five citizens dead. Seventeen injured. And thank God it wasn't more than that. Storms up and down the coasts. Wildfires in the heartlands."

The resolve required to sit there, still and silent, made Rielle's shoulders burn. She refused to break or blink. Her tears could build all they liked.

Tal glared at his casting, arms stiff at his sides. Rielle allowed him his seething silence for a full minute before she decided enough was enough.

"Will I have the chance to defend myself," she asked, "or am I to bear you yelling at me without complaint?"

Tal looked back at her. "What right have you to complain?"

"You don't own me, Tal," she snapped. "No one does, Sun Queen or no. Not Audric, not Queen Genoveve, not the Archon." She rose, lifting her chin. "I *did* save Styrdalleen, yes, and every one of its citizens, from a wave that would have dragged them all into the sea. And by doing that, I proved myself to the Borsvall people, to Prince Ilmaire and Princess Ingrid, to their magisterial council. Even to the Borsvall Obex."

With that, Rielle crouched beside the chest and undid its four bronze latches. She opened the lid and stepped back, allowing Tal to look for himself.

He approached, frowning. The moment he laid eyes upon Grimvald's hammer, his expression eased open, as if he were witnessing dawn for the first time.

Before he could speak, Rielle hurried on. "Jodoc Indarien, speaker of the Obex in the Sunderlands, thinks I may need the castings of the saints in order to repair the Gate. That their castings hold the memory of the Gate's creation, and that by using them, I could follow those memories, reproduce their actions, and make the Gate stand strong once more."

Tal said nothing, still staring at the hammer in disbelief.

Rielle watched his face, craving some kind of sign that he accepted her and what she had done. That he was proud of her, that this strange new rift between them was fleeting and meaningless.

"I know we should have told you our intentions when we left Carduel," she said quietly. "Audric had received an urgent letter from Prince Ilmaire, and we could not delay going to Borsvall. If we had, I'll remind you, the capital would have been destroyed. And Lu was convinced that it was safer for me to stay away from Carduel, for I had just..."

She swallowed. She had not yet told Tal about Corien, and wasn't eager to, not with her nerves so frayed. "Well. Lu thought we should stay away from Carduel for a time, given our encounter with those assassins, and I trust her. I trust both of them. I could have asked them to return, or forced them to, if it came to it. But I didn't want to go back there and face all of those people who hated me."

Tal glanced at her. "Many in Carduel that day did not hate you."

"But some did, and they tried to hurt me for it. They could have hurt my friends. Can you blame me for running away?"

Tal shook his head. "You're the Sun Queen, Rielle. You have a duty to your people. You have a responsibility to be a stable, comforting force during times of peace, and a standard-bearer, a warrior, in times of strife. You can't simply fly away on Atheria whenever it pleases you."

At the mention of Atheria, Rielle's tears broke through her defenses. She dashed a hand angrily across her eyes.

Tal softened. "Audric told me about her. I'm sorry." He came to her, hesitated, then kissed her forehead and each of her cheeks.

Rielle closed her eyes, leaning into his touch. "Didn't I do well? Despite everything I did wrong, I did some things right. I know I did. Please tell me I did."

Tal's voice was thick. "Rielle. What you accomplished in Borsvall was remarkable."

She opened her eyes, relieved, to find him watching her closely. The way he held himself, the new flare in his eyes as he watched her face, was not something she had seen before. A rogue thrill, jittery and bewildered, skipped across her navel.

"Our spy saw you stop the wave with his own eyes," Tal went on. "I received his report three days ago, and I've read it dozens of times over. Rielle, I don't understand how you did what you did. It shouldn't be possible for one human to control such an immense force all on her own."

Rielle beamed. "I don't think I could have without all your years of interminably boring lessons to draw upon."

Tal smiled wistfully. "I'm not sure my lessons did you any good."

"Oh, come now. Surely you don't mean that."

"Books and recitations, praying at the feet of statues." Tal scoffed. "You are beyond such things, Rielle, and always have been. Your father and I were deluding ourselves to think a few prayers could ever contain you."

The unexpected mention of her father dislodged Rielle's sense of calm. For a moment, she could hardly speak. A wild desire broke open against the walls of her chest. Suddenly, she wanted to confess everything about what had really happened on the day of the fire trial. To see the shock on Tal's face and confront his disgust. To unburden herself of a secret that seemed to be growing a mind and will of its own.

Instead, she forced out words that were not a lie, but certainly not the whole truth. "I miss him. He hated me, and yet..." She laughed a little, marveling at her own performance. "I miss him every day."

Tal hesitated, then reached for her cheek.

A slight knock on the door. Tal's hand dropped. He moved away, turning toward his desk. "Yes?"

A young, scarlet-robed acolyte entered, bobbing her head nervously. Her eyes went immediately to the open crate. Rielle stepped in front of it, glaring.

"Pardon me, my lady," the acolyte said, "but I bring a message from Her Majesty the queen. She requests that you come to her sitting room at once."

"Ah," Rielle muttered. "Time for more yelling."

Tal cleared his throat with a pointed look.

"Please tell the queen I will—"

"My apologies, my lady," interrupted the acolyte, looking rather stricken, "but I bring another message, from His Royal Highness the prince. It says…" The acolyte unraveled a slip of paper. "Please tell Lady Rielle that 'at once' means 'at once,' and not 'when you and Tal have finally stopped shouting at each other.'"

Rielle tossed a grin Tal's way. He returned an echo of it, half-formed.

"Well, then. I suppose I should hurry." She moved toward Tal, placed her hand on his. "May I leave the hammer with you? Your office has always been a safe place for me. I would feel comforted if I knew it remained under your watch."

Tal lifted her hand to his lips. "Of course."

Rielle searched his face, but found nothing reassuring. He would not meet her gaze, his mouth set in a bitter line. Without warning, Corien's coy words from long weeks before returned to her:

*Shall I tell you what secrets I sensed in that pretty blond head of his?*

Rielle fled to the hallway to join her guard, Tal's kiss imprinted on her hand and a foreign bramble taking root in her gut. "Evyline?"

The woman stared straight ahead at the wall, flanked by two other members of the Sun Guard. "Yes, my lady."

"It appears we've been summoned."

"It appears so, my lady," Evyline said stiffly.

As they began walking, Rielle glanced sidelong at the head of her guard. "For how long will you be angry with me, Evyline?"

Evyline relented slightly. "I estimate for only a day or two longer, my lady."

Rielle grinned, relief loosening her shoulders. A few more exchanges with Evyline, and she would shake off her strange meeting with Tal like old feathers. "Quite right, Evyline. That seems only fair."

Rielle approached Queen Genoveve's sitting room with no small amount of trepidation, for she could hear raised voices from all the way down the corridor—the queen's, and Audric's.

She stopped at the sitting room doors, which were thick enough to muffle the queen's words, if not their vicious sentiment.

Evyline cleared her throat. "I don't think staring at the doors will make the shouting stop, my lady."

Rielle rolled her eyes. "I wonder if your tendency for insubordination will ever lose its charm, Evyline."

"Unlikely, my lady," said Evyline mildly, "for I have had an excellent tutor."

Rielle swallowed a smile, took a deep breath, and pushed open the doors.

Queen Genoveve turned at once. "I marvel, Lady Rielle, at the length of time required for you to travel here from the Pyre, all those many miles away."

Rielle was too startled to reply. In the weeks since leaving for their tour of Celdaria, the queen's appearance had drastically altered—her cheeks hollowed, her mouth thin and pale, her once meticulously groomed auburn waves now flying tangled about her head. She was still lovely, in the dramatic Sauvillier fashion, but there was a thorny quality to her now, a brittle energy, that spoke of sleepless nights and restless, unsatisfied days.

Rielle bowed low, her travel-muddied skirts gathering stiffly on the rug. "Forgive me, my queen. I came as quickly as I was able."

Genoveve gestured irritably. "You're getting mud on my carpet. Next time you come before me, make sure you change into something suitable first."

With great effort, Rielle refrained from commenting that if she had taken the time to find clean clothes, she would have been even later to their meeting. "Yes, my queen. Of course."

Audric, his expression grim, helped Rielle to her feet. He gently pressed her palm; she squeezed back, grateful. She was not unaware of Genoveve's sharp eyes upon their joined hands.

"I was just telling Mother about our time in Borsvall, and in the

Sunderlands," Audric began, his voice carefully even. "And about our conversations with Jodoc Indarien."

"Yes," Genoveve interrupted, "and I would like to hear your version of events, Lady Rielle, before we proceed."

With that, the queen sat on a nearby divan, settled her arms on the cushions, and crossed one leg over the other.

Rielle glanced at Audric, uncertain.

"I'm waiting, Lady Rielle," said the queen. "We've all been waiting, thanks to your impetuousness. While I, and the rest of the country, grieved our king's death, you dragged his son and heir off to an enemy territory, with no regard for his safety or for our traditions of mourning."

"Mother, as I've told you," Audric said sharply, "it wasn't Rielle who urged us to leave Carduel. It was me, and Ludivine."

"There was an incident during our stay in Carduel," added Rielle, "involving four men who attempted to kill me."

She pushed on before the queen could interrupt and told the whole story—from Carduel to the abandoned village on the outskirts of Styrdalleen. The tidal wave, and finally the Sunderlands.

"We were hoping, my queen," Rielle said, glancing at Audric, "that you would have information about where Saint Katell's casting might be located, or how to approach the Celdarian Obex about—"

"Absolutely not." Genoveve moved to a small table, where a spread of tea and cakes sat on gold-rimmed platters. "Jodoc Indarien was right when he told you that you should have to find these castings on your own, without aid. To be frank with you, Lady Rielle, I'm not sure that even then you would deserve to possess them."

Audric's voice cut the air like a taut wire. "Mother, you're not listening to us. The Gate is *falling*."

Genoveve turned her back on them to fill her cup. "I'm well aware that the Gate is falling."

"Then you must also be aware," Rielle said, stepping toward her, "that I am the best hope we have of mending it."

The queen laughed. "That's rich, Lady Rielle, as you've just told me how you in fact have weakened it."

Rielle swallowed an assortment of uncouth replies. "Yes, my queen. I was rash, and frantic. I acted too quickly, and I don't intend to do so again, now that I understand the true might of the Gate."

"And you have, of course, never given any of us reason to mistrust you," said the queen, taking a sip of her tea.

"No other human is powerful enough to repair the Gate, my queen," Rielle insisted. "No other *hundred* humans are powerful enough. I *must* find the castings of the saints as quickly as possible." She hesitated, then steeled herself. "Is your personal grudge against me worth sacrificing the safety of your entire kingdom?"

Rielle sensed Audric moving slightly toward her, as if preparing to jump to her defense, but Rielle kept her eyes fixed on the queen. Genoveve took a final sip of her tea before returning her cup to its saucer.

"Personal grudge?" she said quietly. "How small a thing you make it sound. My beloved niece was betrothed to my only son and heir, an arrangement engineered by my family, and the family of my late husband, when Ludivine was a mere infant. For years, this agreement defined the relationship of our two houses. It established a bright future, for our families and for the country. The House of Katell bonded with the second most powerful House in the realm."

The queen turned, her eyes cold and terrible, outlined by shadows of grief. "And then you seduce my son, tempting him into your bed like some common street whore, and throw everything into ruin."

Audric's voice came low and furious. "Mother, you will apologize to Rielle right now."

"Or what, Audric? You'll kill me? You'll run away with her and abandon your birthright? Go live a free life in the forests, fucking like peasants?"

The shock of such crude words falling from Genoveve's lips made Rielle want to burst out laughing.

Beside her, Audric's body snapped with tension. "Mother, how could you speak like this?"

"How could I? How could *I?*" The queen's mouth trembled. "How could you embarrass me and shame me as completely as you have done? And so soon after your father's death. Abandoning your cousin, abandoning me, and all for this girl who lied to us for years, whose power *we* cannot understand or trust?" She gestured at Rielle. "She said herself that she is rash and unthinking. This is the creature into whose hands you want to thrust the fate of our world?"

"She is not a creature," Audric snapped. "She is a human being. And she has demonstrated through the trials that—"

"The trials." Genoveve scoffed. "Trials most likely designed in her favor, thanks to the influence of Lord Belounnon and his weak-willed sister, and that lover of his, who would most likely do anything to keep him happy and in her bed—and not in Rielle's."

Rielle could keep quiet no longer, her cheeks burning. "How dare you. Those are Grand Magisters you're talking about. Tal, Sloane, and Miren have nothing to do with me, nor with Audric or Ludivine. They have served your country loyally for many years, and they do not deserve your disrespect."

The queen stood in silence for a moment, then moved toward Rielle and took her chin in one cool hand, appraising her.

Audric stood rigid nearby. The air around him popped like the snap of burning wood, painting dust motes gold as embers.

"To think that I pitied you," the queen whispered. "To think that I sat and prayed with you the night before the metal trial. That I was desperate for your safety."

She released Rielle, her mouth pulled thin and her eyes bright. She returned to her tea with unsteady hands. "I promise you this, Rielle. You'll find Katell's casting only when I have been laid cold and lifeless in my waiting tomb—or when my husband rises from his."

## — 15 —

# ELIANA

*"The Nest is a continuing problem, but one I'm not sure we will ever rid ourselves of—or that we should. Its presence brings smugglers, murderers, gamblers, and even angelic wraiths into our country, but the advantage of that lies in their private soldiers, their networks of villains and thieves that reinforce our own military efforts. These scoundrels and killers will protect our country as fiercely as we do, if only because their beloved Annerkilak lies within its borders."*

—A report from Commander Lianti Haakorat
to Kings Eri and Tavik Amaruk of Astavar

When Zahra had told her that the Nest was an underground market, Eliana had thought she meant in the figurative sense—illegal dealings, illicit substances, violence and depravity.

But the Nest was, in fact, truly underground, a subterranean city that existed in a series of caverns beneath the mountains on Vintervok's northern border.

Eliana and Harkan stood in the shadows behind a damp stone outcropping furred with lichens. Below them stretched an elaborate spread of contradictions—craggy rock formations above and below, flanking the city of Annerkilak like rows of misshapen brown teeth. Walking paths paved with polished jade tiles. Four-story apartment buildings boasted manicured roof gardens that crawled with shadows Eliana couldn't define. Ornate roof spires stretched feebly toward the high cavern ceilings that disappeared into darkness. Tiny galvanized lights hung on wires that had been strung across the cramped tiled roads, from shop front to shop front. The softer light of gas lamps pooled in courtyards and behind windowpanes, and a low roar of sound punctuated the tableau—cheers and shouts, clashing strains of music played on strings and horns, the bray of a donkey, an infant's furious wail.

Throughout the city, massive columns of stone stretched from the ground up into darkness, displaying elaborate carvings of both humans and angels. The saints, brandishing their castings. Angels, wings spread wide. Godsbeasts, claws and fangs bared.

"Angelic *and* human art?" Eliana asked, rubbing heat back into her trembling arms. They had swum through nearly two miles of narrow flooded passages to find the Nest, climbed through cramped caves only wide enough to admit one person at a time—Harkan first, Eliana behind him. Now, the cold cave air cut through her drenched clothes like knives.

"The battle lines so starkly drawn above don't matter as much down here," Zahra said, "not when the partnership between human gangsters and angelic wraiths has proven so fruitful for both."

"So a city of thieves and criminals has figured out how to live together peacefully down here while the rest of us on the surface tear each other to pieces," Harkan observed wryly. "Perhaps we ought to take notes. Bring back suggestions to the kings."

"Collaborative art notwithstanding, this is not a city at peace," Zahra warned. "Do not let down your guard."

Harkan touched Eliana's arm. "Are you all right?"

Eliana snapped open her eyes. She hadn't realized she had closed them while they spoke, that she was leaning heavily on the boulder to her left.

"You need food." Harkan rummaged through the small oilskin bag he'd strapped to his torso and withdrew a slightly damp strip of dried pork. "Here. Eat this, and sit down."

Eliana waved him away. "Stop pestering me. I'm fine."

"You can't do anything if you can't walk. Don't be foolish."

"Don't speak to me like that."

Harkan blew out a sharp breath. "You barely controlled that fire in your room. Do you think you'll be able to do so again, if you end up having to use your power while you can hardly hold yourself up?"

Eliana grabbed the meat from him and tore off a furious chunk. "There. Happy?"

"Honestly, El. Are you eight years old? I'm trying to help you—and by doing so, help Navi. That's why we're here, isn't it?"

To that, she had no reply. He wasn't wrong, and she hated that, how he'd made her feel as small and guilty as a misbehaving child.

Almost as much as she hated the power that had forced her into this half-alive, half-wild state. Hungry and tired, frayed at the edges.

She didn't tell him what she was truly thinking, for she was afraid that if she did, both he and Zahra would turn her around and force her back through the caves to the palace.

She didn't tell him that she was afraid to eat even a few bites, for what if that quenched too much of her hunger? What if that left her softened and incapable of summoning her power when they needed it most?

If this was how her mother had existed, it was no wonder she'd gone mad and joined the angels.

*I don't think humans are meant to possess this kind of power*, she told Zahra. *We're too small for it.*

*You are hardly small, my queen*, Zahra said after a moment, but she didn't sound convinced. Then a feeling of someone wringing their hands crept into Eliana's mind. *I shouldn't have brought you here*, Zahra said softly. *I should never have told you about it.*

*And thereby condemned Navi to an unspeakable death?* Eliana shoved the rest of the meat into her pocket. *You did exactly as you should have. And if you try to force me back, I'll never forgive you for it.*

Zahra fell into a miserable silence.

"Using your mind-speak again?" Harkan asked. "Whispering secrets you don't want me to hear?"

"Yes," Eliana said simply, moving past him and ignoring his mutinous look. "Let's do the job and get home."

Harkan's voice was thin and quiet in the dark. "Just like old times."

—◆—

With Zahra's guidance, they worked their way slowly through the strange streets of Annerkilak. To avoid detection by the wraiths who ruled the Nest, Zahra had shrunken her presence to a mere palm-sized shadow in Eliana's pocket, her thoughts so faint that Eliana had to strain to understand them.

*Stop here*, Zahra instructed, and Eliana obeyed, gently touching Harkan's arm as they passed the mouth of an alleyway where a sullen vendor had set up shop—a sagging cart laden with startlingly beautiful statues carved from various precious stones. Saint Marzana, in ruby. Saint Ghovan, in diamonds and pearls. A topaz idol of the Emperor, his eyes of glittering obsidian.

At Zahra's bidding, Eliana purchased an idol of the Emperor while Harkan flirted with the vendor.

They moved on, the idol a sharp and unwelcome weight in her left hip pocket. Her tired mind imagined its tiny stone fingers poking the flesh of her thigh, insistent and grinning. She resolved to dispose of it as soon as possible.

*Turn there*, Zahra ordered, directing them toward an archway that led to a plaza gurgling with fountains—one in the center, an ivory-white angel with water trickling from her eyes as tears would. Others in each corner— weeping angels all. Some despairing, some furious. Some in prayer; others in combat, with writhing humans caught beneath their boots. The water from the fountains collected in a series of shallow, square pools, where bathers lounged and drank.

*Why are we here?* Harkan tapped against Eliana's wrist—the old, wordless language they had devised while growing up in Orline.

*Because,* Zahra replied, *two strangers appearing out of nowhere and swiftly heading straight for the wraith nest will attract suspicion. We must be cautious. The moment they detect me, we're finished.*

Eliana relayed her answer to Harkan, tapping her fingers against his own.

He subsided, his expression tense.

They traveled through the city in such a fashion for what felt like hours— wandering through shabby neighborhoods on the perimeter of the Nest, where the streets were narrow and hushed; and then in and out of buildings crammed with markets stuffed into parlors and kitchens, like eccentric houses opening up their rooms for perusal by prospective buyers. Vendors shouted prices from behind their carts. Shoppers whispered furtively in corners, counting through damp purses of coins. Eyes liquid and dilated from fresh drops of lachryma; breath sweet and stale, bodies teetering.

And then, at last, her own body so stiff and tense she felt brittle, bleached, a bald mountain stripped of all woodland, Eliana sensed Zahra's thoughts directing her toward a grand building across the road—circular, dark, quilted with windows lit amber from within.

Zahra's fear poured through Eliana's mind, slow and viscous.

"Is that it?" she murmured for Harkan's benefit.

Zahra sent the feeling of a nod. "The hive, they call it."

Then her presence stiffened, a shock of surprise. She pressed herself into the rigid flat of Eliana's palm.

"We must move quickly." Her low voice held a new urgency. "Sarash is on her way."

Eliana tensed. "Sarash?"

"A wraith?" Harkan asked.

Zahra's affirmative came with sharp, cool pressure against the fleshy part of Eliana's thumb. "If she arrives before we are safely away, there will be very little I can do to protect you from her. The other wraiths are lustful, easily distractible. Not Sarash." She cursed then, softly, an angelic vulgarity. "Last I was here, it seemed she would not return to Annerkilak for some weeks."

"How long do we have?" Eliana asked.

"An hour. Perhaps a little more."

Now Harkan was the one to curse.

A wave of exhaustion moved swiftly through Eliana, but she did not allow it to fell her. Her vision danced, careening. She clenched her fists and teeth, willed her sight steady. "Take us inside."

—◆◇◆—

Nearly an hour later, having successfully infiltrated the hive's lower levels thanks to Zahra's whispered instructions, they raced through a dark, clean honeycomb of basement tunnels. The walls were damp with the same black cave water through which they had swum, and small galvanized lights flickered and buzzed, haphazardly illuminating their path.

As Eliana ran, Harkan silent and swift beside her, she recited the steps of their mission as if intoning the verses of a prayer—get to the stores where the wraiths hoard their drugs. Medicine to treat the wounds and illnesses of their slaves, recreational substances like anodynum and lachryma.

Poisons.

Antidotes.

Then she recited the Lissar words Zahra had taught them as they crept through the upper levels of the hive—backs pressed flat against the tapestried walls, boots treading carefully down corridors slick with polished mosaic tiles. Lissar: the most basic of the angelic languages. Far easier than Qaharis and Azradil, Zahra had said, before Eliana hissed at her to shut up. Lissar might have been easier, but Eliana still found the unfamiliar words difficult to remember. Remy was the one with the gift for languages, with the memory like a steel trap.

But she could not think of Remy in these tunnels.

She had to fly through them unfettered, cycling through the Lissar words over and over, in case Zahra had to unexpectedly leave, create a diversion upstairs, give them time to complete their mission alone. She had to keep her mind as clear and sharp as it had once been as the Dread.

Upstairs, the wraiths held court in a series of darkened lounges, lit by galvanized lights in multicolored glass casings. Wild footsteps and whirling dance reels, performed on wailing pipes and frantic fiddles, floated down through the hive's many floors—a faint spectral refrain.

Eliana pushed herself faster, ignoring the exhausted buzz in her head and the cramp pinching her side. She sent a fleeting thought to each of her castings and felt nothing in return. Her eyes stung with frustration. Harkan was right; she should have eaten, she should have slept. All her work, all her self-torment, and for what? For two castings that remained a mystery to her and provided no comfort.

She recalled the sensation of the flames lining the rafters in her room— how their heat had pulled at her, how her castings had felt tugged forward by an urgent, ruthless hunger. She had created the flames, and yet they had been of something else too—not just of her own will, but of something else's.

She had felt, in that moment, that she was a mere vessel. A conduit between the power in her blood and the flames overhead, licking for a taste.

Would there ever come a time when she could use her power and not feel as if it was using her?

Zahra pressed against her fingers, her touch so faint and careful that it could have been a mere twitch of nerves. *Later, my queen. We can talk about that later.*

Eliana's tears muddied the dark corridor. With each thin breath, her abused body protested. *Promise me.*

*I promise. Once Navi is safe, you will be able to think more clearly.*

Eliana didn't dare to hope that could be true. It had been so long since she had been able to think clearly, since she had felt in control of her own tired mind, that she hardly remembered what it felt like.

"Here," Zahra instructed, her voice small, contained, and they turned a corner, obeying her.

Eliana sensed her fear of speaking too loudly while within these walls, of existing too completely. She had explained it to Eliana: How easily would you find an unfamiliar aberration of the skin on the back of your hand? A sight you knew intimately and saw every day?

It would not take long. And so the wraiths would easily be able to catch her scent, if she wasn't careful—an aberration in their hive. An unwelcome visitor.

At the end of a narrow stone corridor, they flew down two sets of stairs and then through a labyrinth of passages dimmer and lower-ceilinged than the rest. At last, their path deposited them before a black door set in the wall, one of several such doors in a corridor that stretched several yards in either direction. At one end of the hallway stood an archway that led to darkness.

At the other end, a wall of stone. A dead end.

Harkan withdrew a set of lock picks from his pocket and knelt, prepared to work while Eliana stood guard, Arabeth in hand. Her castings were dim and quiet.

But the door was not locked.

Instead it stood slightly ajar, a faint artificial light beyond.

Harkan froze, shoulders tense.

Eliana stared at the door, her heart pounding so fast she could feel it in her forehead.

*Zahra?*

*I don't know,* Zahra replied, fainter now than she had been before. *Quickly. Inside. I'll keep watch at the door. She is close.*

Wraiths could be careless, Zahra had told her during their swim, distracting Eliana's thoughts from the cold and the dark with information that would have made Remy's eyes shine like stars. The wraiths of Annerkilak weren't Empire soldiers, efficient and disciplined. They were gangsters, dulled by debauchery and spoiled with power. They could have come downstairs to retrieve a fresh jar of lachryma and been so drug-addled that they'd carelessly left the door open.

Whatever the reason, Eliana didn't have time for debate.

She held her breath, tightened her hand around Arabeth, and stepped past Harkan into the room.

It was larger than she'd expected—deep and wide, lined with dozens of tall shelving units. A smooth black ladder on wheels stood attached to each one. The floor was stone, but polished smooth. Galvanized lights— harsh and white, buzzing faintly—hung from the ceiling rafters in an orderly grid. Neatly labeled white tins lined each shelf, their labels marked with angelic writing. Lissar.

They moved quickly along the shelves, scanning the unfamiliar lettering. The air was cool, but so still Eliana felt suffocated by it. She drew a hand across her sweaty forehead, squinting up at the ocean of angelic markings overhead.

"Nothing here," Harkan muttered, hurrying past her to the next aisle of shelves.

They searched in silence for long moments that felt as vast as ages, and then, at last, a particular word caught Eliana's eye.

She climbed a nearby ladder to the fourth shelf up, where a row of rectangular tins labeled *zapheliar* sat in neat stacks.

*Zapheliar*—the angelic word for crawler, Zahra had told her. And if she was interpreting the markings correctly, it seemed that there were variations of the antidote, perhaps for different forms of crawlers.

She cursed, hesitated for a moment, and then grabbed one of each. She turned on the ladder, whispering softly for Harkan.

He was already there, holding open his bag at the base of the ladder. She tossed the tins down to him—eighteen in total. They were lighter than she'd expected and rattled oddly, as if they contained items made out of alien material.

"Is that all of them?" Harkan asked.

"I saw nine variations. Grabbed two of each."

Harkan fastened his bag shut and looked around the room, frowning as if chasing a sound he couldn't pinpoint, and Eliana had just started to climb down, a question on her lips, when the air in the room changed.

She looked down just in time to hear Zahra cry out a warning and see a slender metal net shoot out of the darkness—a spider's web, gilded silver. Copper plates snapped open from its heart, like wings unfurling, and Zahra screamed at the sight of it, the sound of her unrestrained terror one of the most frightening Eliana had ever heard.

Harkan drew his sword; Eliana jumped down to the floor, brandishing Arabeth. Distantly, she thought of her castings, but they remained dark, useless. Everything was happening too quickly for her to focus her thoughts and summon anything but panic.

Instead she watched, horrified, as Zahra's faint dark form diminished, sucked violently into the spinning copper contraption. Then the awful thing snapped closed and clattered across the floor with a hollow metallic racket, where it quaked, buzzing, as if it now housed a swarm of bees. It was a flat octagonal box, glinting and copper-plated, small enough to fit into Eliana's palm, and from within it came a distant wail that sounded faintly like it could belong to Zahra—but a smaller, frightened version of her that Eliana hardly recognized.

She darted forward, grabbed the box, and shoved it into her pocket. Harkan was at her side at once, his expression ferocious. His free hand hovered over his coat pocket, where Eliana knew a bombardier waited, ready to be uncapped and thrown.

"Show yourself," she demanded of Zahra's attacker. "What did you do to her?"

"Such indelicate manners," came a woman's voice. Silken. An amused sort of boredom. She entered the room slowly, her gait supple and unhurried, and dragged the blade of a long, curved sword across the floor. She was golden-skinned, tall, slender, her hair a net of shining bronze knots. She wore a high-collared, square-shouldered gown of indigo and gold— one sleeve dark, the other woven with golden thread. The gown fell to her heels, leaving slits on each side for her trousered legs to move freely.

Her eyes flickered from an inky black, like those of an imperial general, to brown, to gray, and back to black. An ever-shifting cascade of ill color.

Eliana recognized her at once. The sensation of the woman before her matched the rising currents of fear Zahra had been sending her only moments before.

Sarash. It must have been.

"Yes, that's me," Sarash said, her words lazy and smooth. She nodded at Eliana's pocket, where the strange box now rested. "It was a mistake to trust her. Too weak to claim a body for more than a few moments at a time. Too small-minded to both protect you from my friends upstairs and also sense danger coming. Until it's too late."

She stopped, tilting her head. Her eyes shifted to gray and stayed there.

Eliana's stomach dropped. She recognized that look. All at once, she was back in the outpost in Ventera. Beneath her, Lord Morbrae sat rigid and gray-eyed in his chair.

Harkan shifted. "Eliana," he muttered. "What's happening?"

"Eliana," Sarash said, her voice changing. Now it was no longer simply her, speaking. It was someone else, too—a voice Eliana recognized.

Her mouth went dry, the fingers of her right hand clenching around Arabeth's hilt. Her grip pressed her casting hard against her palm.

The Emperor. *Corien.* He was speaking to her through this wraith, from half a world away.

Sarash's gaze dropped to Eliana's hands. A tiny smile played at her mouth. "A pity," came her double voice—woman and man. Near and far. "Your mother didn't need those."

Then, with no further warning, Sarash attacked, the blade of her sword cutting a mean grin through the humming galvanized light.

Eliana and Harkan lunged to meet her.

The wraith moved like a dancer, coattails flying. She blocked every jab of Eliana's dagger, every thrust of Harkan's sword. Eliana flung Arabeth at her heart. Sarash dodged it, and the blade went skidding across the floor.

Then Harkan threw one of his small knives, catching the exposed juncture of the wraith's neck and shoulder. She roared in fury; her form quaked, shifting, and then realigned itself. Harkan's dagger went clattering away into the shadows.

Sarash recovered quickly. Grinning, sword raised, she ran at Harkan. Their swords crashed silver, and then Harkan spun away from her, avoiding a deadly swing. Eliana ran after her, daggers flashing—Whistler and Tuora. Harkan stayed quick on his feet as Sarash volleyed between him and Eliana.

The wraith whirled, slammed Harkan's sword out of his hands, and sent it flying across the floor. Then she knocked Harkan off his feet with an elbow to the face. She did not stab him; she wanted to play. She laughed as he staggered off, blood gushing from his nose.

Eliana darted forward. Sarash knocked Whistler to the floor, but then Eliana ducked under her arm and thrust Tuora into Sarash's gut.

The wraith howled, then spun around, ripped the knife from her belly, and let her sword fly.

The blade caught Eliana on the shoulder—not a deep cut, but a cut nonetheless. She cried out, stumbling, and then Harkan shouted her name. He tossed Arabeth to her, but Sarash smashed it out of the air with her sword. Eliana grabbed Harkan's discarded sword from the ground and jumped to her feet right as Sarash attacked.

They moved together between the stacked shelves, swords spinning. Eliana's skin was drenched with sweat, her weakened muscles pulsing with fire.

Then, at last, Sarash growled and tossed away her sword. Eliana faltered, caught off guard, and swung hard for Sarash's torso.

But the wraith caught her blade with both gloved hands and held it fast. Eliana fought to jerk the sword from her grip, but Sarash would not budge. She backed Eliana against the wall, blood darkening her sleeves and her eyes flickering black-gray.

"I'll find you, Eliana," came her voice—half Sarash, half Emperor. Livid, and strangely tender.

A wave of revulsion swept through Eliana's body, scraping hard against her bones.

Without warning, her castings flared savagely to life.

A jagged force erupted from her palms, an explosion of light like the birth of a new star. It blinded her. She saw a solid field of white. The ground shook underfoot. She could not feel her fingers; instead she felt only a blazing, biting heat. Smoke stung her throat. At the rim of her vision, orange light snapped and flickered. The hairs on her arms stood rigid, and her mouth felt suddenly parched, as if all the moisture had been sucked from the air.

Whatever had happened, it sent Sarash flying. She collided with the nearest stack of shelves, toppling it. A cascade of tins rained down upon her, and she scrambled away, dazed, just before the shelves themselves teetered and crashed to the floor, pinning her beneath them.

She howled in rage, her scream more the Emperor's than her own. Eliana felt immobilized by the sound. It scrabbled for her with unseen fingers. It wrapped itself around her throat, voracious.

"El, move!" Harkan shouted, then grabbed her arm and pulled her back with him, toward the door. As if through a fog, Eliana watched him, his mouth and chin streaked with blood, uncap a bombardier and throw it at Sarash. They ran from the explosion, Harkan pulling her on, out into the corridor, up the steps, into the winding basement corridors.

But she could hardly breathe, her ears ringing, and no matter how insistently Harkan pulled her onward, she couldn't keep up with him. Smoke clogged her lungs, stung her eyes, and that orange light still flickered at her eyes, chasing her. It wasn't until they were upstairs in one of the abandoned lounges—the air thick and sweet, lachryma-stained rags littering the tile—and then tumbling out onto the street that Eliana understood what was happening.

She had unleashed a fire. Massive and hungry, it had already consumed the wraith's hive, and was climbing higher, faster, zipping through the tiled roads of Annerkilak, climbing up the sculpted stone pillars, reaching for the roof gardens. Faster than ordinary fire, tenacious and unnatural. It roared, it devoured. Her ears filled with screams, with the crashing groan of buildings collapsing beneath the weight of the fire's rage.

She searched dizzily for Harkan. There, very near—his skin gleaming with sweat and blackened with ash. He was pulling her on, from light into darkness, from the inferno of her fire to the cool black of the outer caves. People were pushing past them, fleeing the flames, climbing up staircases cut into the cave walls, cramming themselves into tunnels, jumping into boats that would take them down subterranean rivers out to the sea.

Eliana stumbled and caught herself on the rocks below. Her hands slammed against stone. Dazzling pain ricocheted from her palms up her arms, burning tears from her eyes.

"My hands," she whispered, too afraid to look at them.

Harkan pulled her up, coughing. The air was full of smoke. It suffused the entire vast chamber, a toxic black cloud blotting out all light. Eliana looked over her shoulder once and glimpsed the massive terror of the fire she had created. Flames crawled to the stone sky above. Spitting tongues of fire trailed after her, marking her path. Explosions rattled the caverns, echoing each of her frantic breaths—the fire, perhaps reaching storage rooms full of smuggled explosives.

They ran until they were climb-crawling alone through damp, sloping tunnels of stone. The pain in her hands was extraordinary. She wanted to sit and scream over them, but Harkan wouldn't let her stop. She concentrated on the weight of the horrid copper box in her pocket, the slap of Harkan's bag against her side.

She didn't understand what had happened to Zahra. She couldn't imagine what they would do if the antidotes they had stolen didn't save Navi. Her mind was a roar of impossible questions, each of them exhausted.

They stopped running. Harkan put a hand on her arm. He coughed, a terrible, harsh sound.

"Hold your breath," he instructed, and she did, and the distant explosions stopped rattling the walls.

Then he said, "We're going to swim now." His voice was taut, worried. "Follow me, all right? Stay close."

Eliana nodded and jumped after him into the water that she knew, thanks to a vague nudge of memory, would lead them back to Tameryn's cave. When her scorched hands met the water, her castings hissed. The still black water bubbled, frothing.

A voice followed her as she swam, unmuddied by the water's depths and the weight of the mountains above. She couldn't understand the words, but she understood their sentiment, and the accompanying feeling of rage that gnashed its teeth at her toes.

And worse, a sense of loss and frustration so immense, so profound and old, that the sensation punched her chest in two and sent her clawing up to the surface, gasping for air in the darkness.

# ~ 16 ~

# RIELLE

*"Some scholars refuse to discuss what lies within the pages of the book you are about to read. Certain holy figures would even declare it profane. But what we write is something the saints believed to be true: it is possible to reach beyond the elements to a deeper layer of the empirium. What lies there, we don't yet know. But perhaps, someday, when Aryava's Queens come at last, we will have the answer."*

—*Beyond the Elemental* by Kerensa Garvayne and Llora Maralia of the First Guild of Scholars

*R*esurrection.

The word moved constantly about Rielle's mind—sometimes skittering, erratic. Distracting. Sometimes it slithered, sly and slow, and she could almost forget it was there.

At night, when she managed to sleep, in the warmth of Audric's arms, the word whispered to her, sibilant and insistent. More than a sound—a sensation.

Sometimes it came in Corien's voice, so faint that in her dream-addled mind, she had to strain to identify it.

She knew what the word meant, of course, in the broadest sense: to bring back to life that which was once dead.

But what kept her awake at night, what sent her haunting the royal libraries so often that the librarians began setting aside a workspace for her, sunlit and stocked with cake, was the sense of what resurrection could mean beyond that.

Restoring wounded flesh to its original wholeness.

Healing a painful scar that marked a friend's arm.

Knitting together a new body out of an old one.

—◇—

And then a change occurred. A bend in a wooded dark path, a shift in the ground underfoot.

It began with prayers.

The Archon had suggested it, and Audric and Ludivine readily agreed with him. Rielle would pray, in public, in a different temple every night, alongside the people of the city, and prove her piety. Her devotion to the saints. Her earnest love of Celdaria. By doing so, she would perhaps quell some of the unrest that had remained, simmering, since the fire trial. Since Ludivine had come back from death, while the other victims had not.

But this plan quickly went awry, for whenever Rielle prayed, Corien took the opportunity to visit her.

—◇—

The first evening, kneeling at the feet of Saint Tameryn, with the Archon at her side and the temple roof open to the pale-violet sky above, Corien arrived softly.

*What a good Celdarian you are,* he murmured, his voice like the press of a petal against her nape. *What a dutiful child of Katell.*

Rielle gasped at his sudden nearness, too startled to disguise her shock.

The harsh sound was a crash in the quiet temple, with its gentle fountains and the shuffle of slippered feet across obsidian tiles. Citizens gathered on the prayer steps, their candles flickering before them, looked up—wide-eyed and curious, frowning and amused.

The Archon, beside her, eyes still closed, robes a sea of white around him, murmured, "Is there something wrong, Lady Rielle?"

"No, nothing," she replied. "I apologize for the disruption."

Corien's laughter haunted her prayers like shadows.

&#9670;

The next evening, the Archon walked with her, arm in arm, through the softly lit courtyards surrounding the Holdfast, lush with greenery and the dim glow of whistblooms.

She, Audric, and Ludivine had told him, of course, everything that had transpired in the Sunderlands, but that was too sensitive a topic to speak of in the public gardens. So they discussed nothing of consequence, meandering toward the temple at a pace that made Rielle want to scream.

In the plain, earthen rooms of the Holdfast, surrounded by barefoot worshippers with their toes in the dirt, she prayed, a secret black hope in her heart.

Corien answered with a wordless vision: A wintry landscape, sharp with mountains so monstrously tall that Rielle knew it could be nowhere in Celdaria. Herself, climbing a snowy passage toward a dark mountaintop château, barefoot and freezing, her toes black with frostbite.

Horrified, she tried to shake loose the vision, but it would not release her.

*Here*, Corien whispered. *Here, Rielle.*

Tears in her eyes, she searched through the whirling snow and found him in a soft green clearing, sitting by a fire. She cried out, stumbling toward him. He opened his arms to her and wrapped her in the fur lining of his cloak.

She pressed her face against his chest. His lips touched her hair. In his arms, she bloomed, warming. The pain in her toes faded, and so did her fear.

*Where are you?* she asked, afraid to know the answer.

*Come find me*, he replied, and then he was gone, along with the fire and the foreign winter.

Rielle knelt in the dirt, her breath coming high and fast, a sheen of sweat coating her skin.

The Archon regarded her with one raised eyebrow. "In all my years, Lady Rielle, I have never seen someone pray quite so violently."

She smiled at him, her jaw aching with tension. "Such is the strength of my devotion, Your Holiness."

◆

Corien did not speak to Rielle the third night, in the Firmament, nor on the fourth night, in the House of Light.

Each moment of silence sent her tired thoughts spiraling. What were his intentions? Where was he hiding? He was playing a game with her. He had a plan, and she could not see it.

In the House of Light—Audric's temple, the temple of sunspinners and the Lightbringer, the temple of the Sun Queen—Rielle knelt on a gold-fringed cushion before a marble statue of Saint Katell and bore down on her prayers with a vengeance.

Corien wouldn't speak to her? He would tease her with horrifying visions, with the tender touch of his voice, and then abandon her? Fine. She would pray, then. She would pray as no one had prayed before.

Except that praying had never come naturally to her. It required a quieting of the mind she found tedious and nearly impossible. Over the years she had forced herself to learn—at first out of fear of her father, then out of love for Tal, and then, at last, because she had to begrudgingly admit that praying *did* help focus her mind. Praying kept her power docile, her mind smooth as a river stone.

Her mind was anything but smooth that night. Corien had dropped an anchor into her, hooked himself to her thoughts, and the ripples of that grew, and grew, until her prayers roared and wailed.

Later, feeling wild, Rielle went to Audric. She led him upstairs, to the fourth floor, where a small sitting room overlooked the northern ballroom. She whispered her desires to him, elated when he gently pressed her back against the velvet curtains. She kissed him until her lips were sore. She tugged at his trousers.

"Someone will hear, my love," he murmured, his kisses trailing down her neck.

She threaded her fingers through his curls, held him to her. If he didn't hurry, she would fly apart. "Let them hear," she gasped, and hoped Corien could hear most clearly of all. "Let them all hear how I love you."

—◆—

The next evening—sore, delirious with exhaustion, smiling to herself in a way that was not entirely appropriate for a temple—Rielle allowed the Archon to help her into the warm water of the Baths, and together, they prayed to Saint Nerida.

Overhead, worshippers walked the three open mezzanines of the Baths, the slender stone columns lined with heavy sprays of purple blossoms. Fountains spilled softly into the praying pools; the quiet trill of birdsong floated down from the rafters.

Rielle was comforted, her mind quieter than it had been in days.

O *seas and rivers!* she prayed, drawing her hands through the smooth water. O *rain and snow! Quench us our thirst, cleanse us our evil. Grow us the fruit of our fields. Drown us the cries of our enemies!*

She had barely finished reciting the words when Corien arrived.

His words snapped like tinder. *How are you feeling today, my dear? Tired? Aching?*

Rielle opened her eyes. Night had fallen. The temple was empty. Snow fell through the open ceiling, quiet and even, dusting the surface of the water.

She shivered. Her thin prayer robes clung to her, crusted with ice.

"Are you going to talk to me, truly?" she called out. "Or just play games and send me nightmares?"

Behind her, a soft splash. She turned to see Corien approaching her through the water, in a dark robe of his own.

"This is no game to me," he said, his voice low and thin. He reached her more quickly than he should have been able to. Her head spun, and her foot caught on a slab of ice. She stumbled; he caught her wrist, held her against him.

"Release me at once," she commanded.

He obeyed, his breath puffing in the frigid air. He bowed. "Forgive me. *Sun Queen.*"

Suddenly she found herself blinking back tears. "I don't understand you. You're frightening me, and I hate you."

"You don't," he said at once. "Though you wish that you did."

"Why are you tormenting me? Because I burned you that day?"

He laughed. "You could burn me a thousand times, and I would still want you for my own."

She shivered from the cold, from the frightening beauty of his voice. "Why do you want me? Because I can tear down the Gate for you? Because you can use my power to destroy my race?"

Corien reached for her face, then paused. "May I touch you, Rielle?"

She let out an impatient cry and captured his face in her hands. "There. I've touched you myself. Now, answer me!"

His pale gaze seemed suddenly tired to her eyes, and ancient. He turned into her touch, pressed a kiss to her palm.

"Come find me, darling child," he whispered against her wrist, "and I'll tell you everything you wish to know, and more."

Then he was gone. The water was warm again, the evening light a cheerful violet, the temple halls humming with prayers.

"My lady," said a nearby worshipper, wide-eyed, "are you all right? You're crying."

"Sometimes my power moves me to tears," Rielle replied, her voice thick, her hands trembling under the water. "For it is a gift from God, from the empirium, and it brings me indescribable joy."

—◇—

Her feet carried her automatically to Audric's room that night, but when she found him, she could not bear to wake him.

He slept peacefully, sprawled across the bed, his face soft and his curls in disarray. A book lay open on his stomach—*The Great and Terrible*

*Legacy of Our Blessed Saints.* Three others sat on the bedside table. Papers and pens, small scraps of paper marking pages of import. He had been reading for her, taking notes for her.

She went to him, eyes burning, throat aching, and kissed his brow. He stirred softly, but slept on.

She fled, her body taut and aching. She wished she did not love him so completely. If she didn't, she would not have hesitated to wake him.

—◆◆—

Instead she went to Ludivine, telling her baffled guards to wait outside. They had grown used to her nighttime wanderings, had become marvelously discreet, but she knew her mood was frantic, crazed. Evyline must have sensed it.

"My lady," she began quietly as Rielle knocked on Ludivine's door. "If there's something I can do to help you, please let me know of it."

*Lu, I'm coming in.*

"Please, not now, dear Evyline," Rielle said tightly and then hurried inside.

Ludivine was sitting up in bed, her hair a golden cloud that fell to her waist. Her nightgown's loose sleeves exposed the terrible blue map of her blightblade scar—blue, and growing. Slow but inexorable, it reached for her neck, climbed down the bend of her side.

"What's wrong?" She started to rise, her worry buffeting Rielle's mind like ocean waves.

"Stay there," Rielle snapped. "Please. And don't you know? Haven't you looked?"

"I've been granting you space during your evening prayers, as you requested."

"He keeps talking to me," Rielle said, pacing. "He's trying to tell me something, I can feel it, but I don't know what it is. He kissed my hand tonight, and I wanted him to kiss me more than that. He's been visiting me during my prayers. Maybe he knows you're leaving me alone during that time. Maybe he doesn't like that I pray and wants to distract me."

She stopped, fists clenching and unclenching. "I went to Audric, but he was asleep. I couldn't bring myself to wake him. What would I tell him? That Corien was touching me? That my body is afire for him? 'Make love to me, Audric, and try not to think about the fact that the hand touching you bears the stamp of Corien's mouth.'"

Ludivine said softly, "Rielle, please come here. You're shaking."

Rielle obeyed at once. She crawled onto Ludivine's bed and then onto her lap, her vision a frantic field of tears. She cupped Ludivine's face in her hands, drinking in the sight of her grave, pale face.

"When I was younger, I loved you for a time," she whispered, her thumbs stroking Ludivine's cheeks. "I loved you as more than a friend, more than a sister. The feeling came and went, as these things do, I suppose. And when it came, I thought of you often. I still think of you, sometimes." She leaned against Ludivine, dragged her hands down her body. "Please, Lu, I feel like I'm going mad. My head is spinning. I can hardly breathe."

"Rielle, listen to me," Ludivine said, her compassion blossoming gently in Rielle's mind.

But Rielle didn't want to listen. She wanted someone to drive this wildness out of her; she wanted to erase Corien's touch from her skin. She slammed the feeling of her own desperation back at Ludivine, uncaring and grasping, and then bent low to kiss her.

For a moment, Ludivine allowed it. Her body softened, melting into the frantic hook of Rielle's arms. Through the feeling of Ludivine's worry came a soft pulse of curiosity, of delight.

Then, just as quickly, she pulled away, her cheeks flushed. "Rielle, listen to me."

Rielle let out a sharp sob, reaching for her. "Please, don't stop. I'll go mad if you do."

"*Rielle.*" Ludivine's voice was stern. She caught Rielle's wrists and held them to her heart. "I love you, my darling, but this will not help you. It might, for a time, and then you would feel just as frightened, just as frayed. And," she added gently, "you would have to tell Audric, and that conversation would be uncomfortable, I think."

"Audric wouldn't mind," Rielle argued. "In fact, he and I have spoken of asking you—"

"I know," Ludivine said with a small smile. "And we can discuss that, all of us, and it would delight me to love you both in that way. But this is not the moment for that, and you know it."

For a moment, Rielle remained perched stubbornly in Ludivine's lap. Then exhaustion came for her. She moved away, hugging one of the pillows to her chest, and turned her back on Ludivine. Curled into a tight, tense bow, Ludivine's fingers gently unwinding the knots in her hair, Rielle glared at the fire across the room until, at last, her body began to relax.

"I think," she mumbled, as sleep crept closer, "that we should begin in Kirvaya. We'll retrieve Marzana's casting."

"Oh?" Ludivine said, still stroking Rielle's hair. "Why Kirvaya first?"

Too tired for words, Rielle pushed images of Corien's recent visions toward Ludivine's mind—the high, foreign mountains. The snowy passage, the ice crusting the water of the Baths. The warm clearing, green and impossible in the heart of a blizzard, like the very same clearing in which, long ago, Saint Marzana had found her godsbeast—a great bird with feathers as brilliant as fire.

# ELIANA

*"My darling Nerida, it has been far too long since I have seen your face. Please, come to Astavar before the moon turns. I have a gift for you, and if you like it well enough, perhaps it will convince you to stay forever at my side. My nightmares of the Deep continue. Only when I'm with you do they spare me. Savrasara, Nerida. Come home to me."*

—A letter from Saint Tameryn the Cunning to Saint Nerida
the Radiant, archived in the First Great Library of Quelbani

Eliana burst up through the water in Tameryn's cavern. Her lungs were on fire, but that was nothing compared to the heat of her palms.

She swam and crawled for shore, coughing, and collapsed onto the flat expanse of black pebbles. Her heart pounded between her shaking fingers.

Harkan tried to help her up, out of the water, but recoiled with a hiss. "Your hands are burning. El, God, your castings…"

Woozy, Eliana looked down. Her castings had burned their shapes into the flesh of her steaming hands.

"Do you have the antidote?" she asked, her words fat and faint.

He patted the bag at his hip, his smile tired. "We did it. You did it, El. And Zahra?"

She pulled the tiny copper-rimmed box from her coat pocket, handling it gingerly, as if it would break with too much pressure. For all she knew, it might—and then what? Would Zahra be free? Or would breaking the strange box somehow hurt her?

Eliana sat back heavily on the shore, digging at the box's smooth copper edges with shaking fingers. But there was no catch she could see, no lid to pry open. The box was insubstantial in her fingers, a container constructed of metal light as leaves. She pressed the heel of her boot into it, hesitated, then slammed it against the rocks underfoot.

"Goddammit," she gasped, her efforts sending blazing jolts of pain from her wounded hands up her arms and into the joints of her shoulders. "What is this thing?"

"El." Harkan knelt before her, stilling her hands. "Remember, we did this for Navi. She'll live now."

"And Zahra?" Eliana blinked back tears. "What will happen to her?"

"You'll free her. We'll engineer a way to open it." He hesitated. "Maybe Simon will know what it is. He'll have insight."

"What if we can't open it?" She couldn't look at him, could only glare wearily at the ground. "What if, when I try with my castings, I hurt someone? Or Zahra? You saw what happened back there. You saw what I did. How many people did I just burn, back in the Nest? How many weren't able to escape, simply because I can't control this power I didn't ask for?"

He didn't reply; his silence held volumes.

Then a new voice joined them from the shadows.

"And if the wraiths of Annerkilak follow you here and kill everyone in this castle as vengeance, it will be your fault."

Eliana looked over Harkan's shoulder to see Simon approaching, a few Astavari soldiers behind him.

She bit her tongue and met his furious blue gaze in silence.

"Hello, Simon," Harkan said, fumbling for his words. "We were just—"

"I know exactly what you were doing. Are you injured?"

"Slightly. I'm also hungry." She held up her hands for him to see, biting her lip hard to keep from crying out. "Also, these little shits have burned me."

"She needs to see healers," Harkan said. "Or do you intend to hold us down here as punishment?"

Simon ignored him. "Where's the wraith?"

"Zahra." Setting her jaw so hard it hurt her teeth, Eliana held up the box for him to see. "Call her by her name."

His gaze fell to the box in her hands. He frowned. "Is this some sort of joke? What is that?"

And with that, Eliana's heart sank, too swift and hard for her to pretend otherwise. "I was hoping you'd know."

A beat. Then his gaze narrowed. "Are you telling me she's *inside* that?" When no answer came, Simon exhaled sharply. "So now, whatever comes next, we have no wraith to help us. Spectacular news. I hope you're quite proud of yourselves."

"That we managed to steal the antidote that will help Navi heal?" Harkan said. "Yes, actually, I am quite proud of us for that."

Simon gave him a withering look.

Eliana wished Harkan had said nothing, hating how righteous he sounded, how unabashed. Only now, shivering and burned on the shores of Tameryn's lake, did she begin to see the true rashness of what they had done. Her fire could just as easily have consumed the two of them, as well—leaving Remy both orphaned and sisterless. All of that, and what if the antidotes they'd stolen didn't work? What if they could never break Zahra free of her tiny gleaming prison?

Eliana looked away, unable to bear the sight of Simon's glare.

"We'll fill this passage, collapse it," he said, addressing the guards who had accompanied him. "And we'll need twenty guards stationed here, day and night. If anything comes out of the water, kill it. If the thing attacking you looks human and pleads with you for mercy, kill it anyway. Look for the eyes. They'll be black. They can't hide their eyes."

Another guard, looking rather aghast, cleared his throat. "Black eyes, sir...like the Empire generals?"

"Black like angels." Simon glanced at Eliana's burned hands, his mouth twisting. "Come with me before you pass out."

His voice was thin and precise, a needle poised to pierce.

Eliana followed him, wishing she had the energy to argue.

—◆—

Simon sat in a low chair by the hearth while the healers changed Eliana's bandages.

Long hours had passed since they returned from the Nest, during which the healers had declared Eliana's burns quite minor and begun their treatment. They reapplied an acrid ointment to the red lines left behind by the castings' blazing chains, then wrapped clean cloth bandages over the wounds and carefully refastened the castings around her wrists.

One of the healers, a small, stout woman with pale skin, glanced up as she clasped the last of the casting hooks. As Eliana's eyes met hers, a silent current of understanding passed between them.

Eliana carefully pressed the woman's hand between hers. "Thank you, Ilsi. He won't hurt me."

The woman relaxed slightly, but she nevertheless glared at Simon on her way out.

Once alone with Simon, Eliana arranged herself more comfortably on the sofa, allowing the silence to stretch on. She smoothed the folds of the clean tunic the healers had brought; she examined her nails.

At last, Simon spoke. "Did she really think I was going to hurt you?"

"So it would seem," Eliana said coolly.

"She said nothing of the sort. Can you read minds now as well?"

She fixed him with a hard stare. "A woman doesn't need to read minds in order to speak to another woman. We have a language, especially when danger is near."

"I'm no danger to you, Eliana."

"Tell that to Ilsi."

"I would, were she still here."

"You frightened her away with that unattractive glower of yours."

"I would have no need to glower," he said tightly, "had you not run away."

Eliana sat straight and still. "I had no choice. Navi was ill. No one had been able to help her. If I'd asked you for *permission*, you wouldn't have allowed me to go. So, here we are. And soon she will be healed."

Simon scrubbed both hands over his face. "Yes, and Zahra is now incapacitated and useless to us. Having a loyal wraith around to help when we need it would have been my preference, if that matters at all to you."

"It doesn't. And I'll free her from that box soon enough, so worry not. Soon she'll be useful to you again."

He watched her, implacable. "I don't suppose you managed to find out what it is, during this mission of yours? I've never seen metal like that before."

Eliana glanced at the little box, sitting innocently on her bedside table. In the midmorning light, its copper metal shone iridescent—violet and indigo ripples, so deep they looked like furrows, and yet the box's surface felt smooth to the touch.

"No, but I don't care what it is. Once I've recovered, I'll find a way to break it open. She'll be freed, and then you can stop scowling." Eliana paused. "Oh. Wait. That's impossible for you, isn't it?"

"Once you've recovered. Yes, I suppose it's possible that your power could shatter whatever this is. If, that is, you stop tormenting yourself to force some half-formed version of said power. And yes," he added before she could interrupt, "I understood exactly what you were attempting to do with all that nonsense. Not eating, not sleeping. Battering yourself. But everyone was advising me to let you be, including you, so I did, and now that's gotten us here."

She stiffened, drawing back from him. "You are the most discouraging person I've ever met. You declare loyalty to me, you pledge support of me, and yet you criticize everything I do."

"I've tried to advise you kindly, and you ignore my counsel."

She laughed. "Your version of kindness is an interesting one. If you had your way, you'd tell me when and where I can go and not go. You'd direct every moment of my every day."

"That sums it up nicely, yes."

"And this is kindness, to you?"

"Would you rather I sit back and stare at the wall while you dash about risking your life whenever you feel like it?"

"Your gall is astonishing. You are not my keeper, Simon. In fact, it is I who should be determining where *you* go, and what *you* know, as—according to you—I am your queen, and you are my subject. In that sense, I've done nothing wrong. If you were not keen on obeying me, on operating on a plane inferior to my own, then perhaps you should have kept the knowledge of my heritage a secret from me."

Simon's mouth quirked. "Being a queen doesn't mean you can do what you want without consequence."

"It certainly means I can risk my life to save a friend if I choose to."

"You're wrong."

Eliana blew out an exasperated breath. "Who are you to decide such things?"

Simon leaned forward, elbows on his knees. A resting pose, belied by the intensity of his gaze. "Eliana, do you understand the scope of what's happening? This war between humans and angels has been raging for millennia. If we don't stop it, it could keep spreading. Like an inferno, it could consume every world that exists."

Eliana was determined to keep all emotion from her voice. Nevertheless, Simon's casual mention of other worlds shook her. "Zahra mentioned this concept to me. Just how many worlds are there?"

"I haven't the slightest idea. Some theorize the number could be infinite."

"And by sending the angels to the Deep," she said, "we brought them closer to those other worlds."

"Again, in theory. Your point?"

"We created a lie to lure the angels into the Deep, and it was there that they confirmed the idea of other worlds. Zahra said the Emperor won't stop at conquering this world and avenging his people. She said he seeks answers, whatever that means. She didn't tell me before we left. So, if there are other worlds out there now endangered by the Emperor's insatiable desire for conquest, it's our fault. It's the fault of the saints, of humanity."

"Irrelevant," Simon snapped. "What matters is what's happening now, and how we can stop it from getting worse. The only human ever born with enough power to stem the tide of angelic violence was your mother."

Eliana began to protest. "My *mother*—"

"Yes, I know, your adoptive mother was Rozen Ferracora," Simon said, his voice rising to match hers, "but the mother who birthed you, whose blood you share, was Rielle Courverie, the Blood Queen, the Kingsbane, and the sooner you accept that and embrace the power your ancestry has granted you, the sooner we can end this war. We can end the suffering that millions of innocents have endured over too many years to count and put the world right again. I'm not sure how many different ways I can express this to you. By endangering yourself, you're risking not only your life, but the future of the world."

He rose from his seat and stalked away from her, angrily dragging a hand through his hair. The long lines of his body brimmed with an intoxicating gravity. Eliana couldn't look away from him.

Quietly, at the windows, facing the bright midday world beyond the glass, Simon spoke. "If you had died, Eliana, where would we all be? Navi would still be ill, and the rest of us would be more irreversibly fucked than we already are."

His voice was harsh, strained under the weight of some great emotion that Eliana could not define. The sound of it quieted her. She felt cooler, smoothed out. She rose to join him, then stood a few inches to his right. She gazed out the window at the velvet blue canvas of mountains.

"I suppose some children dreamed of being queens," she said quietly, "or doers of mighty heroics. I never did." She gingerly clenched her fists, wincing. But there was a strange kind of solace in the pinch of her castings. "I didn't ask for this. I've said it before, I know, but it remains true, and something I can't put out of mind."

Simon replied at once. "And I didn't ask to be flung away from my home and into the far-off future, all to save a girl who would grow up to wear out my every last nerve."

Eliana's smile came sharply. "Are you saying you were worried about me while I was gone? The hard, fearsome Wolf, fretting in his room like an anxious mother?"

A new silence fell, thick and significant. Eliana kept her gaze fixed on the mountains for as long as she could bear, heat climbing up her neck. Then she glanced at Simon.

He stood utterly still, except for his hands. Clasped at his back, they flexed and clenched once.

"I was worried," he said at last. His voice caught on its own edges. "I haven't felt like that since Fidelia took you from Sanctuary. Only this time, it was worse. At least then I had some idea of where they'd taken you and was confident I could get you out. But this time, I had no idea where you'd gone, and by the time I realized it, with the help of the kings, I had barely enough time to summon a contingent of guards and gather supplies before you returned."

Eliana felt a stab of guilt, of disgusting, delighted pleasure. "You were going to come after me?"

"Of course. Luckily, there was no need." He drew in a slow breath. "Luckily, you came back to us alive and whole. Remy was inconsolable, once he found out you'd left. He blamed himself for it."

*Remy*. His name was an arrow to her heart.

"Did he say as much to you?" she asked. "That he blamed himself?"

"He didn't have to."

Eliana gazed at the mountains, heat gathering behind her eyes. "I was foolish."

"Yes."

"But you see, if it weren't for me, Navi wouldn't have been out in Sanctuary that night. She wouldn't have been abducted along with me. They wouldn't have..." She swallowed, struggling to find her voice. "They wouldn't have hurt her. I had to try to save her." She looked up at him, imploring. "I wouldn't have been able to live with myself otherwise."

"I understand, and I sympathize." He turned to her, and though he hadn't touched her, once his urgent gaze met hers, Eliana felt his nearness as keenly as if he had cupped her face in his hands. "But you can't do it again. Please, don't do it again. Don't leave, don't run. The world needs you." Hesitant, he reached for her arm, and then stopped and set his jaw. "*I* need you, Eliana. Without you, I'm the only true child of Celdaria still living. My life since leaving home that night has been a lonely one. Now that I've known a life with you by my side, I'm not sure I could bear that kind of loneliness again."

His words held her rapt, motionless with surprise. Her mind hardly knew what to make of him like this. She hadn't thought him capable of such softness.

She tried to reorder her thoughts, gestured helplessly with her bandaged hands. "I don't know how to be like her. I've told you as much. That hasn't changed."

"You made it safely in and out of the Nest," Simon pointed out. "You defended yourself and Harkan with your power."

"But what I had to do to get to that point! I barely ate, I barely slept. I can't fight a war like that, and you can't base a military strategy on a girl who has to starve herself to be of any use, and whose power then erupts uncontrollably."

"We'll work on it, together. I promised you that before, and I'll keep promising you until you trust me."

She shook her head. "You believe in someone who doesn't exist, Simon. Whatever you've been waiting for all these years, whatever savior you've created in your mind, I'm not her."

"No," he agreed. "In fact, you're better than what I had imagined."

She laughed, turning away from him. She was so tired that even thinking was painful, and he was bewildering her. "You flatter me."

He moved closer. "Do I strike you as the sort of man who flatters people?"

"If it gets you what you want, yes."

"And what is it," Simon murmured, "that you think I want?"

The sound of his voice pulled her back to him. When she met his eyes, a sharpness came over her, a sweeping stillness. Suddenly she was scorchingly aware of his closeness, the size of his body compared to hers, the bright focus of his gaze.

"I don't *think* I know what you want," she replied softly. "I know it."

And then, her heartbeat coursing fast up her throat, she touched his cheek with the backs of her bandaged fingers. His scars entranced her, silvered etchings across his unshaven cheeks. One crowned his left eye; another bisected his right temple. Once she started touching him, she could not stop. She traced every scar she could find, following the lines of his face that had long been imprinted in her mind.

He closed his eyes, brow furrowed. His left hand gently cupped hers, and when her thumb touched his lips, he opened his mouth slightly, pressed his tongue against it.

"Eliana," he mumbled against her fingers.

The hoarse quality of his voice left her dizzy, impatient. "Yes?"

He opened his eyes, and the frustrating fondness she felt for his stern visage, his battered cheeks, snatched all the air from her lungs. She swayed a little, leaning into him.

At once, his hands dropped to cup her waist. His fingers curled gently in her tunic and his eyes held a question.

She answered by moving closer to him. His body towered over hers, all sinew and heat and murderous grace. He bowed his head to nuzzle his cheek against her jaw, and then moved lower to her neck. His lips brushed her collarbone; his tongue marked the hollow of her throat.

She closed her eyes, tilting her head back. Ignoring the tender state of her hands, she threaded her fingers through his hair. It was finer than she'd expected. She hummed with pleasure.

He mumbled a question against her neck.

Dazed, she found it difficult to answer.

Simon touched his forehead to hers. His hands remained steady at her hips.

"Do you want me to stop?" he asked roughly.

Eliana shook her head. "No. I want you to keep going, but faster." She felt drunk on his nearness, on the impossible reality of this moment. Simon was kissing her—*Simon*—his fingers drawing tender circles on the small of her back. Something raw and vulnerable threatened to split open inside her. The feeling frightened her, but she could not turn away from it. "I want you to kiss me until I forget how angry I am with you."

He smiled, but his gaze was grave and earnest in a way that embarrassed her. He lowered his mouth once more to her neck. "Yes, my queen," he murmured against her skin. "Anything to please you."

A knock on the door, sharp and efficient, made Eliana jump.

Simon cursed robustly under his breath. "I will kill whoever is standing on the other side of that door."

She laughed a little, shaky, blood roaring in her ears. She placed her hands against his chest, steadying herself.

"Yes, what is it?" she called out, her voice only somewhat shrill.

"Begging your pardon, my lady," came the voice of her guard, Meli, "but I've come with a message from Princess Navana's healers. They request your presence in her rooms at once."

Eliana glanced at Simon, uncertain how to leave him. Her body ached for more of him—and yet, now that they were separated, she started to feel foolish for allowing him to kiss her. The press of his mouth on her skin had pushed her into a land that was strange to her, dangerous and wild.

A quick smile passed over his face. "Go."

She hesitated for only a moment longer, then hurried out of the room.

◆

As she sped through the halls of Dyrefal, Eliana's mind filled with worries. It hadn't been long enough for the antidote to take effect. The message was only a summons and had carried no news. They would have told her if Navi were well and awake. They were waiting to break her heart until she was there in person, standing beside Navi's empty bed.

By the time she reached Navi's rooms, Eliana's body was a flurry of panic. She pushed open the door and flew inside.

"Navi?" She hurried through the anteroom—plush blue carpets, cheerful paintings of stars and gilded night-clouds. "Are you all right? Is she all right?"

She emerged into the bedroom and saw Navi sitting up in bed, propped against a pale mountain of pillows and being spoon-fed broth by a beaming nurse.

One of the healers hurried over and dropped to his knees before Eliana. He kissed her hands and then, pink from his collar to his hairline, stumbled back to his feet. Another healer stood by the window, hands clasped at her neck, grinning tearfully.

"Begging your pardon, Lady Eliana," said the first healer, clumsy and bowing. "But the medicine you brought us... I don't know where you found it, or how, and I don't care. It was bizarre, my lady. A clear tube, a silver needle—the strangest mechanism! Angelic, I assume? But, no matter. My lady, it has worked. It has *worked*."

He gestured at the bed, but Eliana was already there, barely restraining herself from flying into Navi's arms.

"Navi, are you..." Her voice fissured. "Is it really..." She shrugged, laughing. Joy held her immobile. "Navi, can I—"

"I am myself again. Weak, hungry, and myself." Navi smiled tiredly up at her. Dark tendrils still faintly framed her face, foreign and cruel under her fuzzy cap of black hair, but her eyes were clear and sharp and her own. Some of the rich golden-brown color had returned to her previously wan skin. She gently dismissed the nurse fussing at her side.

"If you don't come here at once," Navi said, holding out her arms, "I will banish you to the Kaavalan Passage, and you'll have to hunt seals and penguins and sew a cloak out of bear pelts, and your teeth will rot and fall out, one by one."

Eliana laughed. Carefully, she curled up beside Navi, wrapped her arms around her torso. Her throat tightened when she felt how thin her friend had become. She said Navi's name again and again, and then, like a tower of children's blocks stacked too high, the tension held in her chest gave way. She began to cry, her limbs heavy with fatigue, though she didn't recognize her own tears until she felt Navi's gentle fingers stroking her braid.

"You're so dramatic," Navi said kindly. "I'm the one who should be crying. Oh, my dear Eliana. My dear, my dear."

Navi scooted farther down into the pillows, held up the edge of her soft gray quilt as the healers and nurses left the room. Eliana crawled beneath the blankets and cradled Navi against her, cupping her shorn head as she would a child's. She kissed her forehead, her cheeks and temples.

"I missed you," she whispered, and then they said nothing else, legs and arms locked together, warm and cocooned. Sleep came for them gently.

—◆—

They fell in and out of sleep for days, waking only to eat and talk, to stretch their limbs on the terrace outside Navi's rooms, and then returning to bed once Navi started to tire, which happened quickly.

Eliana was content to hide there for as long as Navi required. No one dared bother her, holed up in Navi's rooms as she was. Not even Simon.

Then, on the evening of the fourth day, Remy finally arrived.

A soft knock announced his presence, and even before the guards outside spoke, Eliana knew him by the sound of his knuckles against the door. Stiffly, she climbed out of Navi's bed to stand at the nearest window, her body clenched tight from toes to shoulders.

Navi watched her, eyes soft. "He will forgive you, Eliana."

She could not find it in her to reply. When Remy entered and rushed merrily across the room toward Navi's bed, his arms full of books, Eliana's heart recoiled in its cage. She was suddenly all too aware of her fleshiness, her obviousness. How impossible it was to hide herself, no matter how rigidly she stood.

Even so, Remy didn't notice her until he had lowered the stack of books onto the floor and embraced Navi, his face bright and open.

Then his eyes met Eliana's, and everything about him—the spark in his eyes, the verve of his skinny limbs—closed and diminished.

They stared at each other across Navi's bed. Eliana regretted skulking near the curtains like a caught thief. She stepped back into the light, unsure of her own tongue.

"Hello," she said. "It's good to see you."

She cringed even as the words left her lips. *It's good to see you?* As if he were a mere acquaintance. But the distance between them, the days of silence, had left her unsure of how to talk to him.

"I didn't know you'd be here," he said, his voice hollow. "Simon didn't tell me you'd be here."

And yet Simon must have known she was here. She wasn't sure whether to feel grateful or annoyed that he had staged this little reunion.

"Well," she said stupidly, "here I am." She waited a beat, then dared to add, "I've missed you, Remy." Another beat. A drawn breath, clenched fists. Bracing herself. "I'm so sorry."

He frowned, considering her. There was a seriousness to his face, a gravity that had not existed before he had learned the truth of Rozen's death. It was as if he had aged months, even years, since learning the truth—faint shadows under his eyes, a hard thin set to his mouth.

"You didn't tell us where you'd gone," he said, his words clipped. "You're always doing that. You're always leaving and not telling us where you've gone."

"There's a market underground," she began, unsure what else to say. "They call it the Nest, and it's in the heart of Vintervok, deep beneath the mountains. They have—"

"I know what you did, and where you went. Harkan told me. He told me about Zahra too."

Eliana's hand flew automatically to the pocket of her tunic, where the box containing Zahra rested.

Remy crossed his arms over his chest, folding into himself. "Can I see it?"

She withdrew the box from her pocket, held it out flat on her palm.

He crept closer, examining it—and maybe, Eliana thought, examining her casting as well. She hardly dared breathe; he was closer than he'd been in days. Her eyes filled. She wanted to reach for him, draw him into her arms, bury her face in the soft, hot tangle of dark hair on the crown of his head.

"Is it hurting her to be in there?" he asked quietly. A moment of silence passed before he looked up at her, his gaze bright.

Eliana shook her head. "I don't know. I hope not."

Remy's mouth wavered. He hesitated, swaying a little, as if ready to meet her halfway and end this horrible stilted vastness between them. Eliana's breath caught in her throat.

Then he moved away, turning his back on her.

"I have to go," he said, shoulders drawn up tight. He gestured at the books. "Navi, those are for you."

Eliana started forward. "Remy, wait, please—"

But he hurried out of Navi's apartment, not looking back. The bedroom was quiet until Navi said quietly, "Come here, Eliana. You look like you're going to fall over."

But before Eliana could catch her breath, or even think of moving—for if she moved, she would shatter, her tears would erupt and leave her empty of all light—a deep-throated roar exploded across the mountains outside Navi's windows.

Three short, sharp blasts, followed by one longer blast. The urgent rhythm repeated, loud enough that Eliana felt it in her chest.

A horn of some kind?

Navi froze, her expression stricken.

"What is that?" When Navi didn't respond, Eliana rushed out onto the terrace, searching the skies. "It's coming from the northwest, I think."

And then, her castings flared to life against her bandages, hot and urgent. She gasped, still unused to the feeling and her palms still tender beneath their bandages.

"Navi?" She backed away from the terrace railing, the stone beneath her vibrating with each thunderous blast. "What does it mean? What's that sound?"

Navi reached for Eliana's hand, her eyes lighting up with the same grim fire they'd shown the first night in Lord Arkelion's maidensfold, when she'd strangled Eliana's adatrox attacker with her necklace.

"It's the Horn of Veersa," Navi said, her voice thin and hard. "It means enemies have been sighted on the Kaavalan Passage. It means invasion."

# ⟶ 18 ⟵
# RIELLE

*"Well, it's done. I'm a king, and I've never felt more ill-fitting in my own skin. Crowns are for warriors, like Ingrid, or charming diplomats, like Runa, or for great men who, most irritatingly, seem to do everything well. Like you, my maddening friend. Crowns are not for me. I'm a scholar, not a ruler. And yet here I stand, pretending smiles for my advisers, while Ingrid runs off to the Grenmark to investigate the most recent attacks there. At one of our outposts, Castle Vahjata—thirty-one soldiers dead. Two left alive. Oddly, that seems to be the pattern. Whenever an outpost is attacked, two are left alive to share the same story of shadows that attack unseen in the night. Soldiers left twisted and bone-white in the snow. Villagers left defenseless and terrified. And this is the land of which I am now king. Audric…I am frightened. What is it that's coming for us all?"*

—A letter written by King Ilmaire Lysleva to Prince Audric
Courverie, dated December 5, Year 998 of the Second Age

Every morning, while on the road to Kirvaya, Rielle scanned the skies for Atheria's silhouette and saw nothing but clouds.

When they bedded down in the evenings, sore and sweaty after a hard day's riding, their wingless horses wearily snuffling through the grasses nearby, Rielle held herself together until safely ensconced in the tent she shared with Audric, their escort of three dozen guards standing watch outside the canvas.

There, miserably, she wept, feeling like a child whose puppy had gone missing, and when she first confessed as much to Audric, he simply kissed her brow, her cheeks, her salty mouth. Smelling of horse and sweat and the bright summer tang of warm stone, he held her until she quieted. He murmured reassurances into her hair and patiently combed out every snarl with his fingers.

One night, after he had soothed her tears, she lay beside him in their nest of furs and watched him quietly. The night air had grown cold so far north, but Audric's bare chest was warm, and she gratefully clung to the solid heat of him.

"Why do you love me?" she murmured after a time.

He smiled, his eyes closed. "Because your kisses bring me to my knees. Because you excel at rubbing the knots out of my shoulders."

"I'm quite serious," she replied, only realizing at that moment how desperately she needed to know the answer.

Audric turned to face her. He touched her cheek, tucking a strand of hair behind her ear.

"Because we are well-matched," he said. "Like the sun and the moon. Like day and night. I am the shore and you are the sea, my darling. The wild, wild sea—ever-changing and mighty. I need your passion, and you need something steady to come home to. An anchor, warm and sunlit."

He paused, an embarrassed smile tugging at his lips, his gaze half-lidded and bleary. "When I'm tired, I become rather poetic, it seems."

"And I love you for it." Rielle kissed the skin beneath his eyes, shadowed from lack of sleep and reddened from the bitter wind of the western Kirvayan plains. She held his weary head to her breast until sleep turned him heavy in her arms.

Then she sent a thought to Ludivine's tent, which stood a few paces from her own. *Since leaving home, I haven't slept through a single night without seeing him.*

*I know*, came Ludivine's reply, thin with fatigue. The scar's growth had slowed, but its presence still seemed to sap much of Ludivine's strength.

*Does Audric know?*

*No*, Ludivine said after a pause. *But he wonders. And he worries.*

Rielle tightened her arms around Audric and pressed her lips to his curls. He was as warm as her dreams of Corien were cold. Ice-bitten, black-edged, and frosted with snow, every night they became clearer.

A mountain path. A dark château on white cliffs. A tall, hooded figure in furs, arms open wide as if to welcome her home.

Already the dream was coming, edging into her mind along with the first reaches of sleep.

Rielle squeezed her eyes shut and waited for its arrival—so she could gather clues, she told herself. Each dream brought with it a clearer image of whatever wintry mountain Corien was leading her to. It was only logical to welcome the knowledge brought by her dreams. It was, in fact, what Audric wanted. As Sun Queen, it was her duty to investigate.

*Be careful, Rielle*, came Ludivine's faint whisper.

But Rielle was already stepping into the dream snow, her ears ringing with the howl of an eager wind that carried the ghost of her name inside it.

◆◇◆

After three weeks of hard traveling, they arrived in the Kirvayan capital of Genzhar to find it turned gold and glittering in their honor.

It was a city dressed for children of the sun. Amber and ivory silks decorated every shop front. Banners bearing the shimmering sigil of the House of Light hung from burnished towers. White petals and gold-hemmed scarves littered the streets.

The broad central avenue teemed with cheering crowds far larger than any Rielle had ever seen in Âme de la Terre, even at the height of her trials. Amid the raucous din, she picked out her own name, Audric's name, Saint Katell's name. She heard cries of *Sun Queen!* in Celdarian, in Kirvayan, in the common tongue—all amid a clamor of temple bells, the reedy trill of Kirvayan fiddles, the small tin drums of children.

At the avenue's apex, near the base of a long, low building of scarlet stone etched with elaborate carvings of flames, a narrow iron gate stood open to a vast stone yard, beyond which stood Zheminask, the palace of the Kirvayan queen. Several times larger than Baingarde, it was crowned with dozens of elegant white towers, their domes gleaming like fresh coins.

Before the gate stood an entourage, splendid and imposing in fine, embroidered robes that made Rielle feel shabby by comparison, her own clothes rumpled and travel-worn. She lifted her chin as they approached. Once she'd had the chance to bathe and change into one of her gowns, it was these people who would feel shabby in her presence.

Three figures stepped forward to greet them. The first was a tall, dark-skinned man in robes of white and gold, whom Rielle assumed to be the Grand Magister of the House of Light. The second was a guard in attractive but simple garb, with light-brown skin and soft brown eyes. The guard scanned the Celdarian escort for a moment before stepping aside to reveal their third greeter—a girl no older than perhaps thirteen. Her skin was a pale, warm brown, and her hair, elaborately pinned within a ruby-scattered golden net, was white as fresh snow.

Rielle knew her at once. The newly chosen queen, Obritsa Nevemskaya. According to Audric, the girl was something of an aberration. Kirvaya had not had a human queen in centuries. Typically, a young firebrand girl was chosen from the temples erected throughout the country in honor of Saint Marzana—holy schools that groomed girls who had the potential to some-day be appointed queen. Audric assumed the selection of Obritsa had been a strategic choice on the part of Kirvaya's Magisterial Council. What with unrest brewing throughout the kingdom, and small bands of human slaves rebelling left and right, it was wise to appoint a human as queen—especially one who so uncannily resembled Saint Marzana herself.

Audric bowed before the girl, and the rest of their escort followed suit.

But the queen waved them all back to their feet.

"Please, rise," she said, hurrying toward Rielle. Evyline and Ivaine stepped forward to halt her passage.

Rielle barely managed to hide her smile at the expression on Obritsa's face. She doubted this girl queen was used to anything blocking her way.

"Let her pass," commanded Rielle, and when they obeyed, Obritsa approached with a broad smile and clasped Rielle's hands in hers.

"I don't think I've ever been so excited to meet another person in my entire life," the girl said breathlessly, practically bouncing on the balls of her feet. Some of the tension drained from Rielle's body. This aberrant queen was merely a child, excitable and guileless, and would clearly need little urging to do whatever Rielle requested of her—even if said request involved handing over Marzana's casting.

Rielle bowed once more and pressed her lips to Obritsa's hand. The girl grinned, her eyes wide and bright.

"It is an honor to meet you, Your Majesty," Rielle said and then looked sheepishly down at her dust-covered skirts. "I apologize for immediately asking a favor of you, but might we be shown to our rooms? I confess, I feel rather small and shabby in the presence of your loveliness."

"Oh, nonsense!" Obritsa gestured dismissively at her glittering gown. "These fussy old-lady clothes pale in comparison to your beauty, Lady Rielle. Come! You must all rest before tonight's feast. You poor, weary dears. Such a long journey you've had." She clucked her tongue like a fussing mother—or rather, like a child pretending at mothering. Rielle barely swallowed her smile when she noticed the disgruntled expressions the queen's magisters wore. Surely this was not the dignified greeting they had been hoping for.

But Obritsa glided on, ignoring them completely. Still grasping Rielle's hand, as if they were old friends rushing off to gossip, she chattered away, carelessly careening between topics of discussion—features of the palace architecture, the health and happiness of Queen Genoveve, how excited the palace servants were to meet the Sun Queen. For they had all, of course, heard the stories about the trials and that terrible tidal wave that had nearly flattened Styrdalleen. Had Rielle *really* stopped the wave with her own two hands? This hand, the very one Obritsa was holding right now?

Rielle glanced over her shoulder at Audric and raised an eyebrow. He smiled behind his hand, his face lit with amusement.

Ludivine, however, was not so entertained. *Be wary of her. She's hiding something.*

But the sensation of Ludivine's thoughts felt uncertain, faltering, as if she herself wasn't sure of the validity of her own warning.

Rielle put it quickly out of mind. It was a delight to be so fawned over, after the long weeks on the road. If she was to worry about Queen Obritsa, she would do so eventually, but only after she had enjoyed a bath.

◆◇◆

That night, they dined in the palace's largest hall—a grand, lavish space with high, arched rafters, walls rich with tapestries, and what must have been thousands of candles.

They hung from iron chandeliers bolted to the ceilings and in gilded brackets affixed to the walls. Fiery bouquets flickered cheerfully along each long, polished table. Every piece of furniture and span of wall had been decorated in shades of scarlet, gold, and white—a blending of Saint Marzana's colors with Saint Katell's. The overall effect was one of such brilliance that Rielle soon felt a headache pulsing behind her eyes, and wished passionately for bed and the safe cocoon of Audric's arms.

But bed she would not have for some time, for the entire hall of feathered courtiers and wide-eyed servants was watching her, waiting.

The current fashion in the capital apparently centered around a firebird aesthetic, in honor of Saint Marzana's godsbeast. Feathers dyed violet, ruby, bright tangerine, and glittering gold hung from jackets and sashes. They had been woven into braids and gathered into fans.

The sight of them, dazzling and bold amid a room lined with fire, reminded Rielle uncomfortably of her final trial, and how she had transformed the flames trapping Tal into harmless feathers. Many times since that day, she had attempted to perform another such transformation— pens into knives, forks into flowers. But all she had managed was to send the targeted objects bursting into flames or shatter them into pieces too tiny to repair.

And now, with Ludivine's blightblade scar a constant smarting tug on Rielle's senses, the need for her to master this deeper power seemed more urgent by the day. Surely the two ideas were linked—transforming fire to feathers and restoring ruined flesh to its former self.

Akim Yeravet, Grand Magister of the House of Light, cleared his throat. He stood before the table a few paces away, his expression one of barely contained eagerness.

"Lady Rielle?" he prompted quietly. "Are you quite well? Shall I instruct the musicians to begin another dance, and we can proceed in a few moments, after you've had a drink of water?"

Rielle blinked, clearing her muddled thoughts. She, Audric, Ludivine, and the Magisterial Council—as well as Queen Obritsa and her ever-present silent guard—sat on a raised dais at the head of the room, before a table heavy with the dregs of their supper.

Beneath the table, Audric found Rielle's hand. His thumb smoothed a gentle circle against her wrist.

*Right now, Audric is wishing you both could retire to your rooms,* Ludivine said quietly. *He is also thinking how proud he is of you, and how tired he is. How desperately he loves you, and how beautiful you look in the light of all these candles. And how, after spending a few hours loving you, he would very much like to visit the Zheminask archives and ask the librarians for permission to view Marzana's journals.* Ludivine paused, then said slyly, *I did not intrude upon his thoughts enough to know the specifics of* how *he should like to love you, but the general sentiment, I think, is one that would leave you quite satisfied.*

Rielle laughed a little and found the strength to stand.

*Thank you, Lu,* she said. *I needed that.*

*I know.* Then more quietly, accompanied by a gentle press of tender feeling: *Please don't worry for me. The pain of my scar is one I gladly bear.*

Rielle stood, bowed her head to the queen, and then turned to face the room at large.

*Give me time, Lu,* Rielle said firmly. *Soon your pain will flee from me in terror.*

Then she began to speak. "Queen Obritsa. Grand Magisters. People of Kirvaya. Thank you for your generosity in hosting myself, my prince, and my Celdarian family." She hesitated, then extended her hand to Audric. He took it and rose to his feet. She hated making speeches. She silently pleaded with him to find the words that she could not.

Of course, he understood at once.

"We know that these times seem unnerving," he said, his rich voice easily filling the room, "that dark whispers and black rumors shadow your streets, just as they do at home in Celdaria. But we are not afraid of the days to come, whatever they may hold. Your new queen is one of vigor and energy, with a lifetime of work and achievement ahead of her."

Starry-eyed and rapt, Queen Obritsa sat up a bit taller in her too-large chair.

"We have recently rekindled a friendship between our nation and the kingdom of Borsvall," Audric continued. "There is much work yet to be done to rebuild that friendship, but in my view, it is work of great promise, and it will mean that your neighbor to the west will be stronger, steadier, and more able to come to your aid if the need should arise. Across the entire northern span of this great continent—from Celdaria, to Borsvall, to here in Kirvaya—there will stand a united region of friendship, strong enough to weather any storm. And, of course, we now have our Sun Queen."

Audric looked at Rielle, the adoration on his face so unabashed she would have felt embarrassed if she weren't so pleased to see it. "I know you have all heard of her great deeds—first in Celdaria and more recently in the Borsvall capital. And that is only the beginning of her power. Every day, she grows stronger. Every day," he said, his voice softening, "I love her more deeply than I did the day before."

The room murmured, waves of delight and curiosity rippling throughout, and Rielle's cheeks warmed to hear it. She would forever remember the sight of Audric in this moment—lit by the candles flanking their dinner plates; his clean, square jaw freshly shaven; the steady, solid presence of him at her side a tangible force, physical and gentle and *hers*.

Audric turned back to face those gathered in the hall. "We are not afraid. We look to the future with clear eyes, and we urge you to join us in this—to hold hope in your own hearts and to come together in the face of uncertainty, rather than allow it to fracture us."

Rielle beamed up at him, a quiet pride kindling in her chest at the sound of his voice—so similar to the one that murmured endearments against her skin every night, and yet so different, so poised and practiced. The voice of a king. Was it possible to love a person so completely? Could one's heart literally split open under the weight of such feeling? She would have grabbed his coat and kissed him right there in front of everyone if Ludivine weren't insistently poking at her thoughts, begging her to restrain herself.

Instead Rielle turned away from him, lifted her hands to the ceiling, and summoned to her palms all the fire lighting the hall.

Thousands of tiny flames rushed to her, accompanied by gasps and cries from the crowd. She stood, arms outstretched, a skull-sized knot of fire in each hand. She held them there for a moment, the flames quivering and eager, and marveled at the ease of her own power. Her mind felt supple, energized. She felt that she could have run all the way home to Celdaria without breaking a sweat. She could have slammed her palms to the ground and shattered mountains on the other side of the world.

Instead, she exhaled slowly and pushed her palms out as if to nudge open a set of doors.

The fire rushed out from her fingers, silent and spinning, a thousand tiny kernels of light rather than the pointed flames of their previous lives. Fire stars, winking amber. Rielle held her breath, her eyes unfocused. She saw nothing but vague, dark shapes—the tables, the crowd, the tapestries hugging the walls—and connecting it all, a thin, shimmering expanse of gold.

How marvelous, how strange and spectacular, to remember that this beauty of the naked empirium was hers alone to see.

She sighed with pleasure, then flicked her fingers once more.

The fire froze in the air—across the tables, above the feathered heads of the nobility, throughout the room from floor to ceiling—each glittering grain held suspended by Rielle's will.

She barely heard their cheers, their astonished applause, and only at last acknowledged Queen Obritsa because Ludivine urged her to. The girl was beside herself, nearly weeping with enthusiasm. She even embraced Rielle before her horrified guard pulled her gently away.

Rielle spared a thought of pity for her, and for all of them—their blindness, their ignorance and inability. She gazed at the beauty of her own creation and tried to imagine what she must seem like to their eyes. An inhuman creature, perhaps; something indecipherable and colossal.

Something closer to God than they could ever hope to be.

# ELIANA

*"And when the horn of Veersa sounds,*
*Rise, my neighbors, my family, my friends.*
*Rise against the tide of malice;*
*Stand firm on the soil of your homeland."*

—"The Battle Cry of Lady Veersa,"
traditional Astavari war hymn

The doors to Navi's rooms slammed open, the Horn of Veersa's long, low wails so deafening that Eliana felt their hum in her teeth. Her hand flew to Arabeth.

"What will we do?" she asked. "How far away is the Kaavalan Passage?"

Four royal guards entered the room and began helping Navi to her feet.

"Don't worry," she told Eliana, moving stiffly. "The mouth of the passage is over one hundred miles away. We have time to prepare a counterattack."

Leaning on one of her guards for support, she tugged on trousers, boots, a tunic and sweater, and a long coat. She tightened the sash, then grabbed two knives from a drawer in her bedside table and shoved them into sheaths at her belt.

Despite everything, Eliana smiled a little. "You'd never know you were lying here half alive only a few days ago, slowly transforming into a monster."

Navi shot her a wry look. "You're going to anger my guards, Eliana." She glanced at one of the guards in question, a broad-shouldered woman with a square jaw and freckled skin. "Ruusa, you may have to carry me downstairs."

Ruusa nodded once. "I will carry you to the edge of the world, Your Highness."

"What's downstairs?" Eliana asked.

"My fathers' war room," said Navi. "My brother will be there, and Lady Ama. I don't know what we're facing, and any intelligence we receive from scouts will be delivered there. After that..."

Her voice trailed off.

"Your fathers' armies will be able to stop them," Eliana said into the silence, forcing steadiness into her voice. "Astavar has stood free for years, thanks to them."

"Except now we have something they want even more than they've wanted to destroy our kingdom and our people," said Navi, glancing over at her. "We have the Sun Queen."

Eliana had had the same thought. She lifted her chin against the sick swoop of guilt that inflamed her body. "I'll ride out to meet them and surrender myself. That will hold them off for a while, give the rest of you the chance to escape."

"Don't be ridiculous," Navi said crisply. "Whatever you could do to them wouldn't give everyone in Astavar the chance to flee to freedom. And even if it would, I wouldn't allow you to risk yourself in such a way."

"You wouldn't allow me." Eliana followed Navi and her guards out of her rooms. Her castings were warm buzzing nets around her hands. She nearly ripped them off and hurled them out the window. "No one will allow me anything. What if I want to surrender myself? Does that mean nothing?"

"No, it doesn't." Navi paused in the threshold of her sitting room, fixing Eliana with a steady, patient stare. "And I think you know that. I know you don't like hearing such things, but—"

Cannon fire detonated outside, near enough to shake the floor, the door to Navi's rooms, the sculpture of Tameryn and her black leopard on the nearby table.

Another boom followed shortly thereafter, and another, and a third, each one nearer than the last, and the Horn of Veersa kept baying over it all, like a pup howling for its mother. Screams, shouts, and the distant sounds of gunfire began floating in through the open windows in Navi's bedroom.

"That was close," Eliana muttered. "It sounds like they're right at the doors."

Navi looked back through her rooms, her expression suddenly taut with fear. "I don't understand. The passage is over one hundred miles away. How could they have gotten so close unobserved?"

The answer came to Eliana swiftly.

The only way an imperial army could have taken the Astavari lookouts so completely by surprise was if someone had hidden their approach. And the only creature powerful enough to do that was the Emperor himself. But was such a thing possible? Imagining the kind of power required to maintain mental control of that magnitude, and from that distance, made her head spin.

"My lady," Ruusa urged, "we must hurry downstairs. Your fathers will want you to head for the tunnels—"

"I would sooner submit myself once again to Fidelia's laboratories," Navi snapped, "than hide underground while my people face the Empire's guns alone. No, we'll go to the war room. At once."

"I'll meet you there," Eliana said quickly, taking hold of Navi's hands. "I have to find Remy."

Navi nodded. "Of course. On the third floor, in the north wing, there hangs a tapestry of Saint Tameryn in prayer. Behind it is a narrow door. Follow the passage, and when you reach a fork, enter the second hallway from the right. It will lead you to a door flanked by guards. This is my fathers' war room. The guards will allow you entrance without question."

Then Navi squeezed Eliana's hands, pressed a kiss to her cheek. "*Savrasara*, Eliana."

"What does that mean?"

"It's an old Astavari word, one we learned from Saint Tameryn's writings. Roughly translated, it means, *You carry my heart*. An expression of love and of warning. It is a great responsibility, to be trusted with another's heart."

A tingle crept down the back of Eliana's neck. Something terrible was about to happen. She sensed it—a subtle rot in the air, a shift in the angles of the world—and could tell by Navi's knotted brow that she felt it too.

"An odd time to tell me such a thing," Eliana said lightly.

Navi's smile did not reach her eyes. "It's always the right time to say such a thing."

The loudest boom yet detonated, shattering the glass roof that allowed sunlight into Navi's sitting room.

Ruusa's tone brooked no further arguments. "My lady, I must insist."

"Go," Navi whispered, releasing her. "And hurry."

Eliana turned and ran toward the central library, assuming Remy would have gone there for solace after seeing her. Another boom from outside shook dust from the dark rafters overhead, rattled vases on pedestals and the artwork hanging from the walls. The corridors were chaos—servants and castle staff hurrying for shelter, guards running for their posts. The sounds of approaching war, and of people utterly unprepared for it.

And then, in the corridor outside her rooms, Eliana ran straight into Harkan. A detonation, followed by the unthinking shove of a sobbing, wild-eyed servant, knocked them into each other's arms.

For a moment, Harkan held her to his chest. Then he pulled back to look at her, the relief passing over his face so palpable and obvious that Eliana found herself wishing she could love him again as she once had. It was a real-ization that came over her with the force and clarity of a punch to the jaw.

"Where's Remy?" Harkan asked, looking round.

"I don't know. He came to Navi's rooms, we barely talked, and then he left. I'm trying to find him and take him with me to the war room. Navi's there, and the kings."

Then Eliana paused. Harkan's face was strangely closed to her, as if he was striving for the kind of unreadable cool cruelty that Simon wore like an accessory to his everyday clothes.

That same creeping sense of dread came over her—the approach of something inexorable and terrible. "What is it? Harkan, what's happened?"

In the cool midday light spilling through a nearby shattered window, his eyes glinted, bright and full. He muttered, "I'm sorry, El. But there's no time to find him. Forgive me."

Before she could move or protest, he had grabbed hold of her, his grip determined. He grounded himself against the wall as she kicked at him, trying to wrench herself away. But he held fast, and then one of his hands came over her mouth and nose, a soaked, sour rag clutched inside it, and she realized what was happening in the few seconds of furious awareness she had before the blackness reared up to drown her.

Harkan was drugging her, just as Fidelia had done all those weeks ago in Sanctuary.

She screamed out his name, her voice muffled against the rag and the hard grip of his hand.

"I can't lose you, not again," she heard him say into her hair, his voice so choked with tears that he hardly sounded like himself. "I'm so sorry, El."

And then his voice faded, and so did she.

# ✦ 20 ✦

# SIMON

*"In holy lore and sacred art, particularly concerning the saints, the image of the wolf can often be found. Though not a godsbeast, the animal is significant. A pack of wolves raised the orphaned Saint Tameryn, and godsbeasts were often found in the company of wolves. The beast has an affinity for creatures touched by the empirium, but do not mistake it for a guardian. The appearance of a wolf can also mean uncertainty. A precipice. A portent."*

—A footnote from *The Book of the Saints*

When Simon strode into the kings' war room, he knew at once that Eliana wasn't there.

It was a terrible, marvelous thing, to be able to so keenly sense her presence. He was no angel—though as a marque, somewhere in his veins existed angelic blood, dormant and useless, snuffed out by the god-damned Blood Queen along with everything else. He was no angel, and yet back in Orline, after only a few days spent observing Eliana from a distance—before they had sparred in her home, before he had been able to, at last, look her in the eye and see that face of hers, uninterrupted and unimpeded—after only a few days observing her, he had known her. The way she moved through a space, the sound of her footfalls against the ground, the lines between her eyebrows when she frowned.

Her father's full mouth, his serious brow, his dark eyes. Her mother's fierce jaw, the delicate turn of her wrists.

From the first moment he had set eyes on Eliana, he had known her in his bones, in the knit of his muscles, in the roar of his blood. As a boy, he had cradled her tiny infant body in his arms and done everything he could to hold on to her even as the world ripped itself apart at their feet. And now, as a man, her closeness changed the air around him, drawing his senses taut as bowstrings and lighting his skin from the inside out, as if he had consumed a brew of stars that wouldn't stop spinning.

But in the war room, the air remained dull and unremarkable, and he knew she wasn't there even before he scanned the room to confirm it.

Ordinarily, he wasn't one to make a scene, but in that instance, he felt dangerously close to it.

"Where is she?" he said very quietly, and then a soft cry from the far side of the room alerted him to Remy.

The boy ran for him and slammed into his front. Face muffled against Simon's shirt, his arms tight around Simon's torso, Remy mumbled, "Navi said Eliana went to find me, but she hasn't come back. We sent guards to find her."

Simon placed one hand on Remy's head and another on his shoulder. He felt a horrible idea beginning to form. "And where is Harkan, might I ask?"

Navi met his eyes from across the room. "We haven't been able to find him either." Then she paused, her eyes widening. "You don't think..."

"I don't know what I think, but I certainly don't like not knowing where either of them are. In fact, instead of just standing here staring at me, why don't you send out more of your guards to fucking find them?"

King Tavik, bent over a crudely sketched map on the room's central table, straightened with a dark look. "Right hand of the Prophet or no, if you say anything like that to my daughter again, I will have my guards toss you out of this tower."

"I'll help," Navi offered dryly.

Simon ignored the king's glare. "Tell me what happened the last time you saw her."

"She said she needed to find Remy, which I understood," Navi replied. "She left in the direction of the central library."

"Damn it, Navi." Simon turned away, dragging a hand through his hair. "You shouldn't have let her go."

"And what should I have done, exactly? Ordered her not to go after her brother? Bound her in chains and forced her to come with me instead?"

"Yes," he said at once. "That's exactly what you should have done."

Navi rose from her chair, leaning heavily against a broad-shouldered female guard. "Has it occurred to you that your insistence on shaping her path for her might be the very thing that keeps driving her away from you?"

Simon bristled. "I've been exceptionally patient with her."

"Your definition of patience is an odd one, Captain," said Lady Ama mildly, examining the map alongside the kings. "You've been hovering around that poor girl for weeks, brooding and scowling." She raised an eyebrow, glancing up. "Did the Prophet forget to teach you manners?"

"Manners have no place in a world at war," Simon said. "And, yes, Navi, your guards should have bodily restrained her, if necessary. Without her, we have no chance to mount any sort of resistance, or fight the Empire, or turn the tide of war. Without her, we're nothing."

"We've done a fine job on our own in Astavar for decades now," said King Eri. "We've resisted the Empire's fleets—"

"They were toying with you," Simon interrupted. "This is all a game for the Emperor. Until he found Rielle's daughter, his slow conquest of this world was a game, a way to pass the time. Now he's found her, and this is no longer a game. It is a hunt. An obsession. This invasion is only the beginning. He will stop at nothing until he finds her, and when he does—"

A series of explosions shook the room. Remy's hand tightened around Simon's fingers.

The door to the war room burst open, admitting Hob and a servant—a young woman, perhaps a year or two older than Eliana. Her mouth was set in a thin, grim line.

Hob wiped his brow, his dark skin gleaming with sweat and dust. "Tell them what you told me, Perri."

Perri nodded once. "I saw them. Lady Eliana and Harkan. They were talking in the corridor near Lady Eliana's rooms. And then…"

Perri glanced at Hob, hands clasped tensely at her waist.

"It's all right," said Hob. "Go on."

Perri squared her shoulders. "And then I saw Harkan grab hold of Lady Eliana and press a cloth to her face. She struggled, and then went limp. She was still a little bit awake, I think, at least enough to walk beside him. But he directed her movements, as though she wouldn't be able to walk without his help. Her eyes were open but foggy. And Harkan, he looked terribly upset. For a moment, I thought he might be sick. Then they were gone, hurrying down the hallway. I came at once to tell someone, and I found Hob."

Then Perri's brow furrowed. "I'm sorry I didn't go after them. I wasn't sure what to do."

"It's good that you didn't," Navi said gently into the shocked silence, her face hard as stone. "He might have hurt you to get away."

"I will kill him." Simon's anger was so complete it numbed him, reduced him to a man incapable of moving. His mind buzzed and snarled—every instinct he possessed, every lesson that had been beaten into him, flooding him with the desire to inflict violence. "I'll find them, and I'll kill him where he stands."

"Please don't," Remy said, his voice breaking. He tugged at Simon's hand. "We'll find them. They can't have gone far. Harkan was probably just afraid. He wouldn't hurt her. Maybe she was trying to leave again, and he had to stop her."

"She would try to flee, leaving you behind? Impossible."

And then Simon's path became clear to him.

He detached himself from Remy's grip, placed both hands on the boy's shoulders, and leaned down to look him in the eye. Navi would try to stop him from taking Remy, as would Hob, as would all of them.

They would fail.

"Do you trust me?" he asked Remy, gentling his voice. Even in his fury, it was an easy thing to do—to slip into that cunning silver world of lies in which he had been raised since landing in this future, all those years ago.

Behind Simon, the war room doors opened once more, admitting Prince Malik, Commander Haakorat, and two other soldiers, each of them spattered with mud and blood. They hurried to the table, Malik consulting in furious whispers with the kings.

Remy watched them, biting his lip. "Malik doesn't look happy. Do you think the city will fall?"

"Answer me." Simon turned Remy back to face him. "Do you trust me, Remy?"

"El would say I shouldn't," Remy replied after a moment, and then his expression flattened in a way Simon had never seen before. "Which probably means I should."

"Good boy. If we move quickly, we can find them, catch up with her and Harkan before they slip into the wild for good. And if you're there with me, I've got a better chance of either changing his mind or turning her against him."

Remy considered him gravely. "Will you hurt me to get her back?"

Simon only paused for a moment. There was no point in lying to the boy, and telling him the truth, as harsh as it was, would perhaps further engender his trust. "I don't want to, but if I must, I will."

Remy glanced over Simon's shoulder. "Navi's watching us."

"Answer me quickly, then."

The boy's bright-blue eyes locked with Simon's own for a long moment. Then he lifted his sharp little chin, squaring his jaw in the same way Eliana so often did. "I'll do it."

Simon gave him a tight smile. "Hold on to me, and close your eyes. When I run, you run too."

Then he reached into his pocket, withdrew three tiny black smokers, and flung them to the floor. They cracked open with a trio of sharp pops, filling the room with smoke. Hob's deep voice bellowed a curse. Navi called out Simon's name. Guards drew their weapons, coughing, the metallic scrape of their swords ringing in the swirling darkness.

Simon ran, trusting Remy to keep up. At the door, he smashed his fists into the jaws of two guards obstructing their path. Their bodies slumped to the floor. He snatched one of their swords, and a dagger from the nearest one's belt, and thrust the latter at Remy.

The boy grabbed the weapon, and together they fled back through the war room tunnels to a castle full of shattered windows and screaming servants. The sound of nearing gunfire punctuated the air, and Simon refused to think about bullets piercing Eliana's body, or cannon fire blasting her to bits, or how he should have taken her away from this place as soon as she had forged her castings.

Instead, his thoughts glided into the comfortable rhythm of the Prophet's teachings, the years of training and conditioning he had endured in that frigid compound under the mountain, the long, brutal dark his life had been before finding Eliana in Orline. Three soldiers pursued them from the war room. He pulled the revolver from his hip and shot them each through the skull. Remy cried out in protest, but Simon shoved him onward.

With every slam of his boots against the floor, his mind chanted one furious word—a curse, a plea, a prayer.

*Eliana. Eliana. Eliana.*

# NAVI

*"To anyone who may read this, the last writing of my life,
it must be known that I fought for my country alongside
my beloved husband, Eri, and my dear friend Ama. Beside
my commanders, I defended my city with all breath left in
me. My kingdom may fall, but the Empire will soon burn
at the hands of the Sun Queen."*

—A message from King Tavik Amaruk of Astavar,
confiscated by invading imperial forces, September 6,
Year 1018 of the Third Age

Navi could no longer keep quiet.

"We are cowards," she murmured into the darkness, Ruusa's torch the only thing illuminating their path through the tunnels below Dyrefal.

Beside her, Malik said nothing, his tense silence vibrating like the furious echo of a drum.

"You are not cowards," Hob replied. In the torchlight, his dark skin gleamed, night-limned with gold. "You are the leaders of your people, and when the dust settles, they will look to you for guidance. They will find you, wherever you land in the days to come, and help you rebuild."

"I should be out there fighting alongside them," Malik bit out. "Not scurrying away through the darkness like a frightened rat."

"And what good would it do, if you were to die?" Hob ducked beneath a low stone archway. "Two of the royal children dead, and the other three halfway across the world. No kings, no crown. A scattered people, lost and leaderless. It was right for you to leave."

Navi leaned on Ruusa's arm, closing her eyes. Her head rocked as if she stood on the deck of a rolling ship.

Ruusa passed her torch to another guard in their escort. "My lady, shall I carry you?"

"Not yet, Ruusa," Navi replied. "We've a long way to go. Save your strength."

"A long way to go." Malik let out a bark of harsh laughter. "That's one way to put it."

Navi found Malik's hand. "Peace, brother."

He ripped his hand away from her. "Peace! Peace, as our people are slaughtered above us, as our parents give up their lives to allow us time to flee!"

Navi moved unsteadily toward Malik. He met her halfway, catching her arms.

"Navi, you can barely even *walk*," he muttered.

"Listen to me." She searched his face. The glittering sadness in his eyes seized her heart. "I know what you're feeling. I feel it myself. But we cannot allow ourselves to fall prey to our own shame."

Malik shook his head. "Navi, I can't bear to leave them—"

"I know, but we *must*." She cupped the back of his head in her hands, brought his forehead down to touch hers. "This war is not only about the fate of Astavar, and we can't help Eliana if we are lying dead on a battlefield."

"Eliana." Malik spat a curse. "She brought this down upon us."

Navi frowned. "She saved us all, that night in Karajak Bay. She sank the Empire fleet."

"Which ended up meaning nothing." He flung his hand toward the ceiling. "Listen to them, Navi. Listen to our people die. Listen to our kingdom fall. If she hadn't come here—"

"If she hadn't come here, we would have fallen weeks ago. And you won't speak ill of her again, not in my presence. She is on a more difficult path than any of us. I can only pray that, wherever Harkan has taken her, she is able to enjoy a little bit of peace before they find her again."

Malik gave her a sad, tight smile, but before he could speak further, dull booms thundered overhead, muffled by the dense stretches of rock above them. Malik tried to move away, dragging a hand across his face with a small sob, but Navi held him fast.

"Astavar may fall," she said quietly, "but its people will live on, and as survivors flee and scatter, you and I will be fighting to save them, and their Venteran brothers, and their Celdarian sisters." She drew a deep breath, her energy nearly exhausted. "Tell me what we will do."

After a long moment, Malik managed to speak. "We will flee south, to the Vespers."

"And then?"

"We will gather allies as we travel."

"We will collect the lost and the homeless, as many as we can care for, as many as our ship can hold. And we will find more ships, and our numbers will grow, and then none of us will be lost or homeless any longer, for we will have made a new home of our own, a new country."

"We will have built an army to crush the Empire," Malik added, his voice stronger now, more assured.

Navi nodded, her heart bursting with love for him. Their fathers' farewell kisses lingered on her brow. If she inhaled deeply enough, she could still smell Ama's perfume on her clothes.

To honor their sacrifice, she wrestled her tears into submission. They could rise later. "The Empire's foothold in the islands is not as strong as it once was. We may be able to unseat them, if not in Tava Koro, then on one of the smaller islands."

"They'll be distracted, looking for Eliana."

"Quite likely." She gripped Malik's soft black hair, anchored him to her eyes. "We will rally the Vespers to our cause. We will gather ships, weapons, soldiers. And when Eliana is ready to destroy the Emperor—for she will, she *will* destroy him, I believe that with my every breath, my every waking *hope*, dear brother—when she is ready, we will be there, with our army of strays, and we will be at her side, and we will not let her fall."

Malik closed his eyes, tears slipping down his cheeks. "We are not cowards."

"No. I was wrong to have said that." Navi stepped back from him and looked at each of her guards in turn. "We are the light against the darkness, and we must continue to burn brightly, so others may find their way out."

Last of all, she met Hob's gaze. He nodded once and then said, "May the Queen's light guide us."

Navi said a quick, silent prayer that she would not only live long enough to once again fight at Eliana's side, but also to see Hob and Patrik reunited. Not once since he had left Patrik weeks ago at Crown's Hollow had Hob complained about how this fight had separated him from his love, but Navi saw the quiet grief in every line of his face, heard it in every word he uttered.

She touched his arm and offered him a small smile, which he returned with shining eyes.

"May the Queen's light guide us," she agreed, and then, unsteady, refusing Ruusa's silent offer of aid—at least for a little while, at least for a few quiet yards on her own two reborn feet—she turned away from her home for what she knew in her heart would be the last time and sent a silent prayer to whatever ravaged vestiges of the empirium remained in the world.

*Find her.*

*Protect her.*

*Help her believe.*

## → 22 →

# ELIANA

*"When the Sun Queen arrives, she may not look like any-*
*thing you've imagined. She may not know who she is,*
*and she may resent the destiny to which she was born.*
*Be patient with her. Nourish and cherish her. And above*
*all, do whatever you must to keep her safe, even if it earns*
*her hatred."*

—*The Word of the Prophet*

E liana observed her and Harkan's progress through an acrid fog, her
head throbbing.

She knew the drug he had used—a powerful sedative, commonly
known as black lily, that she had, as the Dread, often deployed against her
victims. She was so angry with him for using it on her, and with herself for
not seeing it coming, that despite her muddled senses, fury lit the soles of
her feet afire, grounding her useless body.

She had to lean heavily on Harkan to stay upright. His arm was firm
around her waist as they fled through the castle, down the now-familiar
route toward Tameryn's cavern, and then through a different series of
tunnels that, thankfully, were not flooded and required no swimming.

At last, they emerged into the city, into the chaotic heart of Vintervok.
Explosions tore the streets to pieces, debris clattered down upon the roads
from rooftops shattered by cannon fire. Terrified citizens ran screaming

through the streets, only as many belongings as they could easily carry haphazardly bundled onto their backs—arms full of children, books, sacks of food. There had been no time to prepare; the invasion had risen suddenly like a monster from beneath the earth, and now there was nowhere to run.

The black lily was sinking slowly into Eliana's veins, overpowering her sight, her balance. She let herself fall into the support of Harkan's gait and stumbled alongside him like an animal being led by its master.

Beneath the waves of the drug sloshing through her mind, her rage coiled, waiting.

—◆—

They boarded a ship—the *Streganna*, Harkan murmured against her ear. As they were shuffled into one of the ship's dark holds, along with so many other wailing, sobbing passengers that even in her current state, Eliana felt her skin begin to crawl, Harkan told her what he had done.

"While you were with Navi," he said quietly, "I spent time in the city. I met a man named Arris in a tavern and paid him for passage aboard this ship. They're bound for Meridian. I paid him a healthy sum, stolen from the kings' treasury. I know, I shouldn't have. But, God help me, I couldn't bear to stay there, watching you lose yourself to Simon's plans. Those castings… El, he wanted to fight a war with you as his primary weapon. I can't think that's the destiny you truly wanted for yourself."

She listened to him until she couldn't any longer. Her fury bubbled up, allowing her to speak.

"And Remy?" she managed, her words slow and full of effort. She estimated she had to endure another two hours of the black lily's worst effects, and until then, she would remain inert and cottonmouthed.

Harkan paused. He had found them a quiet corner of the hold—a ratty canvas hammock, a fairly clean patch of floor. He had covered her bandaged hands, her castings, with his own gloves.

"I didn't want to leave him," he replied at last, his voice as thick as her mind felt. "You know I didn't. But if it was a choice between going to find

him and losing our chance of escaping, or getting you out of there safely...
El, I couldn't miss the moment. I had to act."

"You didn't." She tried to glare at him, livid that her eyes insisted on
closing against her will. "You didn't have to do any of this. It was my
choice to stay or go. You took that from me."

He shook his head, dragged a hand over his mouth. "Please, try to
understand—"

"No. I hate you. Understand that. Do you hear me? You've lost me.
You have me here now because you're selfish, and a coward, but actually
you've lost me forever. Know that. Live with it."

Forcing out those words required all the voice she had left. Eyes burning from tears, from the drug, from the battle-ash peppering the skies, she
sank onto the hammock upon which Harkan had situated her and fell into
a throbbing black sleep.

◆◆◆

The Sea of Bones was calm—so the captain insisted, anyway—but Eliana
was unused to traveling on ships and spent their first two days aboard the
*Streganna* curled up on her hammock, miserable and sick with anger. A
pail, one of many, sat on the floor below her; she used it often.

Harkan was not much better, which was a small comfort.

Now that the effects of the black lily had worn off, Eliana was able to
observe their surroundings. The hammocks in the ship's hold were strung
up close to one another, ropes bolted to the rafters. She had counted at
least seventy hammocks throughout the main hold, and not everyone had
managed to claim one. The damp air quickly grew unpleasantly musky.
But though the ship was small, it seemed clean enough, and the hammocks were large and sturdy.

Large enough, in fact, for Harkan to climb inside and join her.

He had been pacing the hold, convinced that movement and talking to
their fellow travelers would distract him from his nausea—and perhaps
supposing that allowing Eliana space would diminish her anger.

But at last he gave up and climbed quietly into her hammock. They had nothing left in their bellies, and though she was so furious with him she couldn't look him in the face, she was too sick to shun him altogether. He was a body, as clammy as her own but solid and familiar, so she clung to him reluctantly, the ship rocking them. Even familiar sounds seemed new and strange within the walls of the *Streganna*'s hull—babies crying, the low murmur of conversation, laughter and the slap of cards, a distant sizzle of cooking meat from the galley.

Eliana groaned into Harkan's hair. "That anyone could think of eating."

"Please don't vomit on me," he said.

"You'd deserve it." She wanted to say so much more than that. She wanted to rise from the hammock and abandon him, stay as far away from him as possible until they made port in Meridian, and then leave him behind forever.

But that distance would have been a mercy, for both of them—and neither of them deserved respite. He had taken her from Remy, from Simon, from the people who needed their help.

And she was terrified by the idea of facing whatever lay ahead alone, even if she had only him for company. Once, after such an egregious betrayal, she would have walked away from him and never looked back.

Once, she had existed without an Empire breathing down her neck, and with her hands free of cages she did not understand.

She slipped her right hand into her coat pocket, touched the cold metal lines of the box that held Zahra. The reminder of the wraith's absence sharpened her anger. Her eyes grew hot at the thought of Zahra floating nearby, cooling her cheeks with the supple dark current of her hand.

"I wonder if Remy died after we abandoned him," she said. "I wonder if he tried to find us, got separated from the others, and died with an Empire arrow through his gut."

Harkan blew out a trembling breath. "El, don't."

"I wonder if he died alone, terrified, wondering why we'd left him."

"Please don't do this."

"Fuck you, Harkan. I'll do just as I please." And then, as the boat pitched hard, her tears rose until she could hardly breathe. She swallowed against the sour tang of her upset stomach.

"I'll never forgive you for this," she said, her face pressed against his neck. An animal rage thrumming under her breastbone longed to tear into his flesh with her teeth, rip his throat from his body, let him bleed out and suffer as she feared Remy might have suffered, alone, in the fallen castle, without his sister there to protect him.

Instead she wept quietly against Harkan's shirt, shrugged away his arm when he tried to comfort her, cursed him viciously every time he said her name. Though his voice was familiar, his body a welcome anchor on this tossing sea, it felt foreign to be so near him. She would never have thought him capable of doing what he had done. She would never have imagined him to be the kind of man to take her will from her, to direct her life as he saw fit rather than allow her to lead it herself, as was her right.

A terrible thought occurred to her: Had the war changed him? Had those horrible long weeks after they'd been separated in Orline done something irreparable to his character?

Or had she never really known him at all?

The feeling sat in her chest like a meal she could not digest. She did not try to dislodge it; she let it molder, barbed, between her ribs.

Sleep did not come easily after that.

—◆—

She startled awake to find Harkan gone.

But someone else was watching her.

A child, standing very near in the dim light, dark eyes wide. Dark-brown skin beneath tight black curls.

The boy stared at her castings.

For a moment, she lay there frozen. And then she remembered: she had taken off Harkan's gloves earlier in the night to allow her bandaged hands a chance to breathe—and had forgotten to replace them.

"What are those?" The child looked up, a sharpness overtaking his expression. "I've never seen those before."

"No, I don't suppose you have." Eliana swung her legs out of the hammock, ready to grab Arabeth. "They belonged to my mother. What do you want?"

The child considered her hands once more. "If I touch them, will they hurt me?"

"If you touch them, *I'll* hurt you."

The child's gaze lifted, appraising her. "My name is Gerren. You snore in your sleep. If you don't stop that, someone will pound your face in, probably."

Then, quick as a kitten, he dropped a folded piece of paper into her palm, ducked under the hammock beside hers, and was gone.

The hold was dim—a few stubby candles throughout and a pale wash of light from the nearest hatch. Eliana opened the paper and squinted to read it.

> Slop room. One hour.
> We know who you are.

◆◇◆

She found Harkan swabbing the portside deck, ignored the irritated bark of the boatswain, and held up the paper for Harkan to read.

He wiped his brow. The rising dawn illuminated the sheen of sweat on his skin.

"What did you tell him?" she said softly. "This man you found who secured us passage. Is this his doing?"

"I told him nothing of significance." Harken frowned at the paper, then marched to the railing and tossed it overboard. "Who brought that to you?"

"A child. Gerren was his name. He saw my castings."

Harkan was aghast. "How? My gloves—"

"I took them off to let my hands breathe, forgot to put them back on, and fell asleep."

"El, you can't be careless like that."

"Don't you dare talk to me that way," she said, though she *had* been careless and was furious to realize it. "I was tired, all right? I'm so tired I can hardly think."

"Maybe if you hadn't driven yourself to the edge of death back in Astavar," Harkan said, "you wouldn't be in such a state now."

She fixed him with a hard glare. "It's astonishing to me that you feel you have any ground to stand on here. I did what I had to do to save Navi."

Harkan rounded on her, his eyes glinting with tears. "And I did what I had to do to save you."

Silence fell between them. Harkan turned away to watch the brightening sea. The sun fattened on the horizon; there was no land in sight.

When he spoke again, his voice was steady. "I suppose we'll have to go meet them, whoever they are. Otherwise this could escalate."

"*I* have to meet them, anyway."

"You can't possibly expect me to let you go alone."

Eliana stilled, the lines of her body drawing tight with the urge to strike. "Let me? You'll want to think very carefully about what you say next, Harkan."

He was quiet for a long time, and when he finally looked back at her, there was a weariness to his expression, a sag of regret.

"I know. I'm sorry. I don't think I'll ever be able to apologize enough. And I accept that. But I also don't think you should do anything alone—not here, not when we disembark. You have a target on your back, now more than ever, and we have no friends here, or anywhere. We have only each other."

The terrible truth of that settled, spinning, into her gut.

She had only Harkan.

And she realized, watching him, that despite everything, she still loved him and always would. He had done something unforgivable, and she would see the memory of that act for the rest of her life, every time she set eyes on him.

But there had been a lifetime of friendship and devotion before that, and though she longed to discard those memories, wipe clean the slate of their history, she couldn't. He was too much a part of her, and she of him. They were braided together, and if she untwined those threads, she would have nothing left to hold on to.

Wordlessly, she helped him finish his chores, and then, together, they climbed belowdecks.

✦

The slop room was down the hall from the galley. Multiple times a day, the cook's assistants dumped rotten food, refuse, and waste through a locked hatch in the slop room floor.

The narrow corridor outside the room was empty. All was silent, save for a raucous shout of laughter from the galley.

Eliana knocked on the door. It opened at once, admitting a foul odor that smelled exactly as she had expected the slop room to smell.

"You're late," said the woman inside—one Eliana had seen in passing aboard the ship. She was young, perhaps two or three years older than Eliana, lithe and reedy in a way that suggested she hardly ever stopped moving. Her eyes were quick and sharp, a honeyed brown to match her skin, which was dusted with freckles. Her long, braided brown hair had been dyed a rich scarlet—though that must have been some time ago, for much of the color had faded.

The woman's gaze fell at once to Eliana's hands. "So what are they?"

Eliana did not blink. "They were my mother's."

"Yes, so Gerren said. But what are they?"

"Odd, that you would care so much about jewelry," said Harkan, at Eliana's elbow.

The woman raised an eyebrow. "They're rather ugly, for jewelry."

"What do you want?" Eliana snapped.

The woman considered Eliana for a moment longer. "Your help," she said and then stepped aside to reveal a man sitting behind her on an over-turned pail. He was pale-skinned, with wild copper hair and a fresh red scar across his face, part of it obscured by a black eye patch.

Eliana stepped back, unbalanced. She felt as though she were lifting away from herself.

"Arris?" said Harkan, sounding surprised. "What is all this?"

"Harkan." The man inclined his head, his voice slow and smooth, deeply amused. "When we met in Vintervok, you didn't tell me what sort of company you keep." He glanced at Eliana, his mouth twitching.

"His name isn't Arris," Eliana managed at last, forcing her shock to release its hold. "It's Patrik. He's Red Crown."

# ⟶ 23 ⟵
# RIELLE

*"Stories from the early days of the Second Age tell us that Saint Marzana, understanding how exhausted and heartsick the scattered people of her homeland were after so many years of war, decided to craft her throne from flames that would never die. Even on the darkest night, the throne would burn brighter than the sun and warm the coldest reaches of even the most desolate heart."*

—*The Fire That Lit the World: A History of the Formation of the Kirvayan Realm* by Blazh Tarasov and Lyudmilla Zakhovna

Rielle awoke in the early hours of the morning from a strangely dreamless sleep to hear Ludivine's urgent voice.

*Rielle, wake up. There's someone here to see you. The speaker of the Kirvayan Obex. We're right outside. I barely managed to stop her from barging in. Wake Audric.*

Rielle's exhaustion vanished. She gently shook Audric until he stirred, rubbing his eyes.

"What is it?" he murmured.

"The speaker of the Obex is here." She climbed out of bed, the cool air prickling her skin, and retrieved her dressing gown from the floor. "Lu's outside with her."

Rielle waited until Audric had pulled on his tunic and trousers and then told Ludivine, *All right. We're decent.*

Ludivine entered at once, her brow knotted with worry. Behind her followed a pale woman with close-cropped gray hair, her skin lined and weathered but her gait strong. She wore layers of snow-dusted furs, carried a walking stick, and brought with her the crisp bite of winter.

The bronze clasp of her cloak bore the sigil of the Obex—a single eye, resting atop the Gate.

"Prince Audric. Lady Rielle." The woman bowed. "My name is Vaska. I speak for the Obex."

"It's quite late, Vaska," said Audric, "and we've been traveling for days. Can this wait until morning?"

Vaska blinked. "No, my lord prince. It cannot wait until morning." She looked at Rielle. "You are here for the casting of Saint Marzana, are you not?"

"Yes, we are," Rielle replied. "Has something happened?"

The woman shook her head. "I cannot speak of it here, my lady. As you know, the Obex is loyal to no one but our sacred task. We are not loyal to the Blazing Throne, nor to the Magisterial Council. And, as I'm sure you also know, this city is one of unrest. You have heard, perhaps, of the elemental children who have gone missing?"

Rielle raised her eyebrows. She felt Ludivine's shock like a tiny shove against her spine. *I didn't know of this.*

"No," Rielle said. "We hadn't heard of missing children."

Audric stepped forward. "How many children? Are there efforts under-way to recover them?"

"Yes, but that is not your concern," Vaska replied. "I mention it only to further illustrate the precarious state of this city, which I'm certain our queen and her advisers are taking great pains to disguise from you during your visit. Now, please, come with me. I do not trust the walls of Zheminask."

Vaska walked toward the doors. When they did not follow, she turned back and stared. "Why do you hesitate?"

"This is all rather untoward," Audric replied. "A single Obex representative, coming for us in the middle of the night, urging us to leave with her and go to an undisclosed location."

Vaska nodded once. "I understand. Unfortunately, I cannot disclose our destination." She paused, her mouth thinning. "Jodoc told us of your angel. Surely she can sense my honesty."

Ludivine glanced at Rielle. Her presence was an uncertain tangle, clinging to Rielle's mind like a burr.

"I sense that you are telling the truth, Vaska," Ludivine said slowly.

*But beyond that, her thoughts are clouded to me in a way I dislike.*

Rielle lost what remained of her patience. "She says your thoughts are clouded to her, which she doesn't very much like."

Vaska's smile was thin. "We Obex have learned much over the years about how to shelter our thoughts from angelic intruders." Her eyes passed over Ludivine as they might have over a discolored spot on the floor. "Now, please come. Every moment delayed is another moment closer to the Gate's destruction. And dress warmly. It has begun to snow."

◆

Evyline insisted upon joining them, along with three other members of Rielle's Sun Guard—Jeannette, Ivaine, and Riva. Rielle did not protest. She did not trust Vaska, who led them out of Zheminask through dim passages far below the palace's ground floor.

Ludivine's thoughts felt like those of a confused but determined child, fumbling in the dark.

*There is something amiss here*, she told Rielle.

*Here, in our midst?*

*Here, in this city. And I cannot determine what it is. Something is obstructing me.*

Rielle had an idea of what that might be. She wrestled her thoughts clear and calm. *Perhaps you are merely tired.*

Ludivine fell stubbornly silent. At last, they passed through a narrow door and emerged onto a rough flat of land dusted with snow. They were behind the palace now, and approaching a series of cliffs.

Five elegant stone bridges connected the land on which Zheminask stood to the mountains beyond. Vaska led them across the leftmost one, then up a craggy path that quickly grew steep, scattered with patches of black ice. The higher they climbed, the harder the snow fell, until Rielle could hardly see her own feet. Soon they were trudging through powdery drifts, Rielle's breath coming high and sharp in her chest, her skin slick with sweat beneath her woolen layers.

She stumbled, clumsy in such frigid cold. Audric caught her at once, his arm strong around her waist.

"We're turning around this instant," he told her, having to shout against her ear to be heard, for the hard wind had begun to howl. "This is ludicrous. We'll fall to our deaths."

But Rielle could not allow that. The wailing wind, the swirling snow, and the black night beyond it—these were remnants of her dreams.

"If you fall, I'll catch you," she shouted back to him, dusting snow from his nose with her glove.

Framed by ice-crusted fur, his face creased with concern. He looked up the slope, which seemed to rise forever into blackness.

"Is there something you need to tell me?" he asked her, not looking at her.

Rielle shook her head. "I'm cold. That's all I can think of at the moment."

He smiled, she thought, though she couldn't be sure. Vaska shouted for them to hurry; stopping on the mountain could mean death. They followed her up, and up, and when at last Vaska called out something Rielle could not understand, gesturing ahead of them through the snow, Rielle faltered and stared.

It was the black château from her dreams.

Built to accommodate the mountain's crags and cliffs, tucked between juts of rock, it hugged the slope in long, flat layers, the rooftops square and sharply peaked, as though each level of the building wore a pair of horns.

*What is it?* Ludivine asked. *You're terrified.*

*I'm not. It's nothing.* Rielle fumbled to draw shut the doors of her mind. Her thoughts felt as ungainly and numb as her fingers. *I'm very cold.*

As she followed Vaska up the path, she searched the snow, her heart pounding so hard she felt it in the soles of her feet.

◆◇◆

They were given rooms in a private wing of the Obex temple—dimly lit, the musky, still air sweetened with incense. The hallways were silent, lined with thick carpets that offered some respite from the bitter cold. A few Obex shuffled throughout, quiet in their thick robes and furred slippers. Hoods drawn, heads bowed, they ignored the exhausted newcomers tracking ice and mud across their floors.

The rooms they were assigned were blessedly warm, an enormous fire roaring in the hearth.

Once Ludivine had left them, and her Sun Guard had stationed themselves outside the door, Rielle stripped off her clothes. Shivering, she retreated to the bed, heaped high with furs, and once Audric joined her, they clung to each other, saying nothing until their bodies had warmed.

"This is a strange place," Audric murmured at last. "I don't like it. I fear we should not have come. Once the storm has stopped, we should leave."

"We need the casting," Rielle argued, her head tucked beneath his. "This is how we find it."

Audric said nothing, his fingers absently combing through her hair in the way she so loved.

*What are you hiding from me?* Ludivine's voice came sharply from her room across the hall. *What are you doing, Rielle?*

*Trying to sleep*, Rielle replied. *Leave me alone.*

But she did not sleep. She lay awake until Audric's breathing slowed and then sent out a single, quiet thought: *I'm here. Are you?*

Corien answered at once. *I am. Come find me.*

She slipped out of Audric's arms and dressed, hardly noticing the cold, not entirely sure if she was dreaming.

*Are you watching me?* she asked, tugging on her stiff trousers, her battered boots.

*Always, Rielle.*

She should have been alarmed, enraged.

She was not.

*I wish I weren't wearing these rags,* she admitted, fumbling to fasten her cloak. *They aren't fit to be seen by you.*

His pleasure arched against her like a contented cat. *You want to look beautiful for me.*

Rielle fled down the corridor, past her oblivious Sun Guard, her gloved hands in fists. The temple had darkened, most of the candles burned to stubs.

*I don't know when I'll see you again,* she explained to him. *I want you to...*

She hesitated. Her face burned and tears tightened her throat.

He finished the thought for her. *You want me to remember you at your loveliest. Oh, Rielle.* He laughed, a silky fall of sound. *Your beauty is beyond anything of this world, whether you appear before me in dirty rags or in a gown woven of stars.*

She hesitated, leaning against a wall. She tried to gather her breathing into a steady rhythm.

*You're feeling frightened,* he observed.

*I am feeling many things.* She realized she had heard nothing from Ludivine. *Have you hurt her? If you have, I'll kill you.*

*No. I am hiding you.* His voice curled, delighted. *The little rat thinks you're asleep.*

*Don't call her that. Her name is Ludivine.*

*That is the name she stole from your friend,* he pointed out. *Her true name is—*

*Not yours to tell,* Rielle snapped.

He relented. *Come find me.*

*Where are you?*

*You know exactly.*

Yes, she did. She crossed one of the temple courtyards, climbed over the low stone railing, sank into a shallow white drift. She trudged on through the snow, following the trail left behind by her dreams.

—◆—

She found him, at last, in a clearing hedged by cliffs. A green clearing, quiet and fresh, empty of snow. Birdsong trilled sweetly.

It was a lie of his creation, and he stood waiting in the middle of it.

"Change it," she said, short of breath as she approached him. She could hardly speak—her side cramping, limbs numb with cold, ribs tight and hot around her heart. "I don't want to see your lies. I want to see the truth."

At once, the warm green clearing disappeared from her mind. Instead, Corien stood before a set of sheer cliffs, at a cave mouth piled high with snow.

He lowered his hood, revealing himself to her—his white face, his pale-blue eyes, snowflakes melting in his hair.

She ran for him, forgetting herself, forgetting the cold and her exhausted body and the fact that she wanted to flee from him as utterly as she wanted to touch him.

He opened his arms to her, just as he had in her dreams, and when she stumbled against him, he enveloped her in his cloak. She clutched his coat; it was stiff with cold. Drunk on his nearness, her head spinning and her knees hardly able to hold her up, she reached for his face, hands burning inside her gloves. She ripped them off with her teeth, let out a soft cry of frustration, and then her bare hands were on his cheeks, her thumbs smoothing over the sharp turn of his jaw.

"You're here," she whispered, smiling through her tears, hating herself even as she rejoiced to feel his body pressed against her own. "You're here, and I'm here, and I shouldn't be." She wiped her face, her hand shaking. "God help me."

"God has no place here," Corien murmured, and then lowered his mouth to hers.

She stretched up onto her toes to meet him, hooking her arms roughly about his neck. He opened her mouth with his tongue, lifted her against him, moved swiftly to steady her against the cave wall. The sharp stone dug into her back, lighting it up with pain. Her heartbeat howled in her ears, drowning out the sounds of the storm, and when he wound his fingers in her hair and sharply tugged her head back, exposing her neck to his hot, seeking mouth, Rielle cried out a wordless plea.

He looked up at her, dark hair falling over his eyes, pale eyes glittering. "Shall I stop?"

Stop? Stopping was unthinkable. Stopping was death. But suddenly it occurred to her how he knew that she liked to be kissed this way, with fingers roughly twined in her hair. Her stomach clenched, and she pushed herself away from him.

"Yes," she whispered. "Please stop."

He released her, watching as she stumbled away, collecting herself.

"You've been spying on us," she whispered, looking back at him. "On me and Audric. Haven't you?"

"Only occasionally." His smile was sharp and unhappy. "I enjoy tormenting myself, it seems."

She wanted to slap him, but if she touched him again, she would not be able to stop. "You're disgusting."

"And your conflict is delicious," he replied, unperturbed. "One moment you despise me. The next, you ache for me."

She clutched her cloak tightly around her body. "I forbid you from spying on us again. My time with Audric is ours alone."

"Very well. You have my word. I'll stay away."

"And you'll allow me to sleep?"

"I never kept you from sleeping," he replied smoothly.

"Every time you enter my dreams, sending me images I don't understand, I wake feeling more tired than I did the day before."

He smiled a little. "I'm flattered that my presence is so distracting."

"I have to sleep, Corien." She crossed her arms over her chest. "I don't know what you want of me, but I'm useless to everyone if I can't sleep."

"I understand," he said at last, grave and soft, "but it's the only time I can see you, Rielle. When you're asleep, and your bustling world is quiet at last."

"That is not my concern." She lifted her chin. "Why did you bring me here?"

"Ah, and here she is once more—Lady Rielle, the Sun Queen. All duty and obligation, chained to her beloved prince." He smiled bitterly. "The joy of imagining him finding you in my arms just now will sustain me for weeks."

"How pathetic you are." Her stomach turned over as the reality of the last few frantic moments settled in her mind. How could she have allowed that to happen? She retrieved her gloves from the floor, her mouth souring. She wiped her lips with her back of her hand as if clearing them of poison. "You're not worthy of him."

"Neither are you, my dear," Corien snapped. "And the sooner you accept that, the happier everyone will be."

He stalked away into the cave's shadows. When he returned, he held a battered bronze shield.

"Take it," he muttered, shoving it at her, avoiding her gaze. "Take it and go to him."

Rielle's palms smarted against the shield's rim. Its thrumming power rushed through her blood, clearing her mind. As her thoughts settled, her vision expanded beyond the physical, beyond the cave and the snow and the shield's ancient engravings. Golden shapes emerged in the depths of her mind—a pale woman with white hair, fire cradled in her palms. She stood before a hole in the sky and plunged her blazing shield into a knot of storms.

"Marzana's casting," she whispered. She looked up at Corien, found him watching her. "Why did you give this to me? How did you steal it from the Obex?"

"I stole it because I am powerful, and they are not," he said. "And I'm giving it to you because I'm tired of waiting." He took her chin in his hands. His pale gaze roamed over her face. It was not easy to hold herself back from him. But the thought of Audric, sleeping in the temple, unaware and innocent, burned tears of shame from her eyes.

Corien released her, his mouth twisting. "Giving you the shield is a show of faith and a demonstration of my devotion. I won't force you through trials. I won't bring you before a crowd and urge you to play with your power like some common street performer. These fools in their temple would have tested you for weeks before allowing you to take the casting. A waste of time, and insulting to you." His hands gripped her face, bringing her close to him, but he did not kiss her again. "I see you, Rielle. I *see* you. And I am not afraid. You will never have to pretend with me. Not ever."

Then he released her. A subtle tremor shifted the air. Rielle stumbled, as if jerking out of sleep. She was alone in the cave with Marzana's shield, and Corien was gone.

—◇—

When she returned to the temple, it was nearly dawn.

She entered by way of the same snow-covered courtyard and trudged upstairs, feeling ill in both body and heart. The shield was heavy; her arms ached, and the muscles in her legs burned from plowing through the endless snow.

Evyline, standing at the door to her rooms, gave a soft cry when she saw Rielle. She hurried over, the rest of the astonished Sun Guard at her heels.

"My lady," Evyline said, "what's happened? We thought you were asleep. What..." Evyline's gaze dropped to the shield. She knelt, kissed her fingers, and brought them to her temple. "Is that the casting of Saint Marzana, my lady?"

"It is," Rielle said wearily, moving past her. "I'll explain later, Evyline. I don't want to wake Audric."

But when she closed the door behind her and stepped into her rooms, she saw that Audric was already awake. He sat on the edge of their bed, his shoulders slumped and the expression on his face one of such sadness that Rielle lost her breath.

Beside him stood Ludivine, hands clasped behind her back. She met Rielle's gaze without shame.

"At last," she said, her voice tight and terrible. "We've been waiting up for you."

# ⊹ 24 ⊹

# ELIANA

*"Contained within the pages you are about to read is a theory only those with bold hearts and bolder minds dare to posit: ours is not the only world. In fact, there are many, and between them stretches the eternal Deep. What horrors from those worlds the angels might unleash in pursuit of their revenge we cannot possibly guess. We must be always on our guard. We must never allow ourselves to rest."*

—*Many Worlds: A Radical Study*,
author unknown

Y es, it's me," said Patrik, obviously and smugly amused. "And this is Jessamyn."

He gestured at the red-braided woman beside him, who nodded sharply.

"I have a proposal for you, Eliana," he said. "A choice. When we make port in Meridian, we intend to raid an Empire outpost a few miles from the shore. Primarily, to distract them from our party of refugees, also aboard this ship, whom we're escorting home to a city called Karlaine. Secondarily, because one should never miss an opportunity to kick the shit out of some adatrox."

Beside Eliana, Harkan shifted. "When we met in Vintervok, you told me our payment would be sufficient for passage. You said nothing about who you really are or your Red Crown affiliations."

"That was before I realized with whom you would be traveling," said Patrik.

Eliana's impatience snapped like fire. "What is this *choice*, Patrik? What do you want from me?"

Patrik leaned forward, elbows on his knees. "You can help us accomplish our goals in Meridian, bringing your considerable talents to the aid of the cause. Or you can die."

"That's not much of a choice," Harkan muttered.

Patrik shrugged. "If you don't agree to these terms, we'll dispatch you before we make port and drop your corpses into the sea. Well." He glanced at Harkan. "Perhaps not the boy, if he doesn't do anything stupid. I don't hate him yet."

Eliana smiled thinly. "But you hate me?"

"Yes."

"Because of Crown's Hollow?" Harkan asked.

"Ah," said Patrik. "So you told him."

"Yes, I told him," Eliana said, "and he understood why I did what I did."

"Oh, I understand why you did it, Eliana. I'm saying I don't forgive you for it. But helping me and my colleagues will go a long way toward repairing our relationship."

"And if I don't agree to help you, how exactly do you imagine you'll manage to kill me?"

"Easily, I expect." He glanced at her hands. "You're wearing bandages. I've watched how you handle yourself while working here on the ship. You're in pain. That's a new thing, isn't it?"

Eliana flinched.

"Yes," Patrik said quietly. "A very new thing indeed for the great Dread of Orline. What happened to you, Eliana? What changed?"

Beside her, Harkan tapped on his thigh.

*No. Silence.*

She could have slapped him. As if she would tell Patrik anything of importance.

"Many things have happened," she answered instead. Then a startling thought occurred to her. "Why didn't you come to Dyrefal? Hob was there. Surely you wondered if he was. You knew we were going to Astavar and that Hob had joined us. Why did you stay away?"

Now Patrik was the one to flinch. "Because if I had gone to Dyrefal and seen Hob, I would never have left his side, not again. I would have abandoned Red Crown for him."

"And now Astavar has fallen, no doubt," Eliana said, imagining driving a knife deeper and deeper into Patrik's heart until it could go no farther. "And perhaps Hob with it."

Jessamyn, leaning against the wall, watched Eliana calmly. "What an awful person you are. I understand now how you could have betrayed Crown's Hollow and left them to die."

Eliana pinned her with a glare. "I was trying to save my family. My brother, my mother."

Jessamyn looked curiously about the room. "Yes? And where are they now, this family of yours?"

Harkan stepped forward. "This really isn't necessary—"

"Gone." Eliana forced herself to speak. She hoped her words hurt Harkan as deeply as they hurt her. "They're all gone."

◆

After their meeting with Patrik and Jessamyn, Harkan disappeared somewhere, looking troubled, and Eliana returned to her hammock to brood. At dawn, she was roused from an ill sleep by the hateful clang of the morning bell. She completed her assigned tasks, and in the evening, she retreated to her hammock, shooed away two giggling girls who lay kissing inside it, and proceeded to brood some more. She slipped her hand inside her coat pocket, absently fingering the lines of Zahra's box.

Then she sat straight up, sending the hammock swaying. She clutched the box tightly for a moment, her palm smarting, and then went searching for Patrik.

She found him sharpening his knives near the bow of the main deck. Torches lit the starboard side, where a group of people drank and sang. One staggered up from his seat, went to the railing, dropped his trousers, and pissed overboard. This elicited a round of applause from the onlookers, one of whom promptly retched onto his shoes.

Avoiding them, Eliana joined Patrik silently, watching him work as the sharp sea wind cooled her cheeks. Five minutes passed before he acknowledged her presence.

"Yes?"

"We'll help you get your refugees to Karlaine," she replied.

"Excellent. I suppose I won't kill you, then. At least not tonight."

She bit back a sharp retort, then held out Zahra's box for him to see. "I'm hoping you'll know what this is."

He glanced over. "And if I do?"

"Don't be an ass, Patrik."

"You're in no position to order me around, Dread."

"Please." She inhaled slowly, deciding to take the risk. "My friend is trapped inside it. Her name is Zahra. She's a wraith—an angel who has decided not to take a human body. She's a Red Crown sympathizer and helped me and Navi escape Fidelia." She paused. "You know them, I assume."

Patrik had stopped cleaning his knives. "I had hoped those whispers were only rumors."

"You were foolish to hope for anything good. Fidelia abducted me and Navi from Camille's safe house in Sanctuary. Without Zahra, I'm not sure Simon could have gotten us out. And now she's trapped in here." She blinked back tears, blaming them on the wind. "I can't open it. I don't know if she's dead. I don't know if she *can* die."

She glanced down at her hands, Harkan's too-large gloves concealing her castings. "I don't know anything," she said quietly, and then held her breath, waiting for Patrik to exclaim, in shock and confusion, what she meant when she spoke of angels and wraiths and other such Old World nonsense.

But instead, Patrik was still for a moment, and then rose to his feet. "Come. You'll want to see this."

◆◇◆

In one of the smaller holds of the *Streganna*, guarded by a woman and a man, both armed with rifles, both of whom nodded and moved aside when they saw Patrik approaching, a beast lay chained to the floor.

And it was alive.

Eliana stood at the door's threshold for a full five seconds before she managed to recover herself and step inside. "What is it?"

Patrik closed the door behind them, leaving them in near-darkness. The only light came from the small gas lamp he carried. "The angels call them cruciata."

She looked at him closely, unsure how to determine what, exactly, he knew.

He saw her expression and rolled his eyes. "Do you think you're the only one to know the truth about the Empire? Granted, I try to keep the truth from as many people as possible, as a kindness. And I didn't believe it myself until Simon convinced me when we first met...what, three years ago now? But, yes, I know that the old stories are true and that angels walk among us."

He picked his way across the room, stepping over the beast's slender tail. Its six legs splayed out on either side of its black, scaled body; its long, chapped tongue unfurled from its mouth like a tired flag.

"This one's called a viper," he said. "See how its body is long and thin, like a serpent's? Vulnerable spots are here, under its chin, and here." He pointed. "Where its back legs meet its belly. Besides that, their hides are nearly as tough as stone. Very hard to kill. But I'd rather face one of these any day than a raptor. At least vipers can't fly."

Eliana crouched, slow and wary. She stared at the creature's clouded yellow eye. Its thin pupil shifted slowly, watching her.

"Where did it come from?"

Patrik raised his eyebrow. "Well, that's the wild part. I'll tell you what Simon told me. That's how we met, actually. He saved me from a viper attack. It was a little one, only half the size of this one. But big enough. Most of them are across the ocean on the eastern continent. They came through the Gate. But every now and then, one of them makes it over here. They're clever. Hard to catch. Soon, I imagine, they'll be everywhere."

"They came through the Gate." A shiver tapped merrily down her spine. "They're from the Deep?"

A sad smile softened Patrik's face. "Hob would do a better job of telling the story. He's like your Remy, you know. Fascinated with these stories, with the Old World, with all the legends I'd long thought were nonsense. But it turns out the world is just as outrageous as those stories say it is."

"So I've discovered," Eliana said hollowly, forcing her thoughts thin and slippery so they could not fix on the memory of Remy.

Patrik glanced up at her. "Simon told me that when the angels were in the Deep, they tried to find a way out, and in doing so, they tore a hole between the Deep and the world beyond it."

Eliana nodded. "Zahra mentioned the idea of other worlds to me."

"He had a name for it. I can't remember." Patrik frowned for a moment. Then his face brightened. "Hosterah. That was its name. The world of the cruciata."

"So when the angels came through the Gate…"

"They brought some of these beasts with them," Patrik finished grimly. "Simon told me the angels are doing everything they can to shove them back into the Deep, keep them from flooding through and overrunning our world. But that seems to be a difficult task, even for them."

Eliana rose, backing away from the beast. Its legs and torso were attached to the planked floor with chains so heavy they had dug deep furrows into its flesh, but she still didn't relish the idea of being near it.

"What does any of this have to do with Zahra's box?" she asked.

"See that?" Patrik pointed at the nearest chain. "Cruciata blood."

Eliana inched closer and, squinting, saw that the chain was indeed wet—but not with any blood that she had seen before. Instead of red, it was a deep, rich blue, like the eastern sky at sundown.

"There's a particular weapon you can forge, using cruciata blood," Patrik said. "It's called a blightblade, and it's lethal to angels. Well, not lethal, exactly, but if an angel is stabbed with one, the angel will get sucked up into the blade and will stay there, trapped, leaving the human body they were inhabiting empty and useless."

Eliana thought quickly. "There must be a huge market for this. People who forge blightblades, sell them to rebel factions. Angels, trying to buy them up so they're hard to find."

Patrik nodded. "And they're hard to forge too. Very tricky process, and only a few ingenious fools have managed to perfect the process. One's in Meridian, a nasty old man named Rufian. Woman who caught this one"—he nodded at the viper—"is a friend of mine. And by 'friend' I mean a woman I got marvelously drunk with in Vintervok two days before I met Harkan. She's mad. She hunts these things and sells them to the highest bidder."

"And this?" Eliana withdrew Zahra's box from her pocket. In the dim lamplight, the metal gleamed its strange copper, each plate layered with violet-and-blue waves so deep it looked possible to dive into the metal and sink forever.

"To be honest, I've never seen anything like that structure," Patrik admitted. "A box instead of a blade. But the metal it's made of… Simon had a blightblade once, and I'll never forget the look of the blade. That bizarre copper color, always shifting and iridescent. Like a bird's wing gone liquid." He nodded at the box in her palm. "It looked just like that."

Eliana went very still. "But when I asked Simon about this, he seemed as ignorant as I was. He told me nothing about it. He acted as though he'd never seen such a thing."

"Well, then," Patrik said after a moment. "I don't know why, but Simon lied."

# ⤙ 25 ⤚

# RIELLE

*"I know you're still in Kirvaya, but my head is full of anxious storms, and writing you helps quiet them. Ingrid brought home a dead beast, Audric. That's at least part of what's been slaughtering our soldiers in the east—and yours as well, I suspect. It is a beast unlike any I've ever seen, made of melded parts. Tiger and bear and bird. And even, I think, dragon. I know, it sounds ludicrous, and Ingrid thinks I'm a fool for entertaining the idea. But its hindquarters are scaled. Tough and spiked, lightly furred. Do you think angels could be controlling these creatures? And how were such beasts created in the first place? We have many questions and no answers. Meanwhile, the attacks continue. Every two weeks, one of my outposts is sacked in the night, the bones of its soldiers left scattered, the snow at its gates painted red."*

—A letter written by King Ilmaire Lysleva to Prince Audric Courverie, dated December 27, Year 998 of the Second Age

Faced with Ludivine's quietly furious gaze and Audric's desolate one, Rielle at first could not speak.

She stood awkwardly, rigid, unsure whether it would be best to proceed as if nothing had happened—as though she hadn't in fact recently been kissing Corien, as though her skin wasn't still tingling, awakened by his touch—or if she should instead go on the offensive, though she didn't feel as if she had much ground to stand on, depending on what Audric knew.

She drew a breath and managed only to say, "Oh. Hello."

Audric's gaze fell to the shield in her hands. Already, the heat of the hearth fire was melting the layer of ice and snow encrusting the metal. Water dripped onto the carpet beside Rielle's boots.

"Is that Marzana's shield?" he asked quietly.

"Yes," she answered at once.

"Where did you get it? And how?"

She wanted to look away from him. If she didn't hide her eyes, he would sniff out her deception. But she forced herself to meet his gaze and decided to provide him a version of the truth.

An altered, merciful one.

"Corien spoke to me tonight," she answered. "He told me to come find him, that he would give me Marzana's casting. That the Obex would insist upon testing me for weeks to determine my worth before granting me the shield. That would be a waste of time, he said, and insulting. And I agree with him on that point."

"So you went to him," Audric said. "And he did indeed give you the shield."

"Clearly," she said before she could stop herself.

Audric's dark gaze flicked sharply up to hers. "Don't snap at me, Rielle. I'm not the one at fault here."

"At fault?" She set down the shield, left it leaning against the wall. "How, exactly, am I at fault?"

*What did you tell him, Lu?*

*I told him you'd gone to meet Corien,* Ludivine replied, *and that you were on your way back.*

*Did you tell him that we kissed?*

*No. And I hope you don't. It will only hurt him.*

Rielle swallowed. *Does he suspect?*

*No.* Ludivine's voice softened. *He isn't angry because he thinks you kissed Corien. He's angry because you put yourself in danger.*

"You told me," said Audric, "you *promised* me, that if we were to do this thing, if we were to pursue Corien and uncover his intentions, we would do it together. You promised me no secrets and no lies."

"I didn't lie," Rielle said quietly. "I didn't want to wake you."

He raised his eyebrows. "You don't honestly expect me to believe that."

"Is it so hard to believe that I would have considered your comfort before all else?"

Audric scoffed and rose to his feet. "Rielle, what's the real reason you left me here while you snuck out into the night to meet our enemy on your own?"

She hesitated, unsure which truth to twist, which lies to speak.

*Careful,* said Ludivine.

*Damn you, Lu, don't tell me to be careful. This is your fault. You didn't have to wake him.*

*I did,* Ludivine replied calmly, *if only because maybe doing so will make you think twice next time about giving in to Corien and striking out on your own, just as he asks you to.*

*It was my choice to go to him. I wanted the shield, and he was ready to give it to me.*

*You wanted the shield,* Ludivine agreed, *and you wanted to see him. You wanted to touch him.*

A sharp, tingling heat rose behind Rielle's eyes. *And what if I did?*

"I left you here because I'm ashamed, Audric, and embarrassed," she burst out, so vehemently ignoring Ludivine that her temples ached from the effort. "Do you know how terrible it is, how uncomfortable, to lie there every night beside you while he whispers in my head? How dirty it makes me feel, how unworthy of you?"

Audric's expression softened. "You could never be unworthy of me."

"I could not imagine taking you with me to meet him," she continued.

"He would have said terrible things to you. He might have tried to hurt you. He might have forced himself on me and made you watch. Alone, I can defend myself against him. But with you there, I would have been distracted. He could have used you to get at me. It was unsafe to bring you."

The more she talked, the more easily the lies fell from her lips. She began to convince even herself. Of course she had left Audric behind to protect him. It was the logical thing to have done.

"My duty, as Sun Queen, is to serve and protect my country," she said, moving toward him. "And you are my country. You are its heir, its future king." She touched his face, the slight shadow of his beard. "Yes, it would have embarrassed me for you to have seen how much he wants me, for you to hear the things he would have said to hurt you. But more than that, I could not put you in that sort of danger. Even if I didn't love you, as the Sun Queen, it would have betrayed everything I stand for."

"But didn't it occur to you that it wasn't safe even for you?" Audric said after a moment. "Didn't you wonder why Lu wasn't there to stop you? He kept her in the dark. She didn't even know you were gone until you were on your way back, shield in hand." He shook his head, stepping back from her touch. "I know it is difficult for you to resist him. I know what he offers you."

Rielle stiffened. "Do you?"

"Yes." He glanced at Ludivine. "Freedom. No rules or cloying traditions, no obligations to church or crown. These are things I cannot offer you, though I wish I could." He looked away, his mouth twisting. "I hate that in your mind I am associated with that which binds you."

"Whatever Ludivine thinks she knows," Rielle said icily, "whatever she's been telling you, I am happy to serve my country. I glory in it, in fact. And I'm insulted that either of you would think otherwise."

"Yes, I know you glory in it. That's not the problem."

"What is the problem, then?"

"You have a duty to protect your country, yes, but you are too important to act recklessly. Just because you are powerful doesn't mean you can put yourself in unnecessary danger."

"Unnecessary!" She flung her hand at the shield. "I did what we came here to do, didn't I? I stood up before all those simpering people, and smiled, and performed for them just as they wanted. Just as *you* wanted."

Audric glared at her. "Diplomacy often requires us to humble ourselves."

"Yes, it must have been very difficult for you to stand there and accept congratulations for how prettily I presented myself to the Kirvayan court."

"My God, Rielle," Ludivine said. "Do you really think so little of him? Anyone who approached with congratulations for him instead of you, he promptly and passionately corrected."

Rielle flushed hot-cold. "Well. I still think I had to humble myself in that hall far more than anyone else had to. And now I'm being punished for it."

"You're not being punished," Audric said, "and if you were, it wouldn't be for that. It would be for running off into a blizzard alone."

Rielle bit her tongue. Any reply she could think of reflected poorly on herself, and the exasperated, frustrated look on Audric's face was not one she enjoyed seeing directed at herself. Tears filled her eyes; if she spoke, they would fall.

With a sigh, Audric returned to the bed, roughing his curls with one hand.

For a moment, the room was silent. Then, once she had gathered herself, Rielle said venomously, "Are you happy, Lu, now that you've engineered this lovely little scene?"

"No, I'm not happy," Ludivine replied. "I'm furious with you, and I'm terrified of how easily Corien can slip between us, how he can disguise your movements from me and deceive your guard. If you had any sense in your head, you would be terrified too."

Rielle threw up her hands. "And yet here I stand, neither seduced nor slaughtered. Yes, it's difficult to resist him. Yes, he is relentless. But I, too, am relentless. My will surpasses his own. And the fact that neither of you trust me in this, after everything we've endured together, is outrageous."

*You're treading on dangerously thin ice, Rielle,* said Ludivine. *The image of you throwing yourself into Corien's arms is fresh in my mind, and my willingness to lie for you goes only so far.*

*You mean so far as it suits your whims and needs.* Rielle viciously shoved her reply at Ludivine. *When it becomes useful for Audric to know how his father died, will you tell him, regardless of what happens to me?*

Ludivine's horror was a quiet, wounded hollowness. *You know I would never do that.*

Rielle turned from the feeling, shutting away the part of her mind in which Ludivine lived.

"You wanted me to do this," she said, approaching Audric once more. "You wanted me to be an operative. To allow him to speak to me, to let him move freely in me and talk to him and try to find out information. His intentions, his movements." She knelt before Audric, gathered his hands in her own. "Isn't that right?"

He regarded her thoughtfully. "And did you discover any such information? Do you know more than you did before you left me for him?"

She bristled, rising. "I have the casting," she said shortly. "That's more important than anything right now, for if the Gate falls, all else is pointless. And I didn't leave you for him. I left you here to carry out my duty. A duty *you* placed upon my shoulders. You instructed me to put myself into harm's way, to make myself vulnerable to a creature who is ravenous for me, because it would help Celdaria. And I was only too happy to do it, because I love you, and I love my home. But you can't have it both ways, Audric. Either I am to be the Sun Queen and do whatever is necessary to protect us all, even if that means risking my life—or I am to sit at home, safe and cosseted, under lock and key. Useless and ornamental."

Audric looked up at her in silence, but the weariness in those great, dark eyes of his told her the truth. He was sorry, and he loved her, and he felt as conflicted as she did.

Before he could manage to say anything that would make her feel worse, anything that would remind her of the awful unkindness she had dealt him in that snow-frosted cave, Rielle rose, her throat aching. "I'll take my breakfast downstairs. Lu, keep watch over that damned shield until I return."

Then she turned away from them both and fled for the solace of the temple's strange, perfumed shadows, her guard at her heels and a knot of shame turning slowly, sharply, gleefully in the pit of her gut.

# ~ 26 ~

# ELIANA

*"Meridian was the first land of the western continent to fall to the Empire. Once a lush, verdant country, scattered silver with lakes and brilliant rivers, each constructed by Saint Nerida's own two blessed hands, Meridian is now a wasteland of razed forests and murky waters. More battered than Ventera, more dangerous than the innumerable, nigh unnavigable islands of the occupied Vespers, Meridian is a husk of its former radiant self. Saint Nerida would weep to see it, and her tears of rage would drown the world."*

—*The Sorrow of Saint Nerida*,
as written in the journal of Remy Ferracora,
November 13, Year 1018 of the Third Age

They made port in a small cove off the northwestern coast of Meridian. An abandoned village awaited them, ravaged by long-ago invasion forces and left a ruin of memory. Its skinny, patchwork docks swayed atop the water, as if a few more stubborn gusts of salty wind might send them drifting off to sea.

The crew of the *Streganna* rowed them to shore in dinghies—Eliana, Harkan, Patrik, Jessamyn, the boy Gerren, and twelve other Red Crown soldiers, in addition to thirty-one refugees.

Once everyone in their party had disembarked, Eliana stood on the shore and watched the dinghies leave, until she could no longer pick out their shapes in the black. It was the middle of a moonless night. The *Streganna* sat dark and quiet, nearly invisible, out on the water. If Eliana hadn't known where to look, her eyes would have passed over it entirely.

Patrik came up beside her, adjusting the weapons belt slung around his hips. "Hello there, Eliana. What horrors are you thinking about?"

His cheerful voice nettled her. "If I told you, you might never recover."

"Fair enough. Let them stay in your black heart where they belong."

They stood in silence, insults and barbs circling through Eliana's head until she felt so laden with them that she had to sit down in the damp, gray sand and brace her tender hands against the ground.

"I wish my heart was black," she said after a moment. "I wish it was hard as polished stone. Impenetrable, incapable of shattering."

Patrik joined her. "If you're trying to make me pity you, I must warn you, it's an impossible task."

"I'm not trying to do anything. I'm pitying myself."

"Your friend Harkan is a good man," Patrik said, glancing over his shoulder. "He's helping the orphans find shelter, distributing rations." He clucked his tongue. "If I were a younger man, and if my heart didn't already belong to another, I might just have to declare my adoration for him. Loudly and passionately. Perhaps on bended knee."

"You'd be disappointed," Eliana said quietly. "He favors women. One in particular."

Patrik placed a mocking hand over his heart. "Please don't tell me it's *you*. The world would not be so cruel as to pair such a man with such a monster."

This time, when the memory of Remy manifested in her mind—*No, he had said, backing away from her, you're the monster*—this time, the pain that followed felt dull, blunted.

*Well done, black heart of mine.*

"The world not cruel?" She laughed, a mere breath of sound. "That's a fine joke, Patrik. And here I thought you had no sense of humor."

For a time, they were quiet. Tireless waves lapped against the shore. Eliana listened to the refugees settling in what remained of the dock houses, the rebels taking stock of their weapons and supplies. Harkan laughed, joined by another. Foreign sounds, even illicit, in such a place.

"I want to tell you our plan for tomorrow," Patrik said, all humor gone from his voice. "Not because I trust you, but because I only have one other truly exemplary fighter here with me, and I'll need you ready. The moment I catch a whiff of any trouble, I'll shoot you without hesitation, and I won't miss."

Eliana nodded. "Is it Jessamyn? The other fighter?"

"Indeed. And if I'm dead by the time you decide to betray us, she'll be the one to kill you."

"Can you tell me one more time, please, what will happen if I betray you? I'm still unclear on that point."

Patrik chuckled darkly. "As I said on the *Streganna*, most of the people in our care are from the city of Karlaine. The Empire presence is weak there. It's a city of minimal strategic importance, not located on any major waterways or roadways. But a straight path to the city is blocked by the Nalora River, some ten miles away from Karlaine. There's a small outpost there, on the west side of the river. The land is flat and open. Sentries could see for miles.

"Our goal is twofold: to provide a distraction while the refugees cross the river and flee to Karlaine. And to raid the outpost, freeing as many prisoners as possible. We'll take the survivors to Karlaine, if we're able, and if not, then we'll trust that our refugees have made it to Karlaine and retreat with the survivors to a Red Crown safe house about thirty miles south of here. It's not ideal. I doubt they'll be in any condition to travel, but at least they'll be out of that laboratory."

Eliana turned to face him, suddenly alert. "What sort of laboratory? Fidelia?"

"Our intelligence was patchy, but yes, I believe so. This outpost exists to guard it."

Then a thought occurred to Eliana, and with it came a warm rush of relief that soothed some of the chaos raging in her mind.

"What is it?" Patrik was watching her. "You've thought of something."

"When Navi and I were held by Fidelia, she was experimented upon and tortured. By the time we fled, her body had begun to change. She suffered for weeks."

Patrik closed his eyes. "I am sorry to hear this. A great pity that she was the one to suffer, and not you."

"You are admirably consistent in your hatred."

"Did she die?"

"No. Harkan and I found an antidote."

Patrik sat up, his expression brightening. "Do you have more of this?"

"We do. He packed what was left in his bag before he... Before we left."

"Will you share it with the survivors we liberate? To assuage what I hope is an all-consuming, ever-present guilt?"

"No," she said lightly, "I thought I would toss it all into the river as we pass by."

Patrik laughed a little, scrubbing his face. "I have had very few joys in this life, and even fewer since being separated from my Hob. Your news is one of them, and I thank you for it."

"Have I improved your opinion of me?"

"Ever so marginally."

"Ah. Progress."

They sat quietly, watching the sea. Then Patrik spoke, his voice gentler.

"Were you separated from Remy during the invasion?" he asked. "Or did you leave him behind deliberately?"

A hot clutch of tears seized Eliana's throat. For several seconds she physically could not answer him.

"Harkan took me," she said at last, her voice a shadow of itself. "He wanted to get me away to safety. He drugged me and dragged me out of the city before the Empire could reach the palace. He was well intentioned, and utterly misguided, and I'll never forgive him for it. I don't know what's happened to Remy. I don't know if he survived the invasion."

Patrik sucked in air through his teeth. "I'm sorry to hear that."

She laughed.

"Truly, I am. That was a grave error on Harkan's part."

"It's probably better this way. Remy will live longer, the farther away from me he remains. I'm not safe."

She sensed Patrik glancing at her hands. "What does that mean?"

"It means many things."

He nodded, gazing out over the water. "And Simon? Was he well when last you saw him?"

"When last I saw him," she said, her voice trailing off as she recalled the way he had looked at her that evening in her rooms. How his mouth had blazed a hot trail across her jaw, her neck.

How furious he must have been—and, perhaps, how frightened—when he'd realized she'd gone missing.

*Now that I've known a life with you by my side, I'm not sure I could bear that kind of loneliness again.*

"Yes." She crossed her arms over her middle, against the chill of the sea. "He was well."

◆

They arrived at the Empire outpost after three days of travel. Caebris, it was called, according to Patrik. A series of squat black buildings huddled against the banks of the Nalora River. Surrounding them stood a high stone wall with slender, square towers at each of its corners.

Eliana scanned the outpost. Flat on her belly, hidden by the scrubby grasses of a low ridge, she waited for Patrik's signal. Night had fallen. A western breeze slithered between the thin, dry stalks of grass that clustered across the flat riverlands.

She glanced once to her left. Several yards away, Harkan waited with Jessamyn and two Red Crown fighters—Dasha and Viri. Small bands of refugees hid in tussocks to her right, not half a mile down the riverbank, where a narrow bridge allowed passage across the river.

Looking at the bridge, Eliana tensed. It was a wide river; the bridge seemed to stretch for miles. Thirty-foot watchtowers stood at each bank. Patrik hoped the havoc they would wreak, once inside the walls, would urge any sentries from their posts, leaving the bridge clear for refugees to flee across. The boy Gerren, who was not made for close combat but was a prodigious marksman, waited near the closer watchtower with his rifle, ready to pick off adatrox from the ground.

A shift of light caught Eliana's eye, drawing her attention back to the outpost. The main doors were opening, admitting a thin wash of torchlight from within. Dark figures moved through the light—some entering, some exiting. Horses being moved, supplies carried and dragged. A shift change.

From a few paces ahead of her, hidden in the grass, came the low call of a quail, followed by a second.

Patrik's signal.

Eliana pushed herself to her feet and ran down the slight hill toward the river. She glanced to her left only once and saw the other attack parties echoing her progress, in groups of two or three. Rebels mostly, but also a few of the refugees who were strong enough to fight and itching for the chance.

Harkan was in the group nearest her, running swiftly through the tall grass—revolver in hand, sword swinging at his side.

She sent a silent prayer into the night to the deceitful saints she had glimpsed in Zahra's vision: *Keep us safe. Help us run swiftly. Light our path.*

Her castings jolted, sharp and hot, startling her.

Immediately, the outpost exploded—a series of detonations along the front wall. Four total, blasting great holes through the wall and the out-buildings. Debris and adatrox alike went flying. An alarm bell clanged from one of the high watchtowers. Shouts and cries of pain rang out from the ruins.

Eliana stopped running, breathless.

Patrik's plan had only called for a single explosion, one of their precious remaining bombardiers thrown at the open doors. The chaos would allow them to fight their way inside, at which point they would detonate two more bombardiers and release a barrage of smokers. Patrik and Harkan and a few of the others would remain outside the laboratory, fighting off adatrox and creating as much confusion as possible with what remained of their ammunition. Eliana, Jessamyn, and their party of four others would enter the Fidelia laboratory. The others would gather as many survivors as possible and help them out of the compound by way of a small auxiliary door that Patrik's scout, Ursula, had discovered during one of her patrols.

And Eliana and Jessamyn? They would slaughter anyone who got in their way, allowing the laboratory prisoners time to get to freedom.

That was the plan. But those explosions did not belong to a bombardier.

They belonged to Eliana.

She felt their echo, tingling in throbbing patches along the underside of her arms.

Her heart pounding, she turned her hands over and back again, examining her palms, then her knuckles, her wrists. It was happening again—her castings, pulling at the empirium unpredictably, just as they had done in her rooms, with those rows of snapping fire, and in the Nest, flames devouring the market like disease.

Zahra's box, stuffed in her coat pocket, began to hum as if the explosions had awoken it.

Eliana clamped a hand over her pocket, wildly hoping that the box would shatter—but it remained intact, and its humming ceased abruptly. She squeezed her eyes shut, trying to calm her racing heart. She should have made her castings larger, stronger. More chains, more metal, entire plates of it, her hands weighed down by layers upon layers, enough to stifle any instincts her traitorous body possessed.

Perhaps then her castings would function as they were supposed to, wrangle her confusion into order, subdue her fear, channel the power she could not seem to control.

"El!" Harkan roared from somewhere in the smoke. "Come on!"

His voice jolted her. She ran.

At the entrance to the outpost, smoke-riddled and scattered with tiny fresh flames, swords rang and shots fired. Eliana pounced on an adatrox guard, Arabeth in one hand and Nox in the other. He swiped at her clumsily with his sword; she ducked, spun, gutted him, and ran on. Another was locked in combat with Viri, a few feet away. Eliana ran for them and plunged Arabeth into the adatrox's back just as he reached for his gun.

"Thank you!" Viri said, panting. A flash of white, a smile in the smoke, and then he was gone.

Eliana ran on toward the heart of the compound. Bombardiers exploded around her; she tried not to count the explosions, tried not to think about their dwindling ammunition supply. Her hands blazed around the hilts of her daggers. She tried to ignore that as well. It meant nothing. It was her burns, still tender, never allowed the chance to heal. It was the heat of the burning outpost around her. There was no danger; her castings wouldn't once again summon unquenchable fire that would devour them all, as it had in Annerkilak.

She found the laboratory at the same time Jessamyn did. They tried the door—heavy and wooden, reinforced with metal bars—but it was, of course, locked. Jessamyn cursed and swiped a hand across her smoke-stained face. The four others in their laboratory team joined them, their sweat-slicked skin caked with dust, but their eyes blazing.

"Stand back," Jessamyn ordered them all. Eliana complied, ushering the others back and noting with an automatic appreciation that came from years of living as the Dread how elegantly Jessamyn moved through a battlefield, how easily she existed in her own body. Eliana hurried the others to shelter behind a neatly stacked pile of bodies, their discolored, chapped skin marred with familiar sores.

Jessamyn joined them, unflinching, though she tossed a horrible glare at the bodies. "This is bullshit," she declared, and then she withdrew a bombardier from her pocket, kissed it, and glanced at Eliana. "Last one."

She tossed it at the laboratory's stone wall. Seconds later, it exploded, the structure giving way with a groan. The entire front wall wavered and collapsed.

Eliana ran for it, Jessamyn beside her and the rest of their team just behind. Inside the laboratory, they met a squadron of four adatrox, the brutes coughing and bewildered, struggling stupidly through the rubble. Eliana dispatched two, gladly falling back into the rhythm of her former life—Arabeth to the gut, Nox to the throat. She whirled, saw Jessamyn yank her own dagger from another guard's belly and then spin to meet the other. She knocked his arm with her elbow right before he fired his gun. The shot went wide and harmless down the corridor. Jessamyn wrenched his arm, breaking it with a horrible snap. He cried out, those dead gray eyes flickering, and then she drew her blade across his throat and watched him drop.

One of the refugees in their party, a solid, kind-eyed woman named Catilla, who was adept with a sword, turned away and promptly got sick on the floor. Another refugee, Jaraq, crouched beside the bodies, swiftly searching their uniforms for keys.

Jessamyn's blazing eyes met Eliana's. She jerked her head at the corridor beyond. "Shall we?"

As the only one to have been inside a Fidelia laboratory, Eliana had drawn a map of the Rinthos facility for the team leaders to examine. If this building was anything like that one, she knew exactly where the prisoners would be kept. If it wasn't, they would improvise.

Jaraq cried out in triumph. "Here!" He tossed a ring of keys at Eliana.

She caught it, nodded once at Jessamyn, then turned and hurried down the corridor. Galvanized lights flickered overhead, their casings shattered. From outside came the distant sounds of battle, fading as Eliana ran deeper into the laboratory, her team close behind her. Rasping, inhuman cries filled the air, sounds that the black animal deeps of Eliana's gut recognized with a horrible lurch.

They reached the first of several metal doors, the number forty-seven painted tidily on a rectangular plate at eye level.

Eliana bent, fumbling with the keys. Her bandaged hands felt suddenly clumsy, and the screams of those trapped in this building wrapped her in a gummy fog that slowed everything except her racing heart. She thought of Navi, couldn't help but think of Navi and wonder if she was dead. If after everything they had done to save her, she had died anyway at the hands of the Empire.

"Let me," Jessamyn snapped, snatching the keys.

Once they were inside, flickering light from the corridor poured into the black room, illuminating a woman in a stained tunic and trousers, barefoot, huddling in the far corner in a pile of her own waste. Her pale skin was cut upon, bruised. Bulbous sores marked her temple, her throat, her left arm. Dark tendrils capped her shaved head, framed her cheeks and brow.

Eliana's heart sank. This woman's transformation had already begun, which meant she would be volatile.

Jessamyn strode forward. "Can you walk?"

The woman's eyes flicked to each in their party. She nodded, bestial in her nervousness. Her hands twitched atop her knees.

Jessamyn grabbed her arm, hauled her to her feet. "Catilla, help her if she needs it."

Catilla hurried forward, guiding the woman out of the room. "I'll have to fight, if we're attacked," Eliana heard her explain. "But don't be afraid. Just stay back, keep yourself safe, and when the fighting's done, keep running. We'll get you out of here."

They hurried from room to room, gathering prisoners where they could and leaving the dead where they lay. Some rooms they left untouched, for at the sound of the keys, the prisoners inside launched themselves at the doors, roaring and howling.

With each abandoned room, Eliana felt a scream building inside her—a scream not of rage but of exhaustion. It was too much, this fight. Too immense, too incalculable. Once, she would have been angry to be in this place, to see its carnage. Now, she proceeded numbly through it, half listening to the whimpers of the seven prisoners they had collected, killing any guards who intercepted them with a numb efficiency.

At the final door—1, read the metal plate—they heard nothing, no roars, no cries of pain. Eliana glanced back at the others. The second prisoner they had freed—an older woman, gray-haired and brown-skinned, leaned heavily against Jaraq. Another stood, clear-eyed and square-jawed, with another, half-conscious prisoner in her arms.

The first prisoner hovered wide-eyed just behind Catilla, clutching her arm.

Jessamyn unlocked the final door and pushed it open. Immediately, a shot rang out. She cursed, barely yanking the door closed in time. The bullet ricocheted off metal. More shots rang out, frantic and unthinking, one right after another, until silence fell once more.

Eliana glanced at Jessamyn. "Leave it."

"They're out of bullets," Jessamyn replied.

"Unless they have another gun."

"We should go," the square-jawed prisoner suggested. "Before others come."

"Please," whimpered the first prisoner, her face pressed against Catilla's sleeve. "Please, go."

Jessamyn hissed a curse and pushed open the door, her revolver aimed to kill. Eliana followed, daggers at the ready.

But neither weapon was necessary. In the far corner of the room, huddled around a bleary-eyed prisoner, were two men. Healthy and fair-skinned, pressed tunics reaching their knees, high collars buttoned primly at their throats. One lowered his revolver to the floor, then raised his trembling hands into the air.

"We are physicians," he said, his voice thin. "We are not soldiers. Please, have mercy."

"Physicians?" Jessamyn spat out. "You mean you're the ones who have been torturing these women."

The man's face crumpled, tears spilling down his cheeks. "No, please, it's not like that!"

"It's exactly like that," the square-jawed prisoner said over Eliana's shoulder.

The other physician, however, did not raise his hands and did not beg. Instead, he fixed Eliana with an icy, scornful glare.

"'We are the ones he calls at night,'" he muttered. "'We are the vessels of his might.'"

Eliana's castings lit up like fire, sending hot spikes of urgency up and down her limbs.

Jessamyn cursed, stepping away from her. "What's that? What are you doing?"

"What's he saying?" Catilla asked, her voice tense.

"'We speak the word that he has prayed,'" he continued, and then his eyes shifted. Their color quavered and paled. "'Upon his wings, our souls remade.'"

Eliana felt what was about to happen before it did, but she couldn't move away. A presence, charged and furious, burst from the mind of the physician on the floor and scrambled, seeking, for Eliana's own. It seized her, held her still in that fetid, dark room. The world shifted, rearranging itself.

She stood once more in the red-carpeted corridor from her dreams. She had not seen it since that long-ago night in Astavar when Navi attacked her. But now, seeing it again, the eternal space felt as familiar as it had then felt foreign. Galvanized lights buzzed along the gleaming, polished walls. Endless rows of doors arched to sharp peaks.

One, at the farthest visible end of the corridor, flew open, admitting a beam of light so bright and white that it terrified her. An instant of that, and the door slammed shut.

Then the next followed, and the next, and the next, each door closer to the spot where she stood—flanked by her reflections in the polished wood, red bubbling hot between her toes. When each door opened, a bright light emerged, accompanied by a sound—faint at first, an unintelligible susurration at the edge of her mind. The doors opened at a faster and faster rate. The cutting white lights they emitted sliced the red hallway into slabs of meat. The hissing sounds became whispers and formed a word.

*Eliana.*

She turned, wrenching her feet from the carpet. She ran, but the doors followed, the lights sizzling at her heels.

*Eliana.*

Far ahead of her, on the right, a door stood open, admitting no light. She ran for it, desperate for the shield of darkness, and tumbled inside. She slammed the door closed, pressed herself against it, turned the latch with shaking hands.

She stood, breathing hard, cheek hot against the cool wood.

Then a hand touched her neck, and another, her wrist.

A voice kissed her temple, ecstatic and familiar. "There you are."

The Emperor.

*Corien.*

Her mother's long-ago lover. Leader of the angels, the immortal destroyer.

He wound his fingers through her hair, tighter and tighter, until her scalp smarted and tears sprang to her eyes. "Eliana, Eliana. A lovely name. Lilting and sweet. I wonder what she would have named you. I wonder if she's watching us, even now." He pulled her back to his body, shapeless in the dark. "Rielle," he howled, voice cracking. "Can you see this? You died for nothing!"

Eliana kicked and clawed at him, groped wildly for the door. She could hardly breathe; she was made of terror and nothing else, no blood, no lungs.

"I have her now," Corien announced, breathless, shrill. "I *have* her, Rielle, and you can do nothing to save her!"

A shot rang out, and then another.

Eliana blinked and was released.

She fell to the floor, gasping. The impact jarred her knees. Her breaths tore ragged paths out of her throat. Her cheeks were hot and wet.

Jessamyn helped her rise. Behind her stood the others, wide-eyed. The first prisoner hid her face in Catilla's arms, her cries pathetic and howling.

"I killed him," Jessamyn said, gesturing at the two dead physicians behind her. "I killed them both."

"The Emperor? Oh, God. Did you? Did you kill him?" Eliana sagged against Jessamyn, laughing through her tears. "Then I don't have to. It's done. It's finished. Isn't it finished?"

"No, Eliana." Jessamyn frowned at her, clear-eyed and steady. "Not the Emperor. Nothing's finished. We have to run."

*Nothing's finished.* Never had two words filled Eliana with more despair.

Shouts from down the corridor made the others turn. The prisoners cried out; one of them burst into tears.

"Can you fight?" Jessamyn snapped, shaking Eliana a little. "Or will I have to do this by myself?"

The cruelty in Jessamyn's voice, the uncaring viciousness, tugged Eliana back to her body. Simon would have done the same. He would not have shown her a moment of compassion, not until the mission was complete.

She nodded, retrieving Arabeth and Nox from the floor. "I can fight. I *will* fight."

Then she pushed past Jessamyn and the staring, huddled prisoners and led the way back into battle.

# ⤙ 27 ⤚

# LUDIVINE

*"Without fire or metal or raging waves,*
*Without shadows that mask or light that saves,*
*Without earth that shatters or wind that flies,*
*Still we burn, and still we rise."*

—The Revolution's Prayer, attributed to Ziva Vitavna,
considered the architect of the human revolution in Kirvaya

Something was wrong in the city of Genzhar, but Ludivine couldn't determine what it was.

All she had been able to deduce was that something was happening in the far north, in the frozen mountain range called the Villmark, where few people lived, and the autumn nights were long and dark.

She knew there were missing children in the Kirvayan capital—elemental children, all of them—and that several people in the palace had allowed them to be abducted. Magisters. Royal advisers. Influential courtiers.

Last of all, she knew that angels were involved. She could sense their faint mental footprints, the dust of them like ash darkening her breath.

Beyond that, she knew nothing.

The scar from the blightblade was affecting her strength, her mind's ability to focus. But this blindness went deeper than that. A veil had been drawn across her angelic sight, specifically engineered to muddy her connection to Rielle, to obstruct her view of the minds living in the capital, and Ludivine knew of only one being strong enough to fashion a barrier so thorough, so unmovable.

For the first time in years, she tried to speak to him herself.

In the dark of her room in the Obex temple, eyes closed, Ludivine steeled her resolve. She breathed in slowly through her nose and out through her mouth, ignoring the faint throb of her scarred arm, then opened her eyes.

*I'm here, Corien. I'm willing to talk.*

Silence answered her. She tried again.

*What of the missing children? What have you done with them? Where have you taken them?*

A thin curl of amusement coiled against her mind. She read the language of it at once, how droll and stupid he found it that she would ask him outright things she knew he wouldn't answer.

He didn't speak to her directly—she hadn't imagined that he would—but she could nevertheless feel his disgust, the force of his hatred so immense that it pushed her from her bed to the floor, to her hands and knees. She trembled on the carpet, fighting with all her stolen human strength to keep her body upright, fighting with her angelic strength to keep Corien from carving open her mind and killing her.

Then he did speak, every word viciously articulated: *At least I show Rielle what I really am, and what I really want. I don't lie to her. Can you say the same?*

After a moment that stretched on, relentless, until she had nearly blacked out, he disappeared.

And Ludivine collapsed onto the rug, tears rolling down her cheeks, because the relief of his absence was absolute, as euphoric as the moment she had escaped the Deep in his wake—and because he wasn't entirely wrong.

She was a creature of lies, just as he was—and too much of a coward to admit it.

But she refused to waste the moment by thinking about the right or wrong of her actions. Instead, she savored the sensation of her aching chest, her tightened throat, the hot tears on her face, the taste of their salt on her lips.

She remembered—before the Deep, when she had still existed in her own, true body—how crying had often felt like a release. She remembered the pleasure of taking lovers, the satisfaction of food in her belly, the warm wash of sunlight upon her skin.

And now, how pale it all was. The unnatural crime of what she had done kept her from experiencing true sensation. From the moment she had taken this body—slipping inside it as Ludivine's last breath had glided out—she had known she would never be happy inside it. Existing in a human body was a shadow of a life compared to what she had experienced before the Deep. The empirium had punished her for it, had punished Corien for it, and would continue punishing them for it as long as they were alive. They had lost their bodies in the Deep, and trying to remake them by taking others that did not belong to them was a misalignment, an evil beyond any measurable crime.

But where Corien would tear apart the world to seek revenge for this loss, Ludivine only wanted one thing—a simple thing, a small thing. She cared nothing for the wings she had lost, the centuries spent rotting in a void, even the fate of her kind.

After all, they were the ones who had done this. They had started the great ancient war, and that war had condemned them to the Deep.

But Ludivine was hardly more than a child, and had been even younger when the Gate was sealed shut. This war had never been hers to wage.

Her tears slowed, leaving her with a lump lodged between her collarbones. Her body felt hollow, stretched thin. She climbed to her feet, wiping her face, and dressed in her gown, her furs, her thick boots. She left the Obex temple for the long, snowy path that would take her to the city.

If she couldn't find out what Corien was planning on her own, she would need a soldier to help her.

Luckily, in the palace just down the mountain, lived someone perfectly suited for the task.

Hours later, in the deep of night, Ludivine entered the luxurious royal apartments of the girl queen Obritsa Nevemskaya.

She watched the child lying in her bed—sleepless, frowning, her posture impeccable and poised even as she lay in her bed.

Ignorant to the angel who had just entered her room.

Ludivine settled in a chair, not yet ready to reveal herself, and brushed against the girl's troubled mind. She had already seen the important things: Obritsa was hardly the silly, coquettish girl she had appeared to be upon their arrival. She was an operative for the human revolution stirring throughout Kirvaya, fighting to unseat the tyrannical elementals who had for so long ruled the country and kept humans enslaved. She had been raised by the leader of said revolution, could make a quick, clean kill with any number of objects. She had been chosen as the queen by the Magisterial Council, who had in turn been convinced to appoint her by one of their own—Akim Yeravet, Grand Magister of the House of Light, himself an ally of the revolution, if only because he saw their victory as inevitable.

All of that would have been an interesting enough story—a human girl, child of radicals, perfectly positioned to facilitate an uprising.

But then there was the delicious little detail that Obritsa was not, in fact, human.

She was a marque.

Ludivine watched as Obritsa rose from her bed and curled up on a chair of scarlet brocade by the fire. She glared at the flames, her thin little mouth pursed with anger. Ludivine caught a glimpse of the terrible red dreams the girl had suffered for the past few nights since she had begun wandering the city, determined to solve the mystery of the capital's missing children for herself. Such violent dreams—red with anger, red with blood. Dreams Obritsa did not understand.

But Ludivine did.

With a delicate shift of thought, she made herself known.

Obritsa straightened, eyes widening. She reached for her ankle, seeking the knife she usually kept in her boot. But she had forgotten her feet were bare, and when she realized this, anger swept through her, so clear and precise that Ludivine could taste it on her tongue. Anger had a particular flavor to it—meaty, acrid, slightly charred.

Then, at last, Obritsa caught sight of her.

"Lady Ludivine?" The girl blinked, blinked again, and then shrank back in her chair, summoning forth a nervous, shy smile. She clutched her dressing gown closed at her throat.

Amused, Ludivine watched her transform.

"Sweet saints," Obritsa murmured, laughing a little, "you're not supposed to be here. I'm hardly dressed, and it's the middle of the night! However did you get past my guards? This is decidedly odd. Wait a moment." She hesitated, exchanging her smile for an anxious frown. "Has something happened to Lady Rielle or Prince Audric? Are you ill? Oh, please tell me, Lady Ludivine. I really cannot bear your silence."

"You're a wonderful liar," Ludivine observed. "You've convinced Rielle and Audric—particularly Audric, because he trusts easily—but you never had me convinced, not for a second."

Ludivine felt Obritsa's quick mind scrambling. The girl fashioned a light trill of laughter. "You're acting rather strangely, Lady Ludivine. I don't know what to make of what you're saying."

"I know you're a marque. If you don't cooperate with me, I'll tell everyone what you really are, and I won't lift a finger to help you when they come for your head."

Obritsa froze, calculations turning in her eyes.

Then her expression hardened. Ludivine smiled. This shrewd, sharp-eyed little wolf was the real Obritsa Nevemskaya.

"How did you find out?" she asked, her voice flat and deadly.

"My family's spies are better than yours," Ludivine replied, "and yours are sloppy."

At the mention of House Sauvillier, Obritsa set her jaw.

"What do you want, then?"

Ludivine's mind stumbled, and without warning, her thoughts, still agitated from Corien's abuse, grew black with despair.

*What did she want?*

What she wanted was to feel something again, to fit inside a body again, to look at Rielle and Audric and not feel those terrible flutterings of fear in their minds—fear of her kind, and of her in particular, no matter how much they claimed to love her, and *did* love her.

The truth was that she wasn't like them, that she had lied to them, that she was an intruder living in the corpse of their beloved childhood friend. That was a reality that could not be undone, but if she could be remade, if she was reborn—not as an angel, but as a creature like them, as *human*—then perhaps their fear would diminish over time.

And she herself would taste again, and see again, and *feel* again—not simply the gray imitation of sense and color that currently defined her existence.

*Existence.* She swallowed against a bitter turn of breath. A kind word for what she endured every day. She fought the urge to touch her scar.

"This city is rotten with dark workings," she said to Obritsa, fighting to regain control of her unsettled mind. "The missing children, the murders. I've tried to investigate what it means and have reached many dead ends. All I've managed to uncover is that three members of your Magisterial Council are involved in the abductions, and that the children are being taken to somewhere in the Villmark, in the region known as Shirshaya."

Obritsa raised a cool eyebrow. "Oh, yes? And which magisters are these?"

"Magisters Yeravet, Kravnak, and Vorlukh."

Obritsa shook her head, her mind struggling to make sense of these revelations. She rose from her chair, arms crossed, and made her way slowly toward her desk, which sat against the southern wall of windows.

"These are incredible accusations," she said. "Why should I believe any of them?"

"Because they are true," Ludivine replied. "And because I know many things I shouldn't. I know you are a tool of the revolution, raised by Sasha

Rhyzov in the lower districts of the city of Yarozma. I know they cut the wings out of your back and regrew your skin. I know they want you to abduct Rielle and use her as a weapon of your revolution, which I find hysterical, since Rielle could flatten this city with a flick of her wrist, if she wanted to."

Obritsa listened, her back to Ludivine, and pressed a tiny brass button on the underside of her desk.

Ludivine nearly rolled her eyes. If she had been a human, perhaps she wouldn't have noticed the movement, and Obritsa would have gotten away with the deception. But Ludivine could feel the girl's mind working ten steps ahead, planning her attack. The button had triggered a channel of active earthshaker magic, and soon Obritsa's devoted guard, Artem, a disguised revolutionary himself, would burst into the room, ready to kill whoever had threatened his charge.

Ludivine reclined in her chair, awaiting his arrival.

"What a fascinating tableau you've painted, Lady Ludivine." Obritsa leaned back against her desk. "Please, do go on."

"I know what you saw the other night in the courtyard of that school," Ludivine continued. "You saw a child kill his teacher and then climb inside a carriage that bore him away into the night. You tried to follow, but couldn't. Shadows confused your vision and blocked your passage, making it seem as though the carriage was traveling much more swiftly than it should have been able to. You thought perhaps this was shadow-caster magic. It wasn't. It was the work of angels, fogging your mind, misaligning your senses."

Ludivine paused, watching Obritsa's face. The girl's control was magnificent; she gave nothing away, though her mind was roaring as Ludivine's words helped her recover memory after horrible memory.

"I know Grand Magister Yeravet grabbed you, drugged you with widow's tears, and returned you to your rooms," Ludivine went on. "You woke up remembering nothing but echoes. The Grand Magister told your guard that he had found you drunk on the street, that you had been sneaking out to taverns. I know you've been enduring terrible nightmares. They are the product of your mind screaming at you to remember the events of that night."

At last, Obritsa's control cracked. She clutched her stomach, her eyes glittering.

She managed one word. "How?"

Then the door to her rooms flew open. The air crackled with dirt-smelling, wood-smelling earthshaker magic. Obritsa's guard, Artem, raised his staff, his eyes blazing. He was an earthshaker, an elemental who sympathized with the revolution and had been recruited by its leaders to guard and protect Obritsa. His devotion to his duty, to Obritsa herself, was pure and clean as fire.

Ludivine sighed, suddenly weary.

*Calm yourself*, she told him, and watched as he froze, all the aggression draining from his body.

*Walk toward the terrace*, she continued, *and proceed outside.*

He lowered his staff to the floor and obeyed. When he opened the terrace doors, a blast of snow and freezing wind gusted a stack of papers off Obritsa's desk.

*Climb over the railing*, Ludivine instructed tiredly, appreciating the usefulness of her angelic blood even as she despised its brutality. *Throw yourself over it.*

Artem walked across the terrace and began to climb over the railing.

"Stop!" Obritsa cried, rushing forward, and Ludivine felt the love rise swiftly inside the girl's body, ferocious and desperate.

"Leave him," ordered Ludivine. "One more step, and I'll tell him to keep going."

Obritsa shivered in the cold, looking childlike at last. "What are you?"

"I'm an angel," Ludivine said, "and I believe others of my kind are building something in the far north, in the Villmark. I need you to go see what it is and report back to me."

So many questions arose in Obritsa's mind that Ludivine felt weighed down by them.

At last the girl managed to speak. "Why can't you do that?"

"I can't leave Rielle. I can't endanger myself and therefore risk her safety. And because whenever I try to look north, something stops me. An obstruction. A taunt. I believe angels are involved in this, and if I try to get too close to them, they'll sense me and stop me. They'll be on the lookout for me. But not for you, if you move quickly and carefully."

Ludivine rose because she could no longer sit still. Giving voice to these things left her feeling frayed, restless, and every moment she spent away from Rielle was a torment she could hardly endure.

"I know this is overwhelming," she told Obritsa. "I also know you are more than capable of not only understanding what I'm saying, but also carrying out this task I'm giving you."

Obritsa glanced over her shoulder to see Artem standing near the railing, motionless.

"Why should I do anything to help you?" she asked.

"Because one of your own magisters drugged you in order to keep his secret," Ludivine replied. "He, and the others, are allowing children to be abducted and taken for reasons they don't understand. All they know is that they have been promised power. They have no loyalty to you, to their kingdom, to the people they serve. They are loyal only to their own desires. You may very well be safer in the Villmark than you are in your own palace."

"You can't possibly be engineering this simply to protect me," Obritsa said scathingly. "Or are angels as stupid as you are cruel?"

Ludivine smiled, glad to hear the girl's fire. She would need it.

"Of course it isn't the only reason, or even the primary one. If you die after helping me, it will cause me no grief. I'm asking you because I can't do it myself, and because your marque power will carry you faster than I could travel. And because whatever's happening in the north could and will affect all of us, if it is allowed to continue."

She hesitated, then decided Obritsa deserved to know. "The Gate is falling, Obritsa. There are many angels in the world, and more will come, if Rielle cannot repair it. They are hiding something in the north, and I need you to find out what that is. Not for my sake, nor for Rielle's, and certainly not for the horrible man who raised you or for his revolution. But for the world. For the entirety of your race."

Ludivine felt Obritsa trying to wrap her mind around these words. "And if I refuse to help you?"

"Then I will slip into your mind as well as Artem's," Ludivine replied, "and send you both plummeting over that railing. I will forge a note, a confessional, in which you betray all your revolutionary friends. And I will smooth over any ripples of doubt, until everyone is convinced of your cowardice."

After a moment, during which Ludivine could feel Obritsa's fury swelling quietly—like Rielle's tidal wave, an immense force barely restrained—Obritsa nodded briskly. "I will help you," she said, "because you have forced me into it. Every day I will resent and hate you for it. Every day I will pray that you do not die, but instead are forced to live forever in misery for what you've done."

*Forever in misery.* Ludivine nearly burst out laughing. If only the girl knew. "I don't blame you. And for my part, I will pray that you come to see the cruelty of those who have raised you and are able to break free of their chains. You deserve better than they have given you."

She glanced at the terrace. *Come inside.*

Artem obeyed, shivering, his shaggy brown hair white with snow. He sank onto the carpet, bracing his body on hands and knees.

Obritsa ran to him, pulled off her dressing gown, and threw it around his body.

"Artem, Artem, my dear." She cupped her guard's square-jawed face, wrapped her arms around his shoulders. "You're here. You're safe."

Then, without warning, violence exploded through Ludivine's mind, accompanied by a furious succession of images—pines weighed down by piles of snow, a half-buried village. Tossed flames. Burning flesh.

"He's here," she whispered, no longer entirely in Obritsa's apartments. Part of her was in the mountains, her mind racing to find the source of these terrible images. "He's *there*. He's hurting them. Oh, God."

"Who?" Obritsa stood. "Tell me at once."

"His name is Corien. The most powerful of my kind." Ludivine searched the far reaches of her thoughts and saw the truth. "He is in the mountains, at a small village. Polestal. He is forcing the elementals there to hurt each other. They are burning."

And suddenly she understood what was happening. It was a trap; it was bait. He had grown impatient, so he would try every method he could think of until Rielle relented.

But she wouldn't relent. Ludivine wouldn't allow her to, even if she had to sit stubbornly in Rielle's mind for the rest of her life, controlling her every movement. A sentinel doomed to endless duty.

"You must take me to Polestal now," Ludivine ordered, clutching her aching arm. The blightblade scar was throbbing as if freshly made.

Obritsa's eyes narrowed. "Why?"

"Because he is doing this to force Rielle's hand," she replied, fighting the slow spread of her terror, "and if he succeeds, we're all dead."

# ~ 28 ~

# ELIANA

*"I have heard tell of beasts that run wild in the night. Horrors from children's stories, thrust suddenly into the waking world. It does not surprise me, that now we must add monsters to the list of terrors wreaking havoc upon our world. I'm convinced we did something terrible, long ago, something ancient and unforgivable, and that these interminable years of war are punishment for it."*

—Collection of stories written by refugees in occupied
Ventera, curated by Hob Cavaserra

In the city of Karlaine, Eliana could not sleep.

She lay on the hard, cold ground, under a pale dawn sky slashed with black pines. They had made camp in a small cluster of vacant buildings on the outskirts of Karlaine, slipping into the city in small groups of two or three, so as not to attract undue attention. The atmosphere in Karlaine was already tense and watchful. The smoke from Caebris stained the horizon, and the explosions had surely been audible to those living in the city.

Eliana closed her eyes. Once, she had been good at sleeping, no matter the time of day or her state of mind. Those days were long gone, and as she lay there, her spine wedged against a tree root, legs and arms tightly crossed, her mind filled with the sounds of battle.

Explosions, possibly of her own making.

Wood shattering, watchtowers collapsing with a groan.

The crackle of flames, the clash of swords, the snick of a blade catching against flesh, the cries of bullets hitting bodies and bodies falling to the ground.

The opening and shutting of doors down an endless hallway—faster, harder, closer. Relentless.

Corien's voice in the dark: *There you are.*

And Jessamyn, watching her curiously: *Nothing's finished.*

Eliana turned onto her side, tucking her thrumming hands close against her chest. Her castings had not quieted since the raid of Caebris, and she still couldn't be sure if they had caused those initial explosions, or if Patrik had abruptly decided to use more bombardiers than just the one, or if, perhaps, Eliana had been imagining the number of explosions she had counted. If she could trust her own mind.

She clenched her fists, ignoring the pain of her healing burns, and closed her eyes. It was an odd, unsettling feeling, to love and hate a thing so passionately and in such equal measure. These castings she had made with her own hands.

These weapons she did not trust, imprisoning her.

She tried to remind herself of a few simple, glad truths.

In total, they had saved nine prisoners from the Fidelia laboratory.

Of the refugees who had traveled aboard the *Streganna*, more than three-quarters of them had survived the battle, and those who hadn't yet left for the city now rested peacefully in this copse of trees and in the little buildings nearby—a stable, a feed shed, two tired cottages, one of which was inhabited by an old man and his husband, who had soap and potatoes and had at once set to work gathering well water and starting a fire.

Jessamyn was alive, and Patrik too.

Harkan slept beside her, curled up on his side and lightly snoring.

But still, Eliana could not sleep. She sat up, rubbing the back of her neck. She could feel the faint echo of Corien's fingers there, groping and grabbing. His hand in her hair, his voice unraveling against her nape.

Her stomach churned; her throat tasted terrible, like dirt and blood and old food. She pushed herself to her feet and wandered camp until she found Patrik, on watch at a low stone wall, facing west. It formed one side of a broad paddock that had long gone untended—scattered with rocks, overgrown and empty.

"We'll have to leave by noon," he said quietly as she came up beside him. "They'll come for us soon enough."

"We killed all of them," she said, remembering. Once the prisoners were away, she and Jessamyn had returned through the auxiliary door and cut down every physician they could find, every dead-eyed adatrox blundering through the rubble.

"Perhaps," Patrik conceded, "perhaps not. We did well, that's true. You and Jessamyn were quite a team. But the world crawls with the soldiers of the Empire. And I don't trust these woods, these fields." He waved an arm across the horizon. "I keep waiting to see one of the cruciata jump out from the shadows as the one that attacked me did, years ago."

"From what you've told me," Eliana said dully, "that seems unlikely."

"Angels creating monsters of women and armies of monsters," Patrik muttered. "I don't understand them. Why do they hate us so completely?"

"A long story."

He shot her a sharp glance, watching for a long moment. "I suppose you won't tell me?"

"Once I've had a bath and some food, I'll tell you the whole sordid tale."

"I look forward to that. Meantime, we'll leave the refugees with their families. They'll blend in well enough, even after having been gone for months. But the prisoners we'll have to take with us when we leave in the morning. Their presence wouldn't go unnoticed here."

Eliana placed her hands flat in the dirt. Its dry, hard texture was no comfort, and yet she longed to lie down in it and never rise again. "Where will we go?"

"There's a city about thirty miles south of here. Briserra. It's much larger than Karlaine and has a decent Red Crown presence. My friend Edge runs an inn, of sorts. The prisoners will be safe there."

"And us?"

Patrik shrugged. "I don't know where you'll go. You and Harkan have done what I asked you to do. If you leave this very moment, I won't cry about it. Well. I'll cry a little, to lose Harkan. As for me and Jessamyn, Gerren, and the rest, we'll go where we're needed. And we'll keep going until we're either no longer needed or we die."

"I suppose that's it, isn't it? That's all that's left to us." Eliana considered sitting on the wall, but that required too much effort. Exhaustion pressed down upon her, gray and endless, but she knew that if she returned to Harkan and tried to sleep, she would fail. "We fight until we can't fight anymore, and then we die, and none of it will matter anyway. Nothing's changing."

Patrik was quiet for a long time. "When you and Simon came through Crown's Hollow," he said at last, "it wasn't about getting Navi home to Astavar, was it? Or even, really, about finding your mother?"

Eliana laughed a little. "It was for me. I thought that's what I was doing, anyway."

"And what was Simon doing?"

"He thinks I'm the Sun Queen," she said, because she couldn't find the will to think of a lie. "He lied to me so I would leave my home and fight a war for him."

"Are you the Sun Queen?" Patrik gestured at her hands. "Is that what those are for? What did they call them in the Old World? Castings?"

Something inside her gave way. Wherever he was trying to lead her with his questions, she had no desire to follow.

"I can't talk about this," she said, and hurried away through the trees, searching. When she at last found Jessamyn, the girl was sitting in the feed shed by the light of a small fire, braiding her hair into a tight plait.

Blessedly, she was alone.

Eliana shut the door behind her. "What did you see when we were in that last cell?"

"I saw you turn rigid," Jessamyn replied at once. "Your eyes filled with tears, and you kept convulsing as if you were trying to get away from someone, or something, but you couldn't move. Your eyes paled, though not as completely as the physician's. You cried out, terrified of something. I worried that whatever was happening would kill you." Jessamyn tied off her braid and tossed it over her shoulder, her expression keen. "Why? What did *you* see?"

Eliana hesitated, then sat down in the dirt beside the fire. "I'm not sure how to explain it."

"Or if you *should* explain it."

Eliana looked at her sharply. "Perhaps."

"It's not the first time I've seen something like that happen," Jessamyn said, leaning forward to adjust the fire. "An adatrox, or someone working for the Empire, goes fuzzy-eyed and strange. Or in the case of the adatrox, more fuzzy-eyed than usual. And someone nearby collapses, or seizes, or does something out of character to hurt themselves or others."

Jessamyn sat back on her heels. "Do you know what that means? You don't have to tell me, especially if it'll be safer for me not to know. I rather like my shitty life. But do you know what it means?"

"Yes," Eliana said simply.

"Well, that's a comfort, to know that at least someone understands what's happening in this world."

"No, that's not quite right," Eliana said, hugging her middle. "I know what it means, it's been explained to me, but I don't understand it. Or rather, I understand some of it but not all, and what I do understand makes me wish—"

She subsided abruptly, choked by the sudden rise of tears. She worked so diligently to suppress them that her throat ached, ready to split in two.

After a moment, Jessamyn moved to crouch between her and the flames. She took Eliana's hands in her own, callused ones, gingerly inspecting.

"Your bandages need changing," she observed.

"Yes," Eliana agreed.

Jessamyn traced the lines of Eliana's castings with her fingers. "Does whatever you know about this war have something to do with these?"

Eliana nodded. "Yes."

Jessamyn glanced up at her. "Do they hurt you?"

"Sometimes," Eliana said. "Hence the bandages."

"Can't you take them off, even for a little while?"

"I'm afraid to."

"They're dangerous?"

"*I'm* dangerous," Eliana whispered. "I'm a monster, in fact."

"Aren't we all?" Jessamyn pressed Eliana's hands gently together, between her own. "Is it awful," she said with a little smile, "that knowing you're dangerous makes me want to kiss you?"

Not until that moment did Eliana realize how desperately she needed to be kissed—not by anyone who knew her or wanted things of her, but by someone with a gentle touch who expected nothing in return but to be kissed back.

"If it is awful," Eliana replied, leaning gratefully into the warmth of Jessamyn's body, "then I don't care."

Their lips met softly, and Eliana at once felt the tension in her shoulders melt down her arms and out her fingers. She smiled a little against Jessamyn's mouth and gloried in the realization that this was a girl who excelled at kissing.

"You're crying," Jessamyn murmured, gently nibbling on Eliana's lower lip. "Should I stop?"

"Talking, yes," Eliana said, her eyes fluttering closed. "Kissing, no."

Jessamyn hummed a little, delighted. She cupped Eliana's head in her hands, gently bearing down on her to deepen her kisses, slowly, luxuriously, until Eliana's head spun and her skin tingled. When Jessamyn rose to her feet, extending her hand, Eliana took it at once, feeling hazy, and allowed Jessamyn to lead her to the tiny pallet a few steps away—Jessamyn's own shabby coat, arranged over neat piles of leaves and old straw.

"Usually, I'm not one for sex," Jessamyn confessed, once they'd settled on her coat. She studied Eliana's face, brushed Eliana's hair out of her eyes. "But I do like kissing and being held, and there's something about those hands of yours that makes me somewhat interested in the deed, for once."

Eliana's head buzzed. She felt sheltered in the arms of this girl. Jessamyn kissed her throat, and the warmth of her lips banished Eliana's dark thoughts, leaving her golden and soft.

"Then I'll indulge you," Eliana whispered. She hooked her arms around Jessamyn, slid her hands up Jessamyn's shirt, and splayed her caged hands across her bare back.

With a breathy laugh, Jessamyn shuddered. "You've got the idea," she said, and then she shifted atop Eliana, locking their hips together, and began slowly to move.

—◆—

Gunfire awoke Eliana.

She sat straight up, holding her breath.

Beside her, Jessamyn jumped to her feet. She grabbed her gun, slapped on her weapons belt, shoved her knives into their sheaths.

"Come on," she cried before bolting out the door.

Eliana fumbled for her own knives and stumbled outside into a dim morning. A new, cool wind tossed the pines above. Over the distant hills, a storm approached, and a steady rain stippled the ground.

The camp was chaos—refugees running for shelter, Gerren herding a few of the children into a ravine, Patrik shouting orders. The two old men who lived in the cottage had loaded up a battered wagon with the Caebris prisoners. Their shaggy horse stamped nervously, prancing in its yoke, and the wagon itself sagged beneath the weight of too many passengers. The old men snapped the reins, shouting at the horse to move.

Eliana ran toward Patrik's voice. The coming storm muted all other sounds but those of battle. It was a dim world—churning slate-blue sky, swaying black pines, the rocky brown soil, gray piles of dead pine needles. Gunfire pierced the air like spat nails. Eliana ran low to the ground, her boots slapping the earth, and at last found Patrik at the low stone wall where he had stood on watch. He crouched behind it, weapon trained on whatever lay beyond. Harkan and Jessamyn flanked him.

Eliana raced over and slammed against the stone next to Harkan right as a bullet struck the wall, sending sprays of rock flying.

"What is it?" she cried. "Adatrox?"

"And something else," Harkan replied grimly, the rain washing blood from his cheeks.

A chill raced down her spine. "Crawlers?"

Patrik glanced at her, his expression grave and significant. "And beasts."

Eliana peeked over the wall, her nose stinging with the tang of gunpowder—and saw at once what Patrik meant.

Just out of reach of their weapons fire, prowling along the low stone wall at the far end of the paddock, were three dark shapes. Eliana's first thought was mountain lions, for they moved sinuously and had thin tails nearly as long as their bodies.

But then one of them reared its head and let out a horrible, flat cry, like a slow drag of blade against blade.

Eliana's blood ran cold. She'd never heard that sound before, but the look on Patrik's face told her everything she needed to know.

"Cruciata," she whispered.

Jessamyn cursed. "You're sure?"

"What are they?" Harkan asked tensely.

"Vipers," Patrik said. "Their hide is tough, but they're vulnerable beneath their chins, and at the start of their hindquarters, where leg meets belly."

But then came another piercing cry, and when Eliana looked over the wall once more, she saw the three beasts leap over the fence and rush toward them through the woods—just as three others dropped from the trees, wings spread wide. They were small and slender, scaled jewel-green and blood-red, with wide, hook-tipped wings. They sliced so quickly through the air that Eliana felt dizzy watching them.

"Raptors!" Patrik cried, gesturing at the sky. "Shoot them!"

Immediately Harkan and Jessamyn trained their guns on the raptors, but the beasts spun and spiraled, too fast to fix on. Bullets flew uselessly through the air.

Then one of the raptors dove.

"Get down!" Harkan cried.

The others ducked, flattening themselves against the ground, the wall.

Eliana sprang to her feet, grabbed Arabeth from her hip, and stood tall for as long as she dared. The raptor approached in one blink, two—and then, as it neared her, its talons outstretched, its yellow eyes wide and pitiless, she threw herself to the ground at the last moment and rolled away in the mud, barely evading the raptor's grasp. It spun away and turned in the air with a furious shriek.

She pushed herself up and flung Arabeth at the creature's exposed belly. The blade struck true, and though the raptor tried to fly away, it soon faltered, crashing to the ground.

Eliana ran for it, yanked Arabeth from its belly, and turned to face the others, triumphant.

Her stomach dropped to her toes.

Two more raptors swooped down from the trees to chase the fleeing refugees through the remains of camp. They dove and grabbed, flying back up into the trees with their screaming prey clutched in their claws, and then dropped them. Skulls cracked open against stone, terrified screams abruptly silenced.

Gerren ran out from the orphans' ravine, rifle slung over his shoulder. He threw himself down behind a felled, half-rotted tree and fired at every cruciata he could find, but there were too many of them—at least a dozen, perhaps more—and they were too fast to kill, too alien, too *other*. One dropped after Gerren's bullet struck its chest and crashed into the roof of Jessamyn's shed.

But only one.

Another dove for the old men's wagon, grabbed one of the freed prisoners, and returned to the air. It tossed the woman high, caught her in its grinning beaked mouth, shook her viciously until her screams ceased. Another alighted upon the poor frightened horse, sinking its talons into the creature's hindquarters. The old men jumped off, helped the surviving prisoners out of the wagon. They scattered through the woods—some running for the city, others for the wilderness.

The sky was thick with swarming raptors—red and green, deadly jewels against a canvas of gray rain. They weren't alone. Adatrox followed, and others did too—humans loping like apes, like wolves with mismatched legs. Crawlers. Women transformed into monsters.

Gerren desperately reloaded his rifle.

Shots fired from across the paddock every few seconds, keeping Patrik, Jessamyn, and Harkan, and the others pinned behind the wall, in a gathering puddle of mud and blood. The adatrox were using the cruciata as a first offensive wave and the crawlers as a second, making their own kills that much easier. But how could they do such a thing—control women more monster than human and thoughtless violent beasts from another world?

Eliana watched death come inexorably for them through the trees. Sounds fell away; she focused on the in and out of her breath.

An angel had to have been working through the adatrox, using their vacuous minds as a way station to puppeteer both the monsters they had made and the monsters they had awoken in the Deep.

A general, maybe, in an outpost some miles away.

Or the Emperor himself, even from across the sea. Sniffing her out from thousands of miles away.

*I have her now, Rielle, and you can do nothing to save her.*

Eliana stepped back from the wall, her heart pounding in her ears. She half expected the Emperor to walk laughing out of the trees.

*Found you!*

Patrik shouted at Dasha to look left, just before one of the crawling vipers pounced and grabbed her by the throat with a wide mouth of serrated black teeth.

Another viper leapt onto the stone wall and swiped at Harkan with long, webbed claws. Jessamyn jumped up and slashed her knife across its leg. It snapped its head around, screeching. Harkan, on the ground, fired one wild shot into its belly. The beast fell, but not before a lash of its hooked tail caught Jessamyn across her leg.

She collapsed with a cry, clutching her right thigh. Harkan caught her, helped lower her to the ground, pressed his hands against her wound.

"El, do something!" he shouted. "Your castings!"

She looked down at them. They hummed, warm and vibrating, like queer metal spiders come to life on her palms.

Her mind protested: the explosions at Caebris. The fire in the Nest. The storm in Karajak Bay.

The Blood Queen.

The Kingsbane.

*Her blood runs in your veins.*

But her blood, oh, her blood cared nothing about danger or mothers who ended the world. Her blood was rising to meet the hum of her castings, pressing feverishly against the underside of her skin.

Her blood knew what it wanted.

New gunfire rang out—sharp, precise. Eliana looked up. Two raptors fell from the sky. A third. A fourth.

She ran for the wall, crouched next to Patrik, wiped the rain from her face. "Who's shooting? Not Gerren?"

Patrik's eyes were fierce and bright beneath the sopping mess of his hair. He nodded at the paddock's left wall, some fifty yards away. "It's Simon."

# — 29 —

# RIELLE

*"I have begun to wonder, as have Marzana and Ghovan, about the possibility of using our power to heal those who have suffered great injury in our service. They fight for us, for our entire kind, and so they deserve, in return, everything we can give them. God granted us enough magic to perform great natural acts. Is it not therefore an extension of that power to perform the greatest natural act there is? Giving life to that which lacks life? I must believe this is possible. The empirium is limitless, and we are of the empirium. Therefore, we are limitless."*

—Surviving journals of Saint Katell of Celdaria,
May 24, Year 1531 of the First Age

Rielle heard the villagers' screams in her sleep and awoke to the feeling of fire on her skin.

She cried out in horror and scrambled off the bed, pawing at her arms and torso.

"Rielle? What is it?" Audric followed her and tried to catch her hands, but she shoved him away. If he touched her, he would burn.

Evyline and Maylis burst in, the other members of the Sun Guard right behind them.

Rielle realized the fire was an illusion, a dream remnant. Her nightgown clung to her. Though the floor beneath her bare feet felt like winter polished smooth, her body dripped with sweat.

For the space of five shaking breaths, she stood with her face pressed against Audric's chest. He smoothed back the damp knots of her hair.

"It's all right, Evyline," she heard Audric say. "Lady Rielle has had a nightmare."

Then Ludivine's shout came to her, followed by the faint mind-echo of screams.

*Rielle, they're burning! Hurry!*

She let out a tired sob and detached herself from Audric, fumbling through the dark room for her clothes.

Audric retrieved his own. "What is it? What did she say?"

He knew well the various expressions she wore when Ludivine spoke to her. She felt a burst of tenderness to see him dutifully dressing at her side, ready to go wherever she commanded, without question.

"Villagers are burning," she said. "I think there's been a fire."

*No. Not a fire. Corien. He's controlling them. He's too powerful.*

*Where are you?*

*Trying to stop him.*

And suddenly Rielle's mind filled with images given to her by Ludivine: a humble mountain village, a series of stone shelters built into the side of a mountain pockmarked with caves. Four elementals flinging knots of fire. Blackened bodies, lit up where they had fallen, flames persisting even in the snow.

"It's Corien," Rielle said, drawing on her coat. "He's controlling elementals in a nearby village. He's making them burn one another." She was afraid to look Audric in the eye. "I'm sorry. He'll be there, but we must go to them."

"Of course we must." His voice was unreadable. He fastened his cloak at his throat, flung on his sword belt, and grabbed Illumenor. Together they hurried through the temple, the Sun Guard silent and burnished at their heels.

Ludivine gave them information en route. The village was not far, and the Obex had offered them the use of seven shaggy mountain ponies, solid and sure-footed.

*The village is called Polestal*, Ludivine said. *Eighty-seven inhabitants.* She paused. *Now eighty. Seven have died. More are burning, half-alive. Most in the village are elementals. The rest are human slaves.*

Rielle relayed this information to Audric and her guard, shouting through the snow.

"How are these firebrands overwhelming the other elementals?" Audric asked. "Why are they not fighting back?"

*Corien is confusing them*, Ludivine replied. *Scrambling their minds. They cannot focus. Their power cannot find its footing.*

After Rielle explained, Audric cursed passionately. "Why is he doing this? To draw you out, I assume, but why? He's just seen you."

*Why, Lu?*

*His mind is closed to me, my darling.* Ludivine's voice was thin with terror and anger in equal parts. *I'm trying to understand, but I can barely keep my own thoughts focused. He is a great storm, and in his wake it is diffi-cult to even stand upright.*

"Lu doesn't know," she replied.

Audric looked furious. "It's a trap, and we're walking right into it."

"We can't go back, Audric. We can't abandon these people to him."

"Begging your pardon, my lady," Evyline interrupted, "but the lives of a few villagers are not equal to your own."

"Lady Rielle is right," Audric said. "If we abandon innocents to their deaths, all we will have done is make Corien's task easier for him." He glanced back at Rielle, his face framed in fur.

Rielle wished, in that moment, that she could send him a feeling of love, as she would have done to Ludivine.

*Tell him I love him*, she thought. *Please, Lu, tell him how desperately I love him.*

But Ludivine did not respond.

"She's not answering me," Rielle shouted, her chest a flurry of panic. She pushed her pony up a steep path, narrow between two rocky slabs. The beasts were up to their knees in snow, ears flat, heads bobbing with the effort of pulling themselves up the slope.

Then, at the path's crest, a rush of smoke and orange light greeted them. Rielle threw up an arm to shield her eyes.

"My God," Evyline exclaimed, pulling her mount up beside Rielle.

The village of Polestal sat tucked into the crags of the mountain below them—tiny houses carved into the rock, little stone yards and paddocks piled with snow. Skinny black pines stood afire; screams rose through the wintry air. Dark, furred figures chased one another across a charred white canvas. Some flung knots of fire from brilliant castings—pendants, knives, arrows. Others fell, screaming. They clawed through the snow, frantic for escape. They were caught, pounced upon, beaten with flaming fists.

They burned.

Rielle's breath came high and fast. The flames she had manipulated in front of the Kirvayan court were tame. These were different—wild and furious.

She felt a soft pressure on her arm and realized Audric was touching her.

"Are you all right?" he shouted. At his hip, Illumenor blazed.

She nodded and reached again for Ludivine. *Lu, I don't know what to do. I know I managed the fire trial, but this—*

*You know exactly what to do, Rielle.*

*Corien?* She tensed in her saddle, her every sense sharpened. *Why are you doing this?*

His voice rang silver with delight. *Because I can. Because you left me restless and unsatisfied, and one must find a way to take the edge off, mustn't one? But also because I know you can save them, even those who have died. And save them you should, and you shall, unless you want the entire village to burn.*

Rielle's pony shifted uneasily beneath her. *Save them? I can't do that.*

*Of course you can. You transformed those flames into feathers. You command the empirium to weave nets and form shields. You wrangle waves and craft shadows.*

*Yes*, she whispered, her body turning supple and warm as his words washed over her. She closed her eyes, remembering the tidal wave. Stopping the swords at the metal trial and flinging them to the ground, flat and harmless at her feet. Burning Corien in the cave of her father's death.

Stopping the hearts of three men with the bludgeon of her rage.

*So, then?* Corien was before her, in her mind's eye. She saw herself as she could be at his side—unfettered, blazing, and brilliant. A maker of worlds, a granter of life and a dealer of death.

"Rielle, stay with me!" Audric cried, his voice shaking her out of her reverie.

She did not allow herself to look at him. If she looked at him, she would return to him, to her guard, to the weight of the shield waiting for her back at the temple, to the weight of a role that she had had no choice but to claim.

Instead, she jumped down from her pony and plunged into the snow. With a sweep of her arm, she cleared a path for herself to the village. A storm of white flew into the air, momentarily clouding her vision and leaving behind a dark strip of soil and bare rock. She ran, following the path down the slope, ignoring the cries of Audric and Evyline behind her.

The first body she came to was that of a man, she thought, though his features were cooked, mottled. Patches of glistening red skin, strips of white bone, singed clothes and hair. He writhed in the snow, and though it should have quenched the flames that had burned him, the fire persisted. It flickered up and down his body, blackening his skin and the snow beneath him.

Rielle coughed, eyes watering from the smoke. She swept her arm through the air just over his body, dousing the flames, and allowed herself a tiny moment of triumph at the ease with which she'd managed it.

Once, she would not have been able to. Once, the sight of flames had left her stricken and helpless with fear.

*You are stronger than any flame that burns*, Corien murmured.

"Don't be afraid," Rielle said to the man, though she was uncertain if he could hear her. "I'm going to help you."

Then she lowered her hands to his chest, her mouth souring at the gruesome texture of his ruined skin, and set to work.

She breathed in and out, letting her eyes unfocus. In the books she had read with Ludivine and Audric, various discussions of elemental theory had touched upon the possibility of healing, of repair and restoration, even—though much more rarely—the concept of total resurrection.

Such ideas were a natural extension of elemental power, several of the more radical empirium scholars had posited. To summon fire, to manipulate it, a firebrand must call upon their connection with the empirium and rearrange it, like shifting the blocks of a child's creation to craft something new, taller, better. Similarly, a powerful enough elemental would, in theory, be able to delve beneath the surface of the empirium and manipulate not only the elements of the physical world, but also the elements of a physical body.

Instead of water, earth, and metal—blood, muscle, and bone.

*I will need new prayers*, Rielle thought, sifting through the golden layers of this man's ruined body with her mind. *The Bone Rite. The Blood Rite.*

*And the world will need new prayers to worship you*, Corien replied. *The Prayer of Rielle. The Glory of Rielle.*

*You flatter me.*

*Because I know it delights you. Now, focus.*

It was more difficult than stopping a hundred swords in their tracks, more immense a task than corralling a tidal wave. There were so many more layers to be sorted through than there were in a flame or a wave. There were flesh and muscle, joints and ligaments, tendons and bone and blood, and beneath that—

*Oh*, Rielle whispered. *There are so many things in a body.*

*Tell me, my darling girl*, Corien replied. *Tell me everything.*

*There are tiny pulses throughout his skull, and along a strange web that* spans the length of him—his torso, his limbs. Everything. They flash like storms. Her mouth fell open, in wonder. They carry information. They carry sight and sound. Sensation.

What else?

There is a map, underneath all the rest of it. She scooped through the sea of golden light that was the man's body, looking deeper. Infinitesimal beads. They are pure empirium. They build him, like the bricks of a house. No. Smaller than bricks. The miniscule grains of sand, too small for the eye, that make a brick what it is.

Distantly, Rielle felt something move nearby, heard someone calling her name. But she ignored whoever it was because it was far more important to shift around this body's organs and understand how they connected, how they functioned. Like a pack of dumb beasts, pure instinct and meat, all crammed inside one fleshy hot den.

Enraptured, she traced the man's glowing skeleton with her fingers, feeling every knob and ridge, every rolling joint. She saw the ragged shell of his skin, how the fire had burned off its outer layers, and decided that it would be easy to knit this poor man back together. She saw the tiny storms of his body flashing frantically from skull to limb, from skull to belly, and understood how he currently existed in a froth of unbearable agony.

"I will mend you," she whispered. "It's very easy."

Tell me what you're doing as you do it, urged a new voice, small but eager. I want to understand.

The voice shook Rielle, jarring her concentration. Lu?

Leave her be, rat, said Corien coldly. You're ruining everything.

You poison her, Ludivine replied, her voice thick with anger. You will be her undoing, and then all your so-called great work will have been for naught. I will revel in your downfall. I will bask in it.

You are a traitor and a weak-minded fool, Corien snapped, and when she destroys you at last, it will be too kind a fate for you.

Their warring voices sent spikes of pain ricocheting between Rielle's temples, like hot punching fists. But she could not let them distract her. She had work to do.

She bent low over the man, her hands hovering above the shredded map of his skin. There, on his chest—a particularly horrible burn, the wound wide and deep. A discolored web of the empirium, knocked askew. A darkness where there should have been only light.

She would start there. It would be easy. She would place her hands directly over the burn, energizing the empirium in that spot and encouraging its repair, its growth, until the flesh had re-formed. Layers and layers of it, healthy and new. And then she would move on to the next burn, and the next, and the next—

Something jolted her. A terrible, rasping sound she had never heard before in her life sent violent chills down her spine. Her hands were wedged in something. She tried to dislodge them but found she could not move. The light blooming above her fingers was growing, brightening, so brilliant it hurt her eyes.

*Rielle, stop!* Ludivine cried. *Open your eyes!*

Hands grabbed her shoulders, pulled and tugged. A desperate voice called her name.

Rielle blinked, her vision dimming. She was no longer staring at the shifting golden sea of the empirium.

She was staring at her hands, trapped in a misshapen globule of flesh. It was as if some awful monster of skin and pus had arisen from the man's chest and expanded, overtaking half his torso and continuing to grow. It consumed his burns, his convulsing limbs. It encroached on his glistening red mouth, raw and shining, newborn.

His throat had birthed the terrible scream Rielle had heard. He was writhing underneath her, his eyes white and wild. Rielle tugged on her hands, trying to yank them from his body, but they were stuck fast.

She sobbed, frantic, and Audric's voice came to her from somewhere in this terrible black-and-white night—mountains and smoke, snow and ice and the man's eyes, rolling back into his charred skull.

But Audric's voice, steady and familiar as it was, would not help her. Shaking, she returned her mind to the place it had been moments before—in that golden world, in the realm of the empirium. It was like trying to steer a ship through a gale. Her mind resisted. She teetered, gasping, and at last slipped through a wavering crack into that world beyond the veil of the seen.

She saw the pile of flesh, growing from the juncture of her hands.

*Stop it*, she commanded, her mind unsteady. *Unmake it. Unmake it.*

At once, the empirium obeyed. The light that was the man's overgrown flesh scattered, spilling over the sides of his body.

*Unmake it*, Rielle said, over and over, light-headed, watching with glazed eyes as the man's body unfolded and collapsed, the inhuman net of flesh releasing him.

His screams, somewhere in the world outside her mind, abruptly ceased. Her hands were free once more. She pushed herself back from him with a sharp cry and fell against something warm and solid.

Familiar hands caught her. Weak with relief, she allowed them to help her to her feet, but then her stomach lurched, on fire and roiling, and she staggered away from the warmth and retched into the snow.

"Rielle, we have to leave, *now*," Audric said urgently.

She wiped her mouth on the back of her hand, but her lips came away warm and wet. She blinked, bewildered, and looked down at herself.

She was drenched in blood—her hands, her tunic, her boots. She cried out and staggered back, but there was no escaping her own body.

"Rielle," came Audric's tense voice, "we have to run."

"What's happened?" She looked around and saw three things at once.

Surrounding them, a semicircle of hooded, furred figures. The villagers— no longer fighting, no longer controlled by Corien. They stared in horror, in fury. Several were crying, the wind swallowing their wails.

Then there was Ludivine, pushing her way through the crowd.

And the burned man, on the ground in the snow. The man Rielle had tried to heal.

He was a man no longer. He was a collapsed pile of human parts—bones and organs, misshapen knobs of flesh. A sunken skull, hands shriveled and flayed, a faceless mouth of white teeth grimacing at the sky.

Rielle's knees gave out. Audric caught her, holding her close against him as the Sun Guard formed a line between them and the stirring villagers.

"Blood Queen!" someone shouted. A rock flew out from the crowd. Riva deflected it with the flat of her sword.

Another voice took up the call. "Blood Queen!"

Soon it was a chant, a chorus. More stones flew at them. Someone rushed at the Sun Guard, wildly waving a small club. Evyline easily dispatched them, knocking them out with a blow of her sword hilt.

"My lord prince?" she called over her shoulder. "Your orders?"

Ludivine joined them. *Run. I'll distract them.*

Rielle's head spun, her vision tilting painfully. *I'm not leaving you.*

*Return to the temple as quickly as you can. Don't make me force you.*

Rielle hurried up the slope to their waiting ponies, Audric's arm strong around her waist.

*Corien?* Tears clogged her thoughts. *What have I done?*

*All great work must start somewhere*, he replied, his voice blank as untouched snow. Then, without a touch of comfort, he was gone.

━◆━

In the temple stable, the young queen was waiting for them, Marzana's shield at her feet.

"Queen Obritsa?" Audric dismounted. "This is a surprise."

Obritsa stared at Rielle. "What happened?"

"I'm not entirely sure," Rielle replied, her vision swimming as she slid to the ground, "but I think the villagers of Polestal might require some aid from the crown and a visit from your magisters."

The queen's mouth thinned. "You are covered in what must be the blood of one of my citizens, if not more than one. Humor, however black, is not appropriate at this moment."

"I couldn't agree more," Rielle said, and then turned away to press her face against the cold hide of her pony. She had caught a whiff of her own clothes and felt close to losing what remained of her supper.

Audric touched the small of her back, the warmth of his hand a balm. "Obritsa, if you'll permit me to explain—"

"No time for that," she said briskly. "I have my instructions from Ludivine, and I must obey them. I'll have your things sent to your capital, though it will take a few weeks for them to arrive. The other guards in your escort have been sent ahead and will meet you when you arrive."

"When we arrive where?" Audric asked.

"A small forest, some thirty miles from here. I'm afraid that's the limit of my abilities. Come. I've already prepared it."

"Has Lu explained any of this to you?" Audric muttered, as they followed Obritsa into the back rooms of the stable. "Evyline, please carry the shield."

Rielle shook her head, unable to speak—at first because of her raging stomach, and then, when they entered a spacious tack room lined with feed and hay, because she suddenly understood what it was that Obritsa had prepared.

A thread hovered, glowing, in the center of the room. Several threads, in fact, bundled and bound into a shifting, wavering oval. One of the threads stretched longer than the rest, falling across the floor and dimming to nothingness. But as Obritsa approached, the thread brightened, thickening, until it visibly connected her to the circle of light illuminating the room.

Rielle had never seen this sort of magic before, not in person. But as a child, she had been fascinated by the stories and had pored over every grisly, fantastical tale she could find.

Behind them, Evyline swore quietly.

"You're a marque," Audric murmured. "Do your magisters know?"

"My instructions were to send you to safety," Obritsa replied, "not to tell you the story of my life. The threads will deposit you in the Arsenza forest. I suggest you leave for Celdaria as soon as you've rested. Once word gets out of whatever you did in Polestal, you may no longer be as welcome in this country. There are supplies in that bag, enough to last you until Nazastal, where you can purchase horses. I've left a map in the bag as well."

"What about Lu?" Rielle croaked.

"When she arrives, I'll send her after you. I won't leave until she's safely away." Obritsa opened her mouth, then snapped it shut, frowning. She gestured impatiently at the threads.

"I'll go first," Audric said to the Sun Guard, "and then Lady Rielle after me. Evyline, send the others through before you, and follow last of all."

"Yes, my lord prince," Evyline replied.

Audric stepped through the threads' passage without hesitation. The shifting space within the circle swallowed him completely, as if he had plunged beneath the surface of a glittering pool.

"I don't like this, my lady," Evyline muttered.

Rielle hesitated before the humming lights. She looked back at Obritsa, too numb for questions she knew she would later have. "Thank you for this."

"Don't thank me," said Obritsa, her jaw small and sharp. "Instead, save us."

Rielle turned away—from Obritsa, from the memory of the villager's body collapsing at her touch—and stepped through the shimmering threads into a pine forest, where the air was quiet and still.

Audric was waiting there, and she went to him at once. As her guard arrived behind them, one by one stepping softly into the thick carpet of snow, Rielle pressed her ear to Audric's chest, against the drum of his heart, and matched her breathing to his own.

# ⟵ 30 ⟶
# ELIANA

*"She will remake that which has been unmade. She will deal death to those who have dealt death, and she will show no mercy to those who have been merciless. She is a creature of light and a creature of death, as are all of us. But in her heart these extremes are greater, more dangerous, more violent, because she is chained to the empirium, and those bonds scorch her. And so it was for the Blood Queen, and so I now say to you: look upon your Queens with reverence and awe, with fear and with patience, and with pity most of all."*

—*The Word of the Prophet*

Simon.

Eliana's heart jumped into her throat as she searched through the trees.

A fifth shot sounded, and then a shadow passed over them—a raptor, not dead, but wounded and furious. It crashed onto the stone wall, flailed on its back until it righted itself, then grabbed Patrik's rifle with its cracked black beak, and flung both gun and man over its shoulder into the trees.

Patrik's body slammed into the trunk of a nearby pine and slid to the ground.

The raptor jumped off the wall and clambered falteringly toward where Patrik lay.

Eliana pushed herself over the wall, ignoring Harkan's cry of protest, and threw herself onto the raptor's slippery feathered back. It writhed beneath her in the mud, trying to buck her off, but she grabbed a fistful of its feathers, and the clammy reptilian hide underneath, and then thrust her knife into the tender bend under its jaw.

Blood gushed out over her hand, hot and bright blue. As the raptor fell, she jumped off it and then crawled through the mud toward Patrik.

"Patrik?" She wiped the mud from his cheeks. "Please, say something. Are you alive?"

His eyes fluttered open. He squinted up at her through the rain. "Oddly enough," he croaked, "I think that I am."

She laughed a little, prepared to help him rise.

But then she heard a cry, a familiar voice: "El, watch out!"

She looked up just as a viper, crouched on a low branch, leapt toward her with its black mouth wide open.

A sharp rap of gunfire. The creature fell with a shriek. Patrik, panting, rolled out of the way just in time.

Then two more shots. That same voice, now shouting in pain.

Eliana searched through the trees and found him at once: Remy, clutching his belly. Stumbling against a tree, only a few yards from her. Meeting her eyes through the rain and then, with a frightened, small cry, collapsing.

The world stilled.

The sounds of battle faded—gunfire from the adatrox advancing on them, Harkan's shouts, and Patrik crawling toward her through the mud. Raptors shrieking, diving, devouring. Crawlers screeching half-made words. Killing and being killed.

Eliana's legs took her to Remy. Her body was beyond instruction, operating purely on instinct and terror. The buzzing whine in her head was all she could hear. That, and Remy—his high, thin breaths, his keening whimpers. He pressed his hands to his belly. Blood painted them red, spattered his tunic.

Eliana sank to the ground at his side. She said his name, but she couldn't hear her own voice. She touched his face, his torso, and her fingers came away hot with his blood.

Movement jarred her. She looked to her left, saw Harkan on his knees at her side.

"We have to get out of the crossfire!" he shouted, and then, when she didn't move, he scooped Remy into his arms and ran limping for the wall.

Eliana followed, bullets chasing her heels. She scrambled over the slick wall, clumsy and shaking. Jessamyn, belt wrapped tightly around her thigh, helped her the rest of the way over. Patrik lay in the mud beside the wall, his face pale in the rain, arm cradled against his chest at an unnatural angle. He was saying something—they were all saying something—but Eliana understood none of it.

Then hands grabbed her arms, turning her.

Simon. Hair plastered to his forehead, stubbled sharp jaw. Blue eyes, blazing in a sea of scars.

In a rush of sound, the world exploded and returned to her. There was a new noise amid all the rest—ragged, gasping.

"Eliana," Simon was saying, his voice clipped and firm. "Listen to me. You have to save him."

She drew in a breath to reply—she couldn't save him, she was no healer; she was nothing; she was a monster; she couldn't heal, she could only destroy—but instead a cry burst from her lips, and she understood that the ragged sound was herself, that she was sobbing.

A high keening drew her eye to the ground. Remy lay there, his head in Harkan's lap, his face gone white. He whimpered, trembling. Harkan had reached around to press Remy's hands into his own wound. Their clasped fingers were a dark mess of blood.

Harkan looked up, despair writ plain on his face. His eyes locked with Eliana's, and he shook his head.

"Don't look at them," Simon ordered. "Look at me."

She complied, if only because she couldn't bear for another second the sight of Remy's wide, glazed eyes, losing all their light.

"Eliana." Simon held her face steady. "Listen to me. Breathe, and listen."

"He's dying," she sobbed. "Oh, God..."

"Yes, but he doesn't have to. You can save him."

She ripped herself away from him. "You're mad."

"I'm not. Your mother could do it. She could heal scars. She could create whole flesh out of battered wounds. She resurrected angels. And her blood runs in your veins—her blood, and your father's."

She shook her head, crawled for Remy. She gasped out his name.

But Simon yanked her back upright. "*Listen*, Eliana. You are not only your mother's daughter. You are your father's child too, and he was a good man, a brave man. He led armies and held his head high when everyone else had fallen to their knees. He was his kingdom's hope. He was the world's hope. He rode into a war he knew would be his end, and he fought with a sword as bright as the sun. I see him in you every time I look at your face. Eliana."

Simon smoothed her wet hair back from her cheeks. "Do you hear me? He was the Lightbringer, and you are the light."

She looked up at him, the rain carving soft lines down his worn face.

She held up her hands for him to see. Her bandages, wet and shredded, were nearly gone. The raw lines of her burns echoed the web of her castings.

"I don't understand them," she told him, tears choking her. "They frighten me."

"I know."

"I'm not her. I'm *not*."

"No, you're not," Simon agreed. "You're not her, and you're not him either. You're both of them, and you will surpass them."

Remy cried out, his face collapsing in pain.

"El," said Harkan, his voice breaking, "if you can do something, please do it."

Simon caught her hands, wrapping them in his own. Her castings dug into her palms. "You don't have to understand them. You only have to trust them. Now." He released her, shoving her at Remy. "Save him, or watch him die."

Bullets arced over their heads.

Simon shouted over his shoulder, "Can either of you hit even one of your goddamned targets? Take them out!"

But his voice was distant to Eliana now. Slowly, she crawled away from him to kneel beside Remy. He shivered in the rain, all his color a dark puddle on his torso.

"Remy?" She touched his cold face, his thin shoulders. She was crying again and could not stop. "I'm here."

"El," he croaked, gasping. Tears leaked from his eyes. He tried to say something else—his mouth opened and closed—but no sound emerged. With one last heave of breath, his gaze found hers. He smiled a little, his face settling into something peaceful and terrible.

"Not a monster," he said, and then his eyes fluttered shut.

The world wailed in her ears, clearing every last thought from her mind. Her castings leapt to life in a surge of grief. Her blood rose up to meet them, and she welcomed its ascent.

*I am the light.*

In Astavar, she had starved herself, deprived herself of sleep, driven her body mercilessly through exercise after exercise, until at last her mind had cleared enough for her to exist in whatever strange, fevered world had birthed her mother. A golden world that existed beyond the seen, and which she had truly accessed three times now—Rozen's death. Forging her castings. Setting loose that fire in the Nest from which she and Harkan had barely escaped.

Maybe four times? The explosions at Caebris.

And now—now, a fifth.

The tiny metal box that held Zahra trapped lit up in her pocket, straining against its seams.

"Move your hands," Eliana told Harkan, her voice coming out hollow and strange, but he had already begun to do so, for her own hands were ablaze—twin webs of light, blooming. They tugged her toward Remy's body like birds that knew the right way home.

Swept clean, she followed them.

*I am the light.*

She lowered her hands to Remy's torso, on either side of his wound, and then, suddenly, as if breaking through a glass wall to the fire beyond, the world shattered and flashed, incandescent.

The rain was a diamond cascade, the bullets overhead shooting stars across a field of gold. Harkan was a creature of light, as were Jessamyn and Patrik beyond him—though Eliana could see the wrongness of Patrik's broken arm, the gaping black wound of Jessamyn's bleeding thigh. A nothingness in the empirium, a lack, a cosmic hurt.

The longer she gazed at it all, the farther into the gold she sank. Her eyes unfocused, and her vision expanded. She saw the adatrox advancing across the paddock, raptors feeding throughout the camp. Gerren hiding under his fallen tree, hardly daring to breathe. She saw the narrow streets of Karlaine, the wide flat reach of northern Meridian and its eastern mountains, and the grand port city of Festival, situated on a peninsula curved like a horn.

She saw an ocean, brilliant and amber, and across it, a palace in a vast city. On its highest terrace stood a winged, black figure, shivering against the gold of the sky, misaligned and furious.

Simon's voice murmured against her ear. "Come back to me, Eliana."

She obeyed, for that angry black silhouette frightened her.

"I'm not letting go, El!" Harkan cried. "I've got him!"

Her vision shifted, the gold clearing enough for her to see the false, gray world in which her body existed.

Harkan had his arms locked around Remy's, and Jessamyn and Patrik had crawled over from the wall, holding down Remy's legs, and there were figures beyond their circle—at the wall, approaching slowly, weapons lowering. To the left and right, emerging from their hiding places with limps and bruises. A pair of crawlers paused, poised on the wall to attack, and now looking confused, unsettled. A viper and two raptors fled shrieking from the scene, and some deep part of Eliana—foreign to her, and yet the truest part of herself—told her that they fled because they knew now what she was, and what she was about to do.

Remy's body was lifting up from the ground, held in place only by the monumental efforts of her friends, and her hands were buried inside him, joined with him—not by flesh, but by the power in her blood, and the power of the empirium that lived inside Remy, even though he was ignorant of it. A shell of light formed around the place where her hands met his body.

It frightened her. She flinched, crying out. The light dimmed and shrank.

"It's all right," Harkan shouted, eyes wide. "We've got him, keep going. We're not letting go!"

And then Simon spoke softly against her cheek. "I'm not letting go," he said, his hands locked around her wrists. His torso, strong and warm against her back, anchored her to the ground underneath them.

She breathed, trembling, in the nest of his arms, and the earth shook as she shook, and the air drew taut as she strained against her castings. If she did not control their fire, their eager burn, they would plunge both her and Remy into the earth.

"Think of him, alive and whole," Simon murmured, faint but near. "Think of how much you love him. You're doing wonderfully, Eliana."

She obeyed, picturing Remy's face in her mind. A smile tugged at her lips, and Simon's earlier words shone at her through the fog of a dark age. "I am the light."

"Yes," he replied. "You are the light of the world, and you will guide us home."

"With the dawn I rise," she whispered, because Remy loved the saints, their prayers, their godsbeasts, and it felt right to honor that, to use those particular words to reach for the life left in him.

Simon's arms tightened around her. She felt his muscles strain just as hers did, wondered how hard he was fighting to keep them both earthbound.

"With the day, you *blaze*," he told her hoarsely, and then again, and again, passing the prayer back and forth between them, until he lost his voice. He hid his face against her neck, in her hair, and pressed the words into her skin with his mouth.

*I am the light.*

The earth bucked and then detonated, surging out from Remy's body and her own blazing hands.

She blinked, gasping, her eyes dry and afire. The world around her was as it should have been—rain-soaked, gray and dark, acrid with smoke and gunpowder. A thin wave of light flew out from where she sat in the mud. A ripple in the ground echoed its passage, like the shifting of great plates beneath the earth. What cruciata remained fell from the sky, scrambled blind in the mud. Crawlers fled; their screams held human voices inside them.

Remy cried out and shot upright, gulping down great breaths of air.

Eliana fell back from him into Simon's arms, and then she was pushing herself toward Remy and gathering him up against her, crying into his hair. For he was alive, he was alive, and her hands were her own, tingling in the warm net of her castings. She kissed his cheeks, his dear, dark head, and cradled him against her chest, and he did not flinch from her monstrous touch or duck to avoid her kisses. He clung to her, clutching her shirt.

"I love you," he sobbed, his voice cracking. "I love you, El. I love you, I love you."

Eliana could no longer hold herself up, but she could not bear to let him go. Her side stung, and she glanced down to see copper-bright shards scattered through the mud, and she heard Zahra's voice, deep and familiar and full of tears, and she realized the pain in her side was because this thing she had done, this saving of Remy, had broken open the box and freed Zahra.

Woozy, she noticed Harkan wiping his face, heard his broken, relieved laughter. She leaned against him, letting him support them both, her and

Remy. She felt Zahra against her, her cold-water hands cupping Eliana's cheeks. She heard Patrik shouting orders, saw him and Jessamyn and grim-faced Gerren easily picking off the gathered, gaping adatrox—even though they had all dropped to their knees, their hands clasped in supplication. They implored, they begged, but to no avail.

How strange, Eliana thought as she watched them die, that an adatrox should beg. That was not something she had seen before.

And then, another foreign thing: Simon, still sitting where he had held her, staring at a twisting light in the air. Thin and golden, the light stretched from him to a spot some ten feet away and three feet above the ground, and then arched up, endless, until it disappeared into the trees. Simon reached for it with his other hand and, trembling, wound the light around his fingers, directing it to hug his right wrist.

For a moment, the light remained, allowing his touch. Even relishing it, Eliana thought.

Then, flickering, the light faded.

Simon's body sagged. He braced his fists against the mud and bowed his head, breathing deeply.

Zahra let out a low, sad sound. The air near Simon shifted, and Eliana saw the wraith's long black arm touch his bowed head.

Patrik blew out a curse. "What in God's name was that?"

No one spoke for a long moment as the storm rumbled merrily on, oblivious. Then Simon turned, and the look on his face made Eliana ache for him, even as tired as she was, even with Remy newly reborn in her arms. He gazed at her like a man undone, his expression so soft and bewildered, so obviously belonging to the frightened little boy she had seen in Zahra's vision, that it embarrassed her to look at him.

She knew at once what the light had been, though she couldn't begin to understand what that meant, or how it was possible.

"It was a thread," she said softly, answering for him. "A way of traveling through time."

## ~ 31 ~

# RIELLE

*"As Ingrid investigates the origin of these fell beasts, I must prepare for the arrival of a special guest: Lord Merovec Sauvillier. He wishes to pay his respects, in the wake of my father's death. It's been years since a Sauvillier set foot in Tarkstorm. Well, besides Ludivine, of course. But does she count as a true Sauvillier? Forgive me, but I think not. I, of course, won't say anything of her true nature to Merovec, as we agreed. Can you imagine his reaction? He might very well faint. His head might actually pop off. I shall imagine this scenario to soothe my nerves. The fearsome Shield of the North, fainting on my couch. Now there's an image. I hope your travels in Kirvaya are passing without incident, and that you and Rielle are dazzling them all. When you have a moment to write, tell me about the capital. I've long wanted to see the Blazing Throne for myself. Does the new queen truly sit in a cloud of fire?"*

—A letter written by King Ilmaire Lysleva to Prince Audric
Courverie, dated February 1, Year 999 of the Second Age

They waited in the snow for nearly an hour before Ludivine arrived. Queen Obritsa's threads remained steady, a thin oval of light hovering a few inches above the snowy forest floor. They had decided not to make camp and instead to wait for Ludivine. Once she had joined them, they would start at once for Celdaria.

Rielle sat on a fallen tree, hunched in her blood-stiffened furs. She nibbled on a strip of dried venison Evyline had withdrawn from the pack Obritsa had given them, though she had no real appetite—especially not for meat.

But Evyline had insisted, standing over Rielle with her arms crossed and an impressive glower souring her face, until Rielle had finally complied.

Now they waited in silence.

Rielle watched Audric's progress through the trees. He paced, gloved hands clasped behind his back. Rielle wanted desperately to speak to him, to ask him what he had seen as she attempted to heal the dead villager. But the expression on his face was one of ferocious worry—a worry she knew she had caused.

So she nibbled her meat, striving to keep her mind clear and calm. She would not think about the villager, of the ghastly knobs of flesh knitting her hands to his chest. She would not think of how he had unraveled at her touch, the caved-open pulpy mess of him in the snow at her feet.

Nor of how it must have appeared to Audric, the horror he must have felt as he watched the man collapse at her touch.

Would he flinch from her the next time she tried to touch him?

Her stomach clenched at the back of her throat. She closed her eyes, breathing thinly in and out through her nose.

Then, a soft fall into the snow.

Rielle opened her eyes to see Ludivine righting herself, shaking snow from her furs beneath the low branches of a pine. Behind her, the flickering threads collapsed inward before disappearing.

Ludivine hurried to Rielle and helped her rise. "Are you hurt?"

"No. I'm cold and tired."

*And Audric has hardly looked at me once since we left the temple.*

Ludivine smiled tightly, touching Rielle's face. "I'm sorry to have kept you all waiting."

*And I'm sorry*, she added, her interior voice trembling with emotion, *to have awoken you in the first place. We should have let them burn. I knew it was a trap, that the villagers were bait, and yet I allowed you to—*

"Evyline, please give us a moment," said Audric. Then, after the Sun Guard had moved away, he came up beside them. "Please include me in whatever you're saying," he said quietly. "What's happened concerns all of us."

Rielle forced herself to hold his gaze. It would have been better, she thought, if he had showed anger, or fear, or even revulsion. But this quiet patience, the same familiar steadiness she was accustomed to, made her want to melt into the ground with shame.

"Of course," Ludivine said, squeezing Audric's hand. "I was apologizing to Rielle for having awoken you. I knew it was bait, and yet I led her to him all the same."

"And why did you?" he asked.

Ludivine hesitated. Rielle felt a ripple in her mind but could not interpret it.

"Because I pitied the villagers," Ludivine replied. "I could not bear the sight of them tormenting one another at his command."

"And you thought it worth the risk to save them? Even if it endangered Rielle?"

Ludivine regarded him thoughtfully. "Don't you think it was worth the risk?"

Audric was quiet for a time. Then he seemed to sink beneath the question's weight. "I cannot say. And this is what I feared when all of this began. I should not hesitate before sending Rielle into harm's way, especially if it means saving innocent lives, and yet I can't bear the thought of doing so. Especially when doing so leads to Corien."

"I was never in danger." Rielle carefully linked her fingers with his. "He would not have hurt me."

"I'm not worried that he would have hurt you," Audric said. "I'm worried he would have tried to poison you against me further."

She frowned. "Is my mind so weak, in your eyes?"

"No, and you know that's not what I meant."

"It seems to me that it's exactly what you meant."

*Rielle*, Ludivine cautioned, *you are being disingenuous in your argument.*

But Rielle plunged ahead, drawing away from them both. "If you thought me strong enough to resist his advances, you would not worry for me."

"My love, you *are* strong," Audric said, "but there is only so much human strength can do against a being as powerful as he is."

"Ah, but you forget, I am no mere human." Her voice broke a little, remembering the horror of the villager's dissolution beneath her, but she kept her head high. "Or did you not see what I accomplished in Polestal? Is that the work of a creature you think could so easily fall prey to even an angel's will?"

A thick silence descended upon them, echoing the quiet snowfall that had begun as they spoke. Audric studied her, his expression half-hidden beneath the hood of his cloak.

A few paces away, Evyline cleared her throat. "I wonder, my lord prince, if we should begin making our way toward Nazastal. Queen Obritsa encouraged us to make haste."

"Indeed we should, Evyline, thank you," said Audric, turning away from Rielle to adjust his furs. "Lead, and we shall follow."

They proceeded west through the snow, Rielle's heart a blazing nest of contradictions too scrambled to unravel. The snow melted away at each step of her boots, leaving a steaming, half-frozen path behind her.

*You're alarming your guard*, Ludivine said after a moment. *Fara, in particular, is worried you might combust.*

*Then she would do well to leave a wide berth between us, wouldn't she?* Rielle said sharply, concentrating on the sizzling snap of her footfalls, and not on the awful, heavy silence of Audric at her side.

--◆--

They stopped only for a short night in the town of Nazastal, long enough to acquire horses for the next leg of the journey and rest their aching muscles at the rather ramshackle inn—the proprietor of which nearly fainted when he realized that Prince Audric the Lightbringer had just walked through his doors.

The night at the inn passed quietly, and when they left at dawn, the snow had stopped. By midmorning, the expanse of fresh white cast harsh blades of sunlight back up at the sky, but even that did nothing for the bitter cold.

Rielle huddled in her furs, squinting bleakly at the brilliant white ground—until a shadow passed over her, drawing a familiar shape across the snow.

She threw back her hood and raised her arm to shield her face, and when that same shape swooped down between the narrow, shivering pines, she cried out, fumbling to dismount her own shabby horse.

*Atheria.*

Riva's mount, at the head of their caravan, reared up and shied away from Atheria's approach. The other horses followed suit, tossing their heads, rattled by the presence of a godsbeast.

But Rielle cared nothing for their alarm. The beasts could run away into the mountains and never return, for all she cared. It seemed suddenly unthinkable that she was only a few moments ago riding the back of so small and simple a creature.

She ran through the snow toward Atheria's looming dark shape. The chavaile landed on a small swell in the forest floor, padded by several inches of snow. She shook her wings clean before folding them neatly against her body, and Rielle nearly ran at her, nearly threw her arms around her great gray neck.

But a few paces away, she stopped and held out her arms. "Can I, my sweet one?"

Atheria watched her, very still. Her tail flicked once, sharply.

"Careful, my lady," Evyline said.

"She won't hurt me." Rielle took the last few steps slowly. The very air around the godsbeast seemed clearer, honed by her existence. "Even though I hurt her, she won't hurt me. Isn't that right, Atheria?"

Two steps away, the puffs of air from Atheria's nostrils warming her front, Rielle hesitated only once more.

Then the chavaile lowered her head with a tired, rumbling whicker. She nudged Rielle's shoulder with her velvet muzzle, and the tiny, tender touch left Rielle in tears. She wrapped her arms as far around Atheria's neck as she could and pressed her face against her dark mane.

"I'm sorry," Rielle whispered. "Dear Atheria, I'm so sorry for doing that terrible thing to you. I lost my mind, standing there before the Gate. It frightened me. Do you understand that? Will you forgive me for it?"

Atheria shifted from left to right, then huffed out a sharp breath against her back.

Rielle laughed through her tears, tightening her arms around Atheria's neck. The chavaile smelled of snow, musky and wild, and Rielle wondered where her beastly friend had gone these past long weeks, and if she would ever know.

"Well, then," came Audric's voice after a moment, warm and delighted. "There you are, Atheria. You've come back to us after all."

Atheria pushed her head into Audric's palm and closed her eyes. Her long, thick lashes brushed against Rielle's cheek like the fall of soft rain.

Over the slope of Atheria's nose, Rielle met Audric's gaze. "Can we go home now?"

He smiled at her, and though she knew the worry would return to his face once this small joy had faded, she was glad to see it gone for now.

"If Atheria will carry us there," he replied, stroking the chavaile's forehead, "we'll fly home at once."

For answer, Atheria extended her wings to the sky.

◆

The flight home took only days, rather than weeks, and once back in Âme de la Terre, before visiting Tal or reporting to the Archon, Rielle left Marzana's shield in her room, under Evyline's guard. She donned a plain gray hood and slipped out into the city by the half-light of nightfall.

Trying for discretion, unfortunately, was not a thing achievable with Atheria nearby, her long wings dragging against the clean cobbled streets and children chasing after her at a respectful distance. As Sun Queen, Rielle should perhaps have spoken to the children and given them some sort of blessing, sent them running back to their parents with words of wisdom on their tongues.

But she was tired, sore from days aboard even gentle Atheria's broad back. Now that they had arrived home, an awful dread returned to her, a restlessness that settled thickly against her bones. Echoes of the villager's malformed flesh knit themselves across her knuckles and along her palms. She had not heard from Corien since that night in the snow. Each time she remembered how his body, hard and eager, had pressed against her, how his mouth had burned against her skin, she felt the loss of him anew.

*I see you*, he had said. *And I am not afraid.*

And she believed him. More completely than she was sure of anything else, she believed him—and was glad for it.

She knocked sharply on the door to Garver Randell's shop, ignoring the whispers and murmurs of the citizens gathered at the front gate. When the door opened, she hurried inside.

"Please close the door, Simon," she said, retreating into the shop's shadows. "And lock it, if you would be so kind."

"Yes, my lady." The boy hesitated, peering outside. "Should I allow the chavaile to come inside?"

"You absolutely should not," said Garver Randell, entering from the back room with his arms full of rags. "You should, instead, come fold these rags and stir our supper, before it burns against the sides of the pot, and I'm forced to send you once again to Odo's for sandwiches."

Simon grinned. "I love their sandwiches."

"Yes, but my purse does not."

"Atheria won't destroy anything," Rielle said. "She's graceful, despite her size."

"I'm not worried about that as much as I am about her taking a shit on my floors." Garver dumped the rags on the table in the far corner, then turned with a raised eyebrow. "Godsbeasts shit too, don't they?"

Rielle laughed, but that felt dangerous, triggering a tingling heat behind her eyes. She swallowed the sound almost at once. "Everything shits," she replied.

"Ah, the wisdom of the Sun Queen. That's one for the prayer books." Then he squinted, pointing one bandaged finger at her. "You look terrible. Are you ill?"

"You've hurt your finger. What happened?"

"Bah." He waved his hand at her. "Don't waste my time."

"How dare you speak to me that way."

"I treat everyone the same in my shop. Everyone bleeds and everyone dies. Sun Queens and beggars alike."

Rielle drew an unsteady breath. "I've run out of maidsright herbs," she said, which was the truth, and then burst into tears.

Garver's eyebrows shot up. "Sweet saints, what did I say?"

"Nothing," Rielle sobbed. "You didn't do anything. It's just that I've come home from weeks away, and it was terrible in Kirvaya, and wonderful too. I'm so tired I can hardly stand."

"Then sit, for God's sake," muttered Garver, cleaning off a plain wooden bench for her.

She did, gratefully, wiping her face with the hem of her cloak.

"What happened in Kirvaya, my lady?" came Simon's soft voice. He perched on the bench beside her.

"I can't tell you. And the people I *can* talk to about it, I don't want to be around at the moment. I think that's why I came to you. So I could sit for a while in a place where I can forget, for even a short time, that I'm…whatever it is that I am." She looked up at Garver helplessly. "Does that make sense?"

Garver scratched the back of his head, then flung a hand at Simon. "Make sure Lady Rielle has what she needs, while I fold these rags. And if I discover that this is some elaborate plot between you to get Simon out of his chores, I must tell you that my revenge will be unpredictable and immense."

"Here, my lady," said Simon quietly, offering her a clean cloth for her face. "You can eat supper with us, if you want to."

"Oh, can she?" Garver grumbled from the fire. "I suppose you're now the master of this shop, then."

"That would be a comfort, if you have enough for me," Rielle admitted. Then, noticing how Simon kept glancing toward the shop windows, through which Atheria was staring, her breath puffing against the glass, she added, "And I'd be grateful if Atheria could join us."

Simon straightened, his blue eyes lighting up.

Garver snorted. "What, we'll ask her to sit herself down at our supper table?"

"She looks rather lonely out there, is all," said Rielle. "It seems cruel to leave a creature of God outside in the dark."

She shot a sly glance at Simon, who was stifling a smile. When Garver turned to glare at them, they were all innocence. Outside, Atheria let out a pitiful, lonesome cry.

Garver's mouth thinned. "Fine, fine. But it'll be you, Simon, scrubbing the shit off my floor, and not me."

Simon jumped up, ran for the door, and flung it open. Though Atheria hardly fit through the frame, she seemed entirely untroubled by this fact and lowered herself promptly onto the floor by the fire, her bulk taking up most of their dining space.

Garver stared at her, frozen midfold.

Rielle pulled Simon along by the arm, situated herself on the rug beside Atheria's belly, patted the floor so Simon would do the same, and blinked guilelessly up at Garver.

"You see?" she said. "Isn't this much cozier?"

Garver's indignation was so complete that he seemed to have lost all capability of speech.

Rielle turned to Simon with a grin, her tears drying on her cheeks. And as she answered his endless string of questions about the godsbeast, she existed only in that moment, in that humble, tidy shop, with smells of supper filling the air. Thoughts of Kirvaya simmered quietly, harmlessly, at the edges of her thoughts.

And the need for a fresh supply of maidsright herbs fell out of her mind entirely.

# ⟶ 32 ⟵

# ELIANA

*"You'll no doubt scold me roundly for this in your next letter, but as you know, I've long been immune to your ire. Simon has requested I begin teaching him foundational threading practices, and I've agreed, though I've forbidden him to practice without my supervision. You'll say he's too young. And I'll say in response that we were too young for many things, and yet somehow we survived them all. Anyway, the boy has a remarkable talent, and I'd rather he start using it now. His hunger is insatiable. He's like you in that way. You're both gluttons for knowledge and too stubborn for your own good."*

—A letter from Garver Randell to Annick Caillabotte, dated October 4, Year 997 of the Second Age

Rozen had once told Eliana that, for the first few months of Eliana's life, neither Rozen nor Ioseph had been able to sleep through the night.

"We could hardly believe you were real," Rozen had said, smiling at the memory. This had been eight years ago, when Eliana was ten, and Ioseph was home from the war for a brief spell. He had sat on one cushion, on the floor by the fire, and Rozen on another, with Eliana squished between them and Remy asleep beside her, his four-year-old limbs sprawled across their laps.

"We thought we would wake up in the morning, and you would be gone," Ioseph had told her, with a gentle brush of his knuckles against her cheek. "Our daughter. A miraculous thing, you were. A gift from God."

Eliana had wrinkled her nose, indignant. "God isn't where babies come from. Mama told me."

Ioseph's dark eyes had crinkled with laughter. "Well, no. It's not as though God cuts open the sky and leaves a baby in the road for parents to find. But that's what it felt like to us. And so we woke up, several times a night, just to look at you and make sure you were still breathing. That you were real, and ours."

Eliana felt much the same, eight years later, as she sat in the dirt with Remy in her arms. If she slept, she might miss something important. He might stop breathing, as he had done only days before. His stomach would open where she had knit him closed, and he would bleed out while she slept. She would try to heal him again, and her castings would fail her. His body would pale and shrivel before her eyes.

So instead she lay awake, beneath a carpet of stars and a waxing moon, and listened to Remy breathe against her. Her eyes burned from lack of sleep; she had not yet recovered from what she had done in Karlaine. Her mind moved slowly, as if clogged with mud, and her castings still buzzed around her hands, like a faint itch she could not satisfy.

And, of course, because nothing was easy, it was time for her monthly bleeding. She was bloated and aching, and while Jessamyn had offered her a soft fabric stopper from her bag of supplies, it was her last one, and Eliana had refused to take it, choosing to use rags instead.

On the other side of Remy, Harkan shifted in his sleep and let out a snore. Eliana watched him fondly—the softness of his face, how even in sleep he seemed to curl protectively close around Remy.

She carefully slipped out from Remy's arms and shifted him into Harkan's. At the movement, Harkan's eyes opened a crack.

"Don't worry," she whispered to him. "I've just got to take a piss."

Which she did, far enough away from camp to enjoy at least some privacy. Then she wandered back toward where the others slept—Remy and Harkan, Gerren and Patrik, six Red Crown soldiers, and four of the refugees who had come with them to Karlaine: two men, two women. Rogan, Darby, Oraia, Catilla. Patrik had urged them to stay with their families—after all, that was why they had returned to Meridian—but after seeing Eliana bring Remy back from death, they had refused to leave her. They had appointed themselves as her guard, it seemed, which left Eliana even more uncomfortable than her bleeding.

"They mean well," Zahra murmured, appearing as a column of darkness at her side, so insubstantial that it would have been easy to mistake her for a trick of the eye. It would take her some time, she had said, to regain her full strength after being trapped in the blightbox for weeks. That was the word for it, she had explained. She had known of the mechanisms' existence, but had been fortunate enough to avoid encounters with them until that horrible confrontation with Sarash in Annerkilak.

"Them meaning well is not the problem," Eliana replied, crouching at a small brook to wash her hands. Though she desperately wanted to be alone, she didn't have the heart to demand the wraith leave her.

"The problem is that you fear disappointing them," Zahra said.

"The problem is that when they look at me, they don't see me. They see the Sun Queen."

Zahra was a mere glimmer in the night air. "The sooner you accept that these are not two separate things—Eliana and Sun Queen—the happier you will be, and the easier you will find it to exist in your own skin."

"I expect that's true."

"But musings on identity and magic are not what you want to think about at the moment," Zahra guessed, sounding amused.

Eliana shot her a glance. "Rummaging about in my mind, are you?"

"Only glancing."

"Then you must know what I'm wondering. Why do you think Simon lied about the blightbox? He must have known what it was, and yet he acted as though he didn't when we brought you back from the Nest."

"I've thought about that," Zahra replied, "and I've tried to explore his mind to find the answer, but…"

"But you can't, because his mind's a horrible mess you can't sort out."

"Essentially."

Eliana sighed, looking away into the night. "Maybe it's simply that he didn't want to distract me. He wanted to keep me focused on his mission, and not on trying to free you."

"Or he didn't want to raise your hopes. Blightmetals are nearly impossible to shatter."

"Or he didn't want me to waste my power on such an effort."

"That is highly likely," Zahra conceded.

Eliana crossed her arms over her chest and shook her head. For a long moment, she was silent.

Then she said quietly, "I should hate him, I think, or at least distrust him. But I don't. Does that make me a fool?"

"You're not a fool. You're a young woman, and you're tired and lonely, and your heart holds a thousand different aches. And though I have little love for him myself and can't read what's inside his mind, one does not need to be a wraith to see certain things that are true."

A shift of air brushed across Eliana's brow, a soft gathering of tension in the night's fabric: Zahra's kiss. "Go to him," the wraith said gently. "He will comfort you, and that is enough for now."

Then Zahra was gone, and Eliana walked on alone. She avoided Harkan and Remy, made note of Jessamyn on watch at the western perimeter, and searched the night's gloom for Simon.

He sat at the eastern perimeter, at the base of a stubby pine—legs sprawled out, revolver at his left hip, sword resting on a bed of pine needles at his side.

From a few paces away, Eliana watched him, unsure how to approach him. Once, she would have marched over and said something to nettle him so that he would nettle her back, and their exchanged barbs would liven her, clear her fogged mind and distract her from her cramping.

But now she felt newly shy around him. How naked he had looked in the wake of that thread, how newly made and unlike himself, all the hard, cruel lines of his face gone soft.

"I see you lurking," he said, not turning to address her. "Do you need something?"

She rearranged her features into indifference and gingerly settled herself on the ground beside him. She looked out across the grassy fields that shimmered silver-black in the moonlight, from the edge of their woods to the mountains on the horizon.

"I don't need anything," she replied. "It's just that I can't sleep."

"Nightmares?"

"Not this time. I'm afraid that Remy's wound will open as I sleep, and that he'll die and stay dead."

She felt Simon glance at her. "I understand that fear. I suppose it would do no good to reassure you, yet again, that both Patrik and I inspected his abdomen, and there is no danger of that happening?"

"You suppose correctly. I don't trust your eyes in this matter." She held up her palms. Moonlight shone dully along the chains of her castings. "I don't trust these either, or what they did."

"What *you* did, Eliana, was real and true. Remy's alive because of it, and…"

He fell silent, and when she finally dared to look at him, she realized at once that it had been a foolish thing to do, for moonlight suited him far too well, painting his ruined skin silver and gilding each gnarled scar. It had been a long time since she had examined him in a moment of calm. She noticed things she hadn't realized she had missed—his long lashes, his full bottom lip, the weary lines around his mouth and eyes. How desperately he needed a shave and how utterly his unkemptness endeared him to her.

"I've awoken your power, haven't I?" she said, because if she didn't speak, she would touch him, and she didn't think she was ready to touch him, and really, she was too tired to touch him, too uncomfortable and too frayed. "That thread. That's why it appeared."

It was the first time either of them had spoken of the thread, and with those words, Eliana felt something between them both give way and forge itself anew. The night around their bodies stretched and hummed.

"If that is what's happened," Simon said quietly, "then things will change very soon."

She nodded. She had thought of that, though she wasn't yet sure what it meant—how many things would change, and *how* they would change, and what would be expected of her, and if she would agree to it—and she certainly wasn't ready to begin that conversation.

Before Simon could do it for her, she asked, "Can I try to sleep here for a while?"

He frowned at her. "We'll leave in an hour. I want to get a few miles behind us before dawn."

"I know, but until then."

"Why here?"

"Because you calm me," she said simply, her exhaustion too complete to find a clever response.

His eyes searched her face, and then he nodded. He straightened his legs, and then crossed them, then straightened them again, and moved his revolver and sword away from his body, and then looked over at her, frowning once more.

"Should I sit just here?" He began assembling a pile of pine needles, a makeshift pillow. "I'm afraid you won't be comfortable."

"Stop fussing." She shrugged off her coat and balled it up, propped it against his leg, and lay down beside him, resting her cheek on her coat.

Silence fell once more, this one new and fragile. Eliana kept her body stiff, and so did Simon, beneath her cheek, as if both of them were afraid to move, as if moving would shatter the world. When she breathed, she caught the scent of Remy's blood. Her coat reeked with it, and she squeezed her eyes shut against the memory of him, so pale and small in her arms.

"Thank you for not saying anything to Harkan, about what he did," she whispered after a time. "I know you're furious, and I don't care. He wronged me, not you. I've taken him to task for it, and with everything that's happened, I think that's enough. If you attempt to punish him further, you'll regret it."

He was quiet for a long time. "Very well," he said at last. "I'll say nothing, and I'll do nothing."

She let out a slow breath, hoping that would be the end of it. Then, a deep, dull throb, as her cramps surged. She winced, gritting her teeth.

"Are you in pain?" he asked.

"I never experienced the pain that comes with monthly bleeding," she replied. "Not until after my storm, when everything began. Now I can burn and ache and cramp like all the other women of the world. How fortunate for me."

"It's unfair that you should have to bear so much."

"Me? Or women?"

He laughed, a low rumble that made warmth rush sweetly down her body. "Both," he replied.

"And haven't you had to bear unfair cruelties?"

She held her breath, waiting for his response.

It came quietly. "Yes, that's true. But even so, I would take yours from you, if I could."

Then she felt his hand in her hair—gentle, cautious, as if he feared she would bat him away. She closed her eyes as his fingers traced faint lines from her temple into her knotted braid, matted with dirt and blood. But he touched her as if she were pristine, as if her hair were silk. She allowed him this for as long as she could bear, her throat aching, and then she caught his hand and drew his arm down around her, pressing his palm first against her lips and then her heart. She wondered if he could feel its wild drum. If she looked up at him, would she see him looking down at her? And then what? With the stars and the pines above them, and the silvered grasses whispering at their feet, then what?

She could not find the courage for that, and instead allowed him to gently pry apart her fingers to lace them with his own. His warm, callused palm settled against hers, pulse to pulse. With his thumb, he drew circles across the back of her hand, and Eliana followed his caresses down, down, tenderly, gratefully, into a soft and dreamless sleep.

# -→ 33 ←-
# RIELLE

"Much has happened since my last letter. I'll soon be leaving for Belbrion with Lord Merovec's party. Yes, Belbrion. The seat of House Sauvillier. During Merovec's visit, one of the soldiers who had survived a recent attack went mad and killed his compatriot. Then his own neck snapped, and another survivor started shouting in Lissar. I believe these soldiers were possessed by angels. And here is where I confess that I stole a blightblade from the Sunderlands Obex. Along with my castings, I keep this blightblade always on my person. And when I brandished it, the possessed soldier shrieked and collapsed. Merovec witnessed everything, and I believe I impressed him. I will stay in Belbrion for some weeks to browse the Sauvillier archives, which include many arcane texts from the Angelic Wars. So much of what is happening is unclear to me, and knowledge is the surest way to understanding. In addition… Audric, I do not trust Merovec. Your broken engagement with Ludivine is an open wound. I want to stay close to him—for your sake, Audric, my dear friend. Do not worry, but do keep your eyes open."

—A letter written by King Ilmaire Lysleva to Prince Audric Courverie, dated March 15, Year 999 of the Second Age

Rielle awoke to the rap of an urgent knock on her door.

Beside her, Audric groaned and turned away from the sound, tightening his hold on her. "It isn't fair that I should ever have to be anywhere but in this bed with you."

She wriggled in delight against him and called out, "Evyline, you told me I could sleep in this morning."

The door swung open, admitting not Evyline, but Tal.

Rielle scrambled to cover herself, tugging the blanket over her and Audric's bodies. "Tal, what in God's name are you doing here?"

Evyline rushed in after him, looking most aggrieved. "I'm sorry, my lady, but Lord Belounnon insisted."

Tal strode toward the windows, cutting a quick glance at Rielle as he did so. "I'm sorry to interrupt," he said, sounding not very sorry at all, "but you need to see this."

He pulled open the heavy drapes, letting in a wash of morning sunlight, and then turned.

"Eyes front, Tal," snapped Audric, tugging on his trousers. He joined Tal at the windows, and his shoulders tensed.

Rielle retrieved her dressing gown from the floor and hurried over.

A crowd, perhaps one or two hundred strong, pressed up against the iron gates that separated the city from Baingarde's lowest stone yards. Some pounded against the gates with their fists; others waved crimson banners. Through the closed windows, Rielle could hear the muffled sounds of their voices, chanting something over and over.

A chill swept through her. "What are they saying?"

Without a word, Tal opened the nearest window. Outside on the terrace, Atheria stood looking down upon the crowd, her ears pricked and alert. At once, Rielle heard their shouts.

*Blood Queen!*

*Blood Queen!*

She stepped back from the window, immediately returning to the snowy ridges of Polestal. There, the villagers had bellowed the same words at her, their voices hoarse with anger and fear in the wake of what she had done—that man, a pile of blood and bones at her feet.

And now here, in her home, in her own city, the same angry words met her ears.

"Is it the first time this has happened?" asked Audric softly.

"No," Tal replied. "While you were in Kirvaya, it began. Only a few at first, but a larger crowd gathers each day. Ah." Tal pointed grimly. "Here come the resurrectionists."

"The what?" Rielle crept closer, her heart beating fast, and saw a new, smaller group of people, all dressed in white and gold, come rushing down the road. They plunged into the gathered crowd, bellowing things Rielle could not understand, for there was suddenly too much chaos to pick out words. She heard only furious yelling voices, a distant angry din. She watched the crowd scatter and merge—gold warring red. Across the yard ran a small squadron of the royal guard, swords flashing. A frantic bell rang from one of the white towers capping the stone wall.

"You've missed much while on your travels," Tal said. "The *resurrectionists* is what some call them. The name they've given themselves is the House of the Second Sun. Apparently, they formed shortly after Ludivine reappeared, not dead but alive. They have become rather obsessed with you and your work. They walk through the streets, re-creating the scene of Ludivine's death and resurrection, and her reappearance at your anointing."

"My God," Audric muttered, turning away from the window.

But Rielle stepped closer, pressing her fingers to the glass. She smiled a little to see those whirling white and gold robes, locked in angry combat with the red-bannered dissidents. Her defenders.

"And the others?" she asked. "They believe me to be the Blood Queen, it seems."

"The more radical among them have even begun calling for your death," Tal replied. "Often and loudly. Odo has been sending some of his spies to taverns throughout the city and then reporting back to me daily, keeping me apprised of any plots."

Rielle laughed. "Yes, I'd like to see what plots they could concoct that would endanger me for even a moment."

Audric turned, frowning. "This is not something to take lightly, my love. If word comes of what happened in Kirvaya—"

He fell silent.

Tal shut the window. "What happened in Kirvaya?"

Rielle threw Audric an irritated look. "If I'm going to talk about this, I should like to get dressed first."

"Very well." Tal's gaze flitted down her body as he stepped past her toward the door. "Can you both please come to my office, once you've made yourselves decent?"

"Yes," Rielle said, "and Ludivine will join us."

"As will Miren," Tal added.

Rielle felt a surge of annoyance at the mention of Tal's lover, the Grand Magister of the Forge. Telling Tal without an audience would be dreadful enough. "Must she join us?"

"Yes, she must," Tal snapped. "I'm tired of bearing the burden of you alone."

Rielle went rigid, stunned, as if he had slapped her.

Tal's expression shifted at once. He looked at her in horror, as if she had been the one to say that terrible thing. "I didn't mean that, Rielle. You aren't a burden to me."

"If Rielle didn't love you so much," Audric said evenly, "I would break your arm for that. Leave us. Now."

Tal looked as if he wanted to say more, but instead he inclined his head and left them, and once Evyline had gone, Rielle dressed in silence, wordlessly accepting Audric's kiss between her shoulder blades.

But no amount of kisses could erase Tal's words from her mind—particularly because she realized now that they had already existed there, half-made. Tal voicing them aloud had merely solidified them and brought into sharp clarity their twin truth.

If she was a burden to Tal, to any of them, then perhaps that was only fair. For the burden of their humanity, pale and fragile in comparison to her own, something she was expected to imitate and admire despite its smallness, was one she had carried her entire life.

◆◇◆

They gathered in Tal's office after the midday meal—Rielle, Audric, Ludivine, Tal, and Miren. Rielle kept her eyes on the floor as she began to speak, but then, as the story of everything that had happened in Kirvaya tumbled out, she gradually lifted her chin until she was looking right at Tal, as if she were driving her words into his skull, daring him to protest.

When she had finished, with Audric holding her hand and Ludivine's presence in her mind a reassuring softness, like the weight of a sleepy kitten in her lap, the room was silent for a long moment.

Then Miren, leaning on Tal's desk, blew out a breath. Her delicate features, heavily freckled, were tight with worry.

"Well," she said, "the House of the Second Sun will be happy, once they hear of this."

Tal glared at her. "This isn't funny, Miren."

"No, it's not." She crossed her arms across her chest. In the light from the windows, her red curls glinted cheerfully. "How much of this did you know?"

"None of it." Tal dragged a hand across his face. "Not Corien, not the angels or the Gate, and certainly not that Rielle had been experimenting with her power in such a way."

Miren raised her eyebrows. "And here I thought you and Rielle were so close."

"This is not the time or place to have that conversation," Tal muttered.

"And what conversation is that, exactly?" Audric asked.

"A private one," Tal said with a dark look at Miren. "We cannot protect you, Rielle, if you keep secrets from us."

Rielle stiffened. "I need no protection."

"Clearly you do." He rose from his chair, an angry energy crackling around his body like sparks. "This angel, Corien, he gave you Saint

353

Marzana's shield without asking anything of you. Does that not seem suspicious to you?"

*Careful*, Ludivine warned her.

Rielle, her calm unraveling, shoved Ludivine away. *I don't need you to tell me to be careful.*

"In his eyes," she said aloud, "the shield is a gift meant to win my favor."

"So you'll help him tear down the Gate and resurrect the angels," Miren said flatly. "And here you are doing just that—attempting resurrection, killing innocent people in the name of a practice in which you have no reason to indulge."

Rielle swallowed her immediate, angry replies. They had decided to withhold knowledge of Ludivine's true self and her blightblade scar, which had seemed a good idea at the time and now felt like yet another hateful constraint.

"If I can resurrect the dead," she said, "then when war comes, I can heal our wounded. I can bring the dying back from the brink. And besides that..."

She stopped, glaring fiercely at her hands.

"Besides that," said Tal quietly, "you want to explore your limitations, the far reaches of your power."

She looked up at him. The tired, knowing look in his hazel eyes made her straighten, steeling herself against that familiar appeal to her pity.

"If there are any limitations to my power," she said.

Miren's wry voice broke the silence. "It's not exactly reassuring to hear you say things like that."

"Reassuring you is not my responsibility."

"When someone is as powerful as you are, then, yes, it is part of your responsibility to not terrify those around you."

Rielle smirked at her. "You scare rather easily."

"Enough," came Audric's weary voice, quieting them all.

Ludivine cleared her throat. "Perhaps it would be best if Rielle leaves Celdaria for a while, until the city calms a bit."

Tal, leaning heavily on his knees, frowned at the floor. "That's the exact opposite of what should happen. Rielle needs to show her face at the temples. Pray and worship. Use her power in controlled, easily digestible situations that demonstrate she is not to be feared."

"But I am to be feared," Rielle said. "Pretending otherwise helps no one."

"Now you're outright threatening our city." Miren glared at Tal. "You find this acceptable?"

"I'm not threatening anyone. I'm simply stating the truth." Rielle rose, releasing Audric's hand. "I am more powerful than they are, more powerful than anyone. I can do things they can neither imagine nor comprehend." She returned Miren's stony stare. "Implying that we are the same insults their intelligence."

Tal smiled a little. "And insults your vanity."

"Well." Rielle returned his smile. "I wasn't going to say it."

Miren watched them both, her face unreadable.

"It might be wise, in one sense," said Audric, "for Rielle to stay here and earn back the city's favor, but I fear there isn't time for that. The Gate is falling. That is the priority."

Rielle nodded. "We must continue collecting the castings."

Audric drew in a long, slow breath. "*You* must."

She looked back at him, frowning. "What do you mean?"

"We've spoken of traveling to Mazabat next, a journey that would take several weeks. I can't leave again for so long a time, not with things as they are. Angry crowds at Baingarde's gates, and Mother…" He paused, his face closing.

Rielle blinked. He had said nothing of the queen to her. "What's wrong with Genoveve?"

"She's not been the same since Father's death, as you know. I think it would distress her to have me leave again so soon. And if the city can't see your face and be comforted and reassured by your presence, then they should see mine." He smiled sadly up at her. "Though the thought of being parted from you is not one I relish."

Ludivine's panic came swiftly. *No. He can't. He must come with us. The two of you must never be parted. You must always be together.*

Rielle snapped at her. *And why is that? Because you don't trust me to control myself otherwise should Corien show himself again?*

*That's exactly why. Don't pretend stupidity. It doesn't suit you.*

*Nor does your lack of faith in me suit you.*

Nevertheless, Rielle felt a hot swell of shame in her chest, for there was a part of her that feared Audric's absence, and its effect on her, more than Ludivine did. She cupped his face in her hands and bent low to kiss him.

"You are a gift to your people," she told him softly, "and to me."

He pressed a kiss to the heart of her palm. "My light and my life."

"Well," said Tal, rising, "if Audric isn't going, then I am."

Rielle turned at that, heartily enjoying the sight of Miren's stricken expression.

Audric visibly relaxed. "An excellent idea."

*No,* said Ludivine at once.

What remained of Rielle's patience evaporated. *Now what? Must everyone and everything pass your rigorous approval? Why shouldn't Tal go? He's a Grand Magister. He will bring with him the authority and power of the Church.*

Ludivine hesitated. Her thoughts fumbled.

*You're hiding something from me,* Rielle thought. *About Tal?*

*I worry that so much time spent together will not be healthy for either of you,* Ludivine said carefully.

*What in the name of the saints is that supposed to mean?*

But Ludivine, clutching her covered, scarred arm, did not answer, so Rielle shoved a feeling of disgust at her and stepped away, both in body and mind. She joined Tal at his desk and began inspecting his calendar, with him on one side and Audric standing on the other, and Miren sitting alone, quiet and rigid, by the window.

◆

They decided to wait until Rielle's Sun Guard had made the journey back from Kirvaya before leaving again for Mazabat—in part because Audric trusted them more than any of Rielle's secondary guard, and because Rielle refused to make the journey without Evyline.

She spent much of the following three weeks gritting her teeth. Dutifully, she prayed morning and night in the temples, moving to a different one each day. Dutifully, she made appearances at court, demonstrating meaningless tricks of her power for gaping members of the nobility over tea and cakes. Dutifully, she assisted families in the farmlands with the flow of their irrigation, the tilling of their soil, the angle at which the sunlight lit their crops.

At night, she found a fevered sort of solace in Audric's arms and then slept fitfully, waiting for a voice that never came.

——◆——

The morning of their departure, on the second of April, arrived still and cold. A light snow fell against the gray dawn.

Rielle left Baingarde for the Pyre with Ludivine at her side, her Sun Guard behind her, and Atheria circling happily overhead. The chavaile had been restless for days, constantly gazing south toward Mazabat as if examining the wind and preparing herself to fly.

But Rielle could not appreciate Atheria's joy. A faint dread threw stones in her belly. Her skin was still warm from Audric's kisses. It was an effort not to turn and run back to him. She was weary from their sleepless night and sore from how ferociously they had moved together in a way that would have delighted her, had she not several long hours on a horse in her near future.

It had seemed a wise decision, not to travel on Atheria. She would accompany them, of course, and could be used for a quick escape if necessary. But Atheria could only comfortably carry three people, and neither Audric nor Ludivine much liked the idea of Rielle arriving in Mazabat without her guard.

As she walked, listening to the merry chirruping calls of Atheria overhead, Rielle touched her mouth. Her lips were chapped and raw from hours of kissing. She relished their sting, the worn-out ache of her body. She closed her eyes, remembering Audric's touch, gentle and tireless.

Tears pricked her eyes. Yes, it was the responsible course of action for him to stay in Âme de la Terre—and certainly she wanted to go to Mazabat and find Saint Tokazi's casting. But the reality of Audric's absence tore at her. She had asked him to stay behind and not walk with them to the Pyre, fearing it would be too terrible to ride away from him, to watch him grow smaller and smaller in the distance, but this was far worse. Each step away from Baingarde wrenched something loose inside her; each snow-flake leached his warmth from her skin.

She groped for Ludivine's healthy hand and felt calmer at the touch of her fingers.

Then they arrived at the Pyre, shaking loose their snowy cloaks inside the grand gilded doors, and her calm vanished.

Voices came from one of the tiny sitting rooms lining the foyer—Miren's and Tal's.

"We've had this discussion a dozen times," said Tal, "and I don't want to have it again."

"Well, that's a pity," Miren returned sharply, "because we're going to."

"They'll be here soon. I don't want to leave you like this."

"And I don't want you to leave at all."

"I don't know how many times I have to tell you that there's nothing between Rielle and me."

Rielle froze.

"Oh, for God's sake, Tal," Miren spat out. "Stop reducing my very real fears to some sort of petty jealousy. I know very well that there's nothing between you. What I don't know is if you'll be safe around her. Or if you can be around her for so many weeks without falling so deeply inside your own thoughts that we won't be able to get you out again."

"It's not like that," Tal said softly.

"It's exactly like that. Don't insult me. I know you." A shift of sound; Miren perhaps moving closer to him. Then she said, softer, "I know you want to protect her. I know you yearn for God, and that it eats at you to have reached the limit of your abilities. But don't let your search for understanding blind you to the fact that Rielle is dangerous and that danger stalks her like wolves of her own making."

"Love, please don't worry for me." The soft fall of kisses. Tal's hoarse, imploring voice. "Please trust me. Trust Rielle."

Ludivine sensed Rielle's intentions at once. *Rielle, don't—*

But Rielle could no longer listen to them. She marched around the corner, smiling brightly. "Good morning. I do hope nothing's the matter. I thought I heard raised voices."

Tal recovered quickly, with a broad smile Rielle might have believed, if she hadn't heard their conversation. "Good morning, Rielle. Ludivine. Are we ready to leave?"

From behind Rielle, Evyline said, "The horses are packed and ready, Lord Belounnon."

"Excellent." Then he paused. "I wonder if I might have another moment alone with Grand Magister Ballastier before we leave."

"Of course," Rielle said. "God knows you wouldn't want my dangerous self around, putting your conversation at risk."

She turned away breezily, leaving them agape.

Ludivine joined her by the horses. "That was uncalled for."

"It was entirely called for," Rielle said, adjusting her horse's saddlebags, "and I hope she feels terrible. As if I would ever hurt Tal. Honestly, Lu, the way everyone's acting around me lately, you'd think they've forgotten I'm the Sun Queen, Celdaria's sworn protector and guardian. You'd think they've—"

She paused.

Lu finished for her, gently. *You'd think they've decided that the council was wrong, that Bastien was wrong, that the trials meant nothing. That you are not the Queen the Church says you are.*

Rielle's hands trembled as she stroked her horse's neck. *And what about which Queen I say I am? Does that count for nothing?*

Tal emerged from the Pyre, his face clouded. He avoided Rielle's gaze and said quietly, "Miren wishes to speak with you."

She glared at him, brushed past Ludivine, and met Miren just inside the Pyre doors.

Miren rose from her chair, looking paler and smaller than usual. Her freckles stood out starkly against her skin.

Rielle could not stand the sight of her. She peered past her into the Pyre's soft shadows. "Where's Sloane, do you know? Odd, that she wouldn't be here to bid her brother farewell."

"They said their goodbyes early this morning. Rielle." Miren drew a deep breath. "I know you heard what I said."

Rielle watched her, unflinching. "Yes. I did."

"I won't apologize for it."

"I didn't ask you to."

"No, but I understand it might have hurt you to hear me."

Rielle laughed. "I assure you, Miren, it takes much more than the silly, simple fears of a nervous lover to hurt me."

Miren's mouth thinned. "I don't want to fight with you. I only want to say this: I believe everything I said. I believe you are dangerous, in ways we can't yet fathom. Possibly in ways even you can't. I don't envy the life you've been given, but I won't excuse you for any terrible things you may do or have already done. And if you hurt Tal, well…" Miren sighed, looking past Rielle at the gathered horses. Her face changed when she saw Tal, and Rielle's chest ached to see it, for it reminded her of Audric, how his eyes softened when he found her across a room.

"If you hurt him," Miren said, "there's nothing I can do to punish you. You're too powerful for that. But he has devoted many years to your safety, and for your sake, he has borne that alone. He has been afraid for you, and he has loved you. I hope you'll remember that in the days to come—that many here love you, and would give up their *silly, simple* lives for you. You do not exist alone in this world. You are part of something immense and fragile and finite. I hope you can respect that, even as mighty as you are."

Then Miren gave her a tight smile and left her standing alone in the doorway—one foot in a house of fire, the other in a world of ice.

◆◇◆

For one week they traveled south to Luxitaine, and then took a ship—small and narrow, but replete with luxuries—across the Sea of Silarra, which stretched calm and bright between the shores of Celdaria and Mazabat. After a week on the water, Rielle saw the white shores of Mazabat on the horizon, and after a few more hours, the capital city, Quelbani, rose from the waves like a cluster of sculpted pearls.

Their ship anchored several hundred yards from the Quelbani docks, and small dinghies took them to shore. Mazabat had long been an ally of Celdaria. The economy of the two countries largely depended on each other—crops sent south from Celdaria, minerals and metals sent north from Mazabat. Audric had exchanged friendly letters weeks ago with the Mazabatian queens, who had seemed delighted at the thought of a visit from the Sun Queen.

And yet, Rielle felt uneasy as they approached the shore. Though Corien hadn't spoken to her since that horrible night in Kirvaya, she nevertheless felt watched by some vast and pitiless eye. She sent the feeling to Ludivine, keeping her gaze fixed on the shore.

Ludivine did not respond.

Rielle glanced over, frowning. Ludivine sat hunched and tense on her bench, her mouth clamped tightly shut.

"Is it the scar?" Rielle asked quietly beneath the lap of the waves and Tal's cheerful calls from the other boat.

"It's getting worse," Ludivine replied. "More painful." She glanced up with a thin smile. "I'm sorry. Please don't worry. Concentrate on meeting the queens. I'll feel better, I think, once I spend some time in a bed that's not rocking back and forth."

Rielle felt neither convinced nor comforted. This was a new thing and had begun to take shape alarmingly fast while they were crossing the sea:

Ludivine's scar, which had remained unchanged for long weeks, was now spreading and darkening. Already, its tendrils had crept across her ribs and to the hollow of her throat. She had taken to wearing a collection of gauzy scarves around her neck, but soon the scar would spread to her face, which would be much more difficult to disguise without inviting questions.

A shadow passed over them—Atheria, diving down to the surface of the sea. She plunged her head into the water, snatched up a fat silver fish, flipped it up into the air, and caught it once again in her teeth.

From the shore came a chorus of amazed cries. They were close enough now that Rielle could see the royal entourage awaiting them, a glittering chain across the white sand. Sunspinners lined the path from the shore to the queens, thin lines of sunlight arching gracefully overhead in the pale April sky.

"Atheria can take you home," Rielle murmured to Ludivine. "In fact, I insist upon it."

Ludivine's grip tightened around her hand. "Absolutely not. I'm not leaving you."

"Tal's here, and my guard. I won't be in danger."

Ludivine looked up at her, tears bright in her eyes. "You're always in danger, my darling. And so I will always be at your side."

Rielle kissed her cheek, then held her close until their dinghies reached the shallows. Her guards jumped out and pulled the boats ashore, and Rielle had just managed to reach the dry sand when a young woman ran toward them out of the crowd.

Evyline immediately tensed, but Ludivine murmured, "It's all right. It's Princess Kamayin. The queens' daughter and heir."

Then, with a feeling of relieved gladness: *She is overjoyed to meet you, Rielle.*

At a sharp shout from one of the queens, the princess stopped short, a few feet from Rielle, and smiled sheepishly. She was slender and tall and could not have been older than fifteen—her skin a warm, deep brown, her hair a cap of tight black curls. She wore a long white gown under a smart blue jacket, the sleeves rolled up to her elbows and the hem sweeping the sand. Her brown eyes were bright, and around her wrists she wore two thick gold bands, beautifully engraved with leaves and birds. Rielle felt herself move toward them and knew at once that they were castings.

"My mothers are always telling me I shouldn't embrace people until I confirm that they do in fact like to be touched." Kamayin looked hopefully at Rielle. "Can I, my lady?"

Rielle hesitated, but Ludivine only said wearily, *She is just as she appears. Warm and full of love.*

So Rielle opened her arms and smiled. "I would be honored, Your Highness."

Kamayin's face split into a sun-bright grin. She wrapped her arms around Rielle and kissed each of her cheeks, then pulled back to beam at her.

"I know you must be tired after your journey," she said, "but we did prepare a light lunch for you, if you'd like to eat before you go to your rooms." Then she looked past Rielle, and her eyes widened. "Sweet saints, who is that beautiful man talking to my mother?"

Rielle turned. One of the queens had made her way down the shore and was already engaged in an animated conversation with Tal.

Rielle laughed. "That's Tal. He's my teacher, of sorts, and a Grand Magister of our Church."

Kamayin appraised him. "Does he have a lover?"

"Yes, and besides that, I think he's a bit old for you."

"What a pity." Then, her expression brightening, she hooked her arm through Rielle's. "Come on, then. We'll let them talk themselves to death and get first pick of the food." She glanced at Ludivine. "Lady Ludivine, isn't that right? Are you ill?"

"Just tired," Ludivine said with a wan smile, but as they walked up the shore to the city, Rielle could not shake the growing fear that there was more to Ludivine's pain than she was allowing her to see.

◆◇◆

That night, in the spacious rooms the queens had given her, Rielle lay in her bed, luxuriating in its clean white linens.

Her skin still tingled from the pleasure she had given herself a few moments earlier. She had enjoyed one of her favorite fantasies—herself, wrapped in Audric's arms, and Ludivine's, too, both of them loving her with unwavering focus. But she could not find the dreamy peace that usually came afterward.

Instead, her thoughts buzzed with worry for Ludivine, and she couldn't stop wondering where Corien had gone. Here she was, far from home, separated from Audric, and Corien was nowhere to be found.

Obviously he would have reasons for staying away—but she couldn't imagine what those would be. She despised the fact of his absence even as she was grateful for it.

She turned onto her side, frowning at the moonlit window. Long ivy plants framed it, their branches swaying gently in the breeze. She opened a feeling of love to the next room—*Lu, are you awake?*—but heard and felt nothing in return.

She swung her legs out of bed, slipped on her nightgown, turned—and was met by a swift, darting shadow. It grabbed her and turned her, wrenching her arm behind her back, and placed a thin, cold blade against her throat.

"Don't move and don't scream," whispered a voice, "or I'll cut your throat in two."

Rielle recognized the voice at once.

It belonged to Princess Kamayin.

# ~ 34 ~
# ELIANA

*"My grandmother told me, and her grandmother told her, that Festival was once the merriest city in the world—a place of light and music, art and beauty. At the turn of each new season, the whole city stopped everything to celebrate, for days and days. Heart-of-the-sea trees once blanketed every hill and field and canyon. They were bred by Saint Tokazi and planted by Saint Nerida herself— one for each human killed during the Angelic Wars. They bloomed in April and shed their petals in September. Even after the Blood Queen's death, the trees regrew. But then the Empire came and cut down every tree that bloomed. My grandmother's grandmother said that for long weeks the air smelled like fire and that the sky went dim and cold."*

—Collection of stories written by refugees in occupied
Meridian, curated by Remy Ferracora

After two long weeks spent creeping slowly across the grasslands of Meridian, the endless meadows and thin, spotty woodlands became a landscape of streams and lakes and larger forests in which the sprawling black trees were draped with white-and-silver moss.

The moss reminded Eliana of home, of Orline, and she was quiet that last day, as everyone was, but she felt, in her exhaustion, that her particular quiet was more miserable than the others. It was a thought she was not proud to think, and yet think it she did, over and over, until her mind turned black and brooding.

They waited in a ravine, beneath a roof of moss-strewn tree roots, while Simon went ahead to let the Keshavarzian family know they had arrived. They were a mother and father and three boys, and they lived on an estate called Willow. It was vast, according to Simon—a grand manor house with dozens of rooms, elaborate gardens, rice fields in the sprawling wet-lands nearby, a private wood of several acres. They had long been friendly with Red Crown and had fed and housed many a rebel on their estate. But they kept their property and their coin through a careful, meticulously engineered deception.

To the outside world, they were Empire loyalists. As Eliana had served Lord Arkelion in Orline, so did the Keshavarzian family serve Lord Tabris in Festival.

Simon therefore had to approach the estate carefully, for they had not been able to send word of their arrival, and the family's private soldiers were stationed around the perimeter.

Crouched beside Eliana, Harkan shifted his weight from left to right. "I can't imagine they'll be overjoyed to suddenly have seventeen more mouths to feed."

"If they're not prepared to help," Eliana said, "they shouldn't be a part of this. They should truly serve the Empire and leave acts of rebellion to Red Crown."

Harkan glanced at her. She felt his gaze inspecting her face, her body.

But Remy, on her other side, was the one to speak. "You don't look good, El."

"Neither do you, darling," she replied with a gentle squeeze of his hand. "In fact, we all look like shit."

"It exhausted you, what you did for me," he said quietly.

She heard the note of guilt in his voice and turned to him at once, cupping his face. "And yet I would do it again, ten times over, if it meant keeping you with me."

"A hundred times over?" he whispered, grinning a little, his eyes shining up at her.

She kissed his filthy forehead. "A thousand times over."

It began to rain, a light shower that pattered like quiet finger taps on the leaves above. She closed her eyes and leaned her head back against the tree roots. She opened her mouth and let the fresh water trickle into her mouth, down her neck, into her hair.

Then Harkan tensed beside her. From a few paces away, Patrik whistled softly, alerting the others to attention.

Eliana straightened, tightening her arms around Remy—but it was only Simon, approaching through the trees. Four soldiers flanked him, their weapons drawn.

"Rise slowly," came Simon's voice. "It's all right. They just want to see that everyone is as I described."

Eliana obeyed, though she hated having to leave the safety of the trees and expose herself and Remy to the hooded gazes of these people she could not clearly see through the rain-soaked shadows.

There was a pause as the soldiers inspected them. The rain began to fall harder; Remy shivered against Eliana's side, and she nearly swore at them, pushed to the edge of her patience.

Then one of the soldiers came forward, lowering their weapon—a woman, of average weight and height, with pale skin and a head of thick black hair streaked with silver. There was a pleasing symmetry to her features and a sharp light of authority in her dark eyes that made Eliana feel instantly more at ease.

"Come on, then," the woman said briskly, gesturing at them to move. "You're fine, you're all fine. Poor things, you're filthy. We'll go in through the back terrace, otherwise my husband, Arzen, will have a fit. I'm Danizet Keshavarzian. I realize that's rather a mouthful. You can call me Dani."

They followed her wordlessly through the woods, Eliana watching with half-awake interest as Dani flitted about the group, taking note of their wounds, their supplies, the state of their clothes and boots.

When Dani reached Eliana and Remy, she clucked her tongue at the sight of them.

"Poor darlings. I didn't realize you would be quite so young." She stripped off her coat, which was sopping wet, and settled it around Remy's shoulders. "I know, it's soaked through, but I can't sit here and look at you shivering and do nothing. Don't worry, there's a fire inside, and Evon's made a stew. We'll warm you up right quick."

Then Dani looked at Eliana, her eyes bright and shrewd. "You're the special one, aren't you? The girl who's destined to save us all."

At those words, spoken so plainly, something raw and brittle snapped inside Eliana's ribs. Tears rose and spilled over before she could do anything to stop them. She realized, blearily, that they had reached the manor house. There was a broad stone terrace, slick with rain and bordered with bright-green ferns. Someone was ushering her inside, where there was warmth, light, the distant smell of cooking food.

Someone had taken Remy from her. She reached blindly after him, but then strong, firm hands were guiding her into a quiet room—also warm, but softer, dimmer. She noticed Jessamyn in the room as well, and Catilla and Oraia, all being helped out of their wet clothes by a kind-faced, round-bellied woman with wild red curls.

"That's Ester," said Dani, gesturing at the redheaded woman. "She's been my friend for so long I call her my sister. She has a daughter, off helping refugees in the Vespers, and another one on the way, God help her."

"Ever the cheerful one, you are," came Ester's wry voice.

"There, now." Dani's voice gentled, perhaps noticing how Eliana had begun to shake. "It's all right, love. Your brother's with that beautiful young man, what's his name?"

"Harkan?" Eliana suggested, wiping the rain and tears from her face. Her hands were black with mud.

"Yes, that's the one. They're fine and safe. You're all safe now, at least for a while."

Eliana nodded, following Dani's instructions: "Step out of your boots, there's a girl. Leave your clothes on the floor. It's fine, someone will take care of them later. Wrap yourself in this blanket, there we are. You'll have to bathe one at a time, I'm afraid. We've such a full house at the moment. Who wants to go first?"

"I'll bathe last," Eliana whispered, clutching the scratchy wool blanket around her body. If she managed to hold it in place, then perhaps she could hold herself together as well, and stifle her still-rising tears. "In the meantime, is there a place I might wait in private?"

Dani led her into a small sitting room of wood-paneled walls. A soft, red rug carpeted the floor, and a fire snapped in a tiny hearth. How marvelous that there was such warmth in this house. So many fires, and none of them were of her own making, or of the enemy.

"Now you sit yourself right here on this chair, love," said Dani. "Rest your eyes, and I'll come fetch you when it's your turn in the tub."

But when Dani tried to step away, Eliana clung to her hand, her cheeks burning with shame and her heart aching to be mothered.

She squeezed her eyes shut, but that was a terrible mistake, for Rozen's face floated there, contorted with pain. *Finish it.*

"Please don't leave," she croaked, and then, when Dani crooned soft words of pity and sat down beside her, Eliana's tightly held control shattered. Hoping the rain would muffle the sound of her grief, she turned into the woman's open arms and wept.

—◆—

Eliana bathed and allowed Dani to help comb the knots out of her hair before braiding it into a single, neat plait. Scrubbed clean, she hardy recognized herself. Dani led her downstairs, where she sat at one end of a long table half-full of people. Too tired to learn their names, Eliana ate in silence. Miraculously, no one bothered her. She devoured two heaping bowls of beef-and-vegetable stew and sopped up the remains with a hunk of warm, crusty bread.

By the time she finished, the room had emptied somewhat. Dani and a young man, whom Eliana assumed to be her son, sat talking quietly at one end of the table. And then, the food in her belly granting her some clarity at last, she realized that Simon sat near her, reclining in his chair, feet propped up on a bench. He held a sheaf of papers in his hands and was reading over them with an impressive frown on his face. As she watched him, another young man who looked very like Dani approached her chair, looking ready to ask her a question—but one cutting glare from Simon sent him scurrying away.

She now understood why no one had bothered her as she ate.

Smiling to herself, she moved closer to Simon. She was glad for his nearness, his silent watchfulness. She was glad for the fact that he had bathed, yes, but that his hair and unshaven cheeks still looked scruffy and unkempt. The urge to touch his face overwhelmed her.

She pressed her hands flat against her thighs. "What are you reading?"

He straightened the stack of papers and placed them on the table before her.

She spent a few minutes reading over them, and with each page, her heart sank a little farther in her chest.

"Astavar is now occupied by the Empire," she said. It felt necessary to force herself to say the words aloud. "Kings Eri and Tavik are dead, and the Lady Ama as well. No word of Malik or Navi or Hob. An estimated three thousand Astavari dead in the invasion."

She returned Simon's papers to him. "I regret that second bowl of stew."

"Astavar would have fallen eventually, regardless of whether you were there or not." He folded the papers into a leather packet and tied the packet shut. "Don't agonize over it, Eliana. There's enough to agonize over without adding to the list." Then he looked up at her, and she did not think she imagined the slight softness on his face. "Are you tired?"

She laughed. "Aren't you?"

"Me? Never." He rose, extending a hand to her. "Has Dani shown you to your room?"

She took his hand gingerly, a sudden swarm of nerves fluttering in her throat. "Not yet. I have my own room?"

"Don't tell Jessamyn. She has to share with Catilla—who apparently is an awful snorer."

They began walking upstairs, by way of a side staircase not nearly as grand as the sweeping one at the front of the house. It was narrow and tall, dimly lit by tiny gas lamps in brass sconces, and Eliana felt that she and Simon, together, did not quite fit in this small a space. She breathed shallowly, so aware of his body beside her own that she felt a lightning storm might spontaneously generate between them.

She closed her fists, directing what frayed energy she could gather at her castings: *Stay silent, little monsters.*

They reached the third floor, and Simon led her down a quiet hallway carpeted with a thick, tasseled rug. Oil paintings hanging along the walls depicted imperial scenes—various black-eyed generals in dress uniform; the Emperor's crest floating in a field of stars; what Eliana assumed must be the siege of Festival, when Meridian had fallen and its rulers had been executed.

The trappings of a family loyal to the Empire.

"You're sure we can trust them?" Eliana said quietly.

"The Prophet says we can," Simon answered. "So I will trust them until I am told otherwise."

As always, the rare mention of the Prophet piqued her curiosity, but she was too tired to form a question. They reached a door at the end of the hallway. Simon opened it, then stood back to let her pass. It was a small but cozy room, with a low, slanted roof and a bed tucked into an alcove, away from the windows. A brazier in the corner glowed softly, and the pile of blankets at the foot of the bed beckoned to her like the arms of a lover.

She blew out a breath, smiling a little. "I feel like it's been ages since I've slept in a real bed." Then she glanced back at Simon, who waited at the door. The sight of him standing there, scanning her room with a little frown, as if he were inspecting its contents and finding them lacking, was dear in a way that frightened her.

"Do you also have your own room?" she said, simply to talk over the sound of her racing heart. But it was a terrible question and only made her heart race faster. She attempted a coy smile that felt all wrong. "In case I start to feel lonely."

His gaze shot up to meet hers. The smile he gave her was strained and small. "I do. At the other end of the hall."

She wanted to turn away from him but felt physically incapable of it. "And Remy and Harkan?"

"Second floor."

"Patrik? Jessamyn?"

"First floor, second floor."

"We've the whole floor to ourselves, then?"

He raised an eyebrow. "There are five other rooms between us. Some of our party, and some who were already here when we arrived."

"Yes, of course." She struggled to maintain her composure, which had once been an easy thing to do. "Well, then. Good night."

"Before I go," he said before she could shut the door, "I have to say this: I know you need rest, and I do, too, but we must begin our work tomorrow. We cannot delay."

*Our work.* So here it was, the thing they had not spoken of in the past weeks of traveling—not since the moment in Karlaine when the thread had appeared at Simon's fingertips. Eliana had been working over the nuances of it in her mind, and now, it seemed, they would have to face it.

"You mean, I must continue practicing with my castings," she said. "And you must practice your threading. You want to send me back in time to Old Celdaria. You want me to confront my mother."

"A confrontation may not be necessary," Simon replied. "And that's one of the things we'll discuss as we work. How will you approach her? What will you say and do? What is our goal in traveling back to that age?"

"To prevent this future from happening," Eliana answered at once, determined to keep the absolute terror she felt at the idea from showing on her face. "To change something that occurred in the past and, by doing so, prevent the rise of the Empire."

Silence fell between them, punctuated by a soft rumble of thunder from the growing storm outside. Simon searched her face for a long, tense beat. Once again, as when she had watched him in Karlaine, his body lit by the gleam of his fading thread, she felt the urge to touch his face.

This time, she did.

He turned into her palm at once, eyes closed, and pressed his lips to her fingers. A single word itched on her tongue: *stay*.

But instead she stepped back from him. She needed rest, and if she asked him to stay, she would not sleep. She would kiss him until her fear of what lay ahead diminished. She would kiss him for hours, and then how would she bear to look at him after that? Already, looking at him made her feel as if the world were shifting beneath her feet.

"Where should I meet you?" she asked. "In the morning."

"Afternoon," he said, not meeting her eyes. "It's already late. We'll need a full night of sleep. After lunch, I'll find you. I'll ask Dani where in the gardens would be a safe, private place to work."

He hesitated, his mouth turning down at the corners. Then he looked once more at her and said quietly, "Good night, Eliana," and left her standing in the doorway, watching his retreating form. When he reached his room, she closed her door and leaned back against it until she had caught her breath. Then she climbed into her bed and nestled into its piles of blankets, watching the rain slide down the windows across the room.

Now that the concept of traveling back to Old Celdaria had been said aloud, her mind raced with questions she desperately did not want to ask but knew she would have to, and soon.

What if Simon sent her to the past, and then he lost his ability to thread, because his reawakened power was new and fragile, and she was left trapped there in a foreign world?

What if she found her mother, and did whatever she and Simon decided she must do, and it failed? What if she had to flee, having made some fatal mistake, and then returned to an unrecognizable future altered by her own misstep in the past?

And if everything proceeded as they hoped it would—if Eliana traveled to Old Celdaria and met her mother, if the Empire never rose, and maybe, if the Blood Queen never fell, and the world was never razed to near-destruction—what then? What would happen to the Eliana of now? To the Simon of now? And to Remy, and Harkan, and Patrik and Jessamyn, and everyone she had ever known and loved?

Would they, and she herself, cease to exist?

Sleep did not arrive for some time, and when it did, it brought troubled dreams that, blessedly, she did not remember upon waking.

## – 35 –
# RIELLE

*"Feel the wind slide round the trees,*
*Listen to the waves eat at the shore,*
*Watch the sun climb up the sky,*
*See the shadows reach always for more.*
*Listen! The old world speaks to you.*
*Wait! The old magic lives in you.*
*Breathe, and do not be afraid!"*

—"Prayer to the Old World," traditional

With Princess Kamayin's blade pressed against her throat, Rielle began to laugh.

"I told you not to make a sound," Kamayin hissed.

"What are you hoping to accomplish here, Your Highness?" Rielle asked. "If I wanted to, I could burn you to ashes."

"Not before I slit your throat. Not even you can conduct magic while bleeding out on the floor."

It was then that Rielle noticed how Kamayin's words trembled with tears. Quickly she clamped down on her furious instincts—*Kill this girl, burn her, punish her for daring to threaten you*—and smoothed the anger out of her voice.

"Why are you doing this?" She waited, listening to Kamayin's tight, shallow breathing. "Someone's put you up to it. Why?"

For a long moment, there was only silence and a distant rumbling—the arrival of a storm.

Then Kamayin's blade began to shake.

"They have him, Lady Rielle," Kamayin whispered at last. "They have my Zuka, and they told me if I kill you, they won't kill him."

"I assure you, if you kill me, or even if you try, nothing good will come of it. My country will wage war on yours, as will Borsvall, and possibly others, and then whatever has happened to your friend will be the least of your many problems."

After a tense pause, Kamayin whispered, "If I release you, will you kill me?"

"The thought has crossed my mind," Rielle admitted, "as it does anytime someone attacks me in my room in the middle of the night and holds me at knifepoint. But, no, I won't kill you. Then your country would wage war on mine, and I have quite enough to worry about at the moment."

At last, Kamayin relaxed and lowered her knife. Rielle stepped away, rubbing her throat, and watched as Kamayin sank onto a low cushioned stool, burying her face in her hands. She looked her age again, a frightened girl.

"How did you get past my guards?" Rielle demanded. *And how*, she thought, *did you get past Ludivine?*

"There's a secret passage that leads into this room," Kamayin mumbled. "Behind the mirror on the wall."

Rielle inspected the enormous mirror in question, pulling it carefully away from the wall, and discovered that, indeed, it masked a narrow doorway and a dark stone passage. She turned back at the sound of Kamayin's quiet sobs.

The girl sat hunched on the stool, her mouth screwed up with the effort of containing her tears. Beyond her, the wide square windows revealed a storm approaching across the Sea of Silarra. Lightning danced atop the waves, striking with an alarming ferocity and frequency. A low rumble shook the floor, the walls, the ceiling overhead.

Rielle tensed, listening. Was that thunder shaking the queens' palace?

Or was it something else? She recalled Jodoc's report in the Sunderlands—the earthquakes in Astavar, the blizzard in southern Mazabat. It had been months since that day, and here they all still stood. No irrevocable disaster had yet occurred.

She walked to the windows and opened one, allowing in a gust of salty air that brought with it the acrid bite of lightning and the bloom of rain. Once again, the strange sensation she had felt when approaching the shores of Mazabat returned to her—the sensation of being watched. And now, accompanying it, was something else. A tug on her fingers, on the crooks of her elbows, on the knobby length of her spine. The charge of the approaching storm? Perhaps.

And yet storms did not frighten her. This feeling did. If she was being watched by a foreign, all-seeing eye, then she was also being urged forward by mighty phantom hands, and she felt they were connected—the eye and the hands, all belonging to the same inexorable body.

Urging her forward. But to *what*?

She turned away from the storm, her temples pulsing with the thrum of her heartbeat. "Who is it that has your friend, Kamayin?"

"The Obex." The princess looked up at her, wide brown eyes shimmering with tears. "They hate you, Lady Rielle. They have no intention of allowing you to take Saint Tokazi's staff. They believe you to be the Blood Queen, and that you cannot be permitted to gather the castings of the saints."

"And they captured your friend to pressure you into killing me."

Kamayin visibly fought for composure. "Yes. Zuka is his name. He is an acolyte in the Holdfast and my dearest friend."

"And if you kill me, they'll release him."

"I know it sounds absurd."

"Indeed it does." She glanced at the bands around Kamayin's wrists. "You're a waterworker, aren't you? Why didn't you use your castings? You could have drowned me in my sleep."

Kamayin hesitated, and in her silence, Rielle found the answer.

"Because you don't want to kill me," she said. "You haven't killed before."

Miserably, Kamayin nodded. "My mothers have ensured that I know how to fight, but the most I've done is break my sparring teacher's nose."

"And if you'd managed to kill me, what then? The Gate would have fallen, with no one left alive capable of repairing it, and the Obex would all die anyway." Rielle waved her hand, turning back to the windows. "They won't kill your friend, Kamayin. They're testing me, and using you to do it. They were hoping I would lash out at you to defend myself, perhaps even kill you, and then I would have proven myself to be exactly what they believe me to be. They were willing to lose their princess if it meant exposing me."

Kamayin straightened, an angry light flashing in her dark eyes—but then, with an explosive smack, something enormous struck the palace, throwing both Rielle and Kamayin to the ground. Every window in the room shattered, spewing shards of glass. Through the empty panes came furious, howling winds and cold spits of rain. Miles of angry flashing clouds roiled across the sky. The sea was a tableau of whitecaps and black waves cresting some twenty feet in the air.

Rielle pushed herself to her feet, dimly noticing Kamayin rising beside her—and the soft buzz of her castings flaring to life.

She touched the princess's arm. "Don't waste the energy fighting this storm. It's of the Gate. You can't stop it."

Another slam against the palace sent paintings crashing down from the walls. The floor tipped as if trying to buck them off. Kamayin staggered, catching herself on the nearest bedpost. Rielle found her boots on the floor and tugged them on.

The bedroom door flew open, admitting Evyline and then, an instant later, Tal, flinging his scarlet magisterial cloak over his shoulders. And Ludivine last of all, gazing in despair at the shattered windows.

*I didn't hear her.* She sent Rielle a feeling of utter terror. *Kamayin. She slipped right past me. She walked through the walls between our rooms, and I heard nothing. I felt nothing.*

Rielle went to her, ignoring the terrible sight of her exposed, scarred arm. *Was it Corien? He's shielded me from you before.*

Ludivine shook her head. She held up her blackened hand. In the storm's light, it glittered like a jewel. *I think it was this.*

Rielle folded the ruined hand into her own. The puckered skin was rough and cold. "I swear to you, Lu, I will make it go away. I'll tear away your scar and crush it beneath the blade of my will."

Ludivine leaned her forehead against Rielle's. "I do not deserve a friend such as you."

Evyline stopped short at the sight of Kamayin. "Your Highness? Begging your pardon, but how...?"

"No time." Tal held out his hand for Rielle. "There are shelters underground. The queensguard will escort us there."

Rielle released Ludivine to glare at him. "I'm not going underground. I'm going to stop this."

"No, you're not. You're going to conserve your power for the task ahead."

"And how do you suppose we'll find Saint Tokazi's staff if Quelbani is buried beneath the ocean?"

"How do you suppose you'll repair the Gate if you're dead?"

Rielle shook her head. "Tal, you don't understand. I won't die. Not today. Not because of this storm."

The sky was alive with lightning; it cast unflattering lines across Tal's stricken face. "How can you possibly know when or how you'll die?"

"I don't. But I know my power, and I know what it can do."

Rielle turned away from him, pulled toward the balcony by a force she could not name. With a sharp cry, Atheria alighted upon it and then ducked into the room, shaking water from her wings.

Rielle smiled faintly, stepping across the rain-soaked, glass-strewn floor to meet her. The chavaile's black eyes watched her approach with unearthly steadiness, her breath steaming in the suddenly frigid air. All sound dimmed— the roar of the sea, the piercing howl of the wind, the shudder and groan of the storm-battered palace. Rielle heard only the resonant chime of her own heart, slowing to meet the drum of Atheria's, and she understood, as she touched the godsbeast's velvet muzzle, that the eye she had felt upon her, and the unseen hands she had felt touching her, and Atheria's drenched wings tender on her back, urging her closer, were one and the same.

She let her eyes unfocus, following the twin beat of their hearts down into the quiet space only they two could see—and suddenly Rielle's eyes streamed with tears, for Atheria glowed before her as hot and golden as the sun.

She looked down at herself, at first to shield her eyes from Atheria's glory, but then because she had to see the truth for herself—and there it was, glowing hot and golden in her own breast. The brilliant light that was the empirium, living inside her blood and bones—*of* her blood and bones—and it was telling her, through the storm, through the great unfeeling eye and the phantom, guiding hands, and Atheria's patient and tired gaze: *Come. Come find me.*

And it was nothing like when Corien crooned to her through her dreams, and it was not even the sweetness of Audric murmuring to her in the haven of their bed.

This voice was cold and pure and many, like the light of stars that burned for no one but themselves. And Rielle knew if she followed it, she would find Saint Tokazi's casting.

This voice was of the empirium, and it was trying to help her.

Tal grabbed her arm and spun her back around to face him, jarring her concentration.

Evyline moved swiftly toward him, her expression ferocious. "Lord Belounnon, release my lady at once."

Tal ignored Evyline, his gaze frantic as he searched Rielle's face. "Take me with you. You're going somewhere, and I won't let you go alone."

She could not even be angry with him. She touched his face, drawing him down to kiss his rain-soaked brow. "My path is not one for you to choose, dearest Tal."

"Please," he said reverently, his hands tender in her hair. "Let me come with you. I beg you. I want..." He swallowed. In her golden clarity, she saw his fragility, his confusion. "I want to understand how you are possible."

Rielle ached for him. Tal would never be able to understand what it meant to exist like this. He would always be separate from the empirium, no matter how often he prayed, no matter how diligently he studied. She pitied him deeply for it. She pitied them all.

She clasped his hand in hers. "Come, then."

Evyline started toward her with a sharp protest, and Ludivine sent Rielle an urgent, faint plea: *Don't take him with you. It's unkind to take him. The more he sees of your might, the more fervently he will despair.*

But Rielle ignored them all. Atheria knelt in the rain, and Rielle climbed onto her back, helping Tal up behind her. He clung to her, shivering, and then Rielle remembered the boy Zuka and found Kamayin watching her thoughtfully from the ruined bed.

"I'll find your friend, Your Highness," she said. "And I'll bring him home to you."

Then she guided Atheria out the window and into the storm.

❖

It was unlike any Rielle had ever seen, and she marveled at it.

The black clouds, miles high. The ferocious lightning cutting through the rain and wind like spears of white fire. Waves crashed against the shore, washing away dunes and tearing trees from the ground. Even Atheria fought to keep them airborne. Rielle lay low against her neck, Tal doing the same against her spine. The storm cracked open the ground, collapsing the pretty, white buildings nearest the shore.

"Well?" Tal shouted against her ear. The rain was cold, and so was the air, unseasonably so. They weren't dressed for this weather. Tal's fingers wrapped around her wrists like cold spiders. "Aren't you going to stop it?"

But Rielle knew she couldn't. Not yet. She read the beat of Atheria's wings and the beat of Atheria's heart and the beat of her own blood. The hands of the empirium were upon her, pulling her away from the sea.

"I can't," she shouted back through sheets of rain. "It's a distraction. We can use it."

"The Obex?" he cried.

She nodded. With the storm raging, the Obex would be afraid, maybe even frenzied. They would not see her coming.

Rielle waited until her mind cleared and found the empirium's cold gaze at once. She felt it hovering above her, all around her, in the deepest pit of her stomach. It stared at the city's heart, where delicately sculpted white buildings swayed amid a profusion of rain-slicked, broad-leafed trees.

She turned Atheria down into the storm, following the path of the terrible, ancient instinct with which she had been born.

◆◇◆

It did not take long to find them.

They were hiding in the Holdfast—the largest of the city temples, with great domed roofs that stood firm against the storm's onslaught. Trees and mountains had been carved into every inch of the exterior walls, and in the lightning, wind, and rain, the carvings shimmered and shifted as if they were alive.

Ludivine managed to send Rielle gasping surges of feeling. Through their connection, which seemed fragile and frayed as it never had before, Rielle felt a sensation like drowning.

*Lu, please rest,* she sent back to her gently. *Leave us to our task.*

*I'm sorry,* Ludivine replied, and her grief, her anger at her own inca-pacity, nearly overwhelmed Rielle. *They chose to hide in the Holdfast because it is the largest of the temples, the one most likely to withstand the storm. They have the boy. Zuka. They are furious and afraid. They have barricaded themselves—*

But then Ludivine cried out in pain and fell silent.

Rielle shuddered, and Tal shouted a question at her, but she could not find the voice to answer him. Instead she drove Atheria down toward the domed roofs, her vision a frantic, searing red, and with a quick thought and a stab of anger, she tore a great hole in the western wall of one of the topmost floors, through which Atheria dove.

Inside, those who had taken shelter in the Holdfast ran away from the collapsed wall, screaming and shouting. A robed acolyte and two others lay bleeding, having been caught by the flying stone.

Tal's hands tightened around Rielle's waist. "Tell me what's happening. Tell me you know what you're doing."

She hardly heard him. She scanned the soaring ceilings, the columns wrapped in stone vines, the gleaming wooden floors now covered in dust and rain. She listened to the vibrations of the air in this temple—the whispers and footfalls of everyone inside it, the bright pulsing innards of the empirium that turned in every leaf, every dark chamber.

Tal touched the inside of her wrist. "You're glowing," he said, but his voice came to her dim and clouded, and—*there*.

The Obex were below them, barricaded in classrooms on the fourth floor.

Rielle thought to Atheria, *Go*, and Atheria obeyed, plunging over the nearby railing and down into a circular atrium framed in greenery. Once they had landed on the fourth level, on a dark stone floor painted with golden leaves, Rielle dismounted and stormed toward the nearby wooden doors. They marked the entrance to the temple school, and the empirium told her—pricking her flesh with tiny white-hot needles of information—that the doors had been barricaded shut with great wooden planks, and piles of desks and chairs.

The gall of these Obex. The stupidity and the arrogance, to think such obstructions could stop her. Fury cracked through her body like a whip. She hurled it at the doors, and they flew open, flung off their hinges. The barricades went spinning away—chairs shattered, wooden planks reduced to splinters.

At the far end of the classroom huddled the Obex—thirteen in total, pale and dark, men and women, and all of them gaping at her, as if they were *surprised* that she could have found them, that she could have destroyed their pathetic excuse for a defense. One of them shoved forward a pale, wide-eyed boy—Zuka, the princess's friend. An offering, perhaps, a plea for mercy.

"Run fast," she told the boy. "And don't look back."

He obeyed, slipping on the polished floor, and once he'd gone, a glimmer caught Rielle's eye. She turned and saw a slight, brown-skinned woman frantically weaving several threads into a circle of light—the pet of the Obex, their indentured marque, doubtless trying to provide them an escape.

Rielle laughed. With a flick of her wrist, she broke the woman's neck. She collapsed, soundless; her threads vanished.

Behind her, Tal called her name, but Rielle had eyes only for those who had so foolishly thought they could best her. She stormed toward the Obex, knocking their knives and arrows from the air. She caught the light and wind and shadows hurled from their castings, knotted it all into pure blinding energy in her palms, and sent it careening back at them. Her power slit their throats, flung them back against the wall, dove inside their screaming mouths and burned them from the inside out.

And when she had finished, finally arriving at the far side of the room, where they all steamed and bled and crisped on the floor, she found on the floor a long wooden staff, thickly carved with the sigils of all seven temples. She retrieved it and rose to her feet. She admired its craftsmanship, how easily she wielded it, how nicely it fit in her hands.

And then, a flicker in the world around her—a familiar shift that sent her heart racing with anticipation.

This time, when Corien appeared, he was on his knees before her. His dark cloak pooled on a gleaming black floor. Beyond him were windows, a landscape of mountains and ice.

His pale eyes were bright as moons. "Darling child," he whispered, "you are a vision in red."

And then Rielle looked down at herself and saw that again, as in Polestal, her hands, her boots, her skirts were drenched in fresh blood.

The sight was startling enough to bring her back to herself. She blinked, stumbling back from Corien, but then he was no longer there, and she was staring instead at the classroom's wreckage. The blood painting the walls. The steaming, charred marks where her fire had scorched the floor.

*Even without me urging you on, this is who you are.* Corien's voice came, distant and gentle. *This is what you're capable of, and I accept that.*

Then he was truly gone, and without the comforting weight of his mind in hers, Rielle felt unmoored.

The room was silent, far from the chaos of the storm beyond its walls. She turned to find Tal, his face gone white. She put up her chin, staring him down, for there was something new in that quiet gaze of his—new, and fearful.

"I have the casting," she said to remind him that she had done what she was supposed to do, that there was nothing wrong with having killed these people. They had stolen a boy; they had threatened her life, and Kamayin's too. They would have kept the staff from her and, by doing so, would have doomed the world.

But with her fading rage came the wretched return of her humanity. Her mouth soured with the smell of blood, and her stomach turned hot with shame.

She went to Atheria and leaned against her for a long moment, breathing in the storm-sharp scent of her wings.

"All great work must begin somewhere," she whispered, repeating Corien's words, but the godsbeast remained still, and that stillness was no comfort. A moment longer, and the pull of the empirium had faded from Rielle's limbs. She was small and dim again; she was human once more.

"Why would it direct me to this place," she asked, her voice low and rough, "and tell me to do these things that I've done, and then afterward leave me alone in shame and confusion?"

Tal came to stand beside her. "The empirium?"

"Yes. It spoke to me. I *heard* it. It told me..." But then she fell silent, for in the new awful quiet of this room, she began to doubt herself. *Had* she heard the empirium? Or had it been her own murderous instinct driving her on? Or had it been Corien all along, directing her to do this thing, to kill these people, to take the staff, because he was, as he had confessed, impatient? Had he disguised his thoughts as those of the empirium?

She touched her temple, which had begun to ache. *Lu, are you there?*

Ludivine sent her a wordless, faint feeling—so gentle, so understanding, that Rielle's eyes filled with tears.

She turned away from Tal and climbed aboard Atheria.

"We'll tell them that the Obex threatened me and you," she said hollowly, once Tal had climbed up behind her. "We'll tell them that they threatened Zuka and Kamayin. It was self-defense. It won't be a lie."

"No," Tal said after a moment. "It won't be a lie."

He placed a gentle hand on her wrist, but that only made her feel worse, for her arms were covered in blood, and yet he touched her as if she were holy, a sacred thing to be worshipped.

And there was still the Gate's storm to be dealt with.

Wearily, she said to him, "Hold tight to me," and urged Atheria back out into the night.

◆◆◆

Then, two days later, as Rielle and Ludivine lay quietly by the windows in Rielle's rooms, watching earthshakers and windsingers clear the sunlit beach of debris, a letter from Audric arrived.

Rielle opened the note with joy in her heart, soothed by the sight of his familiar, meticulous penmanship.

Ludivine looked up at her from her pillow, frowning. Her lips were white and chapped. The blightblade scar had begun to creep across her jaw.

"Odd, that he didn't simply send a message through me," she observed.

"He tried to, but couldn't reach you," Rielle said, reading over his words, and then her stomach dropped, and she had to read one particular sentence several times before her mind would believe it.

"What is it?" Ludivine asked, struggling to sit.

Rielle looked up at her, the implications of what she was about to say settling like bricks upon her shoulders. "Queen Genoveve," she whispered, "is dying."

# 36

# ELIANA

*"And so I declare, in agreement with the other saints and with the authority of the governments we have established to bring order to our brave new world, that any surviving marques—that is, the offspring of humans and angels— are now considered enemies of the state, sentenced by nature of their treacherous blood to immediate and swift execution, and that anyone with knowledge of a marque's whereabouts and identity must surrender this informa- tion at once, or else suffer the same fate as these dangerous creatures whose tainted magic we cannot trust and must therefore extinguish."*

—An international decree written by Queen Katell the
Magnificent of Celdaria, dated February 17,
Year 6 of the Second Age

I t's like a web," whispered Remy, leaning close. "That's what Simon told me."
He sat beside Eliana on a low stone bench in the gardens of Willow, beneath one of the trees for which the estate was named. There was a small stream nearby. The gardens were full of them, little trickling rib- bons that kept the foliage lush and the flowers bright. Tall wetland grasses shivered in the afternoon breeze, and wild clumps of perfumed blooms bobbed happily along the dirt footpaths that wove through the trees.

They were alone except for Simon, who stood across a tidy clearing of clover and small white flowers, facing away from them. His shoulders were high and square, his fists clenched at his sides.

Even after two days of working with him, alternating between practicing small, focused tasks with her castings and watching him attempt to thread, Eliana could still hardly bear to look at him. His embarrassment and discomfort were palpable. His restless presence itched at her. She had asked him if he would prefer privacy, but he insisted it was important to have her near, as she had been when his power first resurfaced.

So here she was, sitting on her bench, trying desperately to resist the urge to either run from him or run *to* him and make him look at her. She would tell him not to be embarrassed, that she thought his threading was beautiful. She would take his face in her hands and hold him until his shoulders relaxed.

But instead she stayed solidly put.

"A web?" she asked.

Remy nodded. "I asked him a lot of questions last night, right before bed. Probably about fifty questions altogether. We had a long talk."

"I'm sure he enjoyed that," Eliana said, stifling a smile.

"Not at first, but he did eventually." Remy drew his knees to his chest. "He loves talking about traveling. About who he used to be."

There again was that terrible ache in her chest. *Who he used to be.* She doubted she would ever be able to shake the guilt of knowing that, were it not for her, he would not have been thrust into this strange, anchorless life. But then what? They would have both been in Old Celdaria when her mother fell, and most likely they would have been obliterated along with so many others.

Was this, then, the kinder future? A life of war and servitude to some faceless Prophet?

"Tell me what you mean," Eliana said with some difficulty. "About it being a web."

"He said that underneath the surface of the world," Remy said, "the world we can see, there's another world."

"The realm of the empirium," Eliana said, nodding.

"Yes, only marques can sense it in a way others can't. Not even you can, El, because you don't have angel blood. Marques can sense the billions and billions of threads connecting every person and place and moment. It's all connected. Every person is connected to every moment. Every place is connected to every other place. And marques are the only ones who can navigate all of that." Remy blew out a breath, bouncing a little where he sat. "Thinking about it makes me dizzy."

Eliana remembered what Simon had said during their first hour in the gardens the day before. "To get where you want to go," she added, "or *when* you want to go, you simply have to find the right thread and follow it."

"Easy, right?" Remy snorted and rested his chin on his hand. "I'm glad I don't have to do it."

She smiled a little, glancing up at Simon. He hadn't moved, except for his arms. Those he held out before him, loose and easy, like an artist, only instead of sculpting a figure from clay, he was pulling light out of nothing—a long, hair-thin light, bright enough to illuminate the entire gloomy clearing.

Eliana held her breath, watching him draw first one, then two, then three threads close to his chest. He cradled them there, as if spooning light into the cavity of his torso. But then the threads flickered. They brightened, dimmed, and vanished.

The clearing plunged back into gray.

Simon spat a curse, his body tensing once more. He dragged both hands through his hair and walked toward the clearing's edge.

Steeling herself, Eliana rose and went to him. He turned at her approach, his face a furious storm of misery.

"I can't hold any of them for longer than a few seconds," he said.

"I know," she replied. "I saw."

"I haven't even tried to find a thread in time. I've only tried little threads, ones that would take us back to the house if we followed them. But even those I can't manage." He looked away, his jaw working. "Once, this was easy. It felt like breathing. And now it's like clawing my way through a swamp determined to drown me."

For a moment, she watched his face in profile—his straight nose, the pucker of his ruined skin, the ferocious bright-blue of his eyes in the gray light.

"Well," she said, "you *have* been working at it for two whole days now, after eighteen years of your power lying dormant. I can't imagine why it hasn't all come crashing back to you at once. Eighteen years is hardly anything, after all."

A tiny smile played at the corner of his mouth. "You're mocking me."

She grinned up at him. "I am." And then she touched his cheek and made him look at her. "I think it's beautiful when you thread. Every time it happens, I lose my breath."

"They're spotty," he said, his voice softer now. "The threads are fragile. They hardly hold."

"To you, maybe. To me, they're miraculous."

"They're useless if they can't carry you where you need to go."

"All great work must start somewhere," she said, and then shivered a little, for she hadn't intended to say those words. They'd surfaced as if someone had reached inside her and tugged them out. She touched her throat, frowning.

"Yes, that's true," Simon said, "but unfortunately we don't have time to sit here for ages while I recover my abilities."

Remy marched over, his boots squishing in the mud. "You know what you should do," he announced, stating it half like a question.

"Ah, yes," Simon said, "I'd forgotten you were the threading expert here."

Remy crossed his arms. "I'm serious."

"I know." Then he ruffled Remy's hair with a little smile, and Eliana's heart jumped into her throat. She had to step back from them, put distance between herself and Simon's body.

"The first time you threaded," said Remy, "was when Eliana healed me. And you were holding on to her, and she was using her power. So"—he shrugged—"just do that again."

Eliana stared at him. "We can't possibly re-create that moment. You would have to be dying again."

"Well, not that *exact* moment. But you've been doing lots of little things with your castings—moving branches, flooding streams. Maybe you need to do something bigger." Then Remy examined Simon's face. "Maybe you should try healing him this time instead."

Eliana could hardly contain her surprise, and yet the idea made a certain sense. She looked to Simon, letting her eyes roam over the ravaged landscape of his face, what she could see of his arms.

He looked as though someone had slapped him. "No," he said, backing away from her. "I won't allow it."

"It could work though," Remy insisted. "Your whole body's been beaten up. You told me you're always hurting."

Eliana frowned at him. "What does that mean?"

"Never mind," said Simon, shooting a glare at Remy. "I'm fine."

Remy rolled his eyes. "He told me just last night. He said, 'Will you please, for the love of all that is good in this world, leave so I can go to bed, because my body is screaming at me and soon I'll be screaming at you.' And then I asked what that's supposed to mean, and he said that he's always in pain because of his training with the Prophet." Remy paused, looking smug. "And then I went to bed."

Silence fell between them. It took Eliana several long beats before she could look at Simon again. When she did, she saw that he had closed his face to her. He was all Wolf now—cold and hard, jaw square.

"Don't do that," she said quietly. "Don't pretend with me."

His smile was sharp. "Isn't that what we do, Eliana? We pretend, you and I."

"Not anymore. If you're going to send me back in time, if we're going to attempt this madness, then you're going to look me in the eye and tell me only truths." She glared up at him. "Are you in pain?"

For a long time, he said nothing. Then something in the lines of his body relented.

"Yes," he said tightly. "Always."

"Because of the Prophet?"

"And many others."

Her throat ached at the sight of him standing there, battered and brave, bearing his pain in silence. "Will you tell me, someday? Will you tell me what happened to you?"

He caught her hand in his and pressed a kiss to her palm. "I hope I'll have the time for it," he said against her skin, and then he turned away from her, leaving her swaying a little in his absence.

Remy gave her a shrewd look. "I'll leave you alone, then, for a while. If that would be helpful?"

Eliana made a face at him, which he enthusiastically returned. And then, once he was gone, she took a deep breath and turned around to find Simon watching her thoughtfully.

"Well?" She gestured at his face. "Can I try?"

"I don't know what I'd be without my scars," he said quietly. "They remind me of what I've done, and what's been done to me."

"And don't you want to forget at least that second part?"

He shook his head. "No. My anger fuels me. Without my pain, I'm nothing."

"I don't believe that. We are more than what's been done to us. We are more than our anger. And I think we have to try this. Or, we can sit out here watching your threads fade again and again and wait for the Empire to find us."

It had begun to rain, hardly more than a light mist, and the thin silver curtain of it painted the clearing a queer iridescent shade, as if the light were coming from within the raindrops themselves, and not from the clouded sky.

Simon nodded curtly. "Fine."

They sat on the ground, in a dry patch beneath a broad oak draped with ropy white moss. Eliana's nerves took root in her belly. She made a show of arranging herself in the grass, and when she looked up again, Simon was watching her, his eyes guarded and grave.

Before she lost her courage, she took his face in her hands and closed her eyes, and then, after she had grown used to the unbearable intimacy of it—their knees touching in the grass, his cheeks rough under her palms, his breath moving the ends of her hair—she said quietly, "Hold on to me. Like you did in Karlaine."

At once, he slid his hands up her arms, cradling them gently. As though a broken circle had been completed, she felt calm settle within her. Linked securely to him, she focused all her thoughts and energy into the twin sleeping suns of her castings. They began to vibrate, awakening against his skin. She felt herself shifting, gliding, as if slipping between two cool layers of the world, cut away from each other to create a space for her between them. Her jaw relaxed and her tongue softened. She was liquid and warm; she hummed along with her castings.

"Does it hurt?" she whispered.

"Not yet," he said dryly.

She smiled a little, and when she opened her eyes, her vision was a hazy gold, but Simon's eyes—that brilliant, burning blue—cut through the shimmer to lock on to her.

Each time she accessed her power, it became easier to fall into the realm of the empirium. To let her mind loosen and stretch, to direct her vision to peel away the veneer of the human world. How precious it was, how simple and fragile, the shell upon which they all walked and fought and loved—wind and water, earth and flame. And beneath that, a diamond world, a glittering country. The true golden vastness that had existed, always, and would continue to exist, always, no matter what empires ruled the world or what queens rose and fell.

She shuddered, letting out a cracked breath. For as she slipped inside the roaring river of her power, letting its currents bear her farther and farther away from where her body sat in the dirt, she began to see Simon, truly see him, as she never had before. Just as she had seen Remy, and Patrik, and Jessamyn, in that horrible pasture in Karlaine. The light they carried, the light that made them. Creatures of the empirium, all. Jagged and lacking where wounds had carved bits of them away.

"Oh, Simon," she whispered, for now she saw the light of him, how he blazed and teemed. And even more clearly, she saw the hurt that had been dealt him. As she had seen Jessamyn's wounded legs and Patrik's broken arm, so did she now see the scars mapping Simon's body like a snarl of shadows encasing the sun. Scars up and down his limbs, his abdomen, his face and chest. Even more brutal, the cruel lattice of his back, where the marque wings had once lived. And these weren't even the worst of his scars. Those lived in his mind—pulsing and wicked, a thick black web so dark it surpassed her understanding.

But she felt them through the golden reach of her power. She felt the jarring pain of every blow, the cut of every blade, and what each had done to his tired mind.

"What is it?" His voice came to her softly. "What do you see?"

She shook her head and leaned forward, gathering him closer. Her forehead met his.

"Please tell me I'm not hurting you," she said, tears clogging her voice.

"You're not." His hands slid up her arms to cup the back of her head. "I'll tell you if you do."

"I see everything that's been done to you. Every lash, every cut and cruelty. I can't even understand all of what I see. Simon." She said his name again and again, as if every utterance could restore a stolen piece of himself. "Simon, I'm so sorry."

"Don't cry for me." He pressed a kiss to her cheek, to the corner of her mouth. "Please don't."

But she would cry, and she would help him. She couldn't possibly do it all at once in this garden, and maybe not ever. Those scars in his mind— they were too deep for her to soothe. She sensed the truth of that. They were too cruel, had been carved too skillfully. Maybe, if she had years to study her power and practice. But that was time they did not have.

Still, she moved her hands down his face. She traced soft lines with her fingers, drawing paths through the golden sea of the empirium, and pressed her palms against the broad, solid plane of his chest. She found a gnarled scar that had been carved across his breastbone—jagged and wide, uglier than the others.

A cruel cut from Rahzavel's blade, inflicted upon Simon weeks ago, just before their battle against the crawlers in Karajak Bay. In a shuddering, liquid-gold flash, she saw the Invictus assassin's grinning white face bearing down on her. She felt the blade piercing her own chest as it had pierced Simon's, carving away skin and muscle. She heard Simon's terrible, ragged howl, and a second scream—Rahzavel's—mocking him.

"No," she whispered again and again, drawing her fingers up and down the scar slowly, until she knew the map of it. Until it was as familiar to her as the bones of her own hand. Then she pressed her palms against it—twin suns against one dark hurt. She poured all the energy she could summon into him, into the lack where Simon should have been, and then, trembling, she felt his hands in her hair.

"Eliana," he said, his voice thick, "open your eyes. *Look.*"

She did, feeling supple and faint, her vision clearing just enough to see what Simon saw.

Threads—a dozen of them, perhaps more. Bright and unwavering. They hovered in the branches just overhead and in the cool misting air around them and in the tangled grass. Immediately Eliana sensed their strength, their steadiness. How they yearned for Simon's power as her own castings longed for hers.

Slowly he released her, reaching for the threads, and his face was open and soft, as it had been in Karlaine, and this time Eliana did not look away. She watched him until the burn of her eyes became unbearable. She blinked, wiping her wet face with unsteady fingers.

And then Simon murmured, "Go. Through that passage, there."

He had woven the threads into a shimmering hoop of light. It outlined a shift in the air, a discoloration. One of the threads, the brightest, clung to his palm.

"Where does it lead?" she asked.

"To the house." His focus was remarkable and carried a weight, as if a net of steel wires bound him to the threads shimmering before him. His voice was soft and deep, sleep-colored. "It's all right. It's quite safe. I can feel its strength." And then he glanced at her, once, and she would never forget that unguarded expression on his face—how in awe he was of what was happening and how completely he understood that it was her doing.

"Go, Eliana," he said quietly. "I'll hold on to you. It will feel like walking into winter, for a moment, and then out again."

She stood, shaky, hating that it was necessary to walk away from him, and as she stepped through the ring of shifting light, the reality of what had happened truly registered. It was *her* power that had made this possible. Her strength, her focus.

*Your father was the Lightbringer*, Simon had said, *and you are the light*.

And here she was, proving this to be true. Her power could destroy, but it could also restore. It could heal and illuminate. She could summon storms, but she could also mend hurts. Her power was full of rage, and yet capable of extraordinary tenderness, a dichotomy of darkness and light existing as one.

An immensity of relief overcame her as she stepped out into one of the mansion's sitting rooms, where Harkan sat with Remy by the fire, mending torn shirts.

Remy was on his feet at once, grinning. "I told you it would work," he told her, and then he was leading her to a chair beside Harkan. "Is Simon coming?"

"In a moment, I expect," murmured Eliana tiredly.

Remy jumped to his feet and hurried toward the receiving hall.

As Eliana watched Simon's light fizzle out across the carpet, she shook her head, laughing a little. "I'm no Blood Queen," she whispered. She sat back in her chair and breathed away the threads' lingering chill. "I'm not her."

Harkan set down his mending. "Of course you're not," he said, giving her a small smile. "I could have told you that."

"Yes, but I think I'm finally, truly realizing it. That I'm my own self, and not her. I have power, yes, but I shouldn't always be afraid of it."

"I'm glad for you. Truly." He reached for her hand, then hesitated.

She took his instead. "It's all right. You can touch me."

His smile seemed to shrink with every passing second. "I feel as though I can't anymore. You're so far from me now. You feel beyond me, and mighty in this way I don't understand."

"And if I am beyond you?" Eliana watched him steadily. "Does that mean we can't even be friends? Will you drug me again?"

He pulled away from her, his face raw with shame. "I'm sorry, El. I wish I was more, for you. I wish I was better at this. I wish I hadn't…"

His voice dropped into silence.

Eliana swallowed against a hard knot of hurt. She had not been prepared for this conversation, nor for the terrible, distant sadness on Harkan's face. She knew so well the way he held himself, the subtle ways he wore his despair. But then the front door opened and shut, and a few seconds later, Simon was storming into the room, Remy at his heels.

Simon stopped when he saw her, and then he smiled, a broad, easy grin. It was something she had never seen before on his face—such a real, true expression of unabashed happiness. For a moment she could hardly feel her own body. She was only a shapeless, fizzy, foolish joy, watching Simon smile.

"It worked," he said, breathless, and then he went to her in two long strides, and she was rising to meet him. His arms came around her, tight and strong, and she pressed her face against his shirt, breathing in the rain on his collar and the sweat on his skin. In his arms, she nearly forgot herself. She nearly tilted up her head to kiss him.

But Remy, and Harkan. And the open door, which could admit visitors at any moment. If she was going to kiss him, she wanted the kiss all to herself.

So she stepped back from him, her fingers lingering on his sleeves, and when she turned to find Harkan, schooling her face into something more neutral, something less giddy, he was gone.

—◇—

That night, Eliana could find neither sleep nor a sense of calm. When she closed her eyes, she saw an overwhelming assortment of images—the memories Simon's scar had held, of his torture at Rahzavel's hands. The threads hovering at his fingertips. The web of wounds in his mind.

Harkan's empty, brave smile.

Opening her eyes was no better, for the first thing she saw was the door, and she knew that past the door was the hallway, and at the end of that was Simon's door. Was he sleeping, or was he also lying awake, his brain as frenzied as hers?

A few minutes more, and she sat up, swung her legs out of bed. She got up, then sat back down. Then she rose again and went to stand crossly by the window, staring out into the wet woods.

It would be easier, she thought darkly, if he came to her, since she apparently could not find her courage.

Just when she had decided to climb back into bed and find relief in the touch of her own hands, a shape manifested in the corner of her room—black and vague, flickering in and out of itself.

Eliana's hand went to Arabeth, ready on her bedside table. "Zahra?"

"Oh, my queen," came the wraith's distorted voice, still not as strong as it had once been, before her imprisonment in the blightbox. She dropped to the floor. The insistent pressure of her shifting form pulled on the air, bringing Eliana to her knees.

She touched the chill empty shadow of the wraith's head, her streaming dark hair. "What is it? What's wrong?"

A knock on the door interrupted them, and when Eliana opened the door, she found Simon on the other side, glowering, and past him, the house bustling to life as people left their rooms, tugging on boots and coats.

"What's happened?" Eliana demanded.

"Red Crown scouts have arrived with news," Simon replied. "Empire forces are coming north from the southern regions of the continent. Reinforcements, and unexpected ones. Our intelligence said nothing about this. They'll be here in less than two weeks."

Eliana's skin turned cold. "They know I'm here," she said, seeing the truth in his eyes. "They're coming for me."

# 37

# RIELLE

*"I've now spent weeks ensconced in the Belbrion archives—
and once I gained the trust of their head librarian, Quinlan,
I even gained access to a different, superior library. I have
sworn not to give you further details, except to say that these
archives belong to a rather eccentric woman named Annick,
whose intellect and character I trust completely. She and
Quinlan are lovers, and while Annick was at first unhappy
to welcome me into her home, we have become fast friends,
due to a shared fascination with texts on the empirium. And
this I must tell you, Audric, before anything else: During
my weeks of study, I have come to understand that, whatever
happens, we must trust Rielle. The prophecy, this talk of a
Sun Queen and a Blood Queen…it is folly. Humans aren't
all goodness or all badness, and reducing Rielle to this
choice—presenting her with two impossible and inhuman
extremes—is a terrible cruelty, and it will be our undoing.
We must allow her to live a life of her own making."*

—A letter written by King Ilmaire Lysleva to Prince Audric
Courverie, dated May 9, Year 999 of the Second Age

Rielle had insisted they arrive back in Âme de la Terre on foot, rather
than flying straight to Baingarde on Atheria, but there were problems

with that plan—namely, that she had flown back quickly with only Tal and Ludivine and had therefore left the Sun Guard behind to make their journey by more conventional means.

And then there was the problem of the city itself.

Word must have traveled that she would be making her way home from Mazabat. People must have been waiting at their windows, watching for Atheria on the horizon. For when the godsbeast touched down at the edge of the city, in the tall, thin grasses of the Flats, there was already a crowd waiting on the lake bridges encircling the city. They stood along the central roads that wound lazily northward from the outer districts, toward Mount Cibelline and Baingarde, built upon its slopes. They leaned out of windows and clustered on rooftops.

Not the entire city, not by half, but still many thousands.

And they were shouting her name—not the name with which she had been born, but the names they had given her.

"Blood Queen!" they cried.

"Lady of Death!"

"Kingsbane! Kingsbane!"

That was one Rielle hadn't heard before, and one that made her feel sparkling and hot, as if she'd stepped too close to a cliff's edge and caught herself, right at the last moment. The giddy feeling of having barely avoided disaster.

She held her head high and did as Audric had instructed her in those early days of her national tour. She waved and smiled, ignoring the jeers, the furious cries. No one threw anything at her—perhaps not even the angriest among them dared test her—but they waved crimson banners. They thrust sun pendants at her, the golden surfaces once pristine and now dark with red paint. They crowded close, an aggression in their nearness. The air popped like the heat of a hungry fire.

"We must get you to the castle," Tal muttered. He wore Saint Tokazi's staff around his torso on a leather strap, much of it hidden beneath his cloak. "Take Atheria and go."

She shot him a look. "I won't be cowed. I won't run from them. They can't harm me."

Ludivine sent her a feeling of urgency. *I agree with Tal. Your presence merely serves to provoke them.*

*Then provoke them I shall.* Rielle caught the eye of a ferociously glowering man, his face puckered with hatred. She flashed him a dazzling smile. He spat at her feet, and she smiled even more brightly.

"Where's my mother?" someone cried as Rielle stepped off the bridge and entered the city proper.

"Bring them back!"

*Those who died at the fire trial,* said Ludivine.

*Obviously.* Rielle squared her shoulders. *I will say something to them.*

*No. It's neither the time nor the place for that.*

*It's the time and place when I say it is,* Rielle snapped. She would stop in the market square up ahead, she decided. She would stand on the steps and address them all, tell them she had been studying resurrection, that she had been guiding her power down a path that would someday mean an end to death. No more soldiers killed mysteriously in the cold north. No more unforeseen attacks that would leave dozens dead.

She picked up her muddy skirts and made swiftly for the market steps. Someone spat at her; someone did, at last, throw a fistful of mud that hit her boot. Tal called for her to stop, but she ignored him. He grabbed her wrist and she wrenched her arm free.

*Rielle, this isn't the way,* Ludivine said, but the feeling of her thoughts was weak.

They were, all of them, weak.

Rielle climbed the steps and turned to face the crowd with her head held high.

But before she could speak, there came a sound to her right, beyond Tal. She whirled and saw a man marching forward out of the crowd, his dagger flashing.

Astonished not that someone would try to kill her, but that they would do it so stupidly, she watched him coldly.

Atheria darted between them, rearing up with her front legs flying. Her wings cast immense shadows across the square.

Those nearest the chavaile cried out and jumped back, but the man—wild-eyed, grim-faced—tried to dart around her. Atheria's ears flattened. With a hiss, she bared her long, black teeth.

"It's all right, Atheria," Rielle said. "He can't hurt me."

Atheria subsided at once, and the man pushed past her. Tal lunged forward to intercept him instead, but with a flick of her wrist, Rielle stopped him, freezing his body midstride.

And then she saw the man's dagger flying at her—a decent enough throw with good aim, but still she stifled a laugh at the sight of it, and only because she thought, at the last moment, that Audric would advise her against laughing with so many eyes upon her.

Instead she raised her fingers and stopped the blade in the air. It dissolved to infinitesimal specks of metal and bronze and floated away in the wind.

Then, gently, Rielle flattened her palm and forced the man to his knees. In the tense silence of the watching crowd, she approached him. She stood over him, watching him tremble, and relished the sight of his terror until two tears squeezed out of his limpid eyes, painting tracks down his cheeks.

"As Sun Queen," she announced, her voice ringing out clear and strong, "I am and will continue to be merciful. Even to the murderous and treasonous among you."

Then she bent to kiss the man's forehead, her throat clenching in disgust at the grimy, slick texture of his skin. Without another word, she left him kneeling there in the dirt, held out her arm for Ludivine, and continued up the city streets toward Baingarde. The silent crowd parted before her. Rielle did not allow the man to rise until she had reached the temple district, where the sounds of prayer song washed her mind clean of anger.

Audric was inside his office, in a meeting with the Lady of Coin and the Lord of Letters and three other advisers, all of whom bowed their heads and swiftly left upon Rielle's arrival.

Once they were alone, her exhaustion rose up like a river swell, and when Audric came around his desk, she met him halfway. His arms came around her tightly, his hands soft in her travel-dusted hair. She closed her eyes and pressed her cheek to his chest until the sensation of her fatigue was not so overwhelming.

"A month apart is too long, my love," he said. He kissed her hair, her cheeks, and then her mouth, then led her to the sofa against the windows. He sat in the cushions, and she climbed into his lap. He held her in silence, stroking circles between her shoulder blades until she found the will to speak.

"They were waiting for me," she whispered against his collar, breathing in the scent of his skin, his hair. "Thousands of them, on the bridges and in the streets."

"I know." Audric's voice was steady. Even without Ludivine to help her, Rielle sensed the quiet force of him, like a physical thing in her mind, soothing all her worries. "I hope you aren't angry I didn't come to meet you."

She looked up at him. "Why should I be?"

"I thought it would be best for you to handle the situation on your own." His soft gaze met her own. "God, how I missed your face."

She kissed him, long and slow, and then, drowsy, subsided against him. "They hate me," she said after a moment.

"Not all of them do," he replied.

"Even some is too many. Why should they fear me? Why don't they love me?"

"You know the answer to that."

She frowned against him. "If they'd only step back a little from their anger and their fear of things they don't understand, they'd see that there's no danger in me. I don't want to hurt them."

"I think, given time, they will see this well enough." Then there was a pause, and when Audric spoke again, his voice was grave. "I received a letter from Queen Bazati. She told me what happened with the Obex."

Rielle stilled. "Did she?"

"She said they attacked you, and Princess Kamayin's friend, as well."

"That's true."

"She said you killed them. Every single one of them."

She pushed herself back from him. "That's also true."

"Wouldn't incapacitating them have worked just as well?"

"They deserved to be punished," she said at once. "Not only for attacking me and Zuka, the boy, but also for endangering the lives of everyone in the world by trying to keep the staff from me." Then, worried that this reasoning was still too cold for him, she added, "And anyway, they attacked us—me, Tal, the boy. It was self-defense."

Audric nodded thoughtfully. "Yes. That's what I thought."

"Then why ask me?"

"I wanted to hear you say it. I wanted to see the light in your eyes as you said it."

She stiffened. "Because you wanted to ensure that it wasn't simply bloodlust that made me kill them? That my power hadn't gotten the better of me?"

"That's not what I meant, darling."

But she sensed it was in fact what he had meant, and she couldn't even be angry at him for it, though she wanted to be. She pushed herself off the sofa, avoiding his gaze.

"Well, then," she said. "Perhaps I should pay a visit to your mother."

"She's sleeping just now. I'm loath to wake her."

"What exactly is wrong with her? In your letter, you didn't say."

He frowned at his feet. "I'm not sure, and neither is Garver, nor any of the royal healers. I worry that..."

He paused.

She went to him, reaching for his hand. He squeezed it gratefully.

"I worry that it's a matter of her no longer wishing to be in this world," he began again. "She hardly eats. She barely sleeps. Terrible nightmares plague her. She talks of nothing else but Father. Him, and you."

That startled her. "Me?"

"She talks madness, Rielle." Audric looked up at her, his dark eyes solemn. "She says you can't be trusted. She says everything that happened at the fire trial was your fault. I told her that's ludicrous. I told her an angel was behind the attack. I reminded her of the Sunderlands and the Gate. She refuses to listen to reason."

Rielle forced herself to look right at him. "She must miss Bastien terribly."

"Yes, but it's more than that. My mother is a rational being. I've never imagined her to be the kind of person who would let herself waste away like this."

"Grief is a terrible thing," Rielle forced out, her mind faintly buzzing as it retrieved memories of the fire trial against her will—Bastien's and Lord Dervin's still bodies, flat on the ground. Her own father, his eyes fluttering shut as he sang to her. "You have never seen your mother suffer a loss as terrible as this. My own mother's death altered my father forever."

Audric nodded to himself, brow furrowed. She sat down beside him, letting the moment of their shared loss stretch between them. Pretending, for his sake, that she felt her grief as keenly as he felt his. She kept very still, forcing her mind blank and clear, until the truth of her terrible lie dimmed.

At last, Audric sighed and rubbed his hands over his face. "There's something else."

Rielle looked up sharply at the change in his voice.

"Has Lu told you?" he asked. "About her brother."

"Merovec? No. Why?"

He blew out a long breath. "He arrives in three days for a two-week visit. He wants to pay his respects to Mother, as he hasn't seen her since Father's death or the death of Lord Sauvillier."

Rielle raised her eyebrows. This was unexpected. "Why didn't you tell me this in your letter?"

"I assumed he would have written Lu, or else she would have somehow sensed his intentions. Though she's not truly his sister, the body she possesses was, and I thought…" He gestured, a slight sadness falling over his face, as it always did when either of them spoke of Ludivine's true nature. "I thought she might have known already."

"No. She didn't, and she said nothing to me." She hesitated. "Lu's not well, Audric."

"The blightblade scar?"

"It's spreading. It's interfering with her ability to read thoughts and communicate with me."

He stood. "And her ability to protect you from Corien."

She would never grow used to the sound of Corien's name falling from Audric's lips. It was like trying to shimmy into a gown that did not quite fit.

"Yes," she replied. "That too."

He was quiet for a long moment, staring out the window. When he turned back, his face had slightly closed to her.

"Then you must practice, I suppose, and continue studying," he said. "If Ludivine isn't healed, then you'll be left defenseless against him."

"Don't use that word." She rose, watching him return to his desk. "I'm not defenseless. We've discussed this before."

"I know." His voice was hollow, weary. "I shouldn't have said that. I'm sorry. You aren't defenseless. I only meant that, with Lu, you're more protected than you are alone. You have an adviser in her, and she offers you counsel I cannot." He gave her a small smile. "And I know it would please you to heal her. I know you want to help—her, and all of us."

In an instant, she had forgiven him. The quiet love on his face warmed her. It was trite to compare his ardor to sunlight, and yet every time he looked at her, that was what she felt—a warm, spreading glow from her scalp to her toes. He was the sun to her hungry earth. He was the steady voice in her mind that spoke to her when she didn't feel steady at all.

She went to him and climbed once more into his lap. He welcomed her easily, clinging to her softness as she settled against him. He whispered her name, his eyes drifting shut at her touch, and this time when she kissed him, she did not stop.

—◆—

Merovec arrived at three o'clock in the afternoon, three days later, and the whole city came out to greet him.

From her rooms, as her maids dressed her, Rielle watched his progress through the city. Evyline, at the door, kept clucking her tongue. They would be late.

But Rielle did not relish the idea of standing there at the castle gates, twiddling her thumbs while Merovec took his time wandering through the city. She changed her gown four times before settling on one she deemed suitable—a velvet gown of deep plum and forest green, with a wide, swooping neckline that left her shoulders bare and gold trim at the sleeves and skirts. More of a winter gown than a spring one, but she couldn't resist the drama of it—nor the unabashed House Courverie colors. The maids braided some of Rielle's hair back from her face and left the rest falling free in wild, dark waves.

"Ready," she said at last, primly, as she glided past Evyline out the door.

Evyline blew out a sharp breath and followed her, the rest of the Sun Guard falling into formation behind them.

"My lady," Evyline began.

"Yes, my darling Evyline?" said Rielle.

"I don't think it wise to keep Lord Sauvillier waiting. In fact, as a general rule, I think we should scramble to please him."

"Evyline, who is the Sun Queen? Me, or Merovec?"

"My lady," said Evyline, exasperated, "that is not my point. House Sauvillier—"

"Oh, I know all about House Sauvillier," Rielle said, waving her hand. "Money and power and popularity and more land than they know what to do it. Awful, rocky land in the north, where it snows constantly and no one of sound mind likes to live, but it's land nonetheless, I suppose."

"It's just that in the wake of everything that's happened with, ah, His Highness and Lady Ludivine... That is, with the betrothal broken, and your, ah, relationship with His Highness so publicly known..."

Rielle stopped walking. "Evyline, do you think me ignorant of circumstances in my own life? And the political dynamics of my own country?"

Evyline flushed. "No, my lady."

"Well, then. Let's walk on in silence, shall we?"

And so they did, until emerging into the brightly lit stone yard outside the castle doors. A massive crowd had gathered at the lower gates, waving the colors of House Sauvillier—silver, russet, and slate blue. Raucous cheers met Rielle's ears. They cheered for Merovec, for Ludivine. Merrily, they sang the old northern traveling song: "Beware, beware the Sauvillier smile..."

Just before Rielle joined Audric and Queen Genoveve, thin and pale in her mourning gown, Evyline touched her arm, holding her back.

Rielle nearly snapped at her—until she saw the expression on her face.

"I only ask that you be careful, my lady," Evyline said softly. "I do not trust him. And I very much dislike the things I have heard about stirrings in the north."

Rielle relented, squeezing Evyline's gold-gloved hand. "We will discuss this later."

Then, with a twinge of apprehension in her breast, she turned with a bright smile to greet the Shield of the North.

# 38

# ELIANA

*"I've never had many friends. Most people think I'm fool-*
*ish for believing in the old stories and for writing about*
*them and for telling them over and over and changing*
*things about them to make them better. The only person*
*who's never teased me even once is Eliana. She doesn't*
*believe the old stories are true, not anymore, but she lis-*
*tens every time I tell them. I help her sleep by reading them*
*aloud to her. When I cry or get angry because I can't decide*
*on the right words, she holds my hand until I find them."*

—Journal of Remy Ferracora,
July 27, Year 1015 of the Third Age

As the scouts informed the others of what they had seen—a force
of Empire soldiers, thousands strong, moving inexorably toward a
city that held hundreds of such soldiers already—Eliana carefully watched
Simon's face, but it gave nothing away.

All the feeling he had worn recently vanished, a shutter swiftly falling
down over his eyes. When the scouts finished speaking, and Ester had led
them away to be fed and have their wounds tended to, a silence fell over
those left in the room. Simon glanced at Eliana only once, and then turned
away to stand at the far window.

Patrik blew out a breath, his arm bound in a sling. Remy waited, fretting at the edge of his chair, Harkan sitting still and silent beside him. Dani leaned back in her own chair, a thoughtful frown on her face. Jessamyn stood in the corner, leaning on her crutch and glaring at the floor, her faded red hair falling in two neat plaits down her back.

"Well, we clearly need to leave," she said, "and as quickly as possible. We'll go west once the danger has passed, cut south toward Morsia, and avoid the army altogether. Aren't there several Red Crown strongholds along the way? We'll see what they need, help as we can. Perhaps by then we'll have heard news of your Astavar friends and Hob, and can join them in the Vespers."

When no one responded, she glanced irritably at Patrik. "Why aren't you saying anything?"

"If what Eliana and Simon have told me is true," he said slowly, "it won't matter if we run. The Empire is hunting Eliana. They'll find us wherever we go."

"Then here's where we part ways. We go our way. Eliana goes hers. They don't care about us. They'll be focused on finding her. It's the perfect opportunity to do a lot of good while they're distracted." Jessamyn's gaze cut to Eliana, her expression softening slightly. "I'm sorry, Eliana. But there are only so many of us left in Red Crown. We have to protect ourselves."

Patrik shook his head. "I think our priorities must shift."

Jessamyn stared at him. "You mean give up our mission. Abandon the cause and help Eliana instead."

"You saw what she did in Karlaine. You've heard who Simon and Zahra claim her to be. She *is* the cause." Patrik rubbed a tired hand down his face. "If we protect her, if we help ensure she succeeds, we could save many more lives than we could ever hope to on our own."

"Or we could die. And with Astavar fallen, I'm not particularly keen to throw in my lot with some lost princess who may not, in fact, be a princess, and a marque who may or may not be able to travel through time." She looked quickly at Eliana, then Simon. Her mouth thinned. "Sorry. Again."

Eliana gave her a half smile. "I wouldn't want to throw in my lot with me either."

"But she *is* a princess," Remy said, frowning. "More than that, she's the Sun Queen. Haven't you been listening? Don't you know the prayers? And if the Emperor finds her before she's ready to face him, you'll be dead anyway. So why run?"

Jessamyn considered him appraisingly.

"Listen to the boy," Zahra said, smiling. "He's wiser than his age might suggest."

But Jessamyn would not relent. "You said, 'if we ensure she succeeds.' Succeed at what, exactly? Simon will send her back in time, if he's in fact capable of it—and I hate myself a little for saying such a preposterous thing aloud—and then what?"

"I bet you once thought bringing someone back from the dead was preposterous too." Remy's chin jutted stubbornly.

"I'll talk to my mother," Eliana replied, feeling even as she said the words that they were not enough.

Jessamyn's mouth thinned. "Ah, yes. The Blood Queen. She was one for diplomatic conversation, was she?"

"And how would she react," added Dani quietly, "if some girl appeared before her, claiming to be her daughter? She might fear it a trick. She might attack you."

Remy, perched on the very edge of his chair, looked ready to combust. "Queen Rielle would know about marques. She would understand time travel and what they could do. She would believe El. I know she would."

"You didn't know her, Remy," said Patrik tiredly. "You can't say that for sure."

Remy drew himself up, indignant. "But I've *read*—"

"Stories," Jessamyn snapped. "You've read stories, passed down over centuries through the mouths and minds of the few people who managed to survive the Fall, and their descendants, and *their* descendants. Hundreds of thousands of people who could have gotten any number of things wrong. No one here even knew her. No one can say what she would do."

"I knew her," said Simon quietly, still facing the dark window, against which rain had begun to drum. "I knew her, and I still can't guess what she might do. But I know we can't afford not to try reaching across time to her." He turned back over his shoulder, his profile cutting angry lines against the glass. "Unless you'd like to keep on running, Jessamyn, until you're cut down fighting, after which the world will still go on in its misery. You have a chance here to help in a real way."

Jessamyn straightened. "Are you saying the lives I've saved while working for Red Crown meant nothing?"

"No. I'm saying that staying with us, with Eliana, and helping her however you can in the days to come will mean more than whatever you could do elsewhere. We need as many fighters at our side as we can find."

"Forgive me for asking what is probably a silly question," Dani said after a moment, "but how exactly will this work? If it does work. You'll travel back in time and talk to your mother, convince her not to ally with the angels. Yes?"

Eliana's stomach sat in knots. "That's right."

"Let's say you succeed. All those years ago, you change something the Blood Queen did or didn't do. You alter the course of history." Dani paused, glancing at Simon. "What happens to all of us?"

"Anything Eliana does in the past," Zahra said at once, "whether she succeeds or not, will irrevocably alter this future in ways we can't predict. Her mere presence there will change things."

Then Simon added quietly, "And only she and I, being the ones connected to the thread that sends her back, will be the ones to notice any differences once we return."

"You mean, we could end up dead," said Remy quietly, "or somewhere else in the world, or born to different parents, and we wouldn't know any better."

It was not a question, and spoken in Remy's childish voice, his words held an eerie finality.

"Yes," said Simon, that unfeeling mask firmly in place.

"Or something she does could make this future *worse* than it already is." Jessamyn's words cut the room in two. "Isn't that right?"

Simon inclined his head. "It's possible."

An enormous pressure had been building in Eliana's chest, clamping down hard around her lungs, and now it became so unbearable that she had to rise from her chair and walk away from the group toward the farthest window. She stood there, arms crossed, shoulders hunched as if to bolster herself against a gale.

"So I could save us," she said, "or doom us."

"And we must move quickly." Simon's voice brimmed with frustration. "I had hoped we would have more time to work together here, where it's safe. But if we keep progressing at our current pace, the army could arrive before we've had the chance to attempt traveling."

He spoke as though they were the only two in the room—which, Eliana supposed, was his truth. What else mattered to him, besides her safety and his mission to protect her? Certainly not the lives of the other people gathered around them.

Patrik blew out a long breath. "So the question, then, is this: Do we risk everything and perhaps rid the world of the Empire, even if it means rewriting the lives of everyone now living? Or do we risk less and allow the world to continue on as it will, even if that could mean victory for the Empire?"

"Which would mean doom for this world," Zahra added, her voice rippling like dark water, "and for all the others."

"I have very little room in my heart for the safety of whatever distant worlds may or may not exist," said Jessamyn tightly, "when my own is mired in an endless war."

"It doesn't have to be endless." Dani rose from her seat, briskly smoothing out her trousers. "That's what I'm getting from this conversation. We can end it, if we do this right. And I've been living two lives for all my years—a life of rebellion, and a life of false loyalty to a regime that goes against everything I believe in. It's exhausting. If I can end that and send all the godly sparks of myself into a new form in a new, better world, then I'm happy to do it." Dani placed her hands on her hips. "So what's your plan, Captain? Whatever it is, my family and I will help you and Eliana as best we can."

Simon's smile was so small and tired that Eliana's eyes grew hot. There seemed to be no end to her new capacity for crying.

"There's a masquerade ball," Simon said slowly, "in five days' time. Isn't that right?"

Dani nodded. "To open the Admiral's Jubilee."

"What in God's name is that?" asked Jessamyn.

"A weeklong celebration throughout Festival to celebrate both the anniversary of Admiral Ravikant's resurrection and the Empire's conquest of Meridian."

"And the admiral himself is already here in Festival," Dani added. "He arrived earlier this month. Lord Tabris has been feting him for days."

Jessamyn scowled. "Doesn't the admiral of the Emperor's fleet have more important things to do than attend some party?"

Dani raised her eyebrows. "More important than attending a citywide, days-long celebration held in his honor? Not in his eyes, no."

"Ravikant." Zahra's dark form vibrated with anger. "One of the most prideful angels I have ever known. He orchestrated the fleet's assault on Festival to coincide with his naming day."

"The Jubilee is notoriously decadent," Patrik added. "Feasts and concerts and theater performances, day and night. I've heard stories about the midnight revels in particular."

"And I assure you," said Dani, "that every story you've heard, no matter how extraordinary, is true."

"In other words, it's not a party I'm interested in attending," said Patrik cheerfully, "and yet I get the feeling that's precisely what we're going to do."

"The festivities would provide excellent cover for us," mused Simon. "We'd never get to the docks otherwise."

"The docks?" Jessamyn frowned. "You want a ship?"

"That would be our fastest route away from Meridian. And if we can get aboard one and leave before the army arrives..." Distant calculations turned in his gaze. "With the imperial army on the move, I want her as far away from this continent as possible as quickly as possible."

Eliana watched him, wishing she could speak to him alone, that he would tell her what thoughts were turning in that ravaged mind of his.

"Where will we go?" she asked.

He glanced at her. "I don't know. If we do this, we'll have five days to decide."

"And five days to return to Old Celdaria," she added, "if we want to attempt that while we're here at Willow. Secure and guarded."

He inclined his head. "Indeed."

"Unless the scouts were wrong," Patrik added, "and the army arrives sooner than we think. Maybe even before the Jubilee. We may have to move more quickly than we think."

Zahra laughed. "Admiral Ravikant would never allow military action to delay his Jubilee, and he's done so much for the Emperor that I believe he would respect that."

"Even if delaying his party meant capturing Eliana?" Jessamyn asked. "From what you've told me, I find that hard to believe."

And then Harkan, who had been sitting in silence, staring hard at his feet, said quietly, "You'll need scouts stationed around the city borders, watching for the army's arrival. And if they do arrive early, before you've boarded your ship, you'll need teams to head them off and buy you some time."

He stood, his shoulders rigid, and his face held in such a careful, hard way that Eliana's heart clenched. He had decided something, and she wasn't going to like it.

"I'd like to orchestrate that and lead the point team," he said, and then, glancing in Zahra's direction, he added, "With you, Zahra, if you'll come with me. We can set bombardiers, sabotage the army when and where we can. We can't stop them, but we can make things more difficult for them."

"Harkan," Eliana managed at last. "You can't be serious. We're talking about thousands of imperial soldiers altogether—"

"And a coordinated team of fighters could do some damage, if they were smart about it. And we would be." He wouldn't look at Eliana. "I have no power to offer and no understanding of the Old World. And I'm..." He paused, his jaw working, and Eliana ached for him, the pain of his obvious, terrible sadness lodging beneath her breastbone.

He shook his head a little, looked at Simon instead. "I can lead such a team. I want to lead it. I know we could be helpful."

Simon considered him in silence. Then, nodding, he said, "Dani, would any of your people be willing to join him?"

"I've already thought of a dozen off the top of my head," Dani replied at once. "All of them would be happy for the chance, and I know we can recruit more."

Simon nodded. "Very well. Harkan, we'll speak with the scouts while they eat, see what other information we can get out of them."

But before they could go, Eliana caught Harkan's elbow, holding him fast. "And when we do go sailing away to God knows where," she said fiercely, "and you're left behind in Festival, fighting off an entire army, what then? What will become of you?"

Harkan's eyes shone. He gave her a soft, sad smile so familiar it tore at her. "Does it matter?"

Furious with him for suggesting his life was somehow smaller because of her, or that anyone's life should mean less in comparison to her own, she turned abruptly and left the room.

## ~ 39 ~

# RIELLE

*"Merovec Sauvillier (b. December 14, Year 974): the first child of Lord Dervin Sauvillier (b. 943, d. 998) and Lady Marivon Sauvillier (Gouyet; b. 947, d. 981). Elemental: metalmaster. The elder of two siblings (Ludivine Sauvillier, b. 979), Merovec demonstrated himself to possess a great talent for horsemanship and swordwork, in addition to political savvy, often patrolling the Celdaria-Borsvall border with his father. At age fifteen, he helped engineer the Treaty of the Two Rivers. His prodigious prowess on the battlefield—most notably in the Battle at Courroux (994)—earned him immense national popularity, as well as the moniker 'the Shield of the North.'"*

—A Thorough Catalogue of the Great Celdarian Houses of
the Second Age, compiled by various authors

The night of Merovec's arrival, after he and his party of some two dozen soldiers and advisers had been shown to their rooms, Rielle sat on Ludivine's bed, the room lit softly by three candles. Atheria paced nervously on the terrace outside.

On the bedside table sat a book chronicling the saints' futile attempts to use their power to heal injuries at the height of the Angelic Wars. The number of human casualties had pushed them to desperate acts. Each disastrous attempt—a dozen in total—was chronicled in gruesome detail, followed by each saint's assessment of what had happened and what had gone wrong, and how they had decided, after these dozen attempts and after much discussion and study, that it was simply not possible to extend an elemental's power beyond the seven recognized elements. From water and metal to blood and bone.

Rielle had spent every spare moment during the last three days poring over these accounts, until they had imprinted themselves on her mind.

And now she sat with Ludivine's arm in her lap, ready to attempt what the saints had deemed impossible.

As she had done the last three nights, she traced her fingers up and down Ludivine's arm, from the tips of her scarred fingers to the sharp turn of her shoulder, and then up, across her neck and jaw, and down across her ribs and chest, where the newest scar tendrils showed black and blue against her pale skin. After a lifetime of friendship with Ludivine, Rielle knew very well the lines of her body, but this scar was new and still unfamiliar. She wanted to memorize it.

Ludivine watched her quietly, a gray blanket pooled around her hips, leaving her upper body bare for Rielle to work.

"You won't hurt me," came her soft voice.

Rielle avoided her tired, pale gaze. "I'm not worried about that."

"I'm not so unwell that I can't sense your feelings," Ludivine said wryly. "Not when you're this close to me."

Rielle glanced up, noticing how carefully Ludivine held herself, how the bones of her face seemed more pronounced. It was as if she had determined exactly how best to sit to avoid as much pain as possible and was afraid to even breathe too deeply.

"I could hurt you though," Rielle argued, looking away. "That man in Polestal. I could do that to you."

"You won't."

"But I *could*."

"Yes. You could." Then Ludivine lifted Rielle's gaze to hers, one gentle finger under her chin. "But that is where you are mightier even than your power. In it lies the capacity for both destruction and creation, and only you can decide how to guide it."

Rielle was not entirely sure that was true. There had been times— many times, in fact—when her power seemed to easily get the better of her. The shadow trial, when she had launched the shadow-dragon at the Archon. The hills outside Styrdalleen, when only Audric's presence had prevented her from abandoning the Borsvall capital to destruction. The villager in Polestal.

The Obex in Mazabat.

*In those moments*, she thought to Ludivine, unable to voice the terrible question aloud, *was it indeed my power getting the better of me? Because I'm not strong enough yet to control it in moments of duress? Or was my power merely obeying my wishes?* She swallowed. *Was it aligning itself with my true nature?*

Ludivine let her hand fall. "You have so much light in you, Rielle."

"That wasn't my question."

"No." Ludivine sighed. "It wasn't."

Rielle pushed on, suddenly not wanting to know the answer. "Well, I suppose there's nothing left but to try. Match your breathing to mine. It will help."

So had said the notes of Saint Katell, whose efforts at healing a grisly stomach wound had been more successful than the others'—though she had, of course, ultimately failed. That had been the attempt that made the saints resolve to never again try such a thing.

*Healing*, Saint Katell had written, *is clearly not a power elementals are allowed. The empirium does not permit it. It is an unnatural act, and to attempt it is to succumb to one's arrogance and pride.*

Well, Rielle herself was an unnatural act. And pride and arrogance didn't seem like such terrible things if they allowed her to ease the pain of someone she loved.

So she cradled Ludivine's arm in her hands and slowed her breathing, deepening it, until her limbs flushed warm and calm, and the sound of Ludivine's own breaths matched hers. A moment later, her unfocused vision had slipped into the realm of the empirium. Ludivine's bedroom was a soft, golden landscape of slowly shifting light—but Ludivine herself was something else entirely.

Her form was misshapen in this realm. It was recognizably Ludivine, and then became something else, a figure taller and slimmer than Ludivine, with angelic wings spanning jagged from her back, and then it became Ludivine once more. The shift was so rapid that she seemed caught between the two—between girl and angel—and the effect left her looking malformed. The empirium moved rapidly through her body, a frantic wave of white-gold, as if it were a trapped animal trying desperately to escape its cage.

Watching it made Rielle dizzy, her stomach rising. She understood that she was looking at something that should not be—that *Ludivine* should not be.

But even more ill-fitting in the world than Ludivine herself was the scar of her left arm. Just as Rielle had seen the ragged shell of the Polestal villager's burned skin, so could she now see the unmoving shell of light encasing Ludivine's arm. A sickly light, as if seen through a dark veil, and tinged with an angry, alien blue.

A blue that did not belong in this world, Rielle instinctively recognized.

And it was that certainty, that revulsion, that sharpened her mind until it felt as keen and clear as a jewel.

She placed her hands on Ludivine's arm, and it was as though there were two of her—one Rielle, in the land of the empirium, watching the light that did not belong, and another Rielle, distant and dull, touching Ludivine's cracked skin.

*You don't belong here*, Rielle thought—firmly but without anger, for she did not want to provoke the light or hurt Ludivine. Delicately, she knit her fingers along the dimly lit furrows of Ludivine's ravaged arm, and she imagined that with each gentle press of her fingers, she was pushing the scar back into the world from which it came. She was warming a hand stiff with winter. She was banishing death and replacing it with life.

As she worked, Ludivine murmured words Rielle didn't understand—angelic words, judging by their cadence—but she knew they were words of love. Ludivine opened a feeling to her that at first was little more than a distant bloom of warmth, and then, as the night wore on, it became steadier and brighter, until a feeling of such love enveloped Rielle that she felt light-headed and had to beg Ludivine to stop.

Then at last, abruptly, Rielle felt something shift inside her, like the wrench of a strained muscle, and knew it was finished.

She blinked, returning to the human world in which her body sat, damp with sweat. Ludivine was there at once, supporting her with two arms pale and smooth as cream.

*You did it*, came Ludivine's voice—strong now, and clearer than it had been in weeks. *Oh, darling, you are a marvel.*

"Speak to me aloud," Rielle murmured, pressing her face against Ludivine's neck. "I'm too tired for mind-talk."

"Of course," Ludivine said, and then her arms came around Rielle, and she helped her settle among the pillows. Ludivine stroked her sweaty hair back from her brow until her skin had cooled and her wild heartbeat had slowed, and then she said something so unexpected that the true strangeness of it didn't immediately settle in Rielle's mind.

"I always knew you could do it," she whispered against Rielle's hair, her voice trembling with emotion. "I knew from the first time I sensed your power, when I was still trapped in the Deep. I knew you would be the one to deliver me."

A few moments of silence passed while Rielle tiredly sorted through Ludivine's words.

Unable to make sense of them, she shifted to look up at her. "What do you mean?"

Something flickered across Ludivine's face—too fleeting and small for Rielle to pinpoint. Then Ludivine bent low to kiss her brow.

"Audric's coming," she said. "I sent for him once you'd recovered yourself a bit."

She directed Rielle's attention toward the door, and Rielle could not find it in herself to be irritated with Ludivine for taking hold of her mind so firmly, for forcing her away from their conversation. Because, in the next moment, Evyline was knocking on the door to announce Audric's arrival, and then Audric himself was hurrying toward the bed, his weary face alight with a smile that cleared Rielle's thoughts of everything but the desire to touch him, to ground herself against the warmth of his body. She opened her arms to him and welcomed him into Ludivine's bed, greedily accepting his kisses and his words of praise, listening to Ludivine recount to him her accomplishment, until, very soon, Ludivine's strange mention of deliverance had disappeared from her mind—a discarded, distant memory.

◆

The next day, they all gathered for supper in Queen Genoveve's private dining hall—for, of course, Merovec was family. The queen's nephew and Ludivine's brother.

But from the moment Rielle stepped into the hall, she was made all too aware that this meal was about more than simply enjoying time with family.

It was about loyalty.

The room had been draped in the colors of House Sauvillier—navy-blue carpets bordered with silver flowers, a tablecloth of silver-spangled russet, tapestries of snowy northern scenes. Sauvillier colors in Baingarde were not themselves so outrageous, not since Bastien had married Genoveve. But they had never been displayed quite so obviously and at the exclusion of all others.

A quick glance around the room showed Rielle that any trace of House Courverie colors—emerald, gold, plum—had vanished from the space, as if they had never existed.

She found Audric sitting at his mother's side. Her stomach clenched to see Queen Genoveve's mute, gaunt form. Several times over the last few days, she had asked Audric if she could pay the queen a visit, and each time he had suggested she wait until his mother wasn't resting, or until she was feeling a little better, or until her black mood had brightened.

Rielle suspected the truth behind his deflections. Queen Genoveve did not want to see her, and Audric was trying to spare her feelings. A theory supported by how the queen's eyes, across the dining hall, landed on Rielle's face with a subdued, unimpressed sort of hatred, as if she had spotted a bug whose existence had long nettled her.

Rielle looked away, focusing instead on Audric. To anyone else, the tension in his body might not have been noticeable. He was in conversation with one of Merovec's advisers, and he looked entirely interested in what the woman was saying.

But then his eyes met hers, and with that one glance, she understood several things at once. That he, too, had noticed the room's colors. That the pleasantness on his face as he spoke with the adviser was entirely fabricated. And that he would be proceeding with caution through this evening—and hoped Rielle would as well.

A wave of nerves passed through Rielle's body. Evyline's ominous words from the day before returned to her: *I very much dislike the things I have heard about stirrings in the north.*

But if there were truly anything to worry about, Audric's spies would have uncovered it. Ludivine would have been able to read it in Merovec's mind. Whatever rumors Evyline had heard, then, were merely that— gossip that could be dismissed. And Evyline herself tended to worry about anything and everything.

So Rielle put Audric's worried gaze out of her mind and went to Ludivine, who sat beside Merovec with her newly healed left arm hooked through his.

"Lord Sauvillier," Rielle said warmly, settling in the seat beside Ludivine. "I do hope you and your party enjoyed a restful night."

"Indeed we did, Rielle." Then Merovec smiled. "And, please, call me Merovec. As I'm certain I've requested of you before, years ago."

His voice teased her, and his long-lashed blue eyes held a merry light—but then Ludivine sent her a quiet warning.

*Step carefully around him tonight*, she said, the feeling of her thoughts slightly harried.

Rielle tensed. *Why should I? What is he thinking?*

*I can't see it clearly. But I see enough to fear him.*

*But I healed you*, said Rielle. *Why can't you read him?*

Ludivine hesitated, the feeling of her frustration rising in Rielle's mind like the heat of a blooming fire, and she understood at once.

*It's Corien, isn't it?* she said, a tiny shiver seizing her from her toes up to the blush of her neck. *He's hiding Merovec from you.*

One of the castle servants rang the soft dinner bell; others brought in food from the kitchens.

*I wonder*, said Ludivine, her thoughts bitter and sharp, *if someday you might be able to use your power to make my mind stronger than his.*

And with her words came such a feeling of desire, with hatred right on its heels, that for a moment Rielle lost her breath.

*I would never try such a thing*, she said. *I would never risk your mind. Risking your body was more than enough.*

But what a thought it was, the idea of being able to strengthen Ludivine's mental abilities to the point where Corien would no longer be able to touch her, even with all his might.

Rielle wasn't sure if this was a thought that pleased her—or terrified her.

A servant set a plate of food before her. She found Audric's curious eyes across the table, forcing a smile for him, and then, after a few quiet moments of eating and low conversation, Merovec began to speak.

"I've heard such interesting talk in the last few days," he said mildly over the rim of his cup. "News travels quickly even from Mazabat, it seems."

Rielle faltered only slightly as she raised her spoon to her lips.

"What sort of talk is that?" Ludivine's voice teased. "You've always been such a gossip."

Merovec's answering smile did not meet his eyes. "Perhaps that's true.

But this time, it has served me well. Word has reached my ears, Rielle, of your adventures in Mazabat."

Her fist clenched around her spoon. She fought to keep her voice pleasant. "Adventures?"

"Oh, my apologies." Mervoec set down his glass and looked at her. "I meant your cold-blooded murder of thirteen Obex soldiers."

Any lingering conversation vanished, a terrible silence enveloping the room. One of the queen's advisers cleared her throat.

Rielle glanced at Audric. He had not said a word, but his dark gaze was intent upon her.

*I must answer him myself,* Rielle thought to Ludivine. *Allowing either of you to speak for me will weaken me, in his eyes.*

Beneath the table, Ludivine gently squeezed her hand. Her brow remained furrowed, her gaze distant as she stared at the table. Corien, Rielle assumed, was still interfering with her mind.

Rielle raised her chin slightly. "It wasn't cold-blooded murder, Lord Sauvillier. They attacked me, and I punished them for it."

He had not missed her deliberate use of his formal title. She had to swallow a smile at the flicker of irritation on his face.

"I killed them in defense of myself," she continued, "and of Tal, and of the abducted child Zuka. It was, in fact, in defense of everyone who now lives. The Obex intended to keep Saint Tokazi's staff from me. Without it, without all seven of the saints' castings, I will not be able to repair the falling Gate."

Merovec sat back in his seat, holding his drink loosely in one hand. "Ah yes. The falling Gate. The structure of which you yourself worsened, Lady Rielle, according to my friend in Borsvall."

"And what friend is this?" came Audric's low voice.

"King Ilmaire told me much in his recent letter. He is eager for us all to be friends, in the face of whatever darkness looms on the horizon. I don't much want to be friends with a spineless man who can't command the respect of his own country, but my options are limited these days." He looked calmly at Audric. "Once, my lord prince, I would have considered you a friend. Isn't it funny how things can so quickly change?"

Queen Genoveve let out a soft trill of laughter. Her fingers, resting on the table, twitched as if she had been struck on the ribs.

Audric went dangerously still.

"We've discussed this, Merovec," said Ludivine, coming out of whatever half trance she'd been in. "There is no ill feeling between myself and Rielle, or myself and Audric—or between myself and my aunt the queen, in fact. You would do well to remember that, and to remember that you are a guest here."

Merovec lifted Ludivine's hand to his lips and kissed it. "Your spirit is far too generous, little sister."

"If you have something you would like to say, Merovec," said Audric, his voice even and cool in a way Rielle recognized from their most awful arguments, "then, please, say it. We're all family here, after all."

Queen Genoveve rose from her chair and drifted to a side table, where a silver platter of frosted pastries awaited the dessert course. Rielle knew she should have been paying attention to the conversation at the table, but she couldn't tear her eyes from Genoveve's pronounced cheekbones, the birdlike, wide-eyed way she nibbled her cake, what a startlingly slim figure she cut against the candlelit tapestries.

"Family." Merovec laughed a little. "You know, the broken engagement itself wouldn't have angered me. Well, that's a lie. It would have infuriated me, no matter the circumstances. But to betray my little sister for a monster of a woman is a crime I cannot forgive, my lord prince."

"Merovec," Ludivine snapped. "That's quite enough."

The tension radiating from Audric's body moved down the table like a storm across the sky. "You will not speak of Lady Rielle like that. Not in my presence, and not in hers."

"I will speak of her exactly as she deserves," Merovec replied, his voice as mild as if they were discussing the merits of one horse compared to another. "Here is a woman who cannot be trusted, whose power we do not understand. She attacked the Archon during her trials. She killed thirteen in Mazabat and injured even more than that. She hurt God knows how many poor souls in Kirvaya—news of which has perhaps not yet made the long journey west. Her interference at the Gate caused disasters that killed countless more, I'm sure. Deaths we'll never know about, in quiet corners of the world.

"Oh, yes," he added at the expression on Audric's face. "I know everything that you know, my lord prince. My spies are many, and they are thorough. And yet, after everything she has done, here she is, given a place of honor at your table. In our capital. In our temples."

Merovec leaned forward, elbows on the table, the ghost of a smile on his mouth. "And then, of course, she has a place of honor in your bed as well. Tell me, Audric, when she turns on us, will you have the strength to kill her as she sleeps?" Merovec sat back, making a soft *tch* of disgust. "I don't think you do. I think you'll let us all die if it means you can keep on fucking her."

Then, three terrible things:

Audric pushed himself back from the table, a blazing look of fury on his face.

Merovec rose as well, his smile a taunt. Ludivine shot to her feet just after him, gripping his arm. She snapped at both of them to sit down and get ahold of themselves, lest they distress the queen.

And the queen...

Rielle, so distracted that Merovec's words had barely skimmed the surface of her mind, watched Genoveve move swiftly out of the hall, into the corridor outside.

Some instinct, cold and dire, told her to follow. She pushed back from the table, ignoring Audric as he called after her, and followed Genoveve's pale, thin form down the shadowed hallway. The queen walked faster and faster, her gray gown rustling, and looked once over her shoulder.

"Get away!" she cried, gesturing frantically. "Don't touch me! You'll kill me, you'll *burn* me!"

She began to run, and Rielle followed, afraid to get too close but unwilling to let her out of her sight. With a small sob, the queen clamped her hands over her ears and used her shoulder to knock open a door that stood ajar. She raced inside, and Rielle ran after her, into a small sitting room. She heard Ludivine cry out behind her, and running footsteps she recognized as Audric's.

And then, too quickly for Rielle to grab her arm, or even cry out her name, Queen Genoveve crashed through the glass doors of the sitting room terrace, propelled through them as if by some inhuman force. She sobbed, her voice cracking open, "They won't stop! They won't *stop*!" She pounded on her temples with her bleeding fists, and then, reaching for the stars above as if beyond their bright cage lay an escape, she flung herself over the terrace railing and into the night.

—◆—

The world slowed and narrowed, existing only in a few searing points—Merovec racing across the terrace, his once-smug face now a wreck of horror. Ludivine catching Rielle by the arms, saying words she could not hear, not from the numb hollow place into which she had fallen. The queen's advisers, the queensguard, Rielle's own guard, all hurrying through the rooms and onto the terrace and downstairs, shouting orders.

Audric, staring at the shattered doors with a horrible dullness spreading across his face, as if he had been dealt a fatal blow.

Rielle could not bear the sight of his numb disbelief. One parent dead only months before. Now, the other.

She had recognized that bleak desperation in Genoveve's voice, there at the end. And then there were the queen's fists pounding against her temples, her hands clamped over her ears.

A swift heat snapped up Rielle's body.

*You did this.* She reached inside herself, past her shock, and gathered up every rageful feeling she could find. The fury crystallized her mind, her vision, her certainty of what she must do.

Corien replied after only a moment. *I won't lie to you, my darling. I considered it. But as it turns out, I had to do very little.*

Rielle fled the room, her vision a pure, hot crimson. Ludivine shot her a feeling of protest, grabbing her arm. Rielle wrenched herself free and ran on.

*The woman was grieving,* Corien continued as she flew down the stairs, shouting at every wide-eyed guard she encountered to move out of her path.

*And that gave you the right to end her life?* Rielle spat out.

*You're making many awful assumptions. Had it occurred to you that Genoveve had already decided to take her own life by the time I began visiting her?*

Rielle flung open the castle's front doors, guards streaming in and out on either side of her. The queen's body, she deduced from their confused shouts, had been found shattered in the stone yard.

*You lie.* She sent him a vicious wave of anger. *You infected her thoughts. You're trying to break him, and you'll fail.*

*Him? Oh.* Corien's voice was mild. *You mean your cow-eyed lover.*

*My lover, yes, and someday, my husband.* And with that, Rielle flung all her thoughts outward, banishing Corien as best she could, though she could still feel him hovering at her edges, though the effort of resisting him made her stumble.

Guards had gathered around Genoveve's body, shielding her from any onlookers through the castle gates, but at Rielle's approach, they scattered.

She sank to her knees, forcing herself to examine the queen's body—every gash, every crack in her skull. The skewed position of her limbs; the dark pool of blood spreading beneath her. Her still, glassy gaze.

Audric arrived, breathless, tears streaking his cheeks. He let out a horrible ruptured sound at the sight of his mother's body, and then sank to the ground beside her.

"Don't touch her," Rielle commanded, her vision already broadening past the capacity of her human eyes. She was sinking into a sea of furious gold. "Stay away."

Then she bent low over the dead queen and began to work.

She knit in a controlled frenzy, her fingers skimming across each broken bone. She drew golden tracks down the queen's limbs and chest, around the shattered plates of her skull, her snapped limbs. In the bright unblinking eye of her mind, she saw the queen as she had been before Bastien's death—healthy and strong, a true northern beauty with her pale skin and auburn hair. Her straight nose, her eyes pale and sharp as Ludivine's.

This time, when Rielle felt that tight shift deep in her gut, it felt not like a strain of muscle but rather an expansion. She welcomed it, leaning in to its fever. She opened her mind to it and let it consume her, and when it had enveloped her completely in its fire, she carried stars in her hands and held flames under her tongue. She burned cold and clear, and when she opened her eyes once more, it was to a world both familiar and strange.

She smiled a little, sinking back into her body. Beatific, she relished the hum of her bones. She was sapped clean of all worry, all anger and desperation. There was a distant clanging din, battering against the edges of her awareness, but she dismissed it as she would have a buzzing fly.

"I am everything and nothing," she whispered, laughing a little, and when she found Audric's eyes, the look he gave her, quiet and even, tear-bright, was one she could not decipher.

Then Genoveve's trembling body arched up from the ground, blood-stained but whole. Audric darted forward to support her against his chest, and then, wild-eyed, Genoveve shifted, grappling for something unseen. Her eyes met Rielle's, and she let out a horrible scream of anger, so raw that, despite Rielle's euphoria, the sound shook her to her toes.

"You should have let me die," Genoveve said, her voice tripping over her gasped breaths, and then she howled it to the sky: "You should have let me die!" And her hands clamped over her ears once more, and she rocked in Audric's arms.

"She will kill us," she whispered, turning her face into Audric's chest. She moaned and wept. "She will kill us all."

Then that distant din rose, sharpening itself against the queen's keening cries. Rielle turned to greet it, peering curiously across the torchlit yard.

The crowd gathered at the lower gates had been banging their fists against the elaborate wrought iron, slamming their mock castings, their hammers, their knives against the thick stone wall. And now, as Rielle rose to greet them, they quieted slowly, until only a few stubborn murmurs remained.

"Do not be afraid," Rielle called out to them, raising her hands as if to show them she carried no weapons. A useless gesture, but one she hoped would placate them. "I mean you no harm. Your queen was unwell, but I have brought her back to us. Just as I did Lady Ludivine. Just as I will do for any who require it. I am your Sun Queen, and you need not fear me. Do not be afraid."

Then, smiling faintly to herself, she turned away from them and knelt at the queen's side. Genoveve whimpered, struggling to move as far away as she could while still in Audric's arms.

And Audric said nothing, watching Rielle quietly. She had seldom seen his gaze so somber.

She touched his face. "My love," she whispered. She dropped a kiss onto his brow. "Do not be afraid."

Almost immediately, she regretted kissing him. For when her lips touched his skin, the spell of her power shattered. She was left tired and aching, entirely human, and as Evyline helped her to her feet, she became aware of how, for the first time since she had known him, Audric was regarding her with something like fear.

## ✦ 40 ✦

# ELIANA

*"During the longest winter the world had yet seen, as the seeds
of war sprouted slow from the dirt, Gilduin traveled far.
His heart ached for lands unknown. A nettle in his blood
compelled him to travel without rest.
And this ache was one he did not cherish and longed to
be rid of.
And Morgaine remained in her castle, her rule fair and just.
Her eyes were steel and her mind cut sharp and true.
But at night she wept, alone in her tower, and she did not
know that, alone in the desert, on a far white dune,
Gilduin wept for her and tore at his chest,
that he might rend the terrible angry ache from his veins,
and return home to her
and take up his sword alongside her."*

—"The Ballad of Gilduin and Morgaine,"
ancient Celdarian epic, author unknown

That night, as the rain grew to another storm, Eliana lay awake in her
bed, unable to shut off the wild whirl of her mind.

Then a crack of thunder shook her, and before she could think better of
it, she climbed out of bed, heart pounding. The air was chill, the wooden
floor cold against her bare feet, and the sleep shirt Dani had given her
provided little warmth.

But when she opened the door to her room, all thoughts of cold fled from her mind.

Simon was there, his hair rumpled as if he had spent the night running his hands through it, his fist raised to knock.

For an instant they simply stared at each other, and then a stubborn wall inside Eliana gave way at last. Her restless night, the tension of the day, and the awful weight of what lay ahead combined to fell her. Horrified to feel her face crumpling, she leaned in to him, hiding her sharp sob in his sleeve.

His arms came around her at once, and he held her there for a moment in the open doorway. She felt his cheek against hers; he kissed her hair. Then he gently moved her inside the room, shutting the door behind them.

"Is this all right?" he said. "Or should I leave?"

She shook her head against his chest. "Please don't leave me alone. God, I can hardly breathe. I can't sleep, I can't think."

He was quiet for a moment. "You're frightened."

"Yes, and I hate myself for it."

"I'm familiar with the temptation for self-loathing, but in this case it's unnecessary. You have every right to be frightened."

"Are you? Please tell me you are."

"And that will make you feel better?"

"Marginally."

"Well, then. I'll say truthfully that I've been frightened every day, for as long as I can remember."

She pulled away, looking up at his tired face. The room was dark, save for a stub of candle near her bed and the occasional flash of lightning. She wished suddenly for more light, so she could better see the familiar lines of his nose, the map of his scars, his sharp, strong jaw.

"How did you do it?" she whispered. "All the years of fighting, of seeing and dealing awful cruelties. Being trained by the Prophet. The horrors you've endured, things you haven't yet told me about." She touched his chest, over the spot where the scar she'd healed had once lived. She stared at her fingers, suddenly nervous. "How did you live through it all?"

A pause, and then his hands were in her hair, gently guiding her to look up at him. The small smile he gave her was so tender that it filled her body with light.

"I lived through it," he said, wiping her cheeks, "by thinking of you."

His words spread slowly across her skin, trailing a tingling warmth behind them. "But you didn't know me until a few months ago."

"No, but the hope of you...that I knew for years. The hope that I would find you, that I hadn't lost you after all." And then a darkness fell over his face. He released her, his expression closing. "Sometimes I can hardly bear to look at you."

"Because I remind you of my mother?"

"Because every day I wake fearing I'll fail you, and every night I fall asleep wishing..." He dragged a hand across his face, turned toward the window. "Forgive me, Eliana."

Cautiously, she moved closer to him and took his hands in hers. He raised them to his lips and kissed them—her fingers, her wrists, the metal lines of her castings. Her body thrummed to match his every movement, his every breath.

"Forgive you for what?" she asked. And when he didn't answer, she brought his hands to her lips. "What do you fall asleep wishing?"

He murmured her name, and she gently gripped his collar, stretching up to kiss the underside of his jaw.

"Will you properly kiss me at last?" she whispered against his skin. "I've only wanted you to for months."

"When you didn't want to fight me, that is," he said, a smile in his voice.

She tugged at his shirt, her blood blazing with need. "*Simon.* Either kiss me or leave me here to hate you."

At once he bent to kiss the drying tears from her cheeks, the corners of her mouth, her brow, her temples, and then, when she made a soft, angry noise and tightened her fists in his shirt, he slid his hands into her hair and found her mouth with his own.

His kiss sent heat firing through her body, and she rose swiftly to meet it, hooking her arms around his neck. His kisses were long and slow, his arms strong around her, and then, cradling her head in one large hand, he opened her mouth with his tongue. She whimpered, the heat between her legs aching with such sudden desperation that she feared her knees would buckle. She had lain with many men and women—both in her work as the Dread and simply because she loved it—and had spent countless nights in Harkan's bed. This was not new to her.

And yet in Simon's arms she felt as shaky and wild as if she had never been touched in her life.

"Is this all right?" he murmured against her throat, stamping her neck with his tongue.

She laughed, breathless. "If you stop, I really will hate you forever."

"I need you to say it, Eliana." He pressed his forehead against hers. "Tell me to stay."

"Stay," she whispered. She could not bear the intensity of his gaze. She ducked away, nuzzling his stubbled cheek. "Stay, and take me to bed."

He laughed quietly into her hair—a shredded sound, so raw that she had to squeeze her eyes shut against a fresh rush of tears. He said nothing, but he didn't need to. She understood his relief, and felt it herself—a rightness at his touch, a sense of coming home at last. It was as if all the layers of protection she had constructed within herself—against the world, against her power, against the horrible truth of her family—had folded under and vanished.

He hoisted her up easily against him, and when their hips met, she cried out, tightening her arms around his neck. He carried her to her bed and sat on the edge of it. She settled in his lap, cupping his face in her hands. She kissed him until she had to pull away, both of them breathing hard, for her head was buzzing with want, and even with Simon's hands firm on her hips, holding her against him, she wondered if she might float away.

"I don't understand," she whispered against his mouth before kissing his bottom lip, tugging it gently between her teeth. She couldn't stay away from him for long; with each kiss she felt more frantic for him, as if at any moment he might disappear.

"Don't understand what?" he said, his voice ragged.

Shivering, she locked eyes with him and began to circle her hips against his. He cried out sharply and moved one of his hands to her neck, holding her tightly to him.

"Eliana," he said, nibbling at her breastbone, pushing aside her collar with his mouth. "What don't you understand? Much more of this, and I won't be able to think well enough to care."

She held his head to her breasts, keening a little when he began to kiss her there, his mouth hot and his every movement assured.

"Why this feels so right. I've never felt... Not like this." She tried to explain further but couldn't find the words.

"We survived the end of the world, you and I," he said softly, echoing his words from the ice of Karajak Bay. He touched the strands of hair that had fallen loose from her braid. "That's why, love. I feel it too. You and I, we're all that's left of home."

The sadness in his voice robbed her of all remaining sense. Her throat aching, she bent low to kiss him. It was a clumsy kiss, hard and thin as she held back her tears, and soon she had to hide her face in his neck and cling to him, her arms tight around his shoulders.

He held her for a moment, murmuring low, sweet words into her hair, and then he rose to stand with her beside the bed. He began to unbutton her shirt, his eyes holding a question.

She answered by helping him, her fingers trembling first on her buttons and then his own. Soon they had both undressed, leaving only her castings in place around her hands. The abused lines of his body brought tears to her eyes. He was strong and lean, magnificent even for the tapestry of pain cut across his skin, and he stood before her completely unabashed. She touched his torso, his flat belly, his broad chest, and began kissing his scars, determined to soothe every last one of them.

But he stilled her with one hoarse utterance of her name and then whispered, "Please, can I touch you? I've dreamt of this, Eliana. Worshipping you, for hours and hours."

She smiled up at him, raising an eyebrow. "Hours? My, aren't we ambitious?"

"And even that wouldn't be enough for me," he said, helping her gently down, back into the bed's warm nest of blankets. His gaze roamed over her, greedy and bright, followed by the reverent skim of his palms across every dip and curve. She squirmed under his featherlight touch, heat flooding her, and when he moved down to her belly and kissed her just below her navel, her skin taut and trembling under his mouth, he laughed softly.

"You're even lovelier than I imagined," he murmured. Then he laced his fingers with hers, pinning her hands to the bed, and moved down to settle between her legs.

She cried out, her hips arching up against his mouth as he kissed her, again and again, until she was a girl of liquid fire, squirming and mindless, pleading with him for more. Just when she felt herself ready to shatter, he pulled away to kiss her thighs, her belly.

"Damn you," she panted, looking down at him, but the sight of him smiling up at her from between her legs made her reach for him, her head spinning. "Please, Simon. You darling, beautiful man."

"Don't worry, love," he told her, his voice entirely, smugly pleased. "I'm not finished."

And then he returned to her, kissing and stroking her until she was twisting beneath him, grasping wildly at the blankets, at his hands firm on her hips. She wound her fingers in his hair, moving hard against his mouth until, at last, with a sharp, high cry, the heat that had been slowly building inside her crested, drawing her down into a warm sea, golden-dark and thrumming.

She shook beneath him, time gone slow and supple, and then fell limp against the bed, every inch of her body flushed and tingling.

When she opened her eyes at last, she saw him settling beside her and smiled at him, delirious. She turned into his chest, catching her breath.

He held her to him, stroking her hair, and then, when her wild heartbeat had slowed, she scooted up for a kiss, ready to tease him—something about how he would be insufferable now, how he would gloat about his skill with his tongue for the rest of her days—but she stopped when she saw the look on his face. How gently he watched her, how his eyes were warm in a way she knew instinctively no one else would ever see.

"Simon, please tell me you want more," she said, touching his cheek. "Tell me I can have you."

He kissed her hand. "I want as much as you'll give me. I want you for as long as we have left."

His words stabbed her, recalling truths about their future that she did not want to consider—not now, not with the rain against the window, and this soft cocoon of a bed, and his arms around her like they were meant for nothing else but holding her.

She shook her head against his chest, as if that could do anything to defy the horrible fate that had been dealt them, and then she moved up his body and kissed him, until she felt him hard against her belly. She reached down and touched him, relishing his sharp, strained cries, how he clung to her as she kissed his shoulders, his hair. This fearsome weapon of a man, desperate and trembling in her arms.

After a moment he gently stilled her hand, gasping against her neck. "Please," he whispered, "not like that. I need you. Eliana, Eliana." He nuzzled his face against hers, and she sighed happily at the soft scrape of his unshaven cheeks. "Can I?"

For answer she kissed him, sweetly, slowly—until suddenly, sweet and slow were no longer enough, and he was bearing down on her with a groan, his tongue in her mouth and his back slick under her hands. He moved against her, his circling hips sending waves of heat sweeping through her body, and for a moment she gave herself up to the hungry force of him, gasping into his kisses. He nipped gently at her neck, and she hooked her legs around him with a sharp cry. Low and hoarse, he murmured her name, and she shuddered, holding his head against hers.

"Keep talking," she whispered, her eyes drifting shut. "I love hearing you like this."

He laughed softly. "What shall I tell you? How the sight of you in my arms is beautiful beyond my every imagining?" He nibbled at the soft spot behind her ear. "How determined I am to give you every pleasure you desire?" Then he buried his face in her hair and said her name again, a choked little growl.

Dizzy at the rough sound of his voice, her skin humming and hot, she began turning away from him. He released her at once.

"No," she murmured, nestling her back against his front. "Don't leave. Come back to me."

"I'm here." He kissed her temple and wrapped her up in his arms. "Like this, Eliana? This is how you want me?"

She nodded, wriggling her hips against his, grinning to feel him so hard and eager. He hissed into her hair, a breathless curse. He held her in place—one gentle hand around her neck, the other sliding between her legs, teasing her. And then he was inside her, his thrusts slow and deep, and she arched back into him, crying out from the sheer pleasure of it— his arms cradling her, his chest strong against her back, the fullness of him, the heat of him, his fingers stroking her as his hips rocked against hers.

She gripped his arm, digging her nails into his flesh. "Simon," she said, her voice cracking. "Oh, God…"

"Say my name again." His lips were hot at her ear, his own voice strained. "Please, love."

She did, again and again, until she could no longer speak, for the sounds he made as he moved in her were too delicious, too animal and passionate, and her skin was a prickling wash of fire. He pressed his face against her neck, his arms tightening around her. He kissed her throat, her jaw, and then laughed a little, the sound fevered.

"You're beautiful," he said hoarsely. "You're exquisite. My God, look at you."

Then he guided her head back to his, bringing her flush against his body, and kissed her, murmuring her name against her cheek, her lips. And the tenderness of it, the damp strands of his hair against his forehead, the steadiness of his hands, made her chest ache with the beginnings of a terrible loss.

Soon, they would try the impossible.

Soon, she could lose him. She could lose all of them.

"Harder," she whispered, thrilling when he immediately complied. "Faster, Simon." He would drive it out of her; he would make her come apart a second time and wash the building grief from her heart. She gathered her breasts in her hands, sighing and twisting in his arms, smiling a little when he swore against her neck.

He tightened his grip on her, obeying her every whispered command. She tried to say his name once more, but just then her pleasure crested sharply, and the word broke off in her throat as she fell apart in his arms with a soft cry. The sound seemed to push Simon over the edge. He pulled her back hard against him, his fingers digging into her hips, gasping her name, his voice harsh and frayed. He said it again, and again, whispering it into her hair. After long minutes, when they lay trembling in each other's arms, and Eliana's racing heart had calmed enough that she could think once more, she turned around to face him.

He smiled at her, heavy-lidded. He was so dazzling in his happiness that it pained her, like looking too long at a bright sky.

"Hello there," he said roughly. "You're glorious. Did you know that? You look thoroughly kissed."

But she could not manage a smile and hated herself for it. Even after his touch and his kisses, her earlier fear remained. That terrible, hot sadness had lodged in her chest, and she could not shake it.

She touched his mouth, memorizing its shape.

"What is it?" he asked, his expression shifting to one of concern.

The words were there on her tongue, ready to be said: *this was an awful mistake.*

Because now, if and when she did lose him, the loss would cut deeper.

Except, of course, it wouldn't cut at all. If they managed to do this thing and stop her mother, if they rewrote the course of history so that the Blood Queen never fell and the Empire died before it could begin, none of this would have ever happened. She would never have been Remy's sister, or known Harkan, or killed Rozen.

She would never have fallen in love with Simon.

It was the first time she had said the words to herself, and she felt punched by them, knocked breathless and spinning. But they were true, as true as the fact that if she lost Simon, if she lost this life and this future, and everyone inside it, there would be no loss at all. There would be only an erasure.

And that, she decided, was the worst thing she could imagine. Not to lose a beloved thing, but to have it taken from you, to have the experience of it ripped from your heart, leaving no memory behind. To be ignorant of the loss entirely.

"Eliana." Simon smoothed her tangled hair back from her face. "Tell me what's wrong. I see a million worries in your eyes."

"You know exactly what my worries are," she said, and then, before he could respond, she pressed her face against his chest, her arms tucked between them, and whispered, "Stay with me. Please. Stay with me all night."

He was still for a moment, and then drew the blankets up over them, tucking them around her shivering body. He hooked his leg over hers, and the kiss he pressed to her forehead pulled tears from her eyes.

"I'm right here," he said, his hands soft in her hair. "Don't think about anything else but that. Not tonight."

"And tomorrow?" she whispered, unable to contain the question.

He turned up her face to his and kissed her so gently that her heart felt ready to burst.

"Don't think of it," he told her. "Tonight is all that matters right now."

"Tonight," she said, gazing up at him, "we're together."

The expression on his face was open and tender, so unlike the Wolf she had first met months ago in Orline—and yet so familiar, as if she had been looking at him all her life—that she had no choice but to kiss him.

And this time, when they moved together, she faced him, letting his solid weight press her into the bed. Their gazes locked, his hands cradling her face, and she watched him until she couldn't, until the pleasure of his touch pulled her under. She clung to him, trembling, her hands fisted in his hair. She listened to his voice break against her neck and prayed furiously—to the saints, to the empirium, to her own unthinkable power—that they would wake in the morning to find that someone else had come to save the world, allowing them to rest at last.

# ✦ 41 ✦

# RIELLE

*"'When you feel a prickling on the back of your neck,' said the good witch Tahti, 'even when it isn't cold; when you feel that someone is watching you, even when you're alone; when you feel that the strange road you are walking is one you have walked before, in a dream or in a fever. These are the moments, little one. Listen closely to them. These are the moments telling you one of your deaths has been born. They are many, and some are kind, and some are cruel. They wander the world, blind, with fingers deft and clever. Someday, one of your deaths will find you. Someday, one of them will claim you in the name of an ending.'"*

—*Black Wood, White Sky*
a collection of Borsvall children's stories

Rielle sat in a vast, treeless field dusted with snow.

Barefoot, clad only in a thin nightgown, she shivered, holding her knees to her chest. In silence she waited for the footsteps she knew would come, and when they did, crunching against the frosted grass, she smiled to herself but did not turn to face him.

"Why have you brought me here?" she asked.

Corien circled her, hands clasped behind his back. He wore a long dark coat and a fur-trimmed cloak that trailed through the snow.

She did not look at him. She would not look at him.

"Because you wanted me to," he replied.

"I wanted to sleep."

He laughed quietly. "You wanted *me*."

She bit down on her tongue, refusing to look at him. He wasn't wrong—since resurrecting Genoveve, she'd been desperate for his voice, his touch, his reassurance—but she refused to acknowledge this aloud.

"I haven't been able to sleep," she said instead. "Not since I brought her back." The heat of tears rose up her cheeks, but her eyes remained dry. "Garver's given me medicine to help me sleep. But it doesn't work. Nothing works."

He crouched before her, and still she stared past him at the wintry landscape of her mind.

"You would sleep beautifully," he told her, "if you would stop fighting the truth."

"And what truth is that?"

"That staying there with them, with *him*, will ruin you."

She licked her dry lips. "Audric told me Genoveve isn't sleeping either. She screams and screams. She has terrible nightmares, even worse than before. Sometimes I hear her. Sometimes I ride Atheria to the mountains so I won't hear her."

"You tell me this as if I don't already know it."

Finally Rielle glanced up at him, her breath catching at the beauty of him in the pale, cold light.

"What did I do to her?" she whispered. "Why can't she sleep? Why can't I sleep?"

"I've already answered your second question. As to your first…" He shrugged off his cloak and settled it around her shoulders. "Some minds are too weak to bear the glory of resurrection."

"You've infected her. That's what it is. You're driving her mad." She wrapped herself tightly in the cloak, too grateful for its warmth to discard it. It smelled of him—a sharp, spiced perfume, the tang of smoke, the bite of winter.

"I speak the truth of our suffering," he said, watching her without blinking. "The suffering inflicted upon my people by her own. If she cannot bear to hear it, then that is her failing, and not mine."

Rielle glared at him. "Leave her be."

"No," he answered simply. "She must be punished, as they all must be. She is not the first, and she won't be the last."

Rielle pushed herself up from the ground, discarded the cloak, her teeth chattering, and turned away from him, hurrying toward the horizon.

He walked alongside her. "You're shivering."

"An astute observation."

"I'll take us somewhere warmer. Somewhere more comfortable."

And then the world rearranged itself. The frozen landscape disappeared, replaced by a warm, dark room. A roaring fire in an enormous black hearth. A four-poster bed, a long, elegant divan. Furs and tasseled blankets, a table laden with food and drink.

Outside a wall of broad square windows loomed an arctic tableau—snow-capped mountains, an icy valley, the distant glimmer of a frozen sea.

"I've been here before," she murmured. "In a dream. You brought me here before."

He joined her at the window, still and cold at her side. "And I will again—in reality, if you'll allow it."

She scanned the mountains quickly, noting the neat grid of roads carved through the snow, the half-built ships in an ice-scattered harbor. Broad doors cut out of the mountains, deep square pits carved into the earth, all of them glowing orange with firelight.

She tucked the information away into a corner of her mind, feeling clumsy and frantic as she did so, and unsteady on her feet. He would notice her spying efforts. He would know what information she would bring home to Audric.

To distract him, she touched his hand, and he flinched a little, and then drew her fingers through his own.

Their palms met, hers scorching and his icy cold, and suddenly an image flashed through her mind—herself and Corien, arms entwined, his lips pressed against her neck, her hands tangled in his hair.

She tried to control the image, shove it away even as her body responded, her skin prickling, but it was too late.

The world shifted once more, and they were no longer standing beside the window.

They were in his bed, that massive bed in the corner of the room, draped with silk and furs, and he was pressing her into the pillows, his hips pinning her in place, his mouth sucking hungrily at her neck. And it was as if they had been kissing for hours. Her body hummed, supple and slick. Her legs had hooked around his, though she hadn't moved them herself. Her nightgown had ridden up to expose her belly; his hands gripped her naked thighs.

"No," she gasped against his mouth.

"This is what you want," he murmured, his face pressed against her throat. "I know it is. Rielle, I saw it in your mind."

"It was a thought, not an invitation," she hissed, and then shoved him away so hard that he flew across the room, his head cracking against the wall. She forced herself to regard him dispassionately, though her head still spun from his kisses, and her body ached at the loss of him.

"You don't know what I want," she said, her voice rough. "And if you force yourself on me again, I will destroy you."

Then, as he stared at her, dazed, a dark trickle of blood sliding down his temple, the door to his rooms flew open.

Ludivine entered—pale eyes blazing, hair loose and golden, sparking as if made of flame. She wore a square-shouldered gray gown, its brocaded fabric resembling armor, and she carried a gleaming sword.

"Rielle, get behind me," she instructed, her voice tight and hard. "Don't look at him. Don't speak to him."

Corien, slumped against the wall, began to laugh—a rough, gurgling sound that soon cleared. The blood on his face vanished. He stood, drawing a sword that had appeared suddenly at his side.

"How charming," he said. "Is this how you see yourself, rat? Some vengeful savior?"

Ludivine did not answer, glaring at him. "Rielle, behind me."

Rielle, shaking, rose from the bed.

Corien's eyes cut to her, pale and furious. "Really? You're going to obey her? She beckons and you run to her, like a dog to its master."

"You've a funny way of trying to win my heart," Rielle said, catching her breath against one of the bedposts. "You force yourself on me. You call me a dog."

"I'm trying to save you from them." His voice cut thin as a blade. "Why can't you see that? She could, if she wanted to, wake you from this dream. She's closer to you than I am. She's at your bedside, in fact. She could do it, if she tried. But she wants you to see her like this. She wants to impress you."

"Don't listen to him," Ludivine ordered. "He's trying to poison you against me."

Corien gestured impatiently with his sword. "And she wants what I want, the very same thing, only she cloaks her desires in kindness and lies."

Rielle put her hands to her temples. Her mind was too full of their warring words. "Stop," she whispered. "You're hurting me."

"Ask her what really happened to us." Corien approached, pale eyes flashing. "Ask her what your beloved saints did. How they deceived us."

"Shut your mouth, snake," Ludivine spat out.

Rielle squeezed her eyes shut, turning away from them. Her head was a symphony of drums. "Please. I beg you."

"Me, the snake?" Corien laughed bitterly. "I do what I do to save our people. Yes, that's right. *Our* people. You're an angel, too, or have you forgotten? And what you do, you do it for yourself. You think of no one. You've forgotten us all. You care only to save your own stolen skin."

"Stop!" Rielle screamed, sinking to her knees. Their desires battled within her, tearing her thoughts in two. She curled into herself, pressing the heels of her hands against her temples.

Then, hands on her shoulders and lips against her brow.

She looked up, tears streaming down her face, and saw Audric kneeling before her. He was saying something, but his voice was coming to her from distant shores. She glanced wildly about the room. She was home, she was *home*—in Audric's rooms, beside his bed of rumpled plum-colored sheets. The fire still crackled in the hearth. Behind him stood Evyline and two other of her Sun Guard—Jeannette, Fara.

"Audric." Rielle gasped and leaned into him, pressing her face against his bare chest. "Oh, God. Help me. They wouldn't stop. I felt them inside me, and they wouldn't *stop*."

A soft rustling of fabric, a familiar lavender scent. "Rielle," came Ludivine's voice. "I'm so sorry. I was only trying to help you."

"Lu, get away from her, or I will banish you from this city," said Audric, his voice more furious than Rielle had ever heard it.

Rielle shook her head against his chest. "Only you," she whispered, curling her fingers in his hair. "Please, darling. Only you." Her heart beat wildly. She felt Ludivine's presence, very near, but blessedly gone from her mind, and refused to look at her. Her head still throbbed; she could still see the two of them, circling her. Corien and Ludivine, swords raised.

"Evyline," said Audric, "will you please give us a few minutes alone?"

"What is this?" came a new, sharp voice.

Rielle looked up, bleary-eyed and nauseated, to see Merovec enter the room.

"Oh, please don't worry," said Ludivine, hurrying to him with a smile. She kissed his cheek. "Rielle's just had a nightmare is all."

"I've had nightmares, and it's never caused this much of a fuss." Merovec locked eyes with Rielle, his expression flat and cold. "What did you dream of, Lady Rielle? Are your nightmares the same as those you gave my aunt?"

"Rielle did not give my mother nightmares," said Audric firmly. "She grieves the loss of my father."

"And yet, again, I don't wake screaming and half-mad from dreams of my own dead father." Merovec approached, crouching to meet Rielle's eyes. "What are you, exactly?"

"Merovec, that's quite enough," Ludivine snapped.

He ignored her, staring hard at Rielle. "How long until you bring death and madness upon the rest of us?"

"Say one more word to her," Audric said, his voice vibrating with anger, "and I will see to it that you never set foot in this castle again."

Merovec smiled. "Fine, then. I'll say it to you: you share a bed with a monster, my lord prince. And it is of great concern to me that my kingdom's heir continues to exercise such dangerously flawed judgment."

"Merovec, you will leave this room at once," said Ludivine. "You will go to yours and wait for me there."

Merovec raised his eyebrows, glancing back at her. "She's entrapped you too, little sister. She's not your friend. She's a thief and a whore, and she will be our doom."

Evyline strode forward, putting herself between Rielle and Merovec. Jeannette and Fara glowered beside her.

"Lord Sauvillier," Evyline growled, "if you do not obey my prince, my guard will be forced to remove you."

"It's astonishing how many people you've tricked into loving you," said Merovec. "But, Lady Rielle, I see what you are. I see it plainly."

Then, a familiar voice near the door.

"Audric," said Tal, Sloane at his side—her face pale, her mouth thin and hard. "I'm sorry to interrupt, but we have a problem."

Ludivine drew a sharp breath. "They're at the gates."

Merovec looked swiftly at her. "Who is?"

"How many?" Ludivine asked, ignoring him.

"Thousands," answered Sloane quietly.

"How did you know what he was going to say?" Merovec asked Ludivine, his voice brimming with impatience.

Rielle looked over Audric's shoulder to meet Tal's eyes. The lines of his body snapped with tension. He held his hands in fists, as if he wanted desperately to reach for her.

"Who is at the gates, Tal?" she asked.

He drew a slow breath. "Everyone."

◆◇◆

They swarmed the streets outside Baingarde, lining every road and court-yard of the temple districts. They leaned out of windows and gathered on rooftops. They threw rotten food over the castle walls, handfuls of mud and waste. The broad cobbled yards were littered with it. They banged their fists against the iron gates; they climbed the stone walls and were pulled down by the royal guard, hit on the head and bound by their wrists.

But they kept coming, undeterred by the lines of soldiers barricading them from the castle doors, and soon the lower yards were full of them. Lines of soldiers kept them back from the castle itself, but they climbed the fountains of the saints, waving torches and staffs and knives. They pissed in the water. Fights broke out—punches thrown in Rielle's honor, vicious kicks dealt to ribs and skulls by those wearing ragged Sun Queen sigils splattered with red dye.

They jeered and screamed, the people of Âme de la Terre. They shouted names—Rielle, Audric, Genoveve. They called for Merovec. They demanded to hear from the Archon.

Rielle stood at the main doors of Baingarde, held back both by the thick lines of guards standing between her and the city, and by the immense wall of sound that battered against her.

"Blood Queen!" they cried. "Sun Queen! Rielle!"

Their cries became a clamor, an indecipherable din.

And soon, a chant arose above the rest: "Give us the queen! Give us the queen!"

"Are they talking about me?" Rielle asked Tal. "Or Genoveve?"

"I'm not sure it matters," he replied. "I wish you would have stayed upstairs."

"They need to see my face. They need to see I'm not afraid."

Audric was speaking furiously with the commander of the royal army, who had been the second-in-command to Rielle's father—Rosalin Moreau, a pale, stern-faced woman with eyes of slate and white hair cropped close to her head.

"You cannot possibly expect me to believe that hundreds of armed, trained soldiers can be overwhelmed by an unruly mob." Audric gestured sharply at the yard. "Drive them out of here. Get them past the castle walls. Sweet saints, Rosalin, they're nearly at the doors!"

"Do I have your permission, then, my lord prince, to use whatever force is necessary against them?" Commander Moreau asked flatly.

"I urge you not to," Ludivine murmured at Audric's elbow. "That will only give them more ammunition against you."

"What would you have me do, then?"

*I could slip inside their minds,* Ludivine answered. *I could calm them, direct enough of them away that the rest will lose their fire.*

Rielle startled, for she felt not only Ludivine in her mind, but Audric as well—faint, and kept behind layers of her own thoughts and Ludivine's. But he was there, solid and steady, his mind taut and thrumming with worry.

*Are you talking to both of us at once?* Rielle asked.

*It seemed efficient,* Ludivine replied.

Rielle shook herself. Her mind was still raw and tender in the aftermath of her dream. She wished desperately for quiet, that Ludivine would leave and take Audric with her.

*I think she should do it, Audric,* she said instead. *Let her take control of them.*

*Is that what we'll do now?* He looked away from her, his thoughts in her mind terribly unhappy. *We'll use Ludivine to rob our own people of their freedom of choice when we must?*

Ludivine's presence turned impatient. *Can you think of a better idea?*

And then Audric's thoughts sharpened. He turned toward Rielle, and she stepped back from him, for the expression he wore was terrible, so shocked and angry that it transformed him into someone unfamiliar. Still himself, but as if seen through a dark cloud.

He spoke quietly, so only she could hear. "You saw him tonight."

Her stomach dropped. For a wild moment she considered lying.

*He saw,* Ludivine said, her panic arriving swiftly. *Oh, darling, I'm sorry. I didn't think before I connected us all.*

Rielle swallowed her anger, trying to settle her spinning thoughts. "I did see him, yes. In a dream."

"You kissed him." Audric's jaw worked. "Just now, I saw it in my mind."

"Yes."

"You were in his bed. He was touching you."

Rielle's breath left her. "Yes. But I didn't want to. He forced me into his bed. He took control of my thoughts and made them real, against my wishes."

He turned away from her, running his hand roughly through his curls.

She followed him, her throat clenching to see his eyes bright with tears. "Audric, please, you must believe me," she choked out.

"I do believe you," he said, but he avoided her gaze.

"My lord prince?" Commander Moreau insisted. "Your orders?"

Merovec stepped forward. "Let me speak to them. They want to be heard, and I'll hear them. Seeing any of you will only provoke them."

And then a sharp cry arose from out in the yard, followed by several more. The crowd scattered, their angry screams turning to cries of panic.

Rielle hurried to the door, shoving past Evyline to look outside.

Resurrectionists from the House of the Second Sun—dozens of them, clad in white and gold—stood throughout the crowd, holding blades to their own throats. Some had already fallen, blood gushing from the slits across their necks. One by one, the others followed, too quickly for anything to be done, until only one remained. A man, standing closest to Baingarde's doors, his eyes wild. He held a golden scepter in his right hand—its polished shaft glinting in the torchlight, a gleaming, sun-shaped medallion capping the top.

The man caught Rielle's eyes and then, grinning, called out to her, "As you have done for our queen, so we beg you to now do for us. As you promised us, Sun Queen. As you promised, our beloved God and savior!"

Rielle rushed forward, but Evyline caught her firmly around her waist. "Lu, stop him!" she cried over her shoulder.

But he had already drawn his own little blade across his throat. He fell first to his knees and then forward, the scepter clattering across the stone. And the sight of him lying there, choking on his own death, blood pooling beneath his body, shattered what calm Rielle had managed to gather.

She flung herself against the vise of Evyline's arms, screaming and sobbing—for the man's death, for the bodies staining the yard red and the thousands of others trampling each other to get away, back out the gates, back to the streets. And she sobbed for herself, furious and exhausted. She beat on Evyline's arms, and when she would not let her go, she dug deep into her gut, into her palms and the hot turns of her feet, and shoved them all away—Evyline, her Sun Guard, Merovec, the dozens of guards streaming in and out of the doors.

Audric had expected it. He caught Ludivine, and they steadied each other, only stumbling while the others fell.

"And this is allowed?" Merovec pushed himself back to his feet. He flung an arm out at Rielle. "This temper? This unpredictability? You're all fools." He pointed at Audric. "You're the worst of them all. Can you not see what's happening? She has poisoned you first, and soon it will spread to the rest of us."

Ludivine caught his arm, talking too softly for Rielle to hear, but soon Merovec had subsided, his expression slightly bewildered, like that of a child waking from sleep. Together they hurried away. Merovec's guards followed, frowning in obvious confusion.

Audric stared after them. Then he glanced at Commander Moreau. "I want that yard empty and clean within the hour. I want the streets of this city restored to order within two."

The commander nodded. "And those who refuse to leave?"

"I think you'll find that they'll be easily convinced," said Audric darkly. Then he found Rielle; their eyes locked across the room. He moved past her, away from the doors.

"Come with me, please," he said quietly, and then to his guards, "See that Lady Rielle and I are not disturbed."

She hesitated only for a moment. Her instinct was to reach out to Ludivine or Corien, but she refrained, her stomach roiling from the memory of them fighting in her mind.

She followed Audric across the entrance hall, the crowd's cries diminishing behind her and the clanking golden footsteps of her Sun Guard close on her heels.

—◆◇◆—

He led her to the Hall of the Saints, and once their guards had stationed themselves outside and closed the doors behind them, silence fell across the vast room.

Rielle shivered. The cold inside the hall was different from that of her dream. This cold was sterile, marble-eyed. She glanced up at the statues of the saints, the weight of their hard gazes and massive bronze weapons pressing upon her shoulders.

Audric stood at the center of the room, facing the dais upon which his father's throne stood. "I'll need to be crowned king, and soon," he said, his hollow voice echoing softly against the cold floor, the cold walls. "I've delayed it for as long as I could, but that's finished now. Mother's condition is too debilitating, and I don't have hope that she'll ever recover. The queen she was is dead."

Rielle approached him slowly, watching his body sag under the weight of his own words.

"The people need to know the crown is strong," he said quietly.

"Why have we come here?" she asked.

"Because the last time we were both in this room," he replied, "our fathers were newly dead, and you were blessed by the Archon as the Sun

Queen." He turned to her, his expression unreadable. And this was the most troubling thing that had yet happened that night, for ordinarily his gaze was warm and open, his face soft with love for her.

"And you want to remind me of my duty, is that it?" She straightened, hardening herself against him. "As if it is ever far from me, even for a moment."

"You know that I wish it could be otherwise for you."

"And yet you bring me here to shame me."

"Not to shame you. To understand you." He clenched and unclenched his fists. "You said Corien forced you into his bed."

As she remembered that dark room in the mountains, she felt cut in two between a wash of dread and a shiver of delight.

"He did," she replied.

"You said he took hold of your thoughts and made them real, against your wishes."

Suddenly Rielle understood the heart of this conversation. An ill sweep of cold rushed down her body.

Audric watched her, waiting, but she could not find her voice, so he said it for her. "He made your thoughts real. You were imagining the two of you together, in his bed, and he saw that and gave it to you, because he thought it was what you desired."

Rielle shook her head, fresh tears blinding her. She hurried toward him and reached for his hands.

"Audric, please," she said, "you don't understand."

"I think I understand quite well," he said, his voice cracking, the unfeeling mask he wore slipping to reveal a terrible, naked sadness.

And then he seized her arms, drawing her roughly to him. He bent low over her, his breath hot against her face.

"Is this what you want?" He tightened his grip around her wrists. He nipped her bottom lip, a little too hard, and though Rielle hated the look on his face—as if he despised himself, as if he could hardly bear to touch her—she felt herself rising to meet his passion. Her body responded, her blood thrumming with need.

"Yes, this is what I want," she whispered, trying to touch his face, but he wouldn't let her. He kissed her, hard, and wrenched her arms down to her sides, locking her in place. She cried out into his mouth, squirming against him.

"Come here," he said thickly, and then they were stumbling toward one of the broad, polished tables lining the side of the room, in the shadow of Saint Marzana's shield. He yanked the dressing gown from her body, but when she tried to unbutton his own shirt, he jerked away from her.

He shoved her against the nearest table, turning her away from him. He fisted one of his hands in her hair; with the other, he reached around to tease her, and let out a harsh groan against her neck when he found her hot and ready for him.

"This *is* what you want, then," he said, stroking hard between her legs. "To be handled like this. To be used as if you're nothing, as if you can't be hurt."

She tried to twist back and look at him, but he choked out, "No, Rielle," and pushed her down, pinning her against the table with his hand hard around her neck.

And, though she hated herself for it, though she knew it was just what he expected her to do, she came apart with a sharp cry, her thighs clamping shut around his hand. And he didn't wait for her to recover before driving inside her.

"Tell me I'm wrong," he said as his hips slammed against hers. "Please, Rielle. Tell me you don't want him."

"I..." She shook her head, her body buzzing with pleasure even as her heart shattered. "I can't."

"I know you can't." He sobbed a little, somewhere above her. His hands gripped her hips hard enough that she knew she would wear the marks of his fingers for days—and yet his viciousness was what she wanted. She wanted to forget this horrible night. The black fortress in the mountains. Corien's weight flattening her against his bed. If Audric took her hard enough, she would be scorched clean of all shadows, all confusion.

"He'll use you," Audric said. "I know what he offers you, and I understand why you want it. But he doesn't love you, Rielle. He loves what you can do. He loves how you could help him achieve what he wants. That's it. Nothing more."

And he was wrong. Rielle knew it even as she listened to his voice break. Her connection with Corien was more than what Audric claimed. She knew Corien desired her power, and yet his hand had flinched around hers in that cold dreamscape, as if he could hardly believe his luck that she would deign to touch him. And yet he did not ever look at her with fear, even though he knew intimately every deep, dark corner of her mind.

Audric's lips came down upon her neck, sweet and soft, and it was such a familiar touch, so like their usual lovemaking, that all thoughts of Corien flew from Rielle's mind. She began to cry with relief and reached back to hold him, her arm bending awkwardly. She found his hand and squeezed it. She gasped out his name.

He lowered himself upon her, wrapping her in his arms. His cheek was wet against hers. He turned his face into her hair.

"Tell me you love me," he whispered desperately. "Please, Rielle. Tell me, and I'll believe it."

"I love you," she said over and over, and it was true, it would always be true. If Corien disappeared tomorrow, if he lived in her mind for the rest of her days, it would still be true. Even if Audric grew so afraid of her that he turned away from her forever. Even then, she would love him.

He finished inside her, pulling her down once more along with him, and after the deep roar of her blood had quieted, and his sharp breaths against her neck had slowed, she turned around to face him. Gently, avoiding her eyes, he helped her sit on the table. Then he wrapped her in his arms and buried his face in her damp hair.

She welcomed him, curling her shaking legs around his. "It's all right," she whispered, holding him as he wept. She wiped her cheeks on his sleeve, stared blearily past him at Saint Katell's stern visage. "It's going to be all right."

# ELIANA

*"Go fast into the night,*
*Go soft into the fight,*
*Hold on to your heart,*
*And keep your mind bright."*

—Traditional Mazabatian soldier's prayer

Eliana awoke slowly to find herself wrapped in Simon's arms, his face buried in her hair, his light snores coming soft and steady against her neck.

For a moment she allowed herself to enjoy the warmth of him, the peaceful silence of the room. She pretended this was all there was—a quiet bed, a night of kisses upon her skin, Simon holding her securely against his chest.

But soon dawn was painting the black windows gray, and she forced herself to sit up, slipping out from Simon's heavy embrace. She dressed in silence, bare feet on the cold floor, and felt it the moment he awoke. The room expanded to contain the force of him.

"Are you all right?" he asked, his voice hoarse with sleep.

She did not turn to look at him. She couldn't, or she would return to bed and never leave it.

"I'm fine." She buttoned her shirt, rolled the sleeves up to her elbows. "We have much to do today. Time travel, confronting my all-powerful mother. That sort of thing. I'd like to get started."

She heard him rise, and it took every ounce of her control not to turn and watch him dress.

"Do you have a morning-after tonic?" he asked. "I didn't think... I should have asked last night. I should have made certain. I'm sorry."

"Not to worry. I'm perfectly capable of taking care of my own body." Briskly, she ran her fingers through her tangled hair and tied it back into a braid. "I took a medicine two years ago that will prevent me from having children. A woman who worked in one of the Orline Red Rooms gave it to me. There's no need for concern."

Then she moved toward the door and was about to leave when Simon gently caught her wrist.

"I won't be able to concentrate if I think you're angry with me," he said.

She glared at the door. "I'm not angry with you."

"You're clearly not happy with me."

"I'm not happy with anything." And then tears were filling her eyes, and she growled a little and looked up at the ceiling, blinking hard. "I was happy last night. I was so happy I felt reborn. And now it's time for us to try this mad thing, and I'm furious with myself for letting this happen, because now part of me is hoping it won't work. Part of me is hoping we'll fail, because if we do, at least I'll still have you with me."

Simon murmured her name, tenderly, and she turned to look up at him through a glassy film of tears. He bent low to kiss her—her lips, her cheeks, her brow—and she clung to him, and hid her face against his chest when she could no longer bear the touch of his mouth.

"I don't love you," she whispered, the lie bitter on her tongue. "I refuse to love you."

"I know," he said and held her to him, stroking her hair. "I don't love you either."

She smiled a little, her throat aching. She held on to him until the ache became too sharp for her to breathe. Then she pulled away, squaring her shoulders against the sight of him standing there, so near and warm, his hair messy from sleep, and fled downstairs without looking back.

They worked in separate areas of Willow's gardens, separated by a good mile of rain-heavy trees, muddied paths, swollen streams. Simon insisted upon it, claiming that traveling through time was a sensitive, unpredictable act, and that, while he was relearning all he had once known, he wanted no one near the danger of it.

Even if he hadn't requested this, Eliana would have left him to his work. Sitting with him in the gardens, healing the scar on his chest, had helped him recover the feeling of what it meant to weave a solid, stable thread. He was now able to summon them more easily, and so, her part finished for the moment, she wanted to be as far away from him as possible. The sight of him left her undone. She passed him in the hallways of Willow, and his presence pulled at her. She sat across from him at mealtime and felt so desperate to touch him that restraining herself required all her energy.

After a few hours spent practicing various elemental tasks with her castings—Remy providing irritatingly cheerful encouragement from a nearby bench—Eliana marched around the estate until she found Jessamyn sitting in the grass under a sprawling silver oak, cleaning her knives.

"I need to fight something," Eliana announced.

Jessamyn raised her eyebrows, then gestured at her leg. Her crutch stood propped against the tree. "I'm afraid you won't find me much of a formidable partner at the moment."

"Fine." Then a thought surfaced, startling her. "Can I heal you?"

Jessamyn considered her quietly for a moment. "I was wondering if you'd offer that." She set aside her knives and stretched out her wounded leg with a wince. "Do I need to do anything?"

"Just sit quietly."

"Will it hurt you to do it? Will it require too much of your energy?"

"No, and no."

Jessamyn waved a hand at her. "Slow down for a moment and really look at me. Is this all right? Will Simon be angry that you've wasted your strength on me?"

"It's not a waste. You're a good fighter. We'll need you in excellent shape for the Jubilee. And if Simon gets angry, well..."

But the mere mention of him left her feeling muddled. She fell silent, glaring at the ground.

"Would you like to talk about it?" Jessamyn asked mildly.

"About what?"

"About Simon."

"What about him?"

"About how you love him."

Eliana's head shot up, heat rushing to her face. "I don't love him."

"Oh, please. I know that look. I've had that look." Then Jessamyn leaned forward, her eyes sparkling. "Tell me, was he good? Please tell me he was good, even if it's a lie. My heart will break otherwise."

The look on Jessamyn's face was so wicked that Eliana couldn't help but laugh.

"Oh, he was good," she said. "He was good several times over, in fact."

Jessamyn placed a hand to her heart. "Oh, thank God. Dare I ask for elaboration?"

Eliana hesitated. As she thought of how to respond, images from their night together returned to her, and she could no longer find her voice. Heat tingled sharply behind her eyes and nose, and she looked away, mortified.

"Never mind." Jessamyn squeezed her hand. "I'm sorry. I shouldn't have teased." Then, after a pause, she added, "You really do love him, don't you?"

"No," Eliana replied, her voice catching. She dashed her hand across her eyes, set her jaw. "I don't love him."

Jessamyn nodded, squeezing her fingers once more. "Well, then. My leg hurts like a right royal bastard. Can you help me?"

Eliana smiled and blew out a shaky breath. She placed her hands on Jessamyn's wounded thigh and turned her thoughts away from Simon, directing them instead toward the castings nestled in her palms. They awakened, humming, and she slipped into a world of gold.

And that was how two days passed—Eliana using her castings to both practice elemental magic and bring comfort to those at Willow suffering from injuries.

She closed Jessamyn's wounds and stitched Patrik's broken bones back together. She soothed an old pain in Dani's hips, which had long kept her from moving as nimbly as she would have liked, and sat with her eldest son, Evon, whose mind had been battered with far too many traumas. He slept very little, and his muscles were knotted with the tension of perpetually steeling himself against the possibility of some terrible assault. But when Eliana sat with him, stepping into the realm of the empirium to read the scars his body held, he seemed to relax a little, and he began to speak of old hurts she sensed he had never before confessed aloud.

And though it exhausted her to take on new burdens, she refused to stop. There was something reassuring in the work; healing wounds grounded her in a way that summoning fire and water could not. When she manipulated wind or earth, she felt far removed from herself, as if it were not really her body carrying out these remarkable tasks, but rather the ghost of her mother, working through her from death. But sitting with someone in a quiet room to heal their wounds, or using her power to see more clearly the map of pain they carried inside them, reminded her of her humanity, of her own flesh-and-blood fragility. Such a reminder would once have angered and frightened her, but now it reassured her.

She was not her mother. She was neither God nor queen, and she was not the once-invincible Dread.

She was a girl, and she was human.

So she pushed herself on, until nearly everyone on the estate had been tended to. Their hurts seen and heard, their pain soothed.

Nearly everyone—except for Harkan.

She recognized that she had been avoiding him, and that doing so was childish. But what was she to say to him that would be of any comfort?

And anyway, it seemed he had been avoiding her as well. Every time she found him, he was huddling with Patrik or Jessamyn or Dani, consulting with them on various strategies—securing a ship for Eliana, creating diversions throughout Festival, deciding what Red Crown soldiers should be posted where and when on the various routes through the city and in the canyons and cliffs surrounding it.

Two days after her night with Simon, after the evening meal, Eliana decided she could no longer hide from Harkan. He had gone on a long walk through the gardens with Zahra, and Eliana settled on a bench near the wide terrace at the back of the house, waiting for him.

It was nearly full dark by the time they returned. Eliana watched them approach, her stomach twisting. Zahra met her first, swooping down to brush a cold, airy kiss across her brow.

*Be gentle with him, my queen*, the wraith urged, and then she was gone, drifting soundlessly into the house.

Eliana pressed her hands flat against her thighs. "Hello."

Harkan stood at the edge of the terrace, hands shoved in his pockets. "Hello."

She scooted over, making room for him on her bench. "Will you sit with me?"

He hesitated, then obeyed. They sat in rigid silence for a moment before Eliana sighed sharply and took his hand in hers.

He laughed, smoothing his thumb across her fingers. "I'm not good at this anymore. I'm not good at being your friend, and I'm sorry for it."

"I wish you wouldn't be." She drew a deep breath. "I feel like I should be the one to apologize."

"Why is that?"

"Because I can't give you what you want. Because I've changed, and because none of this is fair. Because I feel like it's my fault that we're all fighting and in terrible danger, even though, logically, I know it's not."

"And because you've fallen in love with someone else?"

She turned to look at him. He had said it without judgment or anger. He sat beside her, leaning against the wall at their backs, looking up at the sky. The lanterns flickering around the terrace threw soft, shivering shapes across his skin—white-gold over golden-brown.

"I'll always love you, Harkan," she said quietly. "And I think you know that."

"And I'll always love you." He looked over at her, his eyes soft on her face. "I worry for you."

She bristled. "Because of Simon?"

"No, not in that way. Because of what he wants you to do, and because of how hard you've been working over the last few days. Driving yourself to exhaustion. Do you think I haven't noticed?"

"You've been avoiding me."

He raised an eyebrow. "And you've been avoiding me."

For a moment they stared at each other, and then Eliana began to laugh from the sheer absurdity of it—sitting there, so far away from home, with an angelic army en route to destroy them, and Simon practicing time traveling somewhere in the trees, and Patrik sitting inside by the fire, mending Dani's old gowns for the Jubilee. And the castings on her own hands, alien and beloved, and the power in her veins, and the horrible knowledge of her mother living somewhere in the past, not knowing that soon her grown daughter would appear before her, begging her to have mercy on the world.

It was all absurd, and yet Eliana could not turn away from it. It was her future, and her past. It was the war she had chosen to fight.

Harkan's laughter joined her own, and when they subsided at last, she leaned her head on his shoulder, wiping her eyes. She watched the garden's shadows deepen. She wondered if years of war had altered the shapes of the trees, the colors of the blooms. She wondered what they all would have been, had they grown up in a world not ruled by the Empire, and what kind of girl she would be if they succeeded in changing the course of history. Raised in a castle, child of a king and a queen, what kind of woman would she become? What friends would she make? What lovers would she invite into her bed?

"I'm leaving in the morning," Harkan told her.

She shook away her spinning thoughts. "To prepare for the army's arrival?"

He nodded against her head. "We're forming a perimeter."

"Who will go with you?"

"Catilla, Viri. Evon, Dani's son. Gerren too."

"Gerren." Eliana sighed. "He's too young to be a soldier."

"We're all too young to be soldiers."

"Surely there won't only be five of you."

"No. Thirty, on our team alone. And Simon and Dani have arranged for five other teams to wait stationed throughout the city, standing by to provide you cover as needed."

Eliana's eyes grew hot. "So many. More than I expected."

"They're eager to fight for you," Harkan said quietly. "They heard of what you did in Karlaine. In Astavar too. Sinking the fleet." He pressed his mouth against her hair. "They'd do anything for you, any one of them. They speak of you with tears in their eyes."

"Stop saying these things," Eliana whispered.

"El, you've given them hope."

"Please, stop. I can't bear to hear about their love for me when I very well might end up killing them."

"What shall I talk about, then? How my ass hurts from sitting here for so long? How Darby hums when he takes a shit?"

She offered him a false, slight laugh. "Tell me where you'll go, exactly. Your team. You particularly."

"The less you know, the better."

"Bastard. I knew you would say that." She swallowed hard. "You said your team leaves in the morning. When?"

"Dawn."

Never had a single word sounded so cruel. "As your Sun Queen, I command you to come back to me safely." She tried to make a joke of it, but her voice sounded flat and strange.

"And as your friend," Harkan said, "I beg you to take care of yourself." He drew in a long, slow breath. "El... Simon wants you to fight a war for him, and for everyone, and you've been doing that marvelously, and I've no doubt you will continue to. But please don't push yourself beyond your limits on his account. I know you love him, but I also know he's rather a zealot, and you tend to jump into the role of martyr whenever you can. It's a dangerous combination."

And then, before she could say anything more, before she could work past the lump in her throat, he gently pulled away from her and stood. Facing the gardens, he straightened his coat.

"I don't want to leave you," he said, his voice strange and closed, "but I really must, or I'll lose my mind. I'll say things I shouldn't. I'll beg you for things you can't give. And anyway, Simon is coming, and he looks as though he has something important to tell you."

Then Harkan strode into the house, leaving her to stare helplessly after him.

*Zahra, you will go with him,* she thought desperately into the night, not even sure if the wraith was close enough to hear her. *Keep him safe. Let him know that I love him. I don't think he believes me.*

And then Simon was there, hurrying across the terrace toward her, looking bright-eyed and wild. She realized with a start that she hadn't seen him all day.

His frantic energy pulled her to her feet. He carried with him a cold, acrid smell, like the tang of smoke and the hot buzz of galvanized light.

"You did it," she guessed, reading the oddness in his eyes. "You traveled."

"I did. Not far." He sat heavily on the bench, running his hands through his hair. His voice and fingers shook, though with excitement or terror, Eliana didn't know.

She caught his hands in her own, brought them to her lips, and then, when he would not stop trembling, she swung her legs over his lap and slid her arms around him. She pressed the warmth of herself against him, tucked her head beneath his.

"I'm sorry," he whispered, his arms coming around her. "It's just that I haven't traveled in years. I thought it was lost to me. And now, so suddenly, it's returned, and all at once I must do a thing I never thought I would do again. And if I fail, we're all lost."

"If *you* fail? What about me?" Again, she tried to tease; again her voice emerged shaken. "I'm the one who has to face my mother, not you."

He swore quietly, kissed her hair. "I should be the one comforting you."

"Then comfort me." She pulled away from him, traced the tired lines around his mouth. "Take me upstairs and comfort me, and then we'll sleep."

He kissed her hands. "And tomorrow we'll begin."

She helped him to his feet, this wild man with his blue-fire gaze. "And tomorrow we'll begin," she agreed and led him quietly upstairs, to the room she now thought of not simply as hers, but as theirs, and shut the door behind them.

◆◆◆

At dawn, with the first arms of gray light touching the sky, Harkan's team left the safety of Willow for the rocky grin of mountains circling Festival's southern border. Eliana came downstairs, to the terrace where he had held her, to say goodbye. Mutely she received a gentle embrace from Viri and Catilla, and a fiercer one from Gerren; prayers from soldiers on bent knees; murmurs of thanks and well wishes from those Dani had brought out from the city.

And then, an embrace from Harkan before Eliana was prepared for it—tight and brief, silent, his face pressed into the bend of her neck. Two seconds, her fingers clutching his shoulders, and he was gone, moving off through the trees to join the others.

"Don't make me do this," came Zahra's miserable voice, and Eliana tore her gaze away from Harkan's retreating form to find the wraith drifting at her elbow, small and shrunken. Her dark eyes shimmered at the edges, as if losing cohesion.

Eliana cupped the tight, cold air that held Zahra's face. *Listen to me.*

"No," Zahra said, her voice buckling. She looked away, her cloudy black arms flickering as if distant storms were moving through them.

*Zahra, I command you to listen to me.*

*My queen.* Zahra's thoughts scrambled at the edges of Eliana's mind. *Don't ask me to leave you. Please. Not now. Not when you're about to put yourself in such danger.*

*I have my castings. I have Simon.* Eliana ducked down to meet Zahra's eyes. *And Harkan will have you. Or else he'll be fighting for me out there alone, facing the imperial army alone, and I'll be out of my mind with worry for him.*

Zahra silently shook her head, over and over.

*And that is not the way you want me to meet my mother, is it?*

After a long moment, Zahra at last replied, *No, my queen,* and a knot of tension released in the air, as if something physical had given way.

Then Zahra rushed at her, shrinking as she moved, shifting to the size of a child, and burrowed against Eliana's chest. Pressed so close, Eliana felt the wraith open a feeling of love to her, so vast and sudden that Eliana stumbled, as if she'd misjudged the height of a step. Remy, crying quietly at her side, caught her elbow and steadied her.

*That was from me,* Zahra said, her voice in pieces, *and also from Harkan. You are lucky, my queen, to have such love in your life.*

And then Zahra was gone, darting through the garden like a shadow shot from an arrow, and then they were all gone, slipping fast into the morning. Remy hooked his arm through Eliana's to help her back into the house, which was a lucky thing, for her own mind had gone soft and dark. She managed to put an arm tight around his shoulders and walked with him into the side parlor where Dani had held her, that first rainy night. There, she held him and let him cry against her shirt until he subsided, shivering and half-asleep.

Eliana was glad Simon had stayed upstairs for this. She was glad to share this moment of grief with Remy alone.

She sent a thought along the veins of the empirium she could now always sense at her fingertips, like the phantom echoes of a song that would never reach its finale.

*Watch over him*, she prayed, more fiercely than she had ever prayed in her life. *Watch over them all. Saints. God. The empirium. Whatever you are, wherever you live. May the Queen's light guide them home.*

She closed her eyes. *Give me the strength to burn bright for them, no matter what lies ahead.*

◆◆◆

Simon waited for her in the spot they had chosen—the patch of grass and clover by the tiny silver streams, near the willow under which she had healed his scar.

She joined him wordlessly, Remy's tears still drying on her shirt. She avoided his gaze but felt it nevertheless, a warm pressure kissing her cheeks.

"I'm sorry, Eliana," he said, and then looked ready to say more, but she feared they would be words of comfort, words that would do nothing to ease the pain in her heart or the worry buzzing like wasps through her body, so she hurried to him and pressed a hard kiss to his mouth before he could speak.

He held her for a moment as she breathed, and then took her by the shoulders and looked into her eyes.

"We should not attempt this if you're grieving," he told her.

"I'm always grieving," she replied. "Isn't everyone?"

"You know what I mean." He frowned and looked away into the trees. "This is happening too quickly. We haven't had the proper time to prepare."

"And if we wait any longer, death may come for us before we can try. The Emperor's army marches. Our friends march to stop them. So, we will do this." She moved past him, standing in the center of the clearing. She lifted her chin against the heartbreak flooding her body. "Now. I'm ready."

"Eliana, please, look at me."

"I've been looking at you," she said, her voice fraying. "I've looked at you so many times that I see you when I close my eyes. I can't shake you. I'm going to lose you too, I'm sure. I'll lose Remy and Harkan, and Patrik and Jessamyn, and I've already lost Navi, and I'm tired of knowing this.

I'm tired of living in a world defined by loss. I'm ready to be rid of it. We've gone over our plan a hundred times. Let's begin."

He stood before her, touched her face. "Look at me."

"No," she said through gritted teeth. "I can't bear it."

"Eliana, love. Come on, look at me."

She obeyed, unable to resist the soft pull of his voice.

"I'm not sending you anywhere when you're this upset," he said, his gaze holding her gently. "You need a clear head to talk to your mother. You need to be able to focus."

She knew he was right, and yet if she remained in these gardens for another moment, she would lose all courage. Her sadness would drown her. She closed her eyes, allowing herself another moment of his touch, and then stepped away, wiping her cheeks dry and lifting her chin.

"You will send me back now," she said, her voice steady and cold. "As your queen, I command it. We don't have time to spare, and if you continue to doubt me, I'll consider it an insult."

He watched her for only a moment. Then he turned, every line of his body unhappy, and began to work.

She was familiar by now with the sight of his threads, golden and shimmering, but as he gathered these into a sparking circle, they were joined by new threads, just as long and thin, but made of shadows instead of light. They were a blue-black color, iridescent, each of them churning viciously through the air like curls of smoke from an angry fire. These darker threads snapped and hissed; they fought the tight whirl of Simon's fingers. Sweat beaded on his brow and neck. The force of his work sent him sinking slowly to his knees.

Eliana fought to stay still, the urge to go to him overwhelming. But he had warned her about this, that the process of traveling through time would require much more of him, that it would be startling and perhaps upsetting to see. No matter what, he told her, she must not interfere.

So she waited, her mouth dry and her heart pounding hard in her ears, until at last she heard Simon croak, "Now, Eliana."

Another of his instructions: She must not hesitate. When he told her to go, she must go. He would hold open the thread for as long as she required, but every passing moment would be more difficult. The shape of him kneeling in the grass, threads of light and darkness twisting out from his chest and fingers, began to shift and flicker. His voice came out distorted.

She took a breath, holding their plan in her mind. He would be sending her back to a relatively peaceful time in Celdaria, before the war against the angels truly began. Her mother was nineteen and newly pregnant. Her father, the Lightbringer, was still alive.

She could not wait any longer. She moved past Simon, stepped into the net of his threads, and let them take her.

# → 43 →
# RIELLE

*"Merovec has returned home from your capital and has invited me to supper tomorrow evening. From Belbrion, I've heard of Queen Genoveve's resurrection. I've heard of your tumultuous streets, the crowds swarming to cheer Merovec's name, and that there is no love lost between him and Lady Rielle. So I will tell Merovec what I've learned and read, in hopes that I may gently nudge him toward a friendship that remains elusive—one with you and Lady Rielle, between House Sauvillier and House Courverie. The two greatest houses in Celdaria must be united in friendship and must face the coming war as allies. For I know, as well as you do, that war is indeed coming. The angels' eyes are everywhere, and they are hungry."*

—A letter written by King Ilmaire Lysleva to Prince Audric Courverie, dated October 1, Year 999 of the Second Age

Ten days before Audric's coronation, Rielle awoke at dawn from the feeling of being watched.

Slowly, she sat upright in bed. Beside her, Audric slept peacefully, his arm heavy over her hips. The room was dark; the Sun Guard stood outside, having given them privacy for the night.

Rielle breathed into the dark silence for a few moments, waiting for the feeling to diminish, but it remained—the great invisible eye, watching her just as it had in Mazabat.

The empirium, cold and endless, waiting for her to understand.

She climbed out of bed, following the tug of energy at her breastbone, as if hot fingers were reaching gently for her heart. Quietly she stepped outside onto the terrace, where Atheria waited, ears pricked toward the towering black slopes of Mount Cibelline that dwarfed the castle. In the east, the sun was climbing, but the mountain remained still and dark.

"You hear it too," Rielle whispered. Her fingers sparked when she touched Atheria's soft gray coat, and the godsbeast knelt, shivering, so Rielle could mount her.

Palms flat against Atheria's neck, she whispered, "We've got to follow it."

Atheria's ears swiveled back, listening.

"I know. I don't want to either."

But the itch in her chest was insistent, and golden images she could not understand shimmered thinly at the edges of her vision. The empirium was a stubborn song she longed to shake from her mind.

She directed Atheria up, away from the castle and into the great pine forests that carpeted Cibelline, and with every booming beat of Atheria's enormous wings, the urgent fist in Rielle's heart gripped tighter, until she could hardly breathe. Her blood raced and roared beneath the hot planes of her skin. She scanned the dark net of trees below, trying to shake the gold from her vision. She summoned up shreds of energy from her pinched gut and shoved them out of her hands as if that could dislodge the empirium from her eyes.

"Leave me alone," she whispered. "I just want to sleep. That's all I want, to sleep for a while. Leave us alone."

When Atheria landed at last, in a thin copse of trees at the edge of a broad, grassy cliff, Rielle slid gingerly off her back and sank, gasping, to her hands and knees. She looked up once, searching the forest. She saw nothing extraordinary—only pines shivering in the high mountain winds. Rocks scattered across ridges of earth, rustling blades of grass. She heard the distant, lonely call of a hawk. Gold slipped across her eyes, as if the empirium were replacing the false frame of her body with something splendid and new.

Atheria lowered herself to the ground, covering Rielle with her wings. She stared up at the canopy of feathers, watching in exhausted wonder as each soft barb lit up like a sky of stars, compressed into a single brilliant moment.

Then a wave of light swept over her, pulling her under.

※ ◆ ※

She had experienced such a thing many times before—dreams from Corien that left her restless and sharp-edged, visions from Ludivine that soothed her mind when nothing else could.

This was different.

This, she sensed, was a message sent from the empirium itself.

She was limbless, bodiless. She was her truest self in this realm—a creature of boundless light. She was stardust, luminous and ancient; she was the infinitesimal ash of long-dead worlds.

She floated in a sea of gold, buoyed by churning eddies of light. She hardly dared breathe for fear of splintering them, and anyway, breathing was an act relegated to the world of humans.

There was an endless plain before her, but instead of stretching from horizon to horizon, it stood upright, like a vast mirror. Though she did not understand what she saw reflected on its rippling gold surface, she knew that what she saw was her own self.

She reached out, though she had no arm, and touched the gold-sea glass, though she had no fingers.

The image of her alien self shattered, replaced with something new. A million colors, a million sounds, cycling faster and faster until they were a frightening, terrible blur—pewter and periwinkle, screams of agony and waltzes performed on sweeping strings, mustard skies and jade fields, the red of an opened wound, the high shriek of a child at play, the dazzling blue of lightning arcing through a storm. A bruised sky, mottled and veined, a dark river of screams pouring from its mouth. A green world, peeling away from itself like thin curls of apple skin until only darkness remained. An oppressive darkness, a physical void that sucked the air from her lungs.

Seven faces looked down upon this collapsing world. They were painted in fire and water, in earth and metal and shadow, in snapping wind and in the scorching light of the sun.

Her human eyes would not have understood what she was seeing.

But her true eyes—the eyes the empirium had given her, the ones she carried deep within herself—knew it at once. Ancient lies curdled, putrid, against the roof of her mouth.

And the moment she grasped the truth, the empirium released her.

—◆—

When Rielle returned to the mountain, she lay breathless in the grass beneath a cloudless blue sky, and Atheria was nowhere to be found.

She sat up, her skin humming. She felt her mind rearranging itself in the wake of this vision, as if the very pieces of her skull were being remade.

She held her head in her hands and thought to Ludivine, too shocked for anger, *You knew. You had to have known. Why did you never tell me?*

Ludivine did not respond.

Instead, Corien did. He walked out of the trees and extended his hand to her.

"You do not belong in the dirt," he told her, and she accepted his help only because the ground was cold, and she did not trust her body to stand on its own.

"You're not really here," she said.

"No, of course not. I'm far away, as requested." He gave her a sardonic bow.

"The saints lied to you. I just saw it, in my mind. The empirium showed it to me."

Corien froze, watching her in silence.

She approached him slowly. "During peace negotiations, near the end of the war, they told you they had discovered another world, lying beyond our own. An uninhabited world, where you could create a new homeland for yourselves. Humans, in Avitas. Angels, in this new world. Two races, separated and at peace. And they lied."

She shook her head, laughing, and lightly touched her temples. "You thought you were traveling to a new home. Then you found yourselves in the Deep."

"And bodiless." The color was high in Corien's pale cheeks.

"It was torment for you. I felt it, just now. I lived it. I felt my body being taken from me, as yours was from you."

He rounded on her. "Vision from the empirium or no, you could not possibly understand what it is to have your body truly stripped from you. To lose your beauty and strength, all sense of touch and taste, and be forced to exist as a shell of yourself. And all the while knowing that your true home lies just on the other side of a veil you cannot move past." He took her face in his hands. "Don't you see, Rielle? What I do, I do to save my people. We were banished to a place that is not our home. We have been painted villains by the very people who wronged us."

"And they would not have had to wrong you," she replied, "if you hadn't grown so jealous of our power that you tried to kill us."

Corien's expression turned to stone.

"Yes, I saw that too," she whispered, smiling. "You were the one to start this war, centuries and centuries ago. You started the movement in the angelic cities that caught fire and spread. You thought it was unjust of God to have granted elemental power to beings so much lower than you and your own. You thought us a scourge, an insult to your own existence, a blight on your world. You craved our power for yourself. You're a warmonger. A zealot. You turned your race against mine. If anyone is to blame for what's happened to your people, it's not the saints. It's you, and you alone."

She stepped away; his hands slipped from her face. "You led an insurgency, near the end. You tried to prevent the banishment, but the saints were too strong for you. They forced you through. Kalmaroth. That was your name."

He flinched, as if the word were a struck fist. "Do not ever say that name again," he said, very softly. "It is no longer mine."

"Do you run from it because it reminds you of what you've done?"

He lunged for her, catching her hard by her wrist before she could stumble. She braced herself to burn him if she had to, insults sharp on her tongue.

And then, distantly, past the vision of himself that Corien had created, came a cry from Atheria. Corien's grip loosened. He frowned a little, looking past her.

"Something's wrong," he muttered.

She turned, searching the trees. "Atheria?"

"Something else. Something that should not be here."

He released her from the veil of his mind, but the echo of him remained beside her, like a ghost of her own body. All at once, she saw the world as it was—the pine forest, identical to the one in which Corien had visited her, but darker, still brightening with the dawn. Atheria, standing before her, wings outstretched as if to protect Rielle from an attacker.

And beyond Atheria, a slender young woman—her skin a few slight shades darker than Rielle's own, dark hair gathered in a single braid, eyes wide and brown and strangely familiar. She stared at Rielle as though she were witnessing something unthinkable.

Behind the girl, far back in the trees, shimmered a faint ring of light.

"She shouldn't be here," Corien said again, his presence in her mind one of utter confusion. "She doesn't belong here."

Feeling Corien so bewildered sent fear shuddering down Rielle's spine. "Who are you?" she snapped. "What is your name?"

The girl answered, falteringly, her accent and pronunciation so clumsy that at first Rielle could not understand her.

But then she repeated herself, and this time Rielle heard her plainly. It was a lie; it was some terrible trick of Corien's. Her exhausted mind was breaking at last and could no longer be trusted.

"My name is Eliana," said the girl. "I am your daughter."

# ‐ 44 ‐
# ELIANA

*"Studies authored by practiced marques, and confiscated by the Mazabatian government, emphasize the importance of discretion when traveling. One errant word, one misplaced stone on a path, could alter the course of a future history in infinite ways—some minute, others gargantuan. Even a marque who is vigilant and meticulous when traveling carries the potential for catastrophic devastation in their blood."*

—*Meditations on Time*
by Basara Oboro, renowned Mazabatian scholar

Eliana waited tensely for Rielle to respond, trying to ignore the enormous godsbeast standing between them.

She waited so long that she began to doubt herself. The woman across the wood *was* Rielle, wasn't she? Simon had given her a detailed description, and she could see, on Rielle's face, similar features to her own. Her nose, the clean turn of her jaw, her arched eyebrows.

How utterly strange to see pieces of her own face on this stranger, to know that this person she had never seen before had given her life. Trying to wrap her mind around the concept felt like trying to circle her arms around the entire world.

She stepped forward, hesitant. Remy had taught her key words and phrases in Old Celdarian over the last few frantic days, enough to communicate the essential: *Do not ally with the angels. What you do will bring the world to ruin. The angels will rise and destroy not only this world, but others as well. I can help you.*

She had practiced these sentences until they'd rubbed grooves into her mind. But now, standing here, in this world that was both her own and not, they eluded her.

The air was too thick with magic, too hot and vital, as if it did not quite fit in her lungs. It clogged her throat as she breathed, burning the back of her tongue. Her castings sparked to life, more eagerly than they ever had before. The heat of them smarted against her palms, and she bit back a yelp of pain.

"Mother?" she said. "Can we talk, please?"

For a moment, Rielle stared at her, muttering under her breath in Old Celdarian far too quickly for Eliana to decipher anything but a few scattered words: *Lies. Believe. Kill.*

*Corien.*

Eliana stiffened. "Corien? Is he here?"

Rielle's face changed, her expression shifting from one of bewilderment to something dark and malicious. She spat something in the direction of the godsbeast, and the creature launched itself into the air, clearing the wood. Even before Rielle's arm moved, Eliana felt the pull in the air, the tightening of it. She knew something terrible was coming, that magic would soon hit her, but it was such an immense sensation to be faced with Rielle's wrath that for a moment she couldn't move. Time became a tangible substance, viscous and tacky. She saw the ripple in the air as Rielle's power surged toward her, felt the heat of its passage.

It struck her hard in the gut like the flat of a monstrous hand, burning a narrow stripe across her abdomen.

She fell, the wind knocked out of her. Soundlessly, she gasped for breath in the dirt, and then she felt another surge coming and turned, scrambling to right herself, and thrust out her palms in Rielle's direction.

Her power snagged on the wind, which sent it gusting at Rielle in two sharp points like arrows. Rielle dodged one of them; the other grazed her left shin, making her legs buckle. She fell, catching herself hard on her hands. She whipped her head around, her glare so furious that Eliana felt pinned to the ground.

She raised her hands, brandishing her castings. "I don't want to hurt you," she said, hoping she had found the right words. "I want to talk."

Rielle advanced on her; her wrists flicked sharply. The ground beneath Eliana rippled, throwing her high in the air. Another fist of magic caught her, flinging her back into the trees. She slammed into the trunk of a pine and slid to the ground. She wavered in and out of blackness, and then looked up, head spinning, vision sparking with stars.

Rielle had thrown her some twenty yards deeper into the forest—and twenty yards farther away from where Simon's threads waited. All it would take, he had told her, would be a single conversation. A few words, a look passed between them. A moment of connection. A seed of an idea planted in Rielle's mind—that the angels were the enemy, that joining them would lead everyone to ruin, including herself. That, he had said, might very well be enough to change the future.

But neither of them had expected *this*, and as Rielle stormed toward her through the trees, the earth cresting like waves on either side of her, trees felling themselves at her approach, Eliana realized all at once, with a terrible, sinking feeling in her gut, how rash they had been. How foolish and utterly naive. So tired of fighting and so eager for an ending that they had flung themselves into a conflict they did not fully understand.

"Wait," she cried, scrambling backward over a clump of tree roots. "Please, just listen!"

With a quick turn of her hand, Rielle uprooted the tree against which Eliana sat. The tree went flying, crashing back into the forest, and Eliana fell twenty feet into a clump of brush. She slammed hard into the ground; the impact shook her mind free of its panic.

She let out a harsh, angry cry and pushed herself to her feet, and this time, when Rielle's power came rushing at her, she thrust up her palms, holding them before her like a shield.

Their magic locked, the overwhelming heat of Rielle's crackling against the shaking wall of her own. White-gold sparks flew from her hands. A terrible noise emanated from their interlocked power, like the grinding of metal against stone.

Eliana squinted past the blinding heat between them and caught a glimpse of Rielle's eyes—a sharp, clear green, rimmed with exhausted shadows. And at the outer edges of her irises, twin rings of gold glimmered, spinning fast.

"Listen to me," Eliana cried. "I don't want to hurt you. I must speak to you." Sweat dripped down her back. She felt fevered, her vision turning cloudy and red. And the stripe of burned flesh across her stomach pulsed with such a searing pain that she could barely hold herself upright. But she held fast, her legs shaking, and forced herself to meet Rielle's eyes.

And for a single, still instant, once their gazes had locked, Eliana saw a flicker of emotion pass over Rielle's face. She lowered her arms slightly; the incredible pressure of her attack lessened.

Eliana smiled a little, though the ribbon of pain across her stomach was expanding, brightening like the rising sun.

"My name is Eliana," she cried over the roar of their sparking power. "I can help you."

But then, before she could say more, a foreign presence punched its way into her thoughts. She swayed and fell hard to her knees, and then a familiar voice said to her, *Ah, Eliana. This is not our first time to meet, it seems. How curious.*

Corien. The Emperor. She pushed herself to her feet, looking around wildly. She lost all sense of Old Celdarian and reverted to Venteran. "Where are you?" she screamed. She flung out her shaking hands, aiming them to her left, then her right. "Get away from me! Get out of my head!"

*But it's such a nice head,* Corien said, *and contains so many secrets. Oh, well, now, this is certainly very interesting.* He hummed a little, as if pondering a delicious meal. *This is very interesting indeed. What a life you have led. What interesting company you keep.*

She ran stumbling into the forest, dodging the explosions of Rielle's power. Hot bolts of magic sliced trees in half, sent enormous clumps of earth and rock flying into the air. A stone caught her on the small of her back; two more struck her left calf, the nape of her neck. She swayed, nearly fell. Saint Tameryn's prayer leapt into her mind. Through the pain flaring up her body, she seized onto the familiar words.

*I fear no darkness, I fear no night.*

She whirled, scooped up shadows from the trees, and imbued them with all her desperation and fear. They became a flock of dark birds, knife-winged and knife-beaked, and spun wildly back toward Rielle. Eliana saw her knock them out of the sky as easily as pushing aside a cloud of flies.

She tried again. *With the dawn I rise.*

She wiped sweat out of her eyes, pulled sunlight from the air and flung it over her shoulders. She heard the impact of Rielle's fists, saw each of her sunlit knots flying off into the trees like shooting stars.

*How valiantly you fight,* came Corien's voice, thin with derision. *Your father would be proud.*

Eliana fell, tore open her hands against the ground, pushed herself up. The sweat stinging her eyes; the pain of her stomach, her skull, her legs; the blinding fear of Corien's thoughts pressing against her mind like squeezing fists. She could hardly see as she half crawled up a gentle slope, pulling herself up by her scraped-raw fingers.

And then, at the top, a sight that made her cry out with relief—Simon's threads, some fifty yards away, still circling faintly in the air where she had left them. But were they too faint? Would she step through them and return to a time that was not her own? Would she end up on the other side of the world from him, from Remy, from everyone?

But Rielle was close behind her, striding calmly through the forest, flinging every obstacle she encountered out of her path. And with every passing moment Eliana could feel Corien sinking deeper and deeper into her mind. She hoped the rift in time would shake his hold on her.

She hoped he had not glimpsed the whole of her life.

She took one last look over her shoulder, unable to resist looking once more at Rielle, and then jumped through the threads, crashing hard to the ground on the other side.

"Close it!" she cried.

She forced her eyes to stay open until she felt hands on her shoulders and heard Simon say her name. She breathed in and out, testing the fullness of her mind. Finding that it was her own once more, she let out a sob and reached blindly for an anchor. Simon's hand caught hers, and then he saw the wound on her stomach and swore, and said her name again, urgently. He turned her face up to his, but the sky was too bright, a spinning white canvas of trees.

Her pain ordered her to surrender, and she obeyed.

# ← 45 ←

# RIELLE

*"I'm writing this, desperate. Audric, he has beaten me. My body is in agony. He is moving against you. He has been gathering those loyal to him, planning his attack for months. He asked me for my loyalty, and I said I would be a friend to you both—to House Sauvillier and House Courverie. And he beat me for it. I can hardly breathe. I fought him, but not well. He ripped my castings from me. I barely escaped. I'm hiding now. I'm leaving this letter with a friend who I hope will get it to you faster than any other messenger. Audric, he intends to——"*

—An undated letter written by King Ilmaire Lysleva
to Prince Audric Courverie, confiscated
by Lord Merovec Sauvillier

T he ring of light disappeared shortly after Eliana jumped through it, snapping closed with a sharp nick like the rap of a blade against wood.

Rielle watched the spot where the light had been, following each white-gold spark as it scattered and vanished. And as she stood there, the mad swirl of her thoughts diminished, leaving her feeling hollowed out. From beyond the forest canopy came the cry of Atheria, who circled nervously overhead.

Rielle whirled to face Corien. "What are you playing at? Is this some sort of trick you've designed to punish me?"

He watched the place where Eliana had disappeared, frowning, his gaze distant. "Not a punishment. I knew nothing of this before it happened."

"You're deceiving me. You want to drive me mad."

"I don't."

"You lie."

He finally looked at her. "Not to you, and not about this."

"I hate you." She turned away, touching her blazing-hot temples. "I hate you so much I taste it like poison on my tongue."

He followed her as she walked unsteadily out of the trees. "That girl wasn't some illusion I conjured, Rielle. She was real."

"Stop talking to me. Both in and out of my head." Rielle stepped out into the sunlight, squinting. She whistled for Atheria. "I don't trust a word you say. I don't trust either of you."

"It's wise of you to mistrust the rat. But I'm just as puzzled by what's happened as you are. Well." He paused, his eyes turning distant once more. "Not quite as puzzled, perhaps."

Atheria knelt, and Rielle scrambled atop her. From her high perch on the chavaile's back, she glanced down only once more at Corien, steeling herself against his steady, moon-bright gaze.

"You made a fool of me today," she said tightly, looking out upon the woods she had shredded. "Chasing after some figment of your twisted imagination like a madwoman."

"Rielle, I swear to you—"

"I care nothing for your promises," she snapped. "Not today. And you would be wise to stay away from me until the memory of this day has faded."

Then she turned her back on him and urged Atheria up into the sky.

◆◇◆

They landed on the terrace outside her rooms, and once Rielle had walked shakily inside, she sank to the floor, hugging her middle. She laid her cheek against the carpet and wept—long, ragged sobs that rubbed her throat raw.

Atheria watched from the terrace, wings folded against her body. One anxious hoof pawed against the white stone.

*There you are.* Ludivine's voice rose swiftly. *You can't just run away like that. Audric's out of his mind with worry.*

Rielle could not breathe beneath the weight of Ludivine's relief. It clung to her like a membrane, sticky and gelatinous. She buried her head in her arms, tugging on her hair.

"Leave me alone," she whispered. "Stop talking to me. I can't bear it. I know about the saints, about what they did to you. Their lies, their great deception. You never told me, and now how am I supposed to trust you?" She squeezed her eyes shut. "Do you want vengeance? Is that why you've befriended me?"

*No.*

"You plot against me, right here in my home."

*No.* Ludivine's thoughts were heavy with sadness. *Darling, how can you think this of me? I love you.*

"I can't trust you," Rielle whispered. "I can trust no one, not even my own mind. My skull will crack open. I will split apart."

*I'm sending Audric upstairs.*

"No!" Rielle croaked. "Not him. Not now. Evyline. Send me Evyline, and stay away from me."

Ludivine said nothing more, and a few minutes later, the doors to her rooms opened admit Evyline, Dashiell, and Riva.

"Just you, Evyline, please," Rielle said, and when the others had left, and Evyline had knelt beside her, Rielle turned to her, reaching blindly for her. Her pounding heart would not slow. "Please sit with me, and say nothing."

Evyline settled herself awkwardly on the rug. She clasped Rielle's hand in her own. "Yes, my lady. For as long as you need me."

And for a time, Rielle cried in peace, reassured by the solid, unquestioning weight of Evyline beside her. Through her tears, she watched Atheria's tail flick back and forth, a pendulum of feathered gray.

Then the doors flew open, and all peace was shattered. Audric said her name, striding fast across the room, and Rielle squeezed her eyes shut against the sound of his voice. She could not put the image of the girl Eliana out of her mind. Those huge dark eyes. Her pitiful pleas for mercy.

"Leave us, Evyline," Audric instructed, kneeling beside them.

"No," Rielle whispered. "I need her."

"Stay, then," Audric said at once. He touched Rielle's hair. "What's happened, darling?"

She caught his face gently in her hands, wound her fingers in his soft curls. "Don't leave me. No matter what happens, don't leave me." Fresh tears rose to her eyes; she could not dislodge the sudden, bone-shaking fear that she would lose him.

He locked eyes with her and said softly, "I'll never leave you. You are my light and my life." He kissed each of her palms and then the salty corners of her mouth.

She turned her face up to receive him, like a flower desperate for the sun. "Evyline," she whispered, "you may leave us now."

Once they were alone, he helped her up from the floor and carried her to the chair by the hearth. She settled in his lap, worrying her hands together restlessly.

"You're shaking," he said, stilling her wrists. "What happened to you? Where did you go?"

"I needed fresh air," she lied, for she had no intention of telling him what had happened on the mountain, beyond the fact of Corien sending her an upsetting vision. *Her daughter.* An outrageous, ludicrous deception.

"So you took Atheria and flew," Audric said. "And this upset you?"

She pressed her face to his neck. "The empirium spoke to me. It showed me..."

After a moment, he prompted her. "What did it show you?"

"Horrible things," she whispered. "Things that make me doubt my own mind. Things that make me want to run far from here and never stop running, not until I fly apart."

And if she did, the dark part of her mind whispered, if she did run, if she disappeared into the far world where no one could find her, not even Corien, then Audric could be a king without distractions, and she could be free of his court, his city, the people who wanted her and hated her all at once.

"Stay with me," he murmured, as if sensing her conflict. He touched his brow to hers. "Stay with me, Rielle."

"I'm here," she said, her voice thin, and then she had to duck her head to hide her face from him, for she could not bear to see the love shining so plainly in his eyes. If he looked for much longer into hers, he would see the truth of her laid bare—the lives she had taken. The lies she had told.

The doubt growing like a restless storm in her heart.

Her mind slowly tearing itself in two.

◆◇◆

Rielle hurried out of the Hall of the Saints into one of the surrounding small anterooms, her bewildered guard following her as discreetly as was possible for seven soldiers outfitted in gold-plated armor.

As soon as the door shut behind her, closing away the glittering finery of Audric's coronation, she ran to a corner of the room, sank to her knees, and vomited. Her back to her guard, she wiped her mouth on the edge of her sleeve.

It was not the first time she had gotten sick in the last several days. At first she had assumed the cause was from sheer exhaustion; she had hardly slept these last weeks. Corien visited her every night, and Ludivine hovered always at the edges of her mind, and the streets near the castle filled daily with people clamoring for her death, her touch, her body, her blood. They came from the capital; they came from all over the kingdom, and more arrived every day.

And then there was that vision of the strange girl on the mountain, a memory that walked beside her always. She could not shake it. When she did sleep, she saw the girl in her mind's eye. Her fear, the square set of her jaw.

Rielle closed her eyes, fisting her hands in the fine golden embroidery of her gown. Every night, she laid with Audric in his bed, or hers. Every night, they moved together, each of them utterly wrung out. Their days had been full: preparations for the coronation; endless meetings with advisers, the Magisterial Council, the Archon; reports from their spies on the missing Kirvayan queen, reports from Mazabat on the quakes rattling their southern cities, reports from the Celdarian Obex on the vicious storms tearing across Meridian.

And the Obex themselves were no help at all. They refused to help Rielle find Saint Katell's casting. They refused to introduce her to the marques in their employ and request of them passage to Meridian, or Astavar, or Ventera—one of the kingdoms on the far western side of the world, where Rielle could continue her search for the remaining castings. When she raged at them, they reminded her of those she had killed in Mazabat. When she threatened to kill them as well, they told her calmly that then Saint Katell's sword would truly be lost to her.

"You would save yourselves before you allow me to save everyone else?" she had snapped at them, during one particularly contentious meeting.

Their speaker replied at once. "Lady Rielle, it is our judgment that, as things currently stand, keeping Saint Katell's casting out of your hands is exactly the thing that will save us all."

That night, she had stormed into Audric's room, the walls and windows trembling at her approach. Though her eyes had burned from lack of sleep, and her body had still been sore from the previous night, she found him dozing by the fire, a stack of petitions on the table beside him, and climbed at once into his lap. She woke him up with her mouth and her hips and held onto him tightly as he drove into her. But even then, afterward, as they lay sweating and exhausted, she could not sleep. She returned to that black northern fortress; she ran through unfamiliar dark hallways, both chasing and fleeing the sound of Corien's voice, both ignoring and seeking the comfort of Ludivine's arms.

And the girl on the mountain followed her every day, every night, a tenacious ghost.

Rielle knelt on the carpet, fingers shaking against her mouth. Her head pounded, bolts of pain slicing through her temples. Neither Corien nor Ludivine were ever really gone from her. The sounds of their eternally crashing swords vibrated her every bone.

Her vision flickered gold, then dull. The sounds of Audric's coronation filtered through the closed door—the choir singing the "Song of Saint Katell," the Archon intoning the coronation rites, the buzz and hum of the hundreds of people gathered to watch Saint Katell's golden cloak tied around Audric's shoulders and his mother's crown placed on his head.

Evyline stepped forward carefully. "My lady, what can I do?"

After a moment, Rielle stood. A terrible fear was climbing up her body, warming her sweaty brow. From inside the hall, Ludivine reached out to her, but Rielle ignored the urgent press of her thoughts. She sensed Ludivine moving toward the anteroom, and felt a sudden, frantic urge to get away from her. There was a Ludivine fighting Corien in her mind; there was a Ludivine rushing through the Hall of the Saints. Rielle's mind was full of her and was never her own.

"I need to see Garver Randell," she said hoarsely, fingers pressed against her temples. "Take me there quickly. We cannot be seen."

—◆—

Her guard stood scattered along the street, unobtrusive in common clothes and traveling cloaks. Inside Garver's shop, Rielle told him everything she had been feeling, and then, under cover of a quilt, she lay on a small bed in a back room of his shop, and he examined her.

Simon stood silently beside her, holding her hand, and once Garver had finished and bid her gently to sit up, Rielle saw the look on his face and knew at once what he would say.

"I'm with child," she said flatly. "Aren't I, Garver?"

He smiled a little. "You are, my lady. I'd thought this might happen. It's been some time since you've come to see me. I had the maidsright sent up to the castle, but perhaps it did not arrive."

Rielle stood, shaky. She wiped her sweaty hands on her skirts. "It did.

490

I've just been rather busy of late. I haven't been thinking. I've been care-less. Oh, God." She held her head in her hands. Ludivine pressed against her mind, calling her name over and over. She was hurrying through the city; soon she would be at the shop door.

*Oh, Rielle,* came Ludivine's voice, full of tenderness. *I had been wondering.*

Rielle stumbled out of the room, knocking over a chair.

"Get away from me!" she screamed. She could not bear the sight of Ludivine's face. It would remind her of that northern fortress, her sleep-less nights, Corien's lips against her neck, the awful push and pull of him and Ludivine between her temples. "Lu, if you come here, I'll kill you."

"My lady, please sit down," said Garver, following her. "I won't touch you, but you need to sit. You're not well."

"No, I'm not," she said, laughing a little. "Can you believe it, Garver? Another me." She pressed her palm against her abdomen. Imagining the life growing inside her, picturing some infant copy of herself being set loose upon the world, a sick wave rose hot and swift up her throat.

Simon moved quickly, brought her a pail. She sank to her knees on the rug and emptied what remained in her stomach.

"Two Queens will rise," she said. "Did you know, Garver, that Audric wants to marry me? To show everyone that the House of Courverie has absolute faith in me, he says. That the crown is loyal to me, as I am to the crown. I will be queen then, a real and true queen. I will be both Sun Queen and queen of Celdaria."

"Lady Rielle, please don't cry," came Simon's quiet voice.

"I would wager all the power I possess that my child will be a girl," Rielle said bitterly. "Two Queens will rise. And here we are, rising, bring-ing with us the very doom that Aryava foretold."

"Forget that damned prophecy and listen to me," said Garver, taking her hands firmly in his. "You're breathing too fast and too shallowly. Listen to the sound of my voice, and breathe when I tell you."

She wrenched herself free of him. "One of blood. One of light. Which do you think I am, Garver? Do I have the power to save the world, or destroy it? And which will my daughter be? And would it be kinder to everyone if I turned myself over to the people who hate me and let them destroy us both before it's too late?"

And then, Corien's voice, haggard and horrified: *It's not true. You wouldn't have allowed it to happen. Rielle, please tell me it isn't true.*

She ignored him, hurried out of Garver's shop, found Atheria waiting for her in the courtyard.

"If you're going to ride, do so gently," Garver said, following her. "Otherwise you might miscarry."

A small crowd had gathered on the street, held off by her Sun Guard. A chunk of rotting cabbage hit her temple. A foul, wet glob she could not identify thumped against Garver's hip.

"Get Simon back inside, Garver," she said, "and lock your door." Then she climbed onto Atheria's back, fighting hard against the urge to whirl on the people shouting her name and smash them all flat against the ground.

She buried her face in Atheria's soft gray mane and tried to push out of her mind the image of the girl on the mountain—her trembling words, the brave way she held her chin, how her eyes were as wide and dark as Audric's, her mouth full, like Audric's, and her eyebrows high and arched like her own.

But she could not trust what she had seen. She could trust no one and nothing and certainly not her own thoughts, which briefly considered that the mountain girl was in fact speaking a wild, horrible truth. But her mind rejected the idea at once. It was too immense, too impossible. Thinking of it made her head spin and frightened her so completely that the fear hardly registered. She noticed her terror dully, as if watching the world move from a staggering height, and then turned away from it.

The girl had been a trick of Corien's, a deception crafted to unbalance her.

She sent a swift thought to Ludivine: *Don't tell Audric about this, and then, if you love me as much as you claim, you'll leave me be.*

Then she whispered, "Take me away from here. Fly for hours. Fly until I feel nothing."

She let the godsbeast carry her into the roaring quiet of the sky.

# ← 46 ←

# ELIANA

*"Many of you will want to find me. You will want to see my face for yourself. But you will never find me. I am nowhere and everywhere. I fight for you in the shadows, and in the shadows I will remain, and if you ever did stumble upon me, I would tear your heart from your chest and your tongue from your throat, and the secrets of my face and name would die with you. Do not seek me. Hear me. Follow me. Trust me."*

—*The Word of the Prophet*

Eliana's mind floated in a sea of strange colors: fuchsia, tangerine, ebony, the deep red of her recurring nightmares, the gold of embers, the roiling blue-black of the ocean at night.

A distant voice floated on the waves. It was familiar, this voice, and she did not want to hear it. She sensed it would hurt her, or that it at least hungered to hurt her, or perhaps simply seize her for its own, but she could not move her arms to cover her ears. She had no arms; she had no ears. She was only her battered mind, and a ribbon of pain somewhere below her that grew more brilliant with every passing moment.

Then something grabbed hold of her hard, beneath her arms. She had arms, she realized, with a dull sort of astonishment. She opened her eyes to see the world. Flickering stars floated across her vision. She shook her head to knock them loose.

Pain gripped her head in two brittle hands.

"I'm sorry," said Simon, very near. "I nearly dropped you. I can hardly stand."

Eliana forced open her eyes, though the strange sea beckoned. She saw Simon—the flash of his eyes, blue like a summer sky, like twin hot flames, like sharp-cut jewels.

"Your eyes are like fire," she whispered, reaching for him.

He staggered a little and lowered them both clumsily to the ground.

"Someone get out here and help us!" he roared over her head, and then he smoothed her hair back from her face.

"Let's hope they know us," he muttered, "and that they don't shoot us on the spot."

*What an odd thing to say*, Eliana thought, and then she thought no more.

—◆—

She awoke, clear-headed, to a familiar ceiling. She knew at once that she was in her third-floor room at Willow. Memories of the day rushed back to her: Stepping through the violently lit ring of Simon's threads. Emerging in that black mountain forest, at first utterly disoriented. She had been expecting a castle, a city, a throne room.

And then she had found Rielle.

Immediately, her heartbeat returned to its wild pace from the mountain. She sat up, too quickly, and a sharp pain tore across her abdomen. She touched her stomach and felt the stretch of a bandage beneath her shirt.

"Dani and Remy tended to your wounds," said Simon softly. He sat in a chair beside her bed, so still and shadowed that she hadn't at first noticed him.

She tried to smile but could hardly hold the shape of it. "It seems to happen a lot, me waking to see you sitting at my bedside."

He was quiet for a moment, and then he folded her hand into his and kissed it. "I saw you fighting her, through the threads," he whispered. "I saw you, and I could do nothing to help you. If I moved, the thread would have snapped. I would have lost you again."

"But you didn't. I'm here, and so are you."

He shook his head against her hand. "Things are changed, just as I feared they might be."

"Are we safe for now?" she asked, interrupting him.

"For now, yes."

"Is Remy here, and well?"

"Yes, and he appears to be himself."

She pulled him gently toward her. "Then let's not talk about it just yet. Please, come here. Even if only for a few minutes."

"I'll hurt you," he said, touching her face. "You should rest, lie still."

"I'm not talking about sex," she replied, and then her voice gave out. She felt Rielle's magic striking her body all over again and, even worse, Corien's mind invading hers. His seeking fingers, his smooth, smiling voice.

Simon slipped into the bed beside her, his body a warm shield between her and the rest of the room. Gently, he gathered her against him, and she hid in the shelter of his embrace, ignoring the pain striping her abdomen.

"I can still feel him inside me," she whispered. "I thought I would have lost him, that time would have ripped him out of me. But I still feel him, I think. Or maybe I just can't rid myself of the memory."

Simon was so still that she wondered if he'd fallen asleep. Then he said quietly, "Do you mean Corien?"

She nodded against his chest. "He was there. At least, I think he was. I didn't see him, but I heard him. I felt him. I tried to get rid of him, but I didn't know how, and he wouldn't leave." She let out a shaky laugh and spoke quickly, the words spilling out of her. "I don't know half of what she said, or if anything I said made sense to her. Remy should have been there." She wiped her cheeks on Simon's shirt. "He could have helped us speak to each other. And he could have seen a godsbeast. Did you see it? It was enormous."

He began to stroke her hair. His voice was remarkably calm. "I did."

She closed her eyes. The rhythm of his fingers began at last to soothe her.

"I should have listened to you," she whispered, her voice heavy. "You wanted to wait, and I pushed you to send me anyway."

"I was just as eager to try as you were," he replied. "If you hadn't been so distraught, I wouldn't have hesitated."

"So we're both at fault, is what you're saying."

"Well," he said, his lips in her hair, "I don't know that I would go quite that far."

"Are you angry with me? If I were you, I'd be angry with me."

"For someone who doesn't love me, you're terribly concerned about my regard for you."

"Simon." The fragile lightness she'd managed splintered in her throat. She pressed her hands against him, as if to move away, but he caught her gently, stroking her cheeks with his thumbs.

"I'm not angry." His troubled gaze searched her face. "I've never been more terrified in my life."

She chased the distant ghosts in his eyes, the sharp shadows that had not been there the day before, and let him soothe her back into his arms. Soon his soft words were lost to her. She fell quietly into a still, black sleep.

⸻◆⸻

When she next awoke, Simon had already left, the bed beside her gone cold.

She pulled on her boots, wincing as she bent over to tie them. Wondering if she should attempt to heal her wound before heading downstairs, she held her hands out before her and reached for her castings with her mind.

But the mere act of trying for even a scrap of focus sent her head spinning. She sat down hard on the edge of the bed, catching her breath, and tried twice more before giving in to her exhaustion.

"Food," she muttered to herself. "Food will help."

She followed the smell of butter and frying sausages downstairs, and was about to join the others in the dining room when Simon appeared at her side, catching her gently by the elbow.

"Before you go in there," he said, "I should tell you what to expect, now that things have changed."

Something about his voice, the careful way he held his face, sent an icy heat sweeping down her body. "Patrik?"

"He's here and, unfortunately, just as he was."

"And Dani tended to my wounds, you said."

"Yes, Dani is here, and all three of her boys. But her husband was killed long ago, and I wouldn't ask her about it. The estate is only slightly altered, from what I could see. Minor shifts in the landscape. A more elaborate architectural style." He hesitated. "The Jubilee now begins tomorrow evening. Admiral Ravikant's naming day is October fourteenth, rather than October sixteenth."

"Tomorrow," she repeated. And suddenly she couldn't look at him, for the first thought that had entered her mind was not that this would leave them less time to prepare for the Jubilee, less time to recover from traveling and attempt it once more, before being forced to flee the continent— but that she would now have less time to be with *him*. Not as soldiers, but merely as themselves.

It was such a silly thought to have, such a selfish, childish desire in the face of everything else, and yet she was not ashamed of having it. The wildest, most uncaring part of her mind wanted to take Simon and Remy and run away. They would hide in some remote corner of the world and leave the rest of them to their war. She would have Simon all to herself and would kill anyone who tried to take him from her.

"And Jessamyn?" she said, unable to keep the bitterness from her voice.

But Simon did not reply. She looked up sharply, dread painting her arms hot. His silence told her the answer, but she needed to hear him say it.

"Where is she, Simon?" she whispered.

"She's not here," he said at last. "And she never was."

# — 47 —

# JESSAMYN

*"Thoughts of Kalmaroth turn in my sleep. Once, I dreamed of love and stars and unknowable ancient seas. Now, his fury floods my dreams. Sometimes it moves softly, feathering my cheeks. The caress of a paw before a kill. Sometimes it stabs me, and I wake sweating and screaming. We should all fear him—angels and humans alike. His anger will never die. Even if we succeed, his rage will flood the Deep."*

—Lost writings of the angel Aryava

In a shabby apartment in the heart of Festival, sitting before a bay window framed in curtains of faded violet brocade, Jessamyn sharpened her second-favorite sword.

It was long and slender, the obsidian handle worn smooth as a river-washed pebble, and with each stroke of her whetting stone against the blade, Jessamyn ruminated not on the mission that would begin the next day, but rather on how deeply she hated her name.

*Jessamyn.* It was a crude name, a *human* name. It had belonged to her for each of her nineteen years, and she had hated it from the moment she had first understood, at age four, that it was not an angelic name. It had been given to her by her human parents, whom she did not remember and did not care to remember. All she knew of them was that they had offered her to the teachers at the lyceum in order to gain entrance to the Emperor's city. Varos had told her as much, once he had chosen her as his student. They had left her there, he said, on the grand marble steps, in the pouring rain—a small girl with freckled brown skin and brown braids, with no possessions save the clothes on her back.

That, and a name she hated so deeply she could hardly bear to open her mouth long enough to tell the lyceum headmaster for his records.

*Jessamyn.* It carried none of the weight of the angelic languages. Every time she thought it, every time someone uttered it, she felt herself shrinking within its confines like an animal in a narrow cage.

*Jessamyn.* Once, she had begged Varos to call her the name she had chosen for herself—the name she would someday earn by serving His Holy Majesty the Emperor of the Undying as an agent of Invictus. It was a word so precious to her that she let herself think of it only on rare occasion, for fear of wearing the shine off its syllables.

But Varos had refused. After watching her coldly for a moment, he had even struck her across the face, which had sent Jessamyn sobbing into her pillow that night like some kind of *child*—not because she was angry at him, or because of the welt his hand had left on her cheek, but out of sheer, vicious shame.

She had deserved that violence. She had, frankly, deserved much worse. That she had dared to ask such a thing of him was insolence deserving of far greater punishment.

Varos had told her as much the next day, watching her across the table in his apartment as she ate her breakfast in silence. The welt on her cheek had felt like a shining beacon, announcing her shame to the world. One glance at her cheek, and her classmates would know the truth—that she was inadequate, insubordinate, unworthy.

"I should have killed you for asking me what you did," Varos had told her.

Jessamyn had swallowed her food and bowed her head. "Yes, *kaeshana.*"

"But I didn't," Varos said, his voice flat, "because I love you."

At those words—so unexpected, so longed for!—Jessamyn's entire body had tensed. She hadn't had the slightest notion of how to respond. Was she to thank him? Was she to tell him that she would die for him, that learning from him was an even greater honor than the true name she so desired?

Was she to tell him that she loved him in return?

Varos wiped his mouth with his napkin, then moved back from the table to consider her. "Come here."

Jessamyn nearly tripped over herself in her haste to obey. She knelt at his side, lowering her head.

But Varos lifted her chin, forcing her gaze up to his and inspecting her face. His beauty robbed Jessamyn of all sense—his sculpted, slender body; his smooth skin, tan and golden from their recent trip to the Vespers, and free of scars, because he was too skilled for that, too careful and cunning; his honey-gold eyes—incongruously soft and beautiful for such a ferocious killer.

Jessamyn trembled under his scrutiny. She had heard of Invictus *kaeshani* taking their students to bed, but not once had Varos ever indicated that he was interested in her in that way—not, at least, until that morning at the breakfast table, his soft eyes roaming over her as if noticing at last that she was nearly a woman grown.

Jessamyn had never been keen on the idea of sex. Her love for Varos was that of a child for its father. But if he chose her, if he wanted her, she would muster up the desire.

"Tell me, Jessamyn," Varos had said smoothly, "who we are."

Jessamyn's pulse jumped in her throat. He was asking her to recite the oath of Invictus—the words she would someday recite before the Emperor himself, when Varos deemed her ready.

"'He has chosen me to guard His works,'" she said at once.

Expressionless, Varos caressed her cheek. "Continue, *virashta*."

The way Varos pronounced *virashta* drew a delicious chill down Jessamyn's spine. Virashta, a ceremonial angelic word, meant "student," but also "cherished" and "terrible," and Varos only uttered it when he felt Jessamyn had done something to deserve it.

"'He has chosen me to receive His glory,'" Jessamyn recited, fighting to keep her voice steady.

Varos's expression softened. He kissed her brow. "'I am the blade that cuts at night.'"

And suddenly, Jessamyn's senses—sharpened for years under his tutelage—told her that she was in danger.

Varos was reaching for the knife in his belt, and he was fast, but Jessamyn was faster. It was why Varos had chosen her for his student all those years ago. Even as a child, she had been hawk-swift.

She grabbed her own knife from her left boot, knocked the weapon out of his hand, and held her blade to his throat. Blazing with triumph, she glared down at him and declared the oath's final line.

"'I am the guardian of His story.'"

Varos had smiled broadly, sending Jessamyn's head spinning. "You'll earn your name yet, virashta."

◆

Now, in the apartment where they waited for the Admiral's Jubilee to begin, Jessamyn heard the door open and shut, and looked up to see Varos enter. He wore common traveling clothes, just as she did. Their Invictus uniforms awaited them on the Admiral's ship.

She stood, bowed her head. "Kaeshana."

He blew past her in silence, reeking of alcohol and smoke.

Jessamyn tried not to care. He had come from the city; he had been performing reconnaissance work. Obviously said work would take him into drinking establishments, gambling parlors, brothels.

And yet, care she did.

She wondered: Had he enjoyed someone's bed during his day in the city? She wouldn't have blamed him for that. Theirs was a demanding, often brutal life, and though they gloried in it, if Varos needed release in the form of sex, then it was not her place, as his student, to judge him.

Still, the thought of him finding comfort with someone other than her rankled deeply. She needed no one else but Varos to feel content and whole. That it might be different for him dredged up the old, skittering fear that she would never be enough for him. That he would never present her to the Emperor and that her desired name would die a silent death inside her.

She watched in silence as Varos stormed through the room. He picked up the plate of food she had prepared for him and flung it against the wall. The plate shattered, shards skidding across the floor.

Jessamyn did not even flinch. She was used to his outbursts and had learned long ago not to react to them.

He leaned against the table, glaring at it. "I have received new orders from the admiral," he said at last. "Instead of moving on the Keshavarzian estate, we are to board the admiral's ship and await further instructions."

Jessamyn opened her mouth, closed it. A treasonous rage flared inside her, and she struggled to contain it. She and Varos were the ones who had discovered the duplicity of Danizet Keshavarzian and her sons—a family Lord Tabris had invited often to dine with him, a family of supposed Empire loyalists who had in fact been overseeing a massive Red Crown operation in Festival for years. The mission to destroy Willow and kill the family of traitors it housed had been assigned to them as a reward for their hard work. And, with Rahzavel dead, Varos was the most decorated member of Invictus, the most beloved. Eradicating the heart of the Red Crown presence in Festival was the reward he deserved.

And if he was kept from it, Jessamyn would not have the chance to prove herself. She would not gain an audience with the Emperor. She would not hear his voice utter her chosen name. And she could not say when another such opportunity would come.

"These new orders come from the admiral?" she managed.

"From one of his lieutenants," Varos muttered. "He would not even take the time to speak to me himself."

"But we are Invictus. We are the Emperor's eyes and ears, his blades. We spent weeks uncovering the Keshavarzians' deception and planning this operation." She hesitated. It was perhaps too bold, to ask the question. "Has the Emperor confirmed these orders?"

"The Emperor has not spoken to me in days. I have even dared to reach for him and have found nothing." His voice vibrated with anger. "He keeps himself from me. I do not understand it."

Jessamyn waited for him to speak again, and when he didn't, she sucked in a breath.

"We are Invictus," she said again, keeping her voice firm and even. "We are not adatrox, mindless and disposable. We do not wait on ships while the glory blazes elsewhere. We take orders from the Emperor, and the Emperor alone, and if the admiral can't honor that, then he is a fool."

Without warning, Varos spun on her. His hand flew hard and fast, striking her on the jaw.

She bore the impact in silence. The pain of his fists had not diminished over the years, but she had learned better how to bear it.

"We are human," he spat out, "and no matter how high the Emperor elevates us in service to him, we will never exceed the glory of his generals, and certainly not that of the admiral. You would do well to remember that. You will not say such things again, or even entertain them in your mind."

Ducking her head, blinking to clear her tilting vision, she whispered, "Yes, kaeshana."

He grabbed her jaw, wrenching up her gaze. He watched her for a long time before releasing her with a scoff. "You claim to desire the Emperor's favor, and yet you force my hand far too often."

She did not cry. Varos had long ago wrung every tear out of her body, leaving none behind. But she burned with anger, and shame, and longed desperately to flee to the mountains outside the city. She would push herself fast down the deadly narrow paths that cut high over the canyon rivers. She would run until she no longer felt the humiliation of his scorn.

"Yes, kaeshana," she said instead, her body rigid.

And then, after a few long moments of silence, he said, "But you aren't wrong."

She stared at the floor, not daring to look up.

"We have indeed spent long weeks preparing for this moment," he continued. "And our victory is so close, our quarry so near, that I can already taste their blood on my tongue. And you, Jessamyn. Look at me."

She obeyed, lips clamped tight. Her heart pounded hard in her throat, its eagerness disgusting her.

Varos smiled at her, the anger slipping from his face, and in that moment Jessamyn forgot every other feeling except for the spark of joy licking up her spine like a hungry flame. She would endure a thousand beatings if it meant he would look at her like that again—her kaeshana, her Varos. Her teacher and her family, and her key to the Emperor's favor.

"You deserve your name, virashta," he said. "And if it means defying the admiral to get it for you, then that's what we shall do."

She knelt at his feet. Too overwhelmed to speak, she simply huddled there, her palms flat against the floor. After a moment, Varos placed his hand on her head, laughing fondly, and told her to clean the mess of his ruined supper.

She obeyed at once, aware of his eyes on her as she worked. And even as her mind spun stupidly with joy, she knew that any defiance Varos displayed was not for her benefit. That he would even consider disobedience showed her how deeply the admiral's dismissal had wounded him. Before anything else, Varos would defy the admiral for himself, to demonstrate to the Emperor that he was not a mere human. That he was something more, and infinitely worthy. That he surpassed the orders all others must obey.

But she cared nothing for his reasons, as long as it meant this mission would end on their terms.

As she worked, her thoughts shifted to the girl Eliana, whom the Keshavarzian family had been housing. Jessamyn longed to hunt her most of all. In her dreams, she was the one to present her before the Emperor. Never mind Willow or Danizet Keshavarzian. Presenting Eliana Ferracora to the Emperor would be a glory unmatched in this world.

But Eliana was the admiral's prey, so instead, Jessamyn recited what she knew of the girl: A child of Ventera. A twelve-year-old brother named Remy. A dead father, killed during the Empire's invasion of Ventera. A dead mother, transformed in one of the Fidelia labs and lost in the icy waters of Karajak Bay when the girl had somehow sent an entire Empire fleet crashing to the bottom of the sea.

She had power, that much was obvious. Power no human deserved.

Power that belonged to the angels.

What the Emperor would do with her once he had her, Jessamyn didn't know, or care—except for a fleeting curiosity she easily dismissed.

The important thing was this: soon, Eliana would be writhing at the Emperor's feet. Perhaps Jessamyn would be fortunate enough to be there, allowed an audience as a reward for a successfully completed mission. Perhaps she would be able to listen to Eliana beg for mercy that the Emperor would never grant.

She shivered to think of it and redirected her thoughts to the present, to the shattered plate, the ruined food, the mission ahead of her, and how she would make Varos proud enough to boast of her wherever he went— his virashta, his brilliant protegée. He would need no one else in his life but her. No lovers, no students.

And Jessamyn would at last earn her name.

# ← 48 ←

# CORIEN

*"In some languages, the word translates to dragon-talkers. In others, it becomes kin of the beast. In the Borsvallic tongue, it is Kammerat, and in that language, its native tongue, means those who carry wild secrets, for the Kammerat—if they are real, if they are not in fact a mere fanciful tale—have long guarded what remains of the great godsbeasts, the ancestors of which carried Grimvald and his soldiers into battle against the angels. All those who have traveled to the high far mountains of Borsvall in search of dragons have died. Some blame the harsh climate. Others, who long for old magic, blame the Kammerat, who guard their holy charges with iron and steel."*

—A footnote from *A Land Cold and Mighty: An Examination of the Legends of Borsvall* by Inkeri Aravirta

In the far north, in the mountain range known as the Villmark, so far north that he could have walked hundreds of miles in any direction and met no one, Corien sat in a scarlet chair, glaring out over the ice.

His rooms were beautifully appointed because that was what he deserved—stone floors, thick rugs, art on the walls, everything polished and pleasingly arranged. Or, rather, they *had* been pleasingly arranged before he'd destroyed them.

He hadn't left his rooms in weeks, not since the day he had realized the newest terrible truth of his life.

Rielle was with child. *Audric's* child.

The moment Corien had realized it, sensing the change in her even from thousands of miles away, across the wide continent between them, he'd stormed out of his fortress—a tall, stark construction of black stone, towering over the military base he'd named the Northern Reach. He raged through the mines, the laboratories, the shipyards. He killed thirty-one human slaves that day, and ten of the abducted elemental children from Kirvaya, and then he disemboweled one of his lieutenants who had grown both lazy and messily brutal since Corien had assigned him the task of overseeing the children's dormitories.

Last of all, Corien had killed two of the Kammerat, the dragon-talkers from Borsvall. Sad-eyed and malnourished, they tended the beasts in their pens and helped dissect their corpses in the laboratories. Killing two of their number was an action Corien immediately regretted, for the Kammerat were useful and necessary in his work with the dragons.

But he had been stupid with rage and hadn't realized he had killed anyone until he crashed into his rooms, drenched in blood and hardly able to see for the tears in his eyes.

He'd slammed the door shut and proceeded to smash everything he could find—every painting, every burgled artifact. Plates and goblets, the mirrors in his bathing room, even the windows that overlooked the Reach.

And then he'd gulped down every bottle of wine in his rooms and collapsed in the chair by the shattered windows.

There he had stayed for weeks, conducting his affairs and commanding the industry of the Reach from the comfort of his chair and the numb shell of his grief.

Snow blew in through the broken windows. Piles of winter and shards of glass littered his once-pristine floors.

Occasionally, he dared turn his thoughts once more to Celdaria, but everything he saw brought him despair—Rielle, in Audric's arms. Rielle, being fitted for her wedding gown. Rielle, examining her body in the mirror, looking for changes that had not yet appeared.

He could not bear looking at her for longer than seconds at a time. The pain of the distance between them was like nothing he had felt since suffering the loss of his body in the Deep.

Then, weeks later, sitting in his glass-dusted, snow-frosted rooms, his head in his hands, his stolen body white and cold and beautiful in his velvet dressing gown, he felt a change in the air of the Reach. A shift.

Even drunk as he was, as dumb with sorrow as he was, it required little effort to stretch the edges of his mind and scan the Reach for the cause of this change.

He saw it at once and straightened in his chair.

How interesting: the Kirvayan queen, Obritsa Nevemskaya, had some-how breached the security of his laboratories. She was stealing from them, in fact, taking a container of the belluorum his surgeons used to keep the dragons docile and dependent.

He watched her, curiosity cutting through the black mire of his thoughts, and when she pulled threads from the air, using them to flee the laboratories and escape into the nearby mountains before his soldiers could stop her, Corien rose from his seat for the first time in days. He walked across the glass and snow to stand at the shattered windows.

His heart that was not a true heart pounded faster in his chest. As much as he could feel delight in this body, and excitement, he felt them now.

The Kirvayan queen was a marque.

For a moment he allowed himself to admire the diligence of her secret-keeping, the thick walls of her mental fortitude. She had been through much, this girl, had endured years of abuse that had left her hardened— though he sensed that, underneath those layers of steel and iron beat a heart that loved selectively but fiercely.

He watched her give the belluorum to one of the Kammerat—a nineteen-year-old man named Leevi. The boy administered the drug to his dragon, a young calf hardly big enough to carry even his scrawny frame. Then boy and dragon lifted off the ground, heading west—for Borsvall, he assumed.

To ask the new king for help, perhaps?

Corien smirked, shrugging off his dressing gown and exchanging it for his shirt and trousers, his long, black coat.

He could just imagine it now. "Oh, King Ilmaire," he said, simperingly, "can you please, oh please come help me rescue my dragon friends? They're being held captive by an army of angels in the far north! They're using the dragons in horrible experiments! You must help us, you simply must!"

Corien snorted. "Good luck with that, boy. Your king's a coward, and you're a goddamned fool."

Then he threw on his cloak and swept out the doors.

—◆—

He had the girl and her guard brought to one of the receiving halls in the fortress itself. She was a marque, after all. She possessed angelic blood, tainted though it was, and deserved better than a holding cell beneath the mountain.

It took her some time to awaken from the blow his men had dealt her, for which he'd made them pay, sinking into their minds until they writhed on the floor and begged for mercy.

"She is not to be beaten or mistreated," he told them coldly, listening to them sob. They were lower angels, hardly powerful enough to maintain grips on their stolen bodies. The sight of them disgusted him. Once, they had been creatures glorious and mighty, before the long dark of the Deep reduced them to *this*.

Now, he sat in a chair opposite Obritsa, watching her eyes flutter open. She was a tiny thing—pale-brown skin, ice-white hair like the long-dead liar Marzana.

"At last, she awakens," he murmured.

Obritsa stared at him, her body tensing. Her eyes traveled to her guard, lying inert on the floor, and then back up. "It's you," she whispered. "I heard you in my mind. You're an angel."

He knelt before her. "My name is Corien. And you are Obritsa Nevemskaya. Chosen queen of Kirvaya. The human revolutionaries in your country call you Korozhka. The Destroyer. It's a delight to meet you, truly. Your mind is sharp and still growing. I appreciate a good mind, especially one with such potential. And you're a marque." He smiled. "That I find most delightful of all."

She lifted her chin, examining his face. Her eyes were pale and bright. "By abducting me, you have committed an act of war against the nation of Kirvaya. If you release us now and allow us to leave this place unharmed, I will take that into consideration when I tell my magisters what you have done."

"Your magisters. Oh, child." Corien cupped her cheek. She did not flinch away from him, met his eyes without blinking. "So much is happening in this world that you do not understand. Your ignorance is charming."

He rose, dusting his hands free of the grime she'd collected on her face. "I have something I need you to do for me. And you'll do it, one way or another. If I have to force you, I can and I will. But I'd rather not. Your half-breed power is unpredictable, and if I take control of your mind, it might affect the purity of your threads. And then where would we be? Smashed into the side of a mountain somewhere. Flung to the bottom of the sea, or forward in time."

The words left his lips before he could think of their significance.

*Forward in time.*

The image of the girl on the mountain returned to him—Rielle's daughter, she had claimed. Her name was Eliana.

And the things he had glimpsed when he touched her mind…

But that was for later. There was to be an order to things, and Obritsa must come first.

The little queen's mind worked quickly. He admired its deftness, how nimbly it moved.

"I'm not taking you anywhere," she declared. "I've seen what you're doing here. You are a fiend who should be put on trial for your crimes. The atrocities you have committed in these mountains will not be tolerated."

He tilted his head, considering her. "And here I thought you were supposed to hate elementals. What do you care if I steal and torture their children?"

The girl had nothing to say to that. He savored the texture of her conflict—years of conditioned hatred for elementals warring against the sheer horror she'd felt after discovering his great work.

"I understand your contempt," he told her, "but you're utterly wrong in it and in everything you just said. You will take me to Celdaria, and you will take Bazrifel as well, and you will take your guard Artem, because I don't trust you not to try something stupid, and if Artem is there, maybe you'll think twice before trying to outsmart me."

Obritsa managed an expression of cool disdain. "Bazrifel. Another angel?"

"Indeed." Corien gestured at her guard, Artem, lying on the floor between them. "He's inside your friend at the moment and having a grand time of it."

Then he told Bazrifel, *Begin*.

Artem's screams began immediately, his body convulsing where it lay, and Obritsa watched him, at first implacable, and then with increasing panic, until her calm broke at last, and she let out a soft, sharp cry. She hurried to the man and sank to her knees beside him. Corien watched them, the two of them huddled on the floor—Artem shuddering, his lips wet with drool; Obritsa holding his head in her lap, smoothing the wet hair back from his forehead.

"Artem, can you hear me?" she whispered to him. "I'm here, Artem, my dear. It's going to be all right."

Artem's eyes opened. He gathered her hands in his, then pressed them to his chest.

"Whatever he wants of you," Artem croaked, "don't do it, Obritsa. Not for me."

Unseen by both of them, Corien rolled his eyes.

"You don't give me orders, Artem," Obritsa replied.

"He cannot be allowed to go to Celdaria. He is after Lady Rielle. He will bring ruin down upon us all."

"Rielle will stop him," Obritsa said. Corien could so clearly see her uncertainty that he nearly laughed. "Audric will gather his armies against him."

"*Obritsa*." Artem struggled to rise. "Let him kill me. Resist him with everything you have."

"I will not stand by while they kill you right in front of my eyes. Don't ask me to do that. You cannot order me to do that. Artem." The tears she had been fighting spilled over at last. "You're the only family I have."

Corien stood quietly for a moment, letting the feeling of Obritsa's love for this man, and his for her, wash over him. A father and a daughter, if not in blood then in heart. Dear friends, singular in the world, who understood each other like no one else did. The loneliness of that—the hopeless fragility of it—struck a raw chord inside Corien's own mind.

He crouched beside them.

"You understand, then," he said quietly. "I can see it in your mind. You've already decided you'll do as I ask, even though part of you feels that is the worst thing you can do, that complying means you lose and I win. Which is true. And you've decided this illogical thing because of love." He smiled a little. "We really are not so different, Queen Obritsa. What I do is also for love. For the love of my people, who have lived for too long in pain. And for the great love of my very long life."

Then he rose. "Will you do as I command?"

Artem kept whispering protests, but Obritsa avoided his gaze, and Corien's too.

"I am not strong enough to send us more than thirty miles at a time," she said quietly.

"In fact, you're stronger than you think," Corien replied, which was the truth. He could clearly see the raw force of her talent, stifled by those who had raised her—feeble-minded humans frightened by things they could neither understand nor possess. "I've seen it myself. You've allowed weaker, less talented people to dictate your limits for you. A tragedy with which I'm intimately familiar."

Obritsa was quiet for a long time. He sensed her praying, which she wasn't good at, because she hated God.

He sympathized.

Her prayers quickly unraveled, and when she looked up at him again, her gaze was hard and full of tears.

"Whenever you're ready," she whispered, "I will begin."

# → 49 ←
# RIELLE

*"I wish it to be known that I protest this union with every-thing I am. I wish it to be known that I will do every-thing within my power to fracture it. For what remains of her life—and I pray that this will be brief and pass swiftly—Lady Rielle will regret the day she restored me to this world. She will regret every smile and kiss she used to seduce my son beyond reason. She will regret every word she has uttered and every step she has taken, and only then, when she lies inconsolable with sorrow at my feet, either dead or dying—only then will I rest."*

—Journal of Genoveve Courverie,
October 27, Year 999 of the Second Age

For days, Rielle watched dully from her rooms as visitors streamed into the city from all over the world, preparing for a wedding she desperately wished not to attend.

Unfortunately, the wedding was her own.

And if she refused Audric now, after agreeing to marry him, it would break his heart. It would humiliate House Courverie and perhaps lead to even more resentment and uncertainty than already existed throughout the realm. And the truth was, she did want to marry him. She wanted to declare to the world—to herself, and to Corien most of all—that she was

Audric's, and he was hers. Nothing had the power to separate them; she wanted that known.

More than anything, she wanted to convince herself that, yes, she could serve for the rest of her life as not only Sun Queen to Celdaria, but as queen to Audric. She had the strength to do it. She would be able to curb her doubts and swallow her protests and stay the course of this life she had been thrust into.

And that seemed to her an odd reason to go through with marrying someone, no matter how much love was involved.

But here she was, on the morning of her wedding, standing on a small platform in her sitting room as her maids and Ludivine's tailors fitted her one last time into what would, she was convinced, go down in history as the most gorgeous gown to have ever been created.

She stared at her reflection in the mirror, drawing comfort from the sight of herself in this elaborate, glittering cloud of a dress. The bodice was dark-gold brocade, shimmering with delicate swirled lines of beadwork. The tiny sleeves perched on the edge of her shoulders, leaving her arms bare. Diaphanous layers of gold, white, and plum chiffon trailed down her arms and far past her fingers to the floor, each piece scattered through with a tapestry of embroidery—white starbursts, plum-colored roses, vines and leaves in Courverie green. Much of the dress was backless, with draped lengths of delicate chains crossing her bare skin—a cool, shifting net of gold. The skirts were a voluminous explosion of silk and lace and chiffon, in the colors of both the Sun Queen and House Courverie.

Ludivine watched her, bright-eyed, in a simple gown of rose velvet cinched at the waist with a slender belt fashioned of golden birds.

"Is it trite and expected," she asked, "to tell you how beautiful you are?"

Rielle attempted a smile. "Perhaps, but not unappreciated."

Even to her own ears, her reply seemed strained. It had been nearly a month since Corien had conjured that awful vision of the girl on the mountain—the girl who called herself Eliana and claimed to be her daughter.

It had been nearly three weeks since Rielle had discovered she was with child.

And during those three weeks, she had barely spoken to Ludivine. Since her vision from the empirium, Rielle had not been able to shake the truth of the angels' banishment from her mind, and she didn't care to speak to Ludivine about it—not about the fact of the banishment itself, and not that Ludivine had kept the reality of it from Rielle, and Audric, for years. Occasionally, Ludivine would dare to broach the subject, gently reaching out to Rielle's mind with a tendril of thought that felt something like an apology.

But Rielle wasn't ready to talk about the saints' great deception and face the terrifying doubts she now possessed—about Ludivine's true loyalty, and what thoughts of revenge might reside deep in her heart. Ludivine had lied about what she truly was. She had chosen not to tell Rielle the truth about the Deep. Whenever Rielle looked at her friend, there now twisted a niggle of doubt in her heart that she couldn't ignore.

And then, of course, there was the wedding to distract her.

It had been a whirlwind of preparations for the wedding itself, the days of feasting afterward, the official church documents the Archon drew up with the help of his secretaries that would bind Rielle and Audric together as king and queen. Fittings with the tailors and meetings for hours every day with the Magisterial Council and the Archon, with the cooks and the decorators. Even with Queen Genoveve.

But Rielle's hopes that Genoveve's opinion toward her would have warmed over the last several weeks since resurrecting her were quickly dashed. Whenever they met, the queen simply stared at her across their tea table, refusing to speak. The old shadows had returned to the delicate skin under her eyes. Her nightmares kept her from more than a few hours of sleep a week. They also, she claimed, robbed her of all appetite.

Rielle didn't doubt that the woman was suffering. She had heard proof of that from Corien. But even with Ludivine helping to soothe her troubled mind, the queen refused to treat Rielle with anything but disdain.

She would not have been surprised if the queen were depriving herself of sleep and food simply out of spite.

And as the castle whirled itself silly with the mundanities of logistics, the city grew and grew.

Word of the wedding spread quickly, and the city soon clogged with visitors. Tent cities sprang up in the Flats, under the bridges, along the shores of the lake. Celebrations raged day and night—as did protests decrying the wedding as the end of peace and the beginning of war.

Factions of resurrectionists from other cities, wild-eyed and beaming, flitted through the city in their white-and-gold robes like birds in mating season, praising Rielle as their one and only salvation. They launched themselves at the protesters that gathered at the castle gates, waving their crimson-spattered brass suns. Minor scuffles broke out every few minutes; deadlier fights ending in injury and death erupted every day. The city guard was stretched thin for several harrowing days, until Merovec arrived from the north with his own soldiers, ready to help where needed.

But even this was a matter of contention, for many in the capital remembered all too well that it had been soldiers of House Sauvillier who had slaughtered their brothers and mothers and neighbors on the day of Rielle's fire trial. Among those uncertain citizens, there were a radical few who continued to challenge the presence of anything related to House Sauvillier in their city. Not even Merovec, with his popularity and his flashing smile, could convince them. They cared nothing for the rumors speculating that those soldiers had been under angelic influence. That knowledge merely served to heighten their hysteria. House Sauvillier was tainted; House Sauvillier was vulnerable to angelic attack.

It was a time of chaos in Âme de la Terre. The perfect time for a wedding, Tal had remarked dryly.

And at least a dozen times each day, Rielle felt herself buckling under the stacked weight of a thousand different expectations. When this happened, wherever she was, she stepped back from whatever conversation or meeting or appointment she was half sleeping through, closed her eyes, and recalled the night of Audric's proposal.

It had been an unremarkable, tender thing, both of them naked and breathing hard in her bed. They'd fallen into it only moments before. Though the endless meetings and the tumult of the riotous streets were wearing both of them out in every other sense, in this, at least, their appetites remained ravenous.

But their lovemaking had changed since that awful, wonderful night in the empty Hall of the Saints. It had begun to take on an air of desperation that Rielle had never felt before. And she knew, when she caught Audric's eyes, when she heard his voice break against her neck and felt his hands tremble around her body, that it was the same for him. Something had shifted, something irrevocable.

That night, after Rielle had caught her breath, a terrible sadness had settled upon her, like the slow press of a boot against her chest. She turned into Audric's arms and caught him looking at her, solemn and bright-eyed, the expression on his face mirroring the hot, sick feeling wedged in her throat.

And suddenly she began to cry. "He hates you," she said, touching his face, "and he hates me for loving you. He'll make you hate me too. Somehow, he'll do it. And then you'll want to turn me away, and I won't be able to bear it."

"Now you listen to me." Audric sat up, pulling her gently into his arms. He wiped her cheeks with his thumbs, made her look at him. "I don't care what he does, or tries to do. I could never hate you. Not ever."

Rielle shook her head. "He'll make you."

"No. Never. I'm yours, and you're mine. No one can change that, not even him." He pressed her hands gently against his chest. "Feel me. I'm right here, and I'm not going anywhere. This is real. My heart, and yours. Never mind Corien, or any war that may come, or this mad city full of people who, frankly, need to have a glass of wine and go to bed for a good long while."

Rielle laughed through her tears. "Or several glasses of wine."

"Really, just send them all to bed forever," Audric declared with a sweep of his arm. "I'm happy to be the king of a sleeping country. That means more time for you, my love." And then he had kissed her, gently, small kisses across her face like the fall of soft rain, and she'd burrowed against him, both of them cocooned in the warm den of her pillows. He'd held her, drawing slow circles across her bare shoulder, and then he'd pressed a kiss to her forehead and murmured, "Marry me, Rielle. I want you with me always. Please, darling."

At that moment, she'd thought of the child she carried and had had to hide her face in his neck to keep from crying anew. Someday, she would no longer be able to hide it. Someday, he would know, and then what? What would the people think of a Sun Queen who could be the mother of a Blood Queen? Already people wanted her dead, and Audric too.

It was a terrible idea, to marry him. To even stay in this city was a risk for everyone who lived there. Someday, Corien would come for her. It was inevitable.

And yet she wanted Audric. She wanted the officialness of it, she wanted a grotesquely grand wedding, at which she would look every one of her detractors in the eye and dare them to try anything. She would wear two crowns—one of sunlight, and one of Celdarian gold. The Archon would place the cloak of House Courverie over her shoulders, and everyone in attendance would tremble before her with adoration and jealousy. They would burn with shame that they had ever decried her, that they had doubted Audric.

"Yes," she had answered, lips pressed against his skin. "Yes, I'll marry you."

◆

*Merovec's coming.*

Rielle blinked out of the memory and realized she was alone in her rooms with Ludivine. The maids and tailors had been sent away, and Ludivine was looking up at her with a strangely wistful expression.

*What is it like?* Ludivine asked. *To love someone so completely in every possible sense? To feel it with every part of yourself?*

"I asked you not to mind-speak to me until I've decided whether or not to trust you again," Rielle snapped. "Now, help me down."

Ludivine offered Rielle her arm, helping her step carefully down from the platform. "It seems I keep doing things that require forgiveness," she said, her voice low. "It's an awful feeling."

"Well, you could stop doing things that require forgiveness."

Ludivine's eyes flared. "And you could help me learn how to do that, I suppose? For you never do anything that's worth apologizing for."

Rielle backed away from her. "How dare you say such a thing to me, when it was you who encouraged me to lie to Audric in the first place, all those months ago."

A sharp knock sounded on the door to her rooms. A moment later, Evyline entered, shutting the door quietly behind her. "Lord Sauvillier is here to see you, my lady."

For a moment, Rielle and Ludivine simply stared at each other. Ludivine was the one to break first, dropping her gaze to the floor.

"We'll speak about this later," she said quietly. "Today is your wedding day, and despite everything, I'm happy for you." She hesitated, then hooked her fingers through Rielle's. Her smile was thin but warm. "I can feel Audric's love for you as keenly as if he stood beside me. The entire castle is suffused with it today. It's like he's a sun newly born."

Rielle felt herself relent, tiny wings of joy fluttering up her body. She squeezed Ludivine's hand in reply. "Well, then I should go to him. But first, tell me what your brother wants."

"He wants to walk you downstairs," Ludivine said. "He thinks it will show everyone in attendance that House Sauvillier supports the crown, even with new bodies on the throne."

"A sentiment in stark contrast to the ones he displayed the last time he was here," Rielle said darkly.

"Perhaps he has had a change of heart."

"Shouldn't you know?"

"With so many people in the city," Ludivine replied, "and so many conflicting passions, it's difficult to read him."

But Rielle heard the hesitation in her voice. "That's not all though, is it? He's hiding something."

"He lets certain thoughts roam freely, and others he keeps locked tightly away." Ludivine frowned. "Merovec is not one for such immaculate mental control."

Rielle stiffened. "I haven't heard anything from Corien in days."

"Neither have I. We should be on our guard."

"Mustn't we always?"

Ludivine's expression softened. "It's my great hope for you that someday you won't have to worry about such things."

Then she kissed Rielle's cheek, and though Rielle still felt uncertain around her—and though she was, honestly, a little afraid of tearing her gown—she drew Ludivine into a fierce embrace.

"You won't leave me to walk alone with him, will you?" she whispered.

Ludivine's voice held a smile. "As long as I live, you'll never have to walk alone."

⟡

Rielle hadn't ever imagined that she would be escorted to her wedding on the arm of Merovec Sauvillier, but the world was a strange place and getting stranger by the day.

Baingarde's doors and windows had been thrown open to the glorious day beyond. The sky was a cheerful, crystalline blue. Flower petals carpeted every courtyard. Banners in Courverie colors snapped from the balustrade of every guard tower. The crisp autumn breeze cooled the sweating brows of noble guests in their finest coats and gowns, and acolytes in their formal robes.

But with the doors and windows open, anyone milling about the castle with their glasses of punch and small plates of hors d'oeuvres could also hear the cries of the crowds gathered at the gates.

As Rielle descended through the castle, the low roar from outside became thunderous. While in the safety of her rooms, she had been determined not to let the hysterical rumblings of idiots disturb her happiness, but that became a more difficult thing to achieve when faced with the stark, messy reality of them.

"Ah, Lady Rielle, please don't trouble yourself with the teeming masses," said Merovec smoothly as they rounded the corner of the north mezzanine onto the grand central staircase. He waved his hand in the general direction of the city. "If I were the sort of man who enjoyed gambling, I'd wager that many people out there today are eager to catch a glimpse of you in your lovely gown. Many more, I would say, than those who would wish to run you out of the city and pray that you never return."

"You've a funny way of putting Rielle's mind at ease, my brother," Ludivine remarked quietly.

"I'm sure Lady Rielle is quite capable of putting her own mind at ease, considering her many talents."

Rielle fixed a smile on her face as they crossed the entrance hall. Each column and banister had been festooned with ribbons of gold and emerald, and the room was packed with whichever guests hadn't merited an invitation to the actual ceremony. They parted at her approach, murmuring behind fans and fingers, gazing appreciatively at her dress. Movement rippled through the crowd as she passed—bowed heads, low curtsies.

The massive doors to the Hall of the Saints opened, admitting a wave of sound. The temple choirs were singing the "Song of Saint Katell," accompanied by a small orchestra of flutes, horns, and chimes.

"Why did you want to escort me today, Merovec?" Rielle asked quietly. "The last time you were here, you were full of hate for me."

"I was," he admitted, "and it will take some time before I can love you as a proper cousin. But my sister has spoken a good amount of sense to me, and my time on the road home to Belbrion after my last visit gave me much opportunity to think and temper my anger."

# -- 50 --
# ELIANA

*"His Excellency Ravikant, Admiral of the Imperial*
*Fleet, Loyal Servant to His Majesty the Emperor of the*
*Undying, invites you to the city of Festival on October 4,*
*to partake in the Jubilee to be held in his honor, to cele-*
*brate His Excellency's naming day, and to commemorate*
*the arrival of imperial forces that did seize this kingdom*
*and began the great work of restoring it to its previous*
*angelic glory. Attendance is not required but is strongly*
*encouraged."*

—Invitation to the Admiral's Jubilee, sent to all citizens
of Festival and surrounding territories September 14,
Year 1018 of the Third Age

The day before the Jubilee passed in a blur of nerves and preparation. Red Crown operatives flitted through the mansion like birds, carrying messages and supplies. Dani's sons clomped upstairs and downstairs, rushing plates of food to everyone working. Rain beat yet again on the windows, which no one was happy about, for mud made everything more easily trackable.

And through all of this, Eliana rested, stewing.

She had been ordered to rest by Simon, and then had scolded him roundly for ordering her to do anything, and then, after he had obeyed her command to leave her alone for a while, she had chastised herself into admitting he was right. She did need to rest. Fighting Rielle had left her considerably drained, as had the trip through time. Her power felt far from her, buried beneath layers of stone. And Simon himself was resting in his own room, which had become a war chamber, everyone hurrying to and from with messages for him, rolled-up maps of the city, weapons to be inspected and approved.

Logically, Eliana knew that the longer each of them rested, the more successful their next attempt to travel back to the Old World would be.

But that didn't make the agony of sitting idly, waiting for time to creep on, any less agonizing.

In the late afternoon, Dani came to Eliana's room and found her cross-legged on the floor, cleaning her knives. Remy sat squashed in an armchair near the window, writing out phrases in Old Celdarian for her to study.

Dani leaned against the door frame. "I'm not sure those knives could get any cleaner if you worked on them for another hundred years."

Eliana had barely glanced up when Dani arrived. It was a strangeness unmatched in her very strange life to adjust to the new reality of the world—Jessamyn gone, Dani's husband gone, the house changed just enough to leave her feeling unbalanced, and no one but her and Simon noticing the difference. Several times during the last few hours, she had had to bite her tongue to keep from pulling Patrik away from his work to sit him down and tell him everything she knew about Jessamyn, curious if it would trigger some faint, warped memory inside him.

But Simon had cautioned her against doing so. It would only confuse things, he warned. It would only further muddy the waters they had already muddied by traveling to the past.

"Time travel has many repercussions, some of which even I don't understand," he had told her, fussing about her room, needlessly straightening furniture and pillows and her strewn-about clothes. "It's not an act to be taken lightly."

As if she took anything lightly in this world. As if she had ever been given the chance to.

She had lost hold of her slipping patience and ordered him out of her room. Never mind that she recognized his needless fussing as a manifestation of energy as nervous as her own. Afterward, she'd stormed across the floor in an ugly temper, unsure where to direct her anger and settling at last on everything. Then her mind, apparently eager to hurt itself, had wandered to Harkan, and she'd had to sit on the edge of her bed, very still, breathing slowly, for it felt like any sudden movement would throw her completely into chaos.

She wondered how he was faring, wherever he was stationed in the city—with Zahra, and Viri and Catilla, and all the recruits that had been assigned to them. Or had those disastrous few moments in the past ruined everything for Harkan's team? Were they at this very moment walking into a trap? Were they already dead?

And now Dani was standing in her door, seemingly determined to strike up a conversation.

"I would really rather be alone right now, Dani," Eliana said, bearing down hard on Nox's curved, flat blade.

"Except for me," Remy added from across the room.

"Except for Remy," Eliana agreed.

"Well, I'm afraid you've got to tolerate me for at least a little while," said Dani. "I've dug up one of my old gowns for you, and it just might fit."

◆◇◆

Eliana had to admit that it was a splendid gown.

A deep crimson across her neck, shoulders, and arms, fading gradually to pure, glittering onyx at the hem. A high neckline in the front, and long sleeves that clung to her arms as if they had been painted there. In the back, the snug bodice opened wide, a broad V that left most of her back exposed and came to a point at the dip of her hips. The fabric was light enough for her to twist easily, but boasted an array of intricate beadwork that caught the light when she turned. Ester and Patrik had sewn various cleverly concealed pockets into the wide skirts, each pocket narrow but deep, for housing her knives. And the skirts themselves flowed and twirled as she walked and spun, allowing for easy movement. The boots Dani had found for her were a bit dull, but supple and sturdy.

She disapproved of only two design elements: the caps of black feathers on the sleeves, and the fact that the beadwork spanning the gown had been sewn in the shapes of feathers as well.

"Can we at least remove the sleeve feathers?" Eliana said, ruffling them with a frown. "They're rather angelic."

"That's the idea." Dani bustled about, instructing Ester where to pin and pointing out what needed adjusting. "Everyone at these parties tries to reference angels as many times as possible in their wardrobe. It flatters the angels and demonstrates to them that you buy into the whole thing."

"The whole thing?" Eliana asked.

"The Empire. Their perpetual, world-spanning rule. You know. The whole thing."

Ester looked back, mouth full of pins. "Oh, is that what you call it?"

"I could call it other things, but I'm trying to curb my foul language," Dani said.

"Whatever for?"

"You know, now that I think about it, I can't remember why I ever decided that. So, fuck it." Dani put her hands on her hips, inspecting Eliana from hem to hair. "You look beautiful, at least. That's a joy for my tired eyes. We'll have to do something with your hair though. You can't wear that messy braid every day of your life."

Eliana ran her hands down her front, turning left and right in the mirror. She winced a little as she brushed against the bandage under her bodice.

"You could cut it," she mused. "I'm tired of managing it. The moment I take out my braid, it breeds a hundred new tangles. And cutting it might help disguise me a little."

Dani made a thoughtful noise. "Now there's an idea."

"Remember how my hair used to look, back when I wore it short?"

Ester pushed herself upright with a little breathless *oof*, then dropped a kiss on Dani's head. "We could try something like that."

"Yes, I do remember, and stop bending over, you beautiful pregnant fool." Dani waved her hands at Ester. "Go sit down, put your feet up."

Simon entered the room, his eyes locking with Eliana's in the mirror. She resisted the urge to gape at him. He wore a long, black coat that buttoned at the waist over a vest of black brocade, with coattails that fell to his knees. A high collar, a gray cravat. Black gloves; silver cuff links gleaming at his sleeves. High, square shoulders, the architecture of which resembled wings in flight. He had shaven at last, though his hair was still a tousled mess.

When he moved past Eliana, the blazing nearness of his body tugged at her as surely as if he had touched her and pulled her along after him.

"Actually," he said, addressing the others, "I wonder if I might speak to Eliana alone for a moment."

Dani and Ester exchanged glances.

"For a moment?" Dani said, straight-faced. "Or perhaps for an hour or two?"

Ester elbowed her in the ribs and grabbed her arm. At the door, Dani turned once more.

"Just please don't rip the dress," she said. "If you do, I refuse to mend it."

Ester pulled her into the hallway with a choked laugh and closed the door behind them.

In their absence, Eliana could only bear the thick silence for the space of a heartbeat.

"I've never seen you like this," she said. "So clean and fine. I hardly know what to think of it."

Simon smiled a little, then moved toward her and helped her down from the low, flat stool on which she stood. "And then there's you," he said softly, his blue eyes glittering as they moved over her body. He let out a long, slow breath, and for a moment she thought he would say something about her appearance. But then a shadow fell over his face, a darkness unlike any she had seen him wear before, flittering and strange, and he turned away from her. He went to the window and stood rigid before it, looking out over the wet, gray world.

"Patrik was fitting me for my Jubilee clothes just now," he said.

Eliana raised an eyebrow. "Really? I would never have guessed. Isn't this what you always wear?"

"I was standing there, listening to him prattle endlessly on, and suddenly I couldn't be there anymore. I couldn't spend one more moment in that room." His fists opened and closed at his sides. "I had to see you."

"Well, here I am." The longer he stood there, brooding at the window, the greater her uneasiness became. The expression on his face, faintly reflected in the window, was a terrible one.

"Yes, and I can't even look at you," he said. "When I do, I want to abandon all of this. I want to forget my training and my mission, defy the Prophet, run away with you like a lovesick boy."

She moved toward him, her heart skipping against her ribs. She knew she shouldn't delight in his distress, and yet she did, because it mirrored her own—and because he was a man invincible against most things. But not this. Not her.

"Simon," she said, reaching for him. Then she hesitated, lowering her arm. "Do you want me to leave?"

"I *should* stay away from you," he muttered as if to himself. "Until we leave for the Jubilee, I should want you nowhere near me. And yet, here I am."

She gently touched his arm and turned him to face her.

"I don't want you to stay away from me," she said. "How much time do we have left? Less than a day."

"Eighteen hours," he said shortly, "before we leave for Festival."

She had known that number, had been silently counting down with the passage of every hour. But hearing him say it brought tears to her eyes, and the ache in her chest grew, relentless, until it overcame the rest of her body.

He saw her tears and swore passionately, his face twisting into something almost furious, and reached for her. She met him halfway, their kiss hard and clumsy. His gloved hands slid into her braid, his fingers catching on the tangles, and she welcomed each sting of her scalp, because the small, sharp pain reminded her that she was alive, and so was he—at least for this desperate hour, at least for another seventeen after that.

He kissed her there against the wall, beside the window, his hands in her hair, and she pulled hard on his coat, tugging him as close to her body as she could. But it wasn't enough. He was too far from her, and she broke away from him with a frustrated sob. A stupid, frantic voice inside her screamed that if she didn't touch him, right then, that instant, he would disappear from her arms, never to be found again. She fumbled at his clothes, wild for the familiar, rough expanse of his skin. She reached beneath his coat, found his tunic, tugged it loose from his trousers, and when her palms met the warmth of his bare back, she pressed a kiss to his neck and sighed his name.

And then he was tugging up her skirts, lifting her against his hips, and when he entered her, it was swift and hard and everything she craved. She wrapped herself around him and held on, dizzy with him, utterly enveloped in him. His cheek scraped against hers; he whispered her name.

After, as they clung to each other, she pressed her forehead to his, breathing hard, and smiled a little. She touched his damp hair. "I still don't love you," she murmured, hoping it would make him smile, hoping it would soften her own grief.

But the expression on his face was utterly bleak, sharp and empty in a way that frightened her, and she knew it had been the wrong thing to say.

"Simon," she whispered, but before she could apologize, he had taken her face in his hands.

"I need more of you," he said, his voice low and hungry, his gaze roving restlessly across her face. His hands slipped down her body, tugging at her sleeves, her bodice. He buried his face in the bend of her neck, his teeth scraping against her skin. "Eliana, God help me, if I don't have you again, I'll lose what's left of my mind."

And there it was again—that strange, skittering darkness in his voice. An agitation in his movements, a slight manic curl in the laugh he breathed against her cheek.

She thought she understood. Time was hurtling them forward, and neither of them could do anything to stop it.

She kissed him, slow and warm, until he calmed, until her own unease had diminished, and then quietly led him upstairs to their room, where she helped him undress and said with her touch what her words could not.

# ✦ 51 ✦
# RIELLE

*"Oh, the maids did dance, and the maids did sing,*
*And with every word their voices did bring*
*A season of storms and a shiny black wing,*
*A knife of steel and a solid gold ring,*
*A throat painted red and a knotted-up string,*
*And the merry maids sang and stomped and howled,*
*And the moors went black, and their rivers turned fowl."*

—"The Merry Maids of the Marrowtop Moors,"
Traditional Celdarian folk song

Baingarde had never looked lovelier.

It was a chill autumn evening, the stars clear and cold in the sky, but all doors in the castle had been thrown open to the night nevertheless. Every room was alight with candles, every table piled high with steaming platters, and the sheer press of bodies drifting from ballroom to ballroom was enough to keep the air sweltering.

Each of the castle's twenty courtyards had been strung with banners of gold and white, emerald and plum. Tiny brass lanterns hung from the trees throughout the gardens, their flames shivering in the crisp breeze. Bouquets of royal lilies had been delivered from Luxitaine, piles and piles of them placed thoughtfully throughout the castle. Spilling out of burnished copper vases, woven through fresh green vines that had only hours before been plucked from the royal greenhouses and wrapped around the gleaming banisters, they filled the air with a cloying sweet scent that made Rielle's head spin, leaving her faintly dizzy.

And yet still, she danced.

The largest ballroom in Baingarde, surpassed in size only by the Hall of the Saints, whirled with color—brocaded gowns, gleaming in the candle-light; smart suits and pressed coats, their tails flying. At the far end of the room, on a stage bordered with velvet green curtains, an orchestra played merrily through waltzes and folk songs from every region in Celdaria.

One such song—"The Merry Maids of the Marrowtop Moors"—concluded with a dramatic flourish, the violinists sweeping their bows up into the air. Everyone dancing turned and applauded. The orchestra master bowed, her pale cheeks flushed from the heat.

Rielle blew out a breath, laughing from sheer exhilaration, and then beamed up at Audric. Dancing suited him marvelously, and they'd been dancing for nearly two hours straight. She felt drunk on the sight of him, his curls damp, his eyes sparkling.

He caught her staring and grinned. "See something you like?"

She flung her arms around his neck, stretched up onto her toes to kiss him. "I see everything I like," she whispered against his mouth, and then they broke away from each other, laughing, because the dancers nearest them had begun to whoop and holler, cheering them on.

At the edges of her mind crowded too many worries to count—the thousands of people still gathered outside, kept from the castle by lines of royal and Sauvillier soldiers, undoubtedly growing increasingly discontented as Baingarde sparkled on through the night.

The lies of Corien and Ludivine, the ever-present echo of them fighting for her allegiance in some distant corner of her mind.

The phantom girl Corien had created to torment her—her own face, and Audric's, so perfectly combined.

Far away in the Sunderlands, a falling Gate.

And Merovec, parading around the castle, a smile on his face and his mind worryingly closed. Ludivine hadn't been able to stop thinking about that particular strangeness all night. Rielle felt her preoccupation like the persistent buzz of a fly.

But none of that could diminish her happiness. Not on this night. Not in this room.

The orchestra began the opening strains of a new dance, one from the Celdarian heartlands that sent up a cheer throughout the room.

Rielle grabbed Audric's hand. "One more?"

He looked longingly past her at one of the food tables, which the cooks had just filled with platters of fresh pastries. "How many dances will that be?"

"Only seven." She pouted up at him. "Please, darling. I love this one. Then we'll grab a whole cake for ourselves and go hide in one of the sitting rooms upstairs." She moved closer to him, her smile turning wicked. "We'll have our fill of the cake first, and then of each other. We'll look down upon them all as we ravish each other, and they'll just keep dancing, far below us, and none of them will know a thing."

He stifled a groan and rested his forehead against hers. "If you really do want me to stay here and dance, you're going to have to stop talking like that."

She grabbed his hand, grinning, and he spun her out into the floor, everyone nearby making room for them—but before the dance could truly begin, a few flutes and a single violin skipping through the passages of the opening reel, a dazzling bolt of pain exploded through Rielle's skull.

She stumbled, hands flying to her head.

*Rielle?* came Ludivine's voice, a shrill, frightened question, as if she were a child suddenly trapped in a dark room. *Oh, God. No, no—*

Then, without warning, Ludivine disappeared.

It wasn't simply that she was no longer speaking; it was that her presence had been completely wiped clean from Rielle's mind. It was the most disorienting sensation she had ever experienced, as if a crucial piece of her body had been brutally cut away.

She whirled, searching frantically through the crowd. *Lu? What happened? Where are you?*

"What is it?" Audric caught her arm. Beyond him, guests were beginning to stare.

"Something's wrong. She's gone."

Audric tensed beside her. "What do you mean, she's gone?"

"I mean I can no longer hear her, or even sense that she's still alive."

Then Rielle's mouth flew open, a soundless exclamation of pain. The pounding of her head was spectacular. She sensed a tumult, somewhere beyond her. Something to do with Ludivine, something angelic. But it was like being shut out of a room, ear pressed against the door, knowing something was transpiring beyond the solid wood but not allowed to enter. *Unable* to enter. A locked door without a latch. Colossal and immovable.

She held her breath for a moment, struggling to clear her mind of anything but a single question: *Corien, are you here?*

Then there was an outcry from the doors on the far side of the room that led outside to the wide northern terrace and the gardens beyond. Gasps and shouts, cries of alarm, spreading fast. The gathered dancers split and scattered, and through their ranks burst Ludivine—eyes wide, face rigid and white.

She ran straight for Rielle, but Audric darted between them and stopped her, hands tight on her arms. Illumenor snapped white-gold at his hip.

"Lu, say something to me," he said firmly. "With your mouth and your voice. No mind-speak. Tell me who you are."

Merovec shoved his way forward, out of the crowd. "What's the meaning of this? Ludivine?"

Then a slow smile unfurled across Ludivine's face, and Rielle's blood turned cold.

*Corien?* Wild, she searched the room for him. *What are you doing? Release her at once!*

"*You found me,*" said Ludivine. "*Well done.*"

Her voice came split into three parts, a distorted chorus—her own voice, and Corien's, and a third. Unfamiliar and thin. Inhuman. Not even angelic. Something vast and cold.

Audric released her and stepped slowly away.

Merovec stared. "What is this?"

"*Manipulating my father's mind,*" Ludivine continued, "*is not the way to win my heart.*"

With that sentence, the voices changed. Ludivine's voice and the third, unnamed voice remained.

But Corien's voice changed to Rielle's own.

A chill broke out across her skin. She remembered those very words. She had spoken them several months earlier, on the day of her fire trial, in the cave under the hill.

So it continued, the conversation unfurling quickly.

"*Shall I release him, then?*" Corien's voice.

"*Release all of them.*" Her own voice.

"*As you wish.*" Corien said again—as did Ludivine and the third, unknown voice, all of them accompanying each sentence, as if they were three actors in a play, reading the same lines in unison.

Audric glanced back at Rielle, his happiness from mere moments before replaced with a cold, hard anger. "Tell me what's happening. Now."

She shook her head. "I don't know."

But she did know. She was beginning to know.

"*What is the meaning of this?*" Ludivine continued—and this time, horribly, the new voice was that of King Bastien. Small cries erupted across the room. Their late king's voice was coming to them somehow from beyond the moment of his death. "*Why are we all here? Armand?*"

Audric looked as though the floor had fallen out from under his feet. "Father?" he whispered.

From her chair near the doors, Genoveve called out Bastien's name, her voice awful and desperate.

"*I don't know, my king,*" the chorus continued, now joined by the voice of Rielle's father.

Ludivine sank to her knees, pressing her hands flat to the floor. She was breathing fast and hard.

Tal pushed forward out of the crowd. He hurried at once to Rielle, his scarlet-and-gold coat gleaming in the candlelight.

"Do I need to alert the city guard?" His hand was steady at her elbow. "Rielle, tell me what to do."

"He's doing this," she whispered. She looked bleakly up at Tal. "He's going to ruin everything. I don't know how to stop him."

"Corien?"

Merovec's voice exploded. "Who's Corien? Someone fetch the royal healers, for God's sake!"

"Don't leave me." Rielle grabbed Tal's arms. "Whatever happens, don't leave me."

Tal's expression softened. "No one's leaving you, Rielle."

"*Are you hurt?*" Rielle's father again, his voice drifting up from Ludivine's trembling form. "*What's happening here?*"

"*Rielle is leaving you, I'm afraid.*" And that was Corien.

Audric turned to her. "Rielle, what is this? Why is she saying these things?"

But Rielle couldn't answer him, the words wedged in her throat. *Corien, don't do this.* She would not look at Audric. She clung to Tal's sleeve. *I'm begging you.*

*I'm sorry, my darling,* Corien replied at last, and the sound of his voice was both a relief and a torment, for it held no joy or satisfaction. Only a quiet sort of pity. *I do this for the sake of your own happiness.*

*It is not up to you to determine my happiness for me!*

*You're doing a terrible job of it yourself,* he replied. *I've waited long enough for you to see the truth. They will reject you, once they see what you really are. And he will too. He will most of all.*

And then, Lord Dervin's voice, thick with despair: "*I never meant for this to happen.*"

"Tell me what's happening this instant," said Merovec. He stared at Ludivine as if she were in the process of growing a second head. "Is it an angel, speaking through her?"

Rielle's voice, pathetic and small, slid out of Ludivine's throat: "*I thought you…*"

"*That I loved you?*" Corien's voice, tender and soothing. "*Child, I love you more than I can say. I'm doing this for you. If you don't leave them, they will stifle, shame, and punish you for daring to breach the walls they are building around you.*" Then a pause, and Ludivine looked up at Audric, tears streaming down her face. "*Yes,*" she whispered, her neck straining as if she were fighting against her own voice. "*Even him.*"

And then, a vision passed before Rielle's eyes, and as it unfolded, she sensed the strength of it like an earthquake vibrating through her body. Instinctively she knew that everyone in the room was seeing the same thing she was, unfurling before their eyes like shapes drawn through clouds: Herself, standing in that cave, flinging out her arms, an expression of wild ecstasy on her face. A blaze of power erupted from her fingertips to race across the cave, knocking three men to the ground—Lord Dervin. King Bastien.

Her father.

The images came faster and faster. Ludivine, huddled on the ground, continued her horrible narration.

Rielle's shimmering ghost stared at Lord Dervin, King Bastien, her father. All of them dead.

From across the ballroom came cries of alarm, fear, anger. Beside her, Tal whispered, "God save us. Rielle, tell me this isn't true."

But she couldn't. She was helpless in the face of this, her lies spreading across the room like a flood that would end the world.

The vision shifted, and then showed Audric, arriving at the cave. "*Rielle?*"

Herself, huddled beside her father's body: "*Here.*"

And Audric, standing over the corpse of his own father.

Tal turned away, hand over his mouth.

"*I tried to stop him,*" Rielle whispered, walking toward him. "*I'm sorry, I…I burned him. He's terribly wounded, but…it wasn't enough. Audric, I'm so sorry. His name is Corien. He's an angel, Audric. He turned the Sauvillier men against us…*"

Their two forms embraced. *"Thank God you're all right. I thought I'd lost you."*

*"Never,"* said Rielle, wrapping her arms around him. *"Never."*

The vision ended, leaving the room just as it had been—except now, the room was in an uproar. The air sizzled with panic. Shouted questions and curses, keening wails. The kingsguard and Rielle's Sun Guard immediately formed a protective circle around her and Audric, keeping the crowd at bay.

On the floor, Ludivine cried out. Her body jerked as if it had been kicked, and then her eyes cleared. She sucked in a gasping breath and pushed herself unsteadily to her feet.

"They're here." Her voice was her own again, but torn through like shredded paper. She grabbed Rielle's hands. "We must find them before they do anything else. They're close. Here, in the city."

But Rielle could only watch Audric, her body clenched stiff with dread.

"It wasn't like that," she whispered so only he could hear. "It was more than that. He didn't show you everything that happened. I tried to stop him that day. I lost control."

Audric's expression was unreadable. He was looking at her with such focus that she felt flayed, every layer of herself peeled ruthlessly away.

Then he muttered, clipped and cold, "Come with me now," and swept past her, toward the garden doors on the ballroom's northern side, his kingsguard following close behind.

◆◇◆

Deep in the gardens, near the edge of the seeing pools and far beyond the golden reach of the party, Audric finally stopped. His back was to them. He faced the black seeing pools, the catacomb doors beyond them. It was dark and still, so far from the castle, the guests' confused outrage a distant rumble.

"Leave us," he told his kingsguard, and the Sun Guard as well. They obeyed, moving off into the trees until they were alone—Rielle, Audric, and Ludivine.

Rielle felt light-headed, a strange numbness sweeping in constant waves through her body. The only thing she could feel with any certainty was Ludivine gripping her hand.

"I defended you," said Audric at last, his voice soft. "From the beginning, I've defended you."

Ludivine stepped forward a little, putting herself in front of Rielle. "Audric, please, allow me to explain—"

"Oh, I think you've done enough. I think I'll be the one to talk now. That was real, wasn't it? That vision I saw. That was the whole truth. And everyone else saw it as well. I could hear them reacting to it, just as I was."

"It was part of the truth, yes," Ludivine said, "but it's more complicated than what you were shown."

"Oh, please, stop talking, Ludivine. Stop talking this instant." And then Audric turned, his terrible dark gaze falling upon Rielle. "You tell me. *Darling*. Was that the truth?"

She searched frantically for a solution, for the perfect words that would disintegrate this horror and return her life to what it had been only moments before, whirling about the ballroom with him.

Her silence stretched on too long.

"Tell me!" he roared.

She jumped, the fury in his voice crashing against her like glass. She had only a few times in her life ever heard him raise his voice, and each had been in the defense of her or in the throes of loving her.

"It's true," she whispered. "What you saw, what everyone saw, is at least part of what happened."

"Part of what happened," he repeated.

"He didn't show you everything."

"*He*." Audric blew out a soft laugh. "Corien."

She stepped forward, hesitant. "I wasn't trying to kill our fathers. I was trying to stop Corien from hurting them."

"And yet still they died."

"I…" She shook her head, tears rising. "It was the most power I'd ever unleashed. I was terrified. I thought he was going to kill them. I lost my grip on it." She watched him, how he kept his expression cold and hard, and felt the world fall away from her, leaving her suspended in darkness. "You don't believe me."

"I don't know what to believe anymore," he said, his voice empty of all feeling.

"Believe me," she cried, reaching for him. "I love you, and I wouldn't…"

She fell silent, catching herself.

He smiled cruelly at her. "You wouldn't lie to me?"

"I was trying to save them." Her words felt small on her tongue, pale and inadequate. "I lost control."

"And now they're dead," he said flatly. "And now we're married, and now you're queen." He turned away, dragging a hand across his face. "What am I supposed to do now, Rielle? Everyone in there saw. Maybe everyone in the city saw. And I've just *married* you. What do they call you? Those who hate you. The Kingsbane. And now he's proved them all right."

"Stop berating her and listen to me," Ludivine said. "Corien is coming, and he's close. We should be sending out every last soldier to bolster the city's defenses against him. And I should be searching for him rather than standing here keeping you from hurting each other. I suggest we talk about this later."

"Fuck your suggestions," Audric hissed. "We're talking about this right now."

"I told you he would make you hate me." Rielle's voice came out thin and shaky. It was a foreign thing, beyond her control. "He's been waiting for the chance to turn us against each other."

"Well, and he's succeeded beautifully, hasn't he?"

*Tell him about the child*, Ludivine said, her presence shrill and piercing. *Rielle, he must not turn you away.*

*Tell him about the child, and I'll kill you*, Rielle replied.

"I lost control, Audric," she said aloud for what felt like the hundredth time, and she would say it as many times as she needed to. She clenched her fists to steady their trembling. "Please believe me. I was trying to stop Corien. He was threatening you. Don't you remember? You were on Atheria. I saw you. You were in pain. You might have died."

He watched her in silence for a moment. "Yes, I remember."

"So, then." A soft wave of relief butted against her. "What I did was an accident, and I did it while trying to save you."

But Audric remained unmoved. "And then you lied about it. Both of you did."

"Only because—"

"To protect me? Because you thought I couldn't understand what had happened? Because you didn't trust me to help you handle the situation?"

"Because I was afraid," Rielle whispered. "I couldn't bear the thought of losing you."

"And the dead Obex? The villager in Polestal?" His face was closed to her, and that was the thing that was breaking her, the needle sinking slowly into her heart. "The nights you spend with Corien? Is that all because you're afraid of losing me?"

She shook her head, unable to speak.

"And your mother too," Audric pressed on. "You'd lost control, you said. And I believed you. You were only five years old. But a child of that age knows what anger is. You could have stopped yourself, but you didn't want to."

"That's unfair," Ludivine said, her voice low and dangerous. "She had had no training, no teacher to help her. She could not have been expected to contain her power the first time it erupted."

"Unfair, yes, you're right about that. This is all terribly unfair. That you spend your nights chasing another man's love. That you carry in your body the power to destroy us all, and that I've believed this whole time that I could trust you. That I should love you, even now."

Rielle went to him, a sob bursting out of her. "Audric, please, you have to believe me! It was an accident!"

"And how many *accidents* am I expected to forgive?" He shoved her arms away. "Don't touch me!"

She stumbled, and Ludivine caught her. She felt Ludivine reaching for Audric's mind, swift and angry, ready to subdue him, and whirled on her.

"Haven't you done enough?" she cried. "For God's sake, Lu, leave him alone!"

Ludivine stepped back, her eyes twin coins of steel.

"Eager to spin more lies, are you?" Audric said, his own eyes glittering with tears. "You can't resist interfering at every opportunity. You're a snake, and a coward. From the moment I learned you were an angel, I should have resolved to fight you with everything I have in me."

Ludivine regarded him with an eerie calm. "I love you with all my heart, Audric. But if you try to hurt her, I will kill you."

"And the moment I feel you try," Rielle told her, "I'll turn you to ashes."

Audric watched them both, a bitter smile on his face. "My detractors say I've been entrapped by you. That I'm some spineless fool whose mind is soft, easily swayed. I suppose they're right."

"You're neither spineless nor soft," Rielle protested.

He looked away, his jaw clenching. His gaze fell on the seeing pools, and Rielle wondered if he was remembering the same thing she was—their childhood, every beautiful, innocent, ignorant year of it.

*He is*, Ludivine said. *It softens him. Talk to him, now.*

"Audric," Rielle said, moving toward him, hating herself for leaping to obey Ludivine's instructions. But she was desperate; she could feel things moving too quickly in the wrong direction. "Please, look at me. I'm still me. We're still us."

"Our love has been built on lies," he said, his voice choked.

She touched his arm, and he moved away from her. "I told you not to touch me."

She looked helplessly after him. "What can I do? Tell me how to mend this."

And then he let out an awful, exhausted laugh. "You haven't even apologized yet. All of this," he said, sweeping his arm toward her and Ludivine, "and neither of you has apologized. And you ask me how to mend it. No more secrets, no more lies. That's what we said the day they put my father in his tomb. You promised me."

His voice turned ugly. "What a fool I was, to think a promise meant anything."

He began walking away from her, and she ran after him, unthinking and frantic. She grabbed his arm, and he turned and caught her wrist, his grip hard. She refused to be frightened by him; she put up her chin and met his eyes.

"Release her," said Ludivine, storming toward them.

"I defended you," Audric said again, his voice a mere whisper. "Anyone who thought you might be the Blood Queen, the doom we've feared for centuries, I was the first to tell them they were wrong. That you could control your power, that we could trust you, that you would keep us safe. And now you've proven them all right. You're the monster Aryava foretold. A traitor and a liar."

And swiftly, all at once, like the strike of a storm illuminating a dark field, Rielle realized he was right.

Ludivine was saying something, both in Rielle's mind and outside of it. But she was a faint hum of sound, and then Audric was releasing her, dropping her arm as if he were disgusted by it, turning away from her.

In that moment, held numb in a net of despair, she heard Corien speak.

*You're not a monster, child,* he told her, his voice tender with compassion. *You are simply yourself.*

She let out a shaky breath, a half-formed sob, and stepped back from Audric, from Ludivine, from the seeing pools of her childhood. Ludivine tried to stop her. With a blink, a swift flick of her wrist, Rielle sent her flying back into the trees, and Audric too, and Evyline, who'd only seconds before come rushing out of the trees, unable to stay away any longer.

Alone, the gardens ringing from the force of her desolate anger, she felt Corien embracing her mind, shielding her from Ludivine.

*Don't listen to him!* Ludivine cried, and then was silenced.

Rielle slipped into the warmth of Corien's words, reaching desperately for comfort. She turned back once, found Audric lying on his back in the trees. Illumenor blazed to life at his side.

*Come to me*, Corien urged her. *Rielle, hurry. The city won't be safe for much longer.*

She didn't understand what that meant, but she didn't ask. It didn't matter. The city was no longer her concern.

She ran through the gardens, following the thread of his voice. The familiar trees swallowed her; she was blind with sadness, tears tightening her throat until she could hardly breathe. But the patient thrum of Corien's presence illuminated a path, guiding her out.

And as she ran, her despair began slowly, inexorably, turning the corner to anger.

# — 52 —

# ELIANA

*"Every night you will dream of my return, and every nightmare will echo with the pounding of my fists. You fear me, even now. You are right to fear me. I will not rest. I will never rest. I will rise up against you, and I will come with stars blazing at my fingers—"*

—The last recorded words of the angel Kalmaroth

The city of Festival was awash with light.

It sat high on the mountainous shore, looking out over the ocean—an orderly city, built on terraced cliffs that climbed up from the water like mammoth steps to some castle in the sky. The buildings were constructed of white stone, the roofs of overlapping white and gray tile, the roads a soft heather gray like a dove's downy underbelly. Courtyards spilled over with greenery, and abundant sprays of flowers punctuated each neighborhood. The air was warm and salty; gentle waves dark as night left the gray beach streaked with white foam. Beyond the shore, sitting dormant at the vast docks, were several enormous ships, painted orange and gold with torchlight. The Jubilee, it seemed, extended even into the water.

And the brilliance of it all, the sheer splendor—thousands of gold lanterns hanging from every door and window; strings of buzzing white galvanized lights draped from shop to shop and apartment to apartment, capping the roads in brilliant grids. Candles everywhere, dripping wax onto windowsills and wrought-iron gates, smoke from torches and incense pots blackly sweetening the air.

Dani had described what it would look like, had even taken Eliana on a brief tour through the estate to show her oil paintings of past Jubilees. But nothing could have prepared her for the reality of Festival's wildest, brightest night.

The streets teemed with people, a constant parade of bodies sauntering and whirling their drunken way from building to building, each room bursting with parties. Capes, gowns, and long glittering cloaks swept the crowd along, hemmed with feathers dyed azure and gilt and scarlet. Bare arms and legs wrapped around bare backs and hips, each stretch of exposed skin dusted silver and turquoise with shining powder. And on every face, a mask—velvet, hemmed with satin ribbons, rigid and sculpted to resemble animals. Foxes, bears, and birds most of all, their beaks hooked and grinning.

Eliana had attended many such parties at Lord Arkelion's palace back in Orline—but that had been another life, and it had been some time since she'd worn a fine dress, pasted on a false, demure smile, and entered an environment such as this.

And besides, none of Lord Arkelion's fetes had ever approached the size and splendor of this one. A city-sized feast, which Dani had said would last for days, the frenzy of it never diminishing. Through windows thrown open to receive the night air, Eliana caught glimpses of couples in the throes of ecstasy, ballrooms effervescent with color and light, dining halls crammed full of bodies.

And it was nearly impossible to tell, on such a night, which bodies were human and which were angel. Only the black eyes would give them away, and their unusually fluid style of movement, impeccably graceful. But some of the masks had mesh for eyes, and not even angelic bodies were entirely immune to the stupefying effects of alcohol.

Eliana's skin crawled from the noise and from the oppressive heat of so many people packed in such close quarters. Given that, she was particularly grateful for what Dani and Ester had done to her hair. Not long enough to gather into a plait, it was now a short, riotous spill of dark curls, the ends of which brushed her jawline. Remy had taken one look at her, gathered her into a fierce hug, and then whispered that he would miss braiding her hair before parties.

So she had let him help her fashion it into something of a style—two slender braids, starting near her temples, their ends held in place amid her curls with a cluster of black pins. Her mask was black too—soft and velvet, lace-trimmed, with gossamer ribbons that tied at the back of her head. A more delicate, more elaborate version of the mask she had worn as the Dread of Orline. And as she moved through the streets of Festival, it felt like a shield behind which she was only too glad to hide.

She reminded herself that in thirty minutes' time they would have made their way through the choked city streets and be safely aboard a cargo ship called the *Dovitiam*, ready to disembark and leave this continent far behind.

Then Simon touched her elbow, making her pause.

She stopped, bending down to adjust her skirts, and glanced over at him. He stood close by, next to the courtyard wall of a narrow manor house, candlelit sapphire blooms spilling over the stone. Another masked man, whom Eliana recognized as one of their Red Crown scouts, was in conversation with him, neither of their voices audible over the street's jubilant racket.

But whatever they discussed, it couldn't have been good. As she watched, Simon's body sharpened into the shape of anger.

A few seconds later, the scout melted back into the crowd. Eliana watched him go, quickly counting the twelve others in their team—six before them, six behind, stretching down the road like floating links in a chain that seemed suddenly fraught and fragile.

She drew a deep breath to steady herself, met Simon halfway.

"What is it?" she murmured.

He put a hand on her waist and gently pulled her close. Lips against her ear, he said tightly, "New intelligence. The ship isn't here yet. Should arrive in three hours."

Her body went heavy with fear. Any moment, the army would arrive on Festival's doorstep.

"We can't linger on the street," she said at once. "We're too exposed, even dressed as we are. And I'll go mad if we stand here waiting for three hours. Is there a safe place we can wait?"

"No safe places anymore." He wrapped her hand in his. "Follow me."

◆◇◆

A mile down the road, in the easternmost ballroom of Lord Tabris's palace, Eliana made for the second-floor mezzanine.

It was a laborious process that took her the better part of ten minutes, each of which was excruciating. Simon had ordered their team to enter the ballroom separately, in the name of discretion, and now, navigating the crowd, the air ripe with wine and sweat, Eliana had never felt so alone in her life.

A waltz chased her upstairs, the enormous orchestra at the far end of the room playing so loudly that were the room not so packed with revelers, the music would have drowned out everything but shouts. As it was, a steady hum of laughter and conversation floated atop the lilting, somewhat disjointed melody—a waltz, yes, and unexpectedly joyous, but also a bit off-balance, as if composed by someone whose perception of the world were skewed.

Finally, she reached the mezzanine and clung gratefully to the stone railing, each slender pillar carved to resemble wings. She grabbed a glass of red wine from the platter of a servant gliding by and drank it so quickly her eyes watered, desperate for even a thin gloss of calm over her nerves.

Alone, she waited for Simon and thought once more through the outline of their modified plan.

Their team would scatter throughout the palace, ready to move the moment they received word from their scouts of the *Dovitiam*'s arrival. Harkan's team waited in the mountains south of the city, ready to intercept the imperial army and pick off as many soldiers as they could. Two other teams flanked his, ready to assist. Three more teams patrolled the city, from the palace down to the docks, waiting to create diversions as necessary, which allowed Eliana, Simon, and their escort a clear path to the docks. There, they would reunite with Remy and Dani's team, and once aboard the *Dovitiam*, they would all sail for the Vespers—the tropical island country where the water was warm, the islands themselves lush with greenery, the Empire presence scattered and careless. There they would wait, and hide, for as long as they could. Simon would practice threading; Eliana would push her power beyond its current limits. Together, once they were both stronger, they would again attempt to travel back to the Old World.

And on that second attempt, they would not fail. Eliana would not flee or allow Rielle to intimidate her. She would get through to her mother, even if it took days of fighting to accomplish.

At least, that's what she was determined to tell herself, over and over, until she started to believe it.

She forced her breathing into an even rhythm, focusing on the kaleidoscope of dancers below her. It was taking too long for Simon to join her, and her panic had just begun to quietly crest when at last he arrived at her side and placed his gloved hand over her own.

"Too many goddamned people," he muttered by way of apology.

She blew out a breath, so giddy with relief to see him that she drew him down for a kiss.

His hands settled at her waist, and when he lowered his mouth to her neck, the cold lines of his mask pressed against her skin. His mask was as hard as hers was soft, a dull silver metal in the shape of a grinning bull.

Frankly, she hated the look of it. They'd had limited choices, choosing from whatever masks Dani had stored from previous Jubilees, but this particular one was bordering on grotesque.

She did, however, love the coolness of it against her overheated skin.

She slid her fingers into his hair, holding him against her. "Can't we just stay here?" she murmured, and for a moment, his body strong and familiar under her hands, she could close her eyes and pretend they lived in a different world.

Simon pulled back from her, a smile curving beneath the rim of his mask. He raised her hand to his lips. "Come. Dance with me."

◆◇◆

The orchestra favored waltzes, each one merrier than the last, and it wasn't until the fourth one they danced together that Simon came abruptly to a halt.

Eliana nearly tripped over his feet. His hands tightened around her, steadying her, and he stared over her shoulder, his eyes suddenly unreadable.

Someone tapped her arm; she turned, her body tensed to run.

A man clad all in black stood before her, roughly Simon's height, but more muscular, bullish. He gave a low, unhurried bow, sweeping his cloak aside. He had a high, stiff collar, a silver chain about his waist. His mask was shaped like a raven, its iridescent feathers gleaming black-blue. The mask covered his entire face, and its hard black beak muffled his voice, distorting its true colors.

"I've been watching the two of you. You dance exquisitely together." He held out his hand to Eliana—a black glove, the gauntlet rimmed with feathers to match his mask. "I wonder if I might have the honor?"

She cobbled together a coquettish smile. "You flatter me, sir. But I did promise my partner a whole night of dances."

"How selfish of him, to keep a jewel such as you all to himself." He looked past her at Simon. "I think you can understand my disappointment."

And then Simon, his voice smooth and careless, said, "Of course, Admiral." He squeezed her hand once, then released her. "Darling? I don't think you recognized the Admiral. This celebration is in his honor, after all. Surely you can spare him a dance or two."

Eliana's body seemed to fall away from the ballast of her heart. She was a pounding, pulsing thrum of fear. *Admiral Ravikant.* One of the most powerful angels in the world. She wanted desperately to look back at Simon, but instead she curtsied and shot the admiral a dazzling smile.

She struggled to wipe her mind blank. She imagined it as a spotless plate of glass, all polished gleam and clean edges.

"Forgive me, Your Excellency," she murmured. "I didn't recognize you, given your current dress."

"Ah, of course. The danger—and the appeal—of a masquerade ball. And why I cannot resist them." He took her hand, the press of his fingers against her palm like the soft dig of a blade. "Forgive me, child. I don't know your name."

"Scarlett," she said at once, and then grinned a little, biting her lip. "At least for tonight."

He threw back his head and laughed, and then spun her past Simon into the heart of the dance.

—◆—

She focused on her feet. She kept her mind fixed on the admiral's hand holding hers, and his other hand gripping her waist, and on not losing her head completely and tripping over her skirts. The frantic rhythm of her pulse entirely mismatched the orchestra's waltz.

She did not allow herself to think of her name, or of Simon's. Not of Remy, or Patrik, or any of the other hundreds of rebels arranging themselves throughout the city, preparing for her escape.

Each waltz spun faster than the last, more and more dancers falling away, laughing too high and too happily. Eliana could hardly keep up with the admiral's strides, and each time she stumbled, his grip tightened.

"You seem troubled, Scarlett," the admiral observed, after they had passed several dances in idle chatter. "May I ask why?"

She licked the sweat from her upper lip. She had lost count of their dances, lost track of time. How many hours had passed? She would not look for Simon; she refused to even think of him. But her mind was slipping, each spin knocking her a little further out of alignment. She did not feel him teasing for entrance into her mind, as Corien had done, but perhaps Corien hadn't been trying to be careful. The admiral might be capable of wrapping himself entirely around her thoughts, stealthy and sly, before she could notice.

"These waltzes are rather frenetic, Your Excellency," she said, deciding that a little honesty would satisfy him. "I can hardly keep up with you."

"Well, then. We can't have that." He fell quiet for a moment, and then the orchestra halted for the briefest instant before beginning a new waltz—much slower, with sparser instrumentation. A lilting harp, two dueling violins. A single female vocalist.

"There, now." He smiled, his voice curling. "Is that better, Scarlett?"

She wished he would stop calling her that. Each time he did, she worried he would creep closer to the truth.

"You are a generous man, Your Excellency, and a considerate partner," she replied.

"Ah, but Scarlett," he said. "I am not a man."

She didn't know how to respond to that, other than an obsequious apology, a few compliments about his prowess on the dance floor.

He responded to none of it, his silence stretching ominously until the waltz concluded. He stopped in the heart of the ballroom to bow before her.

"It's a pity, Scarlett," the admiral said, brushing his mouth across her hand, "that we didn't have more time together."

His lips did not touch her. Instead, the beak of his mask scraped across her sleeve.

Then the room exploded.

→◆←

Chaos overwhelmed the masquerade.

Revelers shoved past each other as they rushed for the exits, trampling the fallen and tripping over their gowns.

Eliana searched for the source of the detonations, but she could see only smoke and clouds of dust, rivers of people fleeing into the streets. A shoulder whacked her, then an elbow. She staggered, and the next time someone smashed into her, she let her fist fly and knocked them flat. Beneath her gloves, her castings were flaring to life for the first time since returning from the Old World.

When she turned back to the admiral, he was gone.

But Simon was there, shoving his way toward her against the crowd's current, revolver in hand. She met him halfway, and he crushed her to his chest with his free arm.

"Are those ours?" she asked of the explosions. "Our teams must know something."

"Those blasts were angelic," Simon replied, his voice carved from ice. "The army has arrived."

*Harkan.* A chill shook her sweat-slicked body and her chest clenched around her heart. His team would be first in the army's line of fire. She shut her eyes, sent a feeling of love Zahra's way, and hoped it would reach her, that she would send it to Harkan. A message of hope, of thanks.

*Stay alive, Harkan. Fight them, and come find me. We'll wait as long as we can. I'll make them wait for you.*

Simon looked ready to spit fire. "We have to go to the docks. Now. We can't wait for the others."

"Has the ship arrived?"

"We'll find another, if we must," he said darkly. "And I'll cut down anyone who tries to stop me."

Together, they ran.

◆◇◆

Outside the palace, the streets were on fire.

Cannon fire shattered the city to pieces, smashing rooftops to the ground and igniting stored fireworks meant for celebrations later in the night.

Angels in gold chain mail and gleaming armor flooded the streets. They marched down every road, the Emperor's winged crest emblazoning their chests. Burnished wings capped their helmets like horns, and they swept through Festival like a wave. They killed indiscriminately. Bodies littered the ground—bloodstained gowns, slit throats heavy with beads, glittering bodices pierced with arrows. Torches had been smashed, tapestries and feasting tents now consumed with flames.

As Eliana ran, ducking flying debris, keeping close to Simon, her thoughts spun wildly for Harkan.

If the army had arrived, then his team had already engaged them. Maybe they were holding off a stream of them, keeping at least some of them at bay. Maybe they had abandoned their post, sensing the futility of it, and were on their way to join Eliana at the docks.

Maybe he was already dead.

*Zahra?* She sent her thoughts into the chaotic night. *Are you there? Is Harkan alive?*

Simon caught her elbow hard. They'd stopped at the edge of small dunes overlooking the white shore.

The beach was a wide crescent-moon smile, its docks snaking into the water like long rotted fangs. The air was ripe with confusion. The people of Festival who'd managed to escape the streets' bloodbath clamored across the sand, fighting their way toward the docks, swimming out into the shallows. They attempted to climb aboard merchant vessels, cargo carriers, even tried desperately for the Empire warships, resplendent with black-and-crimson sails. They screamed for mercy as the angels cut them down, a ruthless storm of gold pushing out from the city.

Simon pointed at the water, sweat dripping beneath his mask. "The *Dovitiam*. It's arrived."

Eliana saw it—a plain cargo vessel, squat and battered, waiting quietly in the shallows. A runt compared to the sleek warships. But its first mate was Red Crown, and the captain was smitten with her, would do anything she asked.

She started forward, ready to run for it, but Simon held her fast.

"There are too many people crowding the beach," he muttered. "We won't be able to reach it without getting trampled."

Then, cannon fire to their right, and a fresh cascade of gunfire. Eliana turned and saw the ghosts of white cliffs around the rim of the beach—the mouth of a canyon, narrow trails winding down the cliffsides. The spark and glint of weapons, armor, gunshots. Another river of the imperial army, flooding down to the beach from the south.

Eliana reached for Zahra once more, her eyes stinging. *Harkan? Zahra? Please, say something.*

But her mind remained empty and her own.

"We have to run for it," she said, forcing her voice past the terrible fear sprouting tendrils inside her. "The *Dovitiam* is the rendezvous. Everyone will be meeting us there. Remy's there."

"I don't much care about everyone else, if it means safely getting you off this continent," Simon said sharply.

She glared at him. "If you think I'm going anywhere without my brother, you're insane."

"And if you die trying to find him somewhere in all of this?" He flung out his hand at the swarming shore below them. "Everything we've done will have been for nothing. I can't allow you to risk your life for him, or for anyone."

"You can't *allow* me?" She laughed. "I thought by now you understood how this works."

He looked away from her with a foul curse. "I can't see how we'll get through that mob without you getting killed."

Eliana gave him a hard grin and ripped off her gloves. Her castings sparked, ecstatic to be set free. "I know how."

Simon went very still. "You're still recovering from your fight with Rielle. You have to save your energy."

"I think I know my own strength better than you do."

"Your castings are a beacon. Using them will draw the army right to you."

"And will give our people hope," she countered, flinging off her mask. "They'll see my light and run toward it, their courage renewed."

"And then every angel standing will know exactly which boat you're on."

"I'll sink any boat that follows us. I'll summon a storm. I'll summon ten storms."

"You'll exhaust yourself. We'll be attacked somewhere else on the water, and you'll have no defenses left."

She took his face in her hands. "Trust me. I can do this."

Beyond his mask, his eyes were cold and flat in a way that frightened her. For a moment, she couldn't be sure that it was truly him standing there before her.

"Eliana, please," he said, his voice pulled thin with an emotion she couldn't name. "We'll find another way. We'll retreat and regroup."

"There is no other way," she said, and then she turned and ran down the grassy dune to the shore. When she stepped onto the sand, she clapped her hands together, her castings sparking, and then flung her fingers up to the midnight sky, clenched them into fists, and pulled sharply down.

Her palms filled with sunlight, twin blazing gold stars. She tossed them into the air, and they flared to enormous life, lighting up the beach as if it were midday. Then she knelt and slammed her fists against the ground. A bolt of energy sprang to life beneath the sand, flying fast across the beach toward the *Dovitiam*. It knocked everyone it touched off their feet, human and angel alike, clearing a path for her.

She ran, heard Simon following her. "Stay close to me!" she cried over her shoulder.

Gunfire chased them toward the water. Flaming arrows came arcing out of the crowd. But her eyes were trained on the *Dovitiam*, and the sight of it pulled her inexorably forward. *Remy, Remy.* She thought his name with each pump of her legs. She flung up her fists as though blocking punches, knocking every bullet and arrow out of the sky. An angel flung himself into her path, fired his gun. She thrust out her fist, launching a shield of energy that sent him and his weapon flying twenty yards away, into the foaming shallows.

And then they were at the *Dovitiam*'s dock. *May God forgive me,* she said and sent a gust of wind racing across the crowded planks, knocking every citizen running toward the boat toppling into the water.

"Are our people coming?" she shouted to Simon. They were almost at the boat, the gangplank free and open. A figure stood on the deck, waving them frantically on. "Are they following us? Do you see them?"

But Simon did not respond. She heard a grunt of pain and whirled to find him.

It was Jessamyn—Jessamyn, impossibly, and Simon, locked in combat. Daggers flying, bodies whirling fast. Simon had dropped his gun. Jessamyn stomped on his foot, then knocked him in the jaw with her elbow. He staggered back, stunned.

Then Jessamyn turned and saw Eliana. Her left arm and right leg were bleeding; sweat slicked her face. And yet her eyes sparked, and when she ran at Eliana, she was fast, swift with fury, and Eliana, in her shock, didn't have time to properly react.

She barely managed to avoid Jessamyn's jab, ducking just in time. But then Jessamyn's boot caught her in the stomach. She stumbled back, nearly blacking out, and reached for her castings, but Jessamyn was relentless and fell upon her too quickly. She punched her in the jaw, jabbed her hard in the throat.

Eliana fell to her knees, choking—and then she looked for Simon and saw the impossible.

He had recovered from Jessamyn's attack and was standing a few paces from her, facing the beach. He had retrieved his gun and was shouting something at the angels still on the shore. Not in Venteran, nor in the common tongue, but in one of the angelic languages.

She recalled Zahra's instructions from the Nest, those frantically memorized words, searching for the unfamiliar lettering in that basement room full of drugs. She recognized the cadence of what Simon shouted, the harshly lilting syllables.

*Lissar.* He was speaking Lissar.

And the angels on the shore were listening to him.

They gathered around the pier's entrance, shooting their arrows, unleashing volleys of gunfire. Not at Simon, but at a crowd of people trapped between him and the angels.

Gasping for breath, her vision blacking in and out, Eliana at last understood what she was seeing. Time slowed, an endless push and pull between the life she had known and the life she would now lead.

There were Dani, and her three boys, and Ester. Darby, Oraia. Patrik.

They had followed her light to the pier, ready to join her, desperate for the ship that would bear them away to safety. Remy would be somewhere among them.

And now they were being slaughtered.

Each one of them fought desperately to the last—Dani, shielding Ester with her body. Patrik, charging at Simon with a roar. And each one of them fell. Ten. Twenty. Thirty. Red Crown soldiers who had helped plan her escape, who had fought through the city to protect her for as long as possible. Some ran, making a break for the broader beach. Angelic arrows caught them in the back. Any who slipped past the angels' line of fire were picked off by Simon's efficient gunfire.

And Jessamyn kept on, kicking Eliana in the ribs, in the stomach, yelling furiously over her head. Words Eliana didn't understand, and one word, over and over: Varos.

Her vision tilting, Eliana called out Remy's name. Vainly, she searched for him in the darkness. She tried reaching for her power, but it was like trying to navigate the froth of a nightmare. Her mind wouldn't focus, shattered by pain. She shouted for Remy, screamed for Simon to stop.

Then swift footsteps crossed to her. She heard the meaty slap of a fist against flesh, and Jessamyn's abuse abruptly ended. Her head spinning, her lips hot with blood, Eliana lay there half-alive, listening to Simon utter something in furious, rapid Lissar.

Jessamyn fell to her knees before him. She whispered a few reverent words. An apology?

Eliana reached out blindly, her arms trembling. She tried weakly to summon her power. But Simon had been right. She wasn't entirely recovered from fighting Rielle.

And now, after her flight across the beach, her head pounding from the fall of Jessamyn's fists, she could barely make her castings spark.

And now, Simon had done *this*. The pier and the water were littered with the corpses of those who had trusted her to save them.

*Harkan?* She tried to find him once more. She reached for Zahra, her head throbbing. *Harkan, where are you?*

Someone was lifting her, shoving her to her feet. She decided she would make it more difficult for them to move her and gave into the rising tide of her pain.

# ⭠ 53 ⭢
# HARKAN

*"Papa once told me that, when I lay dying—because someday I will, as will we all—I must not think of the things that frighten me, and I must not think of my pain. I must think of everyone and everything I have ever loved, for if I do that, those thoughts will follow me into death, and that far black place will turn bright and golden, as the world long ago used to be."*

—Collection of stories written by refugees in occupied
Ventera, curated by Hob Cavaserra

Harkan knew something was terribly wrong.

He couldn't articulate what, but he felt the wrongness like cruel eyes on his back, pinning him where he lay in the dirt. He couldn't swallow quite right; his mouth was sour and aching, and strangely wet. He was perched at the top of a rocky crest of land, looking down upon a wide slope of shale. He held one of Dani's loaned rifles, and he was picking off imperial soldiers as they marched up through the canyon beneath him, pushing inexorably toward the beach where Eliana's ship awaited her arrival. The *Dovitiam*. A cargo vessel. Serviceable, yes, but not good enough for her.

None of them were good enough for her, and neither was he.

*Not true,* Zahra said gently. *You are unkind to yourself.*

Harkan shook his head, dislodging her. He wasn't yet used to how Zahra's thoughts felt slipping inside his mind, like an old dream he didn't particularly want to remember coming back to life without his permission.

*I must focus*, he told her, though it was harder to form that simple thought than it should have been.

Again, a wrongness.

His team had this wave of soldiers bottlenecked. They were pushing up out of the canyon, and if they reached the cliffs where Harkan's team was positioned, hiding behind boulders, firing shot after shot, reloading, ducking when imperial bullets came slamming into the rocks right over their heads—if the army reached the cliffs, that would be it. They would pour onto the beach. They would flood the shallows, forming a barrier between Eliana and her ship.

Harkan couldn't allow that to happen. No matter what, they had to hold this wave here, in this narrow, white canyon, until Zahra told him that the ship had disembarked, that Eliana was safely away.

He stopped to reload. He looked left—Catilla and Viri, shouting orders at those downhill, providing them cover. He looked right—Gerren, crouched like a cat behind a rock, shooting down soldier after soldier. Never mind that the adatrox kept coming, dozens upon dozens upon dozens of gray-eyed imperial tools. And angels, too, among their ranks. Angels who, when shot, merely picked themselves back up seconds later. Whole again, and strong, with laughing black eyes and cruel smiles slashed across their faces.

Never mind all of that. Gerren was the finest sharpshooter Harkan had ever seen, a thought which made him deeply, unbearably sad.

*We live in a world where children must learn to be killers*, he thought, tears rising to his eyes. *Where girls must grow up to become bounty hunters. Venerated saviors and frightened queens.*

*Harkan, stop shooting*, Zahra suggested. *Set down your gun.*

*I can't*, he told her.

"I can't," he whispered, wiping the dust and sweat from his face. "We must hold them here. We must hold them."

*Hold them in the mountains*, he thought, over and over. *Keep them from the beach. Protect her.*

"Hold them!" he cried. He screamed it until his throat felt ready to tear in two. "Hold them here!"

*Harkan.* Zahra's voice brushed across his brow, and the feeling of her was suddenly so near, so full and present, that he could hear the cracks in her words, despite the gunfire and the relentless rhythm of the army's boots.

A wraith's voice, breaking.

Fear gripped him hard. He tried to breathe through it, but it was too difficult, to breathe. There was a vise clamping his chest. He looked for that strange discoloration in the air, that blurry unevenness that marked Zahra's presence. But he couldn't find her, and he pushed himself up, off the ground, but then she was there, keeping him still. He felt her in his mind—a warm palm, pressing gently.

*What happened?* he asked her, choking on his own throat. *I don't understand.*

*Please, lie still.*

"No," he managed. He fought to raise himself up. He crawled across the hard-packed ground, trampled smooth and flat by thousands of marching feet. Red stains, white sand. His hands were caked with color, ghostly and torn. "What happened?"

He crawled to the cliffs' edge, his vision spotting. And that's when he saw the ruined beach, far below. The charred rut through the sand, stretching from the city to the water, left behind by some great scorching fire. The scattered bodies in the shallows, being pushed gently to shore by waves that knew nothing of death.

That's when he saw the *Dovitiam*, still anchored in the bay, and burning. Someone had set it afire, and the pier connecting it to the shore burned as well. And beyond those flames, the admiral's sleek black ship glided out into the water, chasing the rising moon.

Watching it leave the bay, listening to the sounds of the city called Festival once again falling to angelic swords—being cleansed once more, as it had been years ago; being wiped clean of disloyalty, of traitorous schemes—Harkan took a shuddering breath.

And, all at once, with the cold void of Zahra's hand cupping his cheek, he remembered.

◆◇◆

It had happened only moments before, but an entire lifetime had passed between then and now.

First, he saw the endless tide of the approaching army pushing past their paltry line of defense. Of course they pushed past. That he could have ever thought his teams would succeed in this, that a few dozen mere humans could actually hold back this tireless wave of monsters long enough for Eliana to escape…

*No.* Zahra said this gently, redirecting him. *There isn't time for that.*

He moved on.

Second, the members of his team falling all around him. For a while, for longer than should have been possible, they had held off the approach of dozens of soldiers. The army was flooding into the city from all directions, but Harkan refused to think about that. He must instead focus on this particular section of army, this particular canyon in which he must hold them. The beach below must be kept free and clear until Eliana was safely away.

How foolish he was, to have even for a moment entertained the thought that he would be able to join her before her ship disembarked. How foolish, and how eternally, fatally smitten.

Zahra created distortions in the minds of the army's vanguard, distracting them. She cloaked Harkan's team from view when she could, until at last, after an hour of this, her strength gave out. It was then that his team began to die, one by one. They had to have seen death coming for them; they had to have known when they left Willow that this was the likeliest ending, that none of them would be able to join the others on that ship.

But they didn't run. Harkan remembered this now. He had ordered them to hold fast. He had shouted Eliana's name at them, over and over.

*For Eliana*, he had cried. *Hold fast! Hold them right here!*

And they hadn't run.

*You led them well*, Zahra told him, her voice brimming with pride. The feeling of it warmed his cold limbs.

Third, a man bursting out of the mass of soldiers, making straight for Harkan. He had determined that Harkan was the leader of this upstart group of rebels, this squadron of fools who thought they could prevent an imperial army from doing what they did best.

But they *had* prevented it, at least for a while, at least in this one small canyon.

Had it been enough?

*Was it enough?* Harkan asked, groggy.

Zahra sent him a feeling, a sensation—her own ancient fingers stroking his hair. *I'm right here, Harkan.*

He struggled to remember. Even with Zahra's help, it was difficult. Slippery and elusive.

But he did see it now: the man, running for him. Lithe and swift, an efficient swordsman. Harkan had grabbed his sword and jumped to his feet, meeting the man's blade with his own. They were well-matched for a few moments, nimbly dodging each other's blades—until Gerren fell. Caught in the throat. His eyes widening, surprised. His hand flying to his neck. And then the boy was down, dying fast, and that moment of distraction was enough.

The man's fist smashed into Harkan's jaw, knocking him backward. And then he flung a dagger at him, and it landed hard and true in his gut.

Harkan's body jerked. Through a fog, he remembered the pain, how it was as if fire had shot inside him, spreading outward from his abdomen, as though his veins had been scorched by Eliana's castings. His hands flew to the knife in his belly, and he looked down at it and laughed. Then he sank to his knees, falling hard on his side, and he faintly heard Catilla's voice, urging him to get up, to run, before her voice abruptly ceased.

He remembered scrabbling in the dirt, fumbling for his gun, his dagger, *anything*, because this man, whoever he was, was killing everyone—there went Viri, and the girl Roen, and Qarissa, and Rogan, all of whom Dani had recruited from the farmlands outside the city. And then Harkan saw, through a flash of furious thought sent in despair from Zahra, that this man was named Varos, and that he was a member of Invictus. That he had left Willow in flames and executed every member of Red Crown who remained there.

That he intended to hurry next to the beach and make sure that no rebels on the beach interfered with—

And Zahra realized it at the same time Harkan did, for she was delving frantically through Varos's mind with what strength she had left. She howled when she saw the truth, a terrible, shrieking wail that shook Harkan's bones.

*Simon.*

Simon was leading Eliana not to freedom, but to the admiral.

Simon was not Red Crown.

He was loyal not to the Prophet, if the Prophet was even real. That much Zahra could not see. A figment, a lie? Part of the ruse? Perhaps.

No, he was loyal to one being only, and he intended to take Eliana across the ocean to the doors of his palace.

*The Emperor.*

Zahra howled with rage, but Harkan was faster. His fury crystallized his pain; his despair sharpened his slipping mind.

He pulled himself to his hands and knees, found his rifle. Turned, saw Varos drawing his sword out of Catilla's gut, and fired everything he had left.

Varos fell, his gut shredded.

Another scream pierced the air, as full of sorrow as Zahra's had been of rage.

Harkan, his eyelids fluttering, the pain in his gut traveling up to pound at his temples, found the source—a woman with freckled brown skin, a red-dyed braid. Lithe and dangerous; a soldier, certainly. She stared at Varos's body, frozen with horror, and then a brilliant light flashed from the beach.

The girl turned, shielding her eyes. She looked back once at the slain Varos. Her bright gaze cut to Harkan, and he watched her expression harden, a veil of hatred dropping over her eyes. Then she turned and fled down the cliff paths, joining the imperial army as they converged on the beach.

Harkan dragged himself closer to the cliff's edge, watching this light, this fallen sun, streaking toward the water.

Dimly, he heard Zahra screaming, "I can't get to her! I can't stop her! Stop, my queen! No! *No!*" And he felt Zahra's rage, the fist of it pummeling against some cage that he too, could sense, as if someone had erected an invisible shield between them and Eliana, keeping them immobile while she ran unknowing toward betrayal.

Harkan lay his cheek on the hot stained ground, laughing a little, his eyes stinging from tears and the grit of sand. He listened to Zahra sob and wail, fighting uselessly against whatever force was imprisoning her here on these cliffs of death. Then he closed his eyes, listening to the distant sounds of gunfire from the docks below. Sharp, efficient. One after another.

An impressive marksman.

Better even than Gerren.

◆◇◆

"That's what happened?" he whispered.

Zahra's touch was cool and still against his cheek. *Yes, Harkan. That's what happened.*

*But this*, she added, *this happened too.*

These memories were his own—older, deeper, and dear. So distant that, given the circumstances, he wouldn't have been able to find them on his own.

But with Zahra's help, he did.

◆◇◆

First, seven years old. Passing messages to Eliana, from his balcony to hers. Moving his palm across the flame of his candle so she would see a flashing light from her window. The first time they had written a code between them.

Second, ten years old. His brothers leaving for the war front, after which he had been inconsolable for weeks. His only comfort had been playing games with Eliana on the floor in her bedroom, helping care for Remy when Rozen was out working her mysterious job. At night, lighting candles for the windows. *May the Queen's light guide them all home*, Rozen had said, over their heads—his, and Eliana's, and little Remy's, all bowed together over storybooks, listening with bated breath for a door to open with good news that never came.

And third, fifteen years old. A killer now, at Eliana's side. Reluctant, but devoted. And at last, he had kissed her. That first night, in his bed, both of them trembling with nerves, all awkward angles and sweating brows, and Eliana whispering his name against his neck. He had been afraid to touch her, desperate to touch her. After, his cheek against her chest, listening to her pounding heart, trying to catch his breath. The smell of her in his bed. Burying his face in the pillow she had used. Breathing her in.

—◆—

"Yes," he whispered, smiling a little. His eyes were wet, as was his mouth. "Yes," he agreed, "that happened too."

And then he looked up at Zahra's faint ripple of a face, so odd and unsettling in the air, and knew that he was dying, for how else would he— untouched by the empirium, unremarkable and ordinary—be able to see Zahra's face at last?

How strange that the face of an angel who loved humans would be the last thing he would ever see.

"Will you help her?" he asked. His chest began to seize, his lungs fighting for air that would not come.

"I will find a way," Zahra promised. "Until the world ends, I will fight for her."

"We both will," said a voice—a man, leaning over him. Copper-haired and blood-streaked. His voice torn, heavy with pain.

"Patrik?" Harkan tried to form the word, but it came out garbled. Frustrated, he tried again. His voice failed him.

He felt a warm hand on his cold face. "This fight isn't over yet." A slow breath, puffing against his face. A tiny, furious sob. "God. Harkan. I'm so sorry. We tried. We tried so hard. I'm sorry. You did so well, my friend. You're all right. It's all right."

A burst of fear, sudden and wild. *Zahra?*

*I'm here. Me, and Patrik. He's alive. Some of us are alive. We're here. We will go on.*

*Does she still love me?* Harkan could no longer speak. His thoughts were a whisper, fading. But he needed to know. He needed, he needed.

*Oh, Harkan,* Zahra replied, soft and sad. *She never stopped.*

# — 54 —

# RIELLE

*"This has all happened before, and it will all happen again. In the eyes of the empirium, a war is but a sigh; an age is but a blink. We must not let ourselves be confined by a narrow human understanding of events. We must accept that we cannot understand the world's workings and allow the will of free human decision to evolve unfettered."*

—Children of God: A History of the Empirium

They were calling for her death.

She heard them as she ran—the people of the city into which she had been born, the only home she had ever known. She heard their cries rising like flocks of black birds taking frenzied to the sky.

*Kingsbane!*

*Kingsbane!*

*Kingsbane!*

Their screams for justice, their shouts for her death—they carried her swiftly out of the gardens, through the stable yards and the armories, into the temple districts.

The city bells began to chime, and she laughed a little, wiping the tears from her face. Audric had sounded the alarm. He would perhaps send the city guard after her. Would they shoot to kill? She hoped they would. She would melt their swords and fuse their feet together with the molten metal. She would cut their hands from their arms and let them bleed out beside their useless arrows.

Ludivine was screaming at her, distant and distorted, as if Rielle were hearing her through oceans thick with black water. She gathered up every scrap of energy she could find and shoved it at her, pushing her away. She couldn't see Ludivine, couldn't talk to her, couldn't think of her. For if she thought of Ludivine, she would think of Audric, and if she thought of Audric, she would crumble. The pieces of her would collapse, a toppled, ill-fated construction.

*Rielle, please, don't leave me!* Ludivine's last words, which Rielle pushed away with her tired mind. She was pressing hard against a door, desperate to keep Ludivine far from her, but her body was trembling, she was exhausted and could hardly see—but then Corien was beside her. His eyes were dry and clear, his arms steady. Together they closed the door to the part of her mind where Ludivine lived. He put his hand to the latch and turned the key.

*Almost there*, he murmured, his voice a light on the cold horizon. *Almost free.*

—◆—

The city guard did try to stop her.

They tried, and they failed.

Her father's soldiers, dozens of them. They followed their commanders' shouted orders and ran at her, eyes wide. They knew they would die, that something was terribly wrong. She was the Kingsbane, after all. The Blood Queen. She would cut them down, sure as breathing. She had done it to their late king. They had seen the vision, just as everyone else had.

Rielle swept her arm at them, like clearing a table of debris.

They fell all at once, dissolving, and by the time they hit the ground, they were mere glittering swirls of ash.

She ran through the dissolving echoes of their bodies, choking on ruin.

No one tried to stop her after that.

She stumbled out of the city, running into the mountains. The entire valley was clogged with people, but her path remained clear, untroubled. Corien was helping her, she realized, so suddenly, sharply grateful that she felt faint. Her mind spun around a single, indisputable fact: He was the only one left to help her. The only person living who could look at her and see a girl, and not a monster.

She thought of Garver and Simon, sitting in their little shop, their dinner growing cold as Corien's vision played out across their table. Sweet Simon, watching his Sun Queen crumble before his eyes.

It was just as well for him to see the truth. She had hidden it from him, from all of them, for far too long.

She looked up at the sky only once, called for Atheria only once. But the godsbeast did not come. The sky remained empty, a spill of moonless black.

Furious, she plunged into the trees. So, she was truly alone. The realization settled around her like a suit of armor, slowing her feet. But she pushed past the extra weight, muscles burning.

She was alone. She was alone.

She repeated it to herself, twenty times over. Fifty. One hundred. She would keep repeating it until it no longer hurt her.

She was alone.

But not for long.

◆◇◆

She found him standing in a deep wood.

There was a girl sitting in the grass at his feet—light-brown skin and hair like white silk. Queen Obritsa of Kirvaya, eyes wide and haunted, shadows dark across her tear-streaked face.

An unmoving figure in ragged travel clothes lay beside her, their head resting in her arms. An adult—pale brown skin, a soft cap of shaggy brown hair.

Rielle remembered him too. The queen's bodyguard. Artem, was his name.

But then Corien was opening his arms to her, his face awash with pity, and she crashed into his embrace. She pressed her face to his chest, breathed hard and short against him.

"I'm sorry," he whispered. His hands trembled as he stroked her hair, her shoulders, the ruined tatters of her trailing sleeves. "Look at you. My poor, darling girl. I'm sorry you're hurting."

She opened her eyes and looked past him at the capital. Baingarde shimmered, fire-colored, against the inky backdrop of the mountains. She refused to blink. Her tears turned the city into a blurry, glimmering inferno.

"Don't feel sorry for me," she whispered at last. "And don't apologize. It's good that they know. I'm glad they know. And besides," she added, curling her fingers into the stiff black wool of his coat, "I won't be hurting for long."

## ~ 55 ~

# ELIANA

*"The Sun Queen is selfless and pure. She protects and sacrifices. She never breaks. She is never tempted. She shines and she shines and she shines, and she gives all her light to others and keeps none for herself. That is what many of us have believed. But does that sound like a particularly kind life to you? Does that seem a life that any child of this world deserves?"*

—*The Word of the Prophet*

When Eliana awoke, she was sitting in a chair, her arms and legs bound. It was a plain wooden chair, and she was sitting on the deck of a ship. An enormous ship, sleek and black, with red-and-black sails like mourning veils dipped in blood.

Like the tattered gown that clung to her—sweat-stained, bloodstained, drenched from the spray of water.

Awareness came to her in unsteady waves. She squinted at the horizon. There was Festival, slowly receding, but still close enough that, if she jumped, she could make the swim.

But she couldn't jump without Remy.

She would escape these bindings and find him. Together, they would swim for the shore. They would find another boat, or maybe disappear into the cliffs around Festival. They would reunite with Harkan, Zahra, Patrik.

She reached for her castings—and found nothing. No answering spark of power, no heat flaring to life in her hands. She flexed her fingers. The lack of the chains she had made, the lightness of her palms without the weight of the discs resting inside them, made her stomach heave. Her hands were naked, stripped bare; her power was trapped inside her with nowhere to go.

She looked around, fury sharpening both her vision and her injuries. Her body ached from Jessamyn's blows, spots of pulsing pain lighting a path across her body. She didn't understand why Jessamyn had attacked her, what she had become in this new future, but her questions all disappeared when she saw Simon approach her across the deck.

He had exchanged his Jubilee finery for the sleek uniform of an Empire soldier. A trim, square-shouldered coat that fell to his knees. Red on black, trimmed with gold. The crest of the Emperor on his chest. A gleaming fresh sword at his belt.

And he wasn't alone.

He dragged Remy along with him—one hand gripping his arm, the other holding a knife to his throat.

Eliana's mouth went dry. She recognized that jagged blade.

Arabeth.

That, absurdly, was the thing that made tears spring to her eyes at last.

He had taken her favorite goddamned knife.

"Let him go," she said, her voice hoarse.

"El," Remy said, tear tracks shining on his cheeks. "Don't do anything they say. If they kill me, they kill me. Don't give in. Don't let them win."

"He won't hurt you, Remy," Eliana said automatically.

Simon raised an eyebrow. "Won't I?"

His voice belonged to the Wolf, iced over and unfeeling.

And Eliana realized, slowly, the truth bleeding slow and cold down her body, that he would do it. He *would*. He had killed everyone else. He had stood not twenty feet from her and shot them all down.

Remy began to sob.

"It's all right," she lied, her voice trembling. "It's going to be all right."

She looked away from him, unable to bear the sight of his fear. Instead she focused her rage on Simon's implacable face. Her memories slapped her, merciless—Simon moving inside her, pinning her to her bed. Simon kissing his way down her body. Simon murmuring words of love against her skin.

Her tears came faster. Her mind spun, searching futilely for answers. And still Simon stood there, Remy weeping in his arms. He watched her expressionlessly, as if she were a stranger, as if they hadn't shared a single moment together, much less a bed.

"How did you do this?" she whispered. She wanted to yell at him, curse at him, tear herself from the chair and launch herself at him, claw his eyes from his skull, bash his head in, tear out his guts with the blade he was pressing against her brother's throat. "*Why* did you do this?"

No answer came. Instead, Admiral Ravikant approached from across the deck, still wearing his awful beaked mask. He held his hands behind his back. He stood in silence, observing them all.

Then he said, "Scarlett, you lied to me."

"And you knew it," she said quietly. "You were, what, toying with me? Stalling for time until your ship was ready? Until the army arrived?"

"I'm not going to explain myself to you," he replied. "Instead I want to tell you what's going to happen here. I want you to understand your future."

Away from the crowded ballroom, his masked voice no longer sounded so muffled and strange. In fact, it was almost familiar, though Eliana couldn't identify it. A note of alarm sounded in her mind; a frantic instinct was screaming at her, warning her.

"Who are you?" she whispered. "I know you."

"You will be put into a cell," he said, "until you've showed me that you merit something better. The Emperor has given me permission to treat you this way, because you have proven yourself undeserving of kindness. If you try to attack me, or Simon, or any of my crew, if you make even a single move of aggression, I will begin cutting your brother. I won't kill him. I will cut him, and I will keep cutting him, and I will make you watch. He will beg me to kill him. *You* will beg me to kill him. And I won't do it. I will keep him alive and awake so that he feels every moment of pain. So I suggest you do as I tell you."

Eliana's mind, shattered and grieving as it was, nevertheless had begun to identify the admiral's voice. His stature, the shape of his hands. An ill feeling rose inside her, and kept rising, until her mouth had filled with the urge to be sick.

Then he took off his mask, confirming it.

The face of Ioseph Ferracora stared back at her—a jutting chin, like Remy. Dark hair, pale skin, eyes like two thick drops of black paint.

"No!" Remy cried, his voice splitting open. His sobs were terrible, ragged and squalling, and he tried to turn his face away from the sight of their father, staring at them with angel-dark eyes, but Simon wouldn't let him. Simon, a cruel smile playing at the corner of his mouth, held Remy right where he was.

—◆—

The next few minutes passed in a numb black blur.

Eliana was taken below, led downstairs by half a dozen blank-eyed adatrox. Her wrists were bound with chains, as were her ankles—their chains, and not her own. Her chest ached from the loss of her castings; her grief for them snatched away her balance. She fell down the last two steps, and the adatrox let her. They yanked her back to her feet, dispassionate, brutally efficient.

A door opened before her, wide and yawning. The mouth of a beast, welcoming her inside.

Somewhere above, Remy was screaming protests. She clung desperately to the sound, though each one cut away a piece of her heart.

When he fell abruptly silent, she fell along with him. Her mind dropped into a bottomless pit.

They shoved her inside her room—wooden walls, wooden floor. No windows, a single door. An estimate: ten feet by six feet.

She landed hard on her knees. She sat there, breathing, facing away from the door. A column of dim lantern light passed over her, illuminating a block of the wall.

And then, a silhouette.

She turned to face him. In such poor light, she could not see the lines of his face—only shadows, the barest hint of his scars, the flickering blue of his eyes.

*Your eyes are like fire*, she had whispered to him—once, when they'd only just returned from the Old World, both of them weak and trembling, her abdomen scorched by Rielle's power.

And then again, straddling him on the chair in her bedroom, the last time they had loved each other. His hands on her hips, helping her move, his eyes blazing.

*Your eyes are like fire*, she had told him seconds before he'd kissed her.

"Why?" she whispered. The word sounded pitiful, the confused plea of a child. But it was the question in her mind above all others.

He didn't answer. He said not a word. He closed the door and locked it. She followed his footsteps, moving briskly down the narrow corridor, until they disappeared.

Then she curled into a tight ball, pressed her cheek against the floor, and breathed into the darkness.

# ✦ 56 ✦

# AUDRIC

*"They called him The Golden King. They called him Audric the Lightbringer. They say that he rode into battle against the angels on a chavaile—a godsbeast, a winged horse both terrible and beautiful. They say he was a brave man, a fearsome man. They say he was a man full of despair. They say his heart was full of love for his country, and love for the Blood Queen Rielle, and that when war came, he had no love left for himself."*

—Journal of Remy Ferracora,
January 23, Year 1016 of the Third Age

Audric pushed himself to his feet, his head reeling. He leaned against a nearby tree to catch his breath—just as Evyline let out a sharp cry of warning from behind him.

He turned, ducking just in time to avoid the blow of a sword—the captain of his kingsguard, bearing down on him, his face dark with fury. The man was a metalmaster; his sword moved fast, reading his instincts, flying as if it had a mind of its own.

But Audric was faster.

He dodged another blow, yanked Illumenor free of its sheath, and swung hard. The blade crackled, spitting sunlight. Their swords crashed together, his and his captain's, and then Audric spun away from him, and everything that had happened—the strain of the past months, the horrible vision Corien had sent them, his argument with Rielle—gathered like a battering ram in his heart and pushed out, shattering him.

He thrust all the power he possessed into Illumenor, until the blade shone so bright it hurt his own eyes. The captain reeled back with a cry. Audric advanced on him, squinting through the brilliance of his casting, and sliced the man through from shoulder to hip, cutting him cleanly in two.

He fell to the ground in pieces, his wounds bloodless and smoking.

Audric turned to meet the others, but the rest of his kingsguard had fled, back toward Baingarde. Only the Sun Guard remained—Evyline, Dashiell, Riva. Ivaine, Jeannette, Maylis, Fara.

Evyline, her eyes wet, knelt before him. The others followed suit.

"My king," she said, "I don't know what to say to you right now, except that I am the captain of the Sun Guard, and you are the Lightbringer." She paused, her jaw working. "If my queen is gone, then I will follow you, and serve you, with all my heart, until you order me otherwise."

He placed a hand on her shoulder. "Your queen isn't gone, Evyline. I understand what's happened is upsetting, but I promise you..."

Then the city bells began to chime, distracting him. He peered back at the castle. Had his mother ordered the bells to be rung? And if so, why?

A soft, keening wail sounded from among the trees. Searching, Audric found Ludivine, and the sight of her nailed him to the ground.

She was sitting at the base of a tree, knees drawn to her chest, hands over her ears. As she rocked herself quietly, her body shook with sobs.

"Dashiell," Audric said, forcing the fear out of his voice, "take Riva and find my mother. She's the only one besides me or Rielle who should have the authority to ring the city bells."

"Don't!" Ludivine looked up, wild-eyed. "Stay away from Baingarde. It isn't safe."

Dashiell and Riva paused, glancing uneasily at each other.

"My king?" asked Evyline.

"Stay here for now." Audric crouched before Ludivine. Panic rose in his blood, chilling him. "Tell me what's happened. Where is she?"

Ludivine shook her head. "She's gone," she said, her voice heavy with misery. "She's left us."

He did not understand her. Her words slipped in and out of him. "What do you mean, she's left us?"

"She's gone to him. He's here, he's close. He won't let me touch Rielle. She won't let me touch her. She hurt me. I'm losing myself. I can hardly keep my thoughts in place."

Audric stood, backing away from her. A dull, ringing whine bloomed in his ears. "Fight them. Get her back."

"Audric, I *can't*."

"Then we'll go to her. We'll find her and bring her back to us." He whirled, sheathing Illumenor. "Jeannette, run ahead and have my horse brought to the front yard. Evyline, go with her, order the first line of the city guard to meet us by the castle gates."

"You don't understand," Ludivine moaned.

He glared back at her. "What don't I understand? Speak plainly."

"Audric." She drew in a shaky breath, her eyes spilling over with fresh tears. "She's *left* us."

And then she opened up a feeling to him—an immense, stormy feeling that slammed into him like the first blast of winter.

Rielle's rage, her heartbreak. Her relief, and her resolve. They battered him, even diluted through Ludivine's thoughts as they were. He saw their argument unfurl through Rielle's eyes. His own furious voice, grief and anger shifting his face into a new mask. He felt Rielle's desperation, her hopelessness—and he felt it the moment she decided that he was right.

With each word he uttered, he had helped illuminate her choice.

*You're the monster Aryava foretold.*

*A traitor and a liar.*

Then Ludivine released him, and he fell to the ground, hard, on his hands and knees, and gasped out a sob.

Ludivine crawled to him, took his face in her hands. "Listen to me."

"No," he muttered, shaking his head. "No, no, no…"

"Audric, we cannot linger."

"We'll ride out after her. The bells are ringing. They'll have shut the city gates." He tried to push himself up, away from her, and couldn't find the strength. His chest was cleaving itself in two.

"It won't work."

"I'll find her. I'll bring her back to us."

"She won't listen. She's made her choice."

"You can't know that, Lu," he said stupidly, knowing even as he said it that it wasn't true. He fumbled for her hands. She folded his into her own, pressed them all to her heart. "I love her. It was a mistake. I hadn't had time to think. I was out of my mind, I didn't know what I was saying."

"I know." Her face was worn thin, as if the night had diminished her. "I know, darling."

"We have to do something. We'll send her a message. I'll ride out. I'll follow them wherever they go."

"And the moment he can do so without angering her, he'll kill you."

At last, Audric found the strength to stand. He only half noticed Evyline and the rest of the Sun Guard, looking to him for instructions, but they looked as lost as he felt. He didn't know what to say, how to proceed. He could barely hold himself upright.

"The saints' castings?" he murmured, barely managing it.

"Gone," Ludivine said flatly. "While we were…occupied, Corien's operatives stole them. They're with him now—with Corien, and with Rielle."

Audric nodded, his head heavy and slowly spinning. "I see."

Ludivine touched his arm. "You must prepare yourself to leave. I know it won't be easy. It will feel like defeat."

A trio of figures was hurrying toward them through the shadows. Audric watched them, his hand hovering over Illumenor's hilt. A feeling of dread was beginning to creep over him. The bells, chiming madly, a silver-toned clamor. Ludivine's insistence that they must leave.

And a whole castle, a whole *city*, full of people who had seen the terrible truth that he had seen.

*Don't worry.* Ludivine's presence in his mind rattled, unsteady, and then vanished.

"It's Tal," she whispered. "Sloane, and Miren. I can't speak to you again like that, Audric. It will take me some time to recover."

He relaxed as Tal's face came into view—until he saw the expression he wore, and that all of their ceremonial robes were spattered with blood.

Tal was breathless. "They're taking the castle. Hundreds of our own city guard have joined them, and many who stood against them have already fallen. The Archon has been taken into custody. The rest of the council are under close supervision. We barely managed to get out to warn you." Then he paused, looked around through the trees. "Where is Rielle?"

"It happened so quickly," Sloane muttered, her choppy dark hair cutting harsh lines across her pale skin. Her blue eyes, twins of Tal's, were hard with rage. "It was well-planned. They must have been preparing this for months."

Realization settled upon Audric like silt. "Merovec."

Miren nodded. "All his bannermen from the north. There must be thousands of them, all told. Scattered throughout the city, forming a perimeter along the bridges."

Evyline approached, her face grim. "If this is true, my king, then Lady Ludivine is right. We must leave, now."

"My mother," he said, struggling to gather his thoughts. "Is she all right?"

"Merovec won't harm her," Ludivine murmured. "She'll be safer in Baingarde than anywhere else, once word gets out of what's happened."

Sloane cut furious eyes to her. "Did you know about this, angel?"

"No, she didn't," Audric answered for her, "and I won't hear another word on that subject."

Then he turned away from them. Looking out over the seeing pools, his mind conjured up child ghosts—Rielle, dashing fast across the slick stones; Ludivine, meticulously picking her way across after her; and the echo of his own self, bringing up the rear. Urging Rielle to be careful. Pleading with her to slow down.

He squeezed his eyes shut against the memory of her earlier that evening, standing in despair before him, begging him to look at her.

"Audric, you must leave." Miren's voice was urgent. "He's searching for you, and when he finds you, especially after what happened tonight, what they saw, he will kill you."

"In his eyes, the crown has been corrupted," Ludivine added. "He will not spare you."

"You know of the tunnels under the mountain," said Sloane. "They'll turn you out on the far side of Mount Cibelline."

"My father made sure I could navigate them with my eyes closed," Audric said, and then he drew a deep breath and turned to face them.

He was a son of kings and queens. His family descended from Saint Katell. He was the Lightbringer, the heir of House Courverie. And his kingdom was falling into a state of chaos.

He could not let his grief defeat him. Not yet.

"Miren, I'll need eyes here in the city," he said. "Ostensibly loyal to Merovec, but truly loyal to me. Will you do this?"

Miren glanced at Tal, only a small flicker of unhappiness crossing her face. "Of course, my king."

"And Sloane, if you would join me and Ludivine and the Sun Guard."

Sloane nodded, her jaw set. "Where will we go?"

"To Mazabat. The queens will offer us asylum."

Miren raised her eyebrows. "Even after the incident with the Obex?"

"If Rielle were with us, they might object," Audric said tightly. "But considering the circumstances, I'm confident they'll welcome us."

Tal took two steps toward him, his eyes cold as stone. "Where is she, Audric?"

"She's gone. She's left to join Corien. And I need you to go after her and bring her home. Ludivine will tell you what you need to know." Audric moved away before he could see Tal's reaction. He felt as though he were moving through a terrible fog, each cloudy tendril tugging him closer to the ground. "Meanwhile, Evyline, we'll need horses. The tunnels are large enough for them."

But before he could give further instructions, a soft, sharp cry sounded from the canopy above, and then Atheria appeared, gliding down through the trees. She landed before them in silence and went to Audric with a low, rumbling whicker. He watched her approach with tears in his eyes, and when she bowed her head to press her long velvet face against his, he held on to her, allowing himself a moment to breathe in her scent—cold, clean alpine winds; musk like any horse would have; a bright sharp brilliance, as if her coat held the far burn of stars.

"Take her and go, my king," Evyline suggested quietly. "You and Lady Ludivine, and"—she dipped her head toward Sloane—"the Grand Magister. We'll go through the tunnels. I know of them. Your father the king told me of them when I was appointed to..." She hesitated. "When I was appointed to my current position. We'll join you in Mazabat as quickly as we can."

"No," said Sloane. "I'll stay with your guard, Evyline." She brandished her casting, a slender black scepter capped with a blue glass orb. As it cut through the air, it drew wolf-shaped shadows that then loped off into the gardens, noses to the ground.

Sloane shot Evyline a hard grin. "Just in case you need it."

Evyline returned her smile with a nod. "We would be honored, my lady."

Atheria knelt, wings spread wide, and Audric hesitated only once before climbing onto her back. Ludivine silently climbed into place in front of him, curling her fingers in the godsbeast's mane. Atheria rose, and from his perch atop her, Audric looked down at all of them. Evyline and the Sun Guard, Sloane adjusting her blue-and-black robes at their side. Miren and Tal, pulling away from a passionate embrace. Miren looked up at him, bright-eyed. Tal kissed her forehead, and then she was gone, hurrying back toward Baingarde. Tal watched her go, his face cloaked in shadow.

Audric watched as well, following Miren through the gardens until she disappeared. He listened to the clamor of the city bells, the distant cries of fear and violence, the clash of swords ringing out from Baingarde's open windows.

He let his gaze pass once over Baingarde's towers, the sprawling gardens, the distant gray ghosts of the catacomb doors.

Then, incapable of any grand speeches, he said to them simply, "May the Queen's light guide us home."

Atheria launched herself into the air, and soon she had risen above the trees, dwarfed by the black might of Mount Cibelline and flying swiftly south.

Away from Baingarde. Away from Âme de la Terre.

Away from Rielle, and the home in which Audric had loved her.

# ELEMENTS IN THE EMPIRIUM TRILOGY

————————◇————————

In Celdaria, Rielle's kingdom, the Church is the official religious body. Citizens worship in seven elemental temples that stand in each Celdarian city. Temples range from simple altars in a single, small room to the elaborate, lavish temples of the capital city, Âme de la Terre. Similar religious institutions exist in nations around the world of Avitas. In Eliana's time, most elemental temples have been destroyed by the Undying Empire, and few people still believe in the Old World stories about magic, the saints, and the Gate.

| ELEMENT | ELEMENTAL NAME | SIGIL | TEMPLE | COLORS |
|---------|----------------|-------|--------|--------|
| sun | sunspinner | | The House of Light | gold and white |
| air | windsinger | | The Firmament | sky blue and dark gray |
| fire | firebrand | | The Pyre | scarlet and gold |
| shadow | shadowcaster | | The House of Night | deep blue and black |
| water | waterworker | | The Baths | slate blue and sea foam |
| metal | metalmaster | | The Forge | charcoal and fiery orange |
| earth | earthshaker | | The Holdfast | umber and light green |

| SAINT | PATRON SAINT OF | CASTING | ASSOCIATED ANIMAL |
|---|---|---|---|
| Saint Katell the Magnificent | Celdaria | sword | white mare |
| Saint Ghovan the Fearless | Ventera | arrow | imperial eagle |
| Saint Marzana the Brilliant | Kirvaya | shield | firebird |
| Saint Tameryn the Cunning | Astavar | dagger | black leopard |
| Saint Nerida the Radiant | Meridian | trident | kraken |
| Saint Grimvald the Mighty | Borsvall | hammer | ice dragon |
| Saint Tokazi the Steadfast | Mazabat | staff | giant stag |

# ACKNOWLEDGMENTS

---◆---

What a strange and beautiful and terrifying thing, to finally write the sequel to a book I'd been working on for fourteen years—especially because I had to write it during a difficult time in my life. I couldn't have done so without an army of extraordinary people by my side.

I'd like to thank my agent, Victoria Marini, for her unflagging enthusiasm and support, and for her ability to soothe my anxieties with a simple email. I am also indescribably grateful to my editor, Annie Berger, who helped me wrangle the monstrous first draft of this book into something leaner, cleaner, and certainly meaner. To both of these women I must also extend my thanks for their patience, understanding, and unending compassion when I needed it most.

I could not be happier that these books of my heart have found a home at Sourcebooks. Their passion, diligence, and creativity have made the process of getting *Furyborn* and now *Kingsbane* into the hands of readers an utter joy. My special thanks go to Sarah Kasman, Margaret Coffee, Stefani Sloma, Stephanie Graham, Ashlyn Keil, Beth Oleniczak, Heidi Weiland, Valerie Pierce, Lizzie Lewandowski, Katherine McGovern, Sierra Stovall, Kate Prosswimmer, Danielle McNaughton, Heather Moore, Beth Sochacki, Steve Geck, and Dominique Raccah, as well as

Cassie Gutman and Diane Dannenfeldt. Credit for the stunning covers and interiors for the Empirium Trilogy goes to art director Nicole Hower and illustrator David Curtis, both of whom are phenomenally talented.

I must also thank Lia Chan for her film rights expertise; Heather Job, Aaron Blank, and the wonderful team at Penguin Random House Audio; and Fiona Hardingham, for bringing my characters to life with her incredible performance.

So many booksellers, librarians, and readers have embraced this story and welcomed Rielle and Eliana into their hearts. I am forever grateful to them.

My life is filled to the brim with bright, beautiful souls. I've leaned on a particular few of them especially hard over the last couple of years. Alison Cherry, Lindsay Eagar, Diya Mishra, Mackenzi Lee, Anica Rissi, Anna-Marie McLemore, Katherine Locke, Ken Richardson, Sara Raasch, and Lauren Magaziner, thank you for being my lifelines.

I dedicated this book to Erica Messmer, a friend I feel like I've known my whole life even though in truth I only found her three short years ago. Erica, I love you. Thank you for understanding all the messy black knots of my soul.

As always, to Mom, Dad, Drew, Anna, Ashley, Andy, Kylie, Jason, and Sara—thank you for tirelessly cheering me on. I'm so lucky you're mine.

# ABOUT THE AUTHOR

———◆———

Claire Legrand used to be a musician until she realized she couldn't stop thinking about the stories in her head. Now she is a librarian and the *New York Times* bestselling author of several novels for children and teens, including *Sawkill Girls*, the Edgar Award–nominated *Some Kind of Happiness*, and *The Cavendish Home for Boys and Girls*. A Texas native, Claire currently lives in central New Jersey.

# FIREreads

🔥 #getbooklit

Your hub for the hottest young adult books!

Visit us online and sign up for our
newsletter at FIREreads.com

 @sourcebooksfire

 sourcebooksfire

 firereads.tumblr.com